Acclaim for Lee Boyland's first novel, *The Rings of Allah*.

"**Thank Allah it's fiction, because it will scare the hell out of you!**. Author Lee Boyland puts his extensive special weapons background to use in spinning this completely believable tale of al-Qaeda's next step after 9-11 ... A great action story that is just a bit too possible, this is definitely worth it for action and techo fans alike."

- Military Writers Society of America

"*The Rings of Allah* is an exciting, at times harrowing journey into the future. The novel ensnares the reader and the ending is not for the faint of heart. A must read."

– Joe Weber, *New York Times* best-selling author

"Lee Boyland's story of a nuclear terrorist attack on the U.S. *hit the nail on the head*. A plot that can happen today."

– Retired brigadier general, National Security Agency

"The Rings of Allah" is a fascinating in-depth look into the world of radical Islamic terrorism. The technical knowledge of the author comes through in the minute detail of weapon systems and their use. The book, written in a chronological sequence of the development of the nuclear industry, gives the reader a detailed background of what we are faced with in the future. The plot was believable and the characters realistic as their lives were woven together in a tapestry of intrigue and human drama that pitted the beliefs of radical Islamic terrorists against mainstream American democratic values ... The ending is spell-binding and unpredictable, and will leave the reader with an unspoken sense of what can happen in our country if we don't take action."

– Philip W. Little, Author of *Hell In A Briefcase* and *Hostile Intent*

"Stunning - A Must Read! Frighteningly real! Boyland, the new grand master of the techno-thriller, has given us a compelling page-turner that captures the reader with an avalanche of brilliant detail and well thought out characters complete with personality and quirks. "Rings" captures the reader with the clear possibility of nuclear attacks on U.S. soil by fanatical Muslim terrorists..."

– William DeNisi, author of *Trinity*

"Excellent story. I read it in one day. Ideas for my next book."

– Major General Chuck Scanlon retired, Defense Intelligence Agency

Behold, an Ashen Horse

A Novel

Lee Boyland

With

Vista Boyland

This book is a work of fiction that contains historical persons, places and events. The Soviet Union's atomic bomb program existed. The author created a fictional Little Boy team, and all characters, incidents, places and events resulting from the Little Boy team are products of the author's imagination. A list of main fictional characters is presented at the beginning of the book. Any resemblance between fictional characters in this book and real persons is purely coincidental.

Behold an Ashen Horse

© 2007 James L. and Vista E. Boyland
All rights reserved. No part of this book may be reproduced, stored in retrieval system, or transmitted by any means without the written permission of the author.
© Cover design by Lee Boyland
© Author photograph Vista Boyland

PAPERBACK
ISBN-13 978-1-60145-290-0
ISBN-10 1-60145-290-X

HARDCOVER
ISBN-13 978-1-60145-291-7
ISBN-10 1-60145-291-8

Cataloging Data
1. Behold an Ashen Horse—Fiction. 2. Nuclear
terrorism—Fiction. 3. Technothriller—Fiction. 4.
Caliphate—Fiction. 5. Nuclear war—Fiction. 6.
International relations—Fiction. 7. Middle East—Fiction.
8. Terrorism—fiction.

Booklocker.com, Inc.
2007

This book is printed on acid-free paper.

http://www.LeeBoylandBooks.com

AUTHOR'S FOREWORD

Behold, an Ashen Horse is a story of events occurring after an Islamic terrorist attack using nuclear weapons on five American cities—referred to by Islamic terrorists as their "Day of Islam." It is the continuation of the story told in our first book, *The Rings of Allah.*

Can the U.S. survive such an attack?

Will our economy fail?

What would be the worldwide effect of the attacks?

How would the U.S. seek retribution?

Behold an Ashen Horse is a story that answers these questions.

This is not a book about the Islamic religion—a bibliography of recommended books on Islam is included at the end of the book. Nor is this story an attack on Islam. It is, however, a picture of what could occur if Islam fails to stamp out its fanatics and adjust to the 21st century. The dream some Muslims fanatics have of converting the world to Islam is just that, a bad dream—a nightmare.

Can Islam adjust to the 21st century, or will it force a clash of civilizations? The 2006 elections in Palestine and the potential for a religious civil war in Iraq did not get the century off to a good start. Palestinians seeking to establish a new nation exercised their right to vote by electing a terrorists group as the majority party in their parliament—setting the stage for a civil war between Hamas and Fatah. A Danish newspaper published caricatures showing Muhammad as a terrorist, setting off riots. Unpleasant political cartoons are part of freedom, part of the West's culture. Muslims violently objected to the knighting of Salman Rushdie. Mohammad Ali Hosseini, a Muslim spokesman, portrayed the knighting as an act directed against Islam by Britain. Iran's death warrant for Sir Salman is still in effect, and the bounty for his head has been increased to $150,000. Islam refuses to accept criticism—a totally unacceptable position. If Islam continues to demand the rest of the world accommodate its overly-sensitive feelings, *the clash of civilizations is inevitable.*

Behold, an Ashen Horse is a story that depicts the attitudes, actions and events that could occur after the U.S. was attacked with nuclear weapons—a story of survival and retribution. It depicts the consequences Islam will face if its fanatics ever succeed with their plans. Some of the dialog is anti-Islamic, some of the statements made by characters may be incorrect—a realistic picture of events after an attack. After a nuclear attack, no one will care about political correctness—a position that will have become a thing of the past.

A nation will do what it must to survive—and Americans are survivors. When angered, Americans are fierce fighters and terrible enemies. I suggest skeptics read America's history. Pay careful attention to America's attitude toward the Japanese after December 7, 1941. Domestic Japanese proved themselves to be good and loyal citizens. Will *all* domestic Muslims do the same? Will some start a jihad? Islam's response to the cartoons provides an indication of how some will react.

A nuclear weapons attack will kill and maim millions of U.S. citizens. Our rage will be proportional, beyond comprehension. The power of the United States is not understood by its citizens, or by citizens of the world—especially the Islamic world. With sufficient provocation, the U.S. could annihilate all of Islam within hours.

If this story frightens you, I have accomplished my purpose. We must do what is necessary to prevent *Behold, an Ashen Horse* from becoming prophecy fulfilled. The clash of civilizations must not occur.

Islam is a religion based on the Qur'an and its Prophet—neither of which can be questioned by Muslims. Characters in this book discuss both. Obviously, the discussion is limited; else, this work would quickly turn into a treatise on Islam. The Dead Sea Scrolls have caused much debate in the West. Islam has its equivalent—the Yemeni Qur'an—consisting of some 15,000 sheets written in early *Hijaz* Arabic script discovered in a mosque in Yemen. The scrolls are stored in Yemen's House of Manuscripts, and Islamic authorities are resisting examination by scholars.

Whenever possible local time is used (*i.e.*, 1400 hours or 2 p.m. Friday in Albuquerque, NM is 4 p.m. in Washington, DC, 2 a.m. Saturday in Beijing, midnight in Moscow, and 11:30 p.m. in Tehran).

The reader will encounter certain technical terms used in nuclear physics and nuclear weapons. Simple explanations and definitions are provided in the Appendix.

I wish to acknowledge those who helped me complete *Behold, an Ashen Horse*. My wife, Vista, editor and co-author, breathed life into some otherwise dull scenes, filled out several characters, and re-wrote and improved portions of the manuscript. I wish to thank the following people for their input and for reading and editing the manuscript's many drafts: the Space Coast Writers Guild Critique Group; Dr. Valerie Allen; BG Larry Runyon USA (Retired), for his input and editing; Bill Mick, Clear Channel Radio Talk-show host for comments and encouragement; Reverend Arlie Cole for religious advice;

retired aerospace engineer Jack Wiles for comments and encouragement; Paul Newcomb, whose father built the "Orange Juice Plant" for editing and comments; Professor of English Mary Prier, St. Louis University for comments and editing; and my readers Tim Mobley; Joan Waas; Rita Belefant; Andy Vazquez; and Mary Jane Bang.

Lee and Vista Boyland

Prologue

Al-Qaeda obtained five post WWII era, Soviet nuclear gun-type test devices from a cadre of renegade KGB officers known as *Gruppa*, the Group. Usama bin Laden placed Mohammed al-Mihdar, a Saudi al-Qaeda operative, in charge of the nuclear weapons project—code name "Allah's Rings." Mohammed discovered a talented trainee, Ralph Eid, in an Afghanistan al-Qaeda training camp. Eid, an embittered U.S. citizen of Egyptian descent, was scheduled to complete his Ph.D. in nuclear physics upon his return to the U.S. Mohammed made Eid his protégé and instructed him to seek employment at a U.S. nuclear weapons lab.

Eid secured a position at Livermore National Laboratories where he gained access to early nuclear weapons designs. Al-Qaeda provided Eid funds, in the guise of an inheritance, and Eid formed REM Investments. REM established a chain of radiological diagnostic clinics located in high-rise office buildings in the target cities. Eid devised a scheme to import the five nuclear gun-type devices into the U.S. as "Neutron Induced Gamma Spectrometers," medical research instruments, and installed them in radiation-shielded rooms next to the clinics—effectively hiding them in plain sight.

Never identified as a member of al-Qaeda, Mohammed's other al-Qaeda duties included acting as Usama's secret ambassador with Islam's radical Council of Clerics, the *Shura*, and wealthy contributors. After the September 11, 2001 attack on the U.S., Mohammed lost touch with Usama. Growing increasingly delusional, he began fantasizing he was the most powerful man in Islam. As such, he was certain the *Shura* and its leader, Grand Ayatollah Hamid Khomeini, would appoint him Islam's new caliph, the leader of a new Islamic Empire. At a secret meeting with Khomeini and the *Shura*, Mohammed sold them on his plan to bring America, "The Great Satan," to its knees with his hidden nuclear bombs, and announced that his new name was Muraaqibu al-Khawaatim—"Keeper of the Rings."

America's November 2004 elections ended the unexpected race between the incumbent president and the democratic senator from New Hampshire, Hilda Rodman. Hilda Rodman was elected president and immediately restructured the government—drastically altering military deployments and rules of engagement. Appeasement became America's policy. Massive troop withdraws began in Afghanistan and Iraq—leaving only a small contingent in both countries. Civil war erupted in Iraq between Sunnis and Shi'ites; the Taliban emerged from the mountains and reclaimed Afghanistan; and Hizbullah gained control of Lebanon.

With her presidency in trouble, Rodman responded to growing dissatisfaction with her policies—both in Congress and the military—by appointing retired USAF Major General George Alexander the Secretary of Homeland Security. In an effort to silence her critics, Rodman scheduled an address to a Joint Session of Congress for Friday, May 26th, immediately followed by a celebration on the Capitol Mall. Concurrent celebrations were planned in many cities across America. The story continues as Rodman exits the Capitol building after her address to the joint session of Congress.

The old order changeth, yielding place to new;
And God fulfills himself in many ways,
Lest one good custom should corrupt the world.
– Alfred, Lord Tennyson, "Morte d' Arthur"

Main Fictional Characters

King Ali, King of Jordan.

Khalid Ali, Communications director, Al-Jazeera all-news satellite television station, Doha, Qatar.

Mohammed al-Asad, President of Syria.

George Robert Alexander, 45th President of the U.S., Secretary of Homeland Security, Retired USAF Major General.

John Blankenship III, Lieutenant General, USAF, Deputy Commander of the U.S. Strategic Command.

Isaac Calley, FBI Special Agent, Buffalo Office, SAC Buffalo Office.

Betty Chatsworth, M.D., Acting Secretary of Health and Human Services, Acting Surgeon General, Congresswoman from Iowa.

Cheung Qiang, Admiral, Commander of the Chinese Peoples Liberation Army and Navy (PLAN).

James Chin, Ph.D., Director, Los Alamos Laboratories, Director, Department O Energy.

Barry Clark, Special Agent in Charge of the Albuquerque FBI Office; Director, FBI.

Paul Eckard, CIA Station Chief, Moscow.

Ralph Eid, Ph.D., American born, Egyptian. Father and mother killed in an automobile accident. Ph.D. in Nuclear Physics from the University of California, MBA in Business Administration from Harvard. Cell leader for Allah's Rings in the U.S., and founder and CEO of REM Investments, Inc.

William Fobbs, Publisher, financier, Secretary of Treasury.

Bruce Fox, Lieutenant General, USAF, Commander, NORAD.

Ludwick von Graften, see Alexei Valek.

Boris Glukhih, Gruppa's man in Sarov.

Nancy Hatterson, Venture capitalist, Ralph Eid's girlfriend. Founder of PC Capital.

Jay Henniger, US Attorney, Dallas, Attorney General.

Nora Jacobson, Senor officer, Federal Reserve.

Nicholas Karpov, President of Russia.

Muraaqibu al-Khawaatim, Keeper of the rings. See Mohammad al-Mihdar.

Allan Keese, Secretary of State.

Hamid Khomeini, Grand Ayatollah of the Islamic Empire, Head of the radical *Shura* (the council of radical clerics), Supreme Leader of the Guardian Council, and member of the Committee of Nine.

Sean Kilpatrick, New FBI SAC, San Francisco and Oakland.

Howard Krugger, Rear Admiral, Commander, *Kennedy* Strike Group.

George Landry, Ph.D., DOE representative.

Teresa Lopez, FBI Agent, Buffalo Office, assigned to Director of FBI.

Patricia Manning, Publisher, *Los Angeles Herald.*

Vladimir Melnikov, Director, Russian Federal Security Service (FSB).

Mohammed al-Mihdar, Usama bin Laden's lieutenant, in charge of *Allah's Rings*. Masters degree in International Finance Harvard, and a Ph.D. in Physics from MIT. Director of REM Investments, Inc. Alias:
    Muraaqibu al-Khawaatim (Keeper of the Rings); and,
    Saladin II, Caliph of the Islamic Empire.

Muraaqibu al-Khawaatim, Keeper of the Rings. See Mohammed al-Mihdar.

Enrico, Morani, Catholic Monsignor, Professor of Islamic Studies, member of Inter-Faith Advisory Committee.

Christopher Newman, Acting Secretary of Homeland Security.

Boris Popov, Director, Russian Ministry of Atomic Energy (MINATOM).

Kurt Richards, Governor of New Mexico.

James Ross, Brigadier General, USAF, Press Secretary.

Jim Ryder, Lt. Colonel, Attaché, US Embassy in Qatar.

Saladin II, Caliph of the Islamic Empire. See Mohammad al-Mihdar.

Igor Shipilov, See Valrie Yatchenko.

Harry Simpson, General, USA, Former Chairman of the JCS, Secretary Of War.

Harold Smyth, Reverend, Shining Tabernacle, member of the Inter-Faith Advisory Committee.

Abe Steinberg, Rabbi, member of the Inter-Faith Advisory Committee.

Julian Taylor, Captain, USAF, Executive Office to Col Young, assistant to President Alexander.

Neville Chamberlain-Talbot, Prime Minister of the United Kingdom.

David Tuttle, FBI legal attaché, or legat, Moscow embassy.

Alexei Valek, Colonel, KGB, member of *Gruppa*. Obtained Soviet atomic test devices for Mohammed.
> Alias:　Herr Ludwick von Graften, a retired German industrialist in Venezuela.

Yury Vanin, Major, Russian Federal Security Service.

Robert Vazquez, Admiral, USN. CINC US Strategic Command (USSTRATCOM).

Martha Wellington, Director of the CIA.

Tom, Whitwell, FBI, SAC Buffalo Office.

Gordon Williams, Colonel "Gordi," Michigan Freemen's Militia.

Wu Yang, President, Peoples Republic of China.

Aaron Wurtzel, Prime Minister of Israel.

Paul Xi, American advisor to President Wu.

Yan, PRC, Vice Minister Foreign Affairs Ministry.

Valrie Yatchenko, Lieutenant General, KGB. Leader of *Gruppa*.
> Alias:　Igor Shipilov.

Yosif, Mohammed al-Mihdar's lover, and former live in housekeeper, valet, and chef.

Charles Young, Colonel, USAF. Chief of Staff to President Alexander.

David Zimmer, Captain, USN, CO, USS John F. Kennedy (CV 67).

Islam makes it incumbent on all male adults, provided they are not disabled and incapacitated, to prepare themselves for the conquest of other countries so that the writ of Islam is obeyed in every country in the world … The sword is the key to paradise, which can be opened for Holy Warriors!

– Grand Ayatollah Ruhollah Khomeini, 1979

Part I

The Great Jihad

Chapter 1

Friday

Washington, DC – Friday afternoon, May 26th

Hilda Rodman, the 44th President of the United States, concluded her "Peace In The Middle East" speech to a Joint Session of Congress. Smiling and basking in the glow of a prolonged standing ovation, she remained at the rostrum for several minutes. *The Joint Chiefs and most Republicans are still in their seats. To hell with them, I won,* she gloated and began making her way through the crowded main chamber, autographing programs and kibitzing with supporters. Finally reaching the east exit, she stepped out into the warm, sunny day, and paused to savor her triumph and Washington's beautiful afternoon. Little did she know this would be the last afternoon she would ever experience.

National Security Advisor Sara Blumberg interrupted Rodman's reverie. The time was 3:50 p.m.

"George Alexander is causing a problem," Bloomberg whined. "He's all hot and bothered about some terrorist's tape. Called just before you entered the chamber to give your speech. Wanted to speak to you—raise the threat level. He knew you were going to say there was no terrorist danger. The man's an idiot," Bloomberg sneered, shaking her head, "I intercepted his call and told him to get a grip."

President Rodman chuckled, "Well, he's served his purpose as Secretary of Homeland Security—time for him to go. He's the only Cabinet member who's not here. Look around, all of the Supreme Court Justices, the Joint Chiefs, every senator, and all but two house members are here. His absence will be noted."

As if on cue, a member of Rodman's security detail approached and said, "Madam President, Secretary Alexander has been trying to reach you."

❊   ❊   ❊

The entire eastern seaboard was experiencing good weather. Winds were light and the sky clear. Conditions were forecast to change around midnight, when a severe weather front would arrive from the west.

In the REM warehouse, approximately a quarter of a mile from the

Capitol building, the computer in the hidden nuclear device determined five minutes remained before the programmed detonation time stored in its memory. Heating elements in the sealed neutron generator tubes were switched on.

❊   ❊   ❊

Outside the Capitol building, three senators waited for the President.

"A brilliant speech," one gushed.

"Yes, your plan to increase AIDS funding is right on the target," another added.

"President Rodman, I'd like to sponsor your initiative for Iraqi women's schools. I'll be pleased to introduce a bill in the Senate," the third added.

"Thank you, Tim. My staff will contact you to work out the details," Rodman said, and continued toward her limousine.

General Donald O'Neil, Chairman of the Joint Chiefs, caught up to the president. "Madam President," he said softly, "I've received a very troubling report concerning an al-Qaeda video that was broadcast at 2 p.m. My staff considers the threat valid. Secretary Alexander is at Kirkland Air Force Base. We think a nuclear attack is imminent."

Before the president could reply, Bloomberg snapped, "We've been all through that before. Secretary of Energy O'Riley has determined it is impossible to smuggle a working nuclear warhead into the U.S."

Rodman smiled knowingly at Bloomberg, and the two turned and walked away with no further comment. The general watched the two women's backs, shaking his head in disgust.

❊   ❊   ❊

The hidden nuclear device's computer continued comparing real time to detonation time. When the times matched, the detonation sequence began by closing a relay, introducing a twelve-volt current into the firing circuit. Glowing red-hot bridge wires ignited the propellant charge, creating hot gases. Pressure increased in the brass cartridge case. The cannon's breech and barrel prevented the cartridge case from expanding or rupturing. Only the U-235 projectile could move, and it began accelerating down the barrel toward the U-235 target rings.

Approximately six-hundredths of a second later, the projectile exited the barrel, and entered the hole in the target assembly containing the target rings. Less than one-hundredth of a second later—the projectile completely entered the target rings, forming a solid cylinder of U-235. The neutron generator tubes fired, introducing millions of neutrons from three directions. The result was a supercritical nuclear reaction—an atomic explosion, equal to fifty thousand tons of TNT.

❈   ❈   ❈

Walking toward the presidential limousine, Blumberg continued carping about Alexander, "That fool has the military taking the terrorists seriously."

President Rodman laughed, and was about to reply when a brilliant white light, many times brighter than the sun, appeared directly in front of her.

The fireball vaporized everything within a thousand feet from the center of the detonation. Energy released as gamma, X-ray, and particle radiation caused flammable materials to spontaneously ignite, flesh to char, and metal to melt or soften. The resulting super heated air created a blast wave that decimated the center of the city.

Radiating outward from the fireball, the blast wave created overpressure on surfaces, turning shattered glass into lethal fragments, collapsing walls, and flattening houses and buildings. Solidly constructed government buildings remained standing, but were left gutted and contaminated. As the fireball cooled, it created a vacuum, causing a reverse pressure wave, as air rushed back to fill the vacuum.

By the time the blast wave reached the Capitol building, all exposed living things were dead. All that remained of President Rodman, Professor Blumberg, and others outside of the Capitol building were shadows on the concrete.

Alerted by Alexander's and Young's warnings, key personnel at the Pentagon, Ft. Meade, and Andrews and Bolling AFBs had gone to shelters. Some survived. Not so at the CIA complex, where many were killed or injured by flying glass. The blast destroyed aircraft on the ground at Andrews AFB, Bolling AFB, and Regan National Airport. In-flight aircraft faced a worse fate. The flash blinded many pilots and copilots, and the blast wave destroyed aircraft in the immediate area. Radiation and the EMP pulse disrupted ground to air communications. Aircraft crashes compounded already impossible rescue operations. Surviving aircraft landed at Dulles and other airports.

Similar devastation occurred in New York City, Boston, and to a lesser degree in Atlanta.

The huge storm pounding Chicago spared many lives. When the bomb detonated, airports were closed and most people were indoors. The storm's heavy rain removed radioactive particles from the air.

The large storm front continued eastward, pushing the radioactive fallout from Boston, New York, and Washington out to sea. Fallout from Atlanta followed the path of Sherman's march to Savanna.

Televisions tuned to ABC, CBS, CNN, NBC, FOX C-Span, and BBC lost their pictures. After a few minutes, local stations displayed notices of "Network Problems" and switched to prerecorded programming. No one could determine what interrupted the satellite links. Those trying to call New York or Atlanta received a pulsing busy signal.

Kirkland, AFB, Albuquerque, New Mexico

Secretary of Homeland Security George Alexander, a retired USAF major general, his wife Jane, Colonel Charles Young, and several officers were seated in a conference room watching President Rodman and Goldberg walking toward a limousine. After viewing a video broadcast on Al-Jazeera at noon, all were very worried. Without warning, the television picture turned to static. All eyes turned to look at the clock on the wall. The time was 1400 hours—4 p.m. in Washington—precisely two hours after the start of the al-Jazeera tape.

"Oh my God," one of the officers exclaimed.

"Try another channel," Young ordered.

LTC Cobb reached for the remote and quickly switched through the major network channels. Only one station broadcasting local news had a picture.

Colonel Young's face reflected everyone's anxiety. Picking up the phone he punched the code for the direct line to NORAD.

"North American Aerospace Defense Command, Lieutenant Colonel Osborne speaking."

"This is Colonel Young at Kirkland. Does NORAD have any indication of a nuclear detonation in the U.S.?"

"Hold for Lieutenant General Fox," Osborne replied.

General Bruce Fox came on the line, "Hello Charlie, we're kind of busy right now ... Uh, why are you asking about a nuclear detonation?"

"Sir, did you see the al-Jazeera tape that aired two hours ago?"

"No, and I don't have time for that right now ... Did the tape have something to do with a nuclear detonation?"

"Yes, sir. General Alexander, I mean Secretary Alexander, is with me. I'm putting you on speaker," Young said, punching the speakerphone button. "The Arab on the tape said he'd planted five atomic bombs in five of our cities, and that they would soon be detonated."

"Bruce, this is George Alexander. I considered the video to be a valid threat, and tried to warn the president. Couldn't get past Bloomberg, who thought it was a hoax. We were watching live feed of Rodman on C-Span, when the picture turned to static."

"Damn! Satellites show nuclear detonations occurred in Chicago, Boston, New York, Washington, and Atlanta. That's five, just like the Arab said," General Fox replied, his voice strained. "There is a major storm in Chicago, the city is blanketed by heavy clouds. We are zooming in on Washington. It's my understanding the entire government was there—Cabinet, Joint Chiefs, and both houses of Congress. Is that correct Mr. Secretary?"

"Yes, Bruce, that's correct. I'd have been there too, if my son had not been injured in a climbing accident yesterday," Alexander confirmed.

"Mr. Secretary," General Fox continued, his manner becoming formal, "According to the Presidential Succession Act of 1947, as amended in 2003, you are eighth in line to assume the presidency. At this time I must assume the President, Vice President, Speaker of the House, President Pro Tem of the Senate, Secretary of State, Secretary of the Treasury, Secretary of Defense, and the Attorney General all died in the explosion. Do you have any information that any of these persons were not in Washington?"

A stunned Alexander answered, "No. As far as I know they were all there. Probably outside of the Capitol, waiting for the president to leave."

"In that case, I recognize you as National Command Authority. We'll have teams on the way to DC. We expect severe weather to blanket the entire east coast by midnight."

General Fox paused, then asked, "Sir, what are your orders?"

Oh my God, Alexander thought as he surveyed the expressions of the officers sitting around the table. All were looking at him for guidance. *The last thing in the world I wanted was to become president. Assuming General Fox is correct, I'm going to have to start thinking like the Commander-in-Chief.* The multitude of problems facing the nation flashed before his eyes. Thirty years of military training and command, coupled with his dauntless personality focused his thinking. Without a moment's hesitation, he assumed command.

"General Fox, send a message to all military commands advising them of what has happened. Request them to inform all U.S. personnel worldwide. Inform the Air Force and Navy to start evacuation planning for our personnel in Middle Eastern countries. We must consider the possibility of hostile actions by our enemies—especially Iran, North Korea, and other Middle Eastern countries.

"Issue orders grounding all commercial and civilian aircraft and sealing our borders. Until we sort this out, no one is to leave or enter the country. Only inbound aircraft with insufficient fuel to return to their point of origin will be allowed to land. Instruct the FBI to detain and question all passengers on these flights.

"Issue bulletins stating I have assumed leadership as acting president. My command post will be here, on Kirkland. Include in the bulletins that a state of war exists with unidentified enemies. Our first priority is to establish communications and a chain of command. Next priority will be to obtain precise information on conditions surrounding the blast sites—the levels of radioactivity, extent of destruction, and fallout projections. Only then will we be able to develop plans to care for the wounded and determine who survived in Washington. Fallout projections will be sent to affected states and all federal emergency agencies.

"I must make a statement to the nation in the next few hours. Otherwise we will have full-scale panic." Alexander paused and reached for a nearby glass of water.

"Sir," General Fox said, "I suggest we raise the worldwide alert status to DEFCON-TWO."

"Approved," Alexander replied. *I have the full force of America's military at my command, and by God I'm going to use everything we've got to protect our country from another attack.*

"Pass the following orders to CINC STRATCOM. Tell Bob Vazquez I'm ordering release of tactical nuclear weapons to area commanders—get some ready for use. I want the Navy armed with Tomahawk TLAM-Ns ASAP. Also, order the Navy to arm the carriers with B-61 bombs. The Air Force is to arm B-1s and B-52Hs with AGM-129s. B-2s will be loaded with B-61 nuclear and B-83 thermonuclear bombs. As soon as the TACAMO birds are in the air, he is to establish communications with me here at Kirkland. We want to make sure none of the hot heads will think this is a good time to hit us."

☆   ☆   ☆

The Strategic Air Command (SAC) was disestablished in 1992. The command, control, and communications mission of all elements of the nuclear triad were placed under the U.S. Strategic Command (USSTRATCOM) located at Offutt AFB, Nebraska. Commanded by a four star Navy admiral or Air Force general, USSTRATCOM's mission is to: "Establish and provide full-spectrum global strike, coordinated space and information operations capabilities to meet both deterrent and decisive national security objectives. Provide operational space support, integrated missile defense, global C4ISR and specialized planning expertise to the joint warfighter."

"Looking Glass" missions are consolidated aboard Navy E-6B "Take Charge and Move Out" (TACAMO) aircraft located at Tinker AFB, Oklahoma. The E-6B, a Boeing 707 airframe loaded with high-tech communication equipment, has the ability to communicate directly with the nation's ballistic submarine fleet. Its battle staff, when airborne, is under the command of a flag officer—an Air Force general officer or a Navy admiral.

☆   ☆   ☆

Alexander continued, "Have your staff contact the Air Force, Army, Navy and Marines. Tell them to sort out who's their senior officer and have him or her establish contact with me ASAP.

"Charlie, I need your PR people. Tell them what we know, and have them start drafting a short speech for me. Also, have them contact the local TV stations. Alert them that I will be making a statement to the nation shortly. I will also need a method to communicate with our embassies and foreign governments. Designate one of your officers to set up a conference call with the governors of Illinois, Indiana, New York, New Jersey, Connecticut, Maryland, Virginia, and Georgia." Alexander paused to think, sipping water from his glass, then continued.

"Charlie, have someone contact the local FBI Special Agent in Charge. Give him the following instructions: one, set up communications with other field offices; two, alert all FBI offices and the CIA that we are now at Threat Condition 5, Severe, color RED; and three, instruct all FBI field offices to round-up suspected terrorists and place a watch on mosques—we must assume that there will be more attacks. When he has competed his tasks, he is to report to me in person.

"We need to contact the Director of Los Alamos Laboratory and have him get the Department of Energy in the loop. Have the director establish a chain of command and then report to me. We need response teams at each of the detonation sites.

"The military is to coordinate rescue and medical treatment of survivors. Make all assets available.

"Captain Thomas, call Colonels Combs and Ryder right now and fill them in. Have them contact their counterparts in our embassies in the Middle East. All hell may break loose in their area. We need to get our people out of there."

Alexander slowly looked around the table, then said, "Let's get moving people."

Jane Alexander, sitting next to her husband, watched in fascination as he assumed the awesome responsibility of the presidency. Then she quietly rose and left the command center to be with their children.

Chapter 2

Seated on one side of a long table in a large, spartanly furnished room, Muhammad al Mihdar, now known as Muraaqibu al-Khawaatim, the "Keeper of the Rings," and the *Shura*, the Council of Radical Islamic Clerics, sat viewing six large plasma television screens. Each set was tuned to a different network: ABC, CBS, CNN, FOX, NBC, and the BBC. Iran's Grand Ayatollah Hamid Khomeini, a member of the Assembly of Experts and Leadership Council, chaired the *Shura*. The other members were clerics from Saudi Arabia, Syria, Morocco, Iraq, Libya, Pakistan, Egypt, Afghanistan, and Yemen.

Members of the *Shura* did not know Khomeini was also a member of Iran's powerful, secret Committee of Nine, responsible for approving plans and funding operations of al-Qaeda, Hamas, Hizbullah, and the PLO. He was also the driving force behind the Committee's "12th Imam Project:" a grandiose scheme for the destruction of the Great Satan, paving the way for the prophetic return of the *Mahdi*, the hidden 12th Imam.[*]

The Committee of Nine was searching for a workable plan when Allah smiled upon them. Muraaqibu al-Khawaatim brought the *Shura* his in-place, top-secret al-Qaeda operation, "Allah's Rings," the name a reference to the uranium rings in the atomic devices. Khomeini realized Allah's Rings was the plan they were searching for—the key to creating the Islamic Empire, and converting the world to Islam. As a bonus, Sheikh Mohammad al-Mihdar, now calling himself Muraaqibu al-Khawaatim, was the perfect choice for caliph—a young, fanatical fool he could control. Taking credit for the plan, Khomeini renamed it the "12th Imam Operation" and presented it to the

---

[*] The 12th Imam, the Mahdi, is a figure considered by both Sunnis and Shi'as to be the ultimate savior of humankind. Shi'as and Sunnis differ on the identity of the Mahdi, with Shi'as believing that he was born in 868 CE and has been hidden by God (referred to as occultation) to later emerge to fulfill his mission. Sunnis either believe that he is yet to be born, or that he was born recently and has yet to emerge. Whatever the case, both groups believe that he will bring absolute peace and justice throughout the world by establishing Islam as the global religion. *Wikipedia, the Free Encyclopedia.*

Committee of Nine as his operation.

As the clock reached the programmed detonation time, 11:30 p.m. in Qom, 4:00 p.m. in Washington, all eyes focused on the television screens. Three showed the President of the United States and the National Security Advisor walking toward the president's limousine. Two showed Senators, Congressmen, and other important people milling about behind the president, and the last showed the Supreme Court justices standing together watching the president depart. Suddenly, all the screens went blank, the audio died, and the crackling sound of static filled the chamber. The clerics continued watching the blank screens in rapt silence. A minute later, a BBC commentator explained they'd lost the signal from Washington.

Barely able to contain his excitement, a jubilant al-Khawaatim searched each cleric's face—eagerly seeking an indication they understood the significance of the loss of signal. There was none. *For fourteen years I plotted, schemed, and waited to detonate those bombs—and these stupid old men don't have a clue as to what just happened,* he inwardly raged; until finally, no longer able to restrain his glee, he lost all sense of decorum. Bounding from his seat and rushing toward the TVs, he frantically pointed to the blank screens. "Thanks be to Allah!" he shouted. Then whirling around to face the clerics, he raised his hands, palms up, in a dramatic show of jubilation, and bellowed, "The Great Satan has been brought to its knees." Clapping his hands and gesturing to the clerics to join him, he began to chant, "Praise be to Allah, the Great Satan has fallen. Praise be to Allah, the Great Satan has fallen." But the stoic clerics were unmoved. Other than static and the BBC's commentator, the echo of al-Khawaatim's chanting voice was the only sound in the room.

Al-Khawaatim's chanting faded away, and one of the clerics calmly asked, "How can you be sure?"

Allah give me patience, al-Khawaatim seethed, cleverly suppressing his fury. *It will not do for me to lose my temper.* Forcing a subservient expression, he walked slowly toward the questioning cleric. *Allah deliver me from these technically incompetent fools. I must control myself. I'm so close to becoming caliph. I can't blow it now.* Regaining control and stifling a sneer, he responded with uplifted hands and his most earnest expression, "Excellency, the loss of signal. All the major networks in the Great Satan broadcast from New York, and they all have lost their signal. That means New York has been destroyed. Only the British station—the BBC—is on the air."

Not so easily convinced, Grand Ayatollah Hamid Khomeini replied, "We will wait for official confirmation from a major news network before acting. Once news of the detonations is announced, we will issue our message to the faithful."

Grand Ayatollah Hamid Khomeini was a nephew of Grand Ayatollah

Ruhollah Khomeini, whose return to Tehran, Iran from France in February1979 sparked the Islamic revolution. With President Jimmy Carter's blessing, Khomeini overthrew Shah Reza Pahlavi. Khomeini and his radical followers established kangaroo Islamic courts that tried and executed thousands of educated Iranians and military officers. Khomeini fanned the smoldering embers of militant Islamic hatred into a whirlwind that swept across the Muslim world.

Ruhollah Khomeini founded the Islamic Republic of Iran, and became its undisputed ruler, its Supreme Leader. Khomeini rewarded Jimmy Carter for his support by sacking the U.S. Embassy in Tehran, taking fifty-two American diplomats hostage, and holding them for 444 days. Now, Ruhollah Khomeini's nephew, Hamid Khomeini, led the *Shura*, and was the second most powerful man in Iran—second only to the current Supreme Leader. The Committee of Nine, through Hamid Khomeini, used the *Shura* to thwart Westernization of Islamic lands and promote true Islamic governments. The black turban Hamid Khomeini wore was significant. It identified him as a descendant of the Prophet Muhammad, and as such, a man to be revered and obeyed.

Knowing his fate lay in the Grand Ayatollah's hands, al-Khawaatim struggled to retain his composure. Lowering his head, he bowed in recognition of Khomeini's pronouncement and the *Shura*'s authority. Feigning a smile, he excused himself to make a phone call. The moment the room's large doors swung closed behind him, al-Khawaatim's forced smile turned to a sneer. *Fools*, he fumed and jerked his cellphone from his pocket, "Anyone with half a brain would know what the loss of signals means," he muttered in frustration, while activating the speed dial number for the Al-Jazeera television station. Khalid Ali, the station's director, interrupted the caller's thoughts by answering the phone on the fourth ring.

✫   ✫   ✫

Previously, al-Qaeda terrorist Muraaqibu al-Khawaatim had delivered a videotape to Khalid Ali, with instructions to broadcast it at precisely 9:00 p.m. on Friday, May 26, 2:00 p.m. in Washington, DC. Ali was to tell no one the tape's contents prior to its broadcast. The minute al-Khawaatim left the building Ali called the chairman of Al-Jazeera's Board of Directors, a sheik and member of Qatar's royal family. After viewing the video, the sheik decided he must take the video problem to emir. Only the emir could authorize telling the Americans of the tape's message.

The emir found time to address the matter Friday morning. Friday afternoon Ali received orders to inform the Americans before broadcasting the tape. Ali called the U.S. embassy's military attaché, Lieutenant Colonel

Jim Ryder, USA, and warned him of the video's potentially dangerous content. After several failed attempts to warn Washington, Ryder turned to his Air Force friend, Lieutenant Colonel Sam Combs, assistant military attaché, at the U.S. embassy in Israel. Ryder knew Combs was a confidant of the Secretary of Homeland Security. Surely, he would have the authority to do something about the disturbing threats made in the video.

Not long after his appointment, Alexander decided he did not entirely trust the intelligence reports he was receiving. To remedy the problem he began collecting his own intelligence from military officers assigned to Middle Eastern embassies. Lieutenant Colonel Combs was one of these officers.

Combs attempted to reach Secretary Alexander by phone. It was early morning in Washington. His first call was transferred to Alexander's voice mail. His second call answered by the duty officer, who told him the secretary was unavailable and to submit a report through channels. A friend at the Pentagon told Combs Alexander had flown from Andrews AFB to Kirkland AFB early that morning to be with his injured son. The duty officer at Kirkland AFB transferred Combs to Colonel Charles Young's office. Combs explained to the colonel's executive officer, Captain Julian Taylor, he had urgent, time-sensitive information for Secretary Alexander. Colonel Young received Combs' message, returned his call, and learned a threatening video would broadcast by Al- Jazeera at 1200 hours—2 p.m. EDT in Washington. In the tape, an unknown terrorist claimed five atomic bombs were hidden in five American cities, and would soon be detonated.

Young immediately called Alexander at his motel and relayed the message. Alexander knew Combs would not raise an alarm, unless he thought the threat credible. Anxious to hear what Combs had to say, Alexander, accompanied by his wife, Jane, rushed to Young's office. A conference call was arranged between Alexander, Young, Combs, and Ryder. Ryder emphatically stated he thought the threat on the video was authentic.

It was 1150 hours, ten minutes before the video would be broadcast. In a desperate attempt to issue a warning to President Rodman, Alexander called the president's security detail. Rodman was preparing to enter the House chambers to give her speech to a Joint Session of Congress. The call was transferred to Sara Bloomberg, who hated Alexander for his conservative, hawkish, hard-nosed positions on world affairs. Condescending and nasty as always, Bloomberg immediately blew off the threat by saying she knew about the video—just another bullshit and bravado Arab threat—nothing to worry about. Then she hatefully reminded him that the purpose of the president's speech was to calm the American people, not to scare them. No threat warning would be issued. The threat level would remain at Threat Condition 1, GREEN. Convinced that the potential of a terrorist attack using weapons of mass destruction was real, Alexander ignored Bloomberg, and alerted the military and Homeland Security of the scheduled video broadcast.

When Al-Jazeera aired the video at noon, Alexander, his wife, Young, and several other officers watched the live broadcast in Young's conference room. The opening scene showed a richly dressed Middle Eastern man sitting behind an ornately carved desk, atop which lay a large bejeweled scimitar. For several seconds, the man sat silently staring menacingly into the camera. Finally, he spoke and when he did, English subtitles appeared at the bottom of the picture. Subtitles were provided for one purpose only: the speaker, Muraaqibu al-Khawaatim, wanted nothing to delay his Western viewers' understanding of his message.

The speech began with several minutes of typical terrorist bombast and bravado—the usual shrill, almost frenzied, Islamic bitching, whining, justifying, and boasting about their "Holy Tuesday," 9/11—after which al-Khawaatim momentarily paused and once more sat menacingly scowling at the camera. At last he continued: this time with a lower pitch to his voice and in a more subdued tone—one that was intentionally meant to be ominous and upsetting.

> Over a decade ago, Allah provided al-Qaeda with power to destroy the Great Satan.

Al-Khawaatim declared: his jet black eyes terrifyingly bright with religious fervor and his face expressionless—the face of a stone-cold killer.

> A power that had to be hoarded ... protected ... *secreted*. A power to be placed in the land of the Great Satan. Placed in such a manner that the infidels were *completely unaware* when Allah's gift was put in their belly.

Al-Khawaatim sneered and glared into the camera.

> Allah's power is represented by rings.

Al-Khawaatim raised his arms—palms toward him—the back of his hands facing the camera, displaying a brilliant array of ruby, emerald, sapphire, and diamond rings.

> Allah has chosen me, Muraaqibu al-Khawaatim, to be the keeper of his rings—*Allah's Rings!*

Standing, Al-Khawaatim emphasized his last words with a raised fist.

> With Allah's guidance, I have, over many years, carefully placed Allah's Rings in the land of the Great Satan, in the heart of five large American cities.

> Now, Allah has granted me, Muraaqibu al-Khawaatim, the authority to release the awesome power of his rings ... *The power of the Atomic Bomb!"*

Al-Khawaatim lunged forward. Quickly grabbing the scimitar from the desk with his right hand, he raised it threateningly above his head, sneering into the camera.

Today I have given the command to release the power of the rings.

Still holding the scimitar in a striking position, Al-Khawaatim continued speaking through half-clenched teeth, then dramatically placed the curved sword on the desk.

It is *time* for the faithful to reclaim our lands for Allah.

Time to return our lands to Islam.

Time to cut down rulers who proclaim themselves to be true Muslims, but sell out the interests of their own people: Rulers who betray their nations, and commit offenses that furnish grounds for expulsion from Islam. Rulers who drink alcohol. Rulers who listen to evil Western music. Rulers who forsake the teaching of the Prophet and embrace Western ideas—like the equality of women. One such man is the ruler in Riyadh. He and other false rulers, and the influential people who stand by them—must all be cut down. People who have sided with Jews and Christians, giving them free reign over the land of our two Holy Mosques. These people must be wiped out ... Wiped out now!

In the name of Allah the Most Compassionate, the Most Merciful, I call for the Great Jihad to begin when the power of Allah's rings is unleashed, which will be very soon. Then it will be time to expel ... NO ... TO KILL the infidels in our holy lands.

Time for Palestine ... A Palestine without Jews.

Time for our righteous brothers living in the land of the Great Satan to rise up ... to convert the infidels to Islam ... to impose *sharia*[†] on that godless land.

Those who do not convert must perish.

To my al-Qaeda brothers in America I say, once the power of the rings is released, rise up! Implement your plans. Kill the infidels in Allah's name."

The camera zoomed in on al-Khawaatim, who scowled fiercely for several seconds before continuing.

Once Islam was a great empire. The Prophet brought Allah's words to us, and Islam united us. The first caliph, Abu Bark, began the spread of Islam. Other great caliphs followed. Umar, Uthman, Ali, and Muawiya spread Muhammad's message, may he rest in peace, and increased our empire by jihad. So it shall be again. Under the great Caliph Saladin, our empire stretched from North Africa, to Egypt, to Sicily, to Spain. When our great jihad has achieved its goal, Islam will again be a great power. Even greater than before.

[†] Sharia: In the Islamic state *sharia* (religious law) governs both public and private lives of Muslims. It is based upon (i) Muhammad's recitations (Qur'an); and Traditions, (ii) *Hadith,* and (iii) authenticated hadith, *Sunna.* Sunna and Hadith are the words, speeches, actions, and deeds of Muhammad. Islam is all about Muhammad.

Like terrorists in previous al-Qaeda videos, the Keeper of the Rings continued ranting about jihad for several more minutes. By the time the screen finally faded to white, everyone present believed the man's threat was real. Only one—Alexander, the weapons expert—understood the video's hidden message. At al-Khawaatim's first reference to *Allah's Rings*, the general suspected the rings might refer to a component of an atomic bomb. When the man displayed his brilliant array of finger rings, Alexander was certain the rings symbolized the target rings of a gun-type nuclear weapon: the kind of atomic bomb dropped on Hiroshima, a bomb named the Little Boy. The Keeper of the Rings was telling them gun-type nuclear weapons were hidden in five U.S. cities.

After the video ended, Alexander explained his theory, and asked if anyone knew anything about the terrorist. No one had ever heard of him.

Alexander's intuition told him the attack was imminent. He placed a second call to the president's security detail, only to discover Bloomberg had left orders blocking his calls. In a final desperate move to prevent the looming catastrophe, he attempted to used his authority as Secretary of Homeland Security to raise the Threat Condition from 1 to 5, RED: only to learn that once more Bloomberg had thwarted his efforts. Acting for the president, she'd frozen the threat level at Condition 1, GREEN.

Stymied and infuriated with both the president and Bloomberg, Alexander ordered helicopters with radiation monitoring equipment to sweep Washington, Chicago, and New York. Regrettably, when he gave the order, he learned helicopters were restricted from flying within a mile of the Capitol. One course of action remained. Alexander called the office of the Chairman of the Joint Chief's office and told the duty officer to alert the chairman that a terrorist nuclear attack was imminent. The most probable targets were Washington and New York. Alexander's alert saved many lives.

Options exhausted, Alexander and the group in the conference room settled back to watch the president's address to Congress.

Prior to his devastating attack on America, Muraaqibu al-Khawaatim was known by his real name, Mohammed al-Mihdar: the fifth and favorite son of a wealthy Saudi businessman, who was a close associate of the Crown Prince. Born in Riyadh, Saudi Arabia in 1959, Mohammed was raised in a privileged environment. While still a teenager, he accompanied his father on many business trips to Islamic and Western lands. As a result, he grew to adulthood well versed in the different cultures and ideologies of people from many different lands. He obtained his undergraduate degree in electrical engineering at King Abdul-Aziz University in Jidda. While there, he fell under the influence of a radical Islamic mullah, the prayer leader at his mosque, who converted him to Wahhabism—one of the most radically puritanical sects in

Islam. In fact, he followed much the same path as that trod earlier by Usama bin Laden. Later Mohammed would proudly boast that one of his distant relatives, Khalid al-Mihdar, participated in the September 11, 2001 attack on the World Trade Center in New York City.

In pursuit of his graduate degree, Mohammed moved to America, where he attended Harvard and received his Master's Degree in International Economics. After Harvard, he studied engineering and physics at MIT and obtained a Ph.D. in physics. Highly intelligent, Mohammed was a thin, six-foot tall man with piercing dark eyes, a light complexion, dark hair and beard. When clean-shaven, his changed appearance allowed him to pass as a Westerner. But his al-Qaeda brothers knew he was a man who would slit your throat without hesitation. His mercurial personality could change in a split second, from that of a quiet, soft-spoken, reasonable man, to the epitome of a raving fanatic.

After Mohammed obtained the five Soviet nuclear test devices, Ralph Eid formulated a plan for improving, disguising and importing them into the U.S. Only bin Laden, Mohammed and Eid knew of the plan—Allah's Rings.

Doha, Qatar

"Al-Jazeera," Khalid Ali said, after picking up the phone on the fourth ring.

"Praise be to Allah. I wish to speak with Khalid Ali," the caller said.

"This is Khalid Ali."

"Allah has used the power of his rings," the man announced—a code identifying him as the bearer of the earlier tape. "Praise be to Allah. This is Muraaqibu al-Khawaatim. Soon a second video will be delivered to you. Broadcast the new video ten minutes before morning prayers, and rebroadcast it every hour for the remainder of the day. The person delivering the tape has no knowledge of its content nor of recent events."

Ali's breath caught in his throat when he heard the code words. Struggling to maintain his composure he asked the caller, "Do you wish to make a statement?"

"My statement is on the video. I am but a servant of Allah, doing God's work."

Tormented by thoughts of the unfathomable death and destruction the bombs caused, and America's likely retribution, Ali could not help himself from asking, "Do you have any idea what you've done—what you'll cause to happen?"

"Allah has shown me the path to restore His lands to Islam. Soon the infidels will be gone from our holy lands. Soon the Jews will all be dead. Soon the flag of the caliphate will fly over all lands of the former Islamic empire ... and after that new lands will be conquered. Praise be to Allah," al-Khawaatim said, snapping his cellphone shut. It was almost midnight in Qatar. The dawn of a new day was approaching—a day different from all others.

Opening his cellphone, al-Khawaatim pressed the speed dial number for his lover.

Doha International Airport, Qatar – 11:31 p.m., Friday, May 26th

Seated in one of the many vacant, overstuffed chairs in the airport's deserted first class lounge, Yosif was nervously fingering ivory *sabha*, prayer beads. The flight from Riyadh, his first, had frightened him. His large, soft-brown eyes flitted from an adjacent table, where a manila envelope and cellphone lay, to the clock on the wall, where the second hand hypnotically clicked from number to number on its never ending journey around the face of the clock. He silently repeated his instructions, *I am to wait for my master's call ... Take a taxi to Al-Jazeera's TV station ... Hand the envelope to a person known as Khalid Ali ... and return to Riyadh on the first morning flight.*

Yosif jumped when the cellphone chimed. Fumbling with the small instrument, he answered in a soft, high-pitched voice, "This is the servant of the rings."

"May Allah bless the servant of the rings," Muraaqibu al-Khawaatim softly replied. "It is time for you to deliver Allah's message. May Allah bless you."

"When will you return to our apartment?" Yosif whispered to the caller—a man he knew to be his master—Mohammed al-Mihdar.

"Soon, very soon. Then I'll hold you close and tell you of wonders yet to come," al-Khawaatim whispered with a smile and slowly closed his cellphone.

Al-Jazeera's manager sat in stunned silence after al-Khawaatim broke the connection. *The madman, the fanatic has actually done it*, Khalid Ali thought—*I'm sure he has, because all major TV signals from the U.S. have ceased. BBC is still on the air from London, but cannot explain the loss of signals from America.* Gathering his wits about him, Ali quickly called his boss at home. When the sheik answered, Ali said, "I have just received another call from the fanatic. It appears the maniac has made good on his boast. He's sending me a second tape to be broadcast before morning prayers. Shall I inform the Americans?"

"Yes. Immediately! If even one of his bombs functioned, all hell is about to break loose. May Allah have mercy on us," the sheik replied. "If we do not tell the Americans, they will come for us. Yes, call them now!"

With trembling hands, Ali hung up the receiver. Nervously fumbling through his desk he found the number for the U.S. embassy and quickly called Lieutenant Colonel Jim Ryder. "Colonel Ryder, this is Khalid Ali at Al-Jazeera. Can you t–tell me what has happened in America?" Ali hesitantly asked. "We have lost all TV signals," he concluded, his voice strained with emotion.

"Yes, unfortunately the maniac on the tape made good on his threat. Nuclear explosions have occurred in five of our cities. We appreciated the warning—regrettably, it came too late."

"Colonel, I just received another call from the madman. He's sending me a new tape. This one to be broadcast before morning prayers. You must come over, and we'll view the tape together."

"Thank you, I'm on my way."

As soon as Ali broke the connection, Ryder placed a call to COL Young.

Colonel Charles Young, a fifty year old, five-foot-eleven, 174 pound career officer, was five years younger than Secretary Alexander. They'd served together at Tyndall AFB, where they became good friends.

Ryder's call was put through to Colonel Young. "Jim, tell me you don't have more bad news. We're up to our ears in alligators here."

"Sir. I just received word that Muraaqibu al-Khawaatim is sending a second tape to Al-Jazeera. I've been invited to view it when it arrives," Ryder said. "How bad is it on your end?"

"Bad, Jim, very bad. It appears that a fifty-kiloton bomb went off near the Capitol. All of the government officials, including the president, vice president, Cabinet, Supreme Court justices, Joint Chiefs, and Congressional Representatives were outside the capital building. NORAD has recognized General Alexander as command authority. He is the acting president until the deaths of President Rodman and anyone above Alexander in the succession chain are confirmed. I personally have no doubt he's now the president. We're preparing alert orders to all embassies, and requesting the Navy and Air Force to prepare evacuation plans for all of our citizens in the Middle East. Call me back as soon as you've seen the new tape. If possible, get a copy and upload it at the embassy."

"How much can I tell Al-Jazeera?"

"Nothing about the damage to our government. General Alexander will address the nation in a few hours. Tell them five nuclear detonations occurred in the U.S., but you don't know where."

"Roger that. Can you tell *me* where they occurred?"

"Yes, Washington, Atlanta, Boston, Chicago, and New York. Jim, I have to go. Thanks for the heads up."

Twenty minutes after a jittery Yosif delivered the tape and departed Al-Jazeera, LTC Ryder arrived. Ali placed the tape in the VCR and pressed play. Both men sat in stunned silence watching the image of Muraaqibu al-Khawaatim play out on the screen. When the tape ended, Ryder was deeply worried. He spoke Arabic and understood the terrorist's message. "May I have a copy of the tape?"

"Yes, of course I'll make you a copy right away. After it's broadcast, it will be available on our web site."

With the copy in hand, Ryder departed for the embassy, where the tape would soon be uploaded for distribution to Alexander, the military, CIA, and other embassies. By the time a copy of the tape was downloaded at Kirkland AFB, acting President Alexander was preparing to address the nation. He would not see the tape until after his address.

As soon as Lt. Colonel Ryder departed, Ali alerted all of his reporters and cameramen in various cities in the Middle East to be ready to cover monumental events—beginning with morning prayers. Next he called in all of his employees and prepared to cover events throughout the Arab world.

Qom, Iran – Saturday, May 27th

Forty minutes after the loss of television signals—12:10 a.m. in Teheran—the clerics and Muraaqibu al-Khawaatim gathered before a TV monitor to watch as a BBC news flash confirmed the detonation of five atomic bombs in the U.S. At the end of the BBC alert, the Grand Ayatollah, followed by the other clerics, rose and turned toward a beaming Muraaqibu al-Khawaatim. The Grand Ayatollah spoke for the *Shura*, "Muraaqibu al-Khawaatim, as you are now known, you have accomplished all you promised. We recognize you as Allah's greatest warrior, and as our new *caliph*. Allah has smiled upon you and guided you these past sixteen years. We honor you. Now it is for you to honor Allah by regaining our holy lands. Let the word go forth. The time of the *Great Jihad* is at hand. Praise be to Allah."

"*Allahu Akbar,*" God is great, the other clerics shouted, voicing their approval. Then they chanted, "Death to America, Death to the Great Satan."

Khomeini's staff began sending prepared e-mails to mosques and clerics in all parts of the world. Clerics would sound a worldwide call for the Great Jihad at morning prayers. Secular leaders of the faithful received e-mails instructing them to execute their assignments. Al-Qaeda cells in America, England, France, Germany, and Spain, alerted by Muraaqibu al-Khawaatim's first video, were already beginning to implement their respective plans. Saturday morning, May 27th, a worldwide reign of chaos would begin—a period of history that future historians would call, "The Tribulations."

Chapter 3

Faysal's cellphone vibrated. Removing it from his pocket, he noted the time and realized he had fifteen minutes left on his shift. His boss had warned him about taking personal calls. After a quick look around, he opened the phone and quietly said, "Yes."

"Faysal, have you heard the news? One of our brothers has destroyed the Great Satan's capital—New York city also," said an excited voice he recognized.

"Are you sure?"

"Yes, it was on TV. Al-Jazeera's web site posted a video showing a man who said he would destroy five of the Great Satan's cities. Now the local TV station has reported it has been done."

"Then our time is at hand. Call the others and tell them we'll meet at the mosque at 8 p.m."

Later, Faysal and five members of his cell huddled in a back room of the mosque watching television. Indeed, local TV stations were reporting nuclear explosions in New York, Boston, and Washington, DC. When Secretary Alexander addressed the nation at 8 p.m., the cell members were jubilant. Afterward they logged onto Al-Jazeera and viewed Muraaqibu al-Khawaatim's videotape.

"Who is this Muraaqibu al-Khawaatim?" one asked.

"What does it matter?" another said. "He has done what he promised to do. Allah must surely have guided him."

"The time has come for us to strike. Muraaqibu al-Khawaatim has told us to do so," Faysal said, having made his decision. "We've received no instructions for some time. Now we know why. Allah has called for the Great Jihad and given us a leader, a *caliph*. Now we must act. We must leave immediately for the farm and prepare our weapon. Our primary target has been destroyed. We must choose a new one and act quickly. The Americans will now be on guard." Faysal paused to think, then said, "We'll strike Buffalo at first light."

FBI Office, Buffalo, New York

Teresa Lopez, an FBI special agent assigned to the Buffalo office, was at her desk when word of the nuclear detonations in New York, Boston, and Washington reached the office. An Al-Qaeda videotape was rumored to have been broadcast before the detonations. Confusion and bad information compounded the problem. It was 4:20 p.m. A senior agent was attempting to call the New York and Washington offices. A fast busy signal rewarded his efforts. Other FBI agents were experiencing similar problems throughout the country.

As word of the attacks spread through Teresa's office, she and her fellow agents rushed from their desks to crowd around the TV. First they tried CNN, then FOX. None of the news networks were transmitting anything but static. Between the nerve wrenching sound of static, and the shouting of questions and orders from agents crowded around the TV, the scene in the office was turning into mayhem. A minute later, a local TV personality came on and announced loss of network signal.

Teresa watched in disgust while chaos unfolded around her. No one knew what to do. No one was in control. No one was taking the lead. Teresa thought she knew what to do, but past experience taught her to play the role of follower and suggest someone else to lead. Pushing her way through the increasingly noisy crowd, Teresa found the man who should be in control—Special Agent in Charge Tom Whitwell. The bewildered SAC, a native Bostonian with a pronounced accent, was staring at the TV.

"Tom," she shouted, "Can I talk to you somewhere away from this din?"

"Can't tell yah noythin' more than everyone else knows Teresa. Don't go gettin' you'ah knickahs in a knot. Just settle down and wait fowa awduhs from the highyah-ups," Whitwell shouted back, walking past her toward his office.

"Tom Whitwell," Teresa shouted at his back, "Don't you dare patronize me. You come back here and hear me out. Do you hear me?" *The damn fool is ignoring me.* "Tom Whitwell, do you hear me?"

Deliberately ignoring her, Whitwell continued heading to his office, pushing through the crowd of agents. Teresa continued calling out to the SAC—determined to have the last word. "Tom Whitwell. We must round up all Islamic terrorists suspects now, before they can scatter and cause trouble."

Turning slowly toward Teresa whom he loathed and considered a cowboy—or cowgirl to be politically correct—Whitwell sarcastically replied, "When ah you ever gonna learn. The FBI doesn't go 'round ahrestin' innocent cit'zens, jest 'cause yow'ah thinking they'ah teh'rists. We'll be waiting for awduhs like I said."

Teresa flushed with anger. She'd taken insults and demeaning comments from this overweight, arrogant slob since she graduated from the academy. Two years from retirement, Whitwell—known behind his back as "The Twit"—had taken an instant dislike to Teresa Lopez. A bureaucratic survivor, The Twit didn't think the bureau needed women agents—certainly not a Hispanic one. Now, Teresa had reached the end of her patience. Four years of The Twit's insults were enough.

"Washington, Boston, and New York have been nuked, and you want to wait for 'awduhs,' " she mocked. "Don't you think you should get up 'offa yowah' fat ass and grab these SOBs, before they can kill more Americans?"

"YOWAH *SUSPENDED*," The Twit shouted, his face turning red and his double chin straining against his collar causing his flabby cheeks to flutter.

"Maybe he'll have a heart attack and die," one agent muttered to the others.

Teresa turned, snatched up her purse, and stormed out of the office. She had no intention of following The Twit's orders. Instead, she went home and changed into a dark blue pullover shirt, blue jeans, and Nikes. After eating a hurried dinner, she headed for the local mosque, which she suspected was the center of terrorist activities. *To hell with The Twit. I'll keep this bunch under surveillance by myself. I'm convinced Faysal Mosed is the leader. If he leaves, I'll tail him.*

Albuquerque, NM– 6:45 p.m. Friday, May 26th

A deeply troubled Secretary of Homeland Security, and acting president, George Alexander, completed his address to the nation from the main auditorium on Kirkland Air Force Base. After informing the nation of the attack, and his actions and orders, he concluded with the statement, "The greatness of America is its people. Now is the time we must help each other. America has been sucker punched, but we are not down – and we are definitely not out. In the past great tragedy has united us. So it *will* today. "Good evening, and God bless America," Alexander returned to his new office, the former office of Kirkland's commanding general. Colonel Young informed him about the second al-Qaeda videotape, and that it was ready for viewing in the main conference room. This time the tape contained no English subtitles, and a translator was standing by.

As soon as Alexander took his seat at the head of the conference table, Colonel Young addressed the seated group, "As some of you already know, Al-Jazeera has received a second videotape from the terrorist, Muraaqibu al-Khawaatim, with instructions to broadcast it before morning prayers. A copy was provided to our embassy and distributed to as many commands and friendly governments as possible. This time there are no English subtitles. The tape is clearly aimed at the Muslim world.

"Before showing the tape, I want to introduce Rabbi Steinberg who is fluent in Arabic and will translate for us." The Rabbi rose from his chair in acknowledgment. Alexander nodded a greeting, and Colonel Young continued, "I'll pause the tape as needed, in order for the Rabbi to translate and answer any questions. Before we begin are there any questions?" There were none and Colonel Young pressed the play button on the remote control.

The video began with the image of a thin Middle Eastern man with a neatly trimmed beard. It was the same man and same location shown in the first video. The man sat staring into the lens of the camera for several seconds before speaking: his dark eyes riveting, his malevolent demeanor radiating intensity. Finally, he began,

> In the name of Allah, the most compassionate, the most merciful. Allah has blessed me and shown me the path that has led to the destruction of the Great Satan. Allah entrusted me with the power of His rings and I, Muraaqibu al-Khawaatim, placed these holy rings in the belly of the Great Satan. Following Allah's command, I caused these holy rings to detonate yesterday, destroying five of the Great Satan's largest cities. The Great Satan is on its knees—confounded by Allah's power.

Colonel Young paused the tape so the rabbi could provide a translation. With the exception of Secretary Alexander, the group sat listening in shocked silence to the rabbi. Alexander, who had firsthand experience with Islamic fanatics, expected something like this. After several exclamations of disbelief from the others, Colonel Young again pressed play, and again the Rabbi translated: a process that would be repeated throughout the remainder of the video.

> Allah has given me the burden of reclaiming our holy lands from the infidels; restoring our glorious Islamic Empire; and then expanding Islam throughout the world. As Allah's humble servant, I have accepted this burden, and followed Allah's command to become *caliph*.

The self-appointed caliph rose and picked up the jeweled scimitar from the ornately carved desk before him. Turning with a grand flourish, he used the sword to indicate an Islamic flag displayed behind him.

> I have adopted the flag of the great Caliph Saladin. I will draw on the wisdom of the Prophet, may he rest in peace, and the other great caliphs who followed him—Umar, Uthman, Ali, and Muawiya who spread Allah's word by jihad and increased our empire. Under the great Caliph Saladin, our empire stretched from North Africa, to Egypt, to Sicily, to Spain. When our *Great Jihad* has achieved its goal, Islam will again be a great power. Even greater than before.

Turning back to face the camera, al-Khawaatim placed the scimitar on the desk, then standing erect, he continued.

> In the name of Allah the Most Compassionate, the Most Merciful, I command THE GREAT JIHAD TO BEGIN!

It is time for the faithful to reclaim our lands for ALLAH.

Time to return our lands to ISLAM.

The Messenger told us in the Holy *Qur'an*, surah 36, verse 26 that "Allah made the Jews leave their homes by terrorizing them so that you killed some and made many captive. And He made you inherit their lands, their homes, and their wealth. He gave you a country you had not traversed before."

Now is the time to take back our lands.

Now is the time to cut down rulers who proclaim themselves to be true Muslims, but sell out the interests of their own people. Rulers who betray their nations, and commit offenses that furnish grounds for expulsion from Islam. Rulers who drink alcohol. Rulers who listen to evil Western music. Rulers who forsake the teachings of the Prophet and embrace Western ideas—like the equality of women. One such is the ruler in Riyadh; another is in Amman. They and men like them who are false rulers, and the influential people who stand by them must be cut down. People who have sided with the Jews and the Christians, and given them free reign over the land of our two Holy Mosques must be slain—SLAIN NOW!

It is time for a Palestine without Jews. Destroy the Little Satan. DO SO NOW!

It is time for our righteous brothers living in the land of the Great Satan to rise up and convert the infidel to Islam ... to impose *sharia* in that godless land—first the Saturday people, then the Sunday people.[*] Are we to spare the people of the book—the Bible? No! Allah has told us in surah 5:72, "They are surely Infidels who say Christ, the Messiah is God."

Allah has commanded us in surah 9:29 to, "Fight those who do not believe until they all surrender, paying the protective tax in submission," and in surah 9:112 to, "Fight and kill the disbelievers wherever you find them, take them captive, torture them, lie in wait and ambush them using every stratagem of war."

Those who do not convert must perish.

To my al-Qaeda brothers in America and Europe, I say rise up ... Implement your plans ... KILL THE INFIDELS IN THE NAME OF ALLAH!

Many leaders of Islamic countries, such as the rulers of Saudi Arabia and Jordan and their vile families have strayed from Allah's path. They have become contaminated by Western ways and have defamed the Prophet's teachings. They too must be punished for their sins. The same is true of rulers of other Islamic states. Go forth today! Cast out these vile rulers and establish true Islamic states.

Follow my flag and we shall create the greatest Islamic Empire the world has ever known. Follow my flag and create an all encompassing, compassionate Islamic world.

---

[*] Saturday people are the Jews. Sunday people are Christians.

My words are spoken with the divine guidance of Allah and are the blessed fruit of our Great Jihad.

The tape faded to white, then ended. Rabbi Steinberg completed his translation of the last statement and sat watching the others, wondering what would happen. He was sure they were dealing with a maniac. A fanatic who'd succeeded in setting Islam on a collision course with the West. A man who'd started WWIII. *Is our new leader up to the task? Dear God, provide him the strength, wisdom, and courage to face the awesome task you've given him.*

Looking around the packed conference room, Alexander said, "Comments?" No one seemed able to do more than sit shaking his or her head in disbelief.

In addition to those present, Admiral Robert Vazquez, Commander, U.S. Strategic Command (USSTRATCOM), and Lieutenant General Bruce Fox, Commander, North American Aerospace Defense Command (NORAD) were participating via conference call. Both were viewing copies of the videotape, while listening to the Rabbi's translation.

Finally, the SAC of the FBI Albuquerque district, Barry Clark, simply said, "Shit." A sentiment silently echoed by most of the others.

With no other response forthcoming, Alexander addressed the two senior officers listening on the speakerphone, "General Fox, were you able to comply with my instructions?"

"Yes, sir. After your call, I contacted Admiral Vazquez and filled him in. Colonel Young also called the admiral and briefed him."

"Mr. Secretary," Admiral Vazquez said, "I'm going on record as officially recognizing you as command authority, and acting president. I have complied with your orders as relayed by General Fox."

"Thank you, Admiral. I'm acting as president until it is established no one above me on the succession list has survived. What do you suggest?"

"Mr. President, we're at DEFCON 2, and I have issued alert orders to all commands. The Navy has a carrier strike group in the Mediterranean capable of providing support and helping to evacuate our personnel in the Middle East. They have been ordered to do so."

"Which carrier?"

"The *Kennedy*, sir."

"The *Kennedy*. She's conventionally powered isn't she?"

"Yes, sir, she's one of our two non-nuclear carriers. This is her last deployment, and she poses a severe fuel problem. Insurrections and civil wars appear to have started throughout the area. We don't know who is in charge in most of the Middle Eastern countries. We must assume we'll lose fueling privileges in the Middle East. The *Truman* is in the Indian Ocean, about two days sailing time from the Persian Gulf."

Staring at the speakerphone, Alexander's eyes narrowed while he evaluated his course of action, then began issuing orders. "Admiral, order the *Truman* Strike Group to proceed to the Persian Gulf at flank speed. It will probably be necessary to put boots on the ground to secure a port to evacuate our personnel.

"It may also be necessary to seize a Mediterranean port in order to obtain fuel and supplies for the *Kennedy*. Place the pre-positioned ships at Diego Garcia on alert. Issue alert orders to the XVIII Airborne Corps. I want the Eighty-Second and 101st Airborne divisions ready to deploy to staging areas near North Africa. Get them in position to seize a port with fuel and possibly an oil field and refinery. Order the Air Force to dispatch planes to evacuate our people. Finding an open airport may be a problem. We'll need to position bombers as close as possible to the Middle East."

"Mr. President, what are the rules of engagement?" the admiral asked.

"The United States has been attacked by unknown adversaries. We are at war. Any force opposing us will be considered hostile, and will be *destroyed*."

"Sir, does that include tactical nuclear weapons?" Vazquez inquired, his voice tense.

"Yes, if the area commander determines their use is necessary. I repeat. It must be *necessary*. We have no way of anticipating what will happen anywhere in the world. It's a good bet someone will take advantage of our perceived weakness. When that occurs, we must make an example—so no one else will try," Alexander said, and in so doing established America's new policy.

Alexander scanned the room, looking at each person to determine their understanding of his orders. All nodded in agreement, with one exception. A balding, overweight civilian with wire-frame, trifocal glasses was frowning. When the man realized Alexander was looking at him, he said, "Err … Mr. President." *I guess I must call him that, though I don't accept him as president.* "Uh, won't that send the wrong message to the world community? I mean … shouldn't we allow the United Nations to handle this aggression?"

An exasperated Alexander scowled and asked, "*And you are?*"

Shocked by Alexander's sharp tone and hard look, the man stuttered a reply, "I–I'm Doctor George Landry, from the Department of Energy … representing the Director of Los Alamos Labs … Mr. President."

Fixing Landry with a cold stare, Alexander declared, "Well Doctor Landry. Make no mistake. The United States is at war. Our survival is at stake. The United States has never, and will never, place its survival in the hands of others. We *will* identify and *destroy* our attackers. Nothing less is acceptable. Quit worrying about what the world thinks of us. It's time for the world to worry about what we think of them."

Dr. Landry blanched—his face drained of color. Looking at Alexander in consternation, he nodded to the imposing man sitting at the head of the table—a man now being recognized as president. Landry finally mumbled, "Yes, sir." Knowing all eyes were on him, he shifted in his seat—fully aware of the tension surrounding him.

The others slowly turned their attention back to Alexander, waiting with anticipation for his next statement.

Damn, Admiral Vazquez thought, nodding his head and grinning, *we've got ourselves a leader!*

Several seconds passed, while others silently echoed Vazquez thoughts. No one spoke. It was obvious to all present—Alexander was now the boss. And the boss was going to do everything necessary to save the country. Finally Alexander relaxed, settled back in his chair, and continued in his normal deep voice, "Now, Doctor Landry will you please bring us up to speed on DOE's efforts in the five cities."

"Yes, sir," a jittery Landry replied in a tense voice. "Nuclear Emergency Search Teams are enroute to Chicago, Atlanta, and Boston. Teams have arrived at New York and DC. Doctor James Chin, my director, is coordinating with other DOE facilities. The main problem is getting authorizations to act. With Secretary O'Rippley assumed to be dead, no one wants to assume responsibility for committing major resources," the overweight doctor whined.

Again Alexander's exasperation was apparent. Three hours of sleep in the last two days didn't help his disposition. Impaling Landry with a laser-like stare, Alexander spoke in a slow, measured, cold voice, "Doctor Landry. You'll inform Doctor Chin, and the rest of the DOE employees, that he is acting director. His orders will be obeyed. If you and Doctor Chin are not up to the job, I'll appoint someone who is. *Turf wars will not be tolerated.* Anyone engaging in a turf war—while our country is recovering from these attacks—will, at a minimum, be fired."

Alexander continued to stare at the doctor until he was sure Landry and the others got the message. Satisfied, he continued. "When this videotape is broadcast in the morning, I expect all hell to break loose in the Middle East," Sitting back in his chair, Alexander paused, then asked, "What about here—domestically? Let's hear your thoughts."

The men, mostly military officers, looked at each other. No one knew what to say; yet all had opinions. Finally, Barry Clark answered, "Mr. President, I think we must expect major riots, and the possibility of a Muslim insurgency—a blood bath of unparalleled proportions."

Silence prevailed throughout the room. After voicing everyone's worst fears, Clark continued, "From 2002 to 2004, we were able to closely monitor activities in many mosques. That ended last year with the election of President Hilda Rodman. The FBI suspects some mosques are centers for Islamic fundamentalists—meeting places for al-Qaeda, Hizbullah, and Hamas cells.

We're sure, although we lack sufficient proof for arrests, there are al-Qaeda, Hizbullah, and Hamas cells in the country. These cells may be ready to commit acts of terrorism on command. The videotape may well be that command. I expect some of the radical clerics to whip up their congregations. We may see riots by morning. I recommend placing police and FBI surveillance on all suspected mosques. We should alert local police to be prepared to deal with large scale riots."

Others in the room exchanged quick comments and glances, and then all nodded in agreement.

"Yes, I agree," Alexander said. "Colonel Young, alert the governors to activate their National Guard units. They are to prepare to cope with riots and potential Muslim insurrections.

"Barry, send a similar message to all FBI field offices and local police. Place surveillance on all suspected mosques. Riots, especially Muslim insurrections, must be put down quickly. Use whatever force is necessary. Law and order will be maintained in the country. Next, issue orders to take all suspected al-Qaeda members and sympathizers into custody. Hold them as terrorists—no bail and no lawyers.

"From now on, Colonel Young will act as my chief of staff," Looking at the clock, Alexander closed the meeting, "We'll meet here tomorrow at 0600 hours."

Colonel Young waited until the others left, then approached Alexander, "Mr. Secretary, I'm honored by your confidence in me. I only hope I'm up to the job you've given me. We've obtained temporary quarters for you here on the base. Your wife's there." Young was worried about his exhausted friend. Looking up at the taller man, he said, "Sir, it's 2115. You arrived at 0300, and went directly to the hospital to see your son. You've had only two or three hours sleep in the last two days. You have to get some rest. Tomorrow is going to be off the charts."

"Thank you, Charlie. I have two calls to make before I follow your advice. Please get the President of Russia, Nicholas Karpov, on the phone for me—then President Wu in Beijing."

Chapter 4

Nicholas Karpov, president of Russia for the past forty-five days, was also sleep deprived. Weeks earlier, a brewing scandal with the potential to reignite the cold war, forced major changes in Russia's leadership. Worried about Iran's progress toward developing an atomic bomb, a U.S. congressional committee began delving in to Russia's oh-so-friendly relationship with top Iranian leaders. What the committee found, after weeks of connecting the dots, was not a pretty picture. Russia was directly responsible for Iran's weapons buildup. By providing Iran technology required to produce weapons grade highly enriched uranium and plutonium, Russia had given the fox the keys to the henhouse. Knowing the congressional committee's findings would eventually be made public in a report, Russia's power brokers began scrambling to find a solution before the cold war reignited. The solution was simple: the premier resigned and Russia's president appointed Karpov to replace him. Karpov was selected because of his reputation in the West as a moderate and trustworthy man. Fluent in English, Karpov was well traveled in the West. After Karpov's appointment, the president resigned, and Karpov became the acting president. So far, the U.S. congressional report, scheduled for release in June, remained secret. Now, it may have disappeared with the city of Washington. Russian elections for a new president were scheduled for July. How Karpov dealt with this crisis would determine whether he retained his current job.

Karpov realized Russia could never reach an acceptable arrangement with Islam. Iran was taking all the goodies offered before biting the hand providing them. Karpov's job was to make peace with the U.S. He was informed of the Al-Jazeera video scheduled for broadcast at 10:00 p.m. Moscow time, and viewed the broadcast with several advisors. Muraaqibu al-Khawaatim's demeanor and intensity alarmed him. Before retiring for the night, he ordered an investigation to determine if the mad man's claims could be true. Two hours later, Karpov was awakened and informed of five nuclear detonations in the U.S. One detonation was considerably smaller than the others. *What will the American's reaction be? What would ours be, if the same thing happened here?* he wondered enroute to his underground bunker.

It soon became apparent that the U.S. government's entire command structure was disrupted. The U.S. ambassador in Moscow, a nervous, shallow, political appointee, could not reach Washington and was in a panic. Russia's foreign minister informed him of the attacks.

President Karpov was aware of the immediate danger caused by the destruction of U.S. government. American military commanders have great latitude and authority—more than those of any other nation. Now was not the time to take provocative actions—deliberate or otherwise. Orders were issued to cooperate fully with the U.S. military, to answer questions, to provide all available information; and in short, to demonstrate *by actions* that Russia was not involved in the attack. Two hours after the detonations, word reached Karpov that George Alexander, Secretary of Homeland Security, was being recognized as the acting American president.

Karpov sent for Alexander's complete dossier. Reading the file, Karpov learned that George Robert Alexander was born on November 29, 1953, in Raleigh, North Carolina. A highly intelligent man, Alexander graduated from North Carolina State University in 1975 with a Bachelor of Science degree in Nuclear Engineering, and an ROTC commission as a second lieutenant in the U.S. Air Force. Rising rapidly through the ranks, he retired as a major general in December of 2004 from his post as Deputy Director of the Defense Threat Reduction Agency (DTRA). His prior assignment was Commanding General of the Defense Special Weapons Agency's (DSWA) Field Command located on Kirkland AFB, in Albuquerque, New Mexico.

DTRA was formed by the merger of the On-Site Inspection Agency, the Defense Special Weapons Agency, the Defense Technology Security Administration, and some program functions of the Assistant for the Secretary of Defense for Nuclear, Chemical, and Biological Defense Programs. The civilian director of DTRA reported directly to the under secretary of Defense for Acquisition and Technology. President Rodman selected Alexander to be her Secretary of Homeland Security in March.

Karpov paused to consider the information provided by the file.

A GRU (Soviet military intelligence) report contained a transcript of a story Alexander told at a meeting, about his experiences in Iran, "I was in Tehran, Iran, when over three million Iranians took to the streets to welcome Ayatollah Khomeini. Khomeini stepped from his plane, and the smoldering Iranian revolution exploded through the country. In my nightmares, I can still hear the crowds rampaging through the streets chanting *Allahu Akbar*. Watching the mobs reminded me of a wall of muddy water rolling down a dry arroyo in New Mexico, after a violent rainstorm in the Sandia Mountains. Anyone foolish enough to camp in what appeared to be a dry creek bed would be swept away without warning—just like the mobs were sweeping away the Iranians' freedom."

Interesting, Karpov thought. *He may share my views of Islam.*

The GRU report suggested Alexander may have been romantically involved with a beautiful Iranian girl. Reports indicated he frequently visited her parent's home. The girl and her family were arrested during the upheaval surrounding the revolt—then tried by a religious court, and executed the same day. A note in the file highlighted this event, suggesting it may have influenced Alexander's opinion of, and attitude toward, Islam.

Karpov turned to the history portion of the file.

Alexander's training detachment was pulled out of Iran a few days after the mobs began rampaging through the streets; but not, according to statements he made later, before he saw the true face of Islam. A face he recognized was totally alien to Western philosophy.

Soon after returning to Wright Patterson AFB, Alexander's tour was completed, and he was assigned to the Air Force Weapons Laboratory at Kirkland AFB. He met his future wife, Jane Ellington, at a church function in Santa Fe, New Mexico. They were married a year later.

After completing his tour at Kirkland, Captain Alexander attended Harvard and obtained his master's degree in political science. His next assignment was assistant military attaché in Amman, Jordan. Major Alexander's experiences in Jordan and other nearby Arabian countries probably re-enforced the views he formed in Iran.

Following Jordan, Alexander was assigned to Special Operations at MacDill AFB, where he participated in several black ops. Next came a tour at the Pentagon, where Lieutenant Colonel Alexander was assigned to the Office of the Air Force Chief of Staff. Attracting the attention of the First Lady, he was assigned to the Office of the National Security Advisor in the White House. During this assignment, he learned how things were done in Washington, and gained an understanding of global politics.

After completing his White House assignment, Colonel Alexander became the Air Force Military Attaché in Riyadh, Saudi Arabia, where he gained additional understanding of the Arab and Islamic world. Next came National War College, his first star, and command of Field Command, DSWA.

The file contained several photographs, and Karpov selected two of them: a photo taken at Major General George Alexander's retirement, and his official photograph as Secretary of Homeland Security. Both photos showed a handsome, well-built man with close cropped, salt and pepper hair, wide set piercing blue eyes and a square jaw—a face that showed intelligence and determination. The file indicated that he was 188 centimeters tall and weighed ninety-one kilograms.

The dossier concluded with the statement that Alexander was an impatient man who demanded excellence from his subordinates—a man who brooked no incompetence, nor any bureaucratic nonsense at any level. Known to be a man of his word, all levels of the U.S. and NATO military held him in high regard. The State Department, however, disliked him because he was blunt and didn't pander to foreign officials. General Alexander was a leading expert on special weapons—nuclear, thermonuclear, chemical, biological, and special conventional ordnance—a man who fully understood the power of the U.S. arsenal and how to use it. President Karpov was well briefed on General Alexander by the time America's new leader called.

"Sir, President Nicholas Karpov is on line one," Colonel Young said, standing at Alexander's door.

Picking up the phone, Alexander spoke with authority, "President Karpov, I am George Alexander, Secretary of Homeland Security, and acting president of the United States. We have never met, and I regret having to call you at this early hour. I am sure you know the U.S. has been attacked with weapons of mass destruction—five nuclear bombs to be specific."

"The citizens of Russia and I send our deepest regrets and offer any assistance you may require," President Karpov replied in perfect English.

"Thank you, your concern is appreciated. We're still evaluating our situation. I don't expect an accurate assessment of the damage for several days.

"The purpose of my call is to introduce myself, and to inform you we have raised our defense posture to DEFCON 2. This is a defensive move. I am sure you will understand the reasons. The only information we have, as to who is responsible for the attacks, comes from two videos broadcast on Al-Jazeera. At this time we're working on the assumption we have suffered a terrorist attack."

"President Alexander, we have no information other than the two videotapes you referred to. I pledge to you our full cooperation. We will share with you any information we obtain that will help identify the terrorists. We have already begun sharing information with your military."

"Thank you for your offer and your cooperation. Of course we accept your offer. I want to assure you we have no reason to think Russia—or for that matter China—was in any way responsible for the attacks.

"Our two main concerns are the Middle East and North Korea. I fully expect the United States will soon be engaged in military operations in the Middle East—primarily to evacuate our personnel.

"I want you to clearly understand my orders to our military—they are to completely *destroy* any opposition. I have authorized the release of tactical nuclear weapons to area commanders. It is of utmost importance for you to caution your military not to take any unauthorized provocative actions that could trigger a nuclear counter attack by our forces. Accidents have started wars. Something none of us want to happen."

"Under the circumstances, I would do the same thing," Karpov replied. "I will issue specific orders to keep out of your way. Your reputation precedes you. The United States has proven itself to be a rational country. I take your assurances at face value. Thank you for taking time to call me. It is important for us to maintain direct contact," President Karpov said.

"I'll leave instructions for your calls to be put through with no delay— regardless of the time or circumstances. Good morning, Mr. President," Alexander said, ending the call.

Pressing the intercom button on his phone Alexander said, "Charlie, I'm ready for the second call."

Beijing, Peoples Republic of China – Saturday, 12:15 p.m., May 27th

It was mid-day in sunny Beijing, and President Wu's aide was reluctant to bother China's president for a call from a lowly secretary. The aide was aware of intelligence reports indicating Secretary Alexander was on his way out, and thus was a nobody, not worth President Wu's time. Alexander's call was shunted to Vice Minister Yan who was aware of the attacks on America.

"Secretary Alexander, I am Vice Minister Yan, of the Foreign Affairs Ministry. President Wu is unavailable. I wish to convey President Wu's condolences and sympathy for the attack on your country. How may I be of service?"

"Vice Minister Yan, I am now the acting President of the United States. It appears I am the senior surviving member of our government. I will become president once the deaths of President Rodman and the seven others senior to me are confirmed," Alexander said.

Alexander's statement shocked Yan who thought before responding, *How can this be true? I was briefed he was going to be fired. Yes, the American's do have a law setting succession—*

"The purpose of my call is to introduce myself and to make the People's Republic of China aware of our situation," Alexander continued, interrupting Yan's thoughts. "Five of our cities have been destroyed by nuclear detonations. At this time, we don't know who is responsible. A new spokesman for al-Qaeda has taken credit with two videos—one before the detonations, and one after.

"I have just completed a conversation with Russia's President Karpov. I wish to advise you of the facts I presented to him.

"First, we have no reason to think China or Russia was in any way responsible for the attack.

"Second, I have set our defense condition to DEFCON 2, released control of tactical nuclear weapons to area commanders, and ordered the evacuation of our personnel from the Middle East.

"Third, I have issued orders to destroy anyone who opposes our operations.

"It is very important that you caution your military not to take unauthorized provocative actions that could trigger a nuclear counter attack by our forces. Accidents have started wars … and that's something none of us wants."

A stunned vice minister sat staring at the telephone. How dare some unknown person talk to a representative of the PRC in such a crude, blunt, way? No diplomacy. "Mr. Secretary, you are obviously unacquainted with the proper protocol for communicating with a foreign government. In the future, I suggest you relay your thoughts through your ambassador. We will take them under advisement. Any rash actions by the U.S. could have serious consequences. We are a major power," Yan said in a huffy voice.

Alexander realized he was dealing with a diplomatic puke, a fool with no grasp of the situation. Deliberately pausing for five seconds, Alexander slowly and emphatically responded, "Mr. Vice Minister … you are correct, I am not a diplomat, so I will explain it to you this way. … The United States is at war. … Anyone foolish enough to precipitate a confrontation with us will be destroyed. *Totally destroyed … Do you understand?"*

Yan sat in silence for he could think of no reply. After a long pause, Alexander continued, "The purpose of my call is to prevent such an occurrence. Now, I suggest you relay my message to President Wu. I will call him tomorrow," Alexander said and hung up.

Yan heard the click. He was shocked, distraught, offended. *I've never been so insulted,* he fumed to himself, *I must advise President Wu.*

Alexander instructed Colonel Young to transmit a copy of both conversations to U.S. ambassadors in China and Russia.

Yan called President Wu and informed him of Alexander's phone call. Wu was not concerned with Yan's bruised ego. He recognized the danger of provoking an American reaction—especially a nuclear one. As soon as he was sure he'd extracted all of the details from the nearly hysterical Yan, he called Admiral Cheung, Commander of the Chinese People's Liberation Army Navy (PLAN) and instructed him to stand down, "Admiral, do nothing to provoke the Americans. Their new leader has informed Vice-Minister Yan he does not believe China had anything to do with the attack on his country. Do not give him a reason to think otherwise."

Cheung was not happy with his orders. *Our weak leader allowed himself to be intimidated by some retired Air Force general who was about to be fired from his job. We shall see about that. But … this may provide an opportunity for me to act. Yes … I must be patient and observe our weak president's actions. Patience is indeed a virtue,* a now smiling Cheung concluded.

10 Downing Street, London, England – 9:00 p.m., May 26th

The British government was alerted to the forthcoming Al-Jazeera videotape by their military attaché in Israel. Britain's prime minister, Sir Neville Chamberlain-Talbot, an extreme liberal who'd replaced Tony Blair, viewed the broadcast of the first videotape with his advisors at 7 p.m. He discounted it, scoffing that it was a joke. Two hours later, Talbot said, "Turn on the TV. We can watch the end of President Rodman's speech." At the end of her speech, conversation turned to other matters, while they watched the president of the United States exit the Capitol.

When the TV image of President Rodman walking toward her limousine abruptly changed to snow, and the BBC announced their loss of signal from the U.S., Chamberlain-Talbot's jocular dismissal turned to concern—followed by his first serious twinge of fear. *This cannot possibly be happening,* he thought as a chill raced up his spine. The meeting continued into the early morning hours while they waited for additional information.

MI-6 received a copy of the second video from the U.S. embassy in Qatar, and rushed it to 10 Downing Street. The prime minister and his advisors viewed the second al-Qaeda videotape an hour before acting President Alexander. An English translation was dubbed over the terrorist's voice. When the tape ended, an eerie silence filled the conference room. On any other day, a bombastic tape such as the one just viewed would have solicited heckles and jokes. Now the liberals were, for once, quite speechless. Word of the five nuclear detonations in the U.S., received fifteen minutes later, silenced even the left-wing idealists. Everyone was frightened—afraid, of the unknown future.

"Have we contacted the Americans?" Talbot finally asked.

"No," the Foreign Minister somberly replied. Washington has been destroyed. Their military is on full alert. We are trying to find out who is in charge. I am not sure they know."

"Sir, the situation is very serious," the minister of defense added. "We have reason to believe someone authorized the release of tactical nuclear weapons to U.S. area commanders. We have unconfirmed reports a General George Alexander, the Secretary of Homeland Security, has assumed the presidency. We also have a report he will address his nation later tonight," No one else spoke.

"Does anyone know where this Alexander is?" Talbot asked. Blank stares accompanied by shaking heads provided his answer.

"Suggestions? What are my options?" Talbot asked, his high-pitched voice betraying his fear.

The home secretary thought about raising the possibility of a Muslim revolt, or major terrorists acts in London and other cities, but decided to keep quiet. He was in no mood for another one of Talbot's lectures on the rights of Muslims.

News of Muraaqibu al-Khawaatim's first videotape spread like wildfire throughout Great Brittan's Muslim community. Speculation about the sudden interruption of the BBC's TV broadcast from Washington added fuel to the Muslim tinderbox.

"Do you think al-Khawaatim, the Keeper of the Rings, is responsible?" one Muslim asked.

"If he is, it's time for our jihad," another commented.

"Surely this is Allah's work. Muraaqibu al-Khawaatim must be His messenger," a third added.

"Praise Allah, for He has sent a mighty warrior to lead us," still another said. All agreed, if the Great Satan was humbled, it was time to begin the jihad in England.

As dawn broke in the Middle East millions of Muslims were awake, watching Al-Jazeera television or logged onto its web site. Twenty minutes before morning prayers in Qatar, the announcer stated a second tape from Muraaqibu al-Khawaatim would be broadcast in five minutes.

Chapter 5

Twilight was fading into darkness and the temperature was pleasant. Teresa Lopez was sitting in her sedan, with the windows down, when her cellphone softly played the William Tell Overture. The tune told her it was Isaac. Special Agent Isaac Calley had assumed the task of protecting the talented, beautiful young Teresa from The Twit. A task he often found beyond his ability. Special Agent Lopez and The Twit routinely clashed over issues, and it infuriated him that she was usually right.

"Hello, Isaac."

"Did you hear Secretary Alexander's address to the nation?"

"No. What did he say?"

"It's worse than we thought. Al-Qaeda broadcast a video two hours before the detonation. The man in the video said five nuclear bombs would be detonated—and they were. Alexander appears to be the new president. He's issued orders to protect our national security, closed all airports, sealed the borders, and sent orders to field offices—we got ours from Pittsburgh—take down all known and suspected terrorists cells."

"Well, I guess I've won another round with The Twit," Teresa responded tersely.

"No, no such luck. He's still coverin' his ass. He won't act. Not until he receives an order through the chain of command. Where are you?"

"I'm down the street from the mosque. Faysal Mosed and his merry band of terrorists have all arrived."

"Be careful. I'll join you in an hour."

Three hours later, as the clock approached midnight, Faysal Mosed and his terrorist cell members left the mosque. All six entered a dark-grey van and headed east on I-90. Isaac and Teresa had no problem following them, until they took the northbound exit onto State Road 63. "I think they're heading for the Iroquois Indian Reservation," Isaac observed.

Teresa dropped back, remaining just close enough to keep the van's taillights in sight. Had anyone in the van been paying attention, they'd have noticed the dark sedan tailing them. Fortunately, the terrorists were involved in animated discussion pertaining to their plan to contaminate Buffalo and the Peace Bridge—a major international bridge and border crossing into Canada.

Cresting a low hill, Teresa asked, "Where did they go? I don't see their tail lights."

"Speed up, we're losing them."

After two minutes of driving ninety mph, both decided the van must have turned off.

"Let's go back to where we lost them, and start looking for a turn off," Isaac suggested.

Returning to the top of the hill, Teresa turned the Ford Crown Victoria around and started back. "We were about half a mile behind them when they topped this hill. They must have turned off somewhere between here and the next half mile. Watch for a turnoff on your side and I'll do the same," Teresa said.

Three tenths of a mile later, Teresa spotted a dirt road. "There it is, Isaac. It's almost concealed by the roadside brush." Using the Law Enforcement Control switch, she extinguished the car's lights, turned, and drove across the culvert onto an overgrown trail—two tire tracks barely visible in the pale moonlight. Weed-chocked drainage ditches bordered both sides, isolating the trail from the fallow, weed and brush covered fields. Staying on the overgrown trail was difficult, and both leaned out their windows to see. Finally, the silhouette of a large building, illuminated by the van's headlights, appeared.

"I see a culvert ahead on my side. We can drive over it, hide the car in the field, then reconnoiter on foot," Teresa said as she drove over the culvert and into the tall weeds and brush. Carefully exiting the car to avoid being heard, they moved back toward the trail. Using their hands, they raised weeds flattened by the car entering the field.

"Stay here and watch my rear. I'll use the ditch as cover and move closer to see what they're doing. If I'm not back in thirty minutes, go back to the main road and call this in," Teresa whispered over her shoulder. Crouching low she moved silently in the ditch toward the building. *Damn, the mosquitoes are terrible.*

Half way to the building, a few dim lights came on, barely illuminating the entrance and interior of what appeared to be a barn. Startled by the lights, Teresa froze, then slowly lay down and peeked through the weeds. Listening intently, she could hear voices speaking what sounded like Arabic. Rising on her elbows for a better view, Teresa made out images of two vehicles. The van, parked to the right of the open barn doors, had its headlights on, illuminating the rear of a large box truck, parked at an angle to the entrance. The truck blocked Teresa's view of the barn's interior. From her vantage point, all she could see was the truck's underside and a terrorist's booted feet moving behind it inside the barn.

Cursing softly in Spanish, Teresa snaked forward for a better view.

Reaching a position providing a partial view of the truck's rear and the barn's interior, she was startled when floodlights flashed on inside the barn. Momentarily blinded by the brilliant blue-white light, Teresa ducked her head and froze. Straining to hear approaching footsteps, she flinched slightly at the *harrumphing* sound of an engine starting up inside the barn. Slowly raising her head, she silently sighed with relief. The booted feet were still inside the barn. With the engine's loud noise providing cover, she quickly scrambled forward for a better look inside the barn's brightly illuminated interior.

The noisy engine belonged to a forklift a terrorist was maneuvering to pick up the first of three pallets of boxes. The machine obscured the labels on the boxes, but when it turned to place the pallet in the box truck, Teresa gasped. "*Cristo,*" she whispered, "Dynamite! Enough to blow up half of Buffalo." Shaken by what she'd seen, it took a moment before the frenzied motion of several men at the rear of the barn caught her attention. *What the hell are those guys doing to the rear wall?* she wondered, crawling forward for closer view. Using crowbars, four terrorists were ripping planking away from the barn's rear wall. *There must be something behind the wall. Whatever it is, I bet they plan to use it with the dynamite. Hey, what's that guy in the boots doing?* One set of boots walked around the rear of the truck and into the beam of the van's headlights. *It's Faysal, and he has an AK-47.*

Aware of her bad situation, Teresa tensely watched Faysal swing the AK-47 in an arc in front of the barn. Abruptly turning, Faysal yelled something and another man, also armed with an AK-47, joined him. Receiving orders from Faysal, the man began walking back and forth in front of the barn. *Damn! Time to call this in. I'm out of here.* As soon as the guard turned to walk in the opposite direction, Teresa quickly snaked backwards a few yards into the ditch. After taking a last peek, she turned around, rose to a crouch, and quietly made her way back to her point of entry.

"Isaac ... where are you?" she whispered, clambering out of the ditch. Relived to see him hunkered in the weeds, his white teeth sparkling in the light of the three-quarter moon, she whispered with a smile, "Christ you're hard to see in the dark."

"Bein' black do have 'vantages. Don't it?" Isaac joked, swatting a mosquito.

Teresa chuckled. "They have AK-47s and a truck load of dynamite. We gotta call this in." Quietly entering the sedan, Teresa turned it around and prayed the sagging culvert wouldn't collapse as the heavy car rolled across. After raising the weeds, Isaac hurried across and joined her. "*Madre de Dios,* I hope they don't hear us," Teresa muttered. Reaching the main road, she drove north for a quarter mile, stopped, opened her cellphone, and speed dialed the FBI duty officer.

"I can't help you Teresa. I'm under orders to direct your calls to

Whitwell. I'm afraid he's really after your ass this time," the duty officer told her.

Cursing softly, Teresa jabbed the "End" key on her phone—then sat for several seconds, fuming and staring into the darkness. Finally, facing the inevitable, she grimaced and punched Whitwell's speed dial number. When he answered, Teresa tried briefing him, but Whitwell cut her off, "What the hell ah you doin'. I tol' you, you'wah suspended. Now I'm gonna have you'wah badge. You'wah out of heyah—*GONE*," The Twit hissed. "I've been waitin' a long time fo'wah you to disobey my awduhs, and now you have. Get back heyah immediately and turn in you'wah badge and gun."

Extremely pissed, Teresa gritted her teeth. She'd had enough. Snapping her phone shut, she turned to Isaac, and mocked The Twit, "That idiot just 'awduhed' me to turn in my badge and gun. The country's been attacked with nuclear weapons, and he's only interested in his vendetta. To hell with him. Let's take these bastards down. I'm calling Colonel Butterfield. Maybe we can get help from the National Guard."

By spending many weekends training—on her own time—with the National Guard's anti-terrorist maneuvers, Teresa had established a good working relationship with Guard leaders. Selecting the National Guard listing from her phone's menu, she pushed "Send."

"Second Brigade, 43rd Infantry Division, Captain Timothy Yondell speaking," came the response.

"Tim, it's Teresa. I need to speak with the colonel ASAP."

"Teresa, we just received a warning order. I'm sure you know about New York, Washington, Atlanta, Chicago and Boston being nuked," Yondell said.

"Boston *too*? My God Tim, we're at war—but with whom? Look, I've got six terrorists staked out in a barn, north of I-90 on Route 63. They're loading boxes of dynamite into a truck, and digging something out of a hidden room in the back of a barn. I think they plan to load whatever it is onto a truck along with the dynamite. I need help stopping them. They'll be moving by dawn."

"What's wrong with your SWAT team?"

"Tim, the SAC has fired me for monitoring the mosque without permission from Washington. It's just Isaac and me out here in the middle of a field, with six terrorists armed with AK-47s."

"Hold on while I brief the colonel."

Several minutes later, after what seemed an eternity to Teresa and Isaac, Colonel Butterfield came on the line, "Tell me what you've got Teresa."

Teresa carefully reported the events, starting with tailing the van, and ending with her call to the SAC. "Colonel, I don't know what's behind that wall their tearing down, but whatever it is, I think they plan to load it on that truck, take it somewhere and blow it up. If these fanatics get their truck into the city, there's no telling how much damage they'll cause. We need help right now."

Colonel Butterfield knew Whitwell and appreciated Teresa's position. Under ordinary circumstances, he wouldn't interfere, but these were not ordinary circumstances. "Find a position north of the farm road on Route 63. If they leave, call me immediately. First Platoon of B Company has drawn weapons and ammo. I'll send them now. When they reach Route 63, I'll call you. Meet them south of the farm road. I think an ambush is the best tactic. I'll notify the explosive ordnance disposal and the HAZMAT teams. No telling what's behind the wall. I'll also notify the Highway Patrol and have them block I-90 east, and west of Route 63. Additional support will follow."

Ninety-seven minutes later, Teresa and Isaac met the reinforced first platoon commanded by Captain Timothy Yondell, south of the hilltop where they'd first lost sight of the terrorist's van. Sgt. Merideth and two men with night vision goggles were sent with Special Agent Calley to establish an observation post (OP) near the barn. After a brief discussion, Teresa suggested herding cows, presently grazing in the adjacent field, onto the road—positioning them just over the crest of the hill. Ropes would be rigged across the road to contain the animals. Just before the truck reached the top of the hill, the ropes would be pulled back to allow the cows to flee. The truck would either run into the cows, or stop. Either way Teresa's plan would work. The terrorists would have to get out to move the cows.

Following Teresa's plan, the Guard established firing positions. A squad with a light machine gun, an old LAW rocket launcher, and claymore mines was positioned south of the ambush site. If the truck did manage to get through, their orders were to stop it at all cost.

By 5:45 a.m., the ambush was set. Twenty minutes later, the OP reported the truck was pulling out, followed by the van. Two terrorists were in the truck, and the remaining four in the van. The OP previously reported seeing several cases of explosives loaded onto the truck. Then the forklift removed what appeared to be a very heavy crate from a room concealed behind a false interior barn wall. After the heavy crate was loaded onto the truck, the remainder of the explosives were loaded. One of the terrorists placed detonators in several locations in the explosives, and then connected detonator wires to a box. Once the truck's rear door was locked, the terrorists spread rugs on the ground and knelt on them. Chanting in Arabic, they pressed their heads to the ground and prayed for several minutes.

The EOD team arrived and was briefed. All that remained was for the truck and van to encounter the cows.

A jubilant Faysal turned the overloaded truck south onto Rt. 63. *Today I will go to paradise. Will Allah himself welcome me? Will I meet the brave warriors who gave their lives to destroy the Great Satan's cities? Surely my* *brothers and I will be the most honored of all.* Lost in his fantasy of martyrs, 72[*] virgins, and the luscious taste of tiny sweet dates, dripping with honey, Faysal crested the hill at a high rate of speed. As the headlights dropped, Faysal was snapped back to reality by two startled cows standing in the middle of the road—their woeful eyes shining in the headlights. Faysal blinked, desperately trying to reconcile his fleeting impression of hundreds of cows milling around in the darkness behind the first two. He instinctively stomped the brake pedal, but it was too late. After striking the first cow, Faysal frantically jerked the wheel to the right and drove into the ditch.

Like Faysal, the van's driver was also euphoric over their mission. Caught off guard by the truck's abrupt stop when the van slammed into the rear of the truck, the driver was knocked unconscious. Bloodied and stunned by the impact, the van's passengers were momentarily dazed.

Uninjured, Faysal and Yassin jumped out of the truck, and scrambled up the ditch bank to assess the damage. Once clear of the ditch, both were illuminated with spotlights and ordered by amplified bullhorn to freeze. Yassin, fired a quick burst from his AK-47 at a spotlight, and was cut down by M-16 fire. Faysal attempted to draw a pistol and was severely wounded. The three terrorists in the van saw the spotlights and reacted by exiting it with blazing AK-47s. All were cut down by M-16 and light machine gun fire.

The cows stood frozen by the sound of the truck's squalling tires and the van's subsequent impact. Some skittered backwards on the hard pavement, but most simply stared in consternation at the wrecked vehicles. All that changed when the shooting started. The sound of rifle and machine gun fire panicked the beasts, sending them bolting helter-skelter into the night, bellowing and spraying dung in all directions.

"Stampede," shouted Private Johnson, who was from Wyoming.

"Incoming," added another.

The second squad, entrenched along the fence line, barely escaped being trampled by part of the herd. The remainder escaped by charging down the middle of the road.

"Anyone hurt?" the sergeant yelled once the din of gunfire, thundering hooves, and bellowing died down.

"Only if you count being hit by flying cow dung," someone answered in disgust.

"Johnson, get the hell over there and see to that poor beast in the road. Put her out of her misery, if you have to, but get her off the road. The EOD team has to get past her. The rest of you disarm the driver and make sure the

---

[*] 70 or 72 *houris* (virgins) have become accepted folklore. The author has found several references to *houris* in Paradise in the Qur'an, but no specific number is given.

others are dead," the sergeant ordered, pointing to Faysal lying wounded on the road, his autoloading pistol still within reach.

While the rest of his squad advanced with guns ready toward the terrorist, Johnson hunkered beside the stricken cow. After cautiously poking her with his gun, he gently laid his hand on her, out-stretched, twisted neck. "She's gone, Sarge. I think her neck's broken."

"Good, at least she didn't suffer. Now get on with it. Use a vehicle to move the carcass, then tow the van away, so the EOD team can get to the truck," the sergeant grimaced, grateful one dead cow was their only casualty.

Once Faysal's pistol had been recovered, and he'd been searched for additional weapons, a medic applied a field bandage to his shoulder. A bullet had passed through, leaving a nasty exit wound in his back. The four dead terrorists and the unconscious van driver were also searched and disarmed.

As soon as the van was moved, Captain Yondell called for the EOD team. After cutting the padlock securing the truck's rear door, two senior Army EOD team members checked for booby traps, opened the roll-up door, and entered. Thirty minutes later, they'd disarmed the explosives, removed several cases of 60 percent dynamite, and exposed a wooden crate sitting on additional boxes of dynamite. No wires were attached to the crate.

"It appears the explosives were meant to blow up the crate. I think this is a dispersal device," the lieutenant commanding the EOD team said. "Before we open it, I suggest we bring in radiological and biological experts."

Chapter 6

Saturday

Saturday Morning – worldwide prayers

E-mail messages announcing the detonation of five atomic bombs in the Great Satan, and calling for the Great Worldwide Jihad to begin, were sent by the *Shura*. Attached to each message was a suggested sermon.

In the name of Allah, the most compassionate, the most merciful. Allah has blessed us and given us the power to reclaim our holy lands. The power to have a Palestine without Jews. The power to spread Islam throughout the Western world. The power to establish true Islamic governments—an Islamic Empire.

The Great Satan attacked and destroyed the true Islamic State of Afghanistan. Attacked the Islamic State of Iraq. Desecrated our holy land and sacred places. Supported the Little Satan—the evil Jews in Israel.

Allah has told us in surah 74:26, 'Soon will I fling them into the burning Hell Fire! It permits nothing to endure, and nothing does it spare! It darkens the color of a man, burning the skin! It shrivels and scorches men.'

Allah has kept His promise. With Allah's blessing and guidance, our brother Muraaqibu al-Khawaatim succeeded in planting five atomic bombs in the belly of five of the Great Satan's cities.

By Allah's command, these five atomic bombs have been detonated. The Great Satan has fallen to its knees. It is time for the faithful in the Great Satan and in Europe to rise up and convert the infidels to the true faith. It is time to impose sharia on these godless lands. It is time for the Great Satan to become an Islamic nation. It is time for all infidels to embrace the true faith, to submit to Allah's will, or perish.

Many leaders of Islamic countries have strayed from Allah's path. The rulers of Saudi Arabia and Jordan and their vile families are contaminated with Western ideals. They have defamed the Prophet's teachings. They must be punished for their sins. The same is true of the rulers of other Islamic states. Go forth today and cast out these vile rulers. Establish true Islamic states like Iran—and Afghanistan, now that it is again ruled by the Taliban.

Allah has demonstrated his approval of our Great Jihad, He has blessed the efforts of His servant, Muraaqibu al-Khawaatim. Now it is time for our Palestinian brothers to rise up and slaughter the hated Jews. Now it is time for all brother Muslims to support the Palestinians in their jihad against the Little Satan.

By the will of Allah, today we will begin to throw the infidels from our lands.

With the blessings of Allah, it is time to follow our new caliph. Time to begin doing God's work.

Clerics in many countries began updating sermons to be delivered at morning prayers.

As the time for morning prayers approached, the faithful, many who'd just viewed Muraaqibu al-Khawaatim's second video, began gathering at mosques around the world. While crowds formed, tension crackled in the air like tentacles of static electricity. Then, as the sun moved westward, calls to prayer sounded, and mosques filled to capacity—worshipers overflowing into adjoining streets. Hundreds of millions of Muslims awaited their cleric's pronouncements.

Saudi Arabia – early morning, May 27th

Led by radical clerics, the faithful in Riyadh, Saudi Arabia poured from mosques and headed for the royal palace. Other mobs targeted Western embassies and housing compounds. Surging through the streets, the mobs were reminiscent of Alexander's description of the Iranian revolution, and like rushing muddy water rushing down a dry arroyo, the Saudi mobs had the same effect —nothing and no one stood in the path of their fury.

With deafening chants of *Allahu Akbar,* mobs descended upon the royal palace and Western embassies. Security forces were caught off guard—most of them quickly overwhelmed. Alerted to the pending attack by Colonel Sam Combs, the U.S. Embassy's marine guard was prepared. However, the ambassador placed limits on their defensive capabilities. Only the American and British embassies were on alert, but that only delayed their slaughter for ten bloody hours. Communications were out with the U.S. and British governments. Unable to cope with the exploding situation, the American ambassador froze, choosing instead to wait for Saudi protection. None was forthcoming. For a time the Marines held the gate and walls, but eventually were forced to retreat into the embassy. Unable to halt the frenzied mob, they were finally overrun, and all personnel were butchered.

Another mob attacked foreign housing areas. By nightfall, the Saudi royal family and most foreigners throughout the kingdom were dead. A few survivors found refuge in homes of friendly Saudis. The carnage made the Iranian revolution look tame by comparison. Similar events took place in Iraq, Yemen, Sudan, Tunisia, Algeria, Morocco, Libya, Egypt. Unrest in Pakistan, Turkey, and Indonesia was growing.

Europe – early morning, May 27th

In Paris, government officials were awakened and informed of the attacks on five American cities. No senior French officials had viewed Muraaqibu al-Khawaatim's first video. Nor were they aware of the second one. No offers to help America's ravaged cities were forthcoming. Instead, discussions centered around America's probable irrational response. How, they wondered, could France benefit by playing its usual role as America's chief critic? Discussions were in full swing when morning prayers ended. Inflamed by clerics, several million angry, rampaging Muslims charged from their mosques and swarmed through Paris and its suburbs. Catching French police completely off guard, the mobs began a slaughter unequaled since the French Revolution. Similar uprisings began throughout Europe.

Israel – early morning, May 27th

Israel was better prepared. Alerted by the first al-Qaeda videotape, and the pending broadcast of the second one, Israel's military was on full alert. When U.S. military attaché, Colonel Sam Combs, confirmed five nuclear bomb detonations, Israel ordered a full call-up of reserves. Early Saturday morning, when the first fanatics charged from their mosques in the West Bank and Gaza Strip, they encountered a fully prepared Israeli Defense Force (IDF). This time there would be no restrictions, no liberal press, no American politicians to scream foul. The mobs were mowed down in the streets. Unfortunately this was only the beginning.

The Syrian Army, which was conducting major maneuvers in the south, wheeled west and began an approach toward the Golan Heights and the Jordanian border. It was time for King Ali of Jordan to choose sides.

Egypt – early morning, May 27th

Before dawn in Cairo, a group of army and air force officers awakened Egypt's president. "What is the meaning of this?" he demanded.

"Sir," one of the generals replied, "al-Qaeda has made good on their boast. They've detonated five nuclear weapons in the United States. A worldwide call for the Great Jihad has been issued. Muslims are rising up to retake our sacred lands from the infidels and return them to Islam. We are asking you to order an immediate attack on Israel, while the Great Satan is impotent. Sir—"

"What did you say?" the president shouted, interrupting the general in mid sentence. "Did you say al-Qaeda detonated five nuclear bombs in the United States?"

"Yes, sir. The Great Satan is—"

"*Is what* you fool?" the president shouted, again overriding the general. "Do you think five nuclear bombs can disable the U.S.? Are you *insane*? It will only make them angry. They will be looking for someone to retaliate against. Are you suggesting we volunteer to be nuked?" The president asked, so angry he was shaking.

This was not what the generals wished to hear. Plans were underway. The army and air force were being mobilized for a thrust into Israel. Aircraft were being manned for the first strike. The generals hoped their president would join them. Now it was apparent he would not. While the president shouted at their spokesman, a colonel moved behind him. At a nod from the senior general, the colonel drew his .22-caliber autoloading pistol and fired two hollow point rounds into the back of the president's head.

Egypt would attack Israel from the southwest, while Syria attacked from the north and northeast. The six-day war would be replayed, this time without U.S. interference.

Well, that's what the plan said.

Chapter 7

At 0515 hours Colonel Young, exhausted from staying up all night, knocked several times on Alexander's bedroom door. Finally getting a response from Jane Alexander, he told her through the door, "You must get him up. He has a meeting in forty-five minutes."

Colonel Young had sent a team to Alexander's house north of Santa Fe to retrieve clothes for the general and his wife. Thirty minutes later, Alexander, wearing a light tan suit, entered a staff car for the short ride to a building being transformed into a temporary White House. Inside the building, Alexander stopped at a table in the outer office for a doughnut and a cup of black coffee. Entering the conference room, he took his place at the head of the table. The room was packed with men and women, some in uniform, others in civilian clothes. Several wore rumpled clothing. Most had coffee cups. Stubble was visible on many men's faces. It had been a long, sleepless, night. Alexander took a sip of coffee and studied the expectant faces before him. Calling the meeting to order, he asked Colonel Young, who'd manned the command center all night, to provided a summary of events.

Colonel Young stood, walked to the far end of the conference table and began, "Messages received from American embassies in the Middle East all say they were under attack by mobs. The *Kennedy* Strike Group has only been able to establish contact with American embassies in Qatar, Israel, Jordan, and the UAE. Israel is on full alert and has issued a call-up of reserves. The IDF is engaging mobs storming their borders. There is fighting in the streets in numerous cities in Israel and Jordan. STRATCOM reports movements of the Syrian and Egyptian armies, which probably means a two-pronged attack on Israel. A major Muslim uprising occurred in Paris—apparently a real blood bath. Our London embassy reports Prime Minister Talbot has called an emergency cabinet meeting. They're having problems with their Muslims too."

A couple of startled gasps were heard. Barry Clark nervously worked a pencil through the fingers of his left hand. Concern obvious on his face.

"Have we established contact with the CIA?" Alexander asked in a calm voice.

"Admiral Vazquez has established communication with the CIA and is obtaining direct inputs from them. He requested that they establish who is senior, and have him or her report directly to you. The admiral's deputy is enroute here to establish a direct liaison office. We have satellite feed and military communications have been restored."

"What is the domestic situation?" Alexander inquired.

"DOE has established command posts with the National Guard near each bombed city. State National Guards have blocked highways and ordered people trying to evacuate undamaged areas to return to their homes. Doctor Landry is on his way to Los Alamos to meet with Doctor Chin. The military, Red Cross, Salvation Army, and FEMA are beginning to coordinate their efforts. Local hospitals are swamped. I authorized the Army to send transportable surgical hospitals, tents, blankets and MREs to support the rescue efforts," Colonel Young replied. "FEMA will concentrate on providing shelter for evacuees. The Red Cross and other organizations will help with food and clothing. The Red Cross is organizing a nationwide blood drive. It's too early to determine a death toll. Air Force photoreconnaissance flights over the five cities will begin at 0700. We'll have copies by 1200," Colonel Young answered.

"What about the press. They will want copies. How much can we release, or should we release?" Barry Clark asked, still fingering the pencil in his left hand.

"Good question," Alexander replied. "I have no intention of withholding information from the public. They have to understand how badly we've been hit. On the other hand, we must conceal the extent of the damage from our enemies. President Roosevelt must have faced the same dilemma after the Pearl Harbor attack. What are your thoughts?"

"Sir," Colonel Young responded, "I suggest we release aerial photos and video of the death and destruction in Boston. This will convey the extent of the damage to the public, without providing information on Atlanta, Chicago, New York, or Washington to our enemies."

Clark, and the others at the table nodded in agreement. Alexander paused to take a bite of doughnut. His eyes scanned the men and women seated around the table, searching for signs of repressed comments or disagreement. Finding none, he washed the doughnut down with a sip of coffee and said, "Okay, Boston it is. Good work, Charlie. As soon as this meeting is over, get some sleep. That's an order," Alexander said with a slight smile to soften the order. Then he continued, "It goes without saying that every element of the government will provide all available assistance to the relief efforts. Now we must deal with other serious problems. We probably have a banking and credit card crisis. Banks and credit card companies communication links have been interrupted and they can't process transactions."

"Barry, have you been here all night too?" Alexander asked, noting how tired Clark looked.

"Yes Mr. President," Clark replied, suddenly conscious of the sweat stains under his armpits and his unbuttoned shirt collar and pulled down tie.

"It's still too early for the Mr. President bit," Alexander said with a frown. "Barry, as soon as this meeting is over, detail someone from your office to fill in for you—then *go home* and get at least six hours sleep. Sleep deprivation will cause us to make mistakes. Instruct your office to locate a senior member of the Federal Reserve banking system. Have him or her report to me as quickly as possible." Alexander noticed a sergeant standing at the door and motioned for him to enter.

"Mr. Secretary," the sergeant said, entering the room, "I have New Mexico's Governor on the phone. He is requesting a meeting with you."

"Thank you, sergeant. Ask Governor Richards to come as soon as he can."

Alexander turned back to the participants in the room and continued, "I want to thank all of you for your help, especially those who were here all night. My orders to Colonel Young and Mr. Clark apply to all of you. Turn your jobs over to someone qualified. Go home. Get some sleep. You'll be needed here later, and you must be fit and clear headed. Solving our problems will take a long time. Recovery will depend on forming teams, providing them with the resources and authority to deal with specific problems, and letting them do their jobs. Each of you will have a role to play."

Alexander paused for another bite from his doughnut and a swallow of coffee, then continued. "Now Barry, what has happened domestically regarding the Muslims and al-Qaeda?"

"I received reports, starting at 6 a.m. east coast time, that large crowds were gathering around mosques in Buffalo, Richmond, Tampa, and Miami. In the last hour, I've received similar reports from Detroit, Pittsburgh, Cleveland, Columbus, Oklahoma City, and Tucson. A local TV station is broadcasting from a position near a mosque in Detroit. We're trying to obtain feed."

Tension in the room escalated. Several expressed shock, some anger. Like most Americans, the concept of a revolt by dissidents within the country was unthinkable. Now the unthinkable was happening. After a brief pause to allow the grumbling to subside, Young continued his briefing.

"Nationwide raids by the FBI and local police on known al-Qaeda groups netted a large number of potential terrorists." Clark smiled. "It appears we caught some having meetings—planning attacks. A National Guard unit and the FBI captured a cell near Buffalo with a radioactive dispersal bomb." Clark sighed and frowned. "The bad news is we missed some of the most dangerous ones. In several instances, there was no trace of our quarry. Local police have been very cooperative in most cities, but we've experienced some problems."

"What kind of problems?" Alexander asked leaning forward and placing his hands, palms-down, on the tabletop.

Startled by Alexander's sudden movement, Clark reminded himself that Alexander wasn't a typical Washington bureaucrat. *This man's a serious player. He won't stand for any bullshit,* Clark decided, looking at the intense man who was now president, "The mayors of San Francisco and Oakland prohibited local police from assisting. Both claimed we were violating the accused rights and demanded we go before a grand jury for indictments. The SACs of both cities acquiesced to the mayors and didn't perform any raids."

A scowling Alexander responded, "This is unacceptable. We need a strong agent in charge. Who can you recommend to take over a combined San Francisco-Oakland office?"

Clark thought for a moment then said, "Sean Kilpatrick, in Salt Lake City would be a good choice. His deputy, Roslyn Baker is qualified to take over the Salt Lake office."

Pointing to the telephone, Alexander instructed Clark to call Kilpatrick. Clark opened his notebook, found Kilpatrick's home phone number and quickly dialed it.

Sean Kilpatrick, a large, fit man of forty-five years, was at the kitchen door leading to his garage when the phone rang. Returning to the kitchen counter, he answered the remote phone, "Special Agent Kilpatrick."

"Sean, this is Barry Clark in Albuquerque."

Kilpatrick knew Barry Clark was issuing orders under authority of the Secretary of Homeland Security, a man named Alexander, who appeared to be in line to assume the presidency. He also knew Washington, DC had been destroyed, along with most of the government. For some reason, Alexander wasn't there. Kilpatrick's deputy had followed Clark's instructions regarding terrorists and taken five al-Qaeda suspects into custody. Kilpatrick remembered Clark as a thin man, around five-feet ten-inches, with light brown hair, and a receding hairline—a quiet man who always seemed to be on top of things. The son of a Montana cattleman, Clark was married and had four children. "What can I do for you, Barry?" Kilpatrick said.

"Sean, I'm in a conference room at Kirkland Air Force Base with Secretary Alexander, who is the acting president. I'm going to put you on the speaker phone."

"Mr. Kilpatrick," Alexander said in his usual low, calm voice, "as I'm sure you know, we've been attacked, and we're operating under emergency provisions. I'm organizing the government and taking actions to protect our country. Last night, the SACs in Oakland and San Francisco failed to follow orders to arrest all known al-Qaeda terrorists in their jurisdiction. The mayors of San Francisco and Oakland objected and the SACs acquiesced. You are to proceed immediately to San Francisco, relieve both SACs, and assume their positions. The Oakland office is now part of your expanded office. Barry tells me your deputy, Roslyn Baker, is capable of taking over your position, and so she shall. One of the officers here will contact you and arrange for an Air Force plane to fly you to San Francisco. Once you've relieved the current SACs, you'll attempt to capture all known and suspected Islamic terrorists. If either of the mayors causes a problem, arrest them. Do you have any questions?"

Kilpatrick, a man of action, instantly recognized Alexander as a strong, decisive leader, and began to evaluate the task set before him. After a long pause, he replied, "Only one. Do I report to Mr. Clark?"

"Good question. Yes, Barry Clark will be the acting FBI director until we sort out who is on first base," Alexander said, again demonstrating his ability to make fast, important decisions—a leadership trait that inspired others to follow him. Turning to Clark, Alexander continued, "Barry, call the SACs in Oakland and San Francisco and tell them they're relieved. Their number twos will be in charge until the new SAC, Sean Kilpatrick, arrives. If there are any questions or objections, let me know. Mr. Kilpatrick, if you have no more questions, Barry Clark will call you at your office in an hour to finalize arrangements for your transfer."

"No questions, sir."

After ending the call, Alexander turned back to Colonel Young, "Charlie, arrange for an armed squad of military police to accompany Mr. Kilpatrick to his new office in San Francisco. That will establish his authority. Next, assign one of your officers to contact the FCC and determine who is in charge. Then issue orders for that person to take any necessary steps to reestablish national public communications. We must be able to communicate with our people— keep them informed. Also, I'll need a senior public affairs officer." Alexander settled back in his chair, took another bite of doughnut, with a slug of his now-cold coffee, and surveyed the others in the room. Earlier in the meeting Alexander had observed several new faces and assumed they would identify themselves at the appropriate time.

"Now, logistics. I'll need a building for my headquarters and additional buildings for staff. Suggestions?" he asked looking around the room for answers. In response, a thin Air Force brigadier general stood. "Mr. Secretary, I'm James Ross, and I've taken responsibility for obtaining space for you. The old Sandia Base portion of Kirkland appears to be the best choice. I've directed Sandia Labs to vacate a building. With your approval, we'll relocate your offices to Building 600, a large building with one entrance and no windows. Other buildings will be made available as required. If you approve, we can begin making arrangements immediately."

"Thank you, General Ross. Building 600 will do nicely for my situation room and command center. For now, I'll also keep my current office in this building." Alexander paused to think, *So much to do. I'll need a State Department, a Defense Department, a staff,* then continued, "Concentrate on establishing communications with Admiral Vazquez. Establishing secure communication with his command is a top priority. We'll need a building for an interim State Department, another for Intelligence, and another for Defense. When time permits, I'll select a building to serve as the White House. Kirkland is secure, and the old Monsanto Base tunnels and igloos provide a safe refuge and storage area. For the present, the new capital will be here"

Noting the confused look on several of the civilian faces, Alexander explained, "Monsanto Base was once a national stockpile storage site for nuclear warheads. It's surrounded by several chain link fences. Tunnels go deep into the mountain, and the storage igloos have two-ton steel doors. A perfect bomb shelter should we need one."

Turning back to Colonel Young, Alexander asked, "Is the young captain, your executive officer, here?"

"Yes, sir. Captain Taylor. Shall I get him?"

"Have him report to me as soon as this meeting is over. He's been involved since the beginning, and can assist me while you get some sleep."

Thirty minutes later Captain Julian Taylor reported to Alexander who was sitting behind his desk in shirtsleeves. Standing at attention, Captain Taylor saluted. "No need to salute a civilian, Captain," Alexander said, looking up from a document and smiling at the young captain. "You did a good job coordinating the information from our embassies. I want you to fill in for Colonel Young for the next few hours. First, Governor Richards is on his way here. When he arrives, he's to receive a complete briefing on the situation, everything we know. After he's briefed, I'll meet with him.

"Second, have the FBI locate General Harry Simpson, the former Chairman of the Joint Chiefs of Staff. I want to speak to him when they find him. Then I'll want the Air Force to fly him here ASAP.

"Third, make sure a senior Federal Reserve member is on his or her way here."

"Yes, sir, I'll take care of it. The FBI has located a Ms. Nora Jacobson, a senior executive with the Fed in Dallas. She should be here later today."

"Thank you, Captain. What is your Christian name?"

"Julian, sir."

"Keep me posted Julian. Finding General Simpson is a top priority. Now who has been taking calls from other countries?"

"Colonel Young took most of them. He noted their comments and concerns and told them you would speak with them as soon as possible. Here is his log, sir," Captain Taylor said handing Alexander a three ring binder.

Chapter 8

Jordan – Saturday morning, May 27th

Earlier in the day, in a different time zone, King Ali bin Hussein of Jordan faced a monumental decision. The American embassy confirmed the U.S. had been attacked with nuclear weapons. Now he was being informed of Syria's intention to attack Israel—through Jordan. The young king was furious. *I will not repeat my father's mistake. In June, 1967, he allowed Egyptian and Iraqi forces to attack Israel from Jordon's West Bank. Any country foolish enough to attack Israel, after the United States has been nuked, courts disaster—no, total annihilation. What are these fools thinking? Jordan has finally established good relations with Israel. They've placed me in the position of either joining in the attack, or defending the Jews. Some unknown idiot has taken credit for attacking America. He's proclaimed himself caliph, of all things. Now the radical clerics are beating the war drums. Mobs tried to attack my palace and the Western embassies. They didn't last long, but it turned into a bloodbath. Muslims spilling Muslim blood. If I must choose, my decision must be based upon what is best for my people. Attacking Israel is not only impossible to justify, it would be suicide. I know George Alexander who's apparently America's new president. He's no one to trifle with. If the U.S. government has been destroyed as reported, Alexander has almost unlimited authority—a fact not understood by my distant cousin in Syria. Alexander will use his power to protect his country and its allies. My choice is made. I must prevent Syria from entering Jordan—by force of arms if necessary. I must inform the U.S. and British ambassadors of my decision, and then tell my cousin to stay out of Jordan.*

Syria – Saturday morning, May 27th

Mohammed al-Asad, president of the Syrian Arab Republic, was not pleased to receive King Ali's reply. Syria, a country of eighteen million—seventy-five percent of whom are Sunni Muslims—is slightly larger than North Dakota. It borders the Mediterranean Sea between Lebanon and Turkey. Part of the Ottoman Empire until its breakup, Syria was administered by France until it gained independence in 1946, and became part of the United Arab Republic. In 1963, it became a separate republic under military control.

Mohammed al-Asad succeeded his father, Hafez al-Asad as president on June 20, 2000. A member of the Ba'th party, he was elected president by obtaining ninety-seven percent of the vote.

Remembering his election, al-Asad felt piqued. *Saddam was elected with one hundred percent of the vote and a one hundred percent turnout,* he silently grumbled. *Now that pussy in Jordan wants to play games. It's time to deal with the Western puppet.* Turning to his aide he said, "Instruct the army to proceed through Jordan. Crush any resistance offered by their feeble army. When they have reached the attack point, notify me."

Jordanian-Syrian border – Saturday afternoon, May 27th

Jordan's Army began assembling. Infantry and armor units mobilized toward the Syrian border. Jordan's Air Force launched F-5E photoreconnaissance aircraft to assess the Syrian positions, and F-16s to patrol the border. News of Muraaqibu al-Khawaatim's first video spread like wildfire throughout the military. News of the second tape was spreading. "Why are we facing our Syrian brothers, when we should be doing God's work and killing the hated Jews?" some asked. Mutinies followed, led by radical officers alerted by the *Shura's* e-mails. Forces loyal to King Ali formed to meet the Syrian advance at the border. Learning of the king's decision from their clerics, the large Palestinian population gathered at mosques. The air was filled with calls for a Great Jihad—and civil war.

The Syrian commander encountered more resistance than he expected. Even though outnumbered, the loyal Jordanian forces were putting up quite a fight. A fierce air battle ended in a draw. Outnumbered Royal Jordanian Air Force fighters gave a good account of themselves, downing three MIGs for each F-16 and F-1C lost. The Syrian commander placed a call to his president. "Sir, I am encountering stiff resistance. In order to keep my timetable, I request permission to use the special artillery munitions."

"I wanted to keep them as a surprise for the Jews; however, maintaining the timetable is most important. Permission granted," the president ordered.

On the battlefront, Syrian supply trucks carrying 130-mm and 155-mm projectiles moved forward to deliver their cargo to artillery batteries. Other trucks delivered special 122-mm rockets to pre-positioned launchers. At 1700, the Syrian commander issued the order to fire. 122-mm rockets streaked skyward, then slowly pitched over, following a parabolic path toward the Jordanian armor dug in on a ridgeline. Seeing the smoke trails and expecting high explosive warheads or bomblets, the Jordanian commander ordered the tanks and armored personnel carriers to button up. Instead of explosions, the rocket warheads burst upon impact, creating clouds of lethal vapor that entered the armored vehicles through their ventilation systems. Before victims could react their pupils contracted, vision dimmed and they had difficulty breathing. Seconds later they began drooling, vomiting, and loosing control of their bodily functions. Ultimately their bodies twitched and jerked violently, until after a series of convulsive spasms they suffocated.

In the minutes following the attack, a few frantic calls of "gas" and "gas attack" could be heard or radio nets. As is most often the case, some survived the lethal vapors by donning gas masks, which protected them from the GB/GF nerve gas carried by the rockets. However, masks were no protection against the Syrian artillery's next barrage. As soon as the 130-mm and 155-mm projectiles exploded over their targets, a yellowish cloud of mustard gas burst forth and settled to earth, burning and permanently scaring the skin all gas survivors—leaving many to speculate that some of Saddam's missing WMD's had finally surfaced.

Kennedy Strike Group, Mediterranean Sea – late Saturday afternoon, May 27th

Israel picked up a few of the desperate cries of *gas attack,* as did the *Kennedy* Strike Group. The *Kennedy* relayed the message to USSTRATCOM, which ordered a satellite to be tasked to view the battle raging on the Jordanian border. Analysis of the satellite feed showed rear elements of the Royal Jordanian Army in retreat. Along the Jordanian front, bodies could be seen lying around vehicles. There was no sign of firing from Jordanian positions. The Syrian Army was not advancing: a clear indication that the Jordanian position was contaminated.

Kirkland AFB, NM – Saturday, 27 May

At 1000 MDT, Admiral Vazquez lifted his phone with a direct secure link to Secretary Alexander. When Alexander answered, the admiral said, "Sir, early this morning the Syrian and Royal Jordanian Air Forces engaged in a dogfight along the Syrian Jordan border. Ground fighting began at 0700 hours local time and continued until 1430 hours local time, and then the Syrians withdrew. At 1700 hours local time, the Syrians began a rocket and artillery bombardment. Shortly thereafter, the *Kennedy* picked up radio transmissions from Jordanian units reporting a gas attack. I ordered satellite coverage, which shows bodies scattered around armored vehicles. Rear elements of the Jordanian Army are retreating toward Amman."

"This is a serious development. Are you in touch with Israel?" Alexander asked.

"Yes, sir. They have a major Palestinian uprising on their hands. It's possible the uprising will spread to Jordan, which has a very large Palestinian population—nearly fifty percent. Israel knows Egyptian and Syrian armies are on the move. There was an air battle with the Syrians. So far—much to their surprise—Jordan is fighting Syria."

"It looks like Jordan is on our side. Provide Israel with satellite feed of the Jordanian battle. Any word from our embassies?" Alexander asked, writing notes on a pad on his desk.

"Just those in Jordan and Israel. The Brits are in the same boat. The French have their hands full. Appears they're experiencing a full-blown Muslim revolt.

"Sir," Vazquez said, deciding it was time to press Alexander to accept the presidency. "According to my reports, there are no survivors from the capitol area in DC. I believe it's time for you to be sworn in as president. We must have a commander-in-chief."

Alexander sighed. He knew Vazquez was right, but he didn't want the job. After a pause, he said, "You're right, Bob. It's time. Barry Clark and Charlie Young have been telling me the same thing. Guess I have to agree," Alexander said ending the call.

Raising his voice, Alexander called out, "Julian, come here please."

"Yes, sir," Captain Taylor replied, quickly entering Alexander's office.

"Alert the PR officer and find a judge to swear me in. Admiral Vazquez has convinced me it's time to do so."

"Yes, sir, I'll take care of it." *It's about time. This man will be a great president.* "Governor Richards is at the main gate. He's being escorted here to receive his briefing. Also, General Simpson is somewhere in Key West, Florida. I'll let you know when we make contact with him."

"Good work. Have a plane standing by at the naval air station to bring him here. Also task the FBI to locate Bill Fobbs, publisher of *Fobbs* Magazine. I hope he wasn't in DC or New York," Alexander said, frowning. "I need to speak with him as quickly as possible.

"When the PR folks have set a time for my swearing in, let my wife know. Everyone here can attend, Governor Richards too," Alexander said, indicating he was finished giving instructions by returning to papers on his desk.

An hour later Captain Taylor entered to announced Governor Richards' arrival. Alexander greeted the governor at his office door, "Good morning, Governor. Thank you for coming," he said warmly shaking Richards' hand.

"Good morning, Mr. Secretary. Hell of a mess. What can I do to help?" The governor replied, noting Alexander's firm grip and commanding presence. Richardson, a large well-built man of fifty-two years, wore a tan Western styled jacket, over a light blue shirt with a string tie, dark brown slacks, and snakeskin boots.

"I'm glad you asked," Alexander said, smiling his second smile of the day. "Please join me over here," he added indicating two comfortable chairs arranged for informal conversation.

"I assume you're still plugged in with DOE and know the current status of things," Alexander said once they were comfortably seated.

"Yes, Mr. Secretary. I spoke with Doctor Chin on my way here. He's having difficulty coping. I advised him to follow your instructions. He confirmed no one in the DC blast area survived. That makes you the president. When are you going to take the oath?"

"As soon as the PR boys can get TV and radio people here. Admiral Vazquez convinced me to do so. I'd like you to be present."

"I'll be honored," Richards said with a grin.

"Kurt," Alexander said using Richards' Christian name, "I have to cobble together a government, fight a war against still unknown enemies, repair the country's infrastructure, deal with the international community, and keep the public informed. All are equally important. The only way to do this is to appoint people to deal with specific problems. Banking and credit cards are top priorities. In order to keep the food supply moving and the lights burning, we must be able to pay bills. We can't afford to get bogged down with existing regulations and policies. We have to do whatever's required to solve the problems. I'm looking for William Fobbs. If he survived, I want him to take on the banking and stock market problems.

"I'd like you chair the state governors—be my link to them. Use the other governors as your committee. Form subcommittees to solve problems. Reassure the public—keep them informed. Want the job?"

Richards sat for several seconds, contemplating the enormity of the job. Finally he looked up and said, "I'll do my best, Mr. President."

"Good, you'll have 24/7 access to me. I'm trying to locate Harry Simpson. I'm going to offer him the Secretary of Defense position."

"Harry's a good choice. So is Fobbs. What about State?" Richards asked.

"Don't know. Any suggestions? I need someone with a very strong backbone—definitely not one of the State Department pukes. We're not going to start begging for help and friends. As soon as we have the country under control, I'm going after whoever did this—wherever they are—God help anyone who gets in the way," Alexander said with a determined look. "The nation is still in shock. Soon the people will want blood—and rightly so. We've reports of Muslim riots in several cities. It may get worse. Maintaining order is the first priority—doing so is the governor's responsibility."

"Yes, I received a message last night from Colonel Young, recommending I call up the National Guard. New Mexico doesn't have a problem, but I see your point. Some will take advantage the opportunity to riot and loot," Richards said, frowning.

"Correct. Any such riot, disturbance, or uprising must put down with extreme force. Order will be maintained at all costs," Alexander said, looking Richards in the eye. Satisfied, he continued, "I can provide you with an office here."

Impressed by Alexander's intensity and decision-making ability, Richardson softly replied, "No thank you, sir. I prefer to use my office in Santa Fe."

"Okay, I'll place a helicopter at your disposal."

Richards turned toward the door, and then turned back, "Have you thought about the container ship problem? The country works on the 'just in time principal,' we no longer have large warehouses. If the ports close, we'll run out of food and supplies."

Oh, God, another problem. "What do you suggest?"

"Instruct port directors and the Department of Transportation to keep ports and ground transportation system running. Increase radiation monitoring at domestic ports and increase staff at foreign ports."

"You've full authority to do so. Please take on this task. Do what's necessary."

"Yes, Mr. President," Richards said with a solemn expression. *This man can make decisions, and delegate. If anyone can save us, he can.*

"Sorry to interrupt sir," Captain Taylor said. Your swearing-in ceremony will be held at 1400 hours."

After Governor Richards departed to use a telephone in an empty office, Alexander closed his door, walked to the window, and gazed at Sandia Crest. Never a deeply religious man, the general believed the God of his Sunday school years was real; and mankind had a responsibility to a supreme being to live according to Judeo-Christian scriptural precepts. Each human being has a purpose for living on this earth. "Why," he wondered aloud, "Why God, did I survive, when others far more experienced in world affairs died? Why was I chosen at this pivotal point in earth's history? Is this my purpose for living— to lead our wounded republic from the depths of its sorrow toward once again being mankind's best hope for unity, liberty, and justice for all? Please God, don't let me fail."

Chapter 9

At exactly 2:20 p.m. MDT, George Robert Alexander placed his left hand on his wife's family Bible, raised his right hand, recited the oath of office, and became the 45th President of the United States of America. The Bible had been included with clothes collected from their retirement home. Governor Richards stood on Alexander's right during the simple ceremony conducted in the base auditorium. In addition to military personnel able to leave their posts, Albuquerque's mayor, several elected state officials, and available members of the press attended.

Following the oath of office, President Alexander addressed the press and through them the nation.

"My fellow Americans, I have assumed the office of president and commander-in-chief during one of America's darkest hours. I pledge to do my best to right the wrongs visited upon us." Alexander paused, looked with conviction into the TV cameras, then continued.

"But first, we must put our house in order. Priority must be given to aiding the survivors, restoring order, protecting lives and property, getting our banking system back online, and ensuring continued distribution of food, fuel, and electricity.

"I know everyone is concerned about radioactive fallout. Fallout is carried by the wind. People living downwind of detonations have been told to evacuate. Unless you've been ordered to evacuate, remain in your homes and businesses. Evacuating non-threatened areas results in clogged highways, causes accidents that place an additional burden on emergency personnel, and consumes fuel we cannot spare. Follow instructions broadcast by authorities in affected areas—National Guard, state police, and local governments.

"We *must* conserve gasoline," Alexander said, gesturing with his right hand for emphasis. "Supplies from the Middle East have been interrupted. Start carpools. Use personal vehicles only when absolutely necessary. Panic is now our worst enemy. Please remain calm and follow instructions. Remember the words of President Roosevelt, 'The only thing we have to fear is fear itself.' "

Indicating the men and women in uniform in the audience with a sweeping gesture, America's new president continued, "Our military is doing double-duty, protecting us from attack, and providing disaster relief for the five bombed cities.

"Finding and punishing the culprits responsible for the attacks will come later." Alexander placed his hands on the podium, leaned forward with a determined expression, and stared into the TV cameras. "But have no doubts—*come it will.*"

Alexander's gaze swept over the audience, then he removed his hands from the podium, and continued in his normal, measured, cadence. Viewers saw a large, fit, determined, man with a deep baritone voice, who radiated confidence and authority. A president who commanded respect.

"Muslim riots have occurred and are still raging in some of our cities. They're being dealt with. The extent of the insurrections is still being ascertained. Each state governor is responsible for maintaining order in their state.

"My job is to keep our great nation functioning. To this end I'm appointing the best men and women I can find to take charge of problems and to solve them."

Turning to Governor Richards who stood beside him, the president continued. "Governor Richards of the great state of New Mexico will become my link to all state governors. He will be kept informed of domestic and international events and will in turn keep the other governors informed. They will keep you informed. Listen to the radio and watch TV for information and instructions.

"Our banks are closed because the electronic network they use to communicate with each other was damaged. Repairing this network is a top priority. A member of the Federal Reserve is enroute to Albuquerque. She will be given the task of getting the banking system operational."

Grimly smiling and slightly shaking his head, the president continued, "My ATM card doesn't work either, and my wife, Jane, is just as unhappy about that as you are."

Throwing his shoulders back, with a look of fierce determination, Alexander looked squarely into the cameras and the millions of faces viewing him on TV screens, "We *must* make do with what we have and provide assistance to our friends and neighbors. Soon things will improve. Americans are great innovators. We are always at their best during adversity.

"Good afternoon, and God bless America."

Governor Richards left for Santa Fe at 5:00 p.m. and Alexander returned to his office. Minutes later the direct line from STRATCOM rang. The president and was greeted by Admiral Vazquez, "Mr. President, the situation in Israel and Jordan is becoming critical. The Syrian Army is preparing to attack at dawn, five hours from now. We've established contact with Jordan's king through our embassy. The Syrians used mustard and GB/GF nerve gas. Jordan won't be able to offer any real resistance. There have been mutinies in Jordan's armed forces. Syrian forces in Lebanon are preparing to attack Israel. The CIA reports that Egypt's president has been assassinated. Egyptian forces are approaching the Israeli border. It looks like the battle will begin at dawn."

"Is the *Kennedy* in striking range?"

"Yes, sir."

"Order them to prepare a strike on the Egyptian forces. Take them out." Alexander paused to think, and then continued, "Next, set up a conference call for us with King Ali and Israel's Prime Minister Aaron Wurtzel. Any other fires?"

"Maybe. CIA reports Kim Jung-il has placed his army on alert. He may decide this is a good opportunity for another invasion of South Korea," Vazquez replied.

"Keep an eye on him. I'll discuss this with President Wu when I call him in Beijing. Good work, Bob," the president said ending the call.

Alexander closed his eyes and relaxed for a few seconds, then pushed the intercom button on his phone, "Julian, I'm expecting a conference call from King Ali of Jordan and Aaron Wurtzel. Have you found General Simpson?"

"No, sir, but the FBI has a team looking for him. They're checking charter boats. He may be on an overnight fishing trip," Captain Taylor replied, and added, "Ms. Nora Jacobson from the FED has arrived."

"Send her in, Julian."

Alexander stood to greet Nora Jacobson. She was an attractive woman, about five-foot-three, wearing a white blouse, navy blue slacks, and low heel black pumps. Her gold earrings and necklace complimented her outfit. She appeared to be in her mid forties. "Good afternoon," the president said, standing to greet her.

"Good afternoon, Mr. President. It's an honor to meet you, but I'm not sure why I'm here. The FBI came to my house, told me to pack a bag, took me to the airport, and put me on an Air Force jet. I didn't know where I was going until the plane was in the air," she said, gesturing with her hands. "I can't believe what has happened. How could we have been attacked without any warning?"

"Good question. Have a seat," Alexander said indicating a chair in front of his desk. "So far we've no idea how they pulled it off. All we have to go on is what the terrorist said in his video. If we're to believe him, the bombs have been here for a long time." Alexander frowned, shrugged, sat in his chair, and continued. "Now, as to why you're here. We must get the banks open."

"Yes, I've been thinking about where to begin. It's going to be very difficult. First the Fed will have to determine who is in charge. Then the person in charge will have to meet with the chairpersons of the major banks ... and that may be a problem since most of them were in New York or Washington. Next we'll have to form committees to—"

Nora Jacobson was becoming lost in her thoughts. Her eyes drifting, losing focus. Leaning forward and interrupting, the president said, "As of now, you are in charge of the Fed. I want the banks back on line by Wednesday. You'll direct the banks as to what they must do."

The president's words jolted a very flustered Nora Jacobson back to reality. Lifting her head, she looked at the man sitting across the desk from her. "Mr. President, I can't do that. We have regulations, laws. It would take an act of Congress, and new legislation to authorize what you've requested," Jacobson blurted out, gesturing with her hand.

Another bureaucrat unable to cope with radically new situations, Alexander thought looking at the disconcerted woman sitting in front of him. *No, not unable ... unchallenged. This is a totally new situation for her, for all of us. She needs guidance, and that's my job.* Assuming a fatherly appearance, Alexander lifted his right hand to silence her litany of objections. "Nora, there's no Congress to pass laws. I have suspended regulations. Just get the job done. If you can't do it, find someone in the Fed who can. However, I'm *confident* you can do the job," Alexander said, giving Nora a reassuring smile before continuing. "I'm looking for Bill Fobbs. When I find him, I'll put him in charge of the Treasury. The Fed will report to him." Leaning forward, Alexander continued in a soft, reassuring voice, "Right now, you're the only person I have to work on the problem. The citizens of the country want their banks open. They don't want excuses. I know you can get the job done. Concentrate on what has to be done, then do it. If you've a problem, you can't handle, tell Captain Taylor. I'll get involved if necessary."

Attempting to compose herself, Nora looked up at the president and blurted out, "Mr. Fobbs is in Madrid attending a World Bank meeting, Mr. President." Still trying to assimilate what the president told her, she sat back in her chair: her eyes looking past him, lost in thought, her mind racing. *He's telling me to throw the rulebook out the window. No congress. Yes, he's right. How long will it take to get a new one? What has to be done? Who should I call? Yes, Mr. Fobbs is a good choice—"*

Sensing Nora was drifting again, the president said, "I know you can do it. Captain Taylor will find an office for you. The FBI will assist you in locating people you need to contact."

Captain Taylor entered the room, "Sir, your conference call with the king of Jordan and the prime minister of Israel is ready."

Standing, the president said, "Julian, find Ms. Jacobson an office and introduce her to the FBI liaison. She knows where Fobbs is. Find him, and get him here ASAP," the president said, indicating the meeting was over. As

Julian turned to leave, Alexander said, "Julian, a cup of coffee would be nice." Julian nodded and left.

Returning to his chair, President Alexander reached for his phone, "King Ali, Prime Minister Wurtzel, as you know we have been monitoring events in your area. We all know each other, and this is not the time nor place for politics or diplomacy. I commend Jordan for choosing the high road, and I'm saddened at the price your country has paid for doing so. Our satellites show Syria is preparing to attack in force across Jordan toward Israel at dawn. Syria has used chemical weapons and will do so again. They may also have biological weapons. I assume Israel knows this and plans to take action.

"The Royal Jordanian Army and Air Force cannot win a fight under these conditions. I have a simple suggestion. Ali, evacuate the remainder of your forces and loyal citizens from Amman into Israel. Jordanian forces must immediately start withdrawing toward the Israeli border. When they arrive, they will assume defensive positions with Israeli forces. If you join forces you both may survive."

Alexander's blunt, undiplomatic proposal—offered with no preamble— shocked the young king. He was sitting in his office in Amman reading situation reports from his commanders when asked to join Alexander's conference call. *He is correct. The use of chemical weapons has defeated us. I've lost a major portion of my forces ... my brothers in arms. We'll have our backs to the sea ... however, the U.S. Navy rules the sea. Yes, his suggestion is our best chance ... perhaps our only chance. I hope Israel will accept it.*

Prime Minister Wurtzel knew he too was in a desperate situation. There was no doubt Syria would use chemical weapons against Israel. Jordan's opposition to Syria was the only good news he'd received since the horrible attack on the U.S. The fact that Alexander, with all his problems, was taking time to call with a plan was a life raft in a sea of disasters. "President Alexander, your plan is bold. Israel will welcome our Jordanian neighbors. Can you provide any assistance? I am aware of the attack on the United States, and we send our condolences. Under any other circumstances I wouldn't ask."

It was the king's turn to speak, "Jordan accepts the plan and thanks our Israeli neighbors for their kind invitation."

"Excellent," Alexander said. "I've ordered the *Kennedy* Strike Group to attack the Egyptians before dawn. They won't expect our intervention. Can you handle the Syrian armor?"

Wurtzel answered, "Our neighbor and ally was attacked with weapons of mass destruction. We will reply in kind. Jordanian forces and civilians must get as far away from the Syrian formations as possible by dawn."

"I'll leave it to both of you to work out the details. Rear Admiral Howard Krugger, commander of the *Kennedy* Strike Group, will coordinate with you,"

Alexander said, ending his participation in the conversation. Captain Taylor entered with a hot cup of coffee. Alexander took a sip, and then turned to gaze out the window at Sandia Crest. "May God have mercy on them, on all of us," he muttered to himself.

Taylor, standing in the office doorway, allowed the president a few seconds of solitude before saying, "Mr. President, I have General Simpson on the phone. You've also received congratulatory calls from several heads of state."

"Thank you, Julian. Please thank each caller and tell them I'll return their calls as soon as possible," Pushing the blinking button on his main phone, Alexander said, "Good afternoon, Harry."

"Good afternoon, Mr. President. What can I do to help?"

"Thanks for asking, I need a secretary of defense. Want the job?"

Retired General Harry Simpson, former Chairman of the Joint Chiefs of Staff, expected to be asked to fill a position, but not the top job. *George Alexander is a doer, and because he is, he has enemies in the bureaucracy. None of that matters any more. The heart of the bureaucracy is gone and he's now the boss. God help any whiner who starts with the typical bureaucratic nonsense.* "Yes, Mr. President. I'll give it my best shot. I'm in Key West, and my wife is in North Carolina. She should be safe there."

"As soon as you get here, you can make any arrangements you feel necessary for your family's safety. Send them to Fort Bragg if you like. Jane and I are in Kirkland's Visiting VIP quarters. They're cleaning up a closed general officer's quarters near the old Sandia Base Officers Club for me. There is probably another one you can use. I have a plane standing by for you at the Key West Naval Air Station. Get here as quickly as you can."

"On my way, sir."

"Colonel Charles Young is my acting Chief of Staff, and Captain Julian Taylor is his exec. Charlie will provide you with a briefing as soon as you arrive. You know Bob Vazquez at STRATCOM. Contact him in-flight and get the overall picture. You can get the details over a secure line when you get here. I'll fill you in on other events when you arrive," the president said, ending the call. *One more problem solved, God give me strength.*

Half an hour later, British Prime Minister Neville Chamberlain-Talbot called. "He's extremely upset," Captain Taylor commented, when he informed Alexander of the call.

"Okay, Julian, I'll take his call," Alexander replied, closing a folder with a cover bearing the legend "Top Secret," in large bold letters, followed by "Restricted Data" in smaller black letters. The legend was framed by a border of red stripes. Picking up his telephone Alexander said, "Good evening, Prime Minister."

"President Alexander, first I wish to convey our sympathy and condolences for America's losses. It's beyond my ability to understand how terrorists could do such a dastardly thing. Kill so many innocent men, women, and children," the prime minister began. "Of course you can count on us for support. Anything you need."

"Thank you, Prime Minister, I accept your offer," the president replied. "You're correct, the terrorist's acts are beyond our understanding as Christians and Westerners. That is precisely the problem. We have judged radical Islam by our standards, when they operate under an entirely different code of ethics. From now on, we'll deal with them using methods they understand. We will use their rulebook, since it's obvious they don't understand ours. Can I assume you are up to date on events in the Middle East and the status of our embassies?"

"Yes. It appears most moderate governments have been overthrown. We have lost touch with most of our embassies."

Alexander quickly explained the situation in Israel and Jordan, and his decision to intervene.

"You are certain Syria used chemical weapons?" a very shaken Talbot asked. "You really think Israel will use nuclear weapons in the morning?"

"Yes to both questions," the president replied. "Like it or not, we're at war. At war not with a particular nation, but with a religion—radical Islam. There's no other way to look at it. The Islamic religion is the common denominator of all these events, and it is the common denominator of terrorist attacks for the past thirty-nine years. We are experiencing domestic Muslim insurrections and terrorists attacks. If they have not occurred in England, they probably will in the near future. I've ordered such acts of insurrection to be put down with maximum force.

"We need to stage reconnaissance, rescue, and bomber aircraft in England," Alexander added.

"Mr. President, reconnaissance and rescue aircraft are welcome. Bombers are not. Any military action will be left up to the UN and NATO," Talbot whined.

Alexander frowned, shaking his head in disgust. Talbot was an ardent liberal and appeaser whose reputation mirrored that of his ancestor, Sir Neville Chamberlain. Alexander shifted in his chair, clenched his fist, and replied, "Mr. Prime Minister, the United States has been attacked at home and in the Middle East. We have no intention of turning the matter over to the UN. In fact, the UN was destroyed with New York City. I have no intention of allowing it to be re-born."

"President Alexander, the UN must—"

"NATO may become involved later—*not now*." Alexander said, cutting Talbot off. "NATO was designed to protect members against attack by other countries. We are fighting terrorists with no country. Even if a county is involved, we don't have time to wait for NATO to debate plans and strategy. When our cities were destroyed, the rules changed. There's no longer a fence to sit on. You are either our friend or our enemy—and our enemies are going to be destroyed. We'll base our bombers in England and any other country should the need arise. No is not an acceptable answer."

Talbot felt faint. He didn't know what to say. His advisors, listening to the speakerphone with him, had warned him that America's new president was a hard man; a man who would lash out in retaliation. But Alexander's last statement was more than Talbot could cope with. Things were going too fast. Wringing his hands, Talbot looked around the room at his advisors for support. He saw a wide range of emotions. Some were as shocked as he was. Others were nodding their heads in support of the president's position. Refusing to accept Alexander's statement, the PM asked, "Mr. President, if I understand you correctly, you intend to position bombers in England against our wishes?"

"Yes," the president coldly replied. "We will coordinate schedules with the Royal Air Force. I suggest your Royal Air Force and Navy be integrated into our command structure in order to achieve a unified command."

"I will have to consider this Mr. President," Talbot responded.

"There is no time for consideration, Mr. Prime Minister. Have your commanders work out the details with Admiral Vazquez at the U.S. Strategic Command. We must evacuate our personnel from the Middle East while they're still alive—if they are still alive. Mr. Prime Minister, I have to attend to other urgent business. I'm confident integration of our forces will proceed in an orderly manner. Goodbye and good luck," Alexander said to the badly shaken Talbot.

Talbot sat at the conference table looking at his advisors, his stomach churning and his hands shaking. No one spoke. After a long period of silence, the minister of defense rose and left the room to do what must be done.

Captain Taylor remained standing next to Alexander's desk during the conversation. Awed by what he'd heard, he voiced the question that would soon concern all leaders and most citizens, "Sir, how do we differentiate between good Muslims and bad Muslims?"

Looking up with a sad expression, feeling deep concern and consternation, Alexander said in a hushed voice, "I don't know, Julian, but we must try."

Chapter 10

Ralph Eid and his long time love, Nancy Hatterson, were watching the BBC channel's coverage of Muslim riots and uprisings through Europe, reports of a battle between Jordan and Syria, another air battle between Israel and Egypt, and the destruction of Chicago, Boston, New York, Atlanta and Washington in the U.S. It seemed to Nancy the world had suddenly gone mad. The BBC announcer kept referring to videotapes from some Arab terrorist who first called himself the "Keeper of the Rings," and now caliph. Eid suspected the Keeper of the Rings was Mohammed al-Mihdar, a man Nancy would recognize. She'd had a nasty confrontation with Mohammed during a dinner party in a Boston restaurant. Unknown to Nancy, Mohammed objected to Eid's relationship with her, an infidel, and had ordered Eid to get rid of her. Eid's refusal precipitated an increasingly bitter, ongoing conflict with Mohammed.

Eid's mind was racing. *If it is Mohammed, Nancy will make the connection between him, REM and our diagnostic centers, in each of the cities. Who else, other than Nancy, can tie Mohammed to REM and me? In Boston, Professor Bhatti, the builder, and Doctor Murdock and his wife— they're probably dead. Then there's Doctor Ahmad and some of the employees at Chicago Nuclear Diagnostics. Mohammed visited the Chicago facility in his capacity as a director of REM Investments, but they're probably dead too. Who else could be alive? Tom Braggs? I can't remember if he met Mohammed. Tom said something about leaving for a long weekend. He may still be alive. No—just Nancy. If I can keep her from seeing the videotape, she won't know Muraaqibu al-Khawaatim is Mohammed al-Mihdar.*

But eventually that would prove to be impossible.

✯ ✯ ✯

Now forty-five, Ralph Eid was raised in a Muslim environment in New York City, and spoke fluent Arabic and Farsi. He was a handsome, well-built, six-foot-one, 180 pound man, with black curly hair, dark laughing eyes, a cheerful personality, and winning smile. His skin was light for an Egyptian. His Egyptian born parents adored him, and he was devoted to his mother, who teased him by calling him "My Darling Omar." One of his father's clients had compared his handsome features to the movie star, Omar Shariff.

Fate dealt Eid a bitter hand, when both parents were killed in a 1985 automobile accident on the Long Island Expressway. An eighteen-year-old drunk driver caused their death when his Corvette struck their automobile, sending it into the path of an on coming tractor-trailer. The young man, the son of a powerful politician, was uninjured; and his punishment, a sentence of one hundred days community service, was little more than a slap-on-the-wrist. The event left Eid bitter and angry. After earning his MBA from Harvard, he returned to New York and attempted to take over his father's business, while pursuing his lawsuit against the drunk driver and his family. He found empathy among his Muslim brothers at his mosque. The mullah introduced him to Wahhabism. Driven by anger, Eid embraced radical Islam. Funds exhausted, he sold the business and moved to Oakland, California, to begin studying for his doctorate in nuclear physics at the University of California at Berkeley. His obsession to avenge his parent's death grew. The mosque was the only place Eid could vent, and his bitterness brought him to the attention of an al-Qaeda recruiter. When Islamic radicals at his local mosque urged him to make America's establishment pay for his loss, Eid made a fateful decision. Temporarily abandoning his studies, he traveled to Afghanistan to attend an al-Qaeda training camp, where he met Mohammed al-Mihdar who became his mentor and partner in terror. At Mohammed's urging Eid returned to the U.S., completed his PhD, obtained a position with Livermore National Laboratories, and gained access to some of America's nuclear weapons technology.

Bin-Laden put Mohammed in charge of acquiring five WWII era Soviet nuclear test devices from a renegade KGB officer, Colonel Alexei Valek. Mohammed's revelation that al-Qaeda possessed the devices inspired Eid to conceive a plan to import them disguised as medical research instruments— Neutron Induced Gamma Spectrometers.

Mohammed arranged for Eid to receive al-Qaeda funds—in the guise of an inheritance—which he would use as capital to start a business: one that would provide a safe place to hide the five atomic devices. An instant millionaire, Eid quit his job at Livermore National Laboratories and founded REM Investments, Inc., owned by Eid and "Saudi Investors." Eid, the CEO, began establishing upscale, state-of-the-art, radiological diagnostic centers in the target cities. Each diagnostic facility was a separate corporation, with REM Investments holding the majority of the stock.

A separate suite of research offices was set up next to each diagnostic center. Lead shielding was installed in each research suite and diagnostic center to shield radiation produced by the diagnostic center's instruments, and the neutron induced gamma spectrometer atomic bomb. REM became highly successful, and very profitable. Profits were deposited in foreign banks.

While implementing his plans to hide the devices, Ralph rekindled a love affair from his Harvard years with Nancy Hatterson, a beautiful, five-foot-six, blue-eyed, blonde with a to-die-for figure, who was born in Nebraska, the daughter of a farmer. One of four children, she excelled in school and won a scholarship to the University of Nebraska. After graduating, her parents sent her to Harvard for her MBA.

Nancy was now a successful officer in a Boston venture capital firm. She was happy to have Ralph back in her life and knew nothing of his al-Qaeda connection. From all outward appearances he was the successful CEO of REM Investments, Inc.: a closely held Delaware corporation that owned and operated nuclear diagnostic facilities in Atlanta, Boston, Chicago, and New York. When Ralph encouraged her to quit her job in Boston and move in with him in Livermore, California Nancy readily agreed and started her own venture capital firm, PC Capital, LLC.

Two weeks before the planned detonation date for the five atomic devices, Eid began arming the devices. REM's nuclear diagnostic facilities were located in the upper floors of high-rise buildings, carefully selected to produce optimum locations and blast height for the gun-type atomic test devices. Mohammed joined Eid in New Jersey and they completed arming the New York and Atlanta devices. The fifth device, disguised as a mobile CAT scan unit mounted in a diagnostic trailer, was parked in REM's warehouse near the Capitol building in Washington, DC.

On the Tuesday before the detonations, Eid and Mohammed armed the last device in Washington, DC, and departed from Dulles Airport. Eid returned to the condo he shared with Nancy in San Jose, California. Mohammed flew to Paris. The previous week, after arming the Boston device, Eid called Nancy and suggested they go to their estate in Ensenada, Argentina for a vacation. They departed San Francisco for Buenos Aires, Argentina on Thursday, May 25th, the day before the atomic devices, so carefully hidden by Eid years earlier, detonated. Nancy didn't know her lover was involved in these horrendous acts of terror.

Eid purchased the Argentine estate as a birthday gift for Nancy. Originally, the vast estate consisted of the hacienda and guesthouse—each with a pool—a fine stable of Argentinean horses, and acres of pastureland to support beef cattle and a variety of other livestock. The hacienda was partitioned into spacious timeshare apartments when Eid purchased the estate. Eid subdivided a portion of the pastureland and built a small community of upscale villas. The 5,000 square foot ranch style guesthouse became the couple's vacation home. Remodeled, it boasted a complete workout room and gourmet kitchen with every modern convenience. Nancy, who spoke fluent Spanish, oversaw the estate's staff.

Eid built separate buildings for security personnel, live-in housekeepers, and the gardening staff near the main house. A professional security staff was on duty around the clock, monitoring camera locations throughout the estate, and providing transportation to and from outside locations. A wall surrounded the compound. The landscaped grounds contained private gardens, sparkling fountains, and trellised gazebos overlooking the Rio De La Plata River. Bougainvillea flowered during the warm months. Horse stables and a tack room were located at the rear of the walled compound. An electronic gate, controlled by a security keypad, opened to riding trails and a five-kilometer jogging path that meandered through the surrounding pampas.

In short, the estate was something of a fortress, designed by Eid to be an idyllic paradise. There he and Nancy could escape from the dangers of his other life—a life Nancy knew nothing about—and his growing fear of Mohammed. Long ago Eid planned for the day when he would either be killed, or discovered by the authorities and incarcerated—the reason he could never marry Nancy. She was the only person in the entire world Eid truly loved. Her safety and security was paramount to him. If he were killed or captured, the estate would be her safe refuge. Should he survive and escape being identified as one of the terrorists after the bombs were detonated, it would be their new home. A secret hideaway Mohammed knew nothing about—and Eid planned to keep it that way.

Eid used his own funds, and some of REM's cash to fund several of PC Capital's venture funds. The personal computer revolution was in full swing, and Silicon Valley, near Livermore, was the place to be. Nancy's good looks and brains, combined with Eid's friends at Livermore Labs, made PC Capital a roaring success. Eid, Nancy, REM, and several scientists at Livermore Labs made millions.

Planning for the day he would have to leave the United States and hide from Mohammed, Eid incorporated a foreign company, Argentine Radiological Imaging. Eid owned the company through a law firm in Buenos Aires, and it would be very difficult to trace the ownership to Ralph Eid.

REM had over sixty-four million U.S. dollars (USD) in Swiss accounts. Friday morning, before the bombs detonated, Eid transferred thirty million to Argentine Radiological Imaging. He routed the transfer through New York, Atlanta, the Isle of Man, the Bahamas, and Panama. After the detonations, it would be impossible to trace the money. Upon Eid's death, Nancy would inherit Argentine Radiological Imaging.

✯   ✯   ✯

Nancy got up, stretched, and headed for the bedroom, telling Ralph, "I'll be right back." A few seconds later, the BBC announced it would show both of the terrorist's videotapes in half an hour. Ralph quickly turned the TV off, walked into the bedroom, and called to Nancy who was in the bathroom, "Let's go horseback riding. We need to get away from the TV. No point in watching more of the same bad news. We might as well relax, because we can't return to the states, or even call anyone there. Let's concentrate on keeping our minds off problems we can't solve."

"Okay, you're right. Horseback riding is a good idea," Nancy replied from the bathroom.

Eid returned to the TV room and called security. "Henry, have Frank bring the golf cart around. Nancy and I are going riding. Oh, and Henry, I don't want the news from the U.S. upsetting Nancy. Cut off the satellite dish hook-up to the house for the time being. I'll let you know when I'm ready to turn it back on. You keep track of what's going on. I'll call for updates."

Qom, Iran – Saturday, May 27th

The new caliph spent the day watching TV broadcasts from Al-Jazeera and the BBC. He was elated as he watched Al-Jazeera's interviews from Cairo, Baghdad, Rabat, and other Arab capitals, where the new caliph was mentioned and most often praised. Reports of the massacre of the Saudi Royal Family and the Western infidels thrilled him. He was not surprised when the Western puppet in Jordan sided with the Jews. *My Syrian and Egyptian armies will destroy the puppet king, and then the Little Satan. The Great Satan is helpless*, he gloated. News of the Syrian gas attack on Jordanian troops caused a stir among the radical clerics. Muslims killing Muslims, even traitorous ones, was unpleasant—better to concentrate on killing the infidels. By evening the caliph's euphoria began to wane, and he finally started to think about what he should be doing. Like so many zealots fixated on obtaining a goal, no thought was given to what would be required after the goal was achieved.

Grand Ayatollah Hamid Khomeini was watching his puppet, waiting for this moment. Khomeini spent the last twenty-five years planning for a worldwide jihad to spread Islam over most, if not all, of the world. A young dynamic leader with charisma—one who could be controlled—was required to be the caliph. When Mohammed al-Mihdar brought his plan to the *Shura*, Khomeini realized he'd found his man: one who, as an added bonus, brought with him the means to begin the Great Jihad. All that remained was to wait for the young fool to realize he didn't know what to do next. Approaching the caliph, Khomeini quietly took a seat beside him and watched TV for a few minutes before beginning the conversation, "Allah, and the Prophet, may he rest in peace, have blessed you. Our Muslim brothers are beginning to recognize you as their caliph. Now you must address them, show yourself, tell them what to do next."

"Allah be praised. Yes, those are also my thoughts," the caliph replied, striving to appear confident, "What do you suggest?"

Inwardly smiling, Khomeini continued, "With Allah's guidance, you may wish to travel to Tehran and establish your caliphate there. A suitable palace can be obtained for your use. Then you may wish to use the television to address your subjects. A vast coverage can be arranged for your telecasts."

Relieved by the suggestions, the young caliph agreed, "My thoughts exactly. I agree with your suggestions. When can we leave?"

Maintaining his calm appearance, Grand Ayatollah Hamid Khomeini said, "We can leave within the hour. Now that you have fulfilled your duties as Keeper of the Rings, perhaps you should take a more appealing name."

"Allah be praised. Yes, I have also given this much thought. From now on I shall be known as Saladin the Second."

Even for a stern old man, suppressing laughter required great self-control. The Grand Ayatollah answered with a smile, "*Insha'Allah*, as Allah wills, so it shall be."

Chapter 11

Detroit, Michigan

Tramic, Michigan – Saturday, 6 a.m. May 27th

Word of Muraaqibu al-Khawaatim's second video spread through the Muslim community. The *muadhdhin's* (muezzin's) *adhan*, (call for *Subh* or dawn prayer, the first of five obligatory daily prayers), blared from loud speakers on the mosque's minaret, echoing through the quiet neighborhood. Worshipers packed the mosque, and overflowed into the street. Dr. Kabbani, a respected physician of fifty-nine years, and one of the few voices of reason in the Islamic community, approached the mosque. He intended to ask the *mullah*, the leader of prayers, to pray for the people killed in the explosions and to disavow those terrorists who'd done this terrible deed. *We can no longer make excuses for these barbarians in our religion. If we excuse, or say nothing, the country will turn on us and our religion.* Walking toward the mosque, Dr. Kabbani was shocked to hear the comments coming from the faithful filling the street in front of the building. "Now is the time to force the *kafirs* to accept Allah," one said, referring to infidels.

"Yes, the Great Jihad begins, and we'll convert this vile country to Islam," another said.

"Soon," yet another called out.

"No, no." Dr. Kabbani cried, "A great wrong has been done by radical fools in the name of Allah. We must denounce them. Beg Allah to help the injured and to forgive us for allowing these radicals to use His name—"

In an instant, a group of young students in the crowd turned on Dr. Kabbani, shoving him and spitting in his face. Undaunted by their insults, the doctor attempted in vain to reason with his detractors, whose attack on him only became more violent with each passing moment. Finally with an expression of pure hatred on his face, a young man the doctor had mentored as a boy lunged forward from the group, viciously punched the doctor in the stomach, and screamed in his face, "Go home, old man. You're not fit to join the jihad. Go home you stupid old fool. Pray to Allah for a backbone—for the courage to do His work."

Stunned by the blow, the doctor fell to his knees, while the young man urged on by the crowd, continued to pummel him. Just as the doctor was about to loose consciousness, the voice of the mullah came over the loud speaker, and the young man and his cohorts were swept away by the malevolent crowd, which was rapidly becoming a mob. "*Allahhh-u Akbarr, Allahhh-u Akbarr,*" Allah is the Greatest, they shouted.

A local mobile TV crew had set up across the street from the mosque. The cameraman, standing on top of the van, was slowly panning from left to right. Inside the van, the rest of the crew felt the tension in the air and the mob's growing hostility toward them. Descending to street level, the cameraman continued filming, while cautioning the young, blonde, female reporter, "I think we should move to a safer location."

Intent on covering a story that might get her national exposure, Abby Ladd had no intention of leaving. Tom, the producer, was transmitting live feed to the studio. Worried, Tom called the station manager to advise him of their situation, "Bill, I don't like this. A man on the mosque PA system is working the mob up to a fever pitch. We're dealing with mob mentality. Things can quickly get out-of-hand. Better call the police."

"Yes, I'm watching your feed. I'm going to interrupt the normal program and put you on. Tell Abby we're going live in sixty seconds," Bill Thornton replied. Next, Thornton advised his network—or what was then passing for a network—he had live feed from a mosque where the mob was getting out-of-control. The network picked up his feed, and Abby got her national exposure—fleeting though it was.

A block away, two plain-clothes police officers in an unmarked car were also getting nervous. Officer Butterworth returned to the car after walking around the perimeter of the growing mob. "They're all talking in Arabic," he told his partner, Sergeant Downs. "I don't know what they're saying, but the mood is ugly and getting worse. We'd better call it in." Downs nodded, and Butterworth picked up the mike to call dispatch, "Dispatch, Rover 26."

"Go ahead Rover 26."

"We're two blocks from the mosque. There's a large mob gathering. Their mood is ugly. The preacher is giving some type of sermon over the loud speakers. The mob is responding by shouting something in Arabic. Something that sounds like 'Allah Ackaback.' It looks like things are getting out-of-hand. Send reinforcements, and I recommend you begin preparing for a riot. There's a TV crew across the street. If a riot develops, they're going to be in trouble."

"Can you assist the TV crew?"

"Negative. No way to get to them. The street's packed: hundreds of the rag-heads, all of them lathered up. It looks like they're celebrating the nuke attacks."

"Rover 26, watch the 'rag-head' stuff. Stand by, I'll notify the chief."

Disheveled and winded Dr. Kabbani freed himself from the clutches of the mob and stumbled back to his car. Shocked by his experience, the doctor was unaware of the blood streaming from a cut over his right eye as he drove to his nearby home. Entering his house through the back door leading to the kitchen, he was greeted by his wife, Fatima who was terrified when she saw his condition. "What has happened to you? You're bleeding. Your clothes are torn. Were you attacked by robbers?" she cried out, grabbing a dishtowel from the sink and running to his aid.

"No, Fatima, by fellow Muslims at our mosque, and by my most respected protégé, young Riyadh al-Fulani. He punched me and further dishonored his family by verbally insulting me. 'Go home you old fool,' he shouted after hitting me and shoving me into the crowd. They all jeered when I tried to reason with them. 'Grow a backbone,' Riyadh told me.

"Oh, Fatima, our brothers have gone mad—driven mad by the teachings of radical Muslims who are determined to destroy all infidels in a Great Jihad. A jihad that knows no bounds. It's directed at any and all who oppose its intent—to convert all people to Islam—by force if necessary." The good doctor stopped and looked at the bloody towel, then said, "Fatima, get my medical bag, and a mirror."

Using the mirror to examine his cut, the doctor determined he did not require stitches. After giving his wife instructions on how to treat and bandage the cut, he continued his story.

"I tried reasoning with them, but they were inflamed by the mullah, and by al-Khawaatim's claim to have destroyed five of America's cities with atomic bombs. 'This is now our adopted land,' I told them. 'We must live in peace among people of other cultures and religions. That's what freedom means. That's what America stands for. Don't you see?' I asked them, but they would hear nothing I said. Instead they pushed me, spat on me, and shoved me again. Something struck a terrible blow to my head. I stumbled, but didn't fall. All the time I kept trying to explain we must fit into American society, where government is separate from religion. My words only enraged them, and they pushed me, and kicked me, and called me a Zionist lover. Then someone from the mosque screamed over the loud speakers, 'KILL THE SATURDAY PEOPLE,' our neighbors the Jews. The crowd picked up the command as a chant, and before I knew it I was in the midst of a frenzied mob. Somehow I was able to find an opening in the mob and fled. When I looked back I could see a throng of angry people moving toward the local synagogue." The doctor leaned forward, and placed his head in his hands. A soft moan escaped his lips as he looked up at his frightened wife, who was shocked by the despair evident on his face.

"You would have been horrified at the feral look in their eyes and the things they were saying. They're determined to destroy any and all who oppose them. Their fanaticism and hatred have blinded them to the power and determination of the American people. If Islamic radicals committed this horrendous act of mass murder—destroyed five American cities—all Muslims and Arabic-speaking peoples are at risk. Those of us living in America will all be suspect—simply by virtue of our clothing, the color of our skin, and our dialect. Instead of causing problems, we should be doing everything possible to show support for victims of the attack. But no, those fools are starting a jihad that will focus the anger of all Americans directly on us. If they continue this jihad, I fear our days of peace and freedom under the American flag will end. Worse, this may be the beginning of the end for all of Islam. We must pray to Allah for help."

"There, there, calm yourself and lie down on our bed," Fatima said as she helped the doctor remove his shoes. "I cannot believe that well mannered young man you thought so much of did this to you."

"Neither can I, Fatima. I thought he was one of our best and brightest. A man destined to make a better world for all peaceful, freedom loving Muslims."

"How can our Muslim children who grew up in this free country have developed so much a hatred for it?" Fatima asked.

The doctor sighed and propped himself up against the headboard. "I think the answer lies in part with the lessons being taught in the madrasaes. The impact of some of the radical Islamic teaching on our youth has been the focus of a few, but all too infrequent, discussions at the mosque. Some, like myself, believe we must put an end to such hate mongering, but very few, myself included—I'm ashamed to say—have been willing to join together to force a change. Always the naysayers give the same response, 'Our funding and teaching materials come from Saudi Arabia. We must use the text books they provide.' All too few of our brothers are willing to disturb the status quo, or to speak ill of another Muslim. Even if that Muslim is determined to take a course leading to our destruction—eventually causing Muslims to slaughter fellow Muslims." Holding Fatima's hand he swung his legs over the side of the mattress and sat up. Though still woozy, he felt compelled to pray for his adopted country, his fellow Muslims, and their religion. Continuing to hold his wife's hand, he bent to retrieve prayer rugs from beneath their bed.

"Help me arrange our prayer rugs and join me in prayer," he said. Once the rugs were spread, they knelt together, and the doctor began to pray.

"Allah, forgive our wayward people, for they have committed a grievous sin against you and against all humanity.

"Allah, forgive me for not being more vocal sooner in defense of what is right and our American freedoms.

"Allah, we beg you to use Your omniscient wisdom and almighty power to grant calm and reason to our people.

"Oh, Allah, we beg you to send us a leader who will, with

your guidance, show your wayward children the error of their ways.

"Send us a leader who will restore honor to the great religion given by you to the holy Prophet Muhammad.

"A leader who will save us from falling into the great abyss, bringing about the worldwide total destruction of Islam."

Sadly, for this peace loving, gentle couple, the reason and calm they sought, and the leader they so fervently prayed for, was not to be forthcoming. Instead the violent mob of fanatics would continue perpetrating barbarous acts too horrible for Americans to imagine.

Several miles away from where the mob attacked the doctor, Gordon Williams, "Gordi" to his friends, reported to work at Rex Demolition. Gordi, a stocky, five-foot-eleven, barrel-chested man, was a heavy equipment operator for Rex. He was dressed in blue jeans, heavy work boots, and a khaki work shirt with a heavy gold chain around his neck. As was his custom, he entered the company's main office complex to flirt with the office cuties, grab a cup of coffee, and pick up his work orders for the day. Entering the Rex office, he was surprised to find everyone gathered around the TV watching the morning news. The picture on the screen showed a large crowd of agitated people. Chanting some unintelligible words, the crowd was pushing and shoving a frightened looking well dressed older man who seemed out of place in their midst. "What's going on?" Gordi asked, "Who are those people?"

"A bunch of Muslims in front of a mosque," his boss replied.

"Boy, they sure are some kinda worked up. What's that they're shoutin'? Can't quite make it out. Sure sounds funny. ... Must be their 'rag-head' gibberish," Gordi said with a smirk.

Several people in the office briefly turned to give Gordi a disgusted look, then shrugged and turned back to watch the TV. Gordi was being Gordi. By now the fervor of the crowd was reaching fever pitch. The chanting was growing louder and more strident. Suddenly, for no obvious reason, the mob turned and surged away from the mosque.

In the unmarked patrol car both officers felt the hair rise on the back of their necks. The unruly mob abruptly moved away from the mosque and turned toward their unmarked car. "Uh oh," Sergeant Downs said, and felt the words stick in his throat as he announced, "Here they come! Damn, they look mean. Looks like they're out for blood."

"Dispatch, Rover 26. We've got a riot," Butterworth not so calmly reported.

"Damn it! What the hell are they doing to the TV crew?" Gordi shouted, as the group watched, to everyone's horror, the violent scene playing out on the screen in front of them. First a man in the mob grabbed the pretty blonde reporter by the hair, punched her repeatedly in the face, and knocked the screaming woman to the ground. Then in a show of unabashed brutality, others joined the man in kicking and stomping her, until her screams were silenced, and her body lay lifeless on the street. Those on the fringe of the mob turned on the cameraman, punching him, until he fell to the ground, dropping his live camera beside him. Screaming and shaking their fists, the mob turned on the TV van, and once again took up their menacing chant, *Allahhh-u Akbarr, Allahhh-u Akbarr.* Still live, the fallen camera continued to transmit, showing in horrifying real time the mob's legs and feet as they kicked and stomped the defenseless cameraman. Inside the van, Tom attempted to put up a fight. When the remote transmission died, someone in the Rex office cried out, "They've killed them! Those savage bastards killed them!"

"Great God Almighty! Boss, did you see that?" Gordi asked. "Damn ... we gotta do somethin'! We gotta help put a stop to this madness. Boss, I gotta go. I gotta get my people on this thing 'fore it gets out of hand. Looks like the rag-heads are gonna attack us, and we gotta fight back."

In his other life, Gordon "Gordi" Williams was Colonel Williams of the Michigan Freemen's Militia, and now Colonel Gordi had a war to fight. *Hot damn, I gotta call the militia to active duty,* he thought, starting to place calls on his cellphone as he walked purposefully toward his red "hemi" truck. Gordi was a decorated former infantry sergeant with combat experience gained in the First Gulf War.

At city hall, Detroit's mayor and police chief were also watching the live TV broadcast. In stunned disbelief, they watched as the mob knocked the blonde reporter to the ground, and viciously stomped her to death. The cameraman continued filming the mob, until he too was knocked to the ground.

"My God. This is out of control. Do something," the mayor shouted at his chief of police.

Feeling his ulcer acting up, and realizing he was in over his head, the chief hesitantly replied, "I–I can handle it, if this is the only mob ... but if this is happening at other locations around the city, it's beyond the capability of the police department to control. Better call the governor and ask for help."

Butterworth and Downs had seen the attack on the TV crew from their unmarked car. "Dispatch, Rover 26," Butterworth reported "we're following the mob. The TV crew is toast. They've stomped the female reporter to a pulp and beaten the cameraman and driver to death. Looks like the mob is heading for the synagogue." Officer Butterworth did not understand the last Arabic instructions shouted over the PA system by Abdul, the Hamas cell leader in control of the mosque—*"Kill the Saturday people."*

The first police units arrived at the synagogue ahead of the mob. Quickly donning protective riot gear from their patrol car trunks, officers armed themselves with batons, and teargas guns before forming a defensive line in front of the synagogue. A firefight was not a consideration. The onsite commander, Sergeant McDuff, lifted his bullhorn and ordered the rapidly approaching crowd, *"Halt! ... Stop! ... Come no further! ... Disperse! ... Return to your homes immediately!"*

The mob's chants of *Allahhh-u Akbarr, Allahhh-u Akbarr,* drowned out McDuff's commands.

Riyadh, the young student, who'd attacked Dr. Kabbain, shouted in Arabic, urging the mob forward. His fellow mujahedeen, armed with concealed weapons, were strategically dispersed throughout the mob. Realizing the mob wasn't going to stop, Sgt. McDuff ordered teargas to be fired. Teargas canisters skittered around on the ground, some going into the first rank of the oncoming mob. Undaunted by the noxious fumes the mob surged forward, shouting *"Allahhh-u Akbarr, Allahhh-u Akbarr."*

Greatly outnumbered, the officers realized their peril and drew pistols. "Fire a volley into the air," McDuff ordered.

The sound of pistol fire momentarily slowed the mob's advance by stopping the first rank, but pushed forward by the momentum of bodies behind them, they surged onward. *Now is the time to act,* Riyadh thought, and signaled his mujahedeen brothers to uncover their AK-47's, and open fire on the line of police officers.

Officer Grant, who'd been reporting to headquarters from a patrol car, freaked out and screamed into the mike, "Automatic weapons fire! Our men are down. The mob has assault rifles. Officer down! Officer down! They're killing us—"

A burst from Riyadh's assault rifle silenced Grant's report.

After sitting in stunned disbelief for several seconds, listening to the silent radio band, the chief realized he had to act. Grabbing the mike, he began issuing orders, "Lethal force is authorized. SWAT is to go in with weapons released. All units in the area are to proceed to the scene and render support."

Lieutenant Swathmore, the SWAT team's commander and a combat veteran, relayed the order to his men as their armored vehicle approached what was now a combat zone. Riyadh remembered his Afghanistan training camp lessons. Anticipating the police tactics, he'd properly positioned his fighters. The moment the armored SWAT vehicle stopped, two Hamas fighters stood, aimed their RPG launchers, and fired at a range of thirty yards.

As soon as the first fighter depressed his trigger, an electrical squib ignited the propellant in the grenade's small rocket motor, propelling the fin-stabilized grenade out of the launcher and toward the target. When the pointed nose of the grenade struck the vehicle, it generated an electrical signal, causing the detonator in the back of the grenade to explode. The explosive shock wave began traveling down the explosive charge in the body of the grenade, spraying fragments in all directions. When the wave reached the apex of the copper cone (the shaped charge liner), the cone folded, forming a plasma jet of super heated gases and molten copper that burned a small hole through armor, injecting hot gases and high velocity copper fragments into the vehicle. Death was instantaneous for those inside.

The destruction of the SWAT team's truck, and the line of dead police officers inflamed the mob. Assaulting the synagogue doors, the frenzied rabble battered them down. Inside the temple, those terrorists armed with AK-47's spread out, killing anyone they found and emptying their weapon's magazines into the altar and sacred religious trappings. Finally, bent on total destruction, Riyadh and his followers produced fire bombs from their backpacks and set the building ablaze, before fleeing to maraud through homes in the neighboring community.

Urged on by Riyadh, the mob joined in the blood lust, as door after door was kicked in and terror stricken residents ordered to answer two questions, "Are you a Muslim? If not, do you accept Allah as your only god?" Anyone failing to answer yes to the first question had only seconds to say yes to the second. Terrified citizens, too confused and bewildered to understand the question—much less its implication—were slaughtered on the spot.

Police units arrived in piecemeal fashion and engaged the anarchists, but it soon became apparent the out-gunned police could not stop the carnage. Calls for help flooded the governor's lines—only to find the governor frozen by indecision. The very idea of ordering his National Guard to engage citizens with live ammunition and fixed bayonets was too repugnant.

Other acts of insurrection were occurring at mosques and Islamic centers around the city and throughout the U.S.

Colonel Gordi Williams of the Michigan Freemen's Militia was on his way to the militia's assembly point in a barn north of the city. But first, he must visit Rex Demolition's explosives magazine. It was time to meet the enemy on the field of battle, and his men were ready. Opening his cellphone, he dialed the number for Bob Murt's, *Murt in the Morning*, local radio talk show, identified himself, and told the call screener that the Michigan Freemen's militia was getting ready to engage the rag-heads.

"Our next caller is Colonel Gordi Williams, commander of the Michigan Freemen's Militia," Bob announced in an amused voice. "I understand you're prepared to engage the Muslim jihadists."

"Yeah, Bob, we're gonna waste them SOBs what's killin' our women and children. My men are assemblin' now. Then we're headin' for the Tramic area where the worst killin's goin' on."

"Colonel Williams, don't you think that's a job for the police and the National Guard?" Murt asked in a condescending tone.

"Yeah, it is, but they ain't gettin' the job done. We ain't gonna mess around with tear gas and rubber bullets. We're gonna use the real thing. When we finish there ain't gonna be no more rag-heads in Detroit."

"Aren't you taking the law into your own hands?" Murt replied—an insolent smirk evident in his voice.

"Listen, us real Americans don't have no more time for you *girly-men*. You liberals've been fuckin' up our country long enough. We've had enough of your political correctness bullshit. It's time for you to get with the program or shut up. If you keep spoutin' this liberal bullshit we're gonna come after you next."

Quickly disconnecting Gordi, Bob Murt sarcastically continued, "Well, now we've heard from the red necks. It's a good thing people like Colonel Gordi aren't in the majority," he laughed, before deftly cuing in a commercial.

The station's call-in lines were immediately flooded with calls from men and women praising Colonel Gordi and the militia. The mood of the country was shifting, and the liberal media hadn't gotten the message.

Gordi met John Tankelman at Rex Demolition's explosives magazine. Tankelman was Rex's chief blaster and had access to the explosives. Cases of sixty percent dynamite, along with boxes of electrical and non-electrical blasting caps, spools of electrical wire, time fuze igniters, and detonating cord were loaded onto Gordi's pickup.

After completing their task, the two men continued on to the militia assembly point. When they arrived, Gordi found all of his men were present, plus additional volunteers. Most were dressed in BDU's, purchased at surplus stores. Some volunteers wore hunting clothes and carried an assortment of weapons—everything from pistols and shotguns to high-powered, scoped rifles. The militia men were armed with M-16's, AR-15s, M-1s, M-14s and a couple of old M-1 carbines. Their pistols of choice were .45 caliber and 9-mm semiautomatics. One man had a Smith and Wesson .50 caliber revolver—a real hand cannon.

The Michigan Freemen's Militia consisted of a captain, three lieutenants, a master sergeant, and three platoons: each with three squads of nine men. The captain called the men to attention. Colonel Gordi Williams saluted the captain, then ordered the men to stand at ease. Next, he welcomed the volunteers and assigned them to the platoons. Those with high-powered, scoped rifles were assigned sniper duty in support of the platoons.

Assignments made, Colonel Gordi addressed his men.

"We've trained for the day when our country would need us to defend it. Well, today is that day. Them rag-heads have attacked us. They've blowed up five of our cities. Now, this very minute, their attackin' our city. We can't do nothin' 'bout the nuclear bomb attacks, but we sure as hell can do somethin' about the rag-heads attackin' our city.

"The rag-heads killed our police officers, burnt down the Jew's church, and are goin' through the neighborhoods killin' our friends, neighbors, women, and children. Are we gonna let them get away with this?"

"HELL NO," the men shouted.

"That's right. No way in hell we're gonna let them rag-heads get away with this.

"We're gonna start with their church. They call it a mosque. We're gonna blow it up. Then we're gonna find 'em and kill em. All of em!"

"YEAH, KILL EM ALL," the men shouted.

"Okay, let's go. Follow me to the mosque," Colonel Gordi ordered, then turned and started toward his pickup truck. The assembled troops broke formation and ran to their vehicles. The militia had acquired several Army surplus deuce-and-a-half trucks, with bench seats running down both sides of the cargo area.

Paula Scott, a reporter for WKRI-TV, saw the convoy of Army trucks, pickups and automobiles heading into the city with their lights on, blowing their horns. The sight of the all those men holding rifles in the trucks shocked her so much that she decided to turn around and follow the convoy. Using her cellphone she called her boss, who directed her to stay with the convoy, and report back once she'd determined their destination. Finally managing to catch up, Paula pulled up along side the convoy's last pickup truck. "Who are you, and where are you going?" she yelled to the man in the passenger's seat.

"We're the Michigan Freemen's Militia, and we're goin' to Tramic to waste the rag-heads," the man yelled back.

Dropping back, Paula called in the information. Her boss then directed his mobile TV van to head for the mosque in Tramic to cover the fight. Next, he broke into scheduled programming to announce the militia's destination and purpose. Listeners quickly spread the word to friends and relatives. Soon hundreds of men and women began arming themselves with hunting rifles, shotguns, and pistols. Dressed in hunting gear, work clothes, and in some cases suits and ties, local citizens converged on Tramic to join the fight.

Similar situations would soon occur across the nation.

Chapter 12

President George Alexander was pleased with the accomplishments of the past fourteen hours. General Simpson arrived and was getting settled in. They'd located William Fobbs. He would fly to Albuquerque on an Air Force plane in the morning. Alexander had one important task to complete before he could call it a day. Pushing the intercom button, he said to Colonel Young, "Charlie, please place a call to President Wu Yang in Beijing, China."

Ten minutes later, Alexander was told President Wu was on the line. Picking up his phone, Alexander said, "Good afternoon, President Wu, thank you for your call expressing concern and acknowledging my message."

Like President Karpov, Wu had reviewed General Alexander's file. China's file, however, was not as complete as Russia's. *I do not know enough about Alexander to know how to handle him.* Wu realized his aide blundered when he transferred Alexander's call to Vice Minister Yang. *I must establish a good relationship with him,* Wu decided before graciously replying, "All of China sends its sympathy. We wish a speedy recovery to our American friends. If we can provide assistance please call upon us." *I'll have to develop a sense of the man during our conversation.* Wu spoke passable English, but would wait for his translator before replying in Mandarin. Since Alexander had no translator available, they agreed Wu's translator would provide all the translations.

"Thank you for your concern and kind offer, President Wu. Please understand, I do not have time for proper diplomatic courtesies. Nor do I have a Secretary of State to correctly convey such expressions. I ask you to accept what I have to say without taking offense, because none is intended. It is my intention to explain in simple direct terms our position, and my orders to our military; in order for you to fully understand the actions we will be taking.

"First, I have no reason to connect China with the attacks—nor any reason to think Russia was involved. I've raised the United State's Defense Condition to DEFCON 2, and released tactical nuclear weapons to theater commanders. I urge you to take no provocative actions, which could cause an unintentional engagement between our forces. Our military is on high alert. People are nervous, and nervous people make mistakes. Wars have been started by unintentional encounters."

His words are reassuring, but I sense he is a tough man, a man of action. He is going to be more difficult to control than President Rodman. Possibly more difficult than Bush, Wu thought while Alexander continued.

"At this time we don't know who is responsible for these heinous attacks. We are operating under the assumption it was an act of terrorism. The entire Middle East is in a state of turmoil. We have reason to believe many of our embassies have been attacked. Our personnel may have been killed." Alexander paused to see if Wu was going to respond, then continued.

"Syria has attacked Jordan with chemical munitions. Egypt is preparing to attack Israel. Jordanian troops are falling back toward Israel and will join with Israel in a mutual self-defense pact." Alexander paused to allow Wu and his advisors to consider his words before delivering the rest of the news. "I suspect Israel will use a nuclear weapon against Syria before dawn ... and I have ordered an attack on the Egyptian forces."

Alexander's words shocked Wu. *Damn, that's a problem. The whole area can turn into a holy war, affecting our supply of oil.* Looking around the table, Wu saw expressions of shock and consternation on the faces of his advisors; some were voicing their opinions.

"Our primary concern is protecting Israel and rescuing our people in the area." Alexander continued, listening to the babble of voices in the background. *I'm sure he has his advisors listening, just as I have.*

This has gone too far. Time to rein him in, Wu decided, "We are very concerned about your release of nuclear weapons. What assurances can you provide us that you will not use them? Such a serious development must be brought to the attention of world leaders. We must reconstitute the United Nations."

"President Wu, doing nothing to provoke us, either with words or deeds, is the best way to assure we will not employ nuclear weapons against you. As for the use of nuclear weapons, America will use them when and where we see fit." Alexander paused for a couple of seconds, then continued. "I have no intention of reconstituting the United Nations. The UN has been a disaster since its inception. I *will not* allow it to be reborn" Alexander replied in a firm voice. "As for the opinions of other world leaders ... I have no interest in them."

Alexander took a sip of water and allowed Wu time to digest his words. Receiving no response, he continued. "Soon our people will begin to call for retribution—a retribution we shall have," his last words spoken in a slow, ominous cadence.

"When this is over, it is my hope your great nation will still be our friend and trading partner. However, if you make the mistake of opposing us, you may cease to exist."

"Is that a threat, President Alexander?" Wu demanded in English, sitting forward in his chair. *This man is dangerous. I wonder if he has the power to back his words.* Wu looked around the table at his close advisors. Some wore shocked expressions. Others were angry. Only one, Paul Xi, had a thoughtful expression.

"No, President Wu—a statement of fact," Alexander said with finality, then softening his voice continued, "Now, as I see it you have two major problems related to the current situation. First, Muslim insurrections in your part of the world—not a good thing. I encourage you to deal with them.

"Second, we have reports indicating Kim Jung-il is considering an invasion of South Korea. If he does, we will destroy his capital and army with nuclear weapons. Since Kim is in your back yard, I strongly suggest you deal with him in a manner that ensures neither of us will ever have another problem with him. Korea must be united as a free nation. A united Korea is best for both of our great nations."

His message delivered, Alexander sat back and took another sip of water, allowing Wu time to consider his words. Wu made no immediate reply. Garbled voices were heard in the background—one was shrill. The pause lasted several seconds, while the voices increased in volume.

"President Alexander, I require a few minutes to consider your words. If you do not object, I will call you back," Wu said.

Alexander nodded to himself, "I understand President Wu. I will be available for half an hour. If you require more time, please call me tomorrow."

"Thank you President Alexander," Wu said. After signaling for the connection to the U.S. to be terminated, he turned to his advisors.

One counseled taking a hard stance, "He is bluffing. Do not allow him to get by with this insult. Put our missiles on full alert."

A second said, "If he is not bluffing, an alert will trigger a nuclear attack. Why take such a chance, when he said he does not think we were involved?"

A third pointed out, "President Alexander said he hoped we would still be his friend and trading partner. If he is serious about no more UN, then he is implying we will have a powerful place in the new world. He referred to Korea as being in *our* back yard, and referred to *our* part of the world."

"Who does he think he is to make such arrogant statements," the first interrupted. "We must put this arrogant, upstart American in his place."

"He is the most powerful man in the world," Paul Xi said, entering the conversation for the first time. Xi, a native born U.S. citizen, grew up in New York City, attended Boston College and Georgetown University. After obtaining a masters degree in Political Science from GU, he went to work for the U.S. State Department's China desk. He left government service for a high paying position with a major U.S. corporation, where he became head of their China operations. This position resulted in a friendship with China's current president, Wu Yang. President Wu convinced Xi to become his advisor on U.S. affairs.

Xi continued, "Americans are mercurial, difficult for the oriental mind to understand. Japan made that mistake in 1941 by attacking Pearl Harbor against the advice of Admiral Yamamoto, a man who understood Americans. The admiral was quoted as saying something to the effect that they, Japan, had awakened a sleeping giant.

"More to the point is an American anecdote. A story set in a crowded working man's bar, that poses the question, 'Where can a 400 kilogram gorilla sit?' The answer is, 'Anywhere he wants to.' America's new president is a 4,000-kilogram gorilla. Why? Normally the United States' president is constrained by congress and the courts. Today there is no congress, and the Supreme Court is gone. The U.S. military has accepted Alexander as president, which means President Alexander is the defacto emperor of the United States.

"We must face the fact that the U.S. military can destroy China, destroy Russia, destroy North Korea ... in fact destroy any nation. And Alexander has the power to give such an order. This is not the time to test the resolve of the new American president. If he says there will be no UN, then there will be no UN. My counsel is to secure a seat at *his* table, while the invitation still exists."

President Wu raised his hand silencing further discussion. After carefully considering Xi's words he inquired, "How long does it take to prepare our missiles for launch?"

"They have to be fueled, which requires several hours. It cannot be done in secret because of their satellites," a general answered.

"How long would it take for their missiles to strike us?" the president asked.

"No more than two hours, probably less," the general answered.

Wu considered the general's response, and then motioned to an aid to place a call to President Alexander.

"President Alexander," Wu began, "we also have no wish to start a war by an unintentional encounter. We will take every precaution to make sure one does not occur. I will speak to Chairman Kim Jung-il. As you said, he is in our back yard."

Damn, thought Admiral Vazquez, one of Alexander's advisors, monitoring the telephone conversation. *My new boss really knows how to explain things so there are no misunderstandings.*

Admiral Cheung, Commander of the Chinese People's Liberation Army Navy, remained silent during the exchange. Now he scowled, but said nothing. *The arrogant American president has bluffed our weak leader and Xi, his pissant American advisor.* Then he realized this was the opportunity he was waiting for. *Now is the time for decisive action while the Americans are dealing with the terrorists. Now is the time to subdue Taiwan—bring our renegade province under control. I have no intention of letting this opportunity pass. Yes, crisis can also mean opportunity—perhaps the opportunity to do more than just subdue Taiwan. I must give this careful thought.*

Chapter 13

Sunday

USS *Kennedy,* Mediterranean Sea – 0300 Sunday, 28 May

Rear Admiral Krugger was in the ship's combat information center, the CIC, observing the attack plan unfold. Six experimental Y-85 stealth drones, armed with 500-pound bombs, launched at 0100, were approaching the targets. Each drone would circle a target and send back real time video. Tomahawk cruise missiles would be launched at 0400 hours. Pilots in the ready room were receiving their final briefing. The admiral expected to catch the Egyptian Air Force lined up on the taxiways, waiting for dawn to take off. Just before the cruise missiles reached detection range, the drones would attack defensive radar installations with their 500-pound bombs. Minutes later, the Tomahawks would attack known SAM sites, runways, and planes on the taxiway with BLU-97/B combined effect bomblets. Tomahawks armed with BLU-106 Boosted Kinetic Energy Penetrator submunitions would be used to destroy runways and hardened aircraft shelters. A second swarm of cruise missiles would simultaneously attack Egyptian armor with BLU-97/B bomblets. Fifteen A/F-18E Supper Hornets, armed with Rockeye I and Rockeye II Cluster Bombs, were tasked to follow the Tomahawks, and destroy what was left. Armor formations would be attacked with Rockeye I cluster bombs—a MK-20 clamshell dispenser containing 247 MK-118 shaped charge bomblets. Each MK-118 can penetrate the top armor of a tank. Hornets armed with Rockeye II (CBU-59/B) cluster bombs—a MK-20 clamshell dispenser containing 717 BLU-71/B anti-personnel/anti-materiel (APAM) mini-bomblets were tasked to attack aircraft, SAM sites, light armor, and personnel. APAM bomblets have thick walls designed to produce burning fragments capable of causing fires, and a small shaped charge capable of penetrating the top of an armored vehicle. APAM bomblets would shred the Egyptian aircraft on the taxiway and ignite their leaking fuel. A/F-18F Super Hornets would provide top cover and engage any surviving enemy fighters.

Egyptian naval ships and submarines were the target of a second wave of fifteen F/A-18C Hornets, armed with GBU-15 modular guided MK-84 2,000-pound bombs, and AGM-84 Harpoon anti-ship missiles. Screening ships would engage any surface targets with Harpoon missiles. The strike group's two attack submarines, *George Washington* and *John Paul Jones,* had swept the path before them, and had orders to sink any submarine detected within 150 miles of the strike group.

At 0345, the *Kennedy*'s commanding officer, Captain David Zimmer, ordered the ship to turn into the wind and begin launching aircraft. Cruise missile launches began from ships behind and south of the carrier at 0400. Admiral Krugger and Captain Zimmer remained in CIC monitoring radio transmissions from the attack aircraft.

"Sir. One missile just launched from Israel's Palmachim Air Force Base. Time 0545," said Chief Petty Officer Pamela Gordon, who was monitoring satellite feed covering the Middle East.

Admiral Kruger pursed his lips together, and with a slight shake his head in anticipation of events he knew were coming, replied, "Yes, Chief, I've been expecting it. It should track toward the Syrian armor formations to the north. Any additional launches?"

"Affirmative, sir. There has just been a second launch. First one appears to be tracking toward the Syrian position, the second toward Damascus."

Five minutes later, Aegis radars began tracking the Israeli missiles, and Gordon confirmed missile's targets. Admiral Krugger picked up a microphone and made an announcement over the ship's PA system, "Now hear this, Israel has launched two missiles at the Syrians. I have reason to believe they carry nuclear warheads. The fight has begun, and it's up to us to eliminate the Egyptians. Good hunting and God bless America." Turning to Zimmer, he continued, "Relay this information to the fleet."

"Aye, aye, sir," Captain Zimmer responded.

Gebel al-Basure Egyptian Air Force Base – 0530 Sunday, 28 May

Ali Mohammed was sitting in the cockpit of his Mirage 2000. *It will be dawn in thirty minutes, and I'll be able to follow the orders of my caliph—kill the Jews. I have been blessed by Allah to be given this opportunity. If I am fortunate I'll be with my brothers in paradise this evening, and seventy-two virgins will be nice too.* Ali was one of those intelligent men who'd allowed his blind faith in religion to override logic and common sense. Even so, he could not help but ponder the logic of some of Islam's teaching, especially the seventy-two virgins. Sitting alone in the cockpit, he considered the promise, *If there are seventy virgins, will I only be able to have sex seventy times in all of eternity? Perhaps Allah will allow me to keep the women after they're no longer virgins. Could this be Allah's cruel joke?* A horrendous explosion interrupted Ali's daydreams. Several more followed at various locations around the air force base. Noise from the jet aircraft on the taxi way drowned out the engine noise from the approaching cruise missiles. Still looking for the source of the explosions, Ali was unaware of the cruise missile attack until one passed over his aircraft. He was still staring at the departing dark shape, when a BLU-106 submunition struck his cockpit. Soon he would be able to resolve the paradox of the seventy-two virgins.

Southwestern Syria – Sunday, May 28th

The Syrian commander was also waiting for dawn. His armor and artillery units were in position. There'd been no return fire from the Jordanian positions since 1730 hours the previous day. The commander was confident he had a clear road to the Israeli border. Most of his troops were outside of their vehicles, enjoying the cool morning air, when the command radio crackled. A voice reported, "General, incoming missile from Israel."

"Just one?" the general asked.

"Yes, General," the radar operator replied, "Impact in fifteen minutes."

A very worried general realized his worst fears. *One missile can only mean one thing—a nuclear warhead. We've no intelligence indicating Israel has chemical warheads for their Jericho Missiles.* Turning to the officer standing beside him the general said, "Colonel, issue an attack warning on all radio nets."

In Damascus, President al-Asad was in his command bunker, deep beneath the palace when the first missile alert was received. A few minutes later two missile launches from Israel were confirmed. Seven minutes later the missiles' targets—Damascus and the armored units beginning their attack on Jordan—were confirmed. *It's a bluff. Israel would never dare use a nuclear weapon—especially when the Great Satan is out of the picture*, al-Asad thought, but then assured himself and those under his command by saying, "It's a bluff. Do not concern yourself. Allah will not allow the filthy Jews to use their nuclear weapon—if they really have one. In any event, we're completely safe here." Al-Asad was wrong on both counts.

The Syrian general watched as a glowing point of light in the sky slowly increased in size. It was the Jericho's reentry warhead. *I'll soon know if it's a nuke. Insha'Allah.* One hundred and twelve seconds later the general had his answer. The 200 KT Israeli nuclear warhead detonated over the Syrian formation at an altitude of 300 meters. A light brighter than the sun appeared. The general's vision was gone in less than a hundredth of a second. Before he had time to think about the image being burned onto his retina, he was dead: his body exploded by the energy it absorbed from gamma radiation. Neutrons and gamma radiation penetrated the armor of the Syrian tanks, exposing occupants to lethal doses of radiation. Humans exposed to 600 roentgen equivalent mammal (rem) or greater will experience radiation sickness within the hour. None of the Syrian soldiers would live more than thirty days. Thermal and gamma radiation instantly killed exposed troops and rendered most of the equipment worthless. The Syrian Army was destroyed.

A similar type warhead targeted on Damascus was fuzed for a surface detonation. The shock wave penetrated into the ground, destroying all underground cables, pipes—and of course bunkers. Surface bursts produce more fallout, which in this case drifted to the northwest.

The mortal price of jihad had just increased.

Qom, Iran – Sunday, 7:30 a.m., May 28th

The servant entered the caliph's bedchamber with trepidation. How should one go about awakening a caliph? After all, this was the first time he'd had to do so. Approaching the bed, he found his master, Saladin II sound asleep, with his arms wrapped around his young companion, Yosif. The terrified servant stood by the bed and anxiously called out, "Excellency … Excellency, your presence is requested by the *Shura* … and your generals." After several attempts, the servant succeeded in rousing the new caliph.

Mohammed woke from his deep sleep, momentarily confused by his surroundings. Sitting up in bed, the events of the past week came flooding back to him. *I'm now the caliph, Saladin II, and I'm in my palace. What does this fool want?*

The servant prostrated himself on the floor, and said in a quaking voice, "Excellency, your presence is requested by the *Shura*. I was instructed to tell you it's an urgent matter. I have laid out your clothes. I will assist you in dressing."

"What can possibly be important enough to awake me at this hour?" the caliph said, sarcasm dripping from every word.

"Excellency, I do not know," the terrified servant replied from the floor.

"Is something wrong?" Yosif asked in a sleepy voice.

"Don't concern yourself," the caliph replied, leaning over and kissing Yosif. Then, turning to the servant who was still lying on the floor, the caliph snapped, "*Get up* and make yourself useful."

Thirty minutes later, dressed in rich Iranian garments suitable for a king, Saladin II entered a large room. Seated around an enormous conference table were the members of the *Shura*, and several uniformed men. When he entered, the uniform men snapped to attention. Grand Ayatollah Khomeini indicated Saladin II should take the chair at the head of the table. As soon as he was seated, a servant poured him a cup of dark Arabian coffee. Saladin II, who arrived at the palace the previous evening, had no idea where he was, who the military men were, and why he was summoned. *Everyone is waiting for me to speak, and I've no idea what to say.* The caliph sipped his coffee, attempting to control his growing anxiety.

Concealing his amusement, Ayatollah Khomeini sat quietly watching his young puppet squirm.

Saladin II knew he must respond. *I must say something, but what?* Finally a solution occurred to him, and he simply said, "Begin."

Very good, Khomeini thought. *He learns quickly.*

A military man, wearing a uniform and rank insignias meaning nothing to Saladin stood and began, "Praise be to Allah. Oh, Great Caliph, our battle plan has encountered unexpected difficulties. Jordan did not join in the invasion to crush the Little Satan. Our planned mutiny in the Jordanian armed forces failed, and the king was not assassinated." Beads of sweat were forming on the general's forehead. "Jordanian forces engaged in a battle with the Syrian invasion corps, upsetting the attack schedule. Eventually Syria used chemical weapons to destroy the Jordanian's opposition. A coordinated attack by Egypt and Syria was scheduled to begin at dawn today," the general concluded, attempting to control his knocking knees concealed beneath the table.

Saladin II who'd never contemplated military action—much less considered invasion plans, armies, and schedules—suddenly realized he was supposed to know what to do. Pretending to consider the general's words, he searched for answers. *I must make them tell me what to do. I'll ask questions until an answer becomes apparent.* Glaring at the frightened officer, he snarled, "Egypt's attack *was* scheduled? Do you mean it *didn't* occur according to plan?"

Khomeini chuckled to himself. *If this were not so serious, I would enjoy watching him. He is very quick.*

"Oh, Great Caliph, the Little Satan used nuclear weapons against us this morning. One destroyed the Syrian Army, and a second destroyed Damascus."

Saladin was shocked by the news. It was so simple to order the destruction of the Great Satan's cities. He had never considered Israel having nuclear weapons, much less their using them. "What is the status of the Egyptian attack?" he finally asked.

The general was struggling to maintain a calm demeanor, "Oh, Great Caliph, the cowardly Americans attacked Egypt and disrupted their attack."

"How can this be true?" Saladin demanded, half rising in his chair.

A very good question, the general thought, *since you told us the Great Satan was destroyed—on its knees.* "Excellency, aircraft and missiles from the American aircraft carrier strike group attacked before dawn. The evil Americans caught the Egyptian Air Force on the runways and their armor in the process of moving into attack formations. American aircraft and missiles destroyed Egypt's aircraft, armored formations, and most of their naval ships in the harbor."

Saladin sat quietly, appearing to consider the facts presented by the general. In fact, he was in near panic. *How could this happen? I never realized Israel would, or could, use nuclear weapons so quickly. How could one American aircraft carrier, and a few ships destroy Egypt's air force, armor, and some of their navy? Who could have given them the order to do so, after I destroyed their government?* Questions swirled in his mind while the others stared at him, waiting for orders.

Ayatollah Khomeini realized it was time to take control of the meeting. By slightly raising his hand, he gained everyone's attention. "Allah is testing our resolve. He is seeing if we are worthy. The Little Satan has thrown its two spears, and now it is helpless. Egyptian forces will regroup and then attack and destroy the Little Satan. The commander of the aircraft carrier acted without orders. They have expended their weapons and have no support. It is time to destroy them while they lie helpless in our grasp."

Turning to the caliph, Khomeini continued, "It is time for you to order the Tunisian, Libyan, Iraqi, Syrian and Egyptian navies to attack and destroy this ungodly infidel fleet. One of our submarines is in Egyptian waters and can join in the attack. It can sink the Great Satan's evil aircraft carrier."

Saladin was relieved by Khomeini's suggestion, for he had no idea what to do. "A wise suggestion. Why didn't you suggest it?" Saladin said, turning to stare at the general. "Are you capable of carrying out these orders, or do I need a new general?"

Realizing the futility of arguing, or attempting to explain the dangers of such an attack, the general simply bowed and replied, "It will be as you command, Oh, Great Caliph."

Continuing, Ayatollah Khomeini inquired in a soft voice, "What is the status of the Spanish invasion?" Turning to Saladin, he continued, "*Caliph*, I am sure you remember our plans to invade and conquer Spain—return it to our empire."

"Yes, of course I remember. General, is the plan on schedule?"

Smiling to himself, Ayatollah Khomeini thought, *Yes, he's a quick study ... perhaps too quick. I must keep him on a very short leash.*

"My Caliph," the general replied, the plan is on schedule. Fighters have been crossing the Straits of Gibraltar for the past two weeks. They will attack the Spanish communication system and blow up key bridges and railheads. Our invasion fleet is being assembled in the harbors at Bejaïa, Mostaganem, and Skikda in Algeria. The invasion will begin in two weeks."

VIP Quarters, Kirkland AFB – 2330 Saturday, 27 May

The telephone rang as President Alexander entered his bedroom. Dressed in pajama bottoms, he was still toweling off after a hot shower. Jane rolled over and answered the phone on the nightstand, "President Alexander's quarters."

"Ma'am, this is Brigadier General Ekes at STRATCOM. May I speak with the president?"

"Of course general, just a minute," Jane said, and handed the telephone to her husband.

"This is President Alexander. What can I do for you General?"

"Sir, we've received confirmation from Admiral Krugger. The strike against Egypt was a total success. They're out of business, and we had no losses."

"Very good. Pass my congratulations on to Admiral Krugger and the strike group. Send them a 'well done' from the president."

"Yes, sir, with pleasure. Sir, we've confirmed Israel launched two nuclear-tipped missiles: one at Syrian formations on Jordan's border, and the other at Damascus."

"Yes, I expected them to use nukes. Will the fallout endanger Jordan or Israel?"

"No, sir. The prevailing wind is blowing toward the northwest. Lebanon will be affected."

President Alexander grunted, paused for a few seconds, and then continued, "They're paying the price for supporting terrorism. This is just the beginning. Anything else?"

"Yes, sir. We are unable to contact our silent embassies. Our Islamabad embassy has reported fighting in the streets. The ambassador thinks the fanatics are trying to seize control. If they get control of Pakistan's nuclear arsenal we have a real problem."

"Any reports from India? I doubt India will allow that to happen."

"Sir, the ambassador and the CIA station chief reported their military is on full alert. High-level meetings of the Indian government and military are underway, nothing specific yet. We have unconfirmed reports of major fighting in the Kashmir region. This could be the flash point for a war between India and Pakistan."

"Thank you, general. Order the immediate evacuation of our personnel in Pakistan. General Simpson will be taking charge in the morning, but keep me informed of any breaking crises. Good night."

"Good night, Mr. President."

"Good news George?" Jane Alexander asked.

"Yes, if killing your former allies can ever be good news. Bob Vazquez caught the Egyptian Air Force on the runways, lined up like ducks in a shooting gallery. Israel won't have to worry about the Egyptians for a while. Much worse, Israel used two nuclear weapons against Syria ... and Pakistan may be the next government to be overthrown. If so, India becomes the big unknown factor in our calculus."

Jane shuddered, thinking of the burden her husband was shouldering. An experienced military wife, she knew pressure came with command, but George's pressure was more than any man should have to bear. "Let's go to bed. You need all the sleep you can get." Jane turned off the light, rolled over and kissed her husband, murmuring, "I love you."

"I love you too," Alexander said, then closed his eyes and fell into a deep sleep.

Chapter 14

The first telecasts of the USAF video tape showing the damage to Boston was featured on morning newscasts across the country. A shocked America watched in horror as scenes reminiscent of Hiroshima showed the extent of the damage to Boston. The center of the city consisted of the skeletons of tall buildings, with smoke from numerous fires rising in the air. A reporter, struggling to retain some semblance of self-control, attempted to describe a scene beyond description. "While there is no official death toll, the city was full of people still at work or shopping. The death toll will be in the hundreds of thousands … millions," he reported in a shaking voice.

Reverend Harold Smyth was putting finishing touches on a hastily prepared text for his morning sermon. He'd spent the night listening to world and local news, and writing the most important sermon of his career. His nationwide broadcast from the Shining Tabernacle would begin in one hour. Sipping a cup of strong, black, Gevalia Stockholm Roast coffee, the Reverend decided he was ready.

After meticulously dressing in his clerical vestments—a royal blue silk robe, clergy shirt with reversed collar, and gold embroidered stole—Smyth donned a beautician's cape and sat quietly before a brightly lit mirror. There he had his eyebrows penciled in, blush and powder added to his checks, and his collar-length, blonde hair styled and secured with spray. "Your roots need a touch up sir," the stylist commented, when Smyth stood to remove his cape, "Catch me next week, Sam," Smyth said, and patted the pretty young beautician's cheek. Samantha Richards, one of many devoted Smyth followers, watched in adoration as he turned toward the dressing room door. Raising her hand to touch her cheek, Samantha sighed, waived her brush at his retreating back, and softly said, "God bless you, Reverend."

Leaving his dressing room, Reverend Smyth hurried along a short corridor to the Tabernacle's massive music room and sound studio. A sound technician, wearing earphones, was waiting to attach Smyth's pin microphone and run a sound test. "Give us a word or two Reverend," the tech said, gesturing to a man wearing earphones and watching TV monitors in the sound booth.

"May the Lord bless you and keep you," Smyth said with a smile. The man in the sound booth gave them thumbs up. Leaving the studio, the tech and Smyth entered a stair well, leading to a waiting room, where a swinging glass door opened to the sanctuary's raised dais.

God give me strength, Smyth silently prayed, while looking at the sound tech who was intently watching a wall mounted TV monitor. The tech was listening for the sound booth count down cue to begin.

"Three, two, one, go," the tech said, and swung open the waiting room door, which was concealed from the congregation's view by heavy, gold, velvet, draperies suspended from the ceiling. Beyond the door stood the dais, on which the Tabernacle's intricately carved, gold-gilded pulpit held center stage in front of a 300-voice choir, a five-keyboard pipe organ, and a full symphony orchestra. While the organist played the ministry's theme song, "What a Friend We Have in Jesus," the reverend, now in full view of the congregation and television cameras, walked across the dais, climbed the four stairs to the raised pulpit, and nodded a greeting to the somber, uplifted faces below him. It was 8:59 a.m. The church's enormous nave and balcony were filled to capacity.

Looking earnestly into the lens of the center TV camera, Smyth watched for the signal to begin his message—an illuminated red light on the camera—while the last strains of the hymn softly concluded and the choir took their seats. Cued by the sound tech, the light board operator dimmed the overhead lights in the sanctuary, brought up the spotlights illuminating the pulpit and the footlights behind the low, carved, dais balustrades. The camera's red light came on and presented the television viewing audience with the radiant image of the golden-haired reverend, posed against a glorious backdrop of brilliantly colored stained glass windows. Raising both arms heavenward and looking into the camera with a serious expression, Smyth began the service.

"Welcome, welcome friends to this holy place of worship, on this the most grievous day in America's history. Today of all days, in the wake of the devastating atomic attacks visited on us by Satan's minions, we must call upon our Heavenly Father for guidance. I ask those of you present in the sanctuary, and those in the viewing audience at home, to join me—as one—in a prayer for our nation, and for believers around the world."

Stepping to the side of the pulpit, Smyth knelt on the dais with his hands clasped to his chest in the attitude of prayer. Closing his eyes and speaking in a voice quivering with emotion he raised his face to heaven and prayed.

"Oh, Heavenly Father,

"We, Your earthly children, beseech You to shower Your mercy on our great country, and on Your people around the world who love ... honor ... and worship You. America has fallen

prey to Satan's legions who are rampaging across the earth intent on destroying Israel, Your chosen people, and Your church—the worldwide body of believers. We kneel before You, oh God, HUMBLED in the knowledge that the ancient prophecies of Your great saints are coming to fruition. Yes Father, we see anew, fresh evidence of Isaiah's, Jeremiah's, Daniel's, Christ's, St. Paul's, and St. John's forewarnings.

Raising his arms toward heaven, Smyth continued,

"Lord, false teachers, 'ANTICHRISTS,' in the form of fanatical Islamists, are spewing unbridled hatred, calling for the destruction of Your chosen people, Israel. Cowardly terrorists have repeatedly attacked our great country. A country whose governmental institutions were founded on spiritual values, and whose constitutional freedoms are based on biblical principles. Freedoms that include the right to worship as we please. Freedoms that our forefathers fought for—spilt their very blood unto death—that I might have the right to stand before Your people this day, and speak freely—without fear of being harmed—of my belief in YOUR SUPREME AUTHORITY."

Pausing momentarily to lower his arms, the reverend bowed his head and rested his forehead on his prayer-clasped hands. Suddenly his shoulders shuttered slightly and he slumped forward. Obviously overcome by emotion, Smyth thrust his clasped hands up and away from his forehead, while continuing to pray in halting, plaintive sighs.

"Oh, Father ... we TREMBLE ... not in fear ... but in AWE ... of the knowledge that You have allowed this horrendous atomic attack on five of our cities as a sign. A SIGN sent by You to FOREWARN believers that we are standing on the precipice of the LATTER DAYS ... days before the RAPTURE ... and the great TRIBULATION. Days in which believers must prepare. Prepare for the second coming of our Lord and Savior, JESUS CHRIST."

The congregation remained breathlessly silent: some standing with heads bowed, others watching one of two giant projection screens hanging—left and right front—from the sanctuary ceiling. The television camera pulled in tight and Smyth's anguished face filled the sanctuary screens, and those of millions of viewers across the nation and around the world. Gradually Smyth's countenance changed, as he fought for composure and wiped away the tears spilling down his contorted face.

"While we REJOICE in the prophetic promise of the coming of our Savior ... we FEAR for our CHILDREN, Father. We know not when the Rapture will come, nor when Jesus will return with,

*'His eye of FLAME and FIRE and wearing many crowns' to lead
His vanquishing heavenly army against Satan's earthly nations.
We know only that Your word says we must be PREPARED to
meet our Savior.*

Smyth softened his expression, looked down at his clasped hands, and
lowered his voice to a whisper.

At any time ... In the twinkling of an eye."

Looking up, he continued his prayer.

*"And so we come HUMBLY before You now, oh Father, to
IMPLORE You to impart upon us Your wisdom, and Your
almighty strength to WIN this holy war. For the sake of our
children's children, we ask that You stay Your wrath and forgive
the people of this unworthy nation who have forgotten the price
paid for their freedom.*

*"Hear our prayers, Oh Father, and HELP this humble
servant. SPEAK through my mouth the words of Your Holy Spirit,
that I may impart Your DIVINE wisdom to the Christian soldiers
who are about to enter this holy battle for the hearts and souls of
UNTOLD MILLIONS around the world. In Jesus PRECIOUS
name we pray,*

"Amen."

Slowly rising, Smyth stepped behind the pulpit feeling composed and imbued
of the spirit. Looking directly into the camera's lens, and speaking in a strong,
confident voice, he began delivering his sermon: a sermon historians would
credit as the beginning of America's retribution.

"Yes, my brethren, the false teachers, the ANTICHRISTS,
the same minions of SATAN who misled Israel in Jeremiah's
time, and about whom Christ and St. Paul warned early Christian
churches, are among us today. Here in our country and abroad,
these evil servants of the devil, in the form of fanatical Islamic
Muslims, are bent on the destruction of God's chosen people,
Israel, and of Christians the world over. Satan has begun his war
for supremacy over earth and over Almighty God Himself.

"Through the false teachings of their false prophet
Muhammad, these Muslims, these lying servants of Satan, are
carrying out the dictates of the Qur'an *to kill the infidels*—any and
all who do not convert to their modern day Baal—their evil
heathen God ... Allah.

"They want to DESTROY Christianity!

"They want to DESTROY Judaism!

"They want to DESTROY Western civilization!"

The reverend stormed, pounding the pulpit to punctuate each statement.

"They want to force us to accept their false god, this evil Allah!"

Smyth nodded his head to emphasize the point, and momentarily stepping back from the pulpit to allow the congregation time to absorb the meaning of his statement.

"Who is this Allah?"

Smyth asked and stepped forward to look directly at the camera lens for several seconds, before continuing with a sneer.

"He is the *false* god of a *false* prophet."

"God's great prophet, Jeremiah, preached against false prophets 500 years before our Savior came. God spoke these words through Jeremiah as he preached: 'I have seen also in the prophets of Jerusalem a horrible thing: they commit adultery, and walk in lies: they strengthen also the hands of evildoers … they are all of them unto Me as Sodom, and the inhabitants there of as Gomorrah.

" 'How long will this continue in the hearts of these lying prophets who prophesy the delusions of their own minds? They think the dreams they tell one another will make My people forget My name, just as their fathers forgot My name through Baal worship.' "

Again Smyth paused and let his gaze sweep the huge congregation, while they contemplated his last words.

"Allah is the same kind of vile … unholy Baal god referred to in Jeremiah.

"This evil god, supernaturally spawned through the dreamlike image of the archangel Gabriel—no doubt Satan in disguise—in the delusional mind of Islam's infamous, false prophet, Muhammad.

"Inspired by Muhammad's conviction that idol worship was an insult to Allah, the one and only god, Muhammad's followers chose to believe all who thought otherwise should be made *to listen by force.*

"With blind faith, these barbaric infidels followed an illiterate caravan trader, who by his own admission never worked a miracle in his life, and who most certainly was not visited by the most heralded of angels.

"The actions of Muhammad's followers tell an unholy history. A history written in the blood of any and all who wouldn't follow the teachings of the Qur'an, *an evil book.*

"According to the Qur'an, recognized Islamic texts, and a biography of Muhammad, Allah *condoned* immoral and criminal behavior. Allah *bragged* about being a terrorist, deceiving men, stealing their property, enslaving women and children, having his followers commit murder, torture, and genocide.

"So I ask again, who is Allah?

"Allah appears to fit the description of Satan—as he is described in our Bible. Muhammad, the dreamer, the soothsayer, Allah's supposed messenger, did not write the Qur'an. He couldn't. He was illiterate. His followers wrote down their memories of his recitations on any available materials—called fragments, pieces of paper, palm leaves, stones, animal hides, and on their own bodies.

"After Muhammad's death, Uthman, his third successor—called the 'caliph'—assembled men with memories of Muhammad's teachings, collected the fragments, and had scribes write them down. Stories recorded by the scribes were compiled into books, in no particular order, just mixed together in a haphazard manner. Unlike our Bible, the books had no sequence. After the scribes had written down the all stories and fragments, Uthman ordered that all the fragments be burned. The books, when combined, became the Qur'an, and each book became a chapter, called a '*surah*.'

"Remember, Muhammad was Islam's only prophet. His voice is the only source of the Qur'an. Islam is Muhammad's creation, his authorization from Allah for his actions.

"The Qur'an is filled with repetitive stories. It skips from one subject to another with no explanation or logic. It is so badly written that approximately twenty percent of the verses don't make sense. Muhammad's first revelation is contained in the 96th surah, when chronologically it should be the first. The 2nd surah was the 91st revelation, and the 9th surah was the last revelation. Confusing? It sure is. It fell to later Arabic scholars to try to make sense of it.

"What kind of foundation for faith is that my friends? The Qur'an is a hodgepodge of feel good promises and unholy dictates to believers, who seek paradise in an afterlife. A glorious paradise filled with sumptuous food, and seventy-two virgins for the men. A glorious paradise granted on the whim of a god who condones killing innocents who don't worship him.

"Yes, my friends, their's is an EVIL HISTORY. A history of conquests and wars in the name of their false god, Allah.

"Muslims are an EVIL people, with an EVIL GOD.

"Now by the hundreds of millions, their kind are loose upon the earth. Trained in their mosques and their religious schools—their *ma-dras-sahs*—both here and abroad, to HATE JEWS and CHRISTIANS ALIKE. They have infiltrated our communities.

"Even now, they're among us. Living under the guise of peaceful acquiescence, they are using the very liberties they hate to set about fulfilling one paramount objective ... the DESTRUCTION of our way of life. Their despicable attack has destroyed the heart of our government, and our country's great financial centers.

"Now they want to send us all back to the dark ages, to a life under the control of a religious oligarchy.

"A life in which only one god—Allah—may be worshiped.

"A life in which personal freedoms do not exist.

"A life in which women are nothing more than chattel, to be SOLD ... STONED ... or BEATEN at the whim of their religious police."

Smyth said, visibly distraught and shaking his head in disgust. Then, leaning forward to grab both sides of the top of the pulpit he stormed at the camera lens.

"NOW ... at this very HOUR ... here in America they're doing what they do best ... RAPING ... PILLAGING ... KILLING. They have a fancy word for it. They call it '*JI-HAD*,' which means holy war in their foul language. JI-HAD ... an EVIL ACT ... by EVIL PEOPLE ... in the name of their EVIL GOD, ALLAH!"

Resting momentarily, Smyth mopped perspiration from his brow and reached beneath the pulpit for a glass of water. After taking a long drink and regaining his composure, he continued in his normal voice.

"How has Islam spread? By jihad. By the bloody sword! The Qur'an tells us about jihad in its *surah*. Let me quote from the English version of the Qur'an printed by the Fahd Foundation— that's right, Fahd, like King Fahd of Saudi Arabia. Surah 2:190 says: 'Jihad is holy fighting in Allah's Cause with full force of numbers and weaponry. It is given the utmost importance in Islam and is one of its pillars. By Jihad, Islam is established, Allah's Word is made superior, and Islam is propagated. By abandoning Jihad, Islam is destroyed and Muslims fall into an inferior position.' It goes on to say, 'Jihad is an obligatory duty in Islam on every Muslim. He who tries to escape from this duty, dies with one of the qualities of a hypocrite.'

"Does their jihad have rules, like we have rules of war? Yes, their Qur'an establishes their rules. Surah 9:5, 'Fight and kill the disbelievers wherever you find them, take them captive, harass them," which means torture them, "lie in wait and ambush them using every stratagem of war.' Surah 8:12 says, 'I shall terrorize the infidels. So wound their bodies and incapacitate them because they oppose Allah and His Apostle.' Surah 8:57, 'If you gain mastery over them in battle, inflict such defeat as would terrorize them, so that they would learn a lesson and be warned.' And finally, Surah 8:67, 'It is not fitting for any prophet to have prisoners until he has made a great slaughter in the land.'

"Yes my friends, these are but a few of Allah's rules for his jihad."

Still filled with pious fervor, Smyth stopped again to mop perspiration from his brow. Finally gaining control of his emotions, he asked in a soft voice.

"Did you see yesterday's televised newscast from Detroit?"

Shaking their heads, members of the congregation looked first at one another and then questioningly at Smyth, who slowly looked around the sanctuary, up into the balcony, and back again to camera's lens. Then, forcefully emphasizing each subsequent point he stabbed his forefinger at the camera and stridently continued.

"Their evil jihad is here, here in America!

"Just yesterday, these vicious disciples of the devil murdered that woman reporter in Detroit, STOMPED HER TO DEATH.

"MURDERED her TV crew!

"MURDERED our police!

"Then RAMPAGED through the surrounding neighborhoods ORDERING men, women, and children to convert to their vile religion—Islam—OR BE KILLED.

"And KILL THEY DID! They were commanded to do so by their evil book. Listen to what Surah 47:4 tells them, 'So, when you clash with the unbelieving Infidels,' that's us folks, *Christians and Jews,* 'smite their necks until you overpower them, killing and wounding many of them.' It goes on to say, 'Thus you are commanded by Allah to continue carrying out Jihad against the unbelieving Infidels until they submit to Islam.' "

Leaning toward the camera he squinted his eyes and asked in a half whisper.

"What have our state governments done to stop them?

"Some of them have done NOTHING!"

He shouted in disgust.

"That's right! NOTHING!"

"Some state governments are doing nothing … to stop these … evil Muslims.

"No, it was left up to the citizens to defend themselves. A citizen's militia went to their aid. Other citizens heard about the battle raging in the streets of Detroit, armed themselves and joined the battle. Christians, Jews, and atheists fighting together to defend our faith, or our right to have our faith. Even the right to have no faith.

Then in a voice filled with raw emotion, Smyth continued with tears again spilling down his cheeks.

"Our new president, George Alexander, is doing his best. He is *trying* to put our federal government back together."

The reverend sighed, visibly struggling for composure while perspiration dripped from his face.

"Yes, my friends, Washington ... *our beautiful capital city* ... has been leveled by an atomic blast. The members of Congress, the president, and her Cabinet, all assembled for her speech, were *burned alive in that awful nuclear inferno.* All those poor unsuspecting souls at the celebration on the mall and in the other cities were *blown into eternity.*

"How many died without knowing our Savior?"

Smyth sobbed and grimaced before continuing.

"Our central government was destroyed ... but our state governments are intact. *We have good, Christian, men and women* to take the place of the dead ... but that will take time.

"TIME WE DO NOT HAVE!

He shouted and pounded on the pulpit in righteous indignation.

"A religious war has been forced upon us.

"In the name of the Old Testament God, Jehovah, I call upon you to *gird yourselves*, like the mighty Hebrew warriors of old, for the forthcoming battle.

"Our freedoms ... *our very lives are at stake*. America needs our Christian courage. ... Courage that comes only from faith in the ONE, TRUE GOD ... the God of our forefathers, our God is speaking to us.

"*Today* our faith is being tested!

"*Today* our strength is being tested!

"*Today* we must face the challenge!"

"God instructed Moses to tell the Children of Israel to slay the peoples of the Promised Land ... but they disobeyed. They allowed the seven nations inhabiting the Promised Land to live— the Hittites, Girgashaites, Amorites, Canaanites, Perizzites, Hivites, and Jebusites.

"Living among the people of the seven conquered nations, God's children intermarried with them and worshiped their heathen gods. Over and over again God's children suffered for their disobedience. Finally, driven out of their land into captivity, and cast to the four corners of the earth, God's chosen people suffered the ultimate depravity in the gas chambers of the HOLOCAUST.

"Our country fought a war to free the Jewish people from near destruction at the hands of another antichrist ... Adolph

Hitler.

"NEVER FORGET," Holocaust survivors cry. Yet, now, when once again the Jewish people have a homeland in the place of their ancient forefathers, they stand *faced with the threat of* ANNIHILATION.

"The PLO ... HAMAS ... HIZBULLAH ... AL-AQSA MARTYRS BRIGADES ... AL-QAEDA ... all spawned by the Devil to destroy God's chosen people, and our Christian nation—America—are willing to kill themselves for the unholy Islamic conviction that paradise awaits those who kill in Allah's name.

"Today we must go forth with the Old Testament spirit of Joshua ... Saul ... and David, to fulfill God's commands. Today we must to be prepared to slay the evil decedents of the seven nations—the Muslims living among us.

"Once again I admonish you ... in Jehovah God's name

"Be prepared.

"Gird yourself for battle.

"Go home.

"Be vigilant.

"Protect yourself, your family, your neighbors.

"Take up arms like patriots of old against this most unholy menace that will hesitate at nothing to take both your liberty and your life.

"Know your enemy!

"Satan and his minions are at hand!

"NEVER FORGET the consequences visited upon the children of Israel, when they failed to heed Jehovah's commands as they entered the Promised Land.

"Before you leave this holy place today, I ask you to remember those poor souls who died in the atomic infernos. Get right with God.

"Do not delay.

Smyth paused to calm himself, then moved to the side of the pulpit.

"II Chronicles 30:8-9 tells us: 'Now be ye not stiff necked, as your fathers were, but yield yourselves unto the Lord, and enter into his sanctuary, which he hath sanctified forever; and serve the Lord your God, that the fierceness of his wrath may turn away from you.' "

Looking earnestly at the camera and then around at the congregation below, he gave the altar call,

"If you know that you are not living a God centered life, and you want to have a personal relationship with Christ, now is the time to come forward."

Smyth walked toward the ornate spiral stairs at the front of the dais. Standing momentarily at the head of the stairs he raised his arms to encourage those seeking salvation to come forward.

"Our church counselors are waiting to help you as you make the most important decision of your life. Come now and take on the whole armor of God. The counselors are coming forward to greet you and guide you in making this all important life changing decision."

The music swelled and Smyth smiled at the camera as he placed his hand on the railing the gold gilt staircase and slowly descended to stand before the richly appointed altar table, adorned with two massive brass candle holders flanking a towering brass cross. On the cross, hung Christ's broken, crucified body, a sentinel watching over the reverend as he spoke to his spellbound audience.

"To those Christians present and at home, I counsel you to commit yourself to the cause at hand.

"Be a Christian warrior.

"Jehovah God Almighty wouldn't have us stand idly by and watch, as all that our forefathers died to create and protect is lost to a band of savage heathens.

"Fear not: our God is with us.

"Go forth prepared to smite our enemy.

"Put on the whole armor of God.

"Drive these evil forces from our land."

On either side of Smyth the Tabernacle's counselors stood smiling at the congregation, while the orchestra softly played "Onward Christian Soldiers." After showing those under conviction of the Lord approaching the counselors at the altar, the camera cut away for a commercial offering of free tapes and DVDs of the reverend's message—in return for a contribution in support of his ministry. When the broadcast continued, counselors were shown kneeling in prayer with the large number of individuals, who'd responded to their need for salvation, and Smyth who was giving his benediction.

"I will now conclude this service with a prayer that I ask each of you to silently repeat to yourself.

"When I am finished, the choir will sing the invitation hymn # 432 'Onward Christian Soldiers.' While they do, I ask you once again to commit your life to Christ, and to join our Savior in this holy war for the souls of all mankind."

Bowing his head Smyth offered his prayer.

"Oh Heavenly Father,

"We fear the onslaught of a mighty conflagration.

"Dark days are before us.

"Show us, we pray, Your might.

"Grant us Your wisdom and strength that we might meet and defeat the enemy.

"Help us to prepare a way for the coming kingdom of our Savior, Your precious son Jesus. We beseech You, oh Father, to give courage and wisdom to our new president ... Guide his hand ... Give him Your lightning bolts to strike down the evil Muslims who are among us.

"We await the return of our Savior.

"Oh Father, guide us through the Holy Spirit that we may carry out Your will.

"Fill the brave men and women of this nation with resolve.

"Give them the courage and fortitude to do as you have commanded.

"In Jesus precious name we pray.
Amen."

Chapter 15

Southwestern White House – Sunday morning, 28 May

President Alexander and his staff were in the conference room, watching Reverend Smyth's live television broadcast. Everyone was drinking coffee, and most were eating pastries. The president, dressed in slacks, loafers, and a blue short-sleeved polo shirt, had seen enough. Using the remote to turn off the TV, he looked at General Simpson, now the acting Secretary of Defense, and said, "Just what I was afraid of, Harry. I'm sure there will be many more such sermons preached today. The Muslim backlash has begun. Based upon the reports we've received from different cities, we have multiple insurrections on our hands: terrorists from the mosques, Muslim riots in some of our prisons, gangs from the ghettos, and common criminals taking advantage of the situation to steal and loot. Are the states able to control the situation?"

"Some are—those with tough governors," responded Simpson, a tall, trim, broad-shouldered man with close-cropped gray hair. Having arrived from a vacation in Key West, the general wore the best clothes he'd taken with him—tan twill pants, a blue silk sports shirt, and deck shoes. "The riots are getting out of control," he continued, "CS and rubber bullets aren't enough." It's time to take off the gloves and put an end to this. Otherwise we'll have total anarchy. With the exception of Detroit, volunteer militias haven't made an appearance, but I think they will today. Michigan, especially the Detroit area, is out of control. Did you see the video clip of the news crew being massacred?"

"The one Smyth referred to? No, what happened?" the president asked, sitting upright in his chair.

"A mob of Muslim fanatics, obviously urged on by a well armed sleeper cell, rioted in front of a mosque in a Detroit suburb. They assaulted and killed a mobile TV news crew at the mosque and rampaged into a nearby synagogue where they the used AK-47s and RPG's to decimate local police and the SWAT team called in for back up. With no local law enforcement to stop them they went on a killing spree in surrounding neighborhoods until some local militia took them on. Armed citizens heard about the fight and joined in. Gun battles and house-to-house fighting is still raging throughout the area. We have a full blown war on our hands," an angry Simpson explained.

"How did this get so out of control?" the president asked with a frown, leaning forward.

"The police and National Guard are outmatched and outgunned," a disgusted Simpson answered.

"Outgunned? How can they be outgunned?" Alexander demanded, his temper beginning to flare.

"The governor has restricted them to non-lethal force," Simpson replied.

Picking up the phone and punching the direct line to Governor Richards in Santa Fe, the president waited for the governor to answer. "Good morning, Kurt."

"Good morning, Mr. President," Governor Richards replied, sensing Alexander anger from his tone.

"Kurt, what's going on in Michigan? I understand we have a full-blown insurrection in progress. What's the governor doing, or to be more precise, *not* doing?"

"Mr. President, I've spoken with Governor Watkins, and he's doing everything he can."

"Has he authorized the use of lethal force—live ammunition—and ordered his National Guard to put down the insurrection?"

"No, sir. The governor doesn't believe in using lethal force or in the death penalty. He will never issue such orders," Richards replied, attempting to defend Watkins.

"Kurt, we don't have time for political niceties. Tell him to *get control* of his state, or I'll do it for him. He has six hours—then I'll take control."

"Mr. President, you may not have the authority under our existing laws to usurp the authority of a governor."

"Kurt, our country is in turmoil. I'll take whatever action is required to restore order—whatever it takes. He has six hours. Please relay the message."

"Yes Mr. President. I'll do so immediately."

Replacing the phone in its cradle, a frowning president returned his attention to the meeting. "Okay, what's next?"

Dr. George Landry, the representative from the Department of Energy, cleared his throat to get attention, then offered, "Mr. President, the NEST team assigned to Atlanta reported the bomb's yield was much less than the other four. They now estimate the yield at five to seven KT. It appears to have been a fizzle reaction—a partial yield—the nuclear equivalent of a low order detonation in high explosives." Landry's pronouncement caused a stir. Everyone was talking at once. After a minute the room quieted down and Landry continued, "The downtown area was destroyed, and the area to the southeast contaminated by fallout. Samples of the fissile material have been obtained. Preliminary analysis confirms it's highly enriched uranium-235. The samples will be sent to Los Alamos, Livermore, and Sandia Labs for further analysis, and to determine the source. This will take some time."

"Doctor Landry, where could the terrorists have gotten enough HEU for five bombs?" Barry Clark asked.

"Mr. Clark, several nations could be the source. Besides us, Russia, China, North Korea, Israel, Pakistan, India, Iran, France, England, and possibly Iraq. There was a lot of HEU scattered throughout the old Soviet Union. We recovered six hundred kilograms of HEU from the Ulba Metallurgy plant near Ust-Kamenogorsk, Kazakhstan in 1994. As you know, we're still working with Russia to retrieve HEU." Landry shrugged. "No one ever knew exactly how much there was, so we can never be sure we got it all. In 2003, a Russian-U.S. operation recovered one hundred pounds in Yugoslavia, thirty pounds in Romania, and thirty-seven pounds in Bulgaria—more than enough HEU to make one gun-type nuclear bomb. Our labs will attempt to match the spectrographic analysis, which is like a fingerprint of the recovered uranium, to samples in our database. We should be able to identify the source of the HEU." Everyone was listening intently, and Landry was beginning to feel like he was part of the group.

"Thank you, Doctor Landry. Do you have anything else?" the president asked.

"Yes Mr. President, I have a report on the radioactive dispersal device captured in Buffalo. It was a one hundred fifty pound stainless steel container with Russian markings, containing approximately 40,000 curies of cesium-137." Landry's last statement got everyone's attention.

"Aren't cesium-137, strontium-90 and iodine-131 three of the main radioactive contaminants released from a reactor accident? Where would terrorists get it?" Colonel Young asked.

"DOE is wondering the same thing," Landry replied with a slight shrug.

Alexander was following the conversation while staring out the window—troubled by something tugging at his mind pertaining to cesium-137. Try as he would, he couldn't remember what it was. Frustrated, he pushed back his chair, stood, and began pacing back and forth.

"We received a report from the SAC of the Buffalo office," Landry added. "He's elated with his team. Said he'd been keeping close tabs on the terrorist group for some time. He'd ordered them apprehended, as soon as he learned of the attack on New York."

"Can someone put me in the loop?" Simpson said. "This is the first I've heard of this incident."

"The New York National Guard and two FBI agents captured two terrorists and killed the rest near Buffalo. The terrorists were driving a truck loaded with dynamite, packed around a lead-lined, wooden crate containing the cesium-137 container," Young replied.

"If they'd detonated the device in downtown Buffalo, it would have contaminated the entire city. The cleanup cost would have been enormous and would have required months, if not years," Landry added.

Simpson frowned, then asked "If this was an FBI operation, why was the National Guard involved ... and why only two FBI agents?"

"DOE's report stated it was a Guard operation," Landry said, nodding to the general.

Simpson turned to Young and said, "Charlie, why don't you check into it?"

"Yes, sir," Young replied.

"I'll check into it too," Barry Clark added, frowning.

Still pacing back and forth, Alexander had continued monitoring the conversation. Suddenly he recalled the information on cesium-137 containers. Interrupting, he said, "Charlie, you were right. Cesium-137 is a fission fragment from uranium fission. It has a half-life or around thirty years, and decays by emitting beta particles and releasing heat.

"The Chernobyl reactor meltdown released large quantities of cesium-137. As I remember, the Soviets collected it, put it in metal containers, and used it as a thermal power source to generate electricity. Their scientists used it to conduct agricultural experiments for a project they named Gamma Kolos, or "Gamma Ears." [*] The purpose of the project was to determine if irradiated seeds would produce faster growing plants. Scores of those metal containers were distributed around the countryside—each with enough radiation for a dirty bomb that would contaminate a small city. U.S. and international teams have been searching for the canisters, but the total number of containers produced was never determined. Cesium-137 mimics potassium and accumulates in the muscles. Several woodsmen—I think it was in the Republic of Georgia—found some of the containers on a mountaintop. It was wintertime and they huddled around the containers to get warm. All received severe and in some cases lethal doses of gamma radiation."

"Actually," Landry interjected, "cesium-137 decays to barium-137 by emitting a beta particle. Barium-137 quickly decays by emitting a high-energy gamma ray. Barium-137 has a short half-life, 156 seconds, so it's a common mistake to say cesium-137 emits both beta particles and gamma radiation."

"Do you mean there could be more of these containers here?" Clark exclaimed, rising half way out of his chair. Clark was interested in the potential danger of more dirty bombs, not nuclear physics.

---

[*] Project Gamma Kolos: Small, portable, and containing potent cesium chloride in the form of pellets or, more frequently, a fine powder, devices from the project are extremely dangerous, because they could be easily exploited for terrorism. Cesium-137, a silvery metal isotope used commonly in medical radiotherapy, emits powerful gamma radiation and has a half-life of three decades. *NucNews*, November 11, 2002.

Turning to Landry, Alexander said, "George, you better send out an alert to every state and our allies."

Landry was visibly pleased at being addressed by his first name. He hoped it meant the president was no longer irritated with him. Nodding, he quickly replied, "Yes, sir," suddenly realizing he'd come to respect this Air Force general who was now the president. He had never before been associated with a senior manager who was able to draw the best from others, without worrying about his own ego. President Alexander was secure in his own knowledge and ability, and knew how to call on others when he required knowledge he did not possess. But, he would brook no bullshit or incompetence.

Kennedy Strike Group – 1530 Sunday, 28 May

Admiral Krugger was in the CIC receiving his afternoon briefing from CDR Hull.

"Admiral, the Israeli and Jordanian armies are moving north to mop up the Syrians. Israel is reinforcing its units along the Egyptian border. The Egyptian Army and Air Force have ceased operations and are regrouping after our attack.

"We've received reports—confirmed by satellite photos—that naval units from Egypt, Libya, Tunisia, Iraq, and Syria have sortied. It looks as though they plan to attack us. The Iranian submarine has also sortied," Hull said.

"They must be insane to attack us," Captain Zimmer commented.

Krugger sat up, nodded in agreement, and said, "Issue orders to the strike group to destroy all naval combatant ships approaching our formation. Get a message off to the *George Washington* and the *John Paul Jones* to locate and sink the Iranian sub." Turning to the CAG he continued, "Prepare to attack surface ships."

"Aye, Aye, sir," the CAG replied with a grin.

Dropping low over the water, *Kennedy*'s S-3B Viking laid its fourth row of sonobuoys in the projected path of the Iranian submarine. Increasing altitude, the plane circled overhead while the operator monitored the sonobuoys. Ten minutes later, the operator reported a faint signal from sonobuoy number eleven. Concerned about detection, for he was vulnerable to surface-to-air missiles, the pilot was watching several Egyptian warships sortie from the harbor at Alexandria, some twenty nautical miles to the southeast. Another ten minutes had passed when the operator reported, "Strong signal from number eleven."

"Report the readings. I'm turning toward Alexandria to get a better look at the Egyptian ships," the pilot said.

Fifteen minutes later the copilot identified two frigates, and six fast patrol boats putting to sea. "They look like the new MK III fast patrol boats. I think one of the frigates is a Jianghu class," the copilot reported. "I guess the F-18 jocks missed a few."

"Strong signal from sonobuoy number six in the second row. I have a course and speed," the excited operator reported.

"Okay, call it in. We're RTB," the pilot said, turning the plane toward the *Kennedy.*

After entering the observations from the Viking, target information was passed to the CIC. A strike against Egyptian, Libyan, Tunisian, Iraqi, and Syrian naval units would begin in forty-five minutes. Course and speed of the Iranian submarine was sent to the *George Washington* with orders to sink her.

Chapter 16

Berkeley, CA – Sunday morning, May 28th

Students began gathering on the campus early Sunday morning. The day before, the usual campus radicals had printed and distributed handbills calling for a mass demonstration on Sunday. Several liberal professors in the crowd were encouraging a young hothead leftist student, who was using a bullhorn to inflame the students. Worked up and increasing in numbers, the crowd was fast becoming unruly. When Abdul, a well-known Islamic fanatic, gained control of the bullhorn and goaded the students into a frenzy, a police lieutenant radioed warnings to the city hall. The mayor, who'd already instructed local police to keep a safe distance, ordered them to do nothing to interfere with the students' right of free speech.

The Oakland FBI office received a similar report, and quickly relayed it to Kilpatrick, who was monitoring the potential riot from his San Francisco office. Turning to Tom Gallagher, he said, "Tom, get Oakland's Mayor on the phone."

After passing through two gatekeepers, Gallagher held up the receiver and said, "The mayor is on the line, Mr. Kilpatrick."

Picking up his phone, Kilpatrick introduced himself, "Good morning, Mayor Hippe, I'm Sean Kilpatrick, the SAC of the combined Oakland and San Francisco FBI offices." Not one for small talk, Kilpatrick continued, "I've just received a report stating the student demonstration at Berkeley is turning ugly, and there's no police presence. Why?"

Bristling at Kilpatrick's tone and abrupt question, Hippe responded, "Let me make something clear to you, Mr. Kilpatrick. Oakland is my town and I'll run it as I see fit. You, and your FBI, are not involved and will keep out of my business."

Expecting such a reply, Kilpatrick responded, "Mayor Hippe, your interference with an order to arrest suspected terrorists has allowed an unknown number to escape. There's no telling how much damage they will cause. Because of your obstinate stupidity, your town is at risk of a terrorist attack. Interfere with my orders at your own peril. Now, are you capable of putting down the riot if it occurs?"

Hippe spluttered into the phone—so angry he couldn't reply. Receiving no coherent response, Kilpatrick hung up, and instructed Gallagher to get the chief of police on the phone.

"Chief Dobson, please hold for Special Agent in Charge Kilpatrick," Gallagher said, nodding to Kilpatrick to pick up.

"Good morning, Chief, I'm calling to determine your ability to handle the riot that may result from the student demonstrations at Berkeley. I just spoke with the mayor and didn't receive any concrete assurances."

Chief Dobson, who'd been standing near the mayor when Kilpatrick called was in a quandary. He was under orders from the mayor not to interfere. He'd also received reports regarding large gatherings of Muslims at the local mosque and Islamic Center. Deciding that following the mayor's orders was the best way to keep his job, Dobson replied, "We respect the right of free speech. We don't restrict freedom of expression by students or religious minorities."

"Freedom of speech and expression is not a license for anarchy and insurrection. Are you aware of the Muslim uprisings on the east coast? Islamic terrorists, determined to have a religious war, have attacked our country. This is not the mayor's town. It's now my town. There will be no riots, insurrections, nor jihads here. Now, if you're not up to the job, I suggest you go home and get out of my way," a scowling Kilpatrick said harshly.

Chief Dobson was fuming. How dare this fed talk to him this way. *There are courts and laws preventing this type of heavy-handed action. On the other hand ... the fed is right. We were attacked with nuclear weapons. Our government was destroyed. The new president is a former general. Who really has the power? I'd better hedge my bets.* Looking around to see if anyone was listening, Dobson sheepishly replied, "We ... uh, we only have the week end roster of officers on duty. If a riot does occur ... we won't be able to control it."

"That's what I thought. Very well then, I'll notify the governor and the National Guard. The president has declared law and order *will be maintained*. No excuses or exceptions. Riots or any type of insurrection must be put down with *maximum force*. Examples are to be made, in order to prevent reoccurrences. Concentrate on protecting your citizens ... and be prepared for Muslim riots—insurrections. They call them *jihads*.

"Advise your citizens to remain indoors and to be prepared to defend themselves. There is heavy fighting in Detroit. Private citizens, a militia, and the National Guard are fighting armed jihadists in the city streets."

Shit, our citizens don't have guns. We confiscated them. Shocked by this information, a more contrite Dobson replied, "Thanks for the advice and information. I'll keep your office informed."

"Good idea. Alert your officers to be on the lookout for anything out of the ordinary. The fanatics who escaped Friday night will try to execute their planned attacks. Good luck."

Los Angeles, California – noon Sunday, May 28th

KKPI-TV, Channel-44, finished a live telecast of the rioting, which the National Guard commander had called an insurrection. The telecast was highly critical of guardsmen and police using live ammunition to put down rioters. Yes, Jewish synagogues and Christian churches were being burned and looted, and parishioners raped and killed. But, what concerned the female reporter most was that only men of Middle Eastern descent were being targeted for arrest—in other words, profiled! The fact that the majority of the rioters were Middle Eastern didn't seem to matter to her.

In a suite at the Beverly Wilshire Hotel, three well-known Hollywood actresses were watching the live broadcast. The three had just come from a women's power luncheon in Beverly Hills. "This is outrageous," said the one time war protestor—best known for holding up a Rockeye bomblet, while posing for pictures at a North Vietnamese anti-aircraft battery, not far from the infamous prison, nicknamed the "Hanoi Hilton:" a hellhole where American POW's were being subjected to starvation and horrific torture. Despite her apologies for the incident, most Viet Nam veterans and patriotic Americans despised the aging actress.

"Yes, our governor really is living up to his reputation as the 'Terminator.' Or is it the 'Governator?' " snapped the oldest, an actress and singer known for her big nose, sharp tongue, and ultraliberal views. "Our government is responsible for causing those poor Muslim boys to attack us again. We should be reaching out to them, not shooting them. This is really the previous administration's fault."

"Well, what's being done to the Muslims is bad enough, but worse still is this General Alexander who's appointed himself president. How dare he! We don't have independent confirmation our President Rodman is dead. We must use our celebrity status to urge the public to denounce the imposter and call for a UN investigation," said the third actress, an aging redhead who with her movie star husband were also known for their extremely liberal, leftist, and usually illogical positions.

"You're right," said the first actress, "let's call a press conference." Turning to the second actress, she continued, "Barbara, you're friends with the editor of the *Los Angeles Herald*. You call him. I'll call the TV station. How about two o-clock this afternoon?"

The other two agreed. "Let's get on the phones and round up as much support as we can," Jan, the first actress, said. "Do either of you know where to find Michael Grossgutt?"

"I think he's in France making a film with Shawn Bick," Mary, the third actress, answered.

At two o'clock, Jan, Barbara, Mary and a high profile left-wing attorney, Randolph Clarkson, appeared on a live broadcast from the Beverly Wilshire Hotel. A partially reconstituted news network, formerly based in Atlanta, carried the interview. KKPI-TV's handsome anchor opened the interview, "Good afternoon. I'm Thomas Klein, coming to you live from the Beverly Wilshire Hotel. With me are Barbara Focker, Jan Foite, Mary Lane, and well know attorney Randolph Clarkson." Turning to Jan, he continued, "Jan, you called our station to voice your outrage at the way our police and National Guard are treating the rioters."

Staring into the camera, Jan replied, "Yes, I'm outraged. This is worse than Kent State. I actually saw a guardsman shoot a young man. Our National Guard is nothing more than a Gestapo, and our governor is nothing more than another Hitler. He must be stopped … impeached. The public must demand it." The other two actresses voiced their agreement.

Assuming a serious expression, Klein asked, "But wasn't the man the guardsman shot getting ready to throw a Molotov cocktail through the window of a church full of people?"

"That's no excuse for shooting the poor young man. He was just expressing his anger at being targeted, because he's Middle Eastern, oppressed, and has been humiliated by our government. It's the oppressive government's fault he was so angry. We must address the cause of his anger, not act like storm troopers," Jan angrily replied. "The guardsman should have reasoned with him—discussed the cause of his rage. This storm trooper should be prosecuted for murder."

Turning to Clark, Klein continued, "Randolph, I understand you've filed an emergency injunction in Federal Court to force the governor to order the National Guard to stand down."

"That's right Tom, I expect to argue the motion this afternoon in U.S. District Court. A special hearing will be held in Judge Kerry's chambers. I'm sure we'll shut down this atrocity. Our governor thinks he's still starring in movies. I agree. He has to go. He must be impeached."

Smiling into the camera, Klein said to Clarkson, "Well, it looks like you're standing up for our Muslim minority's rights. We'll report the results of your meeting with Kerry, as soon as he issues his ruling."

Turning to Barbara, Klein continued, "I understand you have serious questions regarding the legitimacy of Secretary Alexander assuming the presidency."

"Yes, Tom. How do we know for certain President Rodman is dead? If she is, there's still the vice president and other Cabinet members. Those folks have to be located and confirmed dead, before Alexander can say he is next in line to assume the presidency. This is nothing more than a power grab by a crazed general. I received a call from a friend in DOE, who told me

Alexander released nuclear weapons. How dare this would-be-dictator endanger us? I'm calling on all rational citizens and all state governors to publicly denounce Alexander. We must turn to the United Nations—ask them to send troops and administrators to take over. Our central government has been disrupted—we need the UN," a frantic, almost hysterical Barbara concluded.

"Are you saying we shouldn't recognize General Alexander as president?" Klein said looking into the camera with his most serious expression. "He's been sworn in and is being accepted as the president by our military and our governor."

"Yes, he's being accepted by radical right-wing conservatives, and of course by our *fascist* military. What else would you expect?"

"We must refuse to recognize Alexander as president. We must call upon the UN to determine who is president. Why, we don't even know for sure if terrorists were responsible for the attacks. The military could have planted those bombs, just like they did on 9/11. After all, they're the ones in control of nuclear weapons. Now they've pulled off the perfect coup," a hysterical Mary Lane interjected.

Turning to Clarkson, Klein asked, "Do you agree with Mary?"

"Yes, perhaps she is correct. We have no confirmation President Rodman and others in line to succeed are dead. Their bodies haven't been recovered and positively identified. It certainly appears as though Alexander used this opportunity for a power grab and must be stopped. I'll file a second motion with Judge Kerry to stay the swearing in of General Alexander as president."

"Well, there you have it," Klein commented with a smirk, as he turned to face the camera. "Stay tuned for KKPI-TV's continued coverage of the public's growing demands for UN intervention in this apparent coup by conservative right-wing radicals."

After the KKPI-TV crew and Klein left, a *Los Angeles Herald* reporter who'd been present for the press conference, remained to interview Clarkson and the actresses. He'd recorded the audio from the live telecast, and planned to use it as source material for a front-page feature in Tuesday morning edition.

Thousands of TV viewers were initially shocked, then infuriated by the interview. Soon angry citizens began converging on both the hotel and the KKPI-TV station. Frantic 911 calls flooded an already overcommitted police department, which sent one patrol car to cover both locations. Alerted to the growing presence of an angry public, the three actresses and Clarkson fled through a rear exit to the hotel's limousine. Led by the ever-present paparazzi angry citizens caught up with the limousine, pounded it with their fists, spat on its windows, and hurled insults at the occupants as they sped away.

"I think you'd better come with me to the courthouse," Clarkson cautioned the frightened actresses.

Driving his own car, a near hysterical Tom Klein had barely escaped the mob at the hotel, only to encounter a second angry crowd at the TV station. *Oh no*, he panicked as he approached the gate to the station's back lot. *I'd better stick close behind the van.*

Klein brought his black Jaguar XK8 to a stop a few feet behind the TV van, while the van's driver waited for the security gate to roll open. Unfortunately for him, the ploy didn't work. The driver had been warned of the increasing large, unruly crowd forming in front of the station. As soon as the gate opened, the driver floored it, sped into the lot, and pressed the remote closing device to roll the gate shut behind him. Startled by the van's squalling tires, Klein froze at the sight of the rolling gate. Instead of racing through the closing gate, he sat there watching a man standing by the gate, holding a baseball bat, and looking at him threateningly.

"There's the SOB that interviewed those three bitches," the man screamed to the crowd in front of the station.

"Get the bastard," someone yelled as the crowd surged toward the Jaguar.

Still frozen in terror, Klein made another mistake. Rather than backing up and leaving—he began blowing his horn.

Before he knew it, the crowd had surrounded him and began to violently rock the Jaguar. Egged on by the man with the bat, who was battering the Jaguar's hood, several men were attempting to upend the car. Everyone was screaming and scrambling to get at him. Some banged on the car's windows with their fists, while others used bricks, until finally someone smashed the driver's window. Stunned and bloodied by the blow from the brick, the handsome reporter screamed in anguish as two burly men pulled him through the broken window. While one attacker held him, the other punched him viciously about the head and torso, "My wife and daughter were killed this morning by those Muslim lunatics you're whining about," the man screamed, "Now I have you, you liberal son-of-a-bitch, I'm going to beat you to death."

As the first attacker tired and slumped over from exertion, a blood-splattered bystander lunged forward and kicked Klein in the groin, "Yesterday, those damn Muslims killed my rabbi and burned my synagogue," he screamed, before turning to the enraged mob. "Follow me! Let's get the rest of these liberal bastards," he screamed, running toward the front of the station, where other rioters had battered down the doors.

Ready for a fight, the mob poured into the building, grabbing employees and manhandling them mercilessly before throwing them out the front door. After beating the manager unconscious, the rioters demolished the station's transmission equipment. Still angry, one of the ringleaders shouted to the others to join him as he left the building, "Now let's find those three Hollywood bitches and hang them!"

The police and emergency responders arrived on the heels of the fleeing rioters and took Klein and the station manager to a nearby hospital for treatment.

Chapter 17

President Alexander, General Simpson, Colonel Young, Captain Taylor, Barry Clark, and Jay Henniger, the U.S. Attorney from Dallas, were waiting for Bill Fobbs to join them in Alexander's conference room. Fobbs and several other Americans had departed Madrid at 0200 on an Air Force plane, and arrived at Kirkland an hour ago. Henniger, a thirty-six-year-old, five-foot-ten, 168 pounds bachelor was the president's newly appointed legal advisor. Good looking, with his neatly trimmed hair and stylish titanium glasses, Henniger was considered one of the brightest attorneys in the Justice Department.

Governor Richards was summing up current events from his Santa Fe office, via the president's speakerphone, "The Detroit area appears to be under control, Mr. President. Unfortunately, I had to threaten the governor—told him you 'd remove him and place the state under martial law. He finally agreed to give the National Guard commander full authority to put down the uprising—a real bloodbath. The hard part was separating the citizens, mixed in with the militia, from the Muslims. In addition to the terrorists, hundreds of citizens were killed or injured."

"Reports of similar events have been coming in from around the country. We must do something to stop this madness," Simpson added.

Barry Clark picked up the discussion, "I agree with Harry. Kilpatrick had to call the governor in Sacramento and have the mayor of Oakland removed. Muslim agitators turned a student rally at Berkeley into a riot. Several other riots broke out around Bay Area mosques. Citizens were unable to defend themselves—no guns—an unknown number have been killed and injured. National Guard troops put down the riots. Several hundred rioters were arrested and at least twenty killed. The governor ordered rioters held at Fort Ord. We're also getting reports across the country of armed citizens attacking Muslims. Something has to be done."

"Yes, I agree," the president said. "That's why Mr. Henniger has joined us. I assume everyone has met Jay." All nodded, indicating they had. "Jay, I requested that you review and prepare recommendations to me regarding President Roosevelt's actions pertaining to the Japanese after Pearl Harbor."

"Yes Mr. President, I've done so and have them with me."

Captain Taylor who'd left the room returned accompanied by two men. "Excuse me, Sir," Taylor interrupted, Mr. Fobbs and Mr. Keese have arrived." The president stood and motioned for them to come in.

"Good afternoon, Mr. President," Fobbs said, approaching the Alexander and shaking his hand. "Thank you for rescuing us. We were all quite concerned. Spain was in total panic. I asked Allan Keese, who was also in Madrid, to join me—thought he might prove helpful. Hope you don't mind."

"Not at all, Bill. You don't object to my using your first name do you? I like to keep my meetings as informal as possible. I'm pleased you brought Allan. I can use all the competent help I can get." Turning to Allan Keese, the president offered him his hand. "Allan, I'll be glad to have you join the team," Alexander said, motioning to two empty chairs on the right side of the table as he returned to his seat. "I'm sure everyone knows who Bill Fobbs is. Allan Keese is a former senator, ambassador, and presidential candidate—a man for whom I have the utmost respect. Now let me introduce both of you to my staff." Introductions completed, Alexander said, "I'm going to ask Barry, Charlie, and Harry to bring you two up to date, while I confer with Jay Henniger."

Alexander and Henniger left the room and walked to the president's office. After both were seated at a small conference table, the president said, "Okay Jay, what've you got?"

"Mr. President, the whole legal situation is murky at best. There's no precedent for our situation—no provisions in the Constitution for the entire government being destroyed. We're sailing in uncharted waters," a very serious Henniger began.

"You're correct," the president said, looking across the table at the young lawyer. "However, I find myself in the positions of a staff officer, who suddenly becomes captain of a ship caught in a terrible storm—the only surviving officer. I've no choice but to take command and do whatever I think necessary to save the Ship of State. To do so, I must use every available resource, draw on any useful information, and emulate successful actions of others who've been in similar situations. For our present situation, I'm turning to President Franklin Roosevelt for guidance. You heard what Simpson and Clark said. The Muslim situation is far worse than the one Roosevelt faced with German and Japanese immigrants. Both nationalities proved to be loyal citizens, and like loyal citizens they obeyed orders. But we're dealing with some Muslims who've proven to be traitors and insurrectionists. Our citizens are mad. They are venting their anger on radical Muslim insurrectionists. Unfortunately, good, law-abiding Muslims are being punished with the guilty ones. For the good of all, I'm obligated to take immediate action," the president concluded, looking directly into Henniger's eyes.

"Yes, I quite understand. Here is the draft proclamation you requested. I based it on: President Truman's Proclamation 2914, proclaiming the existence of a National Emergency; President Roosevelt's Executive Order 9066; and 50 USC 21-22, War and National Defense, Chapter 3 - Alien Enemies, Sec. 21," Henniger said placing several documents on the table in front of the president.

Writing comments in the margin as he read, Alexander carefully reviewed Truman's Proclamation, Roosevelt's executive order, the statute, and the proclamation Henniger prepared for him. When he finished, he looked at Henniger, and said, "We have not declared war, nor have we been invaded. Predatory incursion has been perpetrated against our embassies, and the insurrection is clearly in our territory. Let's return to the conference room. After the meeting ends, please revise the proclamation to declare an extreme national emergency, and war with unknown parties." Alexander pushed the documents across the table to his advisor. Standing, he continued, "I'll need it by early tomorrow morning. I assume you've been provided quarters and an office."

"Yes, sir," Henniger replied and rose to follow Alexander back to the conference room. Alexander took his seat at the head of the table and nodded recognition to Dr. Landry, who'd joined the group in the president's absence. After introducing Henniger and Landry, Alexander turned to Keese and Fobbs and asked, "Are you two up to date?" Both indicated they were. "Bill, I need you to take charge of the Treasury, Fed, IRS, and Stock Markets. Until we add more senior staff, your area will also include Interior and Commerce. We have to keep the economy going, which means moving gasoline, food, and medicine. Banks have to open. Taxes have to be collected to keep the government funded. You've a free hand to do whatever is required."

Taken aback, Fobbs looked shocked. "Mr. President, that's an awful lot of responsibility. I'm not sure you have the authority to grant me such power."

"I understand how you feel, Bill. I've been faced with the same questions for two days. The truth is. I can think of no other way to deal with the current situation. If we stumble or show any signs of weakness or hesitation, our country can be lost. I put Nora Jacobson in charge of the Fed yesterday—told her to get the banks open. She informed us of your whereabouts. Nora now works for you. Get anyone else you need. The rulebook is out the window. The only thing that matters is getting the job done."

Fobbs remained silent, thinking about the awesome task given him. Finally, realizing he was as qualified as anyone to do the job—a job that must be done—he quietly replied, "I accept Mr. President."

Smiling, Alexander turned to Keese and inquired, "What are your thoughts, Allan?"

Allan Keese was speechless—a rare occurrence for him. For the past forty-minutes, he'd listened in horror to the summaries of events. The world was in chaos. How could it have happened in two days? Colonel Young provided him a synopsis of Alexander's conversations with Wu and Karpov. *Wow*, he thought. *The world had changed, and the president's laid claim to the chair at the head of the table ... about time too.* "Mr. President, I don't know where to begin. If I can be of help, count on me."

Alexander smiled for a second time, "Good." Turning to the others, he asked, "Where do you think Allan can do the most good?"

General Simpson, the president, and Bill Fobbs were the only ones present who had any experience with the quick witted, brilliant, black man sitting in their midst. "Why Allan, I've never seen you at a loss for words," Fobbs commented with a grin.

"Neither have I," Simpson added with a chuckle.

While Keese squirmed in discomfort, Alexander considered his needs and Keese's expertise. *He's well versed in world affairs and quick minded, but most important—he stood up for his principles. Although smooth and diplomatic, he takes no bullshit—just the man I need for State,* Alexander decided and let the sparring continue for another minute, before saying in a loud voice to get everyone's attention, "Gentlemen, what is our major management problem? Where are we the weakest?"

Realizing the questions were rhetorical, no one answered. Alexander waited to see if any one would answer, then said with a shrug, "It's obvious. It's my non-existent diplomatic skills. Vice Minister Yan told me so." This brought a laugh from everyone but Keese, whose limited contact with Alexander made him unsure how to take the comment.

"Mr. Keese, I want you to join us as acting Secretary of State. You are just what we need. Today we're a new United States, the most powerful nation in the world, and we're going to act accordingly. No more apologizing. No more begging for allies. Leaders don't beg for approval—they lead by example. Our first priority will be our own interests. Something we've forgotten. It's time to get back to basics," Alexander concluded, looking Keese in the eye and waiting for his reply.

Keese sat very still staring at the table, allowing the enormity of the situation to sink in. Finally, he looked up and replied, "I'll do my best, Mr. President."

Alexander responded with a smile and was about to continue when an Air Force major entered, approached General Simpson, whispered in his ear, and departed. Simpson smiled, looked at Alexander and tapped his knuckles on the tabletop to get attention, "I just received a report from Admiral Krugger, indicating he successfully defeated the naval attack launched against his strike group. The remaining Egyptian capital ships, and the Iranian submarine have been sunk. A large number of smaller attack boats have also been sunk or damaged. After the aircraft are rearmed and refueled, the pilots have orders to take out the enemy ports. Kruger's only concern is fuel."

The room erupted in applause. After things quieted down, Alexander turned to Simpson and Keese, "Harry, locate a port where the carrier can obtain fuel. Your other priority is to determine the status of Americans and other allied personnel in the Middle East.

"Allan, notify all our embassies and foreign governments you're now the acting Secretary of State. Make it clear—the United States is going to do whatever we consider necessary to ensure our survival. Opposition will be crushed. Relieve any of our ambassadors who feel he or she cannot be part of our team. Coordinate with Harry on the fuel for the carrier problem. I prefer to purchase the fuel, but if we can't *we'll take it*."

Turning to Colonel Young, Alexander continued issuing instructions, "Charlie, advise the PR people I'll address the nation tomorrow evening at 2000 hours. They're to issue bulletins to all news media. I expect to have full coverage on all operational radio and TV networks, local stations, and Internet simulcasts." Alexander stood, and said, indicating the meeting was over, "I think that'll do it for now."

As the president left the room, Young signaled Simpson and Clark to stay. "I've looked into the capture of the terrorists in Buffalo. There's something strange about this incident. The Buffalo SAC claims responsibility for the capture, yet only two agents were involved. Colonel Butterfield confirmed his unit made the capture, but wouldn't address the FBI issue."

Barry Clark, who'd not had time to follow up on the incident, asked who the SAC was. When told it was Tom Whitwell, he grimaced while muttering, "Not that damn fool. Do you know who the two agents were?"

"Yes, Teresa Lopez and Isaac Calley," Young replied.

"I know Isaac. Good man." Clark said.

"You know, presidents have always acknowledged heroes, and right now we need some heroes. Why not bring the two agents and the officer responsible for the capture here. Let's try and get them here for the president's address to the nation," Young suggested.

After everyone agreed. Clark added, "Let's include Whitwell. I want to get to the bottom of what happened. We'll find out the straight of things when they arrive."

Southwestern White House – 2030 Sunday, 28 May

Jay Henniger entered the president's office after knocking on the door jam. "Mr. President, sorry to disturb you with more bad news. Christy Gonzalez, the U.S. Attorney in Los Angeles, just called. U.S. District Judge Theodore Kerry held two emergency hearings this afternoon and issued two orders: first, staying your swearing in as president; and second, ordering the California National Guard to cease riot-control activities. Christy said she had less than one hour's notice of the hearing. No one was there to represent California. Randolph Clarkson on behalf of the ACLU made the motions. The actresses Barbara Focker, Jan Foite, and Mary Lang were present and gave testimony to the judge. Clarkson and the three actresses gave a live televised press conference that started a riot—this time the citizens were after them. Christy said she didn't know whom to call with the information. The Los Angeles SAC suggested she call me."

Alexander pushed his intercom button and summoned Barry Clark, who arrived a couple of minutes later. After Henniger repeated the information to Clark, Alexander asked their opinion of the judge.

"Kerry has a reputation as an activist judge. He supports extremely liberal issues with rulings that stretch the law," Henniger answered.

"I've heard several complaints about Kerry turning criminals loose on very thin technicalities," Clark added.

After considering Clark's and Henniger's comments, Alexander made his decision. "Jay, is the draft proclamation ready?"

"Yes, Mr. President. I intended to have it waiting on your desk in the morning."

"Please get me a copy now. While I'm reviewing it, call Ms. Gonzalez and direct her to fly to San Francisco with an appeal to Judge Kerry's orders—all of them. After that notify the 9th Circuit, I expect them to hear her appeal first thing Monday morning and rule on it immediately. Failure to comply will result in their removal from the bench. The country doesn't have time for this bullshit. Make my position clear. Next, prepare my first Executive Order removing Judge Kerry from the bench. I'll sign the order after I sign the proclamation. Ms. Gonzalez, the FBI SAC, and a federal marshal will deliver my Executive Order to the judge. If Kerry caused any further trouble, they're to arrest him for treason or insurrection. Ask Ms. Gonzalez and the Los Angeles SAC to review the interview tape. If any of the actresses, or the attorney, made statements supporting an insurrection, or that may be deemed treasonous, arrest them too—on a charge of insurrection or treason."

"S–Sir, such orders must come from the attorney general," Henniger stammered. "And, Mr. President, there is much dispute about the definition of treason."

Alexander frowned and leaned back in his chair to consider Henniger's comments. *Yes, there has to be a chain of command ... Jay seems to be very capable.* Sitting upright, Alexander said, "Jay, you're correct. You are now acting Attorney General. Draft a definition of treason, covering acts by U.S. citizens who give aid or comfort to the enemy. Keep it general. America can no longer tolerate the left's anti-American activities ... nor for that matter, those of the media. I suspect both entities bear responsibility for the attacks. Our enemy judges us by what we say, more than by what we do. From now on the media will either show their allegiance to our country, or they will no longer be in the news business. By this I mean no restrictions will be placed on reporting the truth. Comments and spin are entirely different matters."

Henniger sat slack-jawed, looking at Alexander in amazement and stunned by the gravity of his new position. Events in Albuquerque moved at light-speed compared the normal routine of last week's events. Ever since stepping off of the plane, he'd been in the center of a whirlwind. Suddenly, he realized he was in the center of history making events: a whole new chapter of American history—no, a whole new book—was being written before his eyes. *I'm in the center of one of the most important events in the history of our country—no of the world.*

Chapter 18

Southwestern White House – 0630 Monday, 29 May

Two local TV stations, one reporter, and one radio station were present in the auditorium. At 5:00 a.m. they'd received word, from what was being called the "Southwestern White House," that an important event was going to occur at 6:30 a.m. Reporters were milling around a table spread with coffee and doughnuts, grousing about the inconvenience of being called in without any explanation at that ungodly hour—especially when everyone knew a presidential address was scheduled for 8:00 p.m. "What's up?" one asked another, who raised his eyebrows and shrugged. No information was forth coming from the military types.

At 0630 hours, 6:30 a.m. to the reporters, an Air Force general entered, walked briskly to the podium, "Ladies and gentlemen, in fifteen minutes the president will sign a proclamation and make a brief statement. Following the president's remarks, you'll be provided copies of the signed proclamation. You are requested to make every effort to disseminate the proclamation's content as quickly as possible. Thank you," the general concluded, and, ignoring numerous shouted questions, left the podium.

At 0644 hours, the general returned to the podium. One minute later President Alexander entered the auditorium and proceeded to a table with one chair set up next to the podium. The general held up his hand indicating no questions. Taking a seat, Alexander opened a folder, picked up a pen, and signed a document, while the event was recorded by digital and TV cameras, and described by both radio and TV reporters. After signing the document, the president rose and walked to the podium. The general quietly collected the portfolio and departed.

"Good morning, ladies and gentlemen. I want to thank the members of the press for coming at this early hour. I have just signed a proclamation declaring a state of extreme national emergency and a state of war. Copies of the proclamation will be available shortly. I've based my actions upon those of Presidents Franklin Roosevelt and Harry Truman who also endured sneak attacks. I'm requesting the media's help in disseminating the proclamation.

"By proclaiming a state of extreme national emergency, and a state of war, I'm activating all extreme emergency powers granted to the president. Provisions of The National Emergencies Act of 1976, requiring approval by

Congress *do not apply*, because Congress has been destroyed." Alexander paused, solemnly gazing at those before him, then, looking into the TV cameras he continued, with a determined expression.

"Our nation is at war with unknown and unidentified enemies. Insurrections have occurred, and new ones continue to flare up.

"Persons participating in riots, looting, or any act resulting in damage or destruction of churches or synagogues will be charged with insurrection. Persons providing aid, comfort, or any type of assistance to our enemies will be charged with treason. The writ of *habeas corpus*, as it applies to these charges, is suspended." This statement caused a stir and a few gasps from the reporters.

"It is the duty of the news media to report the facts, and no censorship will be applied to reporting the truth. Our citizens are aware of the tragedy visited upon us, and they're capable of dealing with the facts. I caution the news media against spinning, slanting, or opining in its reports. Doing so will result in severe penalties." Alexander paused, letting his eyes sweep over the reporters, making eye contact with those looking up. He saw surprise, shock, and disbelief on some faces. *Good. That got their attention.*

With a thin smile, the president ended his statement by saying, "I'm sure you have other questions. Most of them will be answered in my address to the nation beginning at eight o'clock tonight. Thank you for coming."

Ignoring shouts from reporters, President Alexander left the auditorium. The general returned to the podium to address the unruly newshounds, "Ladies and gentlemen, please give me your attention. From now on there will be no shouted questions. Doing so is rude and unacceptable behavior. When asking questions, you'll do so in an orderly manner by raising you hand and waiting to be called upon. Failure to comply with these rules will result in revocation of your press credentials. Copies of the president's proclamation are being made for you. Please remain in the area to receive your press handout." Without further comment, the general turned and departed the room, leaving reporters to their own devices. Most were using cellphones to call in their stories. Ten minutes later a sergeant entered and began distributing copies of a press release.

The Southwestern White House
Kirkland Air Force Base
Albuquerque, New Mexico
May 29th

For Immediate Release

Proclamation of the Existence of an Extreme National Emergency and a State of War.

By George Robert Alexander
45th President of the United States of America
Albuquerque, New Mexico
May 29th

WHEREAS the United States of America was attacked by unknown and unidentified agents of a foreign government and/or terrorists at 4 p.m. Eastern Daylight Time, on May 26th, with weapons of mass destruction, being five nuclear bombs; and

WHEREAS, five American cities, Atlanta, Boston, Chicago, New York, and Washington, DC, were thereby destroyed or severely damaged; and,

WHEREAS, the president, vice president, most members of Congress, all members of the Supreme Court, and the entire Cabinet, with the exception of the secretary of homeland security, were killed in the attack; and

WHEREAS, the nation is faced with a clear and present danger of additional attacks by individuals and/or nations; and,

WHEREAS our embassies and citizens in many areas of the Middle East have been attacked; and,

WHEREAS multiple riots and insurrections are taking place throughout the nation; and,

WHEREAS immediate actions must be taken to defend, protect, and preserve our union:

Now, THEREFORE, I, GEORGE ROBERT ALEXANDER, President of the United States of America, do proclaim the existence of an extreme national emergency, which requires that the military, naval, air, and civilian defenses of this country be mobilized and strengthened as rapidly as possible, to the end that we can repel any and all threats against our national security. The writ of *habeas corpus* for persons charged with treason or insurrection is suspended. The Nation is at war with yet to be identified enemies.

I summon all citizens to: make a united effort for the security and well-being of our beloved country; and to place its needs foremost in thought and action so that the full moral and material strength of the Nation may be readied for the dangers which threaten us.

I summon our citizens, farmers, workers in industry, and businessmen: to make a mighty effort to conserve our resources, especially gasoline and diesel fuel; eliminate all waste and inefficiency; and to subordinate all lesser interests to the common good.

I summon every person and charge every community to make, with a spirit of neighborliness, whatever sacrifices are necessary for the welfare of the Nation, and to help the survivors from the bombed cities to the fullest extent of their abilities and resources.

I summon all state, local leaders, and officials to cooperate fully with the military and civilian defense agencies of the United States in the national defense program.

I summon all citizens to be loyal to the principles upon which our Nation is founded, to keep faith with our friends and allies, and to be firm in our devotion to our Nation and our God.

I am confident that we will meet the challenges that confront us with courage and determination; strong in the faith that we can thereby *secure the Blessings of Liberty for ourselves and our Posterity*.

IN WITNESS WHEREOF, I have hereunto set my hand this twenty-ninth day of May in the year of our Lord ...

GEORGE ROBERT ALEXANDER

Sergeant Rogers met Tom Whitwell, Teresa Lopez, Isaac Calley, Colonel Sam Butterfield and Captain Timothy Yondell when they deplaned at Kirkland AFB. Not knowing the nature of their visit, the group wore business attire: Butterfield and Yondell uniforms, Whitwell and Calley business suits, and Teresa her usual pants suit—this time a light tan one with low-heel, brown shoes. "Good morning," Rogers said, smartly saluting the colonel. Pointing to the blue Air Force van, Rogers continued, "The van will take you to the Holiday Inn Express. You'll have thirty minutes to freshen up. General Simpson and Mr. Clark will meet with you at noon."

"D'ya know why we'ah heeyah?" Whitwell asked in his thick New England accent.

"No, sir. Please follow me," Rogers replied and led them to an Air Force van, where their luggage was being loaded.

At 1130 hours the visitors boarded the van at the motel for the short drive to Kirkland. Fifteen minutes later, the van driver discharged them in front of a four-story office building. An air police airman first class guarding the building checked their identifications, then turned them over to a sergeant, who directed them to follow him. On the fourth floor, the sergeant stopped at a conference room door and asked Whitwell and Lopez to wait inside. Calley and the two officers followed the sergeant down the hall and entered a reception area on the left, where the sergeant informed the woman seated behind the desk, "This is Mr. Calley. He's here to see Director Clark." Leaving Calley in the waiting area, the sergeant escorted the two National Guard officers to the end of the hall into similar waiting area on the right. This time a major was sitting behind the desk. Saluting the major, the sergeant said, "Sir, Colonel Butterfield and Captain Yondell are here to see the general."

Colonel Butterfield and Captain Yondell entered General Simpson's office and saluted. Simpson wore civilian clothes—a blue, short-sleeve dress shirt, striped tie, and gray slacks. Returning the salute Simpson greeted them, "Good afternoon, I trust your flight was uneventful. By the way, you don't have to salute me. I'm a civilian."

"Yes, sir," Butterfield replied. "How should we address you?"

"General for now," Simpson said with a smile, then stood and walked around his desk to shake hands with them. "You're probably wondering why we've brought you here in such a hurry."

"Yes, sir," both men replied, sitting down in the chairs Simpson indicated.

"Tell me about the terrorists you caught … everything. Don't leave anything out," Simpson commanded.

Butterfield reported the details, starting with Teresa's telephone call. Yondell picked up the story and described the ambush, giving credit to Teresa for thinking of blocking the road with cows. Simpson stopped them when they reached the end of the firefight by asking, "Why was there no more support from the FBI? They have a SWAT team."

After a long pause and a stern look from Simpson, Butterfield finally added the details of Teresa's problems with her boss. "So, the only reason the terrorists didn't detonate their radioactive dispersal bomb was Teresa and Isaac disobeying Whitwell's orders, and your actions in support of them," Simpson summarized with a frown.

"Yes, sir, Yondell replied after glancing a Butterfield for guidance.

Simpson studied them for a couple of seconds, then stood, extended his hand and said, "Well done. The reason you're here is to meet the president and be decorated. Your actions are one of the few bright spots we've enjoyed during the past three days. This evening during his address, President Alexander will introduce you to the nation and award Captain Yondell the Silver Star, and you, Colonel Butterfield, the Distinguished Service Medal." Observing their surprised look and anticipating their probable objection, he continued, "You both earned them, and the country needs to see some real heroes. You both did what a good officer should do—use initiative in responding to the situation. You'll return to Buffalo on Tuesday. Now, I've arranged for Major Johnson to show you around, and then take you to the officers' club for a late lunch. Treat any information you become privy to as highly classified. I'll see you tonight."

An apprehensive Isaac Calley was shown into Barry Clark's office. Clark
stood and warmly greeted him, "Isaac, it's good to see you again. It's been,
what, three years since the conference in Washington?"

"Yes, three years next month," Isaac replied, shaking Clark's hand. "I
understand you're now the acting director. Congratulations!"

After a couple of minutes of small talk, a more businesslike Clark got to
the point. "What's the real story on the terrorists capture? It's obvious
something's wrong with the report. Why were you and Lopez the only agents
involved? Come on, Isaac," Clark said, leaning forward, "let's have the whole
story."

Isaac hesitated and stared at a photograph of a B-1 bomber hanging on
the wall behind Clark—a memento of the previous occupant—then lowered
his eyes and shook his head in resignation. *I knew it. We're in trouble. Why
else would they fly us all out here? Damn Whitwell, he's behind this. I really
don't care if I'm in trouble, but I have to protect Teresa. She represents the
future of the agency.* Raising his eyes to meet Clark's gaze, he sighed, "Okay,
here goes ..." and began his account of the night he, Teresa, the New York
State National Guard, and a herd of cows saved the people of Buffalo, NY
from certain disaster. Fifteen minutes later Isaac finished the story.

"So, you think Teresa Lopez is a topnotch agent. She took the initiative
and was primarily responsible for capturing the terrorists. Didn't she violate
Special Agent in Charge Whitwell's orders?" Clark inquired.

"Yes, but I'm just as much at fault. I knew about Whitwell's orders and
chose to support Teresa. In truth, he's been unreasonably hard. He's biased
against women in the bureau—especially Hispanic women. In fact, I should
be the one held responsible, because I'm senior, and I encouraged her."

"Actually, you're both guilty," Clark observed with a penetrating look
that caused Isaac to grimace. "Guilty of doing your job. Guilty of showing
initiative. Both qualities are in demand, and highly appreciated around here,"
Clark added, smiling at Isaac's confused expression. "Our new boss, President
Alexander, demands these qualities. People who demonstrate them will get
promoted fast. Those who don't are gone." Clark concluded and continued
smiling and nodding affirmatively at a perplexed Isaac.

Chuckling softly at Isaac's stupefied reaction, Clark leaned forward and
pressed the intercom button for his administrative assistant, Kathy Watson.

"Yes, sir," came the response on the speaker.

"Kathy, Agent Teresa Lopez is waiting in the conference room. Would
you please ask her to join us?"

Turning to face Isaac and standing, Clark continued, his manner
becoming formal, "Agent Calley, you are now Special Agent in Charge of the

Buffalo office."

Isaac stood too, with his arms hanging loosely at his sides—stunned and unsure how to respond. Finally finding his voice he stammered, "D–did you just say I was the new SAC?"

Nodding his head and smiling, Clark walked around his desk, extended his hand and vigorously shook Isaac's. "I know this comes as a surprise, Isaac, but your heroic actions merit this recognition. Tonight the president will address the nation on television, introduce you and Teresa, and award each of you the FBI Medal of Valor." Clark stopped momentarily, hoping to get a reaction from Isaac, but he was still too surprised to react. Changing the subject to Teresa, Clark attempting to elicit a response. "I understand Teresa's single. If she lives up to your description, I want to transfer her here. Can you spare her?"

The ploy worked and Isaac stammered, "T–thank you. Y–yes, I'm sure you'll find her very capable … and yes … of course I can spare her"

Smiling broadly, Clark said, "Good! Good!" *I must find out more about the cows.* Clark, who grew up around the skittish beasts, was amused by the idea of a cow ambush. *I have to hear all of the details.* "Now, tell me, Isaac," Clark began, chuckling again, "Just who thought up the idea of using cows for a road block? I'd have loved to have seen the look on the terrorist's face when he—"

Kathy Watson's knock on the open door interrupted Clark mid-sentence. Both women wondered about Clark's laughter and the odd look Isaac was giving him. Neither man offered an explanation, and Clark maintained his cheerful demeanor through Isaac's awkward introduction of Teresa.

"Good afternoon, Teresa. We use first names around here." Clark said with a twinkle in his eye, and appraised the serious young woman standing before him. Her dark brown hair was pulled back in a bun. He guessed her height to be five-foot-six. She was wearing a tan pants suit with a white, open-collar shirt, and small pearl earrings—no rings or other jewelry. The simple attire served to emphasize her beauty. Before Teresa could respond, Clark turned back to Isaac and Kathy, and said with a chuckle, "Isaac, we'll have lunch later." Looking at Kathy he said, "Please arrange for Isaac to receive a complete briefing while I talk to Agent Lopez."

"It was Agent Lopez's idea," Isaac said over his shoulder as he exited the office.

Teresa quietly watched the exchange, wishing Isaac hadn't been asked to leave. *What did Isaac mean by saying it was my idea? What in the blazes is going on here? It sure didn't look at though Isaac is in trouble.*

Clark indicated for Teresa to take the chair facing his desk and returned to his seat. Leaning forward, Clark looked at Teresa with a stern expression and began, "Isaac told me the complete story of the terrorists capture. Do you feel you were justified in taking matters into your own hands, and disobeying your superior's orders?"

Yeah, I'm in trouble. Teresa decided to defend her actions and let the chips fall where they may. "Yes. In this case, I believe I did the correct thing. I'm willing to take the blame. Isaac, uh ... Special Agent Calley was only trying to keep me from getting into more trouble. Please, don't blame him. I'm responsible."

Sitting back and rubbing the fingers of his right hand across the slight stubble on his chin, Clark pursed his lips and scrutinized Teresa. Beautiful, striking, intelligent, and confident were words that could easily describe her. *Rugged too ... not afraid to get down and dirty either from the look of her,* Clark thought, looking at the mosquito bites still visible on her face, neck, and hands. "Do you make a habit of disobeying orders?" he finally asked. "Do you disobey Special Agent Calley?"

Teresa looked back at the director. Their eyes locked, "No, sir," she replied, her voice calm. "I don't make a habit of disobeying orders. This was a unique situation. I'd been monitoring the suspected terrorist cell for several weeks. I was certain they were getting set to attack us ... and I was proven to be right. I couldn't allow our country to be hit again because of a petty ... uh, because my boss disliked me." Teresa sat very still, using all her self-control to cover her nervousness.

After studying Teresa for a few more seconds, and reflecting on Isaac's comments about Whitwell and women—Hispanic women—Clark leaned forward and said softly, "Good. Sometimes it's necessary to use your own judgment. Trust your instincts. The trick is knowing when to do so." Settling back in his chair, Clark continued studying the young agent who confidently returned his gaze. After a few seconds, he sat forward and smiled, "Your actions, Agent Lopez, prevented a major catastrophe. President Alexander wants to meet you. He wants to tell the American public about your heroism—your's and Isaac's. Tonight, during his address to the nation, he plans to introduce you and award you and Special Agent in Charge Calley the FBI Medal of Valor."

For once Teresa was speechless. She shook her head in disbelief, struggling to compose herself and fully comprehend what just happened. Her mind raced over the director's last statement, *the president ... the nation ... Medal of Valor. Did I hear right? ... Calley is now the SAC? Jesus. Things sure happen fast around here. What about Whitwell?* After a few seconds, Teresa smiled, stood and reached across the desk to shake Clark's hand. "Thank you, Director Clark. I only did what I was trained to do, and I couldn't have done it without Special Agent Calley's and the National Guard's help. I'll do my best to live up to the confidence you and the president have in me."

Smiling, Clark rose, took her outstretched hand, and squeezed it reassuringly, "I'm sure you will. Now I'll have someone escort you to the rest of your group. Take time to relax and enjoy yourself today and tonight. Report to me tomorrow morning at 8:30 a.m. I want to hear much more about the capture and those cows." He told her while escorting her to the door. Smiling and nodding as she exited, Teresa was sure she heard him mutter, "Cow ambush," and chuckle before closing the door.

As soon as Teresa left, Clark called Simpson. They compared notes. After hanging up, a thoughtful Clark sat for several minutes, before summoning Whitwell to his office.

Tom Whitwell, who'd been sitting alone in the conference room for over twenty minutes, was concerned. Slouched down in a chair, with his eyes half closed, he fretted over his situation. *First, I have to sit here with that Hispanic bitch, and then I'm left here alone. This is all highly irregular. Clark was the SAC of the Albuquerque office. Now he claims to be the FBI's director— appointed by some Air Force general who's been sworn in as president. I thought such appointments required Senate confirmation. How do we know Alexander's really in line to be president? Well, at least I did everything by the book. I'm sure Calley and that arrogant Hispanic bitch, Teresa, are getting their asses chewed. I told Clark when he called I'd given both of them specific instructions regarding monitoring the mosque, and they'd exceeded their orders by following the Arab men. I also told Clark I was very upset, because they saw fit to call in the National Guard without my permission. On the other hand, they did catch the terrorists, and it appears they prevented an attack. Yes, I must be careful how I explain the operation so I get the credit.*

Whitwell's brooding was interrupted by a woman who entered the room unnoticed. "Agent Whitwell, the director will see you now. Please follow me."

Whitwell followed the well dressed, middle-aged woman down the hall, where she entered a reception area on the left, proceeded through an outer office, and, without knocking, entered Director Clark's office. "Director, this is Agent Whitwell," the woman announced.

"Thank you, Kathy," replied Clark who remained seated, "Agent Whitwell, have a seat," he tersely ordered, pointing to the chair Teresa had occupied. Sitting forward in his chair, Clark put his elbows on the desk, rested his chin on his upturned fists, and stared at the fidgeting Buffalo SAC. Finally, several seemingly endless seconds later, Clark spoke, "Agent Whitwell, it's been a long time since we last met. How are you these days?" After a couple of minutes of small talk, Clark sat back, apparently pleasantly relaxed. But suddenly his entire demeanor changed. Scowling and looking through half-closed eyes, Clark abruptly asked, "Agent Whitwell, what is your assessment of the situation?"

Rattled by Clark's question, Whitwell fidgeted in his seat, adjusted his bow tie, and stammered, "Uh … w–what do you mean by the, uh … situation?"

Still scowling, Clark sardonically elucidated, "The situation across the country—Muslim insurrections, riots, acts of terrorism, fighting in the streets, rising anger of the American people … the whole mess. What are your thoughts? What are your recommendations?"

"Uh … uh, uh, well that's uh … above my pay grade." Whitwell responded with a shrug. "Yowah askin' about policy made in Washington. My job's to follow awduhs."

Pursing his lips and squinting ever-so-slightly, Clark silently studied Whitwell for quite some time, before methodically pressing him for information on the foiled attack, "Okay, now tell me about the terrorists. How were they caught?" he asked.

Whitwell, who was eager to tell the story to his advantage, enthusiastically responded. Agents Lopez and Calley were ordered to watch the mosque from a distance. Agent Lopez was ordered to return to headquarters and to turn in her gun. "She'd disobeyed a direct awduh to avoid contact with the men from the Mosque," he rambled on, further aggravating Clark with his thick New England accent, "Agents Calley and Lopez exceeded theyah instructions by followin' the van … without my permission," he whined. "They exceeded theyah authority by ent'rin' private property, and spyin' on those men's activities. The fact they uncovahd a terr'rist bomb plot, in no way excuses theyah vi'latin' the rights of owah Muslim minority."

Exasperated with Whitwell's obvious attempt to suck-up, Clark sarcastically interrupted, "Are you telling me you gave priority to protecting suspected Muslim terrorists' rights, over the lives of American citizens—after we'd suffered five massive nuclear attacks?"

"Uh, n–no," Whitwell stammered, "N–not, uh, exactly … Howevah, the end doesn't justify the means. They should've reported to me. I'd've asked the U.S. attorney t'obtain a warrant to search the mosque and the fahm. Aftah thayt—"

"After that!" Clark snapped, sitting forward and leaning across his desk. "Didn't you know we'd been attacked with weapons of mass destruction? Hadn't you received word to apprehend all known and suspected terrorists? Did you take any steps to apprehend the terrorists?"

"Uh, well, uh, not exactly. Uh, my office received a call from another office relayin' instructions to do so, but we'd not received propah awduhs— either from the New York office—or from headquarters," he added as an afterthought.

"I'm sure that's so," Clark sneered, sitting back in his chair, "since both

New York City and Washington, DC had just been blown to kingdom come."

Clearly angry and glaring at Whitwell, Clark sat rigidly grasping the arms of his chair with his fingertips and rocking back and forth in short jerky motions. It took every ounce of self-control he possessed not to go over the desk and beat the hell out of the man. Except for the bobbing motion of his bow tie each time he swallowed, Whitwell sat stock-still, squinting at Clark, waiting for the storm to pass.

After what felt like an eternity, Clark abruptly ceased rocking and sat forward, causing Whitwell to cringe. "Earlier you answered one of my questions by saying it was '*Above your pay grade*,' " Clark said in a low menacing voice.

Nodding meekly in agreement, Whitwell wrung his hands and nearly jumped out of his seat, when a red-faced Clark unexpectedly slapped his open hands, palms down, on the top of his desk. The explosive sound reverberated around the room almost drowning out Clark's angry reproach, "That appears to be the *only thing you got right*," the director snarled through clenched teeth, "Agent Whitwell you're a disgrace to the agency, *so I'm lowering your pay grade* to an amount more commensurate with your level of competence— entry level agent's pay grade—and placing you on *indefinite* probation."

Whitwell shuddered in response, and hung his head in humiliation. Clark sighed, settled back in his chair, and glowered at Whitwell. Finally shaking his head in disgust, he dismissed the cowed agent, "I have appointed Isaac Calley to replace you as SAC in Buffalo. It's up to him to determine if and when you complete probation, and whether you retire at the lowest pay grade. Now, get out of my sight. Return to your hotel and wait there for Calley's orders."

Teresa Lopez, Captain Timothy Yondell, Captain Julian Taylor, and Major Johnson were sitting at a table in the Kirkland Officers Club enjoying margaritas and a light lunch. Calley was having lunch elsewhere with Clark. Colonel Butterworth had found an old friend. The president had instructed Julian to make sure his guests were being properly entertained.

"The boss liked what both of you did," Julian told Tim and Teresa. "He likes people who show initiative and get things done." *Coming from the president's assistant, that's high praise*, Teresa thought, and was really encouraged by Julian's next comment, "I suspect you'll probably be getting a job offer, Agent Lopez. How would you like to live in Albuquerque?" he asked softly, looking at her intently. Teresa didn't reply, but returned his gaze in a way that caused the young captain to shift slightly in his seat. Stirred by the warmth in her big brown eyes, Julian momentarily looked away—just in case she could read his mind. *Boy, is she hot*, he thought and made a show of reaching for his margarita.

When Julian looked away and made busy with his drink, Teresa continued looking at him and thinking how wonderful his aftershave lotion smelled. Suddenly feeling light-headed she thought, *Madre de Dios, what's wrong with me,* and reached for her own drink, *Could it be the tequila? Or was it what just passed between us?* She wondered and looked at Julian again. This time when their eyes met Teresa felt the blood rise in her cheeks. *Enough of that!* she thought, shaking her head slightly to clear it. *Things are moving entirely too fast,* she decided and returned to business by asking Major Johnson, "Do you really think I'll get a job offer? Director Clark did ask me to report to him tomorrow morning. As for Albuquerque, I haven't seen enough of it to know if I like it or not," she said with a shrug, purposely avoiding eye contact with Julian. *But ... if seeing more of it includes a guided tour by a certain handsome officer, I certainly wouldn't object.* Her thought ended with a sigh.

Major Johnson, who hadn't missed the obvious attraction between the young couple, decided things were *definitely* moving too fast. Before Julian could respond, Johnson interrupted, by bringing Yondell into the conversation. "Tim, the same goes for you," he told the captain. "Are you interested in returning to active duty?" Yondell smiled at the question, "Thanks for the compliment sir, but I was just doing my job. As for returning to active duty, I haven't thought about it. My wife and I both have good jobs in Buffalo. I would have to discuss it with her. Are you making me an offer?" Tim asked with a grin.

"No, just an observation. If you're interested, I'm sure we can find a challenging job for you. We need men with your sense of duty and initiative. Let's finish our lunch and take a quick tour of headquarters. You're going to see just how bad things are, and why we need good people. It will help you make up your mind. Colonel Young is going to host an early dinner for your group here at the club at 1800 hours. The president will stop by to meet you before his address, which begins at 2000 hours. Each of you'll be awarded medals during the address. Tomorrow morning, after your meetings, I'll take you on a quick tour of the city," Johnson said directing his last comment to Teresa.

"Your plane will depart for Buffalo at 1700 hours tomorrow," Julian added, "If I can get away, I'd like to see you off."

Chapter 19

Southwestern White House – 1600 Monday, 29 May

President Alexander sat at his desk reviewing his speech. Pausing for a moment, he leaned back in his chair, closed his eyes, and breathed deeply. Ignoring the sounds of people in the outer office and hallway, he allowed his mind to drift—a relaxation method he'd found helpful over the years, when dealing with seemingly insurmountable problems. Alexander used these brief moments of quiet meditation to strengthen his purpose and focus his energy on tasks at hand. Just at the point of total relaxation, the opening of his office door interrupted him. *God give me strength*, he thought as he heard Young quietly say, "Sorry to interrupt you sir, but I have the latest casualty figures for your speech."

"Thank you, Charlie," Alexander said without opening his eyes, "and, if that's all you have for me please close the hall door, and continue to hold my calls for the next half hour. I cannot be disturbed while I finish preparing for my speech." Sitting forward now and glancing at the paper containing the latest casualty figures, Alexander struggled to control an overwhelming mixture of feelings.

Assailed at first by a sudden feeling of nausea, Alexander swallowed and shuddered briefly as images of millions of incinerated dead flashed through his mind. Memories of WWII newsreel clips and still classified documentary films, showing burned and mutilated bodies in Japan, lingered in his mind— never fading, haunting reminders of the inevitable consequences of nuclear war. *Now my people have been burned alive. It's my country grieving. Our beautiful cities—our capital, Washington—have been destroyed ... So many dead. So many unaccounted for. So many injured and maimed for life— Americans, on American soil with no war declared.* Fighting to control a bitter wave of sorrow, Alexander noticed for the first time the estimated figures for property damage. These numbers paled in comparison to the death toll. *The public will only be interested in one thing. Are we next? How do I tell a nation still in shock ... the horror of it all? How do I reassure the living they're safe from a similar fate?*

In the wake of these disturbing thoughts, Alexander fought the rising tide of fury within him. *I can't let myself be controlled by emotions. I must stay focused. Decisive action is the only remedy for dealing with this horrendous attack. The public must see a government establishing order and protecting them from further attacks.* Alexander squeezed the arms of his chair and gritted his teeth. *I have to get a handle on the situation in the Middle East ... Still no word from the Middle Eastern countries or our embassies.*

Intelligence has confirmed the terrorist taking responsibility for the attacks is now claiming to be caliph of a new Muslim empire. They think the bastard is in Tehran, Iran, and they think Iran has nuclear weapons. I'm sure they do. I've got Allan Keese busy attempting to contact the Iranian government. How much of this information do I dare give to the American public? Do I tell them of consequences we face as a nation, if I don't aggressively pursue action against any nation harboring terrorists, or any nation who attacks our allies or us?

Alexander had long been convinced that throughout history the West's greatest failing was its inability to recognize gathering threats—its unwillingness to do what must be done—until it was too late to prevent war. *Hitler told the world his intentions in Mein Kampf, and no one listened. President Roosevelt was forced to stand by and watch Hitler sweep through Europe. It took Pearl Harbor to wake up the country. When we do act, we usually leave the job half done—Korea, Viet Nam, Cuba, Afghanistan, and Iraq. World War II was the last war in which there were clear winners and losers. Sheiks, princes, emirs, kings, and dictators who fund terrorists are not punished, or otherwise dealt with. If Bush II had been reelected, he would probably have seen the conflict in Afghanistan and Iraq through to the end. President Rodman pulled out of Iraq, and civil war is raging between Sunni and Shia ... More Iranian meddling.* Alexander clenched his hands into fists. *Our small contingent of troops in Iraq is in danger. I just received reports the Sunni group—Lashkar-e Jhangvi—is behind the militancy in Pakistan. If they overthrow the government, a second radical Islamic country will have nuclear weapons, and India will attack. I must try to prevent that from happening. More nuclear exchanges are inevitable.* Swiveling his chair toward the window, Alexander gazed at Sandia Crest and contemplated his course of action.

Auditorium, Kirkland AFB – 1950 Monday, 29 May

Reporters, military and civilian personnel, and state, county, and local officials filled the auditorium. The Kirkland Air Force band was playing Gershwin tunes from a corner to the right of the stage. A section was reserved in front of the stage for the president's Cabinet and guests. In the first row sat Governor Richards, General Simpson, Allan Keese, Bill Fobbs, Jay Henniger, Barry Clark, James Chin and Lieutenant General Blankenship. Seated in the second row were Isaac Calley, Teresa Lopez, Colonel Butterworth, Captain

Yondell, Nora Jacobson, Colonel Young, George Landry, Major Johnson, and Captain Taylor. Other members of the president's immediate office staff occupied the next two rows.

The First Lady, Jane Alexander, wearing a camel colored knit suit, sat in the fifth row with their children: Jim, his leg in a cast, sat on the end, and next to him was his younger sister, Jenna, dressed in a light blue pant suit. As she waited for her husband to enter, Jane reflected on events leading up to that day. A call from President Rodman had brought George out of retirement and taken him back to Washington as Secretary of Homeland Security. Their son, a senior at the University of New Mexico, was injured in a fall trying to climb Sandia Crest. His father left Washington early Friday morning to be with him.

If our headstrong son hadn't cut class to go mountain climbing, I would either be dead or widowed. Jane sighed as she remembered her plans to fly to Washington Friday morning to join her husband for President Rodman's address to Congress. *Now, George is president, and we're living in a general officer's quarters on Kirkland Air Force Base, instead of our lovely retirement home in the mountains. He's been given the task of saving our nation. He can do it, if it can be done—but at what cost. Dear God, I fear the stress could kill him.*

Jane sighed again and turned to look at her daughter, Jenna, who was a freshman at the University of New Mexico. Jane disapproved of Jenna's wearing pants to the event. She wanted her to wear a dress, but Jenna, a tomboy at heart, argued she didn't feel comfortable in dresses. *She's having a hard time coping with all of this. Well, so is everyone else, my darling daughter. I've hardly seen my husband for the past three days. He comes home to sleep, maybe for five hours, then—*a slight commotion running through the audience interrupted her thoughts. The band struck up John Phillip Sousa's "The Washington Post" march, signaling the event was about to begin.

At 7:55 p.m., Brigadier General Ross, who'd introduced the president at the morning press conference, entered from stage left. Dressed in his Air Force dress uniform, Ross walked briskly to the podium and began, "Ladies and gentlemen, honored guests, and members of the press, President Alexander will address the nation at 8:00 p.m. There will be no questions or comments from the audience during the president's address. A brief press conference will be held afterwards. Members of the press should limit questions to clarifications of the president's remarks, and should not ask questions about issues the president has not addressed. Asking redundant or nonsensical questions will result in your being removed and forfeiture of your press credentials. The president will not tolerate the press conference circuses of the past. A second warning—never ask questions pertaining to military deployment, troop positions, nor about any subject capable of providing useful information to our enemies. A final warning—in the past, it has been great sport to leak classified documents and information to news media for publication. The president has invoked all of his war powers—the nation is in a state of war—leaking or publishing classified documents or information will be considered an act of treason and guilty parties will be hanged."

Ross remained standing at the podium, quietly waiting for the stir his words caused to cease. Then, upon receiving a signal from a sergeant at the back of the auditorium, he turned toward stage left. A few seconds later, President Alexander, dressed in a dark blue suit, white shirt, and maroon tie, entered the stage. Turning back to face the audience and the live TV cameras, Ross announced, "Citizens of the United States, ladies and gentlemen, honored guests, and members of the press, the President of the United States." After making his announcement, Ross stepped back and waited for Alexander to approach the podium before departing the stage.

Striding purposefully across the stage, a distinguished looking Alexander, nodded at Ross in passing, and took his place at the podium. Quickly finding the camera with the red light, Alexander stood for a long moment looking decisively into the lens, then slowly and deliberately allowed his gaze to sweep over the audience. For an instant his eyes saw Jane's reassuring expression, and he knew it was time—time for America's newest president to begin his address to the millions of television viewers watching in all parts of the world.

"My fellow Americans, Friday afternoon, the United States suffered the worst surprise attack in the history of mankind. The terrorists, who planned this attack, intended to decapitate our government, and they almost succeeded. I stand before you tonight because of an accident. Thursday, my son, Jim, fell while attempting to climb Sandia Crest. I returned to Albuquerque Friday morning to be with him. Otherwise, my wife Jane and I would have attended President Rodman's address to the Joint Session of Congress.

"Television coverage showed the president walking toward her limousine when the bomb detonated. The Cabinet, the Supreme Court, the Joint Chiefs of Staff, and the entire Congress perished in the blast. Emergency teams dispatched to Washington found no survivors near the Capitol building. Residual radiation killed anyone who survived the initial blast.

"Our Constitution makes provisions for the death of the president. As Secretary of Homeland Security, I was eighth in the line of succession. There being no doubt that those above me perished, I was sworn in as the president on Saturday. The presidency is a job I neither sought nor aspired to—but with God's help and guidance—a job I will do to the best of my abilities.

"My first tasks are to aid the injured, restore law and order, and restore our economy. To do so, I must make hard decisions—decisions some may find disagreeable. That is to be expected. But be assured of one thing; every decision, every action I take will be directed toward saving our great nation—restoring America to its historical place as the home the brave and land of the free. Nothing will deter me from this path.

"Our bravery and our ability to face reality are the very things that have made us free. Tonight I pledge to always keep you informed—whether the news be good or bad. I will not hesitate to divulge distasteful information. We must pull together to recover ... *and we will recover*.

"So, I will give you the bad news first. Initial estimates of the dead and missing from the five cities is now two million five hundred thousand. That number will increase. Our efforts continue to focus on aid to survivors, and the defense of our great nation. Medical facilities around the five cities are overwhelmed. Our military, assisted by civilian airlines and Amtrak, are evacuating some of the injured to other cities with medical facilities. Chicago victims are being sent to Seattle, San Francisco, Portland and other western cities. In order to simplify finding missing family members, victims from each of the bombed cities will be sent to specific areas for treatment. The government will bear the cost.

Pausing briefly to indicate a change of subject, Alexander continued with a determined expression.

"Who is responsible for the attack?

He asked, setting his jaw and glowering at the camera for several seconds, before continuing in a matter-of-fact manner.

"So far, the only available information is the claim by a terrorist who now boasts he is caliph—ruler—of a new Muslim empire. We have not devoted valuable resources toward finding the guilty parties ... but be *assured*, soon we *will* begin to look for them.

"No new terrorist attacks, using nuclear weapons have occurred anywhere in the world. But another such attack cannot be ruled out.

"Europe, like America, is experiencing uprisings, insurrections, and terrorist attacks. Additional attacks using radiological dispersal bombs, chemical, and biological weapons may occur.

"With the exception of Israel and Jordan, we have lost contact with our embassies and personnel in the Middle East."

Alexander paused. His gaze sweeping the audience before returning to the TV cameras.

"Here in America, insurrections and riots are still occurring. Most have been put down. State governors are using their National Guards to establish order. Rule of law will be reestablished everywhere in the next few days. Citizens and militias have responded to the uprisings and defended homes, businesses, and churches of all faiths. We are grateful to them."

Alexander's smile faded, and he placed his hands on the podium and leaned forward.

"However, it is now time for our armed citizens to return to their homes. Militias must either stand down or place themselves under the command of their state's National Guard. It is time to allow local law enforcement, the FBI, and the National Guard to take control. Citizens are out gunned and are dying unnecessarily."

Removing his hands from the podium and squaring his shoulders, the president described several thwarted terrorist attacks.

"Law enforcement has been successful in preventing a number of attacks and in apprehending the perpetrators. Raids conducted by law enforcement, after Friday's attack, netted many terrorists cells. Several attacks have been attempted and thwarted. This afternoon a terrorist cell attempted to attack the Oakland-San Francisco area with a crop dusting plane. The plane, which was shot down by an Air Force F-16, carried anthrax. No one, except the terrorist pilot, was injured. All members of the terrorist cell were captured. No anthrax was released. Other cells still exist, and I call upon all my fellow citizens to be vigilant. Report any suspicious activities to your local police or the FBI."

Pausing for a sip of water, Alexander gazed at the audience of somber faces before him, listening in rapt attention. Realizing it was time for encouragement, he half smiled before continuing.

"I want to thank all the young men and women who have lined up at recruiting offices across the country. Your patriotism and desire to serve exemplifies the American spirit. However, I ask you to wait until we call for volunteers. We are still in the throes of recovery and reorganization. Soon your country will have work for you to do."

The president's solemn expression changed to anger.

"A worldwide Muslim uprising is in progress. Saturday morning, Syria and Egypt, whom we have long suspected of being sympathetic to Islamic terrorism, began an attack on Israel. Syria attempted to advance through Jordan. Jordan resisted, resulting in a battle between Jordanian and Syrian forces. In a despicable attack, Syria used chemical weapons to decimate the Jordanian forces. Still fearless in the face of overwhelming odds, courageous Israeli leaders invited the remaining loyal Jordanian forces and citizens to retreat into Israeli territory. Jordanian armed forces then joined Israeli forces in defending Israel. Sunday morning, just as Syrian forces were forming to attack through the destroyed Jordanian lines, Israel launched a nuclear attack on Syria, which destroyed Damascus and the Syrian Army."

Excited murmurs rippled through the audience. The president lifted his hand and waited for silence.

"While Israel was destroying the Syrian forces, our strike group, consisting of the aircraft carrier *John F. Kennedy* and her escorts, attacked Egyptian forces who were preparing to attack Israel. Using satellite imagery to track Egyptian forces, we were able to destroy their air force on the ground and their armored units as they moved into attack formation. Later, the navies of several Muslim countries attacked the *Kennedy* Strike Group. All of the attacking ships were sunk or severely damaged. Most of the attacking aircraft were shot down, and the enemy's ports and airfields were damaged or destroyed. Our strike group suffered no losses or casualties."

Thunderous applause erupted in the auditorium. Alexander smiled and nodded to the now hopeful faces before him.

"I am in communication with the leaders of other nations. The leaders of China, Russia, and England have immediate access to me. We all agree that terrorists made the attack on America. Most countries recognize defensive action must be taken by any nation that's attacked—including the right to seek retribution. In my conversations with these leaders, I have made clear our intentions and my orders to our military. All have offered condolences. For this we thank them."

Again the audience responded with applause, and again the president nodded his approval. Shifting his weight slightly, he looked resolutely into the cameras before continuing.

"Let me clearly state the mission I have set for our government. All politics and diplomacy aside, nothing shall take precedence over the best interests of our people and our country.

"I may be required to take actions violating existing treaties. We don't have the staff, resources, or time to examine each of our actions as they relate to current treaties; so, I am hereby serving notice that the United States of America is suspending all treaties until this crisis is over.

"It is important for you, our citizens, and all peoples of the world to understand my orders to our military. They are simply this. Any force attempting to attack us, to impede our actions pertaining to the rescue of our personnel, or to interfere with our military actions ... *will be totally destroyed*. Any nation launching an attack on the U.S. or its possessions ... *will be totally destroyed*. Tactical nuclear weapons are being issued to appropriate elements of our military. Authority to use these weapons has been released to senior area commanders. There are *no* exceptions to my orders."

In the wake of his last statement, silence permeated the auditorium, followed by a slow ripple of whispers. Some shifted nervously in their seats. Others—mostly the news media—gave forth with audible, disgruntled expressions of disbelief and distain. Ignoring the outbursts, he waited for the meaning of his words to be fully understood.

"Shipments of oil from the Middle East have been interrupted. Gasoline and diesel fuel must be rationed, and plans to do so are underway. Be assured I am taking action to obtain fuel from other sources."

Quickly checking his notes, Alexander saw it was time to move on to the most important part of his speech—the recognition of heroes.

"Establishing a new government and a command center is important. Albuquerque will remain the capital city of the United States for the foreseeable future. Finding the right people to advise me during this critical time has been a priority. Fortunately, there are those whose prior service to our country has prepared them for these important positions. I have found such people to fill the most important positions. Now, I am pleased to introduce my key advisors, acting Cabinet members and staff. As I do, I ask that they join me here on the stage.

"I'll begin with New Mexico's Governor Richards, whom I've appointed to be my liaison with all state governors."

Richards rose and using the stairs on the left side of the stage joined the president.

"Next, I'll introduce the members of the acting Cabinet.

"General Harry Simpson, the former Chairman of the Joint Chiefs of Staff is now the Secretary of War ..."

Alexander continued until all but one Cabinet member had mounted the stairs and joined him.

"Finally, I'm pleased to introduce, Doctor James Chin, Director of Los Alamos National Laboratories, as our Secretary of Energy."

As Chin rose to join the others, Alexander continued. Pointing to the audience, he smiled encouragingly and said.

"Doctor George Landry, Doctor Chin's liaison to me, is seated in the second row; stand up George. These two men have been directing the Department of Energy's rescue efforts in the five cities."

Applause broke out and Landry turned red with embarrassment and pride. *I never expected to be recognized by the president.*

"Also seated in the audience is Lieutenant General John Blankenship, Deputy Commander of the U.S. Strategic Command. He will be Secretary Simpson's and my link with the Commander of U.S. Strategic Command."

Alexander gestured to Blankenship who stood to be recognized.

"One last introduction. Colonel Charles Young is my chief of staff. Stand up Charlie."

As Young stood and smiled, the president smiled in recognition, then waited to allow the buzz in the auditorium to subside.

"Now, for more good news. A group of terrorists had planned to detonate a large radioactive dispersal bomb—a dirty bomb—in Buffalo, New York, early Saturday morning. The dedication of two FBI agents, and the swift actions by members of a New York National Guard unit foiled the plot. Their quick, decisive action resulted in the capture of two terrorists, and the deaths of the others. I am proud to introduce Special Agents

Isaac Calley and Teresa Lopez. Isaac, Teresa, please join us."
Isaac and Teresa mounted the stage to a standing ovation. Finally the president signaled for quiet.

"Colonel Sam Butterfield, commanding officer of New York State's National Guard, Second Brigade, 43rd Infantry Division, and Captain Timothy Yondell of the same unit. Gentlemen please join us."

The applause resumed and Butterfield and Yondell took the stage, as a smiling president greeted them. Then followed by Governor Richards, the other members of the new Cabinet formed a line and each shook hands with the smiling honorees. Returning to the podium, the president continued.

"Special Agent Lopez, using her own initiative, staked out a mosque and waited for a suspected terrorist group to enter. Later Special Agent Calley joined her and together they followed the terrorists to a remote farm. Agent Lopez crept close to a barn and observed the terrorists loading dynamite and a heavy container onto a truck. Deciding the National Guard was in the best position to respond quickly, Agent Lopez contacted Colonel Butterworth, who ordered Captain Yondell to lead a reinforced rifle platoon to the area and set up an ambush. Agent Lopez ingeniously suggested using cattle to block the road just over the top of a hill at the ambush site. The truck carrying the radioactive material and dynamite was stopped by the cattle, and a fierce firefight ensued. Four of the six terrorists were killed. If the terrorists had succeeded in detonating their dirty bomb, the center of Buffalo would have been uninhabitable for many years."

Again the audience was on its feet, this time shouting and enthusiastically clapping their hands in approval. After a minute or so, the president raised his hands for quiet, and then continued with a broad grin.

"It is now my honor to award Agents Calley and Lopez the FBI's Medal of Valor. Director Clark will you assist me in presenting the honors."

Alexander and Clark walked to Calley and Lopez. Alexander removed a medal from the box Clark was holding and pinned it on Lopez's blazer. The second medal was pinned to Calley's suit coat. Again, the audience erupted with applause. Alexander and Clark shook hands with Isaac and Teresa. After several seconds, the smiling president raised his hands for quiet.

"We're not quite finished. There are still more honorees to be recognized. Secretary Simpson, your assistance please."

Secretary of War Simpson joined the president and ordered, "Colonel Butterfield, Captain Yondell, step forward to be decorated." Alexander removed the medal from the box Simpson was holding, and walked up to Colonel Butterfield who was standing at attention.

"Colonel Butterfield, it is my pleasure to award you the Distinguished Service Medal for your outstanding initiative and quick actions resulting in the apprehension of the terrorists and prevention of another major catastrophe."

The president and SecWar shook the colonel's hand, then moved on to Yondell. Simpson held out a second box for the president.

"Captain Yondell, it is my honor to award you the Silver Star for your outstanding initiative and quick actions as commander of the unit apprehending the terrorists, preventing another major catastrophe. In addition, you and all of the men participating in the firefight will be decorated and awarded the Combat Infantry Badge."

After pinning on the medal, the president and Simpson shook the captain's hand, and the audience was once again on its feet. President Alexander waited for the applause to die down.

"Thank you, and thanks to all of the other unnamed heroes who have helped, and continue to help to save our nation."

Then turning back to the TV cameras and the audience, he concluded.

"Thank all of you for your kind attention.

"Good evening and God bless America."

The president left the stage to thunderous applause, and the stirring beat of Sousa's "Semper Fidelis" march.

All across the nation, citizens watching TV, or listening to the radio, felt a new sense of confidence: a sense that the darkest part of the night had passed; that the coming dawn would bring with it the rebirth of America.

The Caliph's Palace, Tehran, Iran – 6:30 a.m., Tuesday, May 30th

Supreme Leader Grand Ayatollah Khomeini, the ultimate authority in Iran—and now the new Muslim empire—and Caliph Mohammed Saladin II had risen early to watch President Alexander's speech. A meeting of the Iranian Guardian Council, which now consisted of extremists handpicked by Khomeini, was scheduled to begin at 9:00 a.m. The purpose of the meeting was to discuss the progress of the Empire's war, and the results of its latest naval battle with the American carrier strike group.

The Ayatollah was sitting in an overstuffed recliner, watching the American president on a large TV screen. Mohammed fidgeted in a matching recliner positioned next to Khomeini. Both men had been served rich, dark, steaming, hot coffee. A gold tray heaped with pastries and fruit sat on a table between the chairs. Mohammed was beginning to worry. Nothing seemed to faze the damnable Americans. If one could believe what Alexander was saying, the carefully planned Muslim uprisings in the Great Satan were being contained and put down. *How can that be possible after I destroyed five of their cities?* Mohammed wondered. *Alexander just announced they've defeated our naval attack and are attacking our ports, which coincides with reports we've received. Impossible! Damn, I wish I knew how to find Ralph Eid. He always gave me good advice. I wonder what's become of him?*

The sound of applause coming from the TV interrupted Mohammed's thoughts. After listening for a few seconds, he realized Alexander was pinning a medal on a woman. *Oh! She's the bitch that fucked up our dirty bomb plans. I'll remember her.*

After Alexander completed his speech and left the stage, Khomeini turned to Mohammed and said, "Allah still tests our resolve. It is up to us to inspire the faithful to continue our Great Jihad, and to overcome the loathsome infidels. Allah will strengthen us."

Mohammed turned and looked into Khomeini's eyes, which radiated intensity, and once again fell under the old man's spell. "Yes, Allah the merciful will provide us with the strength and strategy to win," he replied. His resolve restored, Mohammed rose and began to pace. When Khomeini got up and indicated he was leaving, Mohammed detained him by saying, "I suggest we watch the comments from the news media, and then the press conference." Khomeini nodded in agreement and returned to his recliner.

KPUK-TV Studios, Hollywood, CA – 7:40 p.m., Monday, May 29th

Frank Lambert and Paula Moore, anchors for NBC news, sat at the news desk in a Hollywood TV studio. Both co-anchors watched as the remote feed of the president's news conference ended. The cameras remained focused on members of the president's entourage—still standing on the stage—then panned to the audience. No one seemed to be in a hurry to leave. Roger Teel, the reporter from the network affiliate covering the president's address, was still describing the event. A signal from their producer alerted Peter and Paula they would be on the air in ten seconds. Both checked their appearances in the monitor, assumed their most solemn facial expressions, and gazed into the center TV camera. The red light came on.

"Good evening, I'm Frank Lambert, and this is my co-anchor Paula Moore."

The camera switched to a close-up of Paula, who glibly changed her solemn expression to a smile, and said, "Good evening." Turning to look at Frank she continued, "Well, General Alexander had a few surprises for us tonight. Didn't he Frank?"

"Yes, Paula. First there was his announcement of the number of killed and missing in the five cities—two million five-hundred thousand."

"So far, Frank ... but he said the numbers would increase."

"Then there was the confirmation of the nuclear attack on the Syrians by Israel. Did you notice he made no attempt to condemn it?"

"To be fair, Frank, Mr. Alexander did say the Syrians used chemical weapons on the Jordanians."

"That's right, Paula, but he gave no details—except to say the chemicals were used on the Jordanian military. That's hardly justification for Israel to use nuclear weapons," he smirked.

Paula frowned, extending her lower lip as she nodded at the camera, and said, "Well, did you notice Mr. Alexander never mentioned the UN?"

"Yes," Frank replied in a low voice and with his most serious look, "and that was *quite* an omission. It appears Mr. Alexander may be ... how did Randolph Clarkson describe him in his motion to stay Alexander's swearing in as president? Oh yes, 'power crazed,' 'a would-be-dictator.' "

"You know Frank, I'm confused," Paula said batting her eyes, "I thought Judge Kerry issued a stay order, *stopping* Alexander's swearing in. It's strange that I haven't heard anything more about it. Let's ask Roger to follow up at the press conference that's about to begin.

"Good idea, Paula. We should also ask Roger to follow up on the use of *live* ammunition to put down the riots. I have reports indicating the shooting and killing of many Muslims, which only further demonstrates Alexander's militaristic tendency to trample down the rights of our Muslim minorities."

"Yes, he appears to be out-of-control. Did you catch the two things he said that indicate he's a megalomaniac? First, he introduced another general as the Secretary of War. Then he told us he had released nuclear weapons."

Frank's reply was interrupted by a signal from the producer. The news conference was about to begin in Albuquerque.

In Tehran, Mohammed jumped up and began clapping. "Now that's more like it. We can always count on the news media to help us." Smiling his sadistic grin, he continued, "It will be great sport to teach that reporter bitch Paula how to be a good Muslim woman."

Khomeini flinched ever so slightly at Mohammed's crude outburst, then lifted his hand and pointed to the TV, "Let us listen to the press conference. We may learn more of the Great Satan's plans from the questions of their news media."

Auditorium, Kirkland AFB

BG Ross walked to the podium in the auditorium and called the press conference to order, "The president will join us shortly for a brief question and answer session. Please keep your questions brief and only address one issue. Wait to be called upon. Shouting questions will result in your removal." Turning stage left, Ross waited for Alexander to enter the stage. At a signal, the center TV camera's red light came on and the president walked onto the stage. "Ladies and gentlemen, the President of the United States," Ross announced, and remained standing at the president's side.

"Thank you for staying," Alexander said, addressing the reporters. "I'll answer a few of your questions, then I must leave to attend to pressing matters. Since I don't know any of your names, I'll point to a person who may ask a question. Please identify yourself, and whom you represent." Alexander looked over the assembled reporters and pointed to a woman at the back, "The lady in the blue dress."

"Thank you, Mr. President. I'm Christine Muller with the *Albuquerque Tribune*. You said Albuquerque would be the temporary capital of the U.S. Could you provide more details?"

"Yes, Christine. Kirkland Air Force Base has the communication equipment and facilities necessary for a temporary government. The city is large enough and has sufficient resources to support our needs. Of course, additional facilities will be required, and there is ample unused land surrounding the city. Relocating to any other city would not have provided sufficient advantages to warrant the effort. Once we've reestablished our government, the process to select the site for a new capital will begin."

Pointing to a man in the middle of the group, Alexander said, "The man in the tan blazer."

"Mr. President, I'm Allan Graham of Clear Channel Radio. You introduced General Simpson as the Secretary of War. Did you mean the Secretary of Defense?"

"No, General Simpson is now my Secretary of War. We've been attacked. We're at war. Therefore, I require a Secretary of War and a War Department, just as President Roosevelt did in 1941. Next Question," Alexander said, pointing to a frumpy older woman, with a blunt cut mop of straight, dyed, black hair sitting in the front row.

"Mr. President, I'm Ellen Thompson, Public Broadcasting Service. I don't understand how you can appoint a Cabinet without approval of the Senate?"

"Ms. Thompson, it's difficult to obtain approval from a body which no longer exists." The president's comment brought several chuckles from the press pool.

Ellen Thompson, not known for tact, common sense, or for her sharp mind, pressed on by asking a follow up question, "Mr. President, don't you think it would be advisable to wait for a new senate to be elected instead of usurping the authority of the legislative branch?"

The president frowned and looked at BG Ross, who quickly answered the inane question, "Ms. Thompson, the president, and for that matter the country, does not have the time, nor the patience for 'what if' questions that raise unimportant or ridiculous issues, which divert attention from real issues." The press corps greeted Ross's sharp rebuke with stunned silence.

Ross nodded to a lieutenant colonel at the rear of the group. Ms. Thompson would never attend another press conference.

The president pointed to a man in an open-collared blue shirt seated in the middle of the left side.

"Mr. President, I'm Roberto Gonzales, representing the AP. With your permission, I would like to ask two related questions regarding the Middle East." Alexander nodded.

"Thank you, Mr. President. First, you said Israel used nuclear weapons against Syria. Are you planning to condemn them?"

"No. Syria attacked Jordan with chemical weapons—clearly establishing their intentions to use them against Israel. Therefore, Israel had every right to use its nuclear weapons in a preemptive strike."

Gonzales' expression clearly showed he was shocked by the blunt answer. Forgetting his second question he blurted out, "Does that mean you'll use nuclear weapons too, since we've also been attacked with them?"

Alexander noted Gonzales' confused look and answered, "Yes." Then with a thin smile, he continued, "However, I don't think that was your second question, so go ahead and ask it."

Regaining composure, Gonzales said, "Thank you, Mr. President. My second question is, since our fleet has been attacked in the Mediterranean, are we at war with some of the countries in that area?"

"Good question Roberto. War is normally conducted between nations. Since 9/11, we've been at war with terrorists who have no country, no territory to defend, no flag, and no uniform. A new kind of war is being fought all over the globe. Governments have been overthrown in the Middle East. We've been unable to establish contact with the governments of any of the countries whose navies attacked our fleet. We've unconfirmed reports indicating Egypt's president was assassinated. So to answer your question, yes, we're at war with unknown adversaries in those countries and in other places." Looking at the group of reporters, the president said, "Last question."

NBC's stringer, Roger Teel was waiving his hand and caught Alexander's eye.

"The gentleman waiving his hand on the right," Alexander said, pointing to Teel.

"Mr. President, I'm Roger Teel, NBC News. Did Judge Kerry in Los Angeles issue an order staying you from becoming president? If so, how can you consider your presidency legitimate?"

Teel's question caused a ripple of excitement and comments from other reporters. Alexander was expecting the question, and calmly replied, "District Judge Kerry, a known activist judge, exceeded his authority by issuing such an order based upon one of several motions filed by attorney Randolph Clarkson. All of Judge Kerry's orders have been overturned by the 9th Circuit

Court of Appeals."

Undeterred by Alexander's terse response, Teel shouted at the president, who was turning to leave the podium. "I understand Judge Kerry, Barbra Focker, Jan Foite, and Mary Lane have been arrested."

Ross scowled at Teel and again nodded to the lieutenant colonel at the rear of the group.

President Alexander turned back to face Teel, "You are correct Mr. Teel. After Judge Kerry's orders were overturned, I issued an order removing him from the bench. Subsequent actions by Mr. Kerry resulted in his arrest for fomenting insurrection. Randolph Clarkson, Barbra Focker, Jan Foite, and Mary Lane were arrested on similar charges related to their TV interview, which as you know incited another riot. That was the last question. Good evening."

When the live feed ended, viewers watching NBC were surprised to see KPUK's weatherman, Ben Schmidt, sitting at the news desk instead of network co-anchors Lambert and Moore. Both had been pulled from the news desk and suspended by the station manager during the president's news conference. KPUK's viewing audience, and viewers from other states, jammed the station's phone lines demanding an apology. After the sacking of KKPI-TV's station by an angry mob, threats made by callers were being taken seriously. As one angry caller put it, "If you don't fire those SOBs we'll burn down your station. Quit tellin' us how to think!"

In Iran, the Supreme Leader Grand Ayatollah Khomeini sat quietly in his recliner, carefully evaluating Alexander's words, demeanor, and bearing. *This is a man to be taken seriously. He's no Clinton. He's worse than Bush. He is a spawn of the devil, and he must be killed before he ruins my plans. Allah will help us take decisive action to turn the tide of events back in our favor.*

Unfortunately for Khomeini, Allah was not listening.

If we abide by the Koran, all of us should

mobilize to kill … .

– Mohammad Khatami, President, Islamic
Republic of Iran, October 24, 2000

Part II

Fist Of Allah

Chapter 20

Tuesday

Rome, Italy – 6 a.m., Tuesday, May 30th

The Mercedes truck pulled onto the shoulder of highway SS-1, approximately three kilometers from the Vatican. A strong wind was blowing from the southwest toward the city. The driver, Fahad, quickly jumped from out the cab and removed the left front tire's valve stem. His partner, Seif, exited the cab's other door, removed the emergency kit, and placed hazard markers in front and behind the truck. Fahad opened the rear rollup door, entered the cargo area and activated a timer set for twenty minutes. Pulling down the door, Fahad secured it with a large padlock. While Seif signaled their pick up van with his flashlight, Fahad inserted a toothpick into the padlock's key slot and broke it off. A black van arrived, and both men hastily entered. Reversing directions the van sped away toward the west.

Seventeen minutes later the timer reached zero and closed a relay, allowing electrical current from a twelve-volt battery to flow through three sets of wires—each leading to an electrical blasting cap inserted in a stick of sixty percent dynamite. One of the blasting caps had been installed in the bottom row of dynamite sticks in the case directly under the wooden crate. The shock wave traveled upward, ripping open the lead lined wooden crate and the large stainless steel cylinder inside. The other two blasting caps were inserted in dynamite sticks at the furthest point from the wooden crate— thereby producing explosive shock waves traveling toward the crate from the cab and tailgate. The effect created a fountain of hot gases shooting skyward, dispersing the radioactive cesium-137 powder high into the strong wind. While police and emergency personnel responded to the blast, a cloud of highly radioactive Cs-137 swept toward the Vatican and Rome. Similar trucks were being positioned in Lisbon, Frankfurt, London, and Paris.

Cs-137 has a half-life of thirty years—the amount of time required for half of the Cs-137 to decay. Many half-lives must expire, before contaminated areas are safe for humans. Cs-137 enters the body by ingestion or inhalation and accumulates in muscle tissue—where it can cause cancer. When it decays, Cs-137 emits a beta particle, an electron formed in its nucleus when a neutron transforms itself into a proton. Beta radiation is only dangerous to humans or animals when it's inside the body. High-energy gamma radiation, emitted by

Cs-137's daughter product, barium-137, is a major hazard. Without an extensive cleanup, areas contaminated by the terrorist's dirty bombs would be uninhabitable for 150 years or more.

In 1095 CE, Pope Urban II called for a Holy Crusade to reclaim the Holy Lands from the barbarian Turks. His actions launched the first crusade the following year. Islam never forgives or forgets. It doesn't matter whether the event occurred yesterday, or 910 years ago. The terrorists were doing God's work. They were instruments of Allah's revenge against the crusader pope.

The Caliph's Palace, Tehran, Iran – 9:30 a.m., Tuesday, May 30th

The Guardian Council had been in session for half an hour, and the mood was ugly. The clerics were furious over the Empire's naval defeat. An admiral, whom they held responsible for the loss of their ships and submarine, was taken outside and shot. While the other officers cowered, Saladin endeavored to maintain his charade as the all-knowing caliph, and Khomeini contemplated his dwindling options. A messenger entered, bowed, and waited for permission to speak. Looking up, Saladin scowled at the messenger and demanded, "What is it? *Speak* up you sniveling fool, while you still have your tongue."

"Oh, Great Caliph," the frightened man said, his voice trembling. "A–A news bulletin just reported a radiation dispersal bomb has contaminated the Vatican and parts of Rome."

"Allah be praised," Saladin shouted and clapped his hands. The arguing clerics ceased their carping and muttered various praises for Allah.

"Allah be praised. The evil crusader pope has been struck down," the cleric from Saudi Arabia shouted.

The military officers relaxed a bit, looked at one another, and collectively thought, *Maybe we won't be shot.*

After the messenger departed, the mood lightened, the clerics' chatter died down, and Khomeini brought up the real issue. "Allah has granted us a small success. But, we still must prove ourselves worthy to carry out His will. The Great Satan has defeated our navies. The Little Satan has not been touched, and Allah grows impatient with us. We must take decisive action to turn the tide in our favor."

"What do you suggest?" Saladin asked, before someone else could ask him the same question.

Everyone in the chamber looked at Grand Ayatollah Khomeini and waited for his next words. After a long pause Khomeini replied, "It is time to use The Fist of Allah."

What the hell is The Fist of Allah? Saladin wondered, finally realizing he was nothing but a figurehead. *I have no knowledge of our capabilities.*

Khomeini is the real power. I must assert myself and learn about our military and its capabilities. I'll order one of the military officers to give me a thorough briefing this afternoon. I know it will upset Yosif, because our afternoon together will be spoiled. Saladin sighed, picturing Yosif's slender, nude body lying on their bed.

At the far end of the table, the military officers cringed at Khomeini's pronouncement. *The old fool,* they all thought. General Aghajari looked down at the table. *He has no concept of nuclear weapons. He thinks having a few nukes gives him ultimate power. Our delivery capability is limited to the four nuclear warheads we acquired from the Soviets. We haven't tested our nuclear warhead design, nor have we flown one on either our Shahab-3 or Raad missiles. We're a year away from being ready for this war. Israel and the United States can blanket us with warheads many times larger than ours.* Aghajari's thoughts were interrupted, when one of the clerics hatefully demanded, "Can you attack the Great Satan's aircraft carrier, and the evil Jews in Tel Aviv?"

Directing his response to Khomeini, General Aghajari cautiously replied, "With Allah's blessing, we could use Allah's Fist to attack the Great Satan's fleet with one of our Kh-55 Granat cruise missiles, armed with its two hundred KT warhead."

Saladin managed to conceal his surprise, and watched Khomeini's face for a reaction. *The sly old fox has been holding out on me. I wonder how long they've had a nuclear weapon? Do they ... No, do we have more than one?* Saladin listened intently as the general continued.

"Tel Aviv could be attacked with our *Shahab-3B* missiles. One, armed with a nuclear warhead, would destroy Tel Aviv and bring the Little Satan to its knees. Additional Shahab-3s with chemical warheads could be used to completely eliminate the hateful Jews."

Ah, so we do have more than one. I'm getting tired of the general directing his comments to Khomeini and ignoring me, Saladin thought. *Time to assert my authority.* "How soon can the attacks be launched?" the caliph harshly demanded.

"No sooner than nine days," the general responded, still directing his comments to Khomeini, "The missile and warhead must be transported to Syria or Lebanon—a difficult task, with the lingering radioactive fallout. Launches must be coordinated in order to obtain surprise." Feeling he had to make one more plea for sanity, he cautiously continued, "Before we initiate a nuclear strike, we must consider the consequences. Many Palestinians will be killed. Israel has already used nuclear weapons, and the U.S. will use them if we do."

Annoyed with Saladin and irritated with the general's last remark, Khomeini's demeanor dramatically changed. Squinting his cunning eyes, and fixing the general with an intimidating glare, he sarcastically responded, "Yes, the evil Jews used their nuclear weapons on Syria, because Syria did not have nuclear weapons. The Great Satan is a coward. It will not *dare* to attack Iran, because we *also* have nuclear weapons." Cutting his eyes at Saladin, he continued with a sneer, "Allah's Fist will destroy the Little Satan and the evil American's ships. The Great Satan will be forced to accept our Islamic Empire as its equal. Do not worry about the Palestinians, they will be blessed and Allah will embrace them."

Following Khomeini's lead, Saladin ordered, "The attack will occur in nine days. Make it so. Inform us the day before the attack is launched."

"Death to America. Death to the Great Satan ..." the clerics chanted.

Saladin's behavior worried Khomeini. *He knows he's nothing more than my puppet. I could see it in his face. Mohammed—I still have difficulty thinking of him as Saladin—is very bright, and he's letting his new title go to his head. In order to keep him under control, I must bring him into my plans. Show him he has an important role to play.* When the meeting ended, Khomeini caught up with the caliph outside the door. Touching Mohammed's sleeve, Khomeini assumed the mantra of a father figure and stroked Mohammed's ego by saying, "You did very well in the meeting. Subjects came up we have not had the opportunity to discuss, and you handled them with aplomb. Come to my chambers at 4:30 this afternoon, and we can discuss my plans and ideas for the future."

"Thank you. It will be my pleasure," Mohammed replied, feigning deference.

As soon as he was out of Khomeini's sight, Caliph Mohammed Saladin II sent a messenger to find General Aghajari with a summons to report to him at 1:00 p.m.

Pyongyang, North Korea – 1:00 p.m., Tuesday, May 30th

The Chinese ambassador said his formal good-bye to North Korea's dictator, Kim Jung-il. Together they had watched President Alexander's address to the United States. Afterward, the ambassador had delivered President Wu's forceful "Stand Down" message to "Dear Leader." Kim was strongly advised to do nothing to incur the wrath of the new U.S. president. "President Wu wishes to inform you he received a call from America's new president, who stated that if you invade South Korea, his country will destroy your capital city and your army." The warning was sufficient to send the little dictator with a Napoleonic complex into an apoplectic rage.

Still reeling from the fury of Dear Leader's outburst, the ambassador contemplated the meeting as he returned to his embassy. *Kim Jung-il is a dangerous man—dangerous because he is obviously mentally unbalanced.*

The temper tantrum he just threw proves it. We'll never be able to trust him. He is too erratic. I believe he will completely ignore President Wu's "advice." Something drastic must be done before he starts a nuclear war.

For his part, Kim continued to seethe over the affront handed him by President Wu's lackey ambassador. Dear Leader thought this was the perfect time to invade the south. Now his main benefactor was telling him to stand down. *I thought President Wu was a nobody, a weak man. Now I'm sure he is. What can he do if I do invade? The Americans are in no position to send troops. What else can they do—nothing. We captured their ship, the Pueblo, and still have it.* "Hee, hee, hee," he snickered aloud, rubbing his pudgy, little hands together. *We made them beg and grovel to get their miserable crew back. Their ship is still tied up to our dock in Wonsan. It makes a great tourist attraction.* Kim's gloating was interrupted by his aide.

"Dear Leader, while you were meeting with the ambassador, his military attaché gave me this envelope. He said I was to hand it to you after they left."

Kim opened the envelope and found a personal letter from Admiral Cheung, the Commander of the Chinese People's Liberation Army Navy— PLAN. After reading the letter, he smiled. *So Cheung also thinks Wu is a weakling, with a pissant advisor. He suggests now is a good time for me to unite Korea. Hmmm ... he plans to invade Taiwan and suggests we coordinate our attacks. Yes ... a good plan. I'll be the Dear Leader of Korea, and Admiral Cheung will be president of China. Yes, a very good idea. I'll order my army to stand down in order to make Wu and Alexander think I'm complying with their orders. I'll wait for Cheung to make the first move. Hmmm ... when I'm ready to attack, why not teach the damn Americans a real lesson? Show the world how weak they are ...* "And how strong I am," he muttered aloud with satanic glee.

Kim Jung-il succeeded his dictator father, President Kim Il-sung as leader of North Korea in 1994. Young Kim never took the title of president. A title reserved for the senior Kim who was known as "Great Leader" by his "adoring" subjects. Instead, Kim Jung-il took the titles of General Secretary of the Communist Party, and Chairman of the National Defense Commission— the real center of power in North Korea. His "adoring" subjects know young Kim as "Dear Leader."

Small in stature with a huge ego and excessive tastes, Kim Jung-il enjoys all-night banquets, heavy drinking, blonde Western women, and strippers— while his countrymen starve. Some of his reported excesses include a collection of sports cars and a 10,000-bottle wine cellar. Propaganda force-fed to Dear Leader's subjects include Kim making a hole in one the first time he hit a golf ball, and running the clays the first time he shot skeet. Kim attempts to appear as a godlike, larger-than-life superman to his subjects.

On a peaceful Sunday morning, June 25, 1950, the North Korean People's Army (KPA) launched a massive predawn attack south across the 38th parallel, the dividing line between North and South Korea. The battle for control of the Korean peninsula—the Korean Conflict—had begun. Armed with Soviet equipment and advisors, and manned with unlimited reserve forces, the KPA's surprise attack quickly overwhelmed the lightly armed Republic of Korea Army (ROK). Fleeing south in full retreat, the ROK forces were pursued by the vicious KPA. On June 27, 1950, the U.S. promised to provide naval and air support to South Korea. General of the Army Douglas MacArthur, Commander-in-Chief, Far East Command flew from Japan to Suwon and drove up to the front lines to see the fighting first hand. Based on his trip to the front, MacArthur cabled Washington for authority to commit ground troops. Calling his decision a "Police Action," President Truman only authorized a portion of the troops MacArthur requested.

President Truman demanded immediate action by the UN Security Council. By June 30th, with the ROK Army in total disarray, Truman finally relented and gave MacArthur authorization to transfer two full divisions from Japan to Korea.

After a futile call for withdrawal of North Korean troops by the UN Security Council, the UN passed a resolution on July 24th establishing the United Nations Command (UNC), with General of the Army MacArthur as commander. General of the Army is a five star rank equivalent to a Field Marshal in foreign armies.

America rushed to disarm at the end of WWII—now they would pay the price for doing so. MacArthur's Far East Command, the Eighth Army and Far East Air Force were drastically under-strength. The Air Force was structured for air defense, not ground support. Only a few medium tanks were in the theater. Anti-tank weapons were all WWII vintage—effective against German tanks, but not against the new Soviet tanks, which crushed German armor at the end of WWII. U.S. forces soon found their rifle grenades, 2.36-inch bazookas, 57-mm and 75-mm recoilless rifles could not kill the KPA's Soviet T-34 tanks. Worse still, there was only enough ammunition in theater to support combat for approximately forty-five days.

Following Truman's orders, MacArthur initially sent two rifle companies, an artillery battery, and a few other supporting units of the 24th Division to back up the ROK forces. Before dawn on July 5th, the 540-man force, later referred to as "Task Force Smith," moved into a defensive position astride the main road near Osan, ten miles below Suwon. Other Units of the 24th Division were moving into delaying positions below Osan. A few hours later, at 0800 hours, Task Force Smith was attacked and overwhelmed by a

KAP division. Making a disorganized retreat, during which all of its equipment—except small arms—was lost, Task Force Smith suffered 150 casualties.

U.S. and ROK forces were driven south to the port of Pusan at the tip of the Korean peninsula. With their backs to the sea they formed the legendary "Pusan Perimeter" around the city. After retreating over a hundred miles and losing several bloody battles, troop morale was low. In a conference with General MacArthur at Taegu, South Korea, General Walton H. Walker, Commander of the Eighth Army, was told his troops could no longer retreat. On July 29th, General Walker issued his famed "Stand or Die" order to the beleaguered defenders, "There will be no more retreating," he told his men. "There's no line behind us to which we can retreat. We're going to hold this line … Stand or Die."

Walker's troops valiantly held the Pusan Perimeter against a massive all-out offensive by the North. Finally on July 31st, to the relief of Walker's men, the first reinforcements arrived. Fierce fighting continued through September 15th as the KPA relentlessly attempted to drive the UNC forces into the sea. General Walker used his Marines as a "fire brigade" to repel breakthroughs and regain lost positions.

In the early hours of September 15th, MacArthur again proved he was a masterful tactician by launching an amphibious landing at Inchon Harbor: a feat many declared was impossible until he did it. Catching the North Koreans with their pants down, the U.S. Marines captured Inchon. Reinforced by the Army, the Inchon force attacked and cut off KPA forces to the south. UNC forces trapped at Pusan broke out on September 16th and began a drive up the Korean peninsula. On September 27th, MacArthur was given permission to cross the 38th parallel and to attack into North Korea. On October 19th, Pyongyang fell.

With the intentions of uniting the country, UNC forces drove north across the 38th parallel through North Korea to its northern border with the People's Republic of China at the Yalu River. Communist China, allied with its North Korean comrades, chose to intervene in support of the now defeated KPA. On October 14th, lead elements of the Chinese "volunteer" 38th Field Army crossed the Yalu from Manchuria into North Korea at Andong. On October 25th, Chinese Communist Forces (CCF) struck China's first blow to support the KPA in their conflict against the ROK and UNC forces. Units of the CCF 39th Army destroyed a battalion of the ROK 6th division near Onjong and began one of the worst battles of the conflict at the Chosan Reservoir. Soon CCF forces engaged UNC troops across the entire northern front. Unexpected CCF intervention was a total surprise to the UNC. Inflicting heavy casualties, CCF forces drove the ROK and UNC forces south.

The bloody war continued until a cease-fire, resulting in an armistice, was signed on July 27, 1953 at Panmunjom. The Korean Conflict—now known as the "Forgotten War"—has never officially ended. United States losses, in one of history's bloodiest wars included: 23,615 Killed In Action (KIA); 4,820 Missing In Action (MIA, declared dead); 7,245 captured (Prisoners Of War, POW); 2,847 dead in POW Camps; and 389 reportedly kept by China or North Korea after all POWs were returned. Over 100,000 UNC and ROK troops were killed in action.

In the aftermath of the Korean conflict, America continued to monitor activities in Communist controlled North Korea. On January 23, 1968, the USS *Pueblo*, a U.S. Navy intelligence gathering ship was standing off the coast of North Korea in international waters. The 173-foot ex-cargo carrier had a complement of eighty-three men and light armament consisting of four .50 cal machine guns. North Korean naval ships approached and demanded the *Pueblo* heave to, stop, and be boarded. When *Pueblo*'s captain, Commander Pete Bucher, attempted to escape, the lead North Korean ship opened fire. After a two hour battle in which one crewman was killed, Bucher surrendered the *Pueblo*—the only U.S. Navy ship surrendered in peacetime since Commodore James Barron surrendered the USS *Chesapeake* to the British in 1807. The USS *Pueblo* remains a commissioned vessel of the U.S. Navy.

One crewmember died in the *Pueblo* attack. The other eighty-two men on board were taken prisoner and confined in POW prison camps. For eleven months they were brutally beaten, starved, and tortured. President Lyndon B. Johnson, up for re-election in November and embroiled in the Vietnam War and domestic problems, did nothing. North Korea returned the crew after the U.S. acquiesced and signed a bogus document admitting espionage—which it later repudiated.

The following year, North Korea shot down an American EC-121 reconnaissance plane, killing its thirty-one-member crew. Again, LBJ took no retaliatory action.

Chapter 21

President Alexander called his morning Cabinet and staff meeting to order. Brigadier General James Ross, who had become the president's defacto press secretary, opened the meeting, "Mr. President, Governor Richards reports the governors are receiving favorable public comments regarding last night's address. Kirkland operators received hundreds of calls from citizens praising your handling of the situation. The country is behind you. My staff is creating a White House web site with an e-mail address."

"Thank you, Jim. You did a good job yesterday." Smiling, Alexander decided to add a personal complement. He had noticed Simpson's new suit the previous evening, and asked Julian where he had gotten it. "I understand you're responsible for getting Roberto to open his Men's Shop at 0600 yesterday to provide Harry with a wardrobe. I wondered where he got his good looking suit." This comment elicited several good-natured comments from the other men. One asked if Ross was now in the men's fashion business. After everyone had a good laugh, it was time to get down to business. Looking at Keese, Alexander asked, "Allan, what's the status in the Middle East?"

"In a word, bad. I've been unable to establish contact with anyone in authority in Iran, Egypt, Saudi Arabia, Libya … none of them. The Emir of Qatar has been some help. It appears Muslim fanatics now control the whole area. Oil shipments from the Middle East and North Africa have ceased. Satellite photos show the oil fields and refineries abandoned." Keese grimaced and slightly shook his head. "The entire region is engaged in a macabre party, celebrating the death of the Great Satan. The world economy is in jeopardy. Europe purchases oil and natural gas from Algeria, Libya, and Egypt. China is also buying oil from the same areas."

"Bill, the oil situation alone can wreck our economy. Combined with losses associated with the attacks, we have to be in trouble. What do you suggest?" Alexander asked.

Since first receiving word of the detonations while in Madrid, Bill Fobbs had been deeply troubled about America's economy. By the time he reached Albuquerque to meet the new president he was convinced the U.S.'s economy was only days away from total collapse. Alexander's determination had inspired him to think outside the box. The president told him to throw the rulebook away and get the job done. At first, the magnitude of the vista the president had opened for him was hard to grasp. Finally, he realized he must do anything and everything necessary to save the nation from financial disaster. With a sigh, he leaned forward and raised his right hand holding up two fingers. "Mr. President, we have two problems—oil and cash. I've personally contacted the oil ministers of Venezuela and Mexico and requested increased oil shipments. Mexico will cooperate. Their national oil company, Pemex, will increase production to help us. We're currently getting 15% of our oil from Venezuela. The oil minister in Venezuela refused to help—until I asked him if he preferred working as a field hand in American's new Venezuelan Oil Company—our replacement for their PDVSA. He finally got the message," Fobbs said with a grin. The last comment prompted laughter from all present.

Relaxing in his chair, Fobbs continued, "Based on Allan's assessment, I suggest seizing refineries and oil fields in the Middle East. Although Europe wasn't attacked with nuclear weapons, their oil supply has been disrupted."

"Seizing oil fields could result in a confrontation with China, and some European countries," Keese interjected, leaning forward.

"Yes," Alexander said. "However, the oil fields are now under Saladin II's control. Anyone who wants to share the oil will have to get on our team. Start planning the seizures. I'll advise leaders of select countries regarding our impending actions. By now, Russia and China should realize they've lost their positions in the area. We're all in the same boat—a boat in danger of being sunk by fanatics."

"Our second problem—cash—can also be solved by seizures," Fobbs continued, again holding up his hand displaying two fingers. This statement elicited quizzical looks from the others. "All the oil rich Middle Eastern nations have huge amounts of cash and gold reserves in foreign banks—trillions of dollars. Since we're in a state of war with the current governments of these nations—Saladin II's Islamic Empire—we'll seize their assets as payment for damages. Most of these countries also hold our debt instruments. Seizing our bonds will allow us to write down our national debt."

No one commented. All were too dumfounded by Fobb's statements. Then, one by one, they began to smile, as they grasped the magnitude of his plan. Alexander sat back in his chair with a sense of relief. *Bill just hit one out of the park.*

Smiling, Simpson said, "When we add the oil revenue from their former oil fields, we should be in good shape. We can pay for rebuilding our cities and industry, without bankrupting our economy. I'll start planning immediately."

"Let's take a coffee break," Alexander suggested.

While the others filed out of the conference room, the president pulled Jay Henniger aside. "Jay, I want you to prepare an executive order for seizures. Work with Bill for financial details, and Alan for the proper diplomatic slant. I've no doubt we're going to piss off the bankers, and some sensitive European officials. So let's make sure we do it with the proper language," the president said, with a sardonic smile. "When the order is ready, I'll hold a press conference and sign it."

"What if they refuse to honor our seizure orders?"

"In that event," Alexander said with a grim expression, "we'll have to explain it to them in a way they'll understand."

Five minutes later, the meeting reconvened.

"What is the status of fuel rationing?" Alexander asked.

"The states' governors are preparing a plan." Young responded. "It'll be implemented tomorrow. Tankers enroute will continue to arrive for the next week or so. Once unloaded, they'll be routed to available sources."

"Okay Barry, it's your turn," Alexander said, dreading Clark's report.

"We had four suicide bombings yesterday. A woman walked into a company picnic in Memphis, and blew herself up. A man did it in a crowded Minnesota mall. Another detonated himself in an Okalahoma City movie theater. The final bomber, another woman, chose the Israeli exhibit at EPCOT, in Orlando, Florida.

"With a few exceptions, Muslim insurrections seem to have been quelled. Now we have the reverse problem. Our citizens are hunting Muslims. They're angry and focusing their fury on the Muslim population. Suicide bombers are only making it worse. Most mosques have been destroyed. Any person wearing anything that looks Muslim is a target. Businesses owned by Middle Easterners are being attacked and looted. Indians are putting signs in their store windows proclaiming they're 'Buddhist' or 'Hindu.' Reverend Smyth's sermon lit the fuze and our citizens' pent-up anger exploded." Clark looked around the room. "Gentlemen we have a religious war in the streets of America. The citizen's backlash has begun, and it must be controlled. Vigilantism must be stopped. Otherwise, anarchists will replace the insurrectionists. It was one thing to use extreme force to put down insurrection. Using it against our citizens is something we can't do." Clark took a deep breath, sighed heavily, and concluded, "We must find a speedy remedy to this situation." The room was quiet. No suggestions were forthcoming.

Finally shaking his head in disgust, Young said, "The Muslims wanted a holy war. Now they've got one. Have any of you seen what's being broadcast on Arab TV?' Everyone shook their heads. "They're showing the sacking of foreign embassies ... brutal stuff ... a woman being stoned, bodies hanging from the top of an embassy's entrance gate. Other footage showed Westerners being chased through the streets by a mob. The mob caught a man and beat him to death. The whole Middle East is one big massacre. When our media picks up the story and broadcasts those pictures, it'll be like throwing gasoline on a fire. Our citizens will turn on any remaining Muslims."

"You're right Charlie," Alexander said leaning forward in his chair, "You've hit on the essence of our dilemma. A dilemma we must solve. Just what, or rather who are we fighting in this religious war—Islam—or fanatical Islamists? How do we tell one from the other?" No one offered any answers. "All right, then how do we find out?"

Still, no one spoke. Finally, Ross hesitantly offered a suggestion, "If we're dealing with a religious war, we need religious advisors." Everyone turned to look at him, realizing he had stated the obvious.

Alexander nodded his approval, "Good idea. We must form a group of religious advisors ASAP. How about the rabbi who provided the translations ... and Reverend Smyth? We need a Catholic, no more than two Protestants, and ... a Hindu and a Buddhist. If we find a moderate Muslim scholar he can advise the religious committee ... advise, but not be a member. Does anyone have any recommendations for committee members?" The president glanced around the room. Young's thoughtful expression caught his attention and Alexander asked, "Charlie, what's troubling you?"

"Sir, I hesitate to ask, but given the response to Smyth's sermon, are you sure we want to have him on this committee?" Silence permeated the room. All eyes were on the president.

"Yes, I'm sure." Alexander calmly answered. "Whether we agree with his religious views or not, he has our country's interest at heart. Sure, he stirred the pot, but from the looks of it there's lots of folks who listen to what he has to say. Not only do they believe in what he preaches, they put their beliefs into practice. Yes he's an evangelist, but not a raving fanatic. He's respected worldwide as a brilliant theologian—a true man of God—who is a recognized authority on Biblical prophecies and principals—principals our country was founded on. We need knowledgeable thinkers, because they're going to have to find an answer to a fourteen hundred year-old problem—and find it in a week.

"Jim," Alexander said to Ross, "get hold of the rabbi. Tell him to assemble the group here by Friday."

Turning to Henniger, Alexander asked, "Jay, do you have the final Internment Executive Order ready?"

"Yes, Mr. President. I sent a copy to Governor Richards. I have copies for everyone here," Henniger replied, passing out copies.

"I'll sign the order after the meeting. It's based on Roosevelt's order for the Japanese. The order requires internment of all Muslims. Each state will be responsible for rounding up and detaining their Muslim population. They'll have to improvise internment compounds—possibly use fair grounds for containment—until they can build permanent ones. Available space at closed and unused portions of active military installations will be made available. Since we're dealing with a religious war carried out by zealots, no Islamic materials, clothing, food, prayers, services nor Qur'ans will be permitted."

Alexander sat back, clasped his right fist in his left hand, sighed, and continued with a sad expression, "All Muslims are not evil, but how can we separate the good from the bad? Our first attempt will be to offer each internee an opportunity to renounce Islam and swear allegiance to the United States. Those who do, and pass the interview process, will be sent to nonrestrictive camps—camps to protect them, until we can integrate them back into our society—with the caveat that any Muslim so swearing will be guilty of treason and/or insurrection if they violate their oath. Fanatics and violent Muslims will be segregated and held in high security areas. Guards will continue the culling process at the regular internment camps. The violent detainees will be sent to special high-security camps run by the military in remote desert areas. After the violent ones have been identified and removed, remaining detainees will be exposed to other religions for educational purposes. No one will be forced to convert to any religion."

"The executive order bans the Islamic religion in the United States?" Jim Ross asked looking up from his copy of the order.

"Yes. I hope our Inter-Faith Advisory Committee (IFAC) can find a better solution, but until they do, all mosques are closed, Qur'ans are to be confiscated, not destroyed. A religion based upon jihad can no longer be tolerated in this country—nor anywhere in the world."

Turning to BG Ross, Alexander said, "Jim, you've done a good job as my spokesman. I'm appointing you Press Secretary. Your first job will be to hold a press conference and announce the Internment Order. Re-emphasize my request for militias to stand down, and for citizens to return to their homes."

Looking around the table, the president asked, "Any other urgent matters?"

"We need to start domestic airline flights," Young said. "I suggest a slow phase-in giving priority to people with emergencies and those attempting to return home. Air travel should be limited to passengers with essential business. The country can't afford to waste fuel."

"Approved. Tell FAA to make it so. Alan, inform our embassies to issue priority certificates to citizens who have an urgent need to return home. Leave our radical troublemakers there. We don't need them back here to add to our problems."

"Are you referring to Grossgutt and his crowd of liberal fools?" Keese asked.

"Yes," the president replied with a scowl.

"Some of our ambassadors won't like that. They may refuse," Keese cautioned.

"Fire them. If there's no suitable State Department replacement in the embassy, make the military attaché the ambassador."

Keese nodded, suppressing a smile. *This is going to shake a few liberal apples out of the tree.*

Simpson indicated he had a couple of issues. "First, we're planning to launch a coordinated assault on a Libyan port to obtain fuel for the *Kennedy* Strike Group. Second, The *Harry S. Truman* Strike Group is standing off the entrance to the Gulf of Oman. Admiral Miller is concerned about Iranian anti-ship missiles and doesn't want to enter the Gulf. He's established contact with the remainder of our forces stationed in Iraq. They've withdrawn to Kuwait. Survivors from Iraq, including civilians and diplomats from several other countries, are with them. The airport is open, but if we send in rescue ships and aircraft, Iran may attack."

"Allan," the president said, "Inform the Iranian government the U.S. will be sending naval vessels and aircraft to Kuwait on a rescue mission."

Turning to Simpson, Alexander asked, "Have we moved our bombers to England?"

"Yes. Most are there. The remainder will arrive in the next few days."

"Good. Begin planning two attacks on Iran—one conventional and one nuclear. If the Iranians interfere, we'll implement one of the attack plans.

"Allan, when the plan is ready, inform the French and Italians of our intent to over fly their airspace. Their full cooperation is expected.

"We'll meet here tomorrow at the same time."

Barry Clark was sitting in his office reading a summary of field office reports when Teresa arrived for her 8:30 a.m. meeting. "Good morning, Teresa."

"Good morning, Director," Teresa replied, no longer so in awe of Clark.

After a couple of minutes of chitchat, Clark said, "By now you should have a feel for the situation. No one's had time to think about how the attacks were accomplished—let alone who the perpetrators were. I need an agent who can concentrate on these questions and go anywhere the trail leads; an agent with initiative and an analytical mind capable of recognizing the grains of wheat in the piles of chaff. I understand you're single with no attachments. Want the job?"

Teresa was stunned. She expected to be offered a job in Albuquerque, but not this job. She sat very still, thinking about the magnitude of the task. Finally, she said, "Thank you, sir, but I don't think I'm qualified. I don't have any idea where to start."

Clark smiled, "If I didn't think you could do the job, I wouldn't be offering it to you. As to where to start, none of us knows. You have to start looking for similarities. Start looking and asking questions. Eventually someone will say or do something that will give you a clue. I need a tenacious bulldog, someone who'll not get discouraged and give up. I think you're that person."

Realizing she was being offered the opportunity to render a great service to her country, Teresa replied, "I'll do my best, sir. Thank you for your confidence in me."

"Good. Return to Buffalo this afternoon. Clean out your office and pack your clothes. I want you to return on the plane tomorrow afternoon. Isaac will take care of packing and moving your household goods. I'll arrange temporary quarters for you. Once you get settled, you can find your own place. You'll report directly to me. Kathy will find you an office. I understand Major Johnson is planning to give your group a quick tour of Albuquerque. Have fun. I'll see you Thursday," Clark said, standing and escorting Teresa to the door.

Teresa was overwhelmed with her new assignment. *Wow, I can't believe what just happened. I thought catching those terrorists would be the greatest thing I'd ever do. Now I have the chance to catch whoever destroyed our cities. I'll catch them—even if it takes the rest of my life.* Lost in thought and hurrying along the corridor, Teresa nearly fell when she ran headlong into a tall, well built, and very handsome uniformed officer. Surprised by their sudden collision, the officer wrapped his arms around the young woman to keep her from falling.

"What in blazes," Teresa sputtered in exasperation as she clasped the front of the officer's shirt. She was on the verge of letting loose a Spanish expletive when she recognized the familiar fragrance of Captain Julian Taylor's aftershave lotion. *Madre de Dios,* Teresa sighed, looking up at him. *He smells wonderful and looks—*

"Good morning, Teresa," Julian said, his grip becoming an embrace, as he looked down into her startled brown eyes. *God, she feels good in my arms, and she's so beautiful. I wonder what distracted her? She didn't see me coming. Something's really bothering her.* He reluctantly released her when a red-faced Teresa suddenly pushed her hands against his chest.

"Oh, I … I–I'm so sorry, Captain Taylor, I didn't see you." Teresa stuttered and nervously adjusted the front of her blouse in an effort to disguise the sensual response touching him aroused in her. *He's hunkier than I first thought. I sure wish he was giving me a private tour of Albuquerque.*

"I guess I was preoccupied. Director Clark just gave me the assignment to find out who placed the nuclear bombs in our cities. I'll be moving to

Albuquerque," she said, looking up with a coy smile.

"When?" Julian asked with a huge grin.

"He wants me to return on the plane Wednesday night. Will you be coming with Major Johnson on the tour this morning?"

"No. The president needs me for other things. But I'll meet your plane Wednesday night," Julian added with a smile.

Entering Alexander's office, Julian was puzzled when the president looked up and said, "Good morning, Julian. You look like you just won the lottery. Want to share the good news?"

"Good morning, sir." Julian replied, trying to understand the reason for the president's comment. "Oh … Uh, I just ran into Teresa Lopez—literally—in the hall." Realizing his shirt was rumpled from the collision, he quickly straightened it. "Director Clark has given her the assignment to find the terrorists who planned the bomb attacks. She'll be moving to Albuquerque," he added with a pleased expression.

The prior evening when Alexander stopped by to meet the awardees at the officers' club, he noticed Julian sitting next to Teresa at dinner. Now seeing the lovesick look on Julian's face, he suppressed a smile. The memory of seeing the two of them together, and of Julian's present ruffled demeanor sparked a conclusion. *I think our normally cool, calm, collected, efficient Julian has a serious case of the hots for Miss Lopez … From the way they were acting last evening, there's some chemistry there. They'd make a handsome couple.* Alexander smiled at the thought. *Clark made a good choice in appointing her. She's young, aggressive, tenacious … not full of preconceived ideas … but does she know anything about nuclear weapons? She must understand the technology in order to figure out how they did it.*

Looking up, the president smiled warmly and said with a twinkle in his eye, "Well, we can't have our new heroine wandering around in a strange city by herself, can we? You're going to have to find time to help her get settled in. She'll need a crash course on basic nuclear weapons. I'm pretty sure we were attacked with gun-type bombs. Why don't you find her and give her a quick tour of the city. Be sure to stop by the Atomic Museum. Both of you pay particular attention to the Little Boy. Have someone explain in detail how it worked. Ask Colonel Young to have her issued a Top Secret Restricted Data security clearance on my authority."

"Yes, sir," Julian replied, with a smile.

Alexander signed the Internment Executive Order at noon. Addressing the reporters at a brief news conference after the signing, the president said, "Brigadier General Ross is now my Press Secretary. He'll explain the Executive Order I just signed. Pressing matters prevent my staying to answer your questions. Thank you for coming." After shaking hands with Ross,

Alexander departed for his office.

Ross explained the Executive Order, then mentioned an inter-faith advisory committee was being formed to address problems caused by the worldwide Islamic jihad, "Until the committee presents its recommendations, any practice of Islam and wearing Muslim attire is forbidden. Mosques are closed, and all Qur'ans will be confiscated."

As expected, some were not happy.

Santa Fe, New Mexico

Monsignor Enrico Morani, an amateur archeologist, was enjoying a well-deserved vacation in New Mexico. He'd spent three days hiking and exploring at Gila Cliff Dwellings National Monument, then driven north to Santa Fe. He was leaving Bandelier National Monument when word of a reported nuclear detonation in Washington, DC was broadcast. Returning to his motel on the outskirts of Santa Fe, he first attempted to call Georgetown University, where he was a professor of Islamic Studies. After eating an early dinner, he returned to his room to watch news reports and pray. The new president's address was carried live on the local NBC affiliate and confirmed Morani's worst fears. Now he was sure the attacks were the work of radical Islam. The next morning, unable to contact anyone in Washington, DC, he went to the Archdiocese of Santa Fe to seek guidance, but there was none to be had. Morani decided to remain at the Archdiocese, until he found a useful task he could perform. While watching the noon news cast, he saw President Alexander sign a document, then introduce Brigadier General Ross as his Press Secretary. Morani wasn't surprised when Ross said Muslims were to be interred. Listening to the general explain the executive order, his mind was filled with thoughts of conflicting religious philosophies. When Ross mentioned the formation of an inter-faith advisory committee to advise the president, Morani realized he had found the task he was seeking. *I must go to Albuquerque and find General Ross and the rabbi.*

Chapter 22

Los Angeles, California – Tuesday morning, May 30th

The *Los Angeles Herald's* front-page story featured a blistering attack on President Alexander. The article challenged his right to be president, his handling of the riots, and his hawkish foreign policies. A special section was devoted to Judge Kerry's removal, his arrest, and the arrest of Focker, Lane, Foite, and Clarkson. The story attempted to portray them as martyrs.

The paper's editorial section was rife with angry letters demanding the immediate cessation of all actions by General Alexander and his "rogue" Cabinet. The editorial called for the UN to remove Alexander, assume control of the country, and oversee immediate national elections. The editor whined about the government's aggressive actions against the Islamic community. According to the editor, the terrorists who blew up the five cities were "misguided and misunderstood … every action Alexander has taken has alienated the Arab Street and our allies." The paper made no mention of the bloodbath occurring in the Middle East—or of its impact on America. No thought was given, nor suggestions offered on ways to keep the country functioning, obtain fuel, finance the government, and pay for the damages. Nor was there mention of the possibility of more aggressive actions against America from other countries. Instead, Alexander was branded a warmonger for attacking Egypt, and Israel was condemned for attacking Syria with nuclear weapons. Notably absent was any mention of Syria's use of chemical weapons against Jordan.

Southwestern White House – 1400 Tuesday, 30 May

Copies of the *Los Angeles Herald* arrived with the noon courier plane from Los Angeles. Alexander scanned the paper. He was furious. After pacing back and forth in his office for a few minutes, he called for a meeting of his Cabinet and staff. Thirty minutes later the meeting convened.

Everyone had a copy of the newspaper. No one wanted to speak first—although all had opinions. Alexander sat at the head of the table angrily tapping his copy of the newspaper with a ballpoint pen: his foul mood apparent from his scowling face and body language. Finally he began, "The *Herald*," he said holding up his copy, "is not reporting news. This is a political attack from a leftist newspaper against our country. The paper attacks me, but in reality they're attacking our country." Alexander waited for comments. Receiving only nods, he noted the angry faces looking back at him.

George Landry, who'd just returned from Los Alamos, sat shaking his head is disbelief. How could a responsible newspaper print such tripe? Laundry considered himself a liberal. Now he realized he was ashamed of being one. As a member of Alexander's team striving to save the nation, he knew the facts. He couldn't understand how any responsible publisher could show such disregard for the good of the country. *They're as bad as the Islamists. The only thing they care about is their own political agenda, and their hatred of the military.* "This is treason," he blurted out.

Although everyone agreed, they were taken aback that Landry would make such a comment. Even the president was surprised by Landry's spontaneous outburst. "Yes, George, it is," Alexander said, still tapping his newspaper with the pen. Carefully studying each face around the table, he noted they appeared to be in agreement. "If we allow them to get away with it, their attacks will continue to escalate. We'll waste valuable time answering wild accusations, when we should be working to save the country. It must stop *now*. Any other comments?" the president asked. There were none.

Shoving the newspaper away from him on the desk, Alexander placed his pen on the table and slowly sat back to consider his options. With an exasperated expression, he turned to Clark, and said, "Barry, have the *Herald's* publisher, editor, and lead reporter brought here. I'll give them an opportunity to explain their actions ... before I deal with them."

"Mr. President," Clark hesitantly said, lowering his chin and raising one eyebrow, "I–I'm not sure we have a legal precedent or authority to pick them up and bring them here."

Alexander studied Clark. *He's right to question my requests. But the truth is—if we want to survive—we may have to break all the rules before this is over.* "Barry, President Roosevelt's actions set the precedent. My admiration for the man grows every day. When World War II began, he had similar problems. He solved his dilemmas by incarcerating the big mouths and loose cannons in St. Elizabeth's Mental Institution for the duration of the war."

Clark bit his lower lip and sat back in his chair to ponder the president's words. *I remember reading something about Roosevelt doing that. Nothing was ever said about it after the war. Of course by then Roosevelt was dead.* Finally he nodded at Alexander and responded, "I'll see to it, sir."

Still looking disgruntled, Alexander reached to pick up his pen, stood, and dismissed the group by saying, "Let's put this behind us and get back to work. We have a nation to save."

SecWar Simpson returned to his office. The business with the paper was annoying, but he had more pressing things to worry about. North Korea's unstable dictator kept coming to mind. *He's been too quiet. By now the little runt should have made one of his ridiculous pronouncements. He's up to something. He has at least two nuclear-armed ICBMs. Is he fool enough to use them? Better safe than sorry.*

At 1545, Simpson walked unannounced into the Directed Energy Directorate's Airborne Laser (ABL) Program office located in building 20200 on Kirkland AFB. Earlier in the day, he'd been hastily briefed on the ABL and its director, Colonel Helen Powell. Her mission—to develop the world's first combat aircraft using a high-powered laser as a weapon. Boeing Aircraft Company was prime contractor to the U.S. Air Force.

Based at Edwards Air Force Base in California, the prototype Airborne Laser aircraft (ABL), designated the YAL-1A, is a modified Boeing 747-400 Freighter. The main laser, a megawatt-class Chemical Oxygen-Iodine Laser (COIL), is designed to shoot down hostile ballistic missiles, during their launch phase, by directing the high-energy laser beam at the missile's fuel tank—causing the missile to self-destruct. The warhead will fall near the launch site, providing an added benefit. Aiming a laser at a rapidly accelerating missile 300 miles away is no easy feat. The COIL cannot be fired at low altitudes, because the dense atmosphere causes the laser beam to diffuse. Therefore, physics dictates that the COIL cannot engage the missile, until it reaches a high altitude. By that time the missile would be traveling at a speed of mach-2 or greater. A laser beam travels at the speed of light— 186,000 miles per second—therefore calculating lead-angle is not a problem. To kill a rising missile, the ABL aircraft must identify a missile launch, and then track the rapidly accelerating missile, until it reaches engagement altitudes.

When Simpson entered the reception area of the colonel's office, the young second lieutenant on duty looked up. Failing to recognize the new SecWar, the lieutenant said in greeting, "Good afternoon, sir. Can I help you? This is a restricted area, sir. May I see your identification?"

SecWar smiled warmly and replied, "I'm General Simpson. Is your project director in?"

Standing quickly and coming to attention, the young officer responded, "Yes, sir, Colonel Helen Powell is in her office. I'll inform her you are here."

"Thank you, Lieutenant."

The lieutenant walked briskly to the colonel's office door, knocked twice and waited for the order to enter. Quickly stepping inside, he told the colonel in a half whisper, "Colonel, there's a man here to see you. He's in civilian clothes, but he identified himself as General Simpson."

"General Simpson, the Secretary of War is here?" the surprised colonel asked, getting up and walking toward the lobby.

"Yes, ma'am," the nervous lieutenant responded as she brushed past him. "I didn't know who he was," he said to her back as she hurried down the hall.

"General Simpson, I'm Helen Powell, the Airborne Laser Program Director. We weren't informed of your visit. It's a pleasure to meet you, sir. Please come into my office."

"Good afternoon, Colonel. You weren't informed, because I just decided to stop by," Simpson said, following Powell into her office.

"Sir, would you care for a cup of coffee or a soft drink?"

"No, Colonel, just a quick chat," he said, smiling at the business-like, fortyish looking woman before him. "Was your test last year successful?" he asked, admiring the impressive display of awards and citations hanging on her wall. *Brilliant woman according to her file ... a Ph.D. in chemistry, and a distinguished Air Force career.*

"Yes, sir, during the launch phase, we destroyed the ballistic missile from 300 miles," Powell said with pride. "We have another test scheduled for September."

Sitting in a chair in front of Powell's desk, SecWar nodded and matter-of-factly inquired, "How soon can you be ready for another test?"

Perplexed by Simpson's unanticipated request, Powell paused, mentally reviewing the myriad of details involved in a ballistic missile intercept test. *Is he joking?* "Sir, I can't give you an answer, until I coordinate with several other commands. Scheduling a ICBM test launch takes time."

Smiling again, Simpson explained further, "Colonel, I'm thinking of a *full scale* test against a nuclear armed ICBM. An unscheduled test," he added, raising one eyebrow. Suddenly SecWar's countenance became somber, "with the missile provided by North Korea."

"O–Oh," a surprised Powell replied, her breath catching in her throat. Slowly shaking her head and frowning, she sat back in her chair to contemplate SecWar's serious expression. Silence filled the room, while the colonel nervously bit her upper lip and frantically sought a rational explanation for Simpson's last statement. *Holy Mother of God! What the hell is going on? At first I thought he might be kidding, but he's talking about a real intercept—not a test. Damn. I've been following the events ... the strong possibility of war in the Middle East ... but I hadn't considered North Korea. Yes, that's it. That crazy bastard Kim Jung-il just might decide to launch an ICBM.*

"General, I assume you mean intercepting the launch of an ICBM from North Korea?"

"You've got it, Colonel. Our world's in a mess ... danger from all sides. We've no direct intelligence indicating Dear Leader plans do such a thing, but being safe is better than being sorry. Now here's what I want you to do," he continued, while removing a folded sheet of paper from his inside coat pocket. Leaning forward he placed the paper on the colonel's desk, "This is an order directing you to immediately transfer the ABL aircraft to Japan—with all support personnel and equipment. I'll ask Colonel Young, the president's Chief of Staff, to issue the orders and coordinate the transfer."

Understanding the seriousness of her new mission, and the chance to demonstrate the effectiveness of the ABL, Powell replied, "Yes, sir. I'll begin immediately. It will be necessary to include contractor personnel. They'll have to fly on the aircraft during missions. Do you have a preference for a location in Japan?"

"No. I'll leave the location up to the Air Force. Northrop-Grumman personnel flew missions during the first Gulf War. I assume Boeing, Lockheed-Martin, and other subcontractor personnel will do the same." Standing and extending his hand to the colonel, SecWar concluded, "Keep me posted on your progress. Get into position as quickly as possible. I'm counting on you, Colonel."

Returning to his office, Simpson called Keyes and asked him to clear the transfer with Japan ASAP. No problems were anticipated in receiving permission. Next he asked Colonel Young to come to his office, explained his concerns, and his decision to transfer the ABL aircraft to Japan.

"Good idea," Young said after hearing the plan. I recommend Misawa Air Force Base, the home of the 35th Fighter Wing. Misawa is located on the northern part of Japan's main island of Honshu, approximately 400 miles north of Tokyo. It's the only combined, joint-service installation in the Western Pacific with Army, Navy, and Marine units—plus Japan's Air Self Defense Force. I'm sure everyone there will welcome an additional layer of protection—even if it is still in development. The base is approximately six hundred miles from the coast of Korea."

"Okay, Charlie, make it so."

Page, Arizona – 4:25 p.m., Tuesday, May 30th

Roland Jefferson, Under Secretary for Border and Transportation Security, Department of Homeland Security, eased the 40-foot houseboat up to the dock at Lake Powell's Wahweap Bay Marina. Jefferson, his wife, Cassandra, and their two boys, Roger, seven, and Joshua, nine, had rented the houseboat for a ten-day cruise. They'd spent the first four days slowly motoring up the lake. Sunday morning found them anchored in a cove near Hole-In-The-Rock. Since departing the marina on Wednesday, they'd neither watched nor listened to the news. When Cassandra turned on the radio Sunday morning to listen to Reverend Smyth, news of the attacks came as a complete surprise. Jefferson quickly discovered his cellphone was out of contact with its network. As soon as the sermon ended, they started back to Wahweap Bay Marina. Low on fuel, they pulled into Dangling Rope Marina and learned the credit card terminal was down. After arguing with the proprietor, Jefferson was finally able to get fuel when a Fish and Game officer inspected his ID and vouched for him. The marina reluctantly accepted Jefferson's personal check. The officer filled the family in on events and recommended not attempting to navigate the lake at night.

Appointed by President Hilda Rodman, Jefferson disliked George Robert Alexander. In fact, he didn't like anyone from the military. Before he left Washington on his family vacation, National Security Advisor, Sara Bloomberg, assured him Alexander was on the way out. Jefferson hoped he would be gone by the time they returned. *Now the SOB is claiming to be the president. He certainly has Smyth's endorsement. I guess I have to contact him. Judging from reports he's running amok. I must try to rally support and get him under control.*

After docking, Jefferson drove to the Arizona State Police barracks in Page. There he identified himself to the desk sergeant and placed a call to Kirkland AFB. The Kirkland operator put him through to Colonel Young. Jefferson explained his situation to Young and received a condensed summary of events. Jefferson decided to drive to Albuquerque the next day. The State Police commander cashed Roland's two hundred dollar personal check, so the family would be able to purchase fuel and food. It was late, and the Jefferson family spent another night on the houseboat to conserve money. The next day's long drive to Albuquerque gave Roland Jefferson time to think. *Now is the time to implement our liberal agenda ... open the borders ... implement Hilda's ingenious educational plans. Yes, turn the country into a gentler society.* Reality had yet to intrude into Jefferson's fantasy world.

Chapter 23

The Caliph's Palace, Tehran, Iran – 1:00 p.m. Tuesday, May 30th

General Aghajari received the caliph's summons with trepidation. He sensed the underlying friction between the caliph and the grand ayatollah. When he arrived at the caliph's private chamber at 1:00 p.m., he found the caliph alone, seated in a comfortable chair in an antechamber of his spacious apartment. On a table beside him was a tray of fruit, a pitcher of iced tea, and glasses.

Making a great show of bowing, Aghajari said effusively, "Praise be to Allah. Excellency, how may I be of service?"

"I require a briefing on my Empire's nuclear weapons program," the arrogant young caliph replied, waving his right ring-bejeweled hand.

Aghajari felt uneasy, very uneasy, as he quickly reviewed pertinent facts in his mind. *Iran's nuclear weapons development program is divided into two parts ... the legal part shown to the IAEC inspectors, belonging to Iran's atomic energy agency ... and the secret weapons part, belonging to the Revolutionary Guard. Iran's supreme leader controlled access to the program. Now Iran is the nucleus of the Islamic Empire, and Khomeini has replaced Iran's supreme leader. Khomeini was a member of Iran's Assembly of Experts who picked the supreme leader, and it was rumored he also belonged to the Committee of Nine. Well, that explains how he became the supreme leader. But the caliph ... Who the hell is the caliph? Where did he come from? Who is really in charge ... the caliph ... or the supreme leader? I must follow both of their orders, until there is a direct conflict.* Bowing again, he replied, "May Allah be praised. Excellency, this is a complicated subject. Where do you wish me to begin?"

"At the beginning, general. Where else?" the caliph snapped with a haughty gesture of his right hand.

Aghajari swallowed hard. *Another arrogant fanatic, who won't understand anything I tell him.* "Excellency, with Allah's blessings, Iran decided to become a nuclear power over twenty years ago. To be a true nuclear power, Iran must control the entire uranium processing cycle—making the nuclear explosive—starting with mining ore and ending with highly enriched uranium. We must also be able to manufacture all the weapon's components. Uranium must be processed in a special manner to make it suitable for an atomic explosion—"

The caliph waved his hand, interrupting the general's childish explanation. "Yes, yes, *I understand*. The uranium-235 isotope must be separated from the other isotopes. There are three practical methods for doing so: gaseous diffusion, centrifuge, or by using a tuneable laser to excite a particular isotope. Do we have *any* of these processes in operation?" the frowning caliph threateningly asked.

The caliph's menacing behavior took the general off-guard. Startled, he drew back in consternation and blurted out, "I did not know you understood these things ... Excellency," he added as an afterthought.

"*Of course I understand*. I have a Ph.D. in physics," the caliph sneered with dismissive wave of his hand.

"O–Oh! P–Please forgive my ignorance, Excellency," the general stuttered, looking at the caliph with newfound respect, and began a more detailed explanation.

"In the late 1980s Iran established a relationship with North Korea and China to obtain missile technology. Later, we expanded the relationships to include processing uranium to make fissile materials. We'd discovered ten different locations of uranium ore in Iran.

"In the mid 1990s we established a relationship with Russia, whose scientists provided us with plans and specifications for a uranium mill. The mill at Saghand converts uranite ore into yellowcake. We have several more producing uranium mines and milling facilities." The caliph nodded and gestured for the general to continue.

"As you know, yellow cake must be converted into uranium hexafluoride to provide a feed stock for the separation process. China provided plans and specifications for the small uranium hexafluoride pilot plant we built in Isfahan. Later, China provided additional plans and assistance building an industrial size hexafluoride plant near Isfahan, which will produce 200 tons of uranium hexafluoride per year. That plant has been in operations for six months. The output is stored in large containers in an underground chamber, awaiting shipment to the separation facility.

"Our scientists chose centrifuge technology to separate U-235. Iran has mastered the art of manufacturing the centrifuge and its components. Only a few nations have been able to do so," the general added with considerable pride. "Doing so required specialized manufacturing machines and processes. Pakistan's Dr. Khan[*] provided drawings for the P-1 centrifuge, and aided us in purchasing the required specialized machines. Our pilot facility was located at the Defense Industries Organization munitions works, at Lavizan-Shian on

---

[*] Dr. A. Q. Khan, a Pakistani known as the father of the "Islamic Bomb," and founder of the Islamic "Bombs-R-Us" network based in Pakistan.

the outskirts of Tehran. After several failed attempts, we determined the P-1 drawings were flawed, and we made modifications. Khan, who has a wealth of information from numerous sources, provided us with drawings and specifications for P-2 centrifuges. A U.S. Congressman[†] obtained information from a traitor and pressured the IAEC to refer our 'illegal activities' to the U.N. Security Council. When IAEC inspectors became suspicious of our activities, we razed the plant in 2003 and moved the 164 modified centrifuges to Natanz."

"Are you telling me Iran can actually manufacture all the components required for a high speed centrifuge? One that spins at 1,000 revolutions per second?" the caliph asked, leaning forward and looking up at the general with an intense expression.

"Yes, Excellency. We obtained all of the required machinery right under the noses of the Great Satan's intelligence services," the general boasted with a chuckle, realizing he was beginning to establish a rapport with the caliph. "It seems they didn't think a Third World nation like ours capable of mastering the technology. The devil Bush II and that meddlesome U.S. Congressman were getting close to uncovering our nuclear weapons program. Thanks be to Allah, Bush II was not reelected. The infidel woman who replaced him accepted our assurances that all of our activities were peaceful." The general, laughed, and the caliph joined him.

"Excellency, do you know the Great Satan's CIA and DIA actually believed a Shia nation like Iran would never cooperate with al-Qaeda, because they're Sunni? What a bunch of fools," the general concluded, and once more, the two shared a hearty laugh.

"Yes, they are," the caliph agreed with an evil smile.

Observing the caliph's demeanor, the general, who was still standing, finally began to relax. The caliph laughed, remembering his early days when he was Mohammed al-Mihdar, Usama's trusted secret ambassador. Looking up at the general, he said, "They never realized Iran assisted al-Qaeda in preparing for Holy Tuesday ... or that top al-Qaeda leaders, including Usama and his oldest son, came here when the Great Satan's attack on the Taliban began in Afghanistan." Mohammed had visited Usama in Iran on several occasions in 2001 and early 2002.

Wondering how the caliph knew these things, the general laughed with his leader, and added, "Then America's infidel woman president ordered their military to leave Iraq, allowing us to start a civil war, and absorb southern Iraq."

The caliph smiled. He was beginning to like the general, and he was tired of having to look up while the general spoke. "Have a seat," he said, pointing

---

[†] Weldon, Curt, *Countdown To Terror*. Regnery Publishing, Inc., 2005.

to a chair near him. "Would you care for a glass of iced tea? A taste I acquired as a student in the United States."

Ah! He lived in America—another piece of the puzzle. "Yes, thank you," the general said, sitting and pouring himself a glass from the pitcher on the tray. After taking a sip, he commented, "Tea with ice is very good. Thank you Excellency."

The caliph smiled at the compliment, then leaned forward and said, "Extruding the centrifuge's aluminum cylindrical body is extremely difficult, as is welding the bearing races to the cylinder's end ... And manufacturing the ring magnets. I had no idea we had this capability," After refilling his glass, the caliph continued, "You've been most helpful by enlightening me on the extent of our weapons development program."

Aghajari smiled and relaxed before continuing, "We have operating centrifuges in one of two underground, bombproof chambers near Natanz. Each chamber has twenty meters of earth and reinforced concrete above it, and can hold a 50,000 centrifuge cascade. Half of the centrifuges are installed in one chamber and are producing highly enriched uranium—enough to make one bomb every three months.

"Our scientists have also produced polonium-210 in a reactor—"

"For the neutron source? The polonium-beryllium reaction," the caliph interrupted, then smiled and laughed when remembering how Ralph had replaced the clumsy polonium-beryllium neutron source for the five Soviet devices, with a modern neutron source custom-made to his specifications by the supplier, *and, Ralph did it with the full knowledge of U.S. nuclear weapons scientists.*

"Yes ... a backup ... for an electronic neutron source," Aghajari answered hesitantly, wondering what the caliph found to be so funny. "We have imported a large supply of beryllium. It's also used as a neutron reflector." Aghajari paused, waiting to see if the caliph had another comment or question. The caliph smiled and nodded for the general to continue.

"We contracted with the D. V. Efremov Institute in St. Petersburg to build a pilot demonstration laser enrichment plant. But ..." the general sighed, then continued with a shrug. "Now, I doubt the new Russian president will allow the Institute to build the full scale plant. *Insha'Allah.*" After taking another sip of iced tea, he continued.

"Implosion weapons require plutonium-239 and explosive lens. We have a large HMX‡ explosives manufacturing plant near Isfahan. It's producing explosive lens for our implosion bombs. Our scientists have been testing implosion devices by using steel balls for the pit," the general said, watching

---

‡ Acronyms. HMX–high melting explosive; RDX–research development explosive; and PBX–plastic bonded explosive.

the caliph to see if he understood. Noting the caliph's intent expression, he continued.

"We have a heavy water production plant and a forty megawatt heavy water reactor under construction at Arak. The reactor will convert natural uranium to plutonium. Of course the Bushier nuclear power reactor will also produce plutonium."

The caliph sat back, smiling, amazed by the advanced state of Iran's nuclear weapons program. *My Empire has the capability to manufacture uranium bombs. Soon the Bushier reactor will have run long enough to produce plutonium for my implosion bombs.* "How many warheads have we produced?"

"Excellency, we have enough highly enriched uranium for ten warheads. North Korea provided plans for two types of warheads. One of each design has been fabricated. One is a simple gun-type device to ensure Iran ... er ... your Islamic Empire, will be able to demonstrate a nuclear detonation. An underground test is scheduled for next month."

"Will the implosion warheads fit on our missiles?"

"Yes, Excellency, they were designed to do so."

The caliph smiled, took a bite from a peach, and said, "Tell me about our missiles."

"Iran purchased twelve Kh-55 Granat[§] anti-ship cruise missiles from Uzbekistan. The Granat is similar to the Great Satan's Tomahawk cruise missile. The missile can be launched from an airplane or a ground launcher and has a range of 3,000 kilometers. Our engineers have reverse-engineered the Granat, and we're now producing them as our Raad cruise missile. Initially we purchased the missiles' engines from France." The general laughed and smiled. "Cruise missile engines were not included in the arms embargo imposed on Iran. We also purchased four nuclear warheads from a Soviet general by the name of ...

"Yatchenko?" the caliph exclaimed, grasping the arms of his chair, and starting to rise.

"Y—yes, do you know him?" Aghajari asked without thinking.

"Yes," Saladin replied smiling slyly and settling back in his chair.

I'm beginning to understand how he became caliph. He may be a fanatic, but he understands technology. Something the ayatollahs do not.

[§] On 18 March 2005 *Financial Times* newspaper of Britain reported that Ukrainian Prosecutor-General Svyatoslav Piskun stated that the Ukraine exported 12 cruise missiles to Iran and six to China in 2001. Piskun told the paper that none of the 18 X-55 cruise missiles (also known as Kh-55 or AS-15) was exported with the nuclear warheads they were designed to carry.
(http://www.globalsecurity.org/wmd/world/iran/x-55.htm)

Perhaps there is hope for us after all. "Two of the warheads are from old Soviet SS-4 missiles that were 'destroyed' as part of a treaty agreement. They can be mounted on our Shahab-3 missiles. The other two are for the Kh-55 Granat. They were *lost* in Uzbekistan. For an additional fee, Yatchenko provides parts and technicians to service the warheads every year."

A smile spread across the caliph's face as he nodded his approval.

Encouraged, the general continued, "Iran and North Korea formed a secret missile development program. We paid North Korea in oil. The first jointly designed missile, the No-dong/Zelzal-3 failed its first test in 1994. Our scientists and engineers realized they needed help. We turned to Russia and they provided technical assistance and a working RD-214 rocket motor from the old Soviet SS-4 MRBM. We test fired the RD-214, improved the design, and we're now producing it as our Shahab-3B, a single stage missile with a range of 1,300 kilometers. North Korea's version is the No-dong-1. We also have an improved two stage Shahab-3D, and a three-stage missile—the *Kosar* with a range of 4,300 kilometers—ready for testing. Its first stage rocket motor is based on the RD-216 rocket motor from the Soviet SS-5 IRBM. Iran manufactures the entire Shahab-3B and will soon manufacture the new Shahab-3D and Kosar missiles. North Korea's version of the Kosar is the Taep'o-dong-2. In addition we also have chemical and biological warheads for the Shahab-3D."

The caliph stood, indicating the audience was over. "A good briefing, General. From now on you will personally keep me informed of all events."

After the general departed, Mohammed sipped his iced tea, very pleased with himself. *I'm sure I now know more about my Empire's weapons than Khomeini does. Something I shall keep to myself. Khomeini may think he has me on a short leash, but I'm not content to be anyone's puppet. We'll just see how his eminence handles me, now that I know as much, if not more, about our capabilities than he does.*

Confident that he now held the upper hand, the caliph continued to brood, *I'm tired of Khomeini manipulating me. I know he disapproves of Yosif, but Allah promised one of my rewards in paradise will be boys of perpetual freshness to serve me—scattered pearls—never altering in age, dressed in fine green silk, adorned with bracelets of silver. Why wait? ... Now it's time for me to assert myself, take control.*

At 4:30 p.m., a cocky caliph entered the grand ayatollah's richly appointed private chamber. Swaggering into the room, he stopped and struck a haughty pose directly in front of "his Eminence," who lounged in an overstuffed, leather chair. A matching chair was positioned at an angle to the Khomeini's. In between was a low, round, ornately carved teak table, atop which sat an oversized brass tray bearing a bowl of fruit, a carafe of coffee, a pot of tea, and gold-rimmed handle-less cups.

Khomeini appeared unaware of the caliph's rude behavior, but the old man's keen eyes missed nothing. He was immediately aware of the change in his puppet's demeanor. Avoiding eye contact, the old man casually placed his empty cup on the tray and motioned toward the empty chair.

While the caliph settled in his chair, a wizened little servant, quietly standing in attendance, came forward to re-fill the ayatollah's cup of tea, but waited for Khomeini's nod of approval, before pouring the fragrant, dark, Arabic coffee into the caliph's cup.

Annoyed by the servant's obvious slight, the caliph sneered at the little man before churlishly demanding, "A spoonful of sugar," to which the little old man quickly complied. An almost imperceptible gesture from Khomeini dismissed the servant, who crept quietly from the room, and closed the door.

Tension electrified the room. Both men sat seething, waiting for their steaming beverages to cool. Still annoyed with the servant, and spoiling for a fight, the caliph reached across the table, picked up a neatly folded linen napkin, and spread the cloth on his lap. Then cutting his eyes around at Khomeini, he began a disgusting display of gorging himself on the fruit—first a juicy peach, then several luscious ripe figs. Smacking his lips and sucking loudly on a peach pit, he deliberately allowed the juice to run down his beard and drip on the cloth—all the while peering at Khomeini, making sure his behavior was annoying him. The old man's slight build evidenced simple eating habits, and he silently watched the gluttonous display with disdain: his wrinkled face expressionless. Finally, after burping loudly and using the fine linen cloth to wiped away the sticky juice from his hands, mouth, and beard, the caliph reached for his coffee, burped again, and leaned back in his chair to enjoy the rich brew.

A stoic Khomeini inwardly grimaced and began the conversation. "May Allah bless you, Mohammed. I hope you do not mind my referring to you by your birth name." Khomeini sighed and raised his eyebrows. "You did very well this morning. It was unfortunate the meeting occurred before you were thoroughly briefed. I asked you here in order to share my vision of Allah's plans with you."

Mohammed half-bowed in his chair, "It's an honor to be an instrument of Allah's will," he said, knowing full well the old man was trying to manipulate him. *I'll play the old fool's silly game a little longer. Sooner or later, he'll tell me his plans. In the meantime, I'll smile and let him think he is still the boss.*

Inwardly smiling at his puppet's overtly fawning display, Khomeini said, "Allah has chosen you as His instrument to unite all of Islam under one banner. And, like our beloved Prophet, may he rest in peace, Allah wills you to spread His word throughout the remainder of the world. The first step in Allah's plan is to establish true Islamic governments—like Iran's—in other

Islamic countries. Starting today, Iraq, Saudi Arabia, Libya, Syria, Algeria, Egypt, Morocco, Tunisia, Sudan, Afghanistan, Azerbaijan, Chechnya, Kyrgyzstan, Uzbekistan, Tajikistan, Turkmenistan, and Uzbekistan will all be governed by a guardian council similar to ours. By the end of the week, Pakistan and Turkey should have eliminated their corrupt government and establish their own guardian councils. All these countries and many more to follow will be part of your caliphate."

"Praise be to Allah," Mohammed replied, lowering his head in mock deference.

"Now the time has come to establish Islam's control over the nonbelievers. Usama bin Laden, may Allah bless him, calculated that the West should pay $300 a barrel for our oil. He said the United States, Europe, and Japan are robbing us. Usama is right. Our Great Jihad has stopped all oil production. It's time for you, the caliph, to order the workers back into the oil fields and refineries. By the time production begins, the infidels will be out of oil. They will do anything to get more. OPEC is no more. Now you, the great caliph of Allah's Islamic Empire, will set the price of oil," the master puppeteer said, deftly pulling his puppet's strings.

Khomeini's words had their desired effect. Mohammed's ego inflated and his face radiated arrogance, as he replied with an evil smile, "Allah be praised. *I* shall schedule an announcement for tomorrow morning. *I* will demand a tribute to Allah be paid by those nations to whom *I* choose to sell oil. Those nations willing to meet *my* requirements will be allowed to purchase oil at $300 per barrel."

Khomeini nodded his approval, sneering to himself, knowing he had his puppet partially under control. "May Allah bless you. By collecting such magnificent tributes in Allah's name, you will be hailed as the greatest Caliph. The power of Allah's Empire will grow beyond our wildest dreams. Imagine the might you will possess, once Pakistan becomes a true theocracy. You will have a source of additional nuclear weapons and delivery systems. No power on earth will dare challenge your new empire ... for Allah is guiding your steps," the grand ayatollah said, stroking Mohammed's ego.

Satisfied with the results, Khomeini became serious and said, "I have been informed the new American president is attempting to save his miserable country. He is a strong man, making a valiant effort. Had such a man not appeared, the Great Satan would have already collapsed. Without oil, in spite of Alexander's efforts, the arrogant Americans will fall to their knees—it will just take a little longer. The Great Satan is attempting to purchase additional oil from Mexico, several African nations, and Venezuela. So is Europe, since all Middle Eastern oil has been cut off. The West can never purchase enough oil to replace the oil our empire previously sold them."

On a roll, and full of himself for pulling one over on Khomeini,

Mohammed laughed his evil laugh. "Allah be praised. Soon the dollar will be devalued and their 'house of cards' financial system will collapse. The Great Satan allowed its environmentalists to block building new oil refineries and oil drilling off its coasts and in Alaska. They haven't built a new nuclear power plant in the last thirty years. Through their greed and stupidity, they have placed their economy in our hands. Now I am going to enjoy strangling them. Within a few months they will be a third-rate country," Mohammed boasted.

Khomeini was tired of Mohammed's bombast and arrogance. It was time to jerk his strings—time to re-establish complete control. "Did General Aghajari tell you a second American carrier group has arrived and is sitting in the mouth of the Gulf of Oman?" Khomeini innocently asked, letting Mohammed know who held the real power, and that he knew everything Mohammed did.

Fuck you! You miserable old goat, Mohammed inwardly raged, and replied with a bland expression, "No. He was briefing me on our nuclear capability." Feigning indifference while he gained control of himself, Mohammed grudgingly accepted Khomeini's dominance. Although it galled him, he cleverly acknowledged the fact by saying, "What do you suggest?"

Mohammed's unwilling capitulation amused the sly old man, who hid his pleasure by serenely saying, "May Allah bless you. Order the second Granat missile with its nuclear warhead to Bandar Abbas. When the time is right, we can destroy both of the Great Satan's aircraft carrier fleets at the same time."

"Praise Allah. I will issued the order immediately," Mohammed said with deference, allowing Khomeini to think he was still under the old man's control.

At 6:30 p.m., Grand Ayatollah Khomeini received a call from Iran's foreign minister. "The Great Satan's Secretary of State has called to inform me U.S. ships and aircraft would be arriving at Kuwait to evacuate the Americans and Europeans. The arrogant infidel had the audacity to warn us not to interfere," the minister boasted.

Khomeini instructed the minister to inform the caliph of the message. *I'll discuss this with Mohammed when we review the announcement he will make tomorrow.*

Chapter 24

President Alexander met Nora Jacobson in the hall. "Good evening, Nora, you're working late."

Smiling, Nora replied, "Good evening, Mr. President. I'm just following your example."

Alexander laughed and wondered about the change in her demeanor. *What's different about her? She's more self-assured. I can see it in her bearing and expression.* "How are you doing with the banks and credit card companies?"

"I'll let you know tomorrow, sir. I've spoken with all the key personnel. Some balked at cooperating," she said with a shrug, "But … I think I explained it so they understood the problem. I've scheduled at conference call at ten tomorrow morning with the key players. Afterward, I can give you a definitive answer."

Alexander encouraged her by patting her affectionately on her shoulder. "Good work, Nora. We'll slay more giants tomorrow," he joked and watched with satisfaction as she strode confidently down the corridor.

At about the same time, in Shaare Emeth Temple in northeast Albuquerque, Rabbi Abe Steinberg sat in his office contemplating the enormous task Ross had given him. He'd spent all afternoon phoning other rabbis, two Catholic bishops and one cardinal, and three Baptists and two Lutheran ministers. Three of his fellow rabbis were trying to locate a Hindu and a Buddhist for the committee. So far, he'd run into a stone wall. The Catholics required guidance and approval from Rome. The Baptists needed approval from their Conventions (northern and southern), and the Lutherans from their Synods. All wanted a specific charter for the committee. Drafting and circulating the charter would require a year or more. Most thought it would take a couple of years to seat the committee and several more years to produce recommendations. No one would consider meeting in two days—let alone meeting the seven-day deadline for recommendations.

"Impossible is the only thing they agree on," Steinberg muttered. The ringing telephone interrupted his thoughts.

"Rabbi Steinberg, this is Reverend Smyth returning your call. I apologize for the delay in getting back to you."

"Good evening, Reverend. Did you see the president's news conference today?"

"The one in which he announced signing the Muslim Internment Order?"

"Yes. The Press Secretary also announced formation of an inter-faith advisory committee to address problems caused by the worldwide Islamic jihad. I've been asked to form the committee. I'd like you to be a member."

Smyth was expecting an invitation to join the committee, but he was surprised to receive it from a rabbi. "When is the first meeting?" the Reverend asked.

"Thursday. The president wants recommendations in a week."

Now Smyth was astonished. *In a week ... Recommendations in a week! They must be crazy.* "Uh, Rabbi Steinberg, there's no way I can travel to Albuquerque by Thursday. I must prepare my sermon. I must preach to my congregation on Sunday ... umm, who else will be on the committee?"

"So far, just us. I expect to recruit more members tomorrow. An Air Force plane can pick you up tomorrow morning. We can make arrangements for your sermon to be telecast from here." Steinberg had no intention of being a one-man committee. "Reverend Smyth, your last sermon galvanized the public. You're respected. Think about the international prestige you'll be accorded, by receiving a presidential appointment and helping to find a solution.

Smyth said nothing for several seconds. *The rabbi's right. It's my duty, my obligation to serve the nation. My congregation will understand and appreciate my efforts ... and my flock will grow.* "All right. I'll be ready to come tomorrow afternoon."

"Good. Thank you. You'll be contacted regarding travel instructions. Bring whatever you require."

Smyth's thoughts were racing. Problems and solutions flooded his agile mind. "I suspect you'll have difficultly recruiting members from the major religions. They'll want to take years and argue over every detail. May I suggest you consider independents? The president of Bob Jones University, for example. Has the president set a minimum number of committee members? What will he do, if we can't form a committee?" Have you—

Interrupting Smyth's string of questions, Rabbi Steinberg said with a chuckle, "I see you grasp the problem. You're correct. The major denominations are talking in terms of years. I'm open to any suggestions. Feel free to contact anyone you think can contribute. President Alexander will work with whomever's available. He'll use anything we suggest. Once you're here you'll understand. We must save our nation. Do whatever is necessary. I'm looking forward to working with you."

Los Angeles, California – Tuesday evening.

Patricia Manning's Hispanic maid opened the mansion's front door. Three serious looking men wearing dark suits were standing there. The tall, well-built man presented his FBI credentials and asked to speak with Ms. Patricia Manning, the *Los Angeles Herald's* publisher and president. "I'm sorry, but Senora Manning is entertaining guests. You must call her secretary tomorrow to make an appointment," the maid replied, attempting to close the door.

Special Agent Francis Zimmerman had his orders. Brusquely stiff-arming the door, he stepped through the entrance and told the startled maid, "Please take me to *Señora* Manning *now*." Special Agent Perez, one of the other two agents accompanying Zimmerman, followed him into the house, further unnerving the wide-eyed maid who stood gaping at two black Ford 500 sedans parked in the circular driveway.

The third agent made no effort to come inside, but further upset the maid by brushing back his jacket to expose his holster and service pistol. Now, thoroughly agitated, the maid looked at Zimmerman, swallowed hard, and slowly closed the door. "*Por favor*, please follow me, *señores*," she said in a quivering voice and hurriedly led the way through the entry foyer and down a long hallway. At the entrance to a crowded ballroom, she stopped and frantically looked around the room. About fifty "beautiful people" were milling about enjoying cocktails from two bars—one on either end of the room. Flanking both bars were tables bedecked with silver punch bowls, crystal bowls filled with roses, and an assortment of lavish hors d'oeuvres. A string quartet played softly in an alcove off the far side of the massive room.

"*Por favor*, please wait here *señores*. I'll get *Señora* Manning." Turning, the maid worked her way through the crush of merrymakers to the center of the room. There, a tall, elegantly dressed woman with beautifully coifed silver hair was holding court, surrounded by several similarly dressed women, and men wearing tuxedos. Waiting politely for a pause in the conversation, the nervous maid leaned close to her employer and softly whispered, "*Perdóneme, Señora*."

Annoyed, Patricia Manning snapped, "What *is* it, Gabriella?"

"*Perdóneme, Señora*, but there's *señores* from the FBI here to see you. *El Jefe* insisted I come and get you," Gabriella said, nodding toward Special Agent Zimmerman standing at the ballroom's entrance. Noticing their hostess's agitation and overhearing the maid's comments, some of Manning's guests glanced in the agent's direction.

"Excuse me, my dears, while I deal with this unfortunate interruption," Manning smirked to her admirers.

Manning walked purposefully through the crowed room to where

Zimmerman and Perez were standing. Zimmerman carefully appraised the haughty woman as she approached them with a disdainful look.

"What is the meaning of this unwarranted interruption? What do you want? Can't you see I have guests? This had *better* be important!" Manning sneered.

"Yes, ma'am. I'm Special Agent Zimmerman with the FBI," Zimmerman replied, calmly showing her his credentials. "I have orders to take you to meet with President Alexander. Please pack a bag. We've no time to waste. We must leave immediately."

Already annoyed by this unexpected intrusion into her powerful, privileged world, Patricia Manning's famous temper flared, "How dare you! I have no interest in meeting with the … that … that *imposter*," she snarled. "Now, get out of my house," she ordered, pointing toward the front door.

Now it was Zimmerman's turn to be annoyed. "Ms. Manning, I have orders to take you to the president. If you don't cooperate, I'll take you into custody. You'll be taken to a holding cell, where you'll remain until the plane departs in the morning. If you don't wish to undergo this embarrassment, you'll do as I have instructed. Change your clothes and pack a bag." Stepping aside to allow her to pass, he added, "It *will* be necessary for me to accompany you to your bedroom. If there is only one door, I'll wait outside."

"Well … *I never*," Patricia Manning sputtered and made as though she would turn toward her guests.

Before she could move, an extremely stern Zimmerman quickly cut her short by stepping to her side and forcefully grasping her arm. Speaking softly, but firmly, Zimmerman cautioned, "Now, Ms. Manning, either we go to your bedroom, or I'll handcuff you right here in the presence of your guests."

Oblivious to the scene playing out at the entrance to the elegant room, most of the revelers continued drinking, eating and schmoozing—undisturbed by Patricia Manning's uninvited guests. While laughter and merriment surrounded her, a still defiant, unyielding Manning remained vehement in her refusal to adhere the agent's demands. Continuing to glare at Zimmerman, the haughty woman failed to notice when a man of medium height approached. Zimmerman, however, was watching the partygoers in the ballroom and saw the man moving toward them. Gently squeezing Patricia's arm, and whispering through clenched teeth, Zimmerman once again ordered, "Now, Ms. Manning … your bedroom."

"Patricia, are you all right?" the man asked, concern in his voice, "Who are these men? What's going on?"

"Sir, this doesn't concern you. Please return to the party," Zimmerman said.

"Patricia, is this man threatening you?"

"Winston, he's an FBI agent," she responded still glowering at

Zimmerman. "He says he's here to take me to see the *imposter*—Alexander. He demands I leave with him right away."

Turning to Zimmerman, Winston said, "I don't know who you think you are, but you are to leave *immediately*. I'll file a formal complaint tomorrow."

"Sir." Zimmerman replied, "Please step aside. Otherwise, I'll be forced to arrest you for interfering with a law enforcement officer."

"What did you say?" Winston demanded, puffing out his chest, his face turning red from rage. "I'm Winston Pollock, managing editor of the *Herald*. I demand to know what this is about."

Zimmerman smiled. "Mr. Pollock, I'm glad we found you. You are also invited to meet with the president tomorrow. We have agents looking for you at your house. Please go with Special Agent Perez, while Ms. Manning changes clothes and packs a bag. One of our agents will take you home so you can do the same."

"I'm not going *anywhere* with you," Pollock stormed.

Guests, startled by the sudden outburst, finally took notice of the scene in the hallway. Curious as to the reason for Pollock's behavior, some began moving toward Manning, Pollock and the two men.

"Hey, what's going on, Winston?" One man called out.

Speaking softly, Zimmerman said to Pollock, "Sir, you're causing an unnecessary scene and bringing further embarrassment to Ms. Manning. Either you go with Special Agent Perez or you'll be arrested. Your choice." Perez placed his hand on Pollock's arm.

Realizing they had little choice, but to do as they were asked, Patricia Manning—always the gracious hostess—smiled reassuringly and said to the approaching group, "Nothing, nothing to worry about my dears, just an equipment problem. Please enjoy yourselves, we may be *detained* for a while," she said waving them away, her diamond rings sparkling.

Turning to Pollock, she whispered with a sneer, "Winston, let's not make a scene in front of my guests. We can call our attorney later. Do as he says." Then, jerking her arm out of Zimmerman's hand, she gathered up the long train of her sequined gown, turned, and stormed down the hall—followed by her terrified maid and Zimmerman.

Stifling his anger, Pollock grudgingly turned to Special Agent Perez and hissed, "*All right*, let's go to my house. I'm sure you know where it is."

Three hours later, Patricia Manning, Winston Pollock, and *Herald* reporter, Tom Jacobson, were escorted to separate rooms at Vandenberg Air Force Base VIP quarters. There they were informed breakfast would be served at 0700 hours the following morning, and they would board a jet for Albuquerque at 0800. Quickly discovering the telephones were disconnected, Manning and Pollock furiously paced back and forth in their rooms. Jacobson, who'd interviewed Barbara Focker, Jan Foite, Mary Lane, and Randolph

Clarkson, and later written several articles about District Judge Kerry and the riots, was uneasy.

Chapter 25

Wednesday

The Caliph's Palace, Tehran, Iran – 10:30 a.m. Wednesday, May 31st.

Sporting a neatly trimmed, full beard, Caliph Saladin II admired himself in the mirror. Dressed in a gold-embroidered white *bisht,* worn over a white silk *thob,* with a green *ghoutra* covering his head, he smiled at his resplendent image. *Yes, I am much better looking than Saladin.* Turning, he strutted onto the stage, postured for the benefit of the TV cameras, and began his address to the world.

"In the name of Allah, the Most Compassionate, the Most Merciful, I, Saladin II, proclaim the birth of our new Islamic Empire.

"My empire includes the former Islamic states of Iran, Iraq, Saudi Arabia, Libya, Syria, Algeria, Egypt, Morocco, Tunisia, Sudan, Afghanistan, Azerbaijan, Chechnya, Kyrgyzstan, Uzbekistan, Tajikistan, Turkmenistan, and Uzbekistan. Soon all Islamic states will join my empire. Allah has predestined that my empire become the greatest Islamic Empire in history.

"The infidels have been driven from our lands. A few remain in hiding, but not for long.

"Soon they will be found and killed.

"Soon our Great Jihad will cause the conversion of infidel nations to the one true faith—or they will perish.

"Soon the Little Satan will be no more. Its lands will be returned to their rightful owners.

"Soon the people of the book will bend their knees to me and pay Allah's tribute—or they too will perish.

"Islam has the world's most potent weapon … *oil* … a commodity nonbelievers will do anything to obtain.

"Now, with Allah's blessing, I am prepared to use this mighty weapon Allah the merciful has given us.

"Now we will introduce the nonbelievers to the true faith.

"Now, as Allah wills, *I alone* will dictate the terms the infidels must meet to obtain my empire's oil.

"Henceforth, China, Russia, and the nations of Europe shall pay a tribute tax of two percent of their gross national product to my empire. Quotas will be established for nations meeting my requirements. The Great Satan will not be allowed to purchase oil until its people convert to

Islam, and they establish a true Islamic theocracy.

The caliph paused, gestured with both hands, and pompously announced with a sneer.

"Effective today … OPEC is dissolved. Now *I*, Saladin II, your caliph shall establish the price of oil. Those nations paying the tribute tax, and meeting other requirements *I* may establish, will be allowed to purchase oil … at $300 per barrel.

"Now, Allah requires my empire's oil workers to return to their jobs. Restart the oil fields and refineries. The day of the infidel has passed."

The caliph paused, took a sip of water, and then fixed his eyes on the camera. Sneering again, he sarcastically continued.

"Yesterday, the evil Great Satan's weakling president *begged* me for mercy … *begged* me for permission to allow his ships and aircraft to go to Kuwait to remove the remaining swine-eating-infidel residue from our lands."

He sighed dramatically and lifting his hands, palms up, assumed a pompous expression.

"*I* have benevolently decided to allow them to do so. But … in return for *my* generosity, the Great Satan will pay a tribute of one million dollars per aircraft and five million dollars per ship. It has three days to complete the removal of its *kafirs*—the filthy Christians, Jews, and pagans—from my lands.

"Praise be to Allah. *My* words are spoken with the divine guidance of Allah and are the blessed fruit of our Great Jihad."

Southwestern White House – 0700 Wednesday, 31 May

President Alexander entered the conference room. His wartime Cabinet and staff were present in person or by phone. BG Ross opened the meeting by showing a videotape of Saladin's broadcast. "This was broadcast at 0100. I saw no reason to awaken anyone." The president nodded his agreement.

Dr. Chin, attending the meeting by speakerphone, commented, "Well, we've been expecting something like this. We're making progress obtaining new sources of oil, but we're nowhere near meeting our needs. Fuel rationing went into effect at 12:01 this morning."

"Does this new Islamic Empire he speaks of replace all the countries he listed?" Jay Henniger asked.

"Good question. If it does, should we recognize the Islamic Empire as a legitimate government? If we do, are we at war with it?" Keese asked.

"Allan, you're going to have to make the call. I find it difficult to believe someone like Colonel Qadhafi would relinquish authority to this Saladin character. There's much more going on than meets the eye. We need hard intelligence," Alexander said.

"Mr. President, speaking of hard intelligence, CIA's Deputy Director of Operations, Martha Wellington, is on her way here. She was attending a meeting in Europe when the attacks occurred. I expect her to arrive this afternoon. I'll get word to her to be prepared to address these issues when she arrives," Clark said.

"Good," Simpson said. "We've selected Libya for our first seizure. It has ports, refineries, oil fields, and pipelines. Even more important, it's on the North African coast. After we invade northern Morocco, England and Spain will control the Strait of Gibraltar, and there will be no choke points to bottle up our ships. Libya will provide us a base of operations from which to control North Africa and the entire Middle East. When we capture Wheelus Air Force Base, our old base at Tripoli, we'll have a major base for air operations."

With his left hand clasping his right fist, Alexander leaned back in his chair. Closing his eyes, he listened intently, while mentally visualizing Simpson's war plan. After a few seconds, he abruptly said, "Operation Torch."

Simpson smiled, "Correct. Only this time we won't be fighting Italians and Germans."

"What is Operation Torch?" Dr. Chin inquired.

"Operation Torch was the name for the World War II invasion of North Africa. The Allies landed in several places on the North African coast. This time we'll start with a quick assault to capture and occupy the northern tip of Morocco, the cities of Tangier and Ceuta Tetouan. Then we'll concentrate on Libya," Simpson answered.

"What's your timetable?" the president asked.

"Call up of the reserves has begun. The Eighty-Second and 101st Airborne Divisions are preparing to move to staging areas in Italy. I've ordered our mechanized infantry divisions in Europe to prepare for deployment to North Africa. Two more carrier strike groups are on the way to reinforce The *Kennedy*. The *Carl Vinson* will arrive in four days, followed by the *Abraham Lincoln*. From Libya, we'll move east and capture Egypt, Saudi Arabia, then Iraq and Iran. The *Truman* Strike Group will seal the mouth of the Gulf of Oman. The Iranian coast is hostile. Until Iran is neutralized, we can't enter the Gulf. The target jump-off date for Libya is Sunday morning."

"Did you have any problems getting permission to stage in Italy?" Young asked.

"No, not after the dirty bomb attacks in Rome, Frankfurt, and Lisbon. Spain's Prime Minister resigned, and now Spain and Portugal want to join Italy, Great Brittan, and us in the invasion. All three get a major portion of their oil and natural gas from the area. After they were attacked with dirty bombs, most have had enough of political correctness. Now they want a piece of the Muslims. They're prepared to send troops and crews to help seize and operate the oil fields and refineries. The German military is with us; however, their government is still trying to decide what to do," Simpson replied.

"How about France?" Young asked.

"France is having the equivalent of a nervous breakdown," Keese answered. "After the jihadists' riots, killings, and mutilations, the dirty bomb in Paris sent them over the edge. The French people are turning on the government and the Muslims. It looks like a replay of the French Revolution. Their economy is in shambles."

"Doctor Chin," Alexander said, "We must be prepared to send our people to Libya and other areas in the Middle East to help operate the oil fields, pipelines, and refineries. Instruct the major oil companies to prepare teams … including specialists in extinguishing oil-well fires."

"Mr. President, they're going to want to know about fees and contracts."

"Tell them they'll receive a reasonable fee. They'll be operating as part of our government, under our protection. If they don't cooperate, they'll be nationalized. We'll sort out the details after we solve our energy problems," the president replied. "Next item. How do we rescue the people in Kuwait? One thing is certain, we're not going to pay a tribute to Saladin II."

Simpson answered, "Sending ships into the Arabian Gulf is suicide. They'll be sitting ducks in the Strait of Hormuz. Our best bet is to air evac with heavy fighter cover. People we can't fly out can form a convoy and attempt to drive west to Jordan. We can provide air support and establish re-supply points along their route. The alternative is a massive military strike against air bases and costal installations in Iran, Iraq, and Saudi."

Alexander frowned. "We're not ready to engage Iran. Start the air evacuation. If Iran interferes, I'll order a nuclear strike. Allan, make sure Iran understands our position." Any problems in Qatar, Oman, or the UAE?"

"No," Keese replied. "So far, they have managed to avoid jihad fever. We're air evacuating all nonessential personnel."

"Good. Jay, do you have the seizure order ready?" Alexander asked.

"Yes, sir. My staff worked all night. So did State's and War's."

Addressing Ross, the president said, "Schedule a news conference for noon. I'll give Karpov and Wu a heads up. Allan, do the same with our key allies." Turning to Barry Clark, Alexander signaled it was his turn to report.

"We've had two more suicide bombings and one truck bomb. The round up of Muslims is underway. Most are behaving. They're scared. Some are belligerent. Many are asking to be allowed to return to their native country. The majority don't understand what's happening—or what caused it to happened."

Alexander sighed. "Most humans are inclined to avoid confrontation by either rationalizing or ignoring the problem. This fatal flaw in human nature is the key to success for most dictators. By the time the people realize what's happening, it's too late—they're slaves. So it is with the Muslims. They've failed to condemn the Islamic terrorists among them. Muslims adhere to a religion that doesn't tolerate criticism from within or without. Now they're paying the price. Once we solve our domestic problems, I see no reason why Muslims who wish to leave can't do so." Slightly shaking his head in resignation, he asked. "Anything else?"

"Yes, sir. The publisher, editor, and one reporter from the *Los Angeles Herald* will arrive at noon. They were picked up last night."

"I'll meet with them here at 1400. Allan, Jay, and Barry will attend the meeting. All right Bill, it's your turn."

"Nora Jacobson has a conference call with the heads of the major banks and credit card companies scheduled for 10 o'clock. I'll be with her, but I'm going to let her handle the call." Alexander nodded his agreement. "Unemployment is the big problem. Companies are starting to lay off workers. Our economy can't take this additional shock. I propose to use the seized funds for payrolls for the next month—in other words, no layoffs. Companies will submit a reimbursement claim to Treasury, to pay workers they planned to layoff. We may have to extend the program beyond one month," Fobbs said.

"A good plan. I hadn't foreseen this problem. I'll order an end to layoffs, when I announce the seizures."

"Sir, this could be opening the door for fraud. It would be easy to falsify records and rip off the government," Clark pointed out.

"Uhmm, your probably right." After pausing to consider the possibilities, Alexander added, "Barry, it will be your job to catch anyone who does. Under the circumstance, such acts could be considered *treason*. The guilty will be punished as examples—a warning to others who contemplate doing the same."

Pyongyang, North Korea – 3:25 p.m., Wednesday, May 31st.

Dear Leader watched the live broadcast of Saladin II's pronouncement. He clapped his pudgy little hands together when Saladin announced the tribute tax. *The time is almost right for the invasion of the south. A few more days ... I must slap the United States too. Make them realize I'm a power in Asia ... Perhaps now is the time to launch a nuclear strike on their west coast ... or Okinawa. It is time to contact the admiral.*

After a long detailed conversation with Admiral Cheung, Dear Leader decided he would strike when Cheung launched his invasion.

Southwestern White House – 1200 Wednesday, 31 May

Brigadier General James Ross, dressed in the uniform of the day, called the press conference to order. "Ladies and gentlemen of the press, citizens, and members of the military, the president has called you here to witness his signing of an Executive Order seizing all assets of Middle Eastern countries that have committed acts of war against the United States of America." Ross raised his hand to silence questions. "After the signing, the president will explain the order. Copies will be provided before you leave." Ross paused for a few seconds before announcing, "Ladies and gentlemen, the President of the United States."

President Alexander, dressed in an open collar white short-sleeved, dress shirt and brown slacks, walked briskly to a table next to the podium. Sitting at the table, he opened a leather bound portfolio, picked up a pen, and signed the document it contained. Closing the folder, he stood and walked to the podium. Ross walked to the table, picked up the portfolio, and departed.

Standing behind the podium, the president's gaze swept the gathered reporters and others in the audience, then shifted to the TV cameras. "Fellow citizens, members of the press, good afternoon. Let me briefly summarize events. Last Friday, terrorists destroyed five of our cities with nuclear bombs. The ensuing worldwide insurrections, jihads, by Muslim extremists and terrorists are still being put down. Syria used chemical weapons against Jordan. Then Syria and Egypt attacked Israel. Israel retaliated with nuclear weapons. Navies from several Muslim nations attacked our carrier strike group in the Mediterranean. Yesterday I ordered the internment of all domestic Muslims."

Alexander paused and squared his shoulders, indicating a change of subject. Taking a deep breath and exhaling slowly, he frowned, stepped forward and grasped the sides of the podium. "Early this morning, Saladin II, the terrorist claiming responsibility for destroying our cities, broadcast a new proclamation. In the broadcast, this cowardly murderer proclaimed himself leader of a new Islamic Empire. This self-proclaimed 'caliph,' or king if you prefer, announced he has dissolved OPEC and set a new price for oil—$300 per barrel for Europe and China. Finally, obviously hoping to force our submission, he stated that *no oil* would be sold to the U.S. unless ... or until we *convert* to Islam."

Many in the audience had not heard Saladin II's proclamation, and Alexander's announcement elicited disgruntled mutterings and some loud expressions of anger. The president paused to allow the comments to subside.

"The caliph of this so-called Islamic Empire claims it includes Iran, Iraq, Saudi Arabia, Libya, Syria, Algeria, Egypt, Morocco, Tunisia, Sudan,

Afghanistan, Azerbaijan, Chechnya, Kyrgyzstan, Uzbekistan, Tajikistan, Turkmenistan, and Uzbekistan. If this is so, then the U.S. is at war with the Islamic Empire. We do know our embassies in Algeria, Egypt, Iran, Iraq, Libya, Morocco, Saudi Arabia, Sudan, and Yemen have been sacked. We also know the navies of Egypt, Libya, Syria, and Tunisia attacked our strike group ... and were destroyed," Alexander added with a thin smile, stepping back again and holding up one hand to quiet the reporters.

"And, we do know the West's supply of oil from the Middle East has been cut off. Secretaries Chin, Fobbs, and Keyes are diligently working to obtain replacement oil with considerable success. Soon we will be able to replace most of the Middle Eastern oil.

Placing his hands back on the podium and leaning into it, he continued with a serious expression, "The cost of the destruction of our cities, the damages done by the insurrection, the losses caused by closing the banks and stock exchange, and resulting unemployment are high.

"Should the American people bear the burden of these costs?" the president scowled, his fists clenched. Raising his right hand, he answered his own question, punctuating each word with his fist, "*I ... think ... not!*"

"The document I just signed is an Executive Order seizing the assets of all Muslim nations that perpetrated acts of war against the U.S. The order includes the assets of *rulers and their families*. Seizures include, but are not limited to the countries of, Iran, Iraq, Syria, Saudi Arabia, Egypt, Sudan, Libya, Algeria, and Angola.

"Seized assets will be used by the U.S. to rebuild our cities ... replace buildings, churches, synagogues, and private properties destroyed in insurrections." Alexander paused to allow the babble of comments in the audience to die down.

"Companies and small businesses have begun laying off employees. I'm ordering all layoffs to stop. I further order all laid off employees to be rehired and lost wages paid. Funds from seized assets will be used to reimburse employers."

Cheers from the reporters, technicians, and the audience interrupted the president. The cheering continued for several minutes in the auditorium and throughout the nation: anywhere a TV or radio was tuned into the broadcast. Alexander smiled and enjoyed a drink of water, while the cheering continued. Finally, he raised his hand asking for silence.

"Details for reimbursement will be announced shortly. Banks are instructed to issue funds for payrolls, guaranteed by the Treasury of the United States.

"Thank you for your support. Good afternoon, and God bless America," the president concluded, turned, and left the room and the cheering crowd.

In the din following the press conference, one reporter commented, "I wonder if the banks will cooperate?"

Another answered, "Would you say no to him?"

Los Alamos National Laboratories, New Mexico

While President Alexander prepared for his noon signing of the Seizure Order, Dr. James Chin was analyzing radiation reports from Atlanta. Because of the partial yield, damage was less than the other cities, and the immediate blast area contained more uranium residue than the other sites. Chin was contemplating proposed decontamination strategies when his phone rang. "Jim, this is Peter. I need to see you, now!" Peter Bronson, Ph.D. was the scientist responsible for processing the radioactive fallout samples obtained from the five cities.

Peter is very excited, I wonder why? "Have you identified the source?"

"Yes, that's why I need to see you."

Chin knew something was wrong. Dr. Bronson was a calm, laidback, never in a hurry scientist. His request for an immediate meeting was out of character. "Okay, Peter, I can see you in ten minutes."

Dr. James Chin, Secretary of Energy and Director of Los Alamos National Laboratories, received his doctorate degree in nuclear physics from the University of California. His lineage traced back to the transcontinental railroad. His great, great grandfather had come to America to work on the railroad, made a modest gold strike at Sutter's Mill, moved to San Francisco, and started several profitable family businesses. Dr. Chin, now fifty-two, stood five-foot-seven and weighed 152 pounds. A widower with three grown children, Dr. Chin devoted all his energy to the Laboratory and now the Department of Energy. Always fastidious about his appearance, Chin was wearing a starched, long-sleeved white dress shirt with a striped tie. His navy blue suit jacket was carefully hung on a clothes tree in a corner of his office.

Ten minutes later, Dr. Bronson entered Chin's spacious office. Without saying a word of greeting, he walked passed the puzzled director to the conference table and placed six folders on it, one beside the other. Bronson, a tall, thin, quiet man of fifty-five years, with graying hair, wore his usual attire—a blue open collar dress shirt, tan Dockers, and black loafers. Opening the folder to his left, he removed two graphs and placed one in front of Chin. "This is a mass spectrometer analysis of the Atlanta samples," he said, handing Chin the graph entitled ATLANTA DEPLETEALLOY. "Note the distribution of U-238, U-236, U-235, and U-234 isotopes."

Chin accepted the graph and studied it. "All right. This looks like a typical depleted uranium graph. No surprise, we expected to find depleted uranium was used as a reflector," he said with a quizzical expression.

Bronson nodded and handed Chin the second graph entitled ATLANTA

ORALLOY. After studying it, Chin replied, "This is highly enriched uranium ... the ratios seem a little off. Is there any indication of plutonium?"

"No. No trace of plutonium has been found anywhere. They were all uranium bombs, and I'm sure they were gun-type." Bronson proceeded to show Dr. Chin an ORALLOY graph from each folder. Taking his time, Chin carefully compared the graphs for HEU samples from each of the five cities. Sitting down, he stroked the side of his face with his fingers as the magnitude of the message the graphs conveyed sank in.

Finally, looking up at Bronson, he said, "I'm sure you've checked these results." Bronson nodded. Wrinkling his forehead, Chin looked down at one of the graphs. "Peter, this can only mean one thing." Looking up he continued in a strained voice, "All of the highly enriched uranium came from the same source. The results are almost identical." Bronson, who was now sitting across the table from Chin, nodded again. "If this is true, Peter, it means the terrorists either purchased a large quantity of HEU from one source ... or ... they obtained weapons. Either way, a nuclear power is involved."

Without saying a word, Bronson opened the last folder and handed an untitled copy of a graph to Chin who studied it, then compared it to each of the other five. Slowly looking up, Chin said, "This is a match. What is the source?"

Bronson, who continued staring at the graphs and nervously rubbing his hands together, finally looked up at Chin, swallowed hard, and whispered, "Joe-4."

"What!" Chin gasped, his face draining of color and his body jerking backward in the chair.

"Jim ... Jim, Are you all right?" Bronson asked, rising and walking around the table to place his hand on Chin's shoulders.

Shaking his head, Chin looked around at Bronson and haltingly answered, "Yeah, I–I'm okay Peter ... just shocked ... Have to call Landry." Rising, Chin walked slowly to his desk, picked up the phone, and speed dialed Dr. George Landry. "George, get up here as fast as possible." Turning back to Bronson, he ordered, "Jim, verify your findings with Livermore and Sandia. Top priority."

The Caliph's Palace, Tehran, Iran – 11:20 p.m., Wednesday, May 31st.

The terrified servant entered the caliph's bedchamber. The room was dark, but he could hear sounds of movement and soft moans coming from the huge bed. Realizing his entrance had not been detected, he stammered, "Oh– Oh mighty Caliph. ... Supreme Leader Khomeini requires an audience with you in your sitting room."

Sounds from the bed ceased, and the caliph bellowed out, "How dare you enter my bedchamber. You shall be beaten, before your miserable head is removed from your miserable body."

Afraid to make a sound, the servant fell prostrate on the floor. Khomeini heard the exchange, came to the bedchamber door, and called out, "Mohammed, there is a *problem*. I must discuss it with you immediately."

Mohammed's temper quickly subsided at the sound of the Grand Ayatollah's voice. After a few seconds, he somewhat sheepishly replied while hurrying to the washbasin, "I'll be with you in a couple of minutes, Excellency."

While the terrified servant rose, quietly withdrew, and saw to the Grand Ayatollah's earlier request for coffee, the caliph cleaned and dressed himself in a large bathrobe. A few minutes later, and still fuming, Mohammed entered the sitting room and found a clearly agitated Khomeini standing by a chair.

Tension filled the room. Both men were out-of-sorts. Mohammed, still impassioned with thoughts of Yosif—and his new young lover, Afashr—was obviously irritated with this intrusion into his privacy. Khomeini was disgusted. He knew full well what debauchery was taking place in the caliph's bedchamber … *you revolting excuse for a leader. If I did not need you, I would see to it you never … but at present, I have more important things to concern me. I'll deal with your transgressions later.* Masking his repulsion, Khomeini lifted his hand in greeting, "Allah's blessings upon you, Mohammed."

So angry he was trembling, Mohammed nearly dropped the coffee cup offered by his quaking servant. *What does the old goat want this time. Coming in here at this hour. It's most likely some piddling thing or*—The intense look in the old man's eyes cut short Mohammed's thought and cooled his temper. "You appear troubled, Eminence. Please be seated. Have a coffee and tell me how can I be of service?" Mohammed said, graciously gesturing to a nearby chair.

Swallowing his rancor, Khomeini ignored the chair and quickly came to the point, "Mohammed, that devil Alexander announced he is seizing the assets of the major oil producing Middle East nations—*including ours*. Can he *do that*?"

Taken aback by Khomeini's news, Mohammed sat down and sipped his strong coffee, his mind racing, searching for an answer. *May Allah curse the swine. Alexander's seizing our assets never occurred to me. How will this affect me … and the REM accounts? I need to talk to Ralph about this. I need his advice. Where the hell is he? He said something about taking his blonde whore to the Riviera.* Finally he responded, "He can try. The United States has already frozen assets, including ours, but I don't remember a case where they kept the seized assets. Did Alexander say what he intended to do with them?"

"Yes. He said he planned to use them to rebuild his godless country. Can he do this? What can we do to stop him?" a very agitated Khomeini asked, finally sitting in the chair.

Knowing he must reply, Mohammad decided on bravado to conceal his uncertainty. "First, we must direct our ambassadors to contact our bank presidents and formally object to the United States' unlawful act," Mohammed answered, thinking frantically. "Then, we must demand that the United Nations intervene. I don't think the banks will honor the Great Satan's demands."

Wishful thinking?

Insha'Allah.

Chapter 26

Bern, Switzerland – Wednesday 8 p.m. May 31st.

With few exceptions, government officials and bankers around the world were stunned and angered when the American president's seizure announcement was telecast. A few countries were given a couple of hours advance notice.

"Only an arrogant American would make such a ridiculous statement," the chairman of the Swiss National Bank muttered.

Earlier in the day, Secretary of State Keese called the U.S. ambassador in Bern, Emerson Winchester IV, to inform him of the president's forthcoming seizure order.

The ambassador told Keese, a man he considered a hothead—and way too fractious to be a good diplomat—the seizure order was insane. "If we ask the Swiss banks to go along with this plan, they'll laugh at us. We'll look like a bully. We're a super power. We must be very careful what we do. We don't want to alienate our friends," he whined.

"We *are* a super power—the *only* super power—and our *allies* would do well to remember it," Keese replied. "Quite frankly, we don't give a damn what they think of us, as long as they do what we ask them to do. Now, it's your job to make the haughty Swiss understand the days of pissing on the U.S. are over. From now on, anyone who does will pay a horrible price. If you're unable to explain this to them, call me and I'll explain it."

Secretary Keese's instructions so unnerved Winchester, he mentioned resigning. In response, Keese quickly said the military attaché would take his place. Oh dear, this would never do. The ambassador became even more upset, when Keese told him the military attaché was to accompany him to his meeting with the Swiss president. Before ending the call, Keese informed the frustrated ambassador auditors were on the way to supervise the transfer of assets to the U.S.

The Swiss government was outraged. Two U.S. chartered Boeing 747s filled with bank examiners, FBI financial experts, and accountants from several large accounting firms had landed at the Geneva and Zurich airports. When custom officials learned the purpose of the visit—to examine the records of all Swiss banks—all hell broke loose.

The Swiss president summoned the American ambassador to his office for an unusual evening meeting. When the U.S. ambassador and military attaché—a Marine brigadier general—entered the president's office, the ambassador was taken aback to find the president standing in the center of the room, flanked on either side by the country's grim faced Chiefs of Finance, Foreign Affairs, Home Affairs, Federal Department of Justice and the Chairman of the Swiss National Bank. Only the Chief of Defense was absent. No one thought he would be needed.

Oh my God, I expected a cool reception, Winchester thought as he struggled to muster a diplomatic smile, *but this has the makings of a disaster. I just know it.* Quickly surveying the angry faces before him, Winchester resisted the urge to wipe away the sudden onset of perspiration from his brow and baldhead. Stepping forward, he formally offered his hand to the Swiss president.

After the obligatory handshake and perfunctory remarks, the flush-faced president said through clenched teeth, "What is the meaning of your government sending two plane loads of auditors to pilfer through our bank records. How *dare* you enter our country, with the presumption you are above obtaining our permission through diplomatic channels?"

"First, we receive a message from your State Department ordering us … *ordering us,* to turn over to the United States all … *all,* funds controlled by named Middle Eastern countries … and those of the countries' rulers and their families. Then, two planeloads of your auditors arrive to oversee the transfers. *Are you out of your mind?*"

Inwardly the ambassador cringed. *This is going to be worse than I imagined.* Before he could frame a reply, the Chief of the Federal Department of Justice jumped into the fray, "You have one hour to turn your planes around and depart Swiss air space. If you do not, I will have everyone on the aircraft arrested, and we will seize the airplanes."

"G–Gentlemen." Winchester stammered, "I implore you. Don't overreact. You must try to understand our situation. We have a new president and Cabinet. I assure you we can find some way to comply with President Alexander's order without taking such extreme measures."

The chairman of the Swiss National Bank puffed out his chest and blustered, "*Do not* over react! It is *you* who are overreacting. You know our banking laws are *sacrosanct.* No one—especially you arrogant Americans—tells us what to do. Now, take your planes and auditors and *go home!*"

Before the ambassador could think of a reply, he was brusquely shouldered aside by his military attaché, "I've heard enough of this bullshit," the large Marine said as he moved forward to confront the president. "All of you sit down and shut up!" Startled by the general's imposing demeanor, the president backed away and retreated behind his desk. Some took seats, while others remained standing, defiantly glaring at the general. The Marine glared back and continued, "On May 25th, the world changed. The rules changed. The days of our fawning over a bunch of self-important Europeans are over. *Think very carefully* about who we are ... *before you utter another word.*" The six-foot-four, 220 pound, barrel-chested Marine slowly looked each of the startled men in the eye—one after the other. They'd never been spoken to in such a manner. Those still standing sullenly found a chair. All looked on in outraged silence.

The general continued, his voice hard as cold steel, "President Alexander has made it clear to all the major powers—Great Britain, Russia, and China— we will brook no interference in our efforts to protect our homeland and our people around the world. We're prepared to use *any* means necessary to accomplish our purpose—including the use of nuclear weapons." The general paused, slowly looking at each man in the room, then continued, "Trampling on the diplomatic sensitivities of a few pompous assholes, like you, pales in comparison to our determination to avenge the atrocities we've suffered."

Walking forward he stopped before the president's desk. Leaning forward, he placed his knuckles on the desktop and stared down into the astonished man's eyes. "Now, you *will* clear our team through customs. In the morning you *will* provide escorts for our teams assigned to each of your banks. Next, you, *Mr. Bank Chairman,*" he said turning his head in the direction of the man sitting forward in a chair immediately to the right of the president, "will instruct each bank to do *exactly* what our people tell them to do—nothing more, nothing less."

The chairman harrumphed before sullenly slouching back in his chair.

"If a bank refuses to open its doors, a B-1B bomber, orbiting over the English Channel will deliver a 750-pound bomb to the bank's front door," the general added, locking eyes with the glowering chairman.

"If we encounter resistance from your military ... you will lose a city," the general concluded, standing erect and directing his last remark to the president. For a full minute, the two men glared at one another, while the seated Swiss muttered to each other and shifted in their seats.

Finally the Swiss president who was sitting back with his hands tightly grasping the arms of his chair slowly leaned forward and said through clenched teeth, "I cannot believe you have the audacity to make such threats."

"*Believe it* ... or you'll quickly get a demonstration," the general barked, and gestured toward the president's phone, before pointedly continuing, "Secretary of State Keese is available to confirm my message."

Shaken and desperately seeking some way to escape the situation, the president's eyes shifted from the general's menacing stare to glance at the men seated on either side of him. "Will you excuse us while I discuss this matter with my advisors," the president said, expecting the two Americans to leave the room.

"There is nothing to discuss," the general replied. "Either you comply, or we take action."

Finally, the Swiss president grudgingly accepted the fact they really had no choice. *The crazy Americans are serious. Their new president is a man determined to recoup his country's financial losses. At present, it seems we've no choice but to capitulate. But others won't allow this travesty to pass. There are too many powerful, moneyed people worldwide who will not stand for this. I'll immediately ask for help from other world leaders,* he desperately thought. Slowly standing, he offered his final bitterly spoken response, "We will allow you to conduct this act of piracy, *but,*" he threatened, "when you leave my presence inform your Secretary of State I intend to bring this matter to the *immediate* attention of the Security Council of the United Nations. We will protest in the strongest terms—"

The general laughed in his face, and turned toward the door before the Swiss president could continue his diatribe. Still laughing, the large Marine brushed past the sweating ambassador, preceding him through the office door. As the two walked down the corridor toward the entrance, the general's laughter echoed in the corridor behind them.

The first transfer of forty-eight billion dollars into the U.S. Treasury account occurred at 10:02 a.m. the next morning, followed by a river of dollars, euros, pounds, yen, and precious metals from banking centers around the world.

Ensenada, Argentina – Guesthouse, Wednesday afternoon, May 31st.

Technical problems prevented restoration of their satellite TV connection—or so Ralph told Nancy. They were following world events by listening to the BBC.

"First, this caliph sets the price of oil at $300 dollars a barrel; a price that will destroy the world's economy. Then, President Alexander ordered seizure of all Arab bank accounts. Ralph, the world is on the brink of self-destruction," Nancy said.

Trying to reassure her, Ralph replied, "Our new president's really something. He's rewriting the international rulebook. I'd never have thought of seizing their bank accounts. If he gets away with it—"

"The international banking system will be thrown into complete turmoil," Nancy interrupted. "The international community will rise up against him."

"Probably not. They all have problems with jihads in their countries. Anyway, who's going to stand up to a superpower ready to use its power?"

"Do you really think so? The U.S. has always been so sensitive to the opinions of the Europeans."

"Well, now we have a president who doesn't give a damn what Europeans think. From everything I've seen, he's a man who'll do whatever he thinks is necessary. You and I are financial people. We think in terms of gross national product, exchange rates, trade deficits, projected income, per capita income, and interest rates. Alexander's made the world aware the ultimate measure of a nation's worth is its power—measured in megatons— and the U.S. is the king."

"Do you think he's going to use nuclear weapons?"

"Of course he will. It's just a matter of when. This man is a chess player. He plans his moves and doesn't allow his opponent to control the board. He's already pulled off several miracles. He's pulling the country together, forming a government, obtaining oil, and now he's solved his monetary crises. I wonder what's coming next?" *And I wonder what Mohammed's doing. If the seizures work, his new empire's going to run out of gas. Now there's an ironic situation.* Ralph chuckled at his own joke. *I hope he never decides he wants to find me.*

"Well, we still don't know how they managed to plant the nuclear bombs in our cities," Nancy observed.

Eid inwardly winced. *Yes, and I hope they never find out. Maybe I'll escape. What am I going to do if they discover REM? Where can I go?* "I'm sure someone is trying to find out how they did it." *Gotta change the subject.* "What's for dinner?"

Los Alamos National Laboratories, New Mexico – 1 p.m. Wednesday, May 31st.

When George Landry deplaned from the Air Force Blackhawk helicopter, he was surprised to see James Chin waiting for him. *Something really hot must be up, to warrant Chin taking time to meet me.* "Good afternoon, Jim."

"Good afternoon, George. I hope you had a good flight," Chin said, shaking hands with Landry. Gesturing for Landry to follow, he turned and walked briskly away from the helipad. "Peter Bronson is waiting for us in my office," he called over his shoulder

Boy, I've never seen Chin so agitated or in such a hurry. This must be very important. Landry looked back at the chopper, *Damn, I hate riding in helicopters. I hope he doesn't make a habit of having me fly up here in one.* Entering Chin's office, they found Bronson seated at the conference table with his six folders. After a quick greeting, Bronson repeated his presentation for Landry.

"I'll be damned," was Landry's only comment when Bronson completed his presentation.

"Yes, I agree," Chin commented. "Livermore and Sandia concur with our findings. We've prepared five packages of information and samples for you to take back. Brief the president as soon as possible. I'll call and tell the president you're on the way back with important information," Chin said, walking Landry to his office door.

As the Blackhawk lifted off, Dr. Chin called Alexander and told him Landry was on the way with an answer to one of their "Who done it?" questions. Chin considered the subject too sensitive even for secure phone lines.

Kirkland AFB – Wednesday, 31 May

The UC-35A, a Cessna Citation 560 business jet, carrying Patricia Manning, Winston Pollock, Tom Jacobson, and Special Agent Zimmerman touched down at 1126. Manning and Pollock were in a foul mood. Two Air Force Security Police Force sergeants and two Secret Service agents met them when they deplaned and escorted the three "guests" to a sparsely furnished in-transit lounge. There they could use the facilities while waiting for their appointment with the president. A television was on so the staff could watch the president's noon announcement.

Manning spent twenty minutes in the women's lounge repairing her makeup and attempting to smooth the wrinkles in her Chanel suit. Admiring her reflection, especially her glittering diamond encrusted gold pin, and matching earrings, she decided she was ready. *I'll show the imposter what the upper class is truly like.*

Returning to the lounge, she found Pollock and Jacobson watching the imposter on TV. She was horrified when he announced the seizure of Middle Eastern bank accounts and assets. "My God," Patricia Manning exclaimed, although she couldn't recall when last she'd attended a church service, "The man's insane. He's acting like a dictator. How will we ever apologize to our friends in Europe?"

"Even worse," Pollock added, "How will the Arab Street react to this … this … Our stealing their money?"

"Winston, start writing an editorial. We must lead the fight to get rid of this maniac. We must get assistance from the UN."

What a bunch of stupid, arrogant, fools, Zimmerman thought, listening to the conversation while gazing at a newspaper. *They really don't get it. Our nation's been attacked by Muslim fanatics. We're having insurrections. Christians and Jews are being massacred in Muslim countries. Our economy's on the verge of collapsing, and all these two idiots can think about is what the Europeans and the Arab Street thinks of us.*

At 1340, a staff car and two air force security police Hummers arrived. A first lieutenant with an air police badge on his left pocket entered the lounge and announced, "Patricia Manning, Winston Pollock, Tom Jacobson please come with me. You have an appointment with the president at 1400 hours."

You nitwit, Manning sneered to herself while walking toward the staff car, *Can't these Neanderthals even tell time properly?*

Pollock was mentally composing his editorial. Tom Jacobson was worried. Agent Zimmerman rode in one of the Hummers. The three guests entered the president's conference room at 1400. Five men sat at the large conference table in front of them, the president in the center. No one rose to greet them. Finally, realizing no one intended to speak, Special Agent Zimmerman identified himself and introduced the three guests.

"Thank you. Please take a seat," a man said, indicating a chair placed along the wall, "I'm Barry Clark, director of the FBI." Turning to his right, he introduced the others sitting at the table, "President Alexander, Attorney General Jay Henniger, Secretary of State Alan Keese, and this gentleman," he said gesturing to his left, "is Colonel Charles Young."

Their faces showing disgust, scorn, and anger, the five men continued to stare at the three in front of them. Manning, Pollock, and Jacobson remained standing, unsure what to do. Jacobson had a sudden urge to urinate. Finally, pointing to three chairs directly across the table from the president, Clark said, "Please be seated."

While the three took their seats, Jacobson was keenly aware everyone at the table seemed to be focusing their displeasure at Manning and Pollock. *What the hell are they so damn worked up about? All we've done is report what people want to hear—or what we think they need to hear. We've the right under the Constitution to do so. I don't set paper policy. I write what they tell me to ... This guy Alexander looks like a serious dude. He's got a craz—*

Before he could finish his thought, Jacobson almost jumped out of his skin when Manning who was sitting next to him stormed out, *"What is the meaning of this?* How dare you have us *arrested* and brought here?"

The men seated across the table continued staring at her for another fifteen seconds. Finally Clark said, "You have not been arrested ... yet. Do you have any idea what you've done?"

"We've exercised our right to freedom of the press. We called upon our citizens to refuse to recognize your authority and to have the UN assume control of our country," she informed Clark, and looking at the president with contempt accosted him next. "We watched your disgraceful announcement. *Seizing* other people's assets. Who do you think you are? Now you've given the Arabs and our European friends another reason to hate—"

Keese interrupted her rant. "*I* am the Secretary of State, and it's *my* responsibility to set the tone of relations with other nations—*not yours*," he said, ice dripping from each word.

Rearing back and sitting as erect as possible, a haughty Manning sarcastically replied, "I don't recognize you as a *legitimate* secretary of state, any more than I recognize *Mr.* Alexander as the president. As soon as we return to Los Angeles, we'll start a campaign to have you all removed. Hilda Rodman is our president, until you show us her body!"

Alexander gazed with renewed contempt at the pompous woman and slowly shook his head. Finally, he spoke, "Ms. Manning, you've just confirmed what I've suspected for some time. You, *the media*, actually believe you run this country. Unfortunately, you've been getting away with doing so for far too long. But that day has passed. Last night, citizens of Los Angeles and the surrounding area entered the *Herald's* building, destroyed all the equipment, severely beat many employees, threw the night editor out a window, and then burned the building to the ground. The local police and fire department were ... unable ... to respond in time," he added with a touch of sarcasm.

"Oh! ... Ooooh, you ... you *fascist!* The paper has been in my family for years," Manning screeched through clenched teeth and, placing her hands on the table, prepared to stand.

Pollock who was also shaken by the president's news knew immediately how Manning would react. Turning quickly in his chair, he reached in front of her to grasp both her arms above the wrists. Slight of build though she was, Patricia Manning was a strong woman, with a history of throwing raging fits when someone opposed her. Restraining her arms and bodily holding her in her seat, Pollock wrestled briefly against her fury while she snorted, shook her head violently, and tried repeatedly to rise.

"Now, now, Patricia, remain calm and stay where you are. All is not lost. We still have a loyal following. We can rebuild," Pollock whispered in her ear, desperately trying to hold her in her seat. Pollock knew—based on years of experience and hours spent cajoling Manning out of her tantrums—she was about to lose control and start throwing things. All they needed was for Manning to attack the president. "Patricia," he hissed, grasping her flailing hands and forcing them down to her lap, "Calm down or we *will* be arrested." Slowly, Pollock calmed her. She remained in her seat, rocking back and forth, crying, moaning, and muttering. Fearful of letting go of her, Pollock continued holding her hands tightly in front of her.

Unaffected by her outburst, the president continued speaking despite Manning's near hysterical state, "Ms. Manning, your loss is regrettable. But I have a job to do. A job I did not seek but had to take. I *am* the president. As such, it's my responsibility to save our nation. I'm doing my best, and so are the men sitting with me. As are all the other men and women in the military, government, and our private citizens. Our great nation has suffered a near mortal wound. It's teetering on the edge of a great precipice. For decades, liberals have attempted to force their agenda, their view of utopia on us. Liberals refused to accept defeat at the polls, blocked legislation and appointments, and learned how to manipulate our judicial system to achieve their objectives. Now, driven by your unbridled hatred, you are demonstrating your intent to use your newspaper to push your personal agenda regardless of the results—an agenda that can topple our nation into the abyss. You either don't care, or your philosophy's so warped you're unable to see the consequences of your actions. If our form of government fails, Islam's new rulers won't be kind to you. No, I assure you—you'll be one of the first to be executed. If you can't see this, or worse, if you don't understand it, then it's beyond my ability to explain it to you," Alexander said with a sigh of resignation.

"I have looked to former presidents for guidance. President Franklin Roosevelt's actions provide me inspiration and precedents. I'm convinced he was one of our greatest presidents."

Still overwrought, Manning, who'd only heard part of what Alexander said, snarled her response, "Well, we can agree on something. President Roosevelt was not only a great president, he was a Democrat, and a *liberal*."

A blinking light on the red phone sitting in front of the president interrupted his reply. Picking up the phone, Alexander heard Captain Taylor say, "Sir, it's Secretary Chin, he says it's urgent."

"Put him through."

"Mr. President, we've identified the source of the fissile material. I don't wish to say more on the phone. Doctor Landry's on his way back with all of the information. I hope you'll be able to see him when he arrives."

"Thank you. I will." Frowning, Alexander hung up the phone.

I wonder what that was all about? Pollock thought. *Is he trying to impress us?*

The others in the room were also wondering what could be important enough to interrupt the meeting. Alexander sat quietly looking at the phone for a few seconds with a thoughtful expression, then looking up he continued. "I'm glad we agree on President Roosevelt. He faced many of the same problems I'm facing, including big mouths and loose cannons. You three are both."

Manning reacted with a sniff and a smirk; Pollock bristled; and Jacobson sank down in his chair.

"If I thought there was any way to make you understand the gravity of our situation, we would try to explain in detail; however, I don't think it's possible to do so. Your idealistic liberal bent prevents you from accepting anything other than your view of the world. If I release you, you'll cause more trouble. Your intentions don't matter—only the consequences do." Pausing, the president looked each of them in the eye. "President Roosevelt's solution to his big mouths and loose cannons was to confine them in Saint Elizabeth's Insane Asylum for the duration of the war."

Pollock visibly winced. Manning continued glaring defiantly at Alexander with an expression of pure hatred. "You wouldn't dare," she snarled.

Jacobson who was well versed on WW II's history shuddered. He knew Alexander wasn't bluffing. *Damn, he means it. He's not only crazy enough to do it—he can do it.*

"My solution is similar," the president continued. "Since you don't understand the nature of our enemy, I'll provide you with an education while you're confined. From here you'll be taken to Camp Alpha, one of our internment camps for the radical domestic Muslim terrorists. You'll remain in Camp Alpha until the war is over."

"You can't do this," Manning gasped and tried to rise again. Pollock had all he could do to hold her down. He continued struggling with her, while Clark, after a nod from the president, opened his cellphone and spoke softly into it. Within seconds the conference room door opened and several FBI agents entered. "Special Agent Zimmerman," Clark said, "you'll take the internees to Camp Alpha, turn them over to the camp commander, and then report back to me. You'll speak of this to no one who isn't already involved."

"Yes, sir."

"I demand to speak with my attorney," Manning screamed and began struggling wildly when Pollock released her to the agent's control. "You'll speak to *no one*," Clark said through clenched teeth. With a gesture of disgust, he ordered, "Get them out of here."

Alexander and the others remained seated during the ensuing disturbance. All were relieved to see the last of their guests: some were even privately amused by the bedraggled spectacle they presented. Manning, her skirt hiked up and her once impeccably coiffed silver hair now flying in disarray, continued scuffling with the agents while she was being ushered from the room. Pollock, white faced and sullen, belligerently followed, flanked on either side by an FBI agent. Jacobson, short of breath and sure he was having a heart attack, stumbled and would have collapsed, if not for quick action by the agent to his left.

After the three detainees departed for their trip to Camp Alpha, located at the old Tonopah base camp in the northern part of the Nevada Test Site, Alexander answered his advisor's unasked question. "The phone call was from Doctor Chin. He's found the source of the fissile material, the uranium-235 used in the bombs. George is on his way here with the information. He didn't identify the source. When he arrives we'll reconvene. Charlie, please ask Harry and Teresa Lopez to join us for George's briefing."

Chapter 27

Kirkland AFB – 1700 Wednesday, 31 May

Monsignor Enrico Morani pulled his rented SUV up to the guard at the main entrance to Kirkland AFB, and lowered his window. During the drive down from Santa Fe, Morani heard the radio announcer bragging about it being the 232nd day of continuous sunshine. *Thank you Father, for this beautiful, clear, sunny, day.*

"How can I help you?" Senior Airman Marie Lynch asked.

"At noon today, General Ross held a press conference on this base. He announced formation of an inter-faith advisory committee. I'd like to contact the general and ask to join the committee."

"Please go to the visitor's building and sign in," Airman Lynch said, pointing to a one-story stucco building with a flat roof. "You'll need to show identification and a rental contract for your truck." While the Monsignor drove to the lot, Lynch picked up the phone and spoke with the staff sergeant inside the visitor's building.

Alerted by Lynch that a visitor wanted to join the IFAC, Sergeant Miller followed instructions and called Major Johnson. Miller was instructed to determine if the man was a clergyman. If so, he was to be sent to the major's office. Inside the building, Morani approached the counter and waited for the desk sergeant to finish his telephone call. Reading the sergeant's nametag, Morani said, "Good afternoon, Sergeant Miller, I'm Monsignor Enrico Morani. I'm interested in joining the inter-faith advisory committee General Ross referenced during his noon press conference."

Well that establishes him as a clergyman. "Yes, sir. Major Johnson is the person to see. Can I see your identification?

The Monsignor handed Miller his District of Columbia driver's license and Executive Car Rental contract. After looking at the driver's license, Miller commented, "I guess you're one of the lucky ones."

"Yes, I was leaving Bandelier National Monument when the bombs went off."

Sergeant Miller handed Morani a sign-in sheet along with a car pass and a base map. "Major Johnson's expecting you. I've marked the route for you. You can park in front of the building. The major's in room 306."

Morani had no problem following the map to Building 20011. After parking in the visitor's space, he entered the building and climbed the stairs to the third floor. Walking down the hall, he found the door to room 306 and entered a large anteroom with several desks occupied by uniformed airmen. To the right of the room was the entrance to a long corridor leading to numerous offices. Acknowledging the visitor's presence, an airman first class stood and inquired, "Father Morani?"

"Yes."

"This way sir. Major Johnson is expecting you."

The airman led Morani down the hall and into an office on their left. When they entered, a well-built officer pushed his chair away from his orderly desk and stood.

"Sir, Father Morani to see you," the airman announced.

"Thank you, airman. You're dismissed," the major said with a smile. Then rounding his desk, he walked to the door with an outstretched hand to welcome his visitor.

The two shook hands warmly. Morani immediately liked the personable major who presented an impressive figure in his white, open-collar shirt with shoulder boards bearing gold leafs. He was Morani's height, six-feet, of similar weight, 180 pounds, and had a reassuringly firm hand shake. *Wow. This is one efficient operation. These fellows really have their act together.*

"Welcome to Kirkland, Monsignor. I'm Carl Johnson. General Ross is not available."

"Thank you. Please call me Enrico. I'm from Georgetown University in Washington, DC. I was in New Mexico on vacation when the attack on Washington occurred."

"Okay. I'm Carl. You're extremely fortunate to be vacationing here. Please have a seat." Johnson indicated a chair in front of his desk, and returned to his chair. "They say something good always comes from something bad. Well, in General Alexander's case, he wouldn't be our president, if his son hadn't fallen in a climbing accident on Sandia Crest. Alexander flew in here Friday morning to see to his injured son, otherwise he'd have perished with the rest of the government."

Catching himself before he could utter the trite "God moves in mysterious ways" cliché, Morani replied, "Then God has blessed us again, for America has always had the right man at the helm in times of crisis. Is the boy all right? Was he badly injured? I've heard no news regarding the accident."

"The young man is fine. Some bruising to the spine and a broken leg, otherwise he's okay." Johnson sat back in his chair and studied the Monsignor. Raised a Southern Baptist, he knew very little about the Catholic Church. *I don't even know if he's a citizen. He did say "us."* "I understand you're interested in the inter-faith advisory committee. We refer to it as the IFAC. Can you tell me a little about yourself? Where you were born and raised ... something about your qualifications?"

"Certainly. I was born and raised in Poughkeepsie, New York. After Seminary, I attended Columbia and Yale. I majored in religious studies. My specialty is Islam. I am ... or was a professor of Islamic Studies at Georgetown University in Washington, DC. I'm an amateur archeologist of sorts. I usually take my vacations working as a volunteer at some site or other—either here or in the Holy Land. When I realized I couldn't return to my post in DC, I sought shelter at the Archdiocese in Santa Fe. I've been staying there for the past four days. When I heard General Ross's radio announcement about forming the ... uh, the IFAC to advise the president on Islam, I thought I might be able to help. So, I packed my meager belongings and came to volunteer. I say meager, because I was here hiking and camping when the murderous attacks took place," Morani said, explaining his casual dress.

Johnson laughed. "Well, Enrico, I'm afraid our BX doesn't stock your kind of uniform. We'll have to find some more appropriate attire for you should future occasions demand it." Both men laughed and Morani felt much more at ease with what promised to be a challenging new phase in his ecclesiastical life.

Getting back to business, Johnson continued, "Rabbi Steinberg is forming the IFAC. I'm sure he'll be delighted to have you join his group. I know he's looking for a Catholic and an Islamic scholar. I'll call him."

Johnson picked up his phone and called the rabbi. A brief conversation ensued. Smiling, Johnson said, "He's on his way. He'll meet you in the visitor's building where you signed in." Standing, he handed Morani his card. "Here's my phone number. If you need anything, call me."

Morani stood and Johnson accompanied him to the portico outside the building entrance. Shaking hands, Johnson said, "Enrico, we have enormous problems. We don't understand the Islamic mind; therefore, we don't know how to deal with them. The president needs sound, practical, advice. And he needs it in a week or less. The major religions, Catholics and Protestants included, are talking about taking years to formulate recommendations to solve problems requiring solutions in a few days. I hope you can help us."

"Yes, I hope so too. Since I've been unable to obtain any instructions from my order, I'll participate as an individual, not as a Catholic." Morani waved good-bye and walked to his SUV.

Johnson started to enter the building, when the implications of Morani's circumstances hit him. Turning purposefully, he retraced his steps back to the SUV. "Enrico," he said through the open window, "Our banking system is still off-line. If you're short on funds, I can pay you as a consultant"

"Thank you, Carl, I have a few dollars left. I plan to stay at the Archdiocese in Albuquerque. However, I may have to take you up on your offer. I don't know if the archdiocese can provide me with funds."

Waiving good-bye, the two parted. *Yes*, the major thought as the watched the SUV turn the corner, *there goes another good man who's in the right place at the right time.*

Thirty minutes later Rabbi Steinberg met Monsignor Morani. The two immediately hit it off, and Steinberg insisted the Monsignor stay at his home.

While Monsignor Morani followed Steinberg through the city to the rabbi's home, CIA's Deputy Director of Operations, Martha Wellington arrived at Kirkland AFB. Wellington had been in Brussels attending a NATO intelligence conference the day the attacks occurred. Barry Clark met her when she deplaned.

"Welcome to Albuquerque, I'm Barry Clark," he said smiling and extending his hand to the robust, fifty-two year old, five-foot-eight woman. In response to his friendly greeting, Wellington said nothing. Instead, she grasped his hand firmly, looked him in the eye, and gave only a simple nod in greeting. *A cool one*, Clark thought, *she's probably very tired*, and dismissed her behavior as jet lag. Acting on long established custom, Clark's discerning eye quickly assessed her appearance for more clues to her personality. Her close-cropped, dark-brown hair, understated black slacks, plain, white, cotton shirt, and low-heel, black shoes bespoke of a woman who was definitely not fashion conscious. *She is*, Clark decided, *quite athletic looking. She's probably proficient in self-defense ... wears little to no jewelry.* The silver studs in her ears and her simple gold wedding band prompted Clark to wonder if her husband was in Washington when the attack occurred. *Best not inquire about that right now. Give her time and she will tell me.* Knowing his first impression was usually correct, Clark concluded Wellington's attitude and austere appearance didn't matter. Her demeanor was definitely all business.

"Thank you, for meeting me. Please call me Martha," Wellington finally said with a tired smile.

"My pleasure. I'm Barry," Clark said, feeling the tension between them lessen. "We have temporary quarters for you in the BOQ. We can provide housing on base, or you can make your own arrangements. Your bags will be sent to your BOQ—bachelor officer quarters—apartment." Clark motioned to a young first lieutenant standing near them with two airmen. The lieutenant acknowledged Clark's comments with a nod.

"The president wants to meet you. Doctor George Landry, SecEnergy's representative, is on his way back from Los Alamos with important information. Landry will brief us when he arrives. You're to be present at the briefing. It will provide you an opportunity to meet the president's team." Clark led Wellington to a sedan, where a driver stood waiting to open the rear door. "We'll wait in my office for the meeting to start. Have you eaten?"

"Yes, thank you, I dined on the plane."

After entering the sedan, Clark decided to broach the subject of her family, "I hope your family was spared the horror of the DC attack. We've lost so many good people—"

"No … My family, my husband Alex, my mother, and our German Shepherd, Prince, perished in our home in the Washington blast," Wellington responded, staring out the window. "Our home was in Arlington, on a hill overlooking Washington … a beautiful view," she sighed. "I'm told the house is gone. I … forgive me, I'm still trying to grasp it all," she whispered, and resolutely stuck her chin out before wryly continuing. "All my possessions are in my two suitcases." Swallowing hard, she concluded, "So, you see, the BOQ apartment will be adequate for my needs."

Touched by the sadness of her story, Clark tried to think of something encouraging to say. "I'm sorry about your family. Many of us lost someone special. I want you to know I'm personally very glad you're here. We need your help. In addition to running the FBI, I've been attempting to manage the CIA: a job I'm totally unqualified to do. I understand you're the senior CIA official, which makes you acting director. The president will determine if you get to keep the job. Are you up to date on current events?"

"Yes, I am." Turning to look at Clark, she said, "I've never met President Alexander. What can you tell me about him?"

Clark rested his head against the back of the seat. For a second or two he allowed his gaze to focus on infinity before continuing, "I met the man last Friday after the attack. I've had a short time to assess him, but feel confident telling you he's a man of honor who's totally dedicated to preserving our nation. He'll allow nothing, nor no one, to get in the way. We're all very fortunate he was here instead of being in Washington. By a quirk of fate, or divine intervention, his son was injured in a climbing accident on Sandia Crest. He flew here early Friday morning to be with his boy.

"When the attacks occurred, he held the position of Secretary of Homeland Security. He'd retired from the Air Force as a two star. His last assignment was Deputy Director of the Defense Threat Reduction Agency. Previously he was Commanding General of the Defense Special Weapons Agency's Field Command located here on Kirkland AFB. He and his wife, Jane, own a retirement home north of Santa Fe. Right now, they're living on base. Their two children, Jim, the son who fell, and a daughter, Jenna, both attend the University here in Albuquerque.

"Alexander knows weapons and is highly respected, by both our military and those of foreign countries. He's a no-nonsense, decisive man who will make hard decisions on the spot, then change them if they prove to be wrong. He believes in giving people a job and letting them do it. If they can't, or won't—they're gone. You'll be expected to say what's on your mind. Don't be afraid to disagree. But once the decision is made, implement it. More importantly, we're *not* encumbered with the old rulebook. The only rule now—our charter really—is to save the nation," Clark concluded.

"Yes, your description matches what I've been heard about him," Wellington commented, nodding her head. Smiling, she added, "Issuing internment orders for all Muslims took balls. So did seizing the Arabs' assets."

Her last two comments elicited a raised eyebrow from Clark. *She's no shrinking violet. Took balls did it? Sounds like she's pretty much on the same page with the rest of us. Let's see how much she really agrees with Alexander's policies.* "The Muslim issue is a great worry for all of us," he said, hoping to elicit more of her opinions on present conditions. "The president has formed an inter-faith advisory committee to help us understand the religious issues. So far the committee has three members and starts work tomorrow. He wants recommendations by the end of next week."

"Are you kidding? Getting religious groups to provide any type of recommendation will take years."

Clark laughed and thought, *We're in agreement on that issue too*, before cautioning her, "Never underestimate Alexander. The man has a way of getting things done. I'm betting we get recommendations next week."

"What about the news media? They'll crucify him. There was a copy of Tuesday's *Los Angeles Herald* on the plane. The paper is after his head."

Clark shrugged, "He's already taken care of that issue. Two hours after copies of the paper arrived, we had a meeting to discuss options. We agreed it was necessary to put an end to these media attacks before they derailed our efforts. Alexander directed me to have the publisher, managing editor, and reporter, who wrote the worst stories, picked up. They were brought here today as the president's *guests*. President Alexander, Secretary of State Keese, Attorney General Jay Henniger, Colonel Young, the president's Chief of Staff, and I met with them at two o'clock this afternoon. You've probably not been informed about the riot at the newspaper, and the building being burned." Wellington shook her head to indicate no. "Well, neither were they. When we told them the incident showed public opinion was against them, they blamed the president for their loss. We made every effort to dissuade them from undermining the good of the county. Unfortunately, we soon discovered our guests were determined to pursue their personal political agenda. Patricia Manning, the *Herald's* publisher, threw a God-awful tantrum. She screamed at us, and declared her hatred for the president and his policies. Then she declared intentions to ask the UN to oust Alexander and to take control of our country. Our attempts to reason with them failed."

Clark frowned, pursed his lips and shook his head. "The president had heard enough. Using Roosevelt's methods as a precedent, he summarily

ordered them confined to his version of St. Elizabeth's Insane Asylum—
Camp Alpha Detainee Internment Camp—for the duration of the war. Alpha
is located on the Nevada Test Site. If they're hot under the collar now, just
wait until they experience those 100-degree plus temperatures, and the
companionship of their fellow interns, radical Islamic detainees." Clark
smiled. "If Manning thinks Alexander is a fascist—that's what she called
him—just wait 'til she gets up close and personal with one of the terrorists.
It'll probably be the nearest thing to hell on earth she'll ever experience."

"Jesus!" Wellington said, envisioning classified intelligence videos she
had seen, showing women being stoned to death in Muslim countries. "Yeah,
old Franklin put 'em in Saint Elizabeth's," she chuckled. *I think I'm going to
like this man Alexander.*

The driver stopped in front of the headquarters building—now the
temporary Southwestern White House. Clark and Wellington got out and
walked toward the building's entrance. A guard requested her identification.
"Colonel Young will arrange for your base ID tomorrow," Clark said as they
entered the building. "We're setting up one building for both the FBI and
CIA. All intelligence agencies will be under one roof. No turf battles will be
allowed. Getting into one is the number one way of getting fired."

Martha Wellington considered Clarks comments, especially the last one.
*I think I just got invited to one hell of a party. Maybe, just maybe, I can do
what needs to be done.*

Ten minutes later, they were settled in Clark's office enjoying a soft
drink. "I've put Teresa Lopez in charge of finding out who planned the bomb
attacks, and how they did it. The chase will probably lead outside the U.S., so
she may cross into your area. Like you, she arrived here today and will also be
staying in the BOQ." Clark picked up his cellphone, punched a speed dial
number, and waited for an answer.

"Captain Taylor speaking," came the response.

"Julian, has Ms. Lopez arrived?"

"Yes, sir. We're at the BOQ. I understand she's to attend a briefing when
Doctor Landry arrives."

"Correct. Martha Wellington, Acting CIA Director's with me in my
office. Can both of you join us?"

"Yes, sir. We're on our way."

"Teresa Lopez? Isn't she the FBI agent awarded the decoration by you
and the president?" Wellington asked.

"Yes. The young captain with her is Julian Taylor. Julian's become one
of the president's assistants. He was Colonel Charles Young's executive
officer. I think there's some chemistry between him and Teresa. Incidentally,
Alexander's given her presidential authority to find the terrorists. I'll make it
clear to her she must also keep you informed of her actions."

Fifteen minutes later Teresa Lopez and Julian Taylor entered Clark's office and introductions were made. "I'm looking forward to working with you Teresa," Martha Wellington said extending her hand to Teresa. "Director Clark's briefed me on your assignment."

"Thank you, Director Wellington. I start tomorrow, but I'm unsure where to begin."

"Actually you're going to start this evening," Clark said. "George Landry is on his way back from Los Alamos with the identity of the source of the fissile material." Before Clark could say more, Kathy opened the door and announced, "Doctor Landry is on his way from the helipad. The president wants everyone in the conference room."

Clark stood and everyone followed him to the conference room, where he introduced Martha Wellington to Alan Keese, Jay Henniger, Charles Young, Jim Ross, and Harry Simpson. Young motioned for Julian to stay. A few seconds later, Alexander entered and smiled at the two women standing together. "Good evening. Welcome to Albuquerque, Teresa. You must be Martha Wellington," he said, walking around the table and offering his hand. "We're glad you made it, Martha. Please accept our condolences on the loss of your family. I've only just been informed of your circumstances. We'll do all we can to help you through this difficult time. Most of us have lost someone close to us. We've been so busy taking care of business, we've had no time to grieve. We've become something of a family—a family dedicated to the cause of saving our nation. So, welcome to our family. You and I have much to discuss. We'll meet after the briefing."

"Yes, Mr. President," Wellington said, thoughtfully appraising the new president. *He's relaxed, calm, sure of himself ... not a pompous ass like so many of the politicians I've had to deal with. Everyone is laid back ... relaxed, no ... comfortable, yes, comfortable with each other. No games. If my information's correct most of them never previously worked with each other. Clark, Henniger, Keyes are civilians while Alexander, Simpson, and Young are military. Even Lopez acts as though she belongs. Interesting.*

"While we're waiting for George to arrive, we're going to put you to work," Alexander said, smiling, as he walked back to his seat. "Who's Saladin II? Where'd he come from? He claims to have formed an Islamic Empire, including Libya. Where's Colonel Gadhafi—and how does he fit into Saladin's grand scheme? Alan's attempted to make contact with the Libyan government to no avail."

"We're going to invade Libya on Sunday. Our plan is to seize their oil fields, refineries, and pipelines," Simpson added.

"Libya is the first step toward seizing all Middle Eastern oil fields," Young added.

"As you can see, Martha, we need intelligence," the president said. "In addition to the Middle East, we're worried about North Korea. Barry will provide you with a complete briefing tomorrow. You'll have access to all of our facilities."

Martha Wellington sat still, digesting the scope of the plans outlined. *Damn, these guys are playing hardball.* "Mr. President, the best information we have—confirmed by Israel—is that Colonel Gadhafi and his family are dead. We don't know who Muraaqibu al-Khawaatim—now known as Saladin II—is, nor where he came from. Every intelligence agency's trying to answer that question. What's your policy in sharing intelligence with our allies? For that matter, who are our allies?"

"Good question. Answer is, we're not sure. Insurrections and attacks are changing the European mindset. British intelligence and military are onboard—but we don't know about the government. For now, use your judgment. You know the players better than any of us," Alexander replied. The others nodded their agreement. Teresa sat quietly observing.

Discussion abruptly ended when George Landry, huffing and puffing with exertion entered the room carrying a large leather catalog case. All eyes were on him as he approached the conference table and pulled out a chair. His remaining hair was in disarray. He looked tired, flustered, and disheveled. He waved hello to the men, greeted Teresa, and gave Wellington, who was sitting across the table from him, a puzzled look. Alexander introduced them, and then said, "You don't look so good George. Are you feeling okay?"

"Yes, sir. I simply hate *helicopters*, and I've had *two* flights today." Landry's comments evoked laughs from some at the table.

Stifling a smile, and trying to put Landry a little more at ease, Alexander got back to business, "George, I understand Los Alamos identified the source of the fissile material."

"Yes, sir," Landry replied and sighing heavily took his seat. Motioning to the pitcher of water on the table in front of him, Landry looked at the president who nodded an okay and waited patiently, while Landry filled a glass, drank heartily, and collected his thoughts. Finally ready to explain, Landry brushed back his tousled hair and began, "As some of you know, the U.S. collects samples from all nuclear tests. The Soviet Union's first tests were at the Semipalatinsk Test Range in Kazakhstan. The range was left unguarded. We were able to obtain soil samples after each test.

"We code-named the first seven Soviet nuclear tests Joe-1 through Joe-7—for Joseph Stalin. The Soviet's first two tests, Joe-1 and Joe-2, were plutonium-239 pit[*] implosion devices, similar to our Fat Man design. Joe-3 was a plutonium-239 pit implosion device with a tamper—an outer shell constructed of depleted uranium. The explosive lens compresses the uranium tamper—a neutron reflector—around the plutonium pit, compressing both. The tamper reflects neutrons back into the supercritical mass, thereby increasing the yield. We obtained samples of the Soviet's plutonium-239 and depleted uranium-238 from the test areas after Joe one, two, and three were detonated."

Landry paused to look around the table for questions. There were none, and he continued, "The Soviet's first attempt to build a thermonuclear device, Joe-4, used what they called, *sloika,* or layer cake configuration. Simply put, a thermonuclear, or TN bomb, is a miniature sun that only burns for a few trillionths of a second. Energy from the bomb is produced by the fusion of the second and third isotopes of hydrogen—deuterium and tritium. Their fusion produces helium, and releases energy and a neutron. Starting a fusion reaction requires deuterium, neutrons, and very high temperature and pressure. Tritium is produced by the nuclear fission reaction. A neutron from the fission of fissile material is captured by a deuterium atom, turning it into tritium. The only practical man-made source of enough heat, neutrons, and pressure required to start a fusion reaction is a nuclear detonation using plutonium-239 or uranium-235.

"Our TN weapons have two or more components. The primary, sometimes called the sparkplug, is a nuclear warhead. The secondary, or TN component, is made from uranium-235 and lithium deuteride. Large TN bombs have two TN components—the secondary and the tertiary. Lithium deuteride is a compound of lithium and deuterium. The secondary of a TN weapon is a sphere constructed from uranium-235 and lithium deuteride. Picture a small, subcritical sphere of uranium about the size of a tennis ball. Now coat the sphere with a layer of lithium deuteride. Add a third layer of uranium-235. Keep alternating the layers and you have a secondary, or what the Soviet's called *sloika* or layer cake.

"We suspected the Soviets had obtained partial information on our thermonuclear bomb designs. Somehow they missed the fact we used a primary to ignite the fusion reaction. Their first attempt to detonate a thermonuclear device used the layer cake configuration as the pit in an implosion warhead. There was no secondary. Joe-4 contained no

---

[*] Pit is a name for the fissionable uranium or plutonium—called fissile material— used in an implosion weapon. A subcritical mass is compressed into a supercritical mass by explosive lens that surround it. A scientist looking at a cross section of an implosion device commented that the ball of fissile material looked like the pit of a peach.

plutonium-239. Detonation of the explosive lens compressed the layer cake producing a uranium supercritical fission reaction, with a limited amount of fusion. What they achieved was a boosted fission bomb—a fission reaction created by implosion, augmented by a fusion reaction—a fission-fusion-fission reaction.

"We use a different method to boost our fission warheads. Boosted fission warheads can achieve yields in the hundreds of kilotons. Joe-4 had a yield of four hundred kilotons, while Joe-3, an implosion fission bomb with a tamper, had a yield of forty kilotons. A true thermonuclear weapon has yields in the megaton range, millions of tons of TNT.

"Why is this important? We obtained samples of natural uranium and plutonium-239 from the first three Soviet tests. Joe-4 used uranium-235 instead of plutonium-239. We obtained our first samples of Soviet highly enriched uranium-235, after Joe-4 was detonated on August 12, 1953." Landry paused to see if there were any questions, then continued.

"Spectrographic analysis provides the ratios—percentages—of various isotopes. A uranium-235 graph shows the distribution of isotopes of uranium, and any other elements present. The ratios of the isotopes—the percent of uranium-233, uranium-234, uranium-235, uranium-236 and uranium-238—will depend upon the source of the uranium ore and the separation process.

"Samples of the fissile material from each of our five cities were collected and analyzed by Los Alamos, Livermore and Sandia. Graphs were compared with our databases. There was no plutonium in any of the samples; therefore, the bombs were constructed from highly enriched uranium. This probably means they were gun-type bombs. However, the yields were larger than one would expect from a gun-type weapon." Landry paused to allow everyone to digest the information.

"The surprise," he said shaking his head, "and it was a big surprise … was that the graphs from every sample collected in our cities were the same. Assuming the five bombs were the work of terrorists, we expected to find the fissile material came from several sources. Not so. The uranium-235 used in each of the five bombs came from the same source. Its purity was 90.84 percent."

Alexander was the first to grasp the significance of Landry's last statement. Frowning, he stood and began pacing back and forth the length of the room, as he was prone to do when thinking. Keese like the others was struggling with the information. Not being a technical person, he knew it was important, but he didn't know why. Finally Alexander stopped pacing, locked eyes with Landry and said, "This means the terrorist either purchased a very large quantity of highly enriched uranium or they obtained weapons. In either case, the source had to be a major nuclear power."

"Oh my God," Keese exclaimed.

"Here we go," Wellington muttered, thinking it marked the beginning of WWIII.

Simpson growled. Henniger, Clark, Lopez, and Taylor were dumbfounded. Everyone was silent for several seconds, some open-mouthed watching the president who resumed his pacing, his lips pressed into a thin line. Having already guessed the answer, Alexander stopped directly behind Wellington. Looking over her head at Landry, he said, "All right, George, drop the other shoe. Who?"

Landry swallowed hard, before blurting out the answer. "The graphs were identical," he winced, "identical with the samples collected from the Soviet's Joe-4 test."

Palpable tension filled the room. Everyone sat in shocked silence. Finally, Wellington tentatively asked the unspoken question on everyone's mind, "Some of the missing nukes?"

"I … we don't know," Landry faltered, and looked dejectedly at the president. "They … they weren't implosion bombs—no plutonium," he explained and sat waiting for Alexander's cue to continue. A nod from the president, who had resumed pacing, elicited more information. "The yields were too large to be what are called 'briefcase' or 'backpack nukes.' Correct terminology would be special atomic demolition munitions, or SADMs. Man-portable devices for use by Soviet Spetsnaz—special units like our Rangers, Special Forces, and SEALs. SADMs are one kiloton or less. They're not city busters.

"We're convinced we were attacked with gun-type weapons, however, the yields were too high for this type of weapon. On the other hand, the yields are too low for a layer cake bomb," Landry concluded, emphasizing the dilemma with a shrug of his shoulders.

Alexander stopped pacing again—this time behind Landry. "Not necessarily," he said reassuringly patting Landry on the shoulders. "You're thinking about a *bomb configuration*. What if they were *devices*? No limitation on size or weight … A gun-type bomb or device requires a neutron source," he reasoned as he started pacing again. His last observation hung in the air. No one commented, because, with the exception of Landry, they really weren't sure what the president was talking about.

Landry pondered the president's comment. "Yes, that could be the answer," he said with growing animation, "We didn't consider a device. You know … it's entirely possible … they could have been test devices—"

"Right," Alexander interrupted and stopped his pacing to think aloud, "But I don't recall anything about the Soviets attempting to duplicate our Little Boy. If they did … could they have stopped for some reason?" he muttered. "Let's review what we know about the history of Soviet's bomb tests," he said, returning to his chair. "As I recall, they didn't test a gun-type device until much later in their program." Looking at Landry, he continued, "Have you made comparisons with their uranium-235 from later tests?"

"The lab checked a couple of samples," Landry replied, "There's no exact match. Doctor Chin has them checking all of our Soviet samples."

Alexander leaned back in his chair, rubbing his hands together and squinting his eyes. "You know, a gun-type device could have a of yield fifty KT, if it had a *large neutron source*." Then, continuing to think, he placed his hand on his chin, rubbing his beard's stubble between his thumb and forefinger before finally asking, "Did you find any trace of polonium-210? That was the type of neutron source used in the fifties and early sixties."

"No polonium ... but if it was a device, why not a *modern* neutron source? ... Or several sources?" Landry asked, picking up on the president's line of thought. "Such sources are now commercially available."

Silence followed Landry's last comment. The president, consumed by the myriad of questions surrounding their situation, was unaware of the room full of questioning eyes trained on him. The stuffiness of the room and exhaustion from a long day's work were causing him to lose focus. Momentarily shaking his head to clear his thoughts, Alexander leaned forward to take a drink of cold water and finally became aware of the puzzled faces in front of him. *Most of them don't have a clue as to what we're talking about. They're waiting for me to provide the answers. Landry is the only one giving me any input. I'm not out of ideas, but I'm really starting to feel fatigued. Got to get the others involved and end this meeting. I need sleep.* Slowly turning to look at Teresa and Julian he asked, "What did you learn about neutron sources when you visited the museum?"

"Uh, two chemicals—beryllium and polonium—were mixed together, causing neutrons to be emitted. Some type of nuclear reaction occurred. We were told this method is no longer used," Teresa replied.

"Two elements ... correct," Alexander said, feeling better now that he had more participation, "The neutron sources used in our current nuclear weapons are quite sophisticated. There are, however, commercial versions sold for oil well logging.[†] Spend some time with George exploring this possibility, Teresa. It's vitally important we get as much data as possible in order to decipher who did this to us and how." Frowning and pressing his lips

---

[†] Well logging is widely used in the oil industry. Nuclear well logging is a method of studying the materials surrounding exploratory boreholes. A tool consisting of a neutron or gamma ray source and one or more detectors is lowered into the borehole. The response of the detectors to radiation returning from outside the borehole depends in part on the lithology, porosity, and fluid characteristics of the material. Characteristics of the materials outside the borehole can be inferred from the response of the detectors.

together, he sat back in his chair. "We're going to have to contact the Russians. I'm going to need irrefutable proof when I confront them with our findings. George, do you have data we can provide them?"

"Yes, sir, I brought five sets," Landry replied pointing to his case.

"Good. Alan, I think I'd better break the news to President Karpov. This is going to get sticky. Do any of you think the Russian government was involved?" All shook their heads, responding in the negative. Alexander continued, "I'll call Karpov first thing tomorrow morning. George, and you too, Teresa, be prepared to depart for Moscow tomorrow. I'm sure President Karpov will require a personal explanation. Afterwards, I expect you'll be meeting with your Russian counterparts."

Surprised by the president's statement, Teresa and Landry looked at each other, then nodded their acceptance of his order.

Alexander smiled at them, then continued, "Alan, please inform our ambassador in Moscow. Ask him to provide support. Same goes for both of you," the president said looking at Clark and Wellington."

Addressing George and Teresa, Alexander said, "In addition to Doctor Chin, copy all of us with your reports. Contact me directly if you find something important. I suspect you're about to go on a treasure hunt."

Alexander closed his leather case, signaling the meeting was over. "Martha, due to the lateness of the hour, let us postpone our meeting until tomorrow morning. I usually get to my office by 0700." Alexander stood. "We'll reconvene tomorrow at 1400 hours."

Julian drove Martha Wellington and Teresa Lopez to the BOQ.

Chapter 28

Thursday

The President's Office – 0700 Thursday, 1 June

Martha Wellington entered the reception area of the president's office at 0700. Captain Taylor, seated at his desk, greeted her, "Good morning, Director."

"Good morning, Julian," Wellington replied with a smile. "Thanks for helping me get settled in last night."

"You're welcome, ma'am. I'll let the boss know you're here. He's asked me to place a call to President Karpov." Taylor walked into the president's office without knocking and announced Wellington. Alexander motioned for her to come in.

Entering the large corner office with a spectacular view of a mountain, Wellington walked to the side of the large desk and Alexander stood to greet her. "Good morning, Martha. Have a seat. Would you care for coffee?"

"Good morning, Mr. President. Yes, I would." Seeing the president nod to Captain Taylor, she added with a smile, "Light cream and half a spoon of sugar."

"Julian is about to place a call to President Karpov. You can listen by putting on the headphones." Pointing to four headphones lying on the conference table near his desk, he continued, "Keese and Simpson will also be listening."

Wellington smiled in reply, got up, and moved to the conference table. Sitting quietly, she studied the room and realized most of the pictures and awards belonged to the previous occupant. She was especially interested in a photo of a large Boeing 747 with a turret under its nose. Finally, she recognized it. *That's the Airborne Laser aircraft. Kirkland is one of our high technology centers. Now I understand why Alexander decided to stay here.* Her thoughts were interrupted, when an airman entered to deliver her cup of coffee.

For several minutes more, Alexander and Wellington sat in silence. She knew Alexander was mentally preparing for a very difficult conversation. *I'm really glad he understands all the technical issues ... gives him great credibility, and no one will dare try to bullshit him. It'll be interesting to see how he handles Karpov.* A minute later, the president's phone buzzed.

Alexander picked up the receiver, listened for a few seconds, and then motioned for Wellington to put on the headphones.

"Good afternoon, President Karpov."

"Good morning, President Alexander. I must tell you, we were surprised by your seizing the bank accounts. Thank you for the advanced notice. You've made quite a few people *very* unhappy," Karpov said with a chuckle. "Is there anything we can do to help?"

"Again, thank you for your offer. Perhaps we will call upon you in the next few days. The oil situation in the Middle East is becoming a problem for all of us. I'm preparing a plan to deal with it. I'll discuss it with you and President Wu when plans are finalized. Acquiring Middle Eastern oil is a worldwide problem requiring a worldwide solution."

"Yes, a serious problem, especially for America and China. I am interested in hearing about your plan. Before we continue, I need to pass on some intelligence I just received. We have unconfirmed reports from a reliable source indicating Iran is installing nuclear warheads on two Granat cruise missiles and on one Shahab-3D missile. The report says one of the Granat cruise missiles is no longer at its storage site and may be enroute to Syria."

"Thank you. I'll alert our commanders." Alexander paused and looked at Wellington who acknowledged the information with a quick wave of her hand. "Mr. President, I am calling you directly to discuss a very sensitive issue. Before I begin, please understand I do not consider you or the current Russian government to be responsible." Alexander, Wellington, and others, listening elsewhere to the conversation, heard Karpov's sharp intake of breath.

"Our Los Alamos National Laboratory has identified the source of the fissile material, the fissionable isotope used in the nuclear weapons that destroyed our cities. All of the bombs were constructed from highly enriched uranium-235. We're certain they were all gun-type nuclear weapons, similar to the Little Boy bomb we dropped on Hiroshima."

"What does this have to do with us?" Karpov's voice was tense.

"Let me review some history and you will understand. Joseph Stalin began the Soviet Union's nuclear weapons program in the 1940s. His purpose was to catch up with the U.S. and become the world's second superpower. Massive resources were channeled into the Soviet program, starting the Cold War.

"Two elements—metals—can be used to create an atomic or nuclear explosion. They are uranium-235 and plutonium-239. Both are very difficult to produce.

"There are two basic types of atomic weapons—gun-type and implosion. Gun-type weapons use a cannon to shoot a piece of uranium-235 into another piece of uranium-235, creating a supercritical mass—a nuclear explosion. Implosion weapons surround a subcritical ball of plutonium-239 with explosives and compress the ball to a smaller size, creating a supercritical mass—a nuclear explosion.

"We tested a plutonium implosion device named 'Gadget' on July 16, 1945. We didn't test our gun-type uranium bomb, the 'Little Boy,' before dropping it on Hiroshima. The second bomb dropped on Japan was a bomb version of our Gadget. We named it the 'Fat Man.'

"The first Soviet atomic weapon named 'First Lightning,' was detonated on August 29, 1949, at the Semipalatinsk Test Site, Kazakhstan. It was a plutonium implosion bomb. So were the next two Soviet tests.

"In the early 1950s the U.S. began developing the hydrogen or thermonuclear weapon. We were conducting a series of tests under the name 'Greenhouse.' The Soviet Union tested its first attempt to build a hydrogen bomb on August 12, 1953. We code named the first seven Soviet nuclear tests the 'Joe series,' for Joseph Stalin. The test I'm referring to was the fourth Soviet detonation, Joe-4. You refer to it as RDS-6

"Joe-4 is important because it used a new design called *sloika*. It was the first Soviet atomic weapon to use uranium-235 as the fissionable material."

Karpov was listening intently. He'd been briefed on nuclear weapons, but never really understood how they worked. Listening to Alexander, some of what he'd been told made sense. *It must be nice to understand the complexities of these bombs. Not to have to pretend to understand and trust the information you are being told is correct. Perhaps someday I can ask him for a more complete explanation.* It was time to say something. "Is the *sloika* design what is important?"

"No, not the design, the use of uranium-235. Uranium is used to build gun-type nuclear weapons. The type of weapons we're sure were used to destroy our cities. Modern analytical instruments can precisely measure the atomic structure of a metal, the elements, and isotopes of the elements making up the metal. A mass spectrometer is used to produce a graph, which is like a fingerprint. After a nuclear detonation, some of the fissionable material, called 'fissile material,' is left, not consumed. We collected samples from all nuclear detonation tests, including the Soviet's.

"Samples have been collected from our five cities and analyzed. The analysis resulted in two surprises. First, all of the uranium-235 used in the bombs came from the same source ... the same fingerprint from each city. If terrorists constructed the bombs, we expected they would have obtained the uranium from many sources. The analysis from each city would be different ... different fingerprints.

"Our second surprise was the source of the uranium-235. All of the analytical graphs, the fingerprints, matched the fingerprint from the uranium-235 used in Joe-4. Fingerprints from later Soviet tests were slightly different." *Now we'll see if he understands. His answer will tell me if he does, and if Russia is involved.*

"President Alexander, I am not sure what you mean," Karpov said, his voice betraying his anxiety. Are you accusing us of supplying the uranium to the terrorists?"

"No. I am not accusing Russia of providing the uranium—the fissile material—to the terrorist. The uranium used in the bombs matches uranium produced in the Soviet Union in the early 1950s. The questions we must answer together are how did the terrorists get large quantities of Soviet uranium? Where did they find it? Is there more?"

Karpov relaxed somewhat. "If this is so, we will certainly cooperate. Can you provide detailed information?"

"Most certainly. I am prepared to send one of our scientists, Doctor George Landry, and an FBI agent, Teresa Lopez, to Moscow to brief you and provide copies of all our information. They're prepared to depart today and to stay as long as necessary to assist in your investigation. They will bring samples of uranium collected from our cities."

"Please send them. We must solve this puzzle as quickly as possible." Karpov said, and paused to quickly read a note about Lopez that his aide had handed him. "Would Agent Lopez be the person responsible for catching the terrorists with the radioactive dispersal bomb?"

Alexander chuckled. It was a good opportunity to break the tension. "Yes, she is very bright. We've given her the task of finding out how the terrorists got the weapons into our country and hid them. I am sure she will be of assistance to your investigators."

"Yes. A young fresh mind may see things older minds have accepted without question. Do you have any idea where to begin the search?"

"Nothing concrete, just a hunch. Our Manhattan Project worked on developing both types of atomic bombs. Did the Soviet bomb development group attempt to develop a gun-type bomb like our Little Boy? We have nothing to suggest they did. However, we have speculated the weapons used to destroy our cities could have been test devices."

Oh no! Not another skeleton from Stalin's closet. Karpov winced. "I will start an investigation, and meet with your Doctor Landry and Agent Lopez as soon as they arrive. You can depend on our full cooperation."

"Thank you, Mr. President. I'll keep you informed of important events. Good-bye," Alexander said, concluding the call. *Now I'm certain Russia had nothing to do with the attack.*

Nice job. Wellington thought. *He's established an excellent relationship with Karpov. This could have resulted in a disaster. I'll make sure my people help Landry and Lopez.*

Alexander's phone buzzed. It was Captain Taylor. "Sir, Bill Fobbs would like to see you."

"Okay, ask him to join us," the president replied.

A few minutes later, Fobbs entered smiling broadly. *Looks like something is going well,* Alexander thought as he stood. "Good morning, Bill. This is Martha Wellington, our acting CIA Director. Martha, meet Bill Fobbs, our Secretary of the Treasury and other domestic agencies."

After the usual pleasantries, Fobbs said, "Nora's conference call yesterday morning with the banks and credit card companies was *very* interesting. At first she met with a lot of resistance. It seems your announcement about seizing the assets had a profound impact. When the second conference call convened, everyone was very cooperative, and creative solutions were found. The bottom line is, some credit card terminals should begin working on Friday. It will take some time to get the complete system on line. Nora did a great job," Fobbs concluded, still smiling.

Credit cards, Wellington thought. *I have been so concerned with my agency, I hadn't thought about credit cards. Yes, they're very important. Very few people carry much cash anymore. So many different problems—I wonder how Alexander keeps his sanity? He's a delegator, and people respond to his confidence in them.*

Young walked in and greeted the group, "Good morning, sir. I received a call from Ronald Jefferson. I assume you know him. He said he was the Under Secretary for Border and Transportation Security, Department of Homeland Security." For and instant, Alexander's face showed anger, and the others noted his expression. "He and his family were vacationing on Lake Powell. Seems they were in a remote area of the lake and didn't find out about the attacks until Sunday morning. He wasn't able to contact anyone until he reached the town of Page yesterday afternoon. They're on their way, and should arrive this evening."

Alexander received the news with a stoic expression. Frowning, he muttered, "He may be the senior executive in Homeland Security." Looking down, he added, "The agency's been doing just fine without a leader." Looking up, he continued, "Jefferson's a political appointee, a *darling* of the former president. His ideas differ from mine. We butted heads on occasion. He opposed my illegal alien policy. Well … we'll have to see if he can cut it. Charlie, have someone see if there's a house available for them. They used to live in Georgetown, so they will need a place to live … and they'll need a motel for tonight."

"Yes, sir. Sergeant Troy will take care of it."

Turning to Wellington, the president said, "Martha, you need some time to get organized. We'll meet in the conference room at 1400. I'll expect an update on North Korea and Pakistan. Also, prepare a list, including the exact geographical location, of every Arabic TV station studio and transmitter in the Middle East.

"Charlie, please show Martha where Barry's office is. He can help her get settled in a temporary office until the intelligence building is ready."

At nine o'clock, Governor Richards called for his daily teleconference with the president. "Mr. President, the seizure of the Arabs' assets and using them to pay wages has boosted the country's spirits. The nation has confidence in your leadership. A couple of governors complained during our afternoon teleconference, but the others told them to grow up and smell the roses." Richards chuckled. "We're getting a lot of questions from the press and citizens regarding oil, and what's being done to obtain a reliable supply."

"Kurt, thank the other governors for their support. The seizures are working. The treasury's banked over two trillion dollars, with much more to come. As to the oil issue, pass the word that plans are underway to solve the problem. Future events will be self-explanatory."

Richards laughed. "I can't wait for your next surprise. North Carolina's Governor mentioned the Eighty-Second Airborne was preparing to leave today for an unknown destination," Richards said, fishing for information.

Alexander grunted, ignoring the question. "We expect to have some credit card terminals activated starting tomorrow. It'll take a while to phase in all areas of the country. Good progress is being made in rerouting the telephone network around the destroyed cities. The Chicago switching station was rerouted, and Boston's should be up by the end of the day: Atlanta by Saturday, but New York and Washington will take longer. Same goes for TV and radio networks. FOX and CBS have functional networks. CNN, NBC and ABC should be ready by Sunday."

"I don't know whether to be glad or sad," Richards commented. "FOX and CBS have been showing scenes from the Middle East. Stuff taken from Arabic television. Arabs cheering and dancing, celebrating the destruction of our cities, and mobs sacking Western embassies, offices, homes. Stoning of what appeared to be Western women ... brutal stuff ... bodies hanging from bridges and gates. Our citizens are calling for blood. The mood is shifting from shock to anger. Our nation wants revenge, nothing less." Richards's last statements hung in the air for several seconds, before he continued. "Internment operations are going better than I expected. The radicals are easy to identify. They're full of what is being called 'jihad fever.' As soon as those with the fever cause trouble, the others get as far away from them as possible. It's been necessary to shoot some of the ones with the 'fever.' Troops guarding them are in no mood to take insults—especially when urine and feces are thrown at them. Are you going to court martial guards for shooting prisoners?" Richards asked.

"No. Not if they had a reason. The radicals *must be ... will be* controlled. We should have shot a few of them at Gitmo. Failure to follow orders, throwing urine and feces, and other rebellious actions is sufficient provocation. Have there been any serious problems with the other group, the cooperative ones?"

"No. In fact it's been quite the opposite. It's our nature to be kind to the unfortunate. The ones who behave and cooperate are being well treated, especially the children. What are we going to do with them?"

"I don't know. Our IFAC starts today. I'm depending on them for ideas."

"How many members?

"Three. A rabbi, a Catholic Islamic scholar, who happened to be here on vacation, and Reverend Smyth. We hope others will join, however, the three may be enough."

Julian Taylor and Teresa Lopez were finishing lunch at the officers' club. Both felt the tug of their mutual attraction. Teresa would leave for Moscow in a few hours. Julian knew of the president's North Africa invasion plans, and the scheduled attack on Algeria. Both were aware of the gathering storm clouds portending a new world war. Soon the U.S. and its allies would be engaged in a battle for North African oil. Pakistan was about to explode in revolution. And North Korea and Iran were wildcards in the table-stakes poker game for world domination. Someone had brought their old WWII recordings and was playing them as background music throughout the club. Somehow, they seemed appropriate for the present. Especially to the young couple who sat listening to the haunting words of " 'Til Then:" a song about lovers parting and one going off to war. Neither of them spoke. They felt no need for words. The song said it all. Would the lovers meet again? " 'Til then." Looking up at Julian through misty, soft brown eyes, Teresa said in a low husky voice, "Let's go to my apartment."

The Caliph's Palace, Tehran, Iran – 9:00 a.m., Thursday, June 1st.

The *Shura* and Saladin were listening to an address by the governor of the Central Bank of Iran. His message was not being well received. "I have spoken with the chairman of the Swiss National Bank. Our assets are frozen, and they are being transferred to the U.S. The Great Satan threatened the Swiss with an attack, if they failed to follow instructions. I was assured the issue would be brought before the UN Security Council. However, there is no Security Council. It was destroyed with the UN building in New York."

"Praise Allah. If the Swiss pigs do not give us our money, threaten them with an attack," one of the clerics yelled, his voice shrill with anger.

Bowing slightly to the upset cleric, the governor replied, "Allah be praised. The Great Satan is a superpower. It can attack any country. We cannot. We do not have missile submarines, bombers, aircraft carriers, a huge navy—"

"We have missiles and nuclear warheads! We are a nuclear power! Threaten them! Tell them we will attack them!" the hysterical cleric shrieked.

Saladin suddenly wished he were somewhere else. Unlike the crazed clerics, he was a modern man: as such, he was starting to grasp the reality of their situation. They had four useable nuclear warheads. Three were committed to attacking Israel and the U.S. Navy. Thinking it was better to be on the offense rather than the defense, Saladin sneered at the agitated cleric and said, "Tuesday you wanted to use our nuclear weapons to destroy the Great Satan's Navy and The Little Satan. Now you propose to use them to threaten the Swiss. What, or whom will you want to use them on tomorrow?" Before the cleric could reply, he continued, "Besides, we've told the gullible Europeans we *have* no nuclear weapons, and they believed us. Now you want to threaten them with our non-existent ones. Do you really expect them to believe such a threat?"

"After we use them, they will know our threat is real," the cleric retorted, vibrating with rage.

"Yes, and we'll have none left to use,"

"How can they know that?" screeched the cleric.

"How can *you* be sure they *don't*?"

Khomeini interrupted the bickering. "Allah will guide us. The greedy Swiss love money. The Great Satan does not keep great sums of money in their banks. We do. Governor, remind the Swiss of this. Tell them our empire controls all Middle Eastern and African oil. If we cannot count on them to protect our money, we will bank elsewhere."

I wonder where 'elsewhere' is? Saladin thought, beginning to understand what being a superpower really meant. *The damnable Americans can reach anywhere. The general was right. America's military power is immense. Even though they were reeling from my attack, they were able to swat the Egyptians like a fly ...* Logic and fanaticism would clash once more, and once more fanaticism would win. *No ... we're Allah's chosen people. He will show us the way. It is our duty to spread Islam from pole to pole. We will prevail.*

"Soon Pakistan will join our empire, and we will have many more nuclear weapons and missiles," Khomeini continued. "After we destroy the Little Satan and the Great Satan's Navy the world will tremble before Allah's wrath."

London, England – Thursday, June 1st.

Prime Minister Talbot sat slumped in his office chair. Events were moving much too fast. *How could the world have changed so much in just a few days? I have been pushed aside. The Americans have taken over. My own people are going along with them. I'm not even being consulted. I was just informed the U.S. moved nuclear bombs into our country, and the Royal Air Force is cooperating. What am I to do?* he fretted.

Britain was in turmoil with Muslim uprisings, suicide bombings, and rampaging rioters. The English people were angry at their government, especially Talbot and his party. Unlike their American cousins, Brits were not allowed to have firearms for protection. The police were out-gunned by insurrectionists. Many citizens were being killed. Finally, the army had to be called out to quell the riots.

The British public was demanding Talbot and parliament grant them the right to defend themselves. The media had suddenly turned on him, as evidenced by today's lead news item. The press and public alike were in an uproar over a court decision involving the right to bear arms. According to London's tabloids, a farmer was serving jail time for shooting two burglars in his house in the middle of the night. Having twice fallen victim to the same robbers, the next time they struck, the fed-up farmer used an "illegal shotgun" on the "bloody sods." One of the robbers was killed, the other injured. For his trouble, the farmer was thrown in jail to await his day in court. At the time, British papers fully agreed with the court's decision to jail the owner for having an illegal gun—much less using it to shoot someone. The burglar eventually recovered from his wounds, and he too was sentenced to jail. To add insult to injury, the farmer received a longer jail sentence than the burglar; and he'd been successfully sued by the dead burglar's family for personal injuries and loss of work. Worse, the liberal British government picked up the tab for the burglar's suit. "Where is the justice?" the public screamed. Their tax dollars were going to support the socialist government's aid to a convicted criminal. While the farmer rotted in jail on appeal, he was being forced to pay the £50,000 judgment. He was in danger of losing the only thing of value he owned—the very property he fought to protect.

All over England, Talbot and his liberal cronies were being vilified. Sanity was returning to the citizens of the United Kingdom.

Talbot's only recent good news was the capture of a truck carrying a radiological dispersal bomb. An observant taxi driver alerted the police, and the truck driver and passenger were captured before the bomb was in place.

We are running out of oil, Talbot worried as he sat wringing his hands, *All shipments from the Middle East, and now Africa, have been stopped. Britain cannot pay £173 per barrel. Our economy will collapse. What am I to do?*

Unlike Talbot, Britain's Air Marshal, Sir James Murrell, knew what needed to be done. U.S. and British fighters were being positioned at Gibraltar and Italian Air Force bases. Royal Marines were embarking for Libya. The Brits' Royal Parachute Regiment was preparing to jump with the Americans on the Libyan pipeline. *Britain's not going to miss this party. Anyone who does will be, as the American's like to say, "sucking hind teat." We may not regain all of our former empire, but I'm going to make damn sure we get some of it back. It will be Operation Torch all over again. I wonder what Rommel, Montgomery, and Patton would think of our new tanks?*

Young Prince Harry was also keenly aware of the situation. *The Prime Minister and Parliament have demonstrated their inability to cope. Unlike the Americans, we have no strong leader, no Churchill, Thatcher, or Blair. Perhaps it is once again time for a strong king—not my father or brother. I must speak with the queen.*

Kennedy Strike group – Thursday afternoon, 1 June

Reconnaissance of the North African coast revealed a gathering of men and ships—many types of ships—at the Algerian harbors of Bejaïa, Mostaganem, and Skikda. Admiral Krugger, using a secure data link, was discussing the reports with Army General Samuel L. Letterman, Commanding General of Operation Flare, the invasion of North Africa. President Alexander had expanded Central Command to include the entire African continent and staging areas in England and Italy. A unified command was essential for success.

"Photos and human intelligence agree, this is an invasion fleet. We believe its purpose is to invade Spain. Their caliph stated his intention to reclaim the Islamic Empire. This appears to be his first step," Krugger said.

"What do you suggest?"

"Obviously their ships and men must be destroyed, which provides us with an interesting opportunity," Krugger observed.

"Opportunity?"

"Yes, sir. An opportunity to conduct joint strike operations before the Libyan invasion—a shakedown exercise with live ammunition."

"Hmmm … I'll consider it. We do need to conduct joint operations. What is your condition?"

"We're low on fuel and ordnance. We've enough to defend ourselves, but not enough to conduct strikes against the Algerian ports. We're saving our ordnance to support our Marines when they land on Sunday. Replenishment ships won't arrive for several more days. The *Eisenhower* and *Enterprise* will be on station by then.

"The caliph's invasion fleet makes a mighty tempting target for the B-52s. Plenty of fighter cover at Gibraltar. I'm sure Spain will want a piece of this. Portugal and Italy may want to join too. I'll lay on a strike for tomorrow evening. I don't think the Algerian fighter pilots know how to fly after dark," Letterman concluded with a chuckle.

"Aye, aye, sir."

West of Albuquerque, NM– Thursday evening, June 1st.

Heading east on I-40, Cassandra Jefferson was at the wheel of their dark-blue Honda Odyssey van, driving down the long hill leading to Albuquerque. She was looking for Exit 145. Tired from her long day, Cassandra was annoyed with her husband. The boys behaved well for most of the trip, but were beginning to get restless. Roger was bored by the never-ending desert. Joshua showed some interest, but soon retreated into his video games. Glancing at her husband, she said, "We have to get some new movies. The boys have memorized the ones we have." Roland grunted in reply, angrily listening to the ringing of an unanswered phone in his Bluetooth earpiece. "Please pay attention and help me find the motel, we're all tired," Cassandra snapped.

Roland Jefferson's cellphone had made a connection with a tower when they approached Flagstaff, then lost contact after passing through Winslow. The cell briefly connected once again at Gallup, but made no further contact until twenty miles west of Albuquerque. Jefferson had used every available minute of phone time to call various offices in his agency. Frustrated with the lack of available tower connections, he spent most of the trip berating the lousy phone service. When he finally got through to a field office, he was enraged over the reports he received. Mexicans crossing the U.S. border seeking employment were being arrested. Designated as illegals, those "poor wretches" were being arrested by his agents and thrown into detention pens. He quickly ordered them released into the local communities. He was further appalled to learn foreign passengers, landing at U.S. airports Friday evening, were being detained and questioned by his airport security agents. He ordered them released and became outraged when most of the airport agents in charge refused his orders. "Sorry, sir, but we're operating under presidential orders," they told him, "Only the president can change them." Some U.S. citizens were also being detained, but that didn't seem to bother Jefferson.

Cassandra who'd done most of the driving was irritated with her husband. He'd subjected everyone to mile after mile of his tirades. All she wanted to do was to find a motel get some dinner and some rest. She had asked him several times to call Colonel Young to ask for a recommendation for a motel. All he wanted to do was use the damn phone to call his people. If she'd not insisted—threatened to throw a fit—he wouldn't have called Young and learned a room was reserved for them at the Holiday Inn. Now all she had to do was find the motel. Her husband was still frantically trying to reach people in his agency. Most had gone home.

They finally reached the motel at 7:30 p.m. After unpacking, the family enjoyed a Mexican style dinner in the motel's restaurant. Cassandra and the boys went to the pool. Roland settled down to watch the news. CBS was showing reruns, so he had to turn to FOX. A network he detested. "What's wrong with CNN?" he grumbled. "Why aren't they on the air?" After thirty minutes of watching Fox News Alerts—especially reports of public support for the president—Jefferson was beyond being upset. When Cassandra and the boys returned to their room she found her husband near hysterics. Unable to calm him, she suggested they go to the bar for a drink, while the boys got ready for bed. "The man's *a maniac*," was the last thing Joshua heard his father say before the door closed.

Chapter 29

Friday

U.S. Embassy, Moscow – Friday, June 2nd.

A low ranking embassy official met Teresa Lopez and George Landry at 5:12 a.m. when they arrived at the Moscow airport. Unaccustomed to overnight flights against the sun, both envoys had a severe case of jet lag.

Teresa slept fitfully during the long flight, dreaming of Julian, and troubled by their hasty affair. Normally cautious about intimate involvements with co-workers, her heady reaction to Julian bewildered her. *He's so different from every other man I've been close to—so open, so thoughtful, so gentle, he takes my breath away ... I'm glad we're going to be separated. I could easily fall in love ... and that's not included in my plans.*

Sleep eluded Landry. Surprised by his presidential appointment, and experiencing a growing sense of pride, he kept asking himself how he'd risen so rapidly from a position of near obscurity, to become a presidential envoy. *Given Alexander's obvious annoyance with my tendency for liberal thinking, why has he entrusted me with this serious undertaking? I'm quite sure his first impression of me was one of disgust. I could see it in his face. But he always treated me with respect. When I did the job he gave me, he showed his appreciation. Now he's sending me to Russia as his representative, with the power of the presidency behind me. I've grown to admire him, and I won't let him down.*

Landry wasn't the only one questioning why someone in his lowly position was being sent on such a serious mission. America's Ambassador to Moscow, Stanford Hubert McGill III, a Rodman appointee, had much the same thoughts. The ambassador was "upset." No one had explained the reason for Landry's and Lopez's visit. *Why would the new president and secretary of state send such low ranking individuals as presidential envoys on an Air Force plane—a C-37 Gulfstream V, no less? Secretary Keese called and told me to fully cooperate with them, and provide embassy accommodations suitable to their status. What is their status? What am I to do with them?* he fumed.

The head of the embassy's FBI unit was also concerned. Only Moscow's CIA station chief, Paul Eckard, grasped the importance of their mission. His old friend, Martha Wellington, had called to inform him of her new position as acting CIA Director, and of the envoy's pending arrival on Friday. She'd said nothing regarding the purpose of their trip.

"They're coming as personal representatives of the president," she'd told him, "You're to accord them high-priority status and to provide all possible assistance."

"What's the new president like?" he asked.

"Awesome," she replied—high praise indeed from the pragmatic Ms. Wellington.

President Karpov was immediately informed when the U.S. Air Force plane arrived from Albuquerque. Although anxious to meet Alexander's envoys, Karpov decided to give them some time to get cleaned up and recover from the flight. At 9:00 a.m., he instructed his assistant to call the American embassy and invite Agent Lopez and Dr. Landry to meet with him at 11:00 a.m.

When McGill took the call from Karpov's assistant, he was surprised to learn how quickly President Karpov wished to meet with the envoys. Arranging an interview with Russia's president normally took weeks of prior planning, and Karpov expected them in two hours. *Such a thing is unheard of. Something's going on here that I'm not privy to. And I intend to find out exactly what it is,* an annoyed McGill decided with a snort. Angrily pressing his phone's intercom button, he ordered his secretary to inform Lopez and Landry they were to report to his office immediately.

A few minutes later, the sources of ambassador's irritation entered his large office. McGill eyed them critically as they approached his desk. *Well at least they're appropriately dressed,* he sniffed, appraising Teresa's navy blue pants suit, white blouse with black tie, and low-heel, black shoes; and Dr. Landry's dark blue suit and conservative striped tie.

McGill made no move to shake their hands, offer them a seat, or even speak to them. Instead he remained seated behind his desk, leaning back with his hands folded in his lap and scowling up at them for several long seconds. "You've been invited to meet with President Karpov at 11:00 a.m. I'll be accompanying you," he informed them with a condescending sneer.

Teresa and George looked at each other, unsure how to handle this unanticipated event. Neither spoke. Teresa frowned.

"Is there a problem?" McGill asked with a hint of a Bostonian accent.

Still frowning, Teresa looked down at the ambassador and responded, "Sir, you are not cleared for our mission. Our orders are to present certain information to President Karpov, and to whomever he chooses to have present."

"I don't allow *spooks* to operate out of *my* embassy," McGill exploded, sitting upright and grabbing the arms of his chair. Pointing to the door, he ordered, "Wait outside."

As soon as the two left, McGill phoned Alan Keese. It was 1:30 a.m. in Albuquerque. Not a good time to call the secretary of state to bitch about the president's orders. Keese, who'd been asleep for an hour and a half, was startled by his ringing bedside phone. Fumbling to turn on the light, he noted the time, frowned, and answered the phone, "Hello."

"Secretary Keese, this is Ambassador McGill in Moscow."

Suddenly wide-awake, Keese feared the worst—something must have happened to Lopez and Landry. Why else would the ambassador wake him at this hour? "What's the problem?" Keese demanded. "Has there been an accident? Have they arrived safely?"

"Oh, no. No accident," McGill curtly responded. Landry and Lopez arrived early this morning. I just received a call from President Karpov's office requesting their attendance at an 11:00 a.m. meeting. When I informed them of Karpov's request, Agent Lopez advised me I was *not cleared* for the meeting. Mr. Secretary, I do not allow *spooks* to operate out of *my* embassy."

Shit! He's another one of Rodman's liberal flunkeys. I should have known. Alan Keese wasn't easily provoked to swear—even mentally. "Ambassador McGill, I clearly recall giving you specific instructions. You were directed to provide the president's envoys every cooperation. Are you telling me you don't *understand* my instructions?" Before McGill could reply, Keese continued, his voice cold as ice, "Let's get something straight. It's not *your* embassy. It's not even *my* embassy. You are in the *president's* embassy, and you are *his* employee. Now, let me make this as simple for you as possible. You will immediately place your automobile and airplane at Lopez and Landry's disposal. Then you will go directly to the airport, board the C-37 for its return flight to Albuquerque. Report to me—for consultations—as soon as you arrive. Special Agent Lopez and Doctor Landry may be staying in Russia for some time. I assume you've provided them with quarters suitable for the president's *personal* representatives. Now, do you have *any more* problems ... or *questions*?"

"Uh ... no," McGill hesitantly responded.

The phone clicked. Secretary Keese had hung up. McGill sat in silence. After several seconds spent fuming and staring at the telephone, he jerked up the receiver and grudgingly ordered his limousine. Still incensed, he huffed into the outer office where Lopez and Landry waited, and said with a contemptuous sneer, "My limousine will pick you up at the main entrance. You'll meet with President Karpov at 11:00 a.m."

Baffled by what occurred in the ambassador's office, Teresa expressed her bewilderment to Landry while they waited for the limousine. Landry, a more experienced bureaucrat, understood, and said he would explain later. The meeting with Karpov lasted over an hour. In addition to the president,

Vladimir Melnikov, Director of the *Federal'naya Sluzhba Bezopasnosti* (Federal Security Service or FSB), and Boris Popov, Director of the Ministry of Atomic Energy (commonly called MINATOM) were present. Melnikov and Popov spoke some English, and Karpov translated when necessary. When the meeting concluded, Karpov graciously escorted them to the door. "Thank you for coming, and for a thorough briefing. Please return to your embassy. We have much to discuss," he said, indicating the other two men. "As soon as we formulate a plan, we will contact you. Meanwhile, enjoy our city."

Southwestern White House – 0730 Friday, 2 June

Alexander's phone buzzed. Lifting the receiver, he heard Sergeant Troy say, "Mr. President, Governor Richards is on line three."

"Thank you, Sergeant," Alexander said and pushed line three's blinking light, "Good morning, Kurt."

"Good morning, Mr. President. I hate to bother you," Richards said with a sigh. "I've received calls from the governors of California, Arizona, and Texas, and the mayors of El Paso, Deming, and Carlsbad. It appears someone has ordered Immigration and Border Patrol to release all detainees. What's going on?"

Alexander inwardly groaned. *It must be Jefferson.* "Kurt, I don't know. I gave no such orders. Inform everyone to disregard any such instructions. Thanks for the heads up. I'll look into it immediately. And Kurt, while I have your on the phone," Alexander said, deciding it was time to tell him about the pending attack. "I have an update—for your ears only—on the international front. Today marks the beginning of our next phase. Bombers from Spain, Portugal, Italy, and Great Brittan will attack several ports in Algeria later today. It seems Saladin plans to invade Spain and Portugal—and neither country has any desire to join his empire. You'll receive more details from my staff. I don't plan to announce our part in the attack—unless word leaks out."

"Can I assume this is the beginning? Other actions will follow."

"Yes," Alexander replied with a chuckle. "It won't be long before the new caliph has other things to worry about.

"Thank you, Mr. President. It's about time. This is what the people have been waiting for. They really trust you. They appreciate what you've accomplished and know you'll set things right, when you're ready. Goodbye."

Hanging up, Alexander scowled, then quickly dialed Young's phone. "Charlie, do you know where Jefferson is?"

"Yes, sir. At the Holiday Inn on the west side of town."

Alexander audibly sighed. "He's issuing unauthorized orders to Immigration and Border Patrol to release detainees. Call him and tell him to stop issuing orders and report to me ASAP."

"Yes, sir."

Cassandra woke to the ringing phone. For a second she thought she was still on the houseboat. Blinking to clear her eyes, she remembered she was in a motel room at the Holiday Inn in Albuquerque. Roland was snoring in the bed next to her, completely undisturbed by the ringing phone. Turning on the bedside table lamp, Cassandra squinted at the clock. It was 7:49 a.m. *I wonder who's calling us at this hour?*

"Hello," she answered.

"I'm calling for Roland Jefferson," a male voice said.

"I'm Mrs. Jefferson. My husband is still asleep. Can I help you?"

"Cass who is it?" Roland Jefferson muttered, barely awake.

"Ma'am, I'm Colonel Young, calling from Kirkland Air Force Base. I need to speak with your husband."

"Hon, it's Colonel Young. He wants to speak to you."

Damn the military. Who the hell does this colonel think he is bothering an undersecretary at this hour? "Tell him to call back in a couple of hours," Jefferson mumbled.

Young heard Jefferson's remark, "Mrs. Jefferson. I must speak to your husband *immediately*."

Jefferson who'd moved close to his wife with his ear near the receiver heard Young's reply. Jerking the receiver from Cassandra's hand, he snapped, "Colonel, this had better be good. You don't bother an *undersecretary* at this hour—unless it's *damned* important."

Young, normally a pleasant man, was pissed. *Now I understand Alexander's reaction. This man is a pompous ass. Well, I'm the president's chief of staff, and that means I don't have to take any crap from this idiot.* "Mr. Jefferson, I'm *ordering* you to cease all contact with the Department of Homeland Security and to report to the president ASAP. Come to the—"

"Who do you think you are, *Colonel*, to give me orders? Colonels *don't* give *orders* to Undersecretaries," Jefferson snapped.

"Well, *this Colonel does*," Young barked back, "This Colonel also happens to be the president's chief of staff and speaks for the president. Now get over to the main gate at Kirkland Air Force Base and identify yourself. You'll be met and escorted to the president. Be there by 8:30 a.m."

Before he could reply, Jefferson heard the dial tone. For several seconds he lay stunned, staring at the receiver, before handing it to his wife.

Cassandra had heard Young's harsh reply and figured, correctly, her husband had blown it. "Nice going. If you're fired, just where the hell do you think we're going to live?"

"He wouldn't dare fire me ... would he?"

A rather contrite Roland Jefferson finally found Kirkland AFB's main gate. The time was 9:27 a.m. The guard directed him to the visitors' building, where he found his escort waiting. After presenting identification and registration, he was given a vehicle pass and instructed to follow the air police vehicle. When he finally arrived at the building, now known as the Southwestern White House, he learned he must wait until the president had time to see him.

While Roland Jefferson cooled his heels, President Alexander was engaged in a telephone call with President Karpov. Karpov thanked Alexander for sending two such competent representatives. Neither one would have any problems interfacing with their Russian counterparts. Alexander told Karpov the ambassador's limousine and aircraft, a V-20B Gulfstream-IV, were available for the team's use: news that caused Karpov to chuckle— rightly surmising Alexander's actions must have totally upset the elitist ambassador and his cronies. "Thank you, I will instruct our people to take full advantage of your generosity. Together, we will get to the bottom of this," he assured the American president.

Next, Alexander explained his plans for the invasion of Libya. "This is our party, and we plan to keep the oil fields. But I assure you, Russia's interests will not be compromised."

Karpov who was well informed about U.S./British troop movements knew military action was imminent, but was unaware the target was Libya. *A good choice. I wonder if they know about the caliph's invasion fleets?* "Mr. President, can I assume you are aware of the Islamic buildup in Algeria?"

Alexander laughed, "Yes, thank you. I don't think it will pose a threat to Spain very much longer. Again, thank you for the information on the nuclear Granat missile. We're looking for it."

"Perhaps we can be of further assistance in this matter," Karpov replied. *The Americans are getting better at keeping secrets. I didn't know of their plans to attack Algeria and Libya. This time their press didn't announce their plans to the world.*

"I plan to call President Wu, as soon as he's up and awake, to advise him of our pending actions in Libya. Once we secure the oil fields and refineries, China will be provided the opportunity to purchase oil at a reasonable price."

"Yes, that should satisfy him … a reasonable course of action. Goodbye, Mr. President." *I don't think he plans to stop with Libya. I'm not only dealing with a new American president, I'm dealing with a new America.*

"Goodbye, President Karpov." Alexander said and pushed the intercom button, "Julian, please send in Mr. Jefferson."

The giant was awake and taking its first step.

Israel – Friday, June 2nd.

Satellites began searching for vehicles transporting the nuclear tipped Granat missile to Syria. Martha Wellington called the CIA station chief in Israel and instructed him to inform the country's Prime Minister of the Granat missile's threat.

Israeli forces began a drive north into Lebanon—burning Hizbullah forces out of their holes and destroying them. Activity at a secret Israeli base in the southern desert increased. Preparations for the unthinkable were underway—a nuclear war with the Islamic Empire.

Before dawn, Jordan's King Ali, accompanied by three members of his security detail, rode their horses into the desert. The young king's mind was troubled by many conflicting thoughts. Like his father, Ali was raised a Muslim, educated in the West, and had one foot in each culture. Now, he was attempting to rationalize his religion with history, current events, and the future he knew was coming. *Fourteen hundred years of conflict ... wars with the West ... conquest by the sword. When Muslims weren't ·fighting the infidels, converting them to our faith by force, we were fighting each other. Yes, the West invaded our lands—the Crusades—claiming them as their own. All of this conflict, bloodshed, over an ancient story about Abraham's two sons and a human sacrifice that did not occur. After we defeated the crusaders, the West left us alone. And what did we accomplish? Not much. Then came the First World War and oil. Oil could have made us a mighty people. Instead, it made our rulers rich and funded the radicals—men with no sense of the world. Small-minded fanatics who want to shape the world into their narrow vision. The West went through the same thing—the Dark Ages— but managed to grow out of it ... while we continue to sink into our darkness. Could my religion be false?*

Ali watched the breaking dawn. The sun turned the few clouds in the dark sky red, triggering a memory from Ali's youth. His father had been a great fan and collector of motion pictures. One movie in particular, *The Four Horsemen of the Apocalypse*, made in 1962, had frightened and impressed the young prince. It wasn't the story that affected him—though it was powerful. No, it was the cinematography. He could still vividly remember the movie's opening scene. A terrible cloud filled the screen, out of which four horsemen rode, one after the other. Then, four abreast, they seemed to gallop right off the screen. He recalled cowering at the thunderous sound of the horses' hooves and the terrifying sight of them appearing to soar off the wide screen above his head. Even now he cringed at the terrible image the riders projected—Conquest, War, Famine, and Death. As he watched the beautiful dawn breaking, in his mind's eye the four horsemen came riding once again out of the red tinged clouds. With their looming image came the foreboding echo of an even more ominous memory—the narrator's words, "Behold, an Ashen Horse! And he who sat on it had the name *Death*."

Kuwait – Friday, June 2nd.

The last chartered 747 lifted off from Kuwait City's International Airport, bound for Mumbai on the west coast of India. F-18E fighters from the *USS Harry S. Truman* swarmed overhead. In all, fifteen large passenger aircraft and two C-5s had landed and evacuated the small U.S. military contingent and civilian refugees from several countries, including France, Great Britain, Japan, China, and the United States. Two Saudi fighters had lifted off, threatening to attack, but wisely chose not to approach. Missile tracking radar at Iran's Bandar Abbas air base, located on the county's southern coast, illuminated the first departing aircraft. The air base commander received a message from the U.S. commander. "Turn off your radar now, or a B-52 bomber orbiting over the Gulf of Oman will launch a nuclear armed cruise missile at your base." Shortly thereafter Bandar Abbas reported a radar failure to the *Shura* in Tehran.

Elsewhere in the world

Considering the present circumstances, citizens in the United States were enjoying a rather peaceful day. Not so in the rest of the world. In Great Britain and southern Italy, a sense of urgency was in the air.

At dusk, aircraft from Spain, Portugal, Italy, and England swept over the Empire's invasion fleet anchored in Algerian ports. Three squadrons of B-52 bombers followed as the clean-up team. The fighter escorts had little to do. Command and control problems between the different country's air forces were worked out. The rehearsal for Sunday's attack on Africa was a success. Algeria's military had been decimated, and the empire's invasion fleet reduced to burning hulks.

When news of the destroyed invasion fleet reached the *Shura* in Tehran, the clerics went wild. They demanded the Algerian commander's severed head, but it could not be found in the rubble of Bejaïa. Only Saladin grasped the significance of the news. *How easily we were defeated,* he worried. As the day wore on, he grew increasingly distressed, but said nothing to the others. Finally, after much bickering and wrangling, the *Shura* took an action Saladin knew boded disaster. Throwing caution to the wind, the enraged clerics demanded that the Granat missile's delivery to the Syrian coast be speeded up. *They're exposing our one ace-in-the-hole*, the caliph silently grumbled, and then quietly slipped away to his apartment.

In his absence, blood lust gripped the *Shura*. "Death to America. Death to the Great Satan," they chanted.

Admiral Cheung monitored the U.S. military buildup in England and Italy. Sitting with half-closed eyes in his comfortable chair in Beijing, he contemplated the situation. *The Americans are getting ready to invade one of the Arab countries to get oil. So far, we haven't determined which one. Saladin, the stupid ass, has placed us in a bad position. Does this bunch of Islamic idiots really think we're going to pay them a tribute and 300 U.S. dollars per barrel for oil? If we back the Americans, we look like their lackey. If we oppose them, Xi, our president's pissant advisor, thinks they won't sell us oil. The good news is, they won't be able to meddle in our affairs while they're busy invading the Middle East. Taiwan will soon be ripe for the plucking.* When news of the attacks in Algeria reached him, Cheung smiled. *So, Algeria is the target. It wouldn't have been my choice—so much for Alexander's military skills. My preparations are almost complete. It is almost time to act. I must motivate Kim Jung-il. He will provide my final distraction.*

In Moscow, Teresa Lopez and George Landry were doing what Americans do best—sightseeing and shopping.

Chapter 30

Saturday

The President's Quarters – Saturday, 3 June

George Alexander had allowed himself the luxury of sleeping until 0730. Now he was enjoying his first breakfast with Jane in their new quarters. Jane insisted on preparing her husband's favorites—fresh grapefruit sections, Eggs Benedict, and Jamaican Blue Mountain coffee. Jim and Jenna were still asleep. Both were unhappy about having to leave the campus because of security issues.

"The house looks great, hon. I don't know how you do it. Sorry I haven't noticed before," Alexander told his smiling wife, "and, as usual, your Eggs Benedict is outstanding."

"I've had plenty of practice nesting, George. And I'm not surprised you haven't noticed. Poor dear, you've only had enough energy to come home and drop into bed. You're forgiven. Now enjoy your breakfast and tell me what you've been up to," she said, while refilling his coffee cup.

While they ate, Alexander brought her up to date on events and plans. She'd heard the news of the attack on Algeria. The media was all over the story. "We've decided to downplay Britain's and our role, and let Spain, Portugal, and Italy take credit for foiling the Islamic invasion. Our B-52 bomber strikes aren't being publicly announced. Ross did a great job of fielding reporter's questions. He said the U.S. was pleased at how well Spain and Portugal defended themselves, and praised Italy for its assistance," Alexander said, smiling as he stirred his coffee. "The press is chafing at the bit, trying to get at what we're planning. For the first time in many decades, America's war plans will be kept secret," he concluded with a chuckle. After finishing his coffee, Alexander's mood abruptly turned somber. Frowning slightly, he pushed his chair away from the table, looked at Jane, and said, "By tomorrow evening they'll have some really big news for their nightly reports." For a moment their eyes locked in recognition of the obvious subject of the media's forthcoming story—war.

Knowing he was about to tell her something she really didn't want to hear, Jane quickly looked away and rose to clear the table. With her back to him, she stood at the sink rinsing dishes, trying to hold back the tears threatening to fill her eyes.

"It starts this evening," he told her, and knew from the way her shoulders drooped he was unavoidably hurting her. Standing, he walked to her, put both of his arms around her waist, and hugged her. "You know I don't want this any more than you do, but it's inevitable. We've no choice in this conflict. There's no reasoning with this enemy. We don't even know for sure who or what we're fighting. We—my senior staff, the Cabinet, and I—have gone over this more times than I can count. That's why we formed the IFAC—to help us understand the nature of the beasts who did this awful thing to us."

Gently placing his hands on her shoulders, he turned her around to face him. Looking lovingly into her tear filled eyes, he tried to find words to console her. "Jane, we knew going into this we'd have to make tough choices. I have some great people advising me, and we have the best military in the world. I don't know how yet, but I do know we will survive. Now, dry your pretty eyes and come sit with me. Let me finish telling you today's schedule, and more about our plans," he said, taking her hand and leading her to the table.

"My staff and Cabinet will meet at noon for a final review. I've asked the three members of the IFAC to join us for a working lunch. After they leave, we'll review the invasion plans one last time."

"Another war," a worried Jane replied, "I'd hoped we were through with war. Will it ever end?" she whispered.

"Only God knows the answer, sweetheart. We've been kicked in the belly, but we're far from being out-of-the-game. It's time for *us* to put some points on the scoreboard. So far we've been playing defense. Tonight's action is our first offensive play. The first phase will be a strike to secure the oil resources we need to pursue the second phase—punishment—which will come later. More than punishment, we must eliminate the threat. In the past we've dealt with enemies who were, to some degree, rational. A peace settlement could be made after they'd been defeated. Now ... now we're facing an enemy who doesn't appear to care about consequences ... death, destruction ... an enemy that ..." He struggled for the right words. "It's ... It's about religion, Jane. It's a clash of civilizations, and only one can survive."

Jane studied her husband as he spoke. *He's aged ten years in the past week. God help him. The weight of the presidency is a terrible burden. He's already served his country well. Why must he be caught up in this turmoil? He'd retired, and we were happy in our home in the mountains. Then that conniving political animal, Hilda Rodman, called him back for more service. Why, God ... to pacify her enemies? Now he's been thrust into the presidency and given a task no man should have. Was he truly chosen to decide the fate of Islam? No man should be asked to do that. Help him, God,* she silently prayed.

For some time they sat quietly. Then, troubled by the burdened look on her husband's face, Jane attempted to break his somber mood, "George, I've been wondering about something. Whatever happened to Ronald Jefferson? You told me he was screwing up again."

Jane's comment snapped Alexander out of his dark thoughts. With a snort, he replied, "Oh, yes, *him*. Well, I finally had time to see him around 1100 yesterday. Do you remember his wife Cassandra? I think you met her at some function."

"Yes, at a picnic. They have two young boys. Cassandra seemed to be the stable one in the family. I really liked her."

"Right. Well his family is here with him. Like so many others, they have no place to go. Their home in Georgetown was destroyed. I told you he was causing trouble by not recognizing my authority. I really wanted to can his pompous ass, but under the circumstances, I couldn't. He has a family. They've lost their home. I couldn't put them on the street. Besides," he said with a chuckle and a wry look, "despite the fact he *thinks* he knows all the answers, he really has no practical experience. So … I decided to provide him some."

Jane laughed. Knowing her husband, she had pretty well guessed what was coming next. "So … what did you *do* with him?"

Alexander smiled and laughing heartily told her, "I assigned him to El Paso to work as a border patrol agent. After a few months in the desert, he'll be transferred to customs. If he learns from the experience, perhaps there'll be a place for him later."

"What about his family?" Jane asked.

"They'll get temporary quarters at Fort Bliss. He'll be paid as a GS-12— more than enough for them to live on."

"Yes, well that should take his ego down a few notches. I hope the marriage survives," Jane giggled, and then becoming serious told him, "George, you really don't look well. I'm worried about your health. Please come home and take a nap this afternoon. I know you're going to be up all night."

Standing and walking around the table, Alexander took his wife's hands and pulled her up into an embrace. Kissing her gently on the cheek, he whispered softly in her ear and patted her bottom, "I'll try, but only if you promise to join me."

"Oh, you! You're incorrigible," she said, smiling at his back as he walked out the door.

Officers Club, Kirkland AFB – 1130 Saturday, 3 June

The working luncheon meeting convened in a private dining room at the Officers Club. The Cabinet, and its newest member, Martha Wellington, were joined by Governor Richards, Lieutenant General Blankenship, Deputy Commander of the U.S. Strategic Command, Rabbi Steinberg, Reverend Smyth, and Monsignor Morani. After introductions and lunch was served, the doors to the room closed, and Alexander addressed the group. "What you hear in this room must remain secret until the events occur," he said, looking at Steinberg, Smyth, and Morani who nodded they understood the order. Satisfied, Alexander continued. "I assume everyone has seen the news reports of the destruction of the Islamic invasion fleet, anchored in Algerian ports, by Spain, Portugal and Italy. We don't plan to make our part public. We want Spain, Portugal, and Italy to take the credit."

The three clergymen nodded, and Governor Richards commented, "Public reaction to the events is favorable. However, citizens and the media are asking when we're going to retaliate for the attack on our five cities. Telecasts of anti-Western violence are really working up the public. They want action."

"Well, they're about to get it," Alexander said with a determined look. "Around midnight tonight, the U.S. will begin a massive bombing attack on Libya, followed by amphibious landings. U.S. and British paratroops will seize refineries, pipelines, and oil fields. At the same time, attacks will be made on military installations in Tunisia, Algeria, and Western Egypt. Our main mission is to capture Libya's oil fields and refineries. The Italians have offered to provide oil field workers. We're assembling a team to take control of the Libya's oil industry. Once Libya is secure, we'll invade and capture Algeria and Egypt, thereby expanding our oil supplies. The oil fields will become our property. Of course, we'll share with other friendly nations."

"Italian, Spanish, and Portuguese troops will follow to guard the refineries and pipelines," Simpson added.

No one spoke. Finally, Governor Richards muttered, "Oh, boy, the public's going to love it."

After a few more seconds of silence, Reverend Smyth asked, "May I make reference to these events in my sermon tomorrow morning?"

"Yes, unless the operation is cancelled. We invited the three of you to join us today to discuss the religious aspects of the war plan. Even though we're technically fighting the Islamic Empire of this so-called caliph, Saladin II, it appears we're actually fighting Islam. What are your thoughts?" Alexander asked the three guests.

Rabbi Steinberg, acting spokesman for the three, responded. "In essence, you're correct Mr. President. We are fighting Islam, which means 'submission' in Arabic. Muslims are given no choice. Their lives are predestined by their God. The Qur'an says in surah 33:36, 'It is not fitting for a Muslim man or woman to have any choice in their affairs when a matter has been decided for them by Allah and his Messenger.'

"We three believe the key to understanding Islam lies in understanding Islamic literature—starting with the Qur'an, which means 'recitation.' A book revered by over a billion people worldwide—many who have never read it, because they're illiterate. But they hold it dear, out of terror instilled in them by imams, mullahs, ayatollahs, and sheikas—their teachers and preachers. Ironically, the very terror Muslims feel is the foundation of Qur'anic teachings. One either submits to Islam and accepts its ideology, or one loses his or her head, dies and goes to hell—convincing fodder for the minds of the young, the impoverished, and the uneducated—don't you think?" The rabbi paused and held up his personal copy of the Qur'an.

"History tells us there have always been drastic consequences for criticizing or mishandling the Qur'an. Islamic tradition is replete with rituals defining how the holy book is to be treated. To a Muslim, the Qur'an is the holiest of holies. It must always be placed on top of other books—never beneath. Nor is one allowed to drink, smoke, or talk when it's being read.

Steinberg placed the book on the table. "While volumes of commentary exist on the Qur'an, rarely has it received the kind of objective historical scrutiny applied to the Bible, Torah, and the sacred books of other religions. Why? First and foremost because orthodox Muslims—especially fundamentalists—believe the book is a divine revelation. And second, because the Qur'an and Muhammad himself expressly forbade his followers to ever question him or the book's content. Islamic history is full of stories about so-called 'heretics' who did. They were horribly tortured, crucified, burned, or beheaded." Steinberg sighed and shook his head.

"Muslims believe the Qur'an is the literal word of the one god, Allah. It can't be questioned. Its wording is letter by letter fixed by Allah. All recitations recorded in the Qur'an were made by Muhammad. He is the only source of the Qur'an.

"Now with your forbearance, I'll provide a quick summary of how the Qur'an came to be in its present form—how Muhammad received his revelations and gave birth to Islam."

Modestly nodding and smiling at his audience, the rabbi began to painstakingly tell the story. "According to tradition, Allah had the Qur'an revealed by the angel Gabriel to one man, Muhammad, who is also referred to as 'the Prophet' or 'the Messenger.' In 610 CE, when Muhammad was forty years old, he claimed to have received his first revelation. While sleeping in a cave near the small Arabian town of Mecca, a caravan oasis and center of pagan worship, Gabriel appeared to him in a dream. According to

Muhammad, Gabriel said the revelations came directly from the one God, Allah. Muhammad was told to recite what Allah said—first to his wife and family, then to members of his tribe. Gabriel's first revelation marked the birth of what would later be known as the *Qur'an*.

"Muhammad received his first eighty-six revelations—the peaceful revelations—while living in Mecca and began preaching Allah's message. But the 'one God' concept upset Mecca's tribal elders. For centuries, Mecca had been collecting a substantial portion of its income from the pilgrims who came to worship 360 pagan rock idols in a shrine called the Ka'aba. Despite local opposition, Muhammad continued preaching Allah's revelations and began converting a number of followers. Some of those converts came from Yathrib, a town 200 miles to the north. In 622 CE, Mecca's tribal leaders finally had enough of Muhammad and forced him and his followers to flee to Yathrib: a journey to that came to be known as the *hijra*.

"Scholars tells us Muhammad was uneducated, which may be true, because no writings of Allah's revelations have ever been attributed to him. His followers either wrote down what he recited, or professional 'rememberers'[*] repeated his recitations for others to hear and record. Those who wrote down the revelations did so on any available materials—pieces of papyrus, animal hides, leaves, stones, even on their bodies. Twenty years after the Prophet's death in 632 CE, Uthman, the third caliph, which means successor to the Prophet, assembled all those with memories of Muhammad's recitations, and collected all the written copies, called 'fragments,' of his revelations. From the collective memories and fragments, Uthman's scribes recorded the stories in documents called *surahs*, written down in the order the fragment or remembered event was presented to the scribe. The scribes produced one hundred fourteen surahs, containing a total of 6,346 verses. When the transcriptions were complete, Uthman had all the fragments burned."

Steinberg hesitated, suddenly frowning and scratching his head. Then drawing his head back slightly, he blinked his eyes several times, as though trying to sort out something that was puzzling him. "You know," he said, "come to think of it, I don't believe any records exist pertaining to the fate of the professional rememberers and those who wrote on their bodies." He paused for several seconds looking at Morani with a puzzled expression.

Impatient with the rabbi's slow, analytical, boring, delivery, and annoyed with his penchant for minutia, Smyth—ever the evangelist—took over the presentation with a more dramatic account. "Yes, well then the surahs were combined into one large book. The one hundred fourteen surahs were

---

[*] Recitations and Hadiths were passed from one person with a gift for memory to another such person. Each has an *isnad*, a record of the persons passing on the story.

recorded in no particular order. Each surah had a different length—depending upon the number of verses—and Uthman had a dilemma," Smyth said with a demonstrative wave of his hands. "How should they be combined? His solution was to sort them by length, and then arrange them in a book in descending order—the longest surah first and the shortest last. Once compiled, the surahs became chapters, and the book became the Qur'an. A book with a text so disorganized it appears the surahs were gathered together like a deck of cards after a game of Fifty-Two Pick-Up," Smyth said with a chuckle—to which Rabbi Steinberg frowned and ever so slightly winced. "Yes ... well," Smyth sighed, "whatever its faults, Uthman's compilation remains the only recognized version of a book revered by over a *billion and a half* people: many of whom have no idea as to the true nature of the book, nor of the true history of the Prophet." Smyth paused for a moment, and was about to go on, when the rabbi leaned forward in his chair.

Giving the reverend a daunting look, Steinberg took up where the preacher left off—this time at a faster pace and with more enthusiasm. "Unlike our Bible and Torah, the Qur'an is based on the words of one man—Muhammad. There is no existing corroboration that his revelations actually occurred. No one else saw the angel and heard his words. And Muhammad offered no proof of his divine inspirations. Consider for a moment the differences between our religious books and the Qur'an. By comparison, the Bible has over forty authors who all wrote a consistent story of the history of man's relationship with a living God—a history spanning fifteen centuries. Islam is based upon borrowed, twisted biblical stories told by one man. A man who claimed he was the prophet both the Jews and Christians were waiting for. When both rejected his claim, Muhammad turned on them, and claimed they had corrupted the true word of God. Muhammad told his followers, Allah had chosen him to correct those corruptions by revealing his true message through the angel Gabriel. The words Gabriel gave Muhammad to recite came—according to the angel—directly from stone tablets in Allah's paradise. They were pure, uncorrupted, absolutely true, and beyond criticism. To question the Qur'an was to question the very words of God and was blasphemous. Allah directed Muhammad to tell his followers their duty was to *unconditionally obey* the holy book's divine commands."

Smyth who was practically trembling with the urge to sermonize couldn't resist interrupting to give his account of the story. "Yes," Smyth interjected, looking around the room to make sure he had everyone's attention, "Well ... uh, you'll no doubt be surprised to learn that Allah's revelations recognized the existence of Jewish and Christian characters in the Bible and Torah. Yes, it's true. In fact, the Qur'an actually contains plagiarized portions from both the Bible and Torah—complete with stories about Adam, Noah, Abraham, Isaac, Ishmael, Jacob, Joshua, Lot, Moses,

Aaron, Johan, David, Solomon, Mary, Jesus, Satan and of course Gabriel. Even more appalling,"—Smyth slapped the table with his hands—"is the fact that our beloved Judeo/Christian stories were taken out of context and told in a *perverted, twisted way.* Why, some, if not most, of Muhammad's recitations are nothing more than justification for his own demonic, hetaeristic, behavior ... *his raping ... his pillaging ... and his murdering,*" Smyth stormed, expressing his righteous indignation by shaking his fist and half rising from his chair.

Almost everyone at the table seemed to be either enthralled or amazed by Smyth's emotional display. Everyone that is, except James Ross. He was annoyed. To him, Smyth's outburst was altogether too reminiscent of evangelical rants he'd been forced to endure as a young man. Smyth's drama and histrionics were slowing down the committee's presentation, and Ross decided to interrupt. "Excuse me Reverend, but I'd like to pause for a moment to summarize what the committee is telling us. If I understand correctly, the Qur'an is a jumble of stories. Unlike the historical accounts told in the Bible and Torah, there is no order to the Qur'an's stories. And you *personally* believe that many of those stories were composed to justify immoral behavior." Ross looked around the table to see everyone but Jay Henniger nodding in agreement.

Monsignor Morani sensed Smyth's emotional expression of his personal opinions may have rubbed a raw nerve, and quickly answered, "Yes, General, that's our opinion. The 'peaceful verses' were recited in Mecca. Muhammad's recitations became increasingly violent and longer after the *hijra.* After reaching Yathrib he turned to caravan raiding and slavery to finance his religion. And, yes, he needed Allah's blessing to do so."

"That's correct," Steinberg concurred. "Aisha, the six year old Muhammad married, is reported to have said to him, 'Truly thy Lord makes haste to do thy bidding.' She was a smart one, and Muhammad's favorite wife. He died in her arms in Medina in 632."

"The Islamic calendar did not begin when Muhammad had his first revelation in 610," Smyth added. "No, it begins in the year Muhammad reached the larger town of Yathrib on September 24, 622. Yathrib is now known as the 'City of the Prophet'—Medina."

"It appears Allah made mistakes, or Muhammad did," Steinberg added. "Allah abrogates some of Muhammad's recitations in later surahs. Thus, Islamic scholars and jurists say the message in the later surahs superceed messages in the earlier ones—in other words the warlike surahs trump the peaceful ones—and the the ninth surah is last one he recited. In other words, the Verse of the Sword, 9:5, wipes out all the peaceful ones."[*]

---

[*] Doctrine of Abrogation, http://www.islamreview.com/articles/quransdoctrine.shtml

Realizing the discussion was drifting, Morani returned to the main topic, "Many non-Muslim critics of the Qur'an have written serious, scholarly documents that concur with Reverend Smyth's opinion. If you wonder why Muslims themselves do not question the book's inconsistencies, the answer is precisely what Rabbi Steinberg told you, *they are not permitted to*. Mullahs, imams, ayatollahs, and sheikas interpret it to suit their purpose. The Qur'an contains many angry passages, which can be used to justify any action or philosophy. In no chronological order, the surahs are, according to some modern day critics: often nonsensical, written in the wrong voice, plagiarized from Jewish writings, repetitive to a fault, full of erroneous scientific and historical observations, violent, vengeful, and most important to some— *immoral*. In fact there are those who agree with Reverend Smyth that Allah's revelations were recited, and the Qur'an ultimately written, for one purpose alone—to justify one man's lust for power, and to condone some of the most ungodly behavior the world has ever known."

Morani grunted and looked around the table. Ross nodded, indicating he was satisfied with the explanation.

Henniger's analytical mind was troubled. "Before you continue," he interjected, "I've been wondering how we can be sure Uthman recorded all the stories."

Morani answered, "We can't. Some were probably lost. There's no way to really know." Smyth and Steinberg nodded their agreement.

Realizing enough had been said about the Qur'an, Morani decided it was time to move on. "Thank you, Rabbi Steinberg and Reverend Smyth. I'll continue the presentation from here by introducing, as succinctly as possible, other sacred Islamic literature.

Islam stands on two legs—one is the Qur'an and the other is the *Hadith*, which means tradition. A Hadith is a report made by one of Muhammad's contemporaries of the Prophet's words, deeds, and attitudes, which are believed to have been inspired by Allah. Accepted collections of Hadith are referred to as *Sunnah*, a custom or practice of the Prophet. Sunnah is based on collections of Hadith compiled in the eight to tenth centuries. It is from these collections that all accounts of the revelations of the Qur'an and early years of Islam are derived.

"Sunnah is primarily the work of four Islamic authors whose works are universally accepted to have profoundly influenced Muslim custom, worship, and law. I'll briefly list the four and their most important works."

"First," Morani said, holding up his hand with one finger extended, "Ibn Ishaq's *Sira*, the Biography of Muhammad, entitled *Sirat Rasul Allah*, written in 750 CE. It is the earliest record of Muhammad's life and the formation of Islam: there is no earlier or more accurate source. Ishaq's *Sira* is arranged in chronological order, which provides a method for placing the jumbled surahs found in the Qur'an in proper order. No known copy of Ishaq's original manuscript exists, but in 830 CE, Ibn Hisham edited and abridged—sanitized might be a better term—Ishaq's *Sira*. In the foreword of Hisham's revision, he explained: 'I am omitting things which Ishaq recorded in this book ... things which are disgraceful to discuss and matters which would distress certain people.' Alfred Guillaume's translation of Hisham's revised *Sirat Rasul Allah* was last published by the Oxford Press in 2002 under the title *The Life of Muhammad*.

Morani paused, raised his hand and extended two fingers. "Abu Muhammad bin al-Tabari's *History of al-Tabari*, the *Ta'rikh*, 870-920 CE, is a collection of Hadith recounted by those who lived close to Muhammad. The *Ta'rikh* is the oldest uncensored history of Islam's formation. In chronological order, it's formatted like the Bible. Tabari had a copy of Ishaq's *Sira*, and referenced Ishaq's original work in his *Ta'rikh.*"

Again Morani paused. This time displaying three fingers. "Imam al-Bukhari's Hadith, compiled between 850-870 CE and entitled *Sahih al-Bukhari*, *The True Traditions*, is considered *Sahih*, meaning genuine collections of Hadith. It's arranged by topic.

"And, finally," Morani said, displaying four fingers, "there is Bukhari's student, Muslim Ibn al-Hajjaj who collected over 300,000 Hadiths between 815 and 875 CE.

"Muslims consider the Sira and Hadith stories genuine accounts of the actions and words of the Prophet. As such, they're considered as sacred, holy scriptures—like the Qur'an—and are also above criticism.

"Hadith stories give us chronological accounts of Muhammad's words and deeds as reported by his Companions. They are the foundation for Sunnah—Islamic rituals, behaviors, laws, and conquests—and give order to the Qur'an's chaotic ramblings and repetitions. In addition to the Qur'an, Islam cherishes and believes these four books are divine revelations of their one god, Allah. Now as we proceed with our presentation it is important to remember Rabbi Steinberg's comments regarding Islam's attitude toward criticism." Morani concluded, and gestured with his hand for Steinberg to continue the presentation.

"Thank you, Monsignor. In the twentieth-century, a few brave former Muslim authors, like Salman Rushdie, author of the *Satanic Verses*, and secularist Ibn Warraq—not his real name by the way—author of *Why I'm Not a Muslim,* wrote critical books and have been vilified. Non-Muslim authors, Craig Winn author of *Prophet of Doom,* and Serge Trifkovic, author of *Sword of the Prophet*, for example, have written scholarly books critical of Islam. Robert Spencer's book, *The Truth about Muhammad*, provides a good summary of Muhammad's life. These authors daring works now enable us to gain insight into the man, Muhammad, and to better understand the insidious ideology of Islam.

"We've prepared a list of several of the most respected authors in the genre," Steinberg continued, picking up copies of the list lying on the table before him. "We're also compiling excerpts from their works to be used in future discussions." The rabbi was turning to hand Governor Richards copies of the list, when he suddenly shook his head, frowned, raised his left hand and forefinger, and said, "Oh. I just remembered. You might like to know that the author Warraq—or whoever he was—was actually an ex-Pakistani zealot who broke away from his faith because of the Ayatollah Khomeini's fatwa, ordering the death of author Salman Rushdie—something Warraq refers to as the 'Rushdie Affair,' and—" Steinberg was about to continue another rambling discourse when he noticed Reverend Smyth roll his eyes and start fidgeting.

Morani also noticed Smyth's reaction, and the impatient expression of several of the others seated at the table. Smiling at the rabbi, Morani gestured toward the governor, indicating the lists needed to be passed on, and said, "For expediency and because the critical works on your list are so complex, I'd like to summarize. The almost universal trend of critical thought, among those brave souls on the list is, to put it bluntly, the Qur'an is an *awful* book— awful in construction, awful in content, and because of its awful intent, *awfully immoral*." Morani paused and looked around the table at the group, noting their fascinated expressions.

"How can this be, you ask, when we've all been told Islam is a peaceful religion? The answer is frighteningly clear. First, we are victims of our own political correctness. Second, we are victims of the paranoid culture of 'multiculturalism' and 'secular progressive' ideas forced on us by the liberal establishment. Third, we are victims of the world's failure to recognize the real message in Islam's so-called sacred literature. We've allowed ourselves to believe the media, and those leaders who knowingly or unknowingly sacrificed the truth about Islam on the altar of their own ideology, or for political gain. They've told us the Qur'an is simply a religious book Muslims memorize and recite—much like we memorize and recite inspirational and comforting portions of our Bible and the Torah.

"We've accepted their statements as truth. And in part it is. Muslims do recite portions of the Qur'an—those portions deemed important by whatever teacher or preacher happens to be present or encouraging them at the time. And they do so over and over—until the recitation becomes a mindless chant, which often has nothing to do with comforting their souls. In radical Islamic mosques the chants may come from Qur'anic surahs that encourage jihadists to ritualize suicide fantasies of: dying as martyrs for Allah; going to paradise; and having beautiful virgins fulfill their every carnal desire. Chants may also be comprised of self-deprecating or violently motivating surahs designed to work the faithful into a rage.

"Perhaps the most deplorable use of memorization and chanting can be found in *madrassahs*, Islamic schools, where young children are required to memorize and chant for hours. It's interesting to note an opinion expressed by Alfred Guillaume who translated Hisham's revision of *Ishaq's* Sira. Ibn Warraq's *Why I'm Not a Muslim* quotes Guillaume as having said, and I paraphrase here, 'the mindless way children are forced to learn either parts of or the entire Koran—some 6,300 verses—by heart … accomplishes this prodigious feat at the expense of their reasoning faculty … and often stretches their memories so that they are little good for serious thought.'

"Taken out of context Islamic recitations may seem to be innocuous. However, consider what happens when the Qur'an is arranged chronologically by using the *Sira*, Muhammad's biography, and the Sunnah. Then the message—*far* from being innocuous—shouts *terrorism, murder, genocide,* and *world domination* by a religion that demands submission from everyone not already bowing to Allah. Yes, this is the ideology of Islam as espoused in the Qur'an and practiced by its author, Muhammad. In fact, for years Muslim clerics have tried to hide the Qur'an's true hostile nature by claiming the book can't be translated, which in itself is laughable. In reality, the clerics don't want the world to know how vitriolic Allah's book really is. They know it's hate-filled, vicious, and anti-Semitic. To quote a passage from Craig Winn's *Prophet of Doom,* one of the books on your list, 'The Qur'an is very nasty; it's dimwitted, demonic, and deceitful. It promotes, immorality and inspires terror.' Winn goes on to say, and others on your list agree—I'll paraphrase here again, 'The Qur'an is quite simply the *rant* of a depraved mad man, a sexual predator, and pedophile whose sick recitations were nothing more than a justification for rape, murder, genocide, and pillage.'

"Muhammad's own biographer Ibn Ishaq, describes the Prophet as being far less than a gentle soul. Ishaq describes Muhammad as being an avowed rapist, warlord, and vicious warrior, who captured goods in raids and demanded tribute from Christians and Jews alike—if they refused to succumb to his religion. After his death, Islam spread across the world like a giant tsunami. Conquered peoples converted or perished. Exceptions were made for people of the book—Christians and Jews—but only if they paid a submission tax and agreed to live as second class citizens under the terms established by Muhammad. Christians are infidels, according to the fifth surah, verse seventeen, which says, 'They are surely Infidels who say Christ, the Messiah is God.' " Morani paused to allow the impact of this statement to register, then continued.

"The collections of Hadith traditions, which I mentioned earlier, play a vital role in dictating Muslim behavior. Each tradition includes a chain of the names of the men and women who passed the story down from one generation to the next. Hadith, arranged chronologically, tell us about Muhammad's deeds and words during his years as a prophet. Muhammed is Islam, and Islam is Muhammad. Muhammad's life is the role model for all Muslims. As Spencer says in *The truth about Muhammad*, 'His [Muhammad's] words and deeds have been moving Muslims to commit acts of violence for fourteen hundred years.' "

Raising his hand for clarification Alan Keese interrupted, "This is all very informative and I appreciate the detail, but I'm curious about one point. How does all this tie in with and explain the Israeli-Palestinian conflict?"

Realizing Reverend Smyth was about to respond, Rabbi Steinberg quickly explained, "One of the major differences between Islam and Judeo-Christian beliefs is the story of Abraham preparing to sacrifice one of his sons. The Old Testament and Torah state that God, the Almighty, was testing the Jewish patriarch Abraham's faith. Gabriel appeared to the old man and directed him to offer his beloved second born son—his legitimate son, Isaac—as a blood sacrifice. Abraham started to obey God's order, but the boy was miraculously saved. At the last moment a ram, caught by its horns in a bush, appeared next to the altar. God spared Isaac by having Gabriel instruct Abraham to sacrifice the ram as a substitute offering. Abraham was willing to give God his most cherished possession. As a reward for his act of obedience, God promised Abraham that the seed of his son, Isaac, would inherit the land of Canaan—the land promised to the Children of Israel when they followed Moses out of Egypt—the land between the Nile and Euphrates rivers."

"*The Qu'ran tells the story differently*," Smyth dynamically interjected, leaning forward in his seat. "It says the event occurred near Mecca, not in Israel. And, the son to be sacrificed was Abraham's first-born son, *Ishmael*, born out of wedlock to an Egyptian slave. Therefore, Ishmael received Allah's blessed inheritance. Why is this important? Because according to history, Ishmael's decedants made Arabia their home. Therefore, Muslims consider Abraham to be the father of the present Arab world. If Ishmael was the son to be sacrificed, then God's covenant and the ownership of the Promised Land belongs to the Arabs—not the Jews. It's their *waqf*, their endowment, and no Muslim can cede any of the land to Israel or any other non-Muslim."

"*This* is the *cornerstone issue* regarding Israel's right to exist," a somber Steinberg added, and all three theologians, quietly nodding their heads, sat looking at their audience.

By then, the others at the table were so engrossed with the story that several of them jumped, when Governor Richards suddenly sat forward in his chair and placed his hands on the table. Frowning at the three clergymen, Richards challenged them by saying, "You've really painted a *harsh* picture of Islam. I must tell you I'm very confused … and frankly … I–I'm astounded." Scratching his head, Richards turned and said to the president, "I keep thinking about what we've been told. Islam is supposed to be a gentle, peaceful religion. There are only a small number of radical terrorists. I don't understand the contradiction."

"*Of course you don't,*" Smyth blurted out. He'd been observing the other's reactions and was incensed by the governor's obvious naiveté. "You've been fed *phony propaganda* by so-called good Muslims and our *own political apologists* for years. I don't mean to offend sir, but when you read the surahs for content, they prove the contrary—for example Allah commands in Surah 47:4, 'O True believers, when you encounter the unbelievers, strike off their heads,' " Smyth said making a chopping motion with his right hand. Catching his breath, he continued, "We'll be giving you some excerpts to read before our next meeting. After reading them, you'll see for yourself Allah's Qur'an clearly approves incest, rape, lying, thievery, deception, torture, slavery, mass murder, and terrorism. In truth, any *good Muslim* by Islamic standards is a *bad Muslim* by our standards. If they subscribe to the tenets of the Qur'an, they have to be bad to be good—or they will go to hell. Our political leaders have been too afraid of inciting violence to tell us the truth. No one wanted to offend the Muslim community. For this reason alone, political correctness may be the end of us, and the price we pay will be our own funerals—"

"I don't believe political correctness is an issue anymore. We're well past worrying about offending," Wellington sarcastically interjected.

"Yes, well, let me read to you a few passages from the Qur'an," Smyth continued, opening his dog-eared copy.

"5:33 The punishment for those who wage war against Allah and His Messenger and who do mischief [mischief means those who don't follow Islam's mandated behavior], in the land is only that they shall be killed or crucified, or their hands and feet shall be cut off on opposite sides, or they shall be exiled. That is their disgrace in this world, and a dreadful torment is theirs in Hell.

"5:55 Whoso of you makes them his friend is one of them.

"9:5, Fight and kill the disbelievers wherever you find them, take them captive, harass them, lie in wait and ambush them using every stratagem of war.

"8:39, Fight them until all opposition ends and all submit to Allah ... Fight them until there is no more *Fitnah,* disbelief in Allah, and all submit to the religion of Allah alone.

"8:12, I shall terrorize the infidels. So wound their bodies and incapacitate them because they oppose Allah and His Apostle.

"8:57, If you gain mastery of them in battle, inflict such a defeat as would terrorize them, so they would learn a lesson and be warned.

"48:29 Muslims must be merciless to the unbelievers but kind to each other.

"Here are some of Muhammad's words taken from the *Sira*, his biography," Smyth added.

"Ishaq: 326 If you come upon them, deal so forcibly as to terrify those who would follow, that they may be warned. Make a severe example of them by terrorizing Allah's enemies.

"Ishaq: 587, Our onslaught will not be a weak faltering affair. We shall fight as long as we live. We will fight until you turn to Islam, humbly seeking refuge. We will fight not caring whom we meet. We will fight whether we destroy ancient holdings or newly gotten gains. We have mutilated every opponent. We have driven them violently before us at the command of Allah and Islam. We will fight until our religion is established. And we will plunder them, for they must suffer disgrace.

"I can go on, but I think you get the picture. Does this sound like a peaceful, loving religion to you?" Smyth asked in all seriousness. "No! These people will *never* be peacefully assimilated into any society—no matter how much they pretend to do so. Let me paraphrase Ayatollah Ruhollah Khomeini who was responsible for the Iranian revolution. His words clearly prove my point.

" 'Islam makes it incumbent on all adult males, provided they are not disabled and incapacitated, to prepare themselves for the conquest of countries so that the writ of Islam is obeyed in every country in the world ... Those who know nothing of Islam and pretend that Islam counsels against war ... are witless. Islam says: Kill all the unbelievers just as they would kill you all! ... put them to the sword ... People cannot be made obedient except with the sword ... the key to paradise. Does all that mean that Islam is a religion that prevents men from waging war? I spit upon those foolish souls who make such a claim.'

"Khomeini's statement quotes directly from the Qur'an and gives an almost verbatim definition of the word *jihad* as it's found in the *Dictionary of Islam*, which says a jihad is:

" 'A religious war with those who are unbelievers in the mission of Muhammad. It is an incumbent religious duty, established in the Quran, and in the Traditions as a divine institution, enjoined specially for the purpose of advancing Islam and of repelling evil from Muslims.'

"We're at war with a religion more evil than any enemy we've ever faced. If we do not confront the reality of this enemy—we are *lost*," Smyth concluded.

A very troubled Governor Richards frowned and asked, "Then perhaps you can tell me Reverend, why do the Islamic governments allow this archaic behavior to continue? Surely they know such a war for global domination won't be allowed in the modern world."

Once more Morani felt compelled to clarify Smyth's remarks, "Islamic countries do not share the Western view of representative government. In most Islamic countries, the people don't participate in government. There the peoples' lives revolve around their Mosques, where they meet, discuss events, and are manipulated by the clerics. The power in any Islamic country lies with the clerics, and they answer to no one. Unfortunately for the world, Islam has neither a Pope nor a protestant equivalent."

"There must be a way to break the cycle," Richards muttered, trying to puzzle out an answer.

Smyth heard the governor's comment, and feeling once more moved of the Spirit—the urge to preach—felt obliged to pontificate, "To break the cycle, the foundation of Islam *must be altered*," he said raising his arms in a dramatic gesture. "First, education of the young must be taken away from the clerics. Religious schools teaching only the Qur'an, and the cleric's interpretation of it, must be eliminated. These schools fill their students with hate and despair. Our news media finally discovered the madrasaes in Pakistan. But they failed to make the connection with the expansive building of Saudi funded madrasaes worldwide, including here in the U.S. Clerics in many of the madrasaes, which are worse than cults, brainwash the children, and fill them with a philosophy of hate. Once the children have been programmed, it's almost impossible to deprogram them. For those who wonder if a Muslim can leave his or her religion, Muhammad answered the question by saying, 'If a Muslim discards his religion, kill him.' This, ladies and gentlemen, is the reality of what we're dealing with."

No one spoke. All were quietly contemplating what they'd heard. Many accepted truisms had been exposed as myths. A clearer picture of the enemy was emerging. Ross considered the reverend a bit too evangelical, but concluded Smyth was correct in his view of Islam. Looking around the table, he said, "Mosques appear to be the center of the problem. We must recognize them as political institutions and deal with them accordingly."

Throughout the presentation, Alexander had quietly observed his advisor's reactions. Unlike most of those present, he was well aware of the facts presented by the committee. He'd seen the face of evil first-hand and knew full well what would be required to destroy it. Now it was time to see if the others fully realized the inevitability of their circumstances. "If I understand you gentlemen correctly, we cannot peacefully co-exist with Islam. Their purpose is to force their religion on the world."

Wellington knew what the president was thinking. She had her ear to the pulse of the world and knew instinctively where Alexander had to take them. It was how they got there that she wasn't sure about. *How far is he prepared to go?* she wondered as she studied him. *I'm with you all the way.* Catching his eye, she said, "I'm convinced that has always been their goal. I remember a draft analysis that was floated, but was never finalized, in the agency several years ago. The gist of the study was that Christendom first clashed with Islam in the form of crusaders, seeking to protect Christian prigrams and free the holy land from heathen worshipers, after three centuries of Islamic conquest. Although the West has long forgotten the crusades, Islam has not. The Crusades continue to be a major hot button in Islam.

"When the Ottoman Empire began to collapse, the West was able to tolerate or ignore Islam and its intolerant fanatics. But oil, the fuel that powered World Wars I and II, changed this. Backward Muslim states were yanked into the 20th Century by Western militaries, oil exploration—and later by big oil companies operating the oil fields. The clash of civilizations re-ignited and is raging today. Enormous wealth was literally dumped into the laps of unqualified, backward, rulers in the Middle East: rulers dominated by Islamic clerics who rejected Western concepts, values, philosophy, and technology—except weapons technology. Suddenly cultures with 9th Century mentalities possessed the funds to purchase 20th Century weapons. It was equivalent to giving two rival ghetto gangs access to automatic weapons, hand grenades, explosives, and even weapons of mass destruction. Like gangs or tribes who unite in an uneasy truce to fight outsiders attempting to enter their territory, Sunnis and Shiites unite to reject Western ideals and culture. There's no room for compromise with Islamic fanatics. Usama bin Laden refers to the Western armies of liberation as crusaders—thereby pressing the hot button. Radicals called the destruction of the World Trade Towers, 'Holy Tuesday.' Now, the destruction or our cities is being called 'The Day of Islam.' "

"So," the president said, giving Wellington a knowing look, "we agree. The clash of civilizations that has been building for fourteen hundred years is upon us." Starting on his left, he slowly looked at each person seated at the table—silently demanding their concurrence or objection. One by one, each nodded his or her agreement.

Simpson, the last person to meet the president's eyes, frowned, nodded his agreement, then raised a question that had been troubling him. "Mr. President, we have a small number of patriotic Muslims in our military. So do some of our allies. Will they disavow their religion and fight fellow Muslims? How will we deal with those who won't?

Simpson's question prompted the others to look at each other in consternation. Somehow they'd all overlooked this problem. After several minutes of discussion, a plan was formulated. The religious committee would prepare a summary of their presentation for military chaplains. Muslim men and women in the military would immediately be assigned administrative duties. Chaplains would meet with each individual and present the government's position. Then each Muslim would be given time to consider his or her options: either they renounced their religion or they would receive an honorable discharge and be interned. It was not a good solution. There was no good solution.

Alexander stood to address the three guests. "This is an emotional issue for all of us. No one wants to actually do what we all know must be done. The committee has made it clear. We have no alternative. We want to thank each of you—Rabbi Steinberg, Reverend Smyth and Monsignor Morani—for your contributions to our meeting. Please keep up the good work. I want you to concentrate on how we should deal with our domestic Muslim citizens."

Turning to Richards, Alexander said, "Kurt, there is no reason for you to stay. We'll be reviewing military plans for the next couple of hours. You may leave with the clergymen. As for everyone else, now is a good time for a break. Let's reconvene in twenty minutes.

A few minutes later, Alexander returned from the restroom, sat in his chair, and stared blankly at a painting of an Indian tribe camped in front of a butte. Oblivious to the comings and goings of others around him, he was the lost in the memories of Islam's violent recent history: the holy war that destroyed Iran in 1979—mobs rampaging through the streets shouting "Allah is the greatest;" the murder of his first love, Sorour, the beautiful Iranian girl and her family, who'd been hauled before a religious court for supporting the Shah, and executed the same day; the embassy bombing in Beirut, Lebanon in April 1983, followed by the truck bombing of the Marine barracks in October—Hizbullah's first victories; the February 1993 truck bomb attack on the World Trade Center, followed by the Black Hawk Down incident in Mogadishu, Somalia the same year; the Khobar Tower's attack in Saudi Arabia, June of 1996; the 1998 American embassy bombings in Africa; the October 12, 2000 attack on the U.S.S. Cole; the 9/11 attacks that failed to convince the American public of the danger of Islam; the killing of four American civilians lured into an ambush in Fallujah, Iraq 2004—their burned, mutilated, bodies dragged through the streets, and left dangling over the road from a bridge; the televised beheadings of American civilians in Iraq; the 2005 Muslim rampage throughout Europe and the Middle East over a cartoon depiction of Muhammad; and finally Friday's attack on our five American cities.

Mentally reviewing the IFAC's report, Alexander was reaching a decision. In his mind, he recalled the most relevant quotes from the Qur'an and Ishaq's *Sira*: *"If you gain mastery of them in battle, inflict such a defeat as would terrorize them, so they would learn a lesson and be warned ... Deal so forcibly as to terrify those who would follow, that they may be warned ... Make a severe example of them by terrorizing Allah's enemies."*

The West has failed in dealing with Islam on Western term. Islam has its own rules and values. Now we must use those same rules and values to deal with them. It's the only way to make them understand. We must use force— force far beyond their own capabilities or comprehension. Shaking his head and sighing deeply, he softly muttered, "So be it!"

Shortly thereafter, the meeting reconvened and continued for another hour, during which final invasion plans were reviewed and approved, and mosques were added to target lists. When the meeting finally ended, an exhausted Alexander returned to his quarters for a much needed nap.

At 2200 hours, the president joined Simpson, Blankenship, Wellington, Young, and Clark in the war room in Building 600. Planes were in the air and the attack would soon begin. Earlier that day, Alexander had approved a special strike.

Chapter 31

Sunday

Over the Mediterranean Sea – 0230 Sunday, 4 June

Lieutenant Colonel Osburn was piloting his B-52H bomber in a racetrack pattern over the Mediterranean Sea. Suddenly his radio came to life. "Backstop 4, Arc Angel." Arc Angel was the controller in a Boeing E-3 Airborne Warning and Control System (AWAC) aircraft, monitoring activity over the Mediterranean Sea.

"Backstop-4, Arc Angel."

"Backstop-4, proceed at max speed to 32.5 N 33.5 E. Final engagement orders and target data will follow."

"Roger. Proceeding to 32.5 N 33.5 E."

"Backstop" was the call sign for nuclear-armed B-52H bombers assigned to orbit over the Mediterranean. Acting on an intelligence tip from the Russians, a U.S. satellite had located and tracked a convoy of Iranian military trucks, through the Kuhha Mountains in western Iran to the village of Khanaqin, just inside Iraq. A Dark Star unmanned aerial high altitude reconnaissance vehicle (UAV) launched from Israel, would arrive over the village in fifteen minutes. Real time analysis would determine if the convoy was transporting the Granat cruise missile.

Thirty-five minutes later, analysts were ninety percent confident the Granat cruise missile and nuclear warhead were in the village. At 0319 hours local time, 1819 hours Saturday evening in Albuquerque, the president approved the launch of one AGM-129A ALCM, Air Launched Cruise Missile, by Backstop-4. At 0341 local time, Lieutenant Colonel Frank Osburn became the first U.S. aircraft commander to launch a nuclear weapon in anger, since 1158 hours, August 9, 1945—when Major Charles Sweeney, piloting *Bockscar*, a B-29 bomber, dropped the Fat Man on the city of Nagasaki. The Fat Man weighed 10,300 pounds, with a yield of twenty-one KT. By comparison, the AGM-129A weighs 3,500 pounds, has with a range of 2,000 nautical miles, and flies at speeds up to 500 mph: its W-80 nuclear warhead was set for ground burst at 200 KT. A high yield ground burst was chosen to confuse the enemy and to maximize the probability of destroying the target.

On August 6, 1945, Japan received and ignored several warnings, before the U.S. dropped its first atomic bomb, the Little Boy, on Hiroshima. Claiming the event was a natural disaster, Japan's rulers refused to believe a bomb destroyed Hiroshima. After the second bomb blast at Nagasaki, denial was futile and Japan surrendered. Other than a two-hour notice designed to create terror and panic, America received no warning prior to the five nuclear attacks on its cities. Lieutenant Colonel Osburn and his crew felt no regrets. All had family or friends in one of the five destroyed cities. They all hoped for the opportunity to inflict more damage on the enemy. In the coming war, no quarter would be given.

At 0552, the village of Khanaqin was transformed into a large radioactive hole. Satellites recorded the event. Military sources estimated the blast to be in the 200 KT range. Two hours later NATO issued a statement, confirming the occurrence a nuclear detonation, but refusing to comment on its origin. A usually reliable source speculated it was an Iranian bomb, because the explosion matched the yield of a warhead believed to have been stolen from the Soviet Union. The stolen warhead could be adapted for use on either Iran's Granat cruise missile or its Shahab-3B or D tactical missile. The deception soon had the desired effect in Tehran.

Great Britain – 0001 Sunday, June 4th

The tumultuous roar of hundreds of jet engines shattered the peaceful night. B-52 bombers lined the taxiway at several British airfields. Nicknamed BUFFs, Big Ugly Fat Fellows, the B-52s were loaded with an assortment of bombs: 500-pound MK-82s, 750-pound M-117s, 2,000-pound MK-84s, and CBUs (cluster bomb units).

As one of the ancient giants lifted off, another began its takeoff roll. Engines screaming as it gathered speed, its drooping wings catching the wind—lifting, straightening—soon the beast would fly.

London and much of England awoke to the tumult. Windows rattled. Roofs shook. Frightened people poured outside to see what the commotion was about. Sitting on the porch of a small house in Coventry, Evelyn turned to James, her husband of sixty-four years, and said in a whisper, "I never expected to see this sight again. Not since 1944, when Bomber Smith's B-17s and Landcasters roared overhead on their way to bomb Germany, have I seen such a sight."

Putting his arm around his frail wife, the WWII pilot gazed at the huge dark shapes silhouetted against the night sky and said in awe, "They're a thousand times more powerful than my old Lancaster." James and Evelyn, the last of the "Great Generation," sat quietly watching the birth or their successors: a new generation of warriors heading off to fight in a new World War.

Like a swarm of angry birds rising to defend their nests, the cloud of dark carriers of death rose thunderously into the night sky. Elsewhere in the dark sky, other birds of prey circled silently ... waiting.

Prime Minister Chamberlain-Talbot cowered in his office.

Prince Harry, standing alone on the ramparts of Buckingham Palace, gazed at the spectacle and softly whispered, "It has begun."

Off the coast of North Africa – 0400, 4 June

Flying at 30,000 feet, four F-16C Fighting Falcons, call sign Probe, turned on their search radars and headed for Libya's coastline at 600 knots. Libyan Air and Defense Command quickly picked up the four fighters on radar, sounded alerts, and manned SAM sites. Thirty miles out from the coast, the F-16s launched two AGM-158 Joint Air-To-Surface Missiles, JASSMs, targeted on the Libya's command center and the palace once belonging to Moammar Khadafi. The missile launch elicited the desired response. Libyan SAM sites turned on their search radars. Sleepy pilots awoke. Several ran toward their fighters.

When the council of clerics assumed control, competent military commanders—those educated in the West and in disagreement with the clerics—were either shot or imprisoned. Those now in command were highly motivated followers of Islam, with no concept of what was about to descend upon them.

"Allah will guide our mighty missiles to destroy the infidel's aircraft," one shouted. Unfortunately for them, Allah forgot to tell them about Wild Weasel radar suppression operations. Oh well, some things are best learned by experience.

After missile launch, Probe flight turned back to sea and resumed their holding pattern seventy miles offshore.

Inland, Wild Weasel F-117A Nighthawk Stealth Fighters circled in lazy racetrack patterns—invisible to Libyan radar. Their flight leader, Lieutenant Colonel Robert Ledbetter, smiled as his threat receiver showed SAM targeting radars lighting off, "Owls, weapons free."

"Two." "Three." "Four."

Each pilot in Owl flight spoke his or her flight number to acknowledge their flight leader's order, and then each turned their radar-invisible, black fighter toward their designated target area.

Using the CP-1001B/C HARM Command Launch Computer (CLC)—an electronic subsystem installed on the airframe to interface with the AGM-88 HARM High-speed Anti-Radiation Missile—Ledbetter selected his targets. Then the CLC entered each target's parameters in the guidance module of a HARM, nestled inside the aircraft's weapons bay.

Developed during the Viet Nam war to replace the AGM-45 Shrike, the HARM is a fire and forget missile. Once launched, the missile requires no further guidance from the aircraft. The HARM's guidance system homes in on the microwave radiation emitted by the selected ground radar—its purpose, to disrupt or destroy the elements of an integrated air defense system. The AGM-88C's improved WAU-7/B warhead contains forty-five pounds of PBXC explosive. After launch, the supersonic missile closes on its target, and the guidance system selects optimum burst height for the warhead. When the warhead detonates, 12,845 preformed tungsten fragments produce a circular fragment pattern on the ground, similar to the pattern of shotgun blast. Ground radars, trailers, communication equipment, and personnel in the fragmentation pattern are destroyed or killed. If a surface-to-air missile is inside the fragment pattern, its explosion is spectacular.

"Weasels ready?"

"Two." "Three." "Four."

"Launch."

Lieutenant Colonel Ledbetter opened the F-117's weapons bay and began pickling off the AGM-88 missiles. Libyan radar operators couldn't believe their eyes. Numerous missiles magically appeared out of thin air on their scopes. The operators were still staring at the tracks on their scopes when the HARM warheads detonated.

"Weasels, report mission completed."

"Two." "Three." "Four."

"Roger Weasels, RTB."

In less than ten minutes, the Libyan surface-to-air defense system was rendered inoperative. Probe flight, armed with HARMs and AIM-9M Sidewinder short-range air-to-air missiles, would continue to patrol the coast, looking for any SAM radars the Weasels missed. After visiting a friendly Texaco—a KC-130 Air Force tanker—they would provide additional fighter cover for the inbound B-52s.

Similar events were occurring in Tunisia and Western Egypt.

At 0300, ships in the *Kennedy* Strike Group, steaming toward the Libyan coast, began launching BGM-109 Tomahawk Cruise missiles. The Tomahawk's, armed with CBU-97 combined effect bomblets, were targeted on Libyan military personnel compounds, equipment, and aircraft on the ground. Missile launches were timed for simultaneous attacks on army and air force bases throughout Libya.

After the F-117s concluded their attack, five highly motivated Libyan pilots managed to reach their fighters before the Tomahawks arrived. Three MIG-21s and two Su-22s raced down the runway at the Uqba ben Nafi Air Base, the former U.S. Wheelus Air Force Base, near Tripoli. With praise for Allah on their lips, the five rose into the air, intent on revenge for the infidel's attack. Turning toward the coast, they formed up to attack the F-16s loitering seventy miles offshore. Arc Angel spotted the fighters shortly after liftoff.

"Predator Lead, this is Arc Angle Three. Are you hungry?"

"Copy that Arc Angel. Predators are always hungry. What's for breakfast?" Lieutenant Colonel Carolyn Murt, flight leader of Predator Flight asked.

"Five fat pigeons lifting off from Uqba ben Nafi. Intercept vector one-seven-three."

"Roger. Predator One and Two engaging. Predator 2, one-seven-three now. Weapons free."

"Click." Major Carl Best, responded, acknowledging the order by clicking his mike.

Five minutes later, Murt, flying the lead F-22A Raptor acquired the Libyan fighters as they climbed through 25,000 feet with their search radars on. "Talley Ho."

"Click."

Search radars in the MIG-21s and Su-22s didn't show the stealthy Raptors, which passed over them, then dived from 36,000 feet, coming up behind the doomed fighters on their "six"—the position directly behind—the blind spot. "Carl, take the two on the right."

"Click"

Both pilots selected Sidewinders and opened their internal weapons bay doors. Slowly reducing speed, the two birds of prey silently closed to 2 kilometers. Murt waited until she had Sidewinder tones for each of the three MIGs, then began launching three of her AIM-9Ms. Keying her mike she said, "Fox-One, Fox-One, Fox-One," announcing the launch of three heat-seeker missiles.

Seeing the flash from his leader's first Sidewinder motor, Best immediately launched two Sidewinders, and broadcast, "Fox-One. Fox-One."

The two pilots watched the five Sidewinders slowly diverge, each tracking one of the Libyan fighters. In an instant, it was over. Murt's first Sidewinder struck a MIG on her left. Less than two seconds later, another MIG exploded in a fireball. Startled, the remaining Libyan pilots realized they were under attack, but were slow to react. Then Best's first missile caught up to one of the Su-22s. The last two explosions occurred so close together the human eye couldn't distinguish which came first.

"Arc Angel, splash five bandits," Lieutenant Colonel Carolyn Murt said with satisfaction, reporting the first kills for the new fighter.

"Roger. Five splashed. Return to patrol area."

"Roger. Lead returning to patrol area."

While Predator flight was maneuvering behind the Libyan fighter, Tomahawks caught the remaining Libyan fighters and fighter-bombers on the

ground at Uqba ben Nafi, Benghazi, al-Kufrah Oasis, Jabal al-Uwaynat, and
the al-Jufrah Army and Air Force base near Hun. The latter, being army
headquarters, received special attention. Most of the personnel at each base
were killed or wounded.

By 0700, the city of Tripoli was alive with angry Muslim men, women,
and children. The previous Sunday, Tripoli's inhabitants had danced in the
street, celebrating the destruction of the Great Satan's cities. Now they were
about to feel America's wrath. Mosques were packed, the faithful overflowing
into the streets. All were listening to sermons damning the Great Satan and
praising Allah. "Death to the Great Satan. Death to America," the throng
chanted.

Then the B-52s arrived, flying too high to be seen or heard. A wall of
explosions began at the edge of the sea and marched rapidly across the city.
Within minutes, Tripoli was reduced to rubble. Only the large Uqba ben Nafi
Air Force Base near Tripoli was spared. Soon it would again be named
Wheelus Air Force Base.

Similar, but smaller strikes were being carried out on the Libyan port
cities of Es Sider, Marsa el-Brega, Tobruk, Ras Lanuf, Zawiya, and Zuetina.

First flights of C-130 aircraft arrived at 0900. The Eighty-Second
Airborne jumped on the ports of Ras Lanuf and Zawiya, capturing refineries
at both cities. The 101st Airborne jumped on the Bu Attifel, Defa-Waha, and
El Sharara oil fields. The British Parachute Regiment captured the points-of-
origin and key stations along the Hassi Berkine, Hassi Messaoud, and In
Amenas oil pipelines. Italian Paratroopers seized the Hassi R'Mel, the point of
origin and transmission points of the natural gas pipeline running north
through Tunisia to Sicily and mainland Italy. Spanish and Portuguese troops
seized key points along the Hassi R'Mel Pedro Duran natural gas pipeline
connecting Hassi R'Mel through Morocco to Cordoba, Spain—where it ties
into the Spanish and Portuguese natural gas pipeline.

Marines from the *Kennedy* Strike Group made amphibious landings and
seized the cities of Tripoli and Tobruk, and the ports of Ras Lanuf and
Annaba. There was little resistance. The ferocity of the aerial attack had
accomplished its purpose. Stunned survivors crawled out of the rubble to find
a landscape reminiscent of Berlin and Frankfurt at the end of WWII. Fanatics
who resisted quickly met Allah. Unlike previous wars, the Americans showed
little pity for survivors. Most American fighters, and many English, Italian,
Portuguese, and Spanish troops carried photos of one of the five destroyed
American cities as reminders of whom they were fighting. Islam was
beginning to reap what it sowed. U.S. reconnaissance aircraft followed the
bombers; however, satellites had already provided evidence of the destruction.
Footage of the destruction would be available for the evening newscasts in the

U.S.

The next day engineers arrived and quickly restored Wheelus Air Force Base to operational status. Soon F-16C Falcons and A-10 Thunderbolts, affectionately nicknamed the "Warthog," would be patrolling the pipelines. Engineers were also restoring other Libyan Air Force bases. Libyan military units that did not immediately surrender were destroyed. Opposition was squashed. Attacks on the pipelines or oil fields resulted in the immediate destruction of all possible points of origin of the attackers. Mosques were being destroyed, Qur'ans burned. All forms of Islam were banned.

Bombings would continue for the next several days. The cities of Algiers, Annaba, Oran, Arzew, and Skikda would be bombed, followed by Tunis and La Skhirra in Tunisia.

By the end of the week, the northern coasts of Algeria, Libya, and Tunisia were conquered. Supply ships headed for the harbors.

Troop ships from Spain and Italy departed for North Africa. Remaining U.S. Armored and Infantry Divisions in Germany were embarking for North Africa. Ships carrying munitions, supplies, and troops also departed from the U.S. and Europe for Algeria and Libya.

Oil and natural gas production was quickly restored and distributed among the participants. The buildup of forces for the conquest of the Middle East had begun.

The Caliph's Palace, Tehran, Iran – 6 a.m., Sunday, June 4th

Once again, the terrified servant entered the caliph's bedchamber and wondered, *How should I go about awakening him this time?* Approaching the bed, he found his master, caliph Saladin II, sound asleep. His two young companions lay next to him. The terrified servant stood by the bed and anxiously called out, "Excellency … Excellency, your presence is requested by the *Shura* and your generals." After three attempts, the caliph stirred.

Saladin woke in a stupor from a deep sleep. *What does this fool want now?*

The servant immediately prostrated himself on the floor and said in a quaking voice, "Excellency, your presence is requested by the *Shura*. I was instructed to tell you it is an urgent matter. I have laid out your clothes. I will assist you in dressing."

Forty minutes later, Saladin entered the conference room. Taking his place at the head of the table, he barked, "Report," at the three generals, who were standing at attention and visibly shaking.

"May Allah b–bless you, oh, Great Caliph," the army general stammered. "Two hours ago we received word of a nuclear explosion near the village of Khanaqin."

"Where is Khanaqin?" a startled caliph asked. *What the hell? A nuclear explosion. If it was the Americans, the explosion would have occurred here.*

"Praise Allah. Khanaqin is a village just across the border in Iraq."

Khomeini sat in silence, allowing his protégé to conduct the interrogation. He too was worried, but had not yet grasped the significance of the report being picked out of the terrified general. *Something is wrong. Why else would the man be so frightened?*

"How could a nuclear explosion occur in a border village? What could be there to cause such an explosion? Why would one of our enemies use a nuclear bomb on a remote village?" the caliph snarled as he hurled questions at the general. "Get on with it. There is more to this. What's the rest of it?"

"Oh, Great Caliph," the general said, his body trembling, "our Granat missile was in the village. News reports say it was a t–two hundred kiloton d–detonation," the general stammered. "Our missile has a t–two hundred kiloton warhead."

Shocked and angry, Khomeini jerked upright in his chair and blurted out, "Are you telling us our *warhead exploded?*" his voice a half octave higher than normal.

May Allah have mercy on me, the general prayed, and bowing to the supreme cleric of the Islamic Empire, attempted to compose himself before continuing. "Praise be to Allah. Excellence, the reported y–yield matches the yield of our warhead. I can see no other explanation."

"How could this happen?" a cleric loudly demanded, then added as an afterthought, "Allah be praised."

Blinking his eyes, and looking at his fellow officers for support, the general replied, "I ... w–we, do not know."

"We must punish those responsible. Allah demands it," another cleric shouted, standing and waving his hands.

"That will be very difficult to do," Saladin said, sneering at the cleric, "since they are now in Allah's hands. As to what caused the warhead to detonate—most likely it was carelessness." Then locking eyes with the standing cleric, he sarcastically asked, "Wasn't it *you* who demanded we speed up the movement of the missile? Haste causes mistakes. Tired men make errors. We can't admit any knowledge of this. After all, we *have* no nuclear weapons ... *do we?*" he hissed through clenched teeth, glaring in disgust at the cleric. *If it was the cursed Americans, they must have known about the missile and attacked it. Could a bomb or missile cause the warhead to detonate? So much I don't know. Damn, I need Ralph. I must find him.*

The meeting was interrupted by a report of the first attacks on Tripoli. Two missiles had struck the command center and Gadhafi's palace. Surface-to-air missile batteries were searching for attackers.

"Damn," The air force general muttered, so softly only the other two generals could hear. "The American's are baiting the fools to turn on their radars. If they do, Wild Weasel aircraft will destroy their radars and control systems." A sudden though occurred to the general, *I wonder if they destroyed the Granat missile?*

While Grand Ayatollah Khomeini and the other clerics turned to Allah for guidance, Saladin wondered if anything else could go wrong. He would soon find out.

Garbled reports trickled in from Libya. The scope of the debacle would not be known until President Alexander's announcement later in the day.

Chapter 32

Starting with early morning reports of large numbers of bombers taking off in England, sketchy news flashes pertaining to military actions were broadcast throughout the U.S. and Europe. From 5:00 a.m. on, the airwaves were filled with speculations and sage comments from "experts." No one really knew what was going on.

At 12:35 p.m. mountain time, special announcement banners flashed on TV screens. Radio programs were interrupted. The President of the United States would be making an announcement at one o'clock.

At precisely 12:59, General Ross appeared on both TV and radio, where he announced, "Ladies and gentlemen, George Alexander, the President of the United States." The president walked to the podium in the same auditorium where previous announcements had been made. Flanking him on either side were SecWar Simpson and SecState Keese. All were dressed in open collar, short-sleeved, dress shirts. All looked tired. When the camera's red light appeared, the president began.

"Fellow citizens, today the United States and its allies took decisive action against the Islamic Empire. The same Islamic Empire claiming responsibility for attacking us and disrupting the world's oil supply." The president paused, staring directly at camera.

"At 8:00 p.m. last night, four o'clock this morning in the Mediterranean, United States forces began an attack on Libya. F-117 fighters eliminated air defenses. Five Libyan fighters were destroyed by our new F-22A Raptors. Ground targets were then attacked by Tomahawk cruise missiles, launched from the *Kennedy* Strike Group.

"At 11:30 p.m., 7:30 a.m. in the Mediterranean, B-52 bombers began attacks on Tripoli and other cities along the North African coast. After the bombers departed, airborne troops from Great Britain, Italy, and the U.S. captured oil fields, pipelines and refineries in Libya and Algeria. Spanish and Portuguese troops secured the natural gas pipeline providing gas to Spain and Portugal.

"U.S. Marines from the *Kennedy* Strike Group landed and captured Tripoli and other cities on the Libyan coast.

"We now control the area and its oil fields, refineries, and pipelines.

"Losses were minimal. Mechanical problems forced two B-52s to make emergency landings." The president paused, then continued with a stern expression.

"You are about to see aerial photographs of Tripoli. Before you do, I want to make something clear. Since the Korean Conflict, America and most of Europe has been fixated on avoiding collateral damage. As a result, our militaries have been unrealistically expected to selectively destroy the enemy, without causing any civilian deaths or property damage. A stupid notion: allowing our enemy—the terrorists—to find sanctuary in crowds, behind women and children, and in mosques ... resulting in the *needless deaths* of our military personnel," the president concluded with a scowl, fury evident in his voice.

Placing both hands on the podium, he leaned forward scowling into the camera lens. "The purpose of war is to impose your will on others ... or to prevent others from imposing their will on you. Wars are won by destroying the enemy's *will* and *ability* to fight," Alexander thundered with a determined look, raising his right fist and gesturing to emphasize his words. "At the end of WWII, the losers knew they'd been defeated. Their cities lay in ruin."

Pausing, Alexander removed his hands from the podium, stood erect, and continued. "When President Harry S. Truman signed the Korean armistice, the North had lost their ability to fight, but not their *will* to fight. We've allowed them to rebuild their ability to fight.

"One of our nation's greatest military leaders, General of the Army Douglas MacArthur, disagreed with Truman on how to prosecute the Korean Conflict, and Truman fired him. General MacArthur offered the nation one final piece of advice regarding war. In his farewell address to Congress on April 19, 1951, he said, and I quote, 'But once war is forced upon us, there is no other alternative than to apply every available means to bring it to a swift end. War's very object is victory, not prolonged indecision. In war there is no substitute for victory.' " Alexander paused, let his gaze sweep the reporters, and then looked directly toward the cameras. "We've forgotten his words, and paid the price for doing so."

Placing his hands back on the podium, Alexander leaned forward, still staring at the TV cameras. "At the end of the first Gulf War, Saddam Hussein lost most of his ability to fight, but not his will to fight, resulting in the second invasion of Iraq. *Again*, we did not destroy the enemy's will to fight. President Rodman decided to abandon President Bush's plans and withdrew most of our forces, including the Fifth Fleet, from the Middle East. The result was a civil war between the Sunni and Shi'ites. Now Iraq has joined our enemy—the Islamic Empire."

Still leaning into the podium, Alexander straightened his arms, squared his shoulders, and said with a stern expression, "This war *will not be left* half-finished. The enemy—who we're still attempting to define—appears to be a religion rather than a nation. This time the enemy's will to fight will be crushed and its ability to fight destroyed." The president continued to stare into the cameras for several seconds, then stood erect and concluded his remarks.

"The pictures you are about to see are shocking. So are the pictures of Atlanta, Boston, Chicago, New York, and Washington.

"The survivors of Tripoli now know defeat. It is for them to reconcile events with Allah's will.

"Good afternoon, and God bless America."

The scene faded and was replaced with pictures taken from an airplane. The coastline flashed by, then the smoldering ruins of what remained of Tripoli. Across America, most citizens regretted it had come to this, but there was little remorse.

After his address, Alexander returned to his office and left instructions he was not to be disturbed. Closing the door, he walked to the window and gazed at Sandia Crest. Several minutes later, he walked to the large map showing North Africa and Saudi Arabia. When he finished studying the map, he returned to his desk, pressed the intercom, and requested a document. Five minutes later, a courier arrived with the document in a locked briefcase. The president signed for the document and asked the courier to wait.

Sitting at his desk, Alexander removed the document from its envelope. The cover displayed a red striped border and the legend "TOP SECRET" printed in red, and Restricted Data printed underneath in black letters. Settling back in his chair, he began scrutinizing the Enduring Stockpile list—the list of nuclear and thermonuclear weapons remaining in the national stockpile. Smiling, he found what he was seeking, and then scribbled a note to himself, "6 B-53s." Walking to the outer office, he returned the document to the courier, poured a mug of coffee, and returned to gaze out his office window. After a few minutes, he returned to his desk, consulted a phone list, and called Reverend Smyth. "Good afternoon, reverend. Can you come to my office for a chat?"

"Certainly, Mr. President."

"Good. I have an idea for a special sermon. Please don't discuss this with anyone."

Reaction to the Libyan attack – Sunday, June 4th

Detroit, Michigan

Colonel Gordi Williams sat perched on a stool in the Pontiac Sports Bar, enjoying a Bud with the usual Sunday crowd. The game they'd been watching was interrupted by the president's announcement. "Hot damn! 'Bout time we stomped on them rag-heads," Gordi loudly announced, beer suds clinging to the stubble on his upper lip. "Boy, I like this Alexander. He don't fuck around. He's got his shit together. We got ourselves a president with brass balls ... 'bout time, too," he told the bartender.

"Yeah," agreed the bearded man sitting two stools down. "I sure 'preciate the way he grabbed them A'rabs money. I like t' lost my job. The Prez knows how to take care of us working stiffs. He's got my vote."

"Hell yes," the bartender chimed in. "I hope he don't stop—hope he mows down ever' last one of them sand monkeys. I've had it up to here," he said with his hand raised over his head, "with them fat, shitty A'rabs."

Spinning around on his stool to face the crowed bar room, Gordi yelled, "What d' you guys think? We got a Prez with balls or what?"

"Hell yes!" came the shouted response.

Memphis, Tennessee

Three generations of the Waltman family quietly mingled with fellow church members in the church annex, waiting their turn at the buffet table. On any other Sunday, the room would be filled with the happy sounds of cheerful chatter. Not so today. No, today, the large meeting room was filled with hushed conversations between worried looking adults. The preacher's sermon had been somber. Taken from the Old Testament, it centered around an "eye for and eye." A few mothers seemed to be holding their little ones a bit tighter than normal.

A deacon interrupted the murmuring congregation with an announcement over the PA system. The president was about to make an important announcement on TV. A hush fell over the crowded room, when the annex's large projection screen TV came to life. Even the children were quiet: they sensed something important was happening. Ladies working in the kitchen abandoned their chores to join others watching the TV in the meeting room. All eyes focused on the large screen, throughout the president's announcement and the subsequent scenes showing America's military operations.

For several seconds after film clips depicting air strikes on Libya ended, the room remained silent. No one moved—not even the children. Everyone stared at the TV screen, shocked by how much damage had been inflicted in such a short amount of time; yet knowing it had to be done, and that more would follow. The voice of the shaken commentator broke the spell. "Well, as you have just seen, the president has begun using our military might to defend our country. Libya can't supply all of the oil we need, but it's a start. I was heartened to see the British, Italians, Portuguese and Spanish in there helping us." The newsman paused for a moment to look down at a sheet of paper handed to him by someone off-camera. When he looked up at the camera his eyes were filled with tears. Swallowing hard and holding the sheet of paper up before him, he said with a slight tremor in his voice, "I have just received the latest casualty figures from the attacks on our five cities. Over ten million of our people are either dead or missing." The announcer paused to gain control of his emotions, then continued with a heavy sigh, "Ladies and gentlemen ... we *must* destroy the people who did this to us."

Those watching in the church's annex sat in stunned silence. No one disagreed with the announcer. Slowly the room came to life, and discussion centered on the president's actions. Most agreed with him, but a few failed to grasp the situation—saying we needed to do "this" or "that" to become less dependent on oil. All but one approved of seizing Islamic assets. The lone dissenter, a well-to-do widow with no children, argued about the law and morality. When asked how she thought the economy could survive without oil to move goods, and money to pay for food and services, she replied with a blank look, "What on earth could affect our great country's economy. I'm certain our friends in Saudi Arabia will make sure we get plenty of oil."

The man who asked the question shook his head, turned, and walked away—followed by others who'd been listening to the conversation.

Perplexed, the lady said to their backs, "Well, for heavens sake ... won't they?"

Similar scenes took place throughout the country. Of course, there were idealists who lived in their fantasy worlds and took freedom of speech to the extreme—and those who'd had enough of them.

Seattle, Washington

Diners filled most tables in the main dining room of the Fairmont hotel. When the hotel manager heard the president would make an announcement at noon, he alerted the dining room staff. The dining room's large screen projection TV was turned on, and everyone watched quietly. After the commentator announced the casualty figures from America's five cities, conversation erupted around the room.

Most diners commented quietly and favorably on the president's actions, however, a loudmouthed party of eight at a circular table became boisterous. A bombastic, baldheaded man wearing an Al Gore, "Stop Global Warming," necktie, leaned back in his chair and looked around at other diners seated nearby, "This is outrageous," he said in a loud voice. "Our warmongering, imperialistic, imposter president is grabbing control of the world's oil supply.

Now the world will really hate us." Turning back to his seven companions, the bald man continued carping about how Alexander had stolen the Arab's money and intended to turn the country into a police state. Several more inflammatory statements followed, drawing hoots of agreement from others at his table.

An obese woman sitting to the right of the bald, loudmouth, stopped slurping her soup and gorging on buttered rolls. Brushing back her mop of wiry hair with her left hand, she raised her right arm and began bad-mouthing the president. With her flabby arm waving over her head, she punctuated every point of her rambling tirade by stabbing the air with the half-eaten roll in her right hand. Alexander was a power crazed general who stole the presidency. Alexander attacked a peaceful Islamic nation. Collateral damage caused by his military actions had killed thousands of innocent people. As her tirade wore on, she became more and more venomous. Finally, she looked around the room and said loud enough for everyone—including the kitchen staff—to hear, "Alexander is a disgrace to our country. He's a child killer, a murderer who should be impeached and imprisoned."

A man in his fifties, sitting alone five tables away, had had enough. After neatly folding his napkin and calmly laying it on the table by his half-eaten meal, he clenched his teeth, lowered his head, and pushed away from the table. Slowly standing, he squared his shoulders and walked over to the round table full of whining wimps. Coming up behind the fat woman, who continued lambasting the president, he grabbed two handfuls of her hair and drove her face down into her bowl of bouillabaisse. Still holding her by the hair, he repeated the action several times, finally breaking the bowl with her head. Then jerking her head back one last time, he snarled, "My wife and family died in the Chicago blast. Get out of here, you liberal bitch before I kill you." Letting go of the woman's hair, he glared at the others seated around the table. Pointing to the exit door, he growled menacingly, "That goes for all the rest of you traitors."

Shouts of agreement and applause erupted from around the dining room.

The Caliph's Palace, Tehran, Iran – Sunday, 11:50 a.m. June 4th

At first the palace had been besieged with reports from Libya, Algeria, and Tunis. Word of the attacks on the Empire's forces, by air and by sea, continued flowing in throughout the morning. By late morning, reports had slowed to a trickle and by noon, they'd completely stopped. The *Shura* did not believe the first reports of walls of explosions marching through the cities. But then came the desperate pleas for help, and finally the pathetic laments, "Allah has forsaken us."

"We must slaughter the crusaders! Put them to the sword! Call down

Allah's wrath!" *Shura* members shouted. Summoning the generals, the enraged clerics demanded the crusaders be thrown into the sea. Those responsible for allowing Libya and Algeria to fall into infidel hands must to be punished. The "I command, therefore it is" philosophy held full sway. None of the military men argued, for to do so meant death. All began plotting their individual plans for escape and wondering—would the Americans allow them to surrender?

Realizing the *Shura* must be placated, Grand Ayatollah Khomeini instructed General Aghajari to arm a second Shahab-3D with the last nuclear warhead, and use it to destroy the crusaders in Libya.

"May Allah bless you, Grand Ayatollah. The Shahab-3D doesn't have sufficient range to reach Libya," Aghajari replied.

Khomeini scowled while the usual hyper, shrill-voiced cleric screamed at the general.

Saladin sneered at the hysterical cleric. *Time to assert myself and put these ignorant fools in their place.* "Praise be to Allah. Our experimental missile, the Kosar, can carry our nuclear warhead. It *can* reach Tripoli."

Khomeini cut his sharp eyes at Saladin, then looked at the general, who nodded his agreement. Smiling with newfound respect for Saladin, Khomeini looked at the generals and said, "Praise be to Allah. He has provided us the means to carry out his will. Arm the Kosar with our last nuclear warhead."

Saladin, wondering why their missile exploded, frowned and voiced his concern, "We had four warheads. One, in transit to Syria, exploded. We don't know why. Are they defective? If they are, will they explode when the missile is launched? We require answers."

"Oh, Great Caliph," the other general replied. *Maybe he isn't such a fool after all.* "A team is on the way to Khanaqin and will arrive late tonight. We may receive a report tomorrow."

"Have them bring the pieces of the bomb back for analysis," the shrill-voiced cleric demanded.

Has the man no concept of what a two hundred kiloton blast is like? Bring back the pieces! The fool is thinking about one of his car bombs, the general thought before replying, "As you command, Excellency."

Ningbo, China – 1230 Sunday, 4 June

Admiral Cheung was in the Eastern Fleet's headquarters: his purpose—to review final plans for the invasion of Taiwan. The admiral and the Eastern Fleet's commander sat watching BBC reports of the attack on Libya. Cheung was surprised at the attack's ferocity. *The Americans have not mounted an attack like this since WWII. Their 'shock and awe' attacks in Iraq were mostly show. They were too concerned about civilian casualties. Not this time. I may have underestimated their new leader. Perhaps I should delay the invasion of Taiwan, until I get a better feel for him.*

Addressing the Eastern Fleet's commander, Chung noted, "I don't think we are ready. Prepare a practice landing on one of the smaller islands. I will be back in two weeks to review your progress."

On his return trip to Beijing, Cheung mulled over his options. *I need to test Alexander's resolve. Kim Jung-il is the perfect foil to use. The crazy little bastard is fool enough to launch an attack on the south. All I have to do is goad him into doing so.*

Ensenada, Argentina – Guesthouse, Sunday, June 4th

Problems with their satellite receiver solved, Ralph and Nancy were watching a rebroadcast of the president's announcement and pictures of Tripoli. The news was full of videos and photos of the attack. They showed a demoralized, cowed populous. The men were shown cleaning up the rubble, while women and children set up housekeeping in tents in hastily prepared compounds. "None of the women are wearing veils or head scarves. Interesting," Ralph noted.

"Yes. I wonder how the women will like their freedom?"

"They won't. They've been raised believing men are superior. I doubt they'll be able to accept equality. Sad, isn't it?"

"Don't you think the educated women will?" Nancy asked.

"Perhaps, but how many educated women do you think there are in Algeria or Libya?"

Nancy watched the TV for several minutes, before asking, "Ralph, do you think the war is about over?"

"No, hon. It has just begun," *And I caused it. What have I done?*

Behold, an Ashen Horse!

And he who sat on it had the name Death.
– Revelations 6:8

Part III

An Ashen Horse

Chapter 33

Embassy residents awoke to news of the attack on Libya. There was no Kremlin condemnation, and the Russian media reported the event in a matter-of-fact manner. George Landry and Teresa Lopez were eating breakfast in the embassy dining room. The room was abuzz with speculation about the attack, and Russia's apparent acceptance of it. George and Teresa refrained from commenting.

When asked for their thoughts, Teresa dodged the question and spoke of their successful shopping trip. Both she and Landry had purchased Russian Karakul wool hats as souvenirs. While Teresa was extolling the softness of the wool to an embassy staff member, Landry was handed a message requesting their appearance at the Kremlin.

"I purchased one for a friend in New Mexico. He tells me the winters can be bitterly cold there," Teresa was saying when Landry handed her the folded slip of paper.

"Please excuse us, we've an urgent matter to attend to," Landry told the others at their table. Teresa quickly read the message, said her goodbyes, and rose to follow Landry from the dining room. "Teresa, we're to be there by 1:00 p.m. Best inform Kirkland and see if they have any up-dates for us before the meeting," Landry told her as they walked toward the communication center.

Later, a very excited Teresa began dressing for the forthcoming meeting. She and Landry were rested and recovered from their initial jet lag, and both were anxious to get on with their investigation. Everything seemed to be happening so quickly. She was having the most wonderful experience of her life, and was about to begin a fascinating adventure.

Standing before the full-length mirror in her dressing room—she and Landry were now in VIP quarters—Teresa reviewed her first meeting with Karpov. *I was tired, a little disheveled, and certainly did not look my best. Today will be different.* Today she was determined to make a good impression. The fawn color of her pantsuit's fitted, fingertip jacket, worn over a cream-colored silk shirt, was a stunning complement to her tawny Latin complexion. Today she chose not to put her hair in a bun. Instead she brushed it back from her face and held it in place with a tortoise-shell hair band. Shiny and somewhat wavy, her brunette locks hung softly behind her ears, barely touching her shoulders—a perfect frame for her lovely features. Never wearing more than the simplest of make up, today she added a touch more blush to her cheeks, and a bit of tinted gloss to her lips. Her dark brown eyes and thick eyelashes needed nothing to enhance their beauty. Simple gold earrings, a matching pin, and medium-heel, brown, kid pumps accessorized her outfit.

"You'll do ... and nicely I think," she said to her reflection in the mirror, then added a puff of Elizabeth Arden's 'Green Tea,' cologne to her wrists before leaving to meet Landry for an early lunch.

When they arrived at Karpov's office, the president greeted them warmly. "Thank you for coming. I hope you have enjoyed our city," he said with a smile, admiring Teresa's stunning appearance. Turning, he led them to the large conference table in his spacious office. "You have already met Directors Vladimir Melnikov and Boris Popov. This is Major Yuri Vanin. He is with our FSB and has an assignment similar to yours, Agent Lopez. Major Vanin reports directly to Director Melnikov and me. President Alexander and I are depending upon you three to help us find the answers to our mutual problem."

Landry and Lopez shook hands with the three men. Teresa appraised the well-built, six-foot plus, blonde, major with sparkling blue eyes. *Madre de Dios, he's handsome,* she sighed and said, "I'm pleased to meet you, Major."

"It is entirely my pleasure," Vanin replied with a smile, admiring the attractive FBI agent. *Zdorava! Great. She's beautiful. This is one American agent I'm really going to enjoy keeping an eye on.* "It is also my pleasure to meet you, Doctor Landry." Vanin, who spoke excellent English with a slight British accent attributable to his tour in the London Embassy, would provide translations when required.

After everyone was seated at the table, President Karpov said, "Our preliminary investigation found no indication of an early Soviet gun-type weapons development program. This doesn't mean there wasn't one. Lavrenti Beria was in charge of the program, and he kept his secrets close. I've ordered an audit of the production of enriched uranium before 1953. The inventory will also be audited."

"The audit will take time," Boris Popov said, picking up the discussion. "Archives are being searched for production and shipping records. The only source of enriched uranium was the Urals Electrochemical Combine, located in the city of Novouralsk, sixty-seven kilometers northwest of Yekaterinburg. In the forties and fifties it was known as Sverdlovsk-44, one of our ten secret cities. While we await the records, you must begin your investigation in another secret city, Arzamas-16, which is now known as Sarov. It's our equivalent of your Los Alamos."

"*Da*." Melnikov added. "Major Vanin will escort you there tomorrow. We will use your embassy's airplane if it is available."

"Yes, sir. The airplane is available. Will security be a problem?" Landry inquired.

President Karpov answered. "I have given orders to provide you with any information pertaining to your investigation. If there is a problem, Major Vanin has authority to grant clearance. If it becomes too sensitive, the major can contact one of the three of us. There will be no interference or unnecessary delays. Are there any questions?"

There being none, the president escorted Lopez, Landry, and Vanin to the door.

"When you find important facts, please return and brief us. Access to data pertaining to this investigation is limited to those of us in this meeting, and Director Chusov in Sarov. And of course those persons President Alexander has cleared in the United States. Thank you for coming."

"Yes, Mr. President," Teresa said. "Thank you for your cooperation and hospitality."

Major Vanin walked with them to the embassy limo. "Agent Lopez, " he said, then added with a smile, "it will be necessary for me to speak with your pilot—to establish a flight plan, and then obtain clearance to land at Sarov. Your aircraft is located at Domodedovo airport, is it not? I suggest we plan to depart at 7:30 a.m. The flight should take an hour and a half. I will arrange for hotel rooms. A car and driver will be assigned to us."

Smiling and looking up at the handsome Russian, Teresa extended her hand and said, "Why thank you, Major. Why don't you come with us to the embassy? I will call the ambassador's office and arrange for our pilot to meet with you when we arrive."

"*Da*, yes, I accept your offer. I will come with you," Vanin replied, pleased at the thought of getting better acquainted with the Latin beauty with the flashing brown eyes. *I would love to run my hands through her lovely hair*. Continuing to hold her soft hand, he wondered as the driver opened the limo door. *She smells of ... I don't quite recognize fragrance ... fresh, clean ... lovely*. Reluctantly releasing her hand, he helped her into the limo, and reached a decidedly pleasant conclusion, *This, I think, promises to be a very ... very exciting investigation*.

Special Agent David Tuttle, the FBI Legal Attaché, or Legat, was decidedly unhappy to learn of the major's unexpected visit. He was meeting with the CIA Station chief, Paul Eckard, when Lopez's call was transferred to him. After approving Vanin's visit he said, "Paul, I'm going to have to speak with Agent Lopez. She has to understand her place. She has no business inviting a Russian FSB officer into the embassy without first clearing it with me. Hell, *she* hasn't even reported to me. I have no idea what she's up to."

"David, I suggest you leave her alone. No one knows why she and this Doctor Landry are here. However, they have met with President Karpov twice. Apparently they have a lot of horsepower."

Looking over his half-glasses, Tuttle asked, "What do you know that I don't?"

"Probably nothing. Director Wellington called me before they arrived. She told me to cooperate with them—and not to ask questions. She implied they were on a secret presidential mission." Then Eckard started laughing. "I heard McGill didn't waste any time stepping on their toes. Now he's in Albuquerque and may not return." Normally very low key, Eckard started laughing and couldn't stop—for he truly despised Ambassador McGill.

Tuttle, who also had no love for McGill, thought it was funny—but not that funny. Finally, Eckard regained control. Still grinning, he said, "I guess you don't know McGill called Secretary Keese and woke him at one thirty in the morning to bitch about not being invited to the first meeting with Karpov." Eckard started laughing again, and finally blurted out the rest of the story between laughs. "It seems our new SecState wasn't real happy about being awakened. Not to mention having to listen to McGill bitch about Lopez and Landry violating his 'no spooks in *his* embassy' policy. First SecState told him it wasn't his embassy. It was the president's embassy. Then he ordered him to place his car and airplane at their disposal. Finally, SecState ordered McGill to go to the airport, get on the plane that brought Landry and Lopez, fly to Albuquerque, and report to him as soon as the plane arrived. I'll be surprised if he comes back." Eckard paused to wipe tears from his eyes. Then, still laughing, he continued, "You had to hear the conversation to appreciate it."

Now Tuttle started laughing. Finally, he said with a sly grin, "How did you get to hear the conversation?"

Eckard stopped laughing long enough to reply with an innocent expression, "Did I say I heard the conversation? Oh dear, I must have misspoken."

Two hours later, the flight to Sarov was arranged. Teresa walked Major Vanin to the embassy's main entrance. "Well, Major, I'll meet you at the hanger in the morning."

Smiling, Vanin replied, "Would you honor me with the pleasure of your company for dinner this evening?

Teresa looked up with a smile and responded without hesitation, "Why, thank you, Major, I would be delighted to join you."

"*Zdorava!* Great! I'll pick you up at 7:00 p.m. *Da svidaniya*, Goodbye," Vanin told her, turned, and walked briskly to his waiting car.

Domodedovo Airport – Tuesday, June 6th

Landry and Lopez arrived at the Domodedovo Airport at 7:12 a.m. The flight crew for the Gulfstream-IV was preparing the aircraft. Major Vanin was waiting for them in the lounge. Teresa and Yury—they were on a first name basis now—greeted each other with warm smiles. The pilot, Hector Denota, entered and walked up to the group. "Good, everyone is here. Is this all of your luggage?" he asked, pointing to three suitcases placed near the door.

"Yes, that's all of it," Teresa replied with a warm smile.

Denota turned to Major Vanin and said, "Flight operations couldn't believe we have clearance to land at the government airport in Sarov. When I filed my flight plan, they called to confirm. I guess we're the first U.S. aircraft to land there."

Vanin smiled. *No, not the first.* Addressing the pilot he said, "Unfortunately, Sarov is still a closed city. Your's and the flight crew's movements will be restricted. Rooms have been reserved for all of us at the Avangard, probably the best hotel in Sarov. You can take your meals at the House of Scientists near the hotel. A tour of the city can be arranged if we have to remain for any length of time. If you leave the hotel area, you must be escorted by security personnel."

During the flight, Vanin provided a history of the early Soviet atomic bomb program. "Stalin formed an atomic bomb development group in 1942. He named a relatively young and unknown scientist, Igor Kurchatov, to lead it.

"Reports of American and British progress spurred Stalin to increase funding for the atomic bomb project. Laboratory No. 2 was established on the outskirts of Moscow in 1943, and Igor Kurchatov was appointed Director. Laboratory No. 2 became LIPAN, then the Kurchatov Institute of Atomic Energy, and is now the Russian Research Center.

"As the progress and importance of the atomic bomb program grew, a political leader was required. Stalin appointed Lavrenti Beria to head the program, which by then was known as the First Main Directorate. Later it became the Ministry of Medium Machine Building.

"Lavrenti Beria was a cruel and feared man. In fact, he was considered the second most feared man in the Soviet Union—second only to Stalin. Only Stalin could question his actions. So, the records will say what Beria wanted them to say."

Smiling, Vanin continued, "Our research was less costly than yours. We were receiving *unauthorized* assistance from some British and American scientists—you called them spies. We knew two types of atomic bombs were being developed at Los Alamos—a plutonium bomb and a uranium bomb.

Our ability to keep secrets was much better than yours or the British. Stalin or Beria, perhaps both, conceived of the idea of secret cities." Noticing Teresa's confused expression, he added, "Yes, truly secret cities. Their names were removed from all maps, directories, and documents. In other words, they ceased to exist. Workers and their families were restricted to the city's boundaries. Mail was delivered to and sent from different locations.

"Stalin and Beria knew about America's July 16th atomic bomb test in New Mexico. But, I don't think they understood its power. After Hiroshima and Nagasaki our program became a top priority. By then the party chiefs understood the importance of producing plutonim-239 and uranium-235. In November 1945, construction began on our plutonium production facility in the Urals—the Mayak Production Association. This facility became another secret city, Chelyabinsk-65. Our first Plutonium-239 was produced in 1948."

Vanin looked at Landry, who nodded agreement, for he was familiar with the Soviet history. Teresa sat listening in rapt attention. She was learning information that wasn't in any of the history books she'd studied.

Vanin continued his story. "In the United States, the Manhattan Project built the Hanford Reactor Works to produce plutonium for your bombs. I believe it covered 600 square miles.

"Separating the fissionable isotope in uranium proved to be a major challenge. Uranium is extracted at the mines and shipped as uranium oxide—commonly called yellow cake. Uranium has several isotopes—atoms with the same number of protons, but different number of neutrons. The fissionable isotope of uranium required for a nuclear bomb has a total of 235 neutrons and protons in its nucleus and is referred to as uranium-235. Yellow cake uranium contains seven tenths of one percent of the uranium-235 isotope."

Landry noticed Teresa's confused expression and tried another approach. "Teresa, think of a Ford automobile dealership. All the automobiles in the showroom are Fords, but the models are different. One is a sports car, another a sedan, still another is a truck. Only the truck is suitable for hauling heavy loads. Isotopes of an element are much the same. One isotope of uranium is suitable for making a bomb, while the others are not."

After thinking about Landry's explanation, Teresa nodded and said, "Thanks George, now I get it."

Landry smiled and continued, "To extract the uranium-235 isotope, the yellow cake is converted to uranium hexafluoride, a highly corrosive gas, which is pumped into a chamber under pressure. A membrane filter is placed on one wall of the chamber. Holes in the filter are so small only a molecule of uranium-235 hexafluoride can pass through. Some of the molecules of uranium-236, or uranium-238, would also pass through the filter, the rest remained in the chamber. To obtain uranium-235 with a purity of ninety percent or greater, thousands of chambers, one after the other, are required.

The arrangement is called a cascade. The Manhattan Project's gaseous diffusion facility built at Oak Ridge, Tennessee was a U shaped building, measuring over a mile in length. During construction, the workers referred to it as the 'Orange Juice' plant. Until the late 1990s, it was the largest processing building in the world."

"Interesting," Vanin said and resumed his narrative, "Construction of our first gaseous diffusion plant also began in 1945. It was located in the Urals at Verkh-Neyvinsk, some fifty kilometers from Yekaterinburg. It became the secret city Sverdlovsk-44." Vanin chuckled then said with a smile, "Well it's not secret any more, but it's still a closed city. All uranium-235 used in what you call Joe-4—our designation is RDS-6—came from Sverdlovsk-44. Depending upon the results of the audits, we may also have to visit there."

Teresa continued to be enthralled with the history being revealed to her. She suddenly realized she knew almost nothing about the Manhattan Project. What she did know she learned during her two-hour visit to the Atomic Museum. Turning to Landry she said, "George, you are going to have to tell me more about the Manhattan Project. It was not covered in high school or college history."

Landry smiled. "Unfortunately, Teresa, that's a sad fact. Our bleeding hearts seized upon the pathos associated with the atomic destruction of two Japanese cities and succeeded in placing the whole country on a terrible guilt trip." *My God, I'm beginning to sound like a conservative!* The thought caused him to pause before continuing. "The Manhattan Project was the greatest scientific, engineering, and manufacturing effort in the history of mankind. It redefined America and created the world's first superpower. We built cities to house workers for facilities not yet designed. The largest electrical generating plant in the country, TVA's Norris Dam, was built at Oak Ridge to power the K-25 gaseous diffusion plant—before the technology was fully developed. As Major Vanin said, we acquired 600 square miles to build nuclear reactors used to convert unanium-238 to plutonium-239—before a self-sustaining nuclear reaction was achieved. The scientific developments achieved by the Manhattan Project were the impetus that made America the technological leader of the free world. Now NASA's space program is doing the same thing. Several books have been written about the Manhattan Project. My favorite is one written in 1967 by Stephane Groueff, *Manhattan Project: The Untold Story of the Making of the Atomic Bomb*. I brought my copy. You can borrow it while we're here."

"I'd like to borrow it, too," Vanin added with a smile. *Perhaps some day a book will be written about our program ... our efforts. Yes, war is bad, but it also drives human advancement.* Realizing his mind was drifting, Vanin said, "*Kharasho*, okay, back to our history lesson. "In addition to secret production facilities, a secret design laboratory was needed. And Moscow was not a sutiable location for one. Sarov, a small town 400 kilometers southeast of Moscow was selected. Kurchatov moved his team there. The lab became Design Bureau-11, and Sarov became the secret city Arzamas-16—our equivalent of your Los Alamos. In fact, the workers sometimes called it 'Los Arzamas,' something Beria did *not* find amusing.

"Today it is again Sarov—and still closed. This afternoon we'll visit the All-Russian Scientific Research Institute of Experimental Physics. We refer to it as VNIIEF. You might consider VNIIEF the successor to Bureau-11—" Vanin was interrupted by the pilot's announcement that they were on final approach to the Sarov airport.

When the group deplaned at the Sarov terminal, they found a small reception committee waiting. Anatoly Chusov, the Director of VNIIEF headed the delegation, along with the senior FSB official, Colonel Girgidov, and an air force major. Director Chusov who appeared to be in his fifties, around five-feet-eleven, of average build, and medium length salt and pepper hair, welcomed them. Colonel Girgidov explained the rules associated with their visit to his closed city. Security personnel assumed responsibility for transporting their luggage to the hotel. The air force major was there to see to the flight crew's needs.

Director Chusov invited Dr. Landry, Special Agent Lopez, and Major Vanin to accompany him in his ZIL limo for the trip to VNIIEF. Once in the limo Dr. Chusov, who spoke passable English, said, "I have assembled a group of scientists to meet with you. None of them were told the real reason for our inquiry. They were told our two countries are preparing a joint documentary on the development of nuclear weapons—a historical film documenting our efforts and achievements. Both nations feel it is time to produce a true history and eliminate all of the myths and half-truths that have circulated for years. A good story, *da*?"

"*Da*, a good cover story," Vanin replied. "Actually making such a documentary is a good idea. We should consider doing so."

The VNIIEF meeting went well. Major Vanin translated for Landry and Lopez. The scientists were actually eager to discuss the early atomic bomb development program. Landry swapped stories with them. Unfortunately, nothing of substance was learned. Too much time had passed. No one with direct experience was still alive. No one remembered seeing records or reports relating to development of an early gun-type atomic bomb. "Has anyone else been here asking questions similar to ours?" Vanin asked.

"*Niet!* No," was the unanimous response.

As the meeting broke up, Vanin had a thought. Catching Chusov's eye, he whispered, "Director, perhaps we should also question retired scientists."

Da, the major is correct. The people responsible for selling the uranium would have done so between 1989 and 1995, when the Soviet Union was breaking up. Chusov waited until all the scientists departed, then said to the major, "A good suggestion. I will have my staff start calling all retired scientists in the area. Finding those who have moved away will take more time. I suggest you stay in Sarov, until we've contacted those who are still here. It should not take very long."

Dr. Nicholas Fedotov and his wife Maria were sitting in the living room of their small house when the phone rang. Maria answered. "I am calling for Doctor Nicholas Fedotov," the female voice said.

"Please wait, I will get him," Maria said and turned to her husband, "It's for you Nickie—a woman. She asked to speak to *Doctor* Fedotov."

Nicholas Fedotov slowly rose and limped to the telephone. He had arthritis in his left knee. Now 74, he retired six years ago. *I wonder who this is. None of my friends would ask for Doctor Fedotov.* "This is Doctor Fedotov."

"Good evening, Doctor, I am an assistant to Doctor Chusov, Director of VNIIEF. He is seeking anyone who has specific knowledge of our atomic bomb development efforts prior to 1953. If you have such knowledge, or if you were contacted in the past by anyone seeking such information, the director wants to speak with you."

Fedotov was puzzled. Why would the director be interested in such old information? "*Niet,* I do not have any specific knowledge. No more than is generally known."

"Thank you, Doctor Fedotov. Good evening."

Fedotov returned to his chair and started to read his book. Maria was curious. "Well, what did she want?

Looking up through his thick lens, Fedotov grunted. Starting to ask what did who want, he finally understood her question, "It was an assistant to Doctor Chusov, Director of VNIIEF, asking about the early days of the atomic bomb program. Did I have any specific information … And, oh, yes, had anyone been asking questions about it in the past?" Fedotov returned to his book.

The next morning, Maria had a thought. "Nickie, you said the woman wanted to know if anyone ever asked you questions about the early atomic bomb program."

"I did? What woman?" His short-term memory was failing.

"Yes dear, last night. You said they wanted to know about anyone asking questions in the past."

"Huh?"

"Do you not remember telling me about some KGB officer from Moscow? Let me think. *Da,* it was the year your mother died—1991. You thought it was funny. He was asking questions about the early atomic bomb program—the first bomb. *Da*, I remember now. You couldn't understand why the KGB was interested in things that happened in the 1940s, when the Soviet Union was falling apart around us."

"Ah, yes. Now I remember." There was nothing wrong with Fedotov's long-term memory. "It was early in the year and very cold—January or February. I remember the man, a colonel I think. He complained about the cold, and the heater in his automobile. *Da*, he was asking questions about one of the ... well about things you do not need to know."

"You had better call Doctor Chusov."

"*Da*, I will do so right away."

Vanin, Landry, and Teresa were leaving the VNIIEF Nuclear Weapons Museum. "Well, now that you've seen all of our secrets," Vanin said with a serious expression, "you must be shot."

"Oh, no." Teresa replied, feigning fear. "If I show you our secrets, will you spare us?"

"I will consider it." Vanin replied in mock seriousness.

Landry laughed. "Well, if you've seen one atomic weapons museum, you've seen them all. Actually, our's is not much different."

The FSB officer who was observing them approached and interrupted their banter. He was confused, because he did not speak English. First the major made what sounded like a threatening statement, and the woman replied with fear. Then the major made what seemed to be another serious remark, and they all started laughing. "Major Vanin, Director Chusov would like you to come to his office at 1300 hours," the confused officer told him.

"Thank you. Inform the director we'll be there," Vanin responded, then translated the request for his two guests.

Watching the three walk away, the FSB officer thought, "*Stranna! This is strange, what crazy business are those two Americans up to? Do I report this?*

Entering the director's office an hour later, the three found Chusov and an elderly gentleman waiting for them at the far end of the large room. "Ah, ha, Doctor Fedotov, our guests have arrived," Chusov said to the old fellow who was sitting next to him in a comfortable chair. Gesturing for the group to come forward, Chusov rose to make introductions, then realized the good doctor was sound asleep and softly snoring.

When Chusov gently shook his sleeping guest's arm to wake him, Fedotov jumped, raised his bald pate from the plush velvet cushion it rested on and mumbled "*Shto, Shto*—What, What." Now awake, he looked up at them through heavy steel rimmed glasses, stroked his neatly trimmed beard and spluttered, "W–What's happening?"

"Our guests have arrived. They want to ask you some questions," Chusov told him and stood to make the introductions. From the look of him, Teresa thought Fedotov appeared to be heavyset, but it was hard to tell while he was seated. When he rose with difficulty to limp forward and greet her, she could see he was her height, five-foot-six, and definitely rotund. Smiling and extending her hand Teresa suddenly found herself caught off guard. For as he drew nearer his most noticeable features—overly large ears sticking straight out from his head, and enormous steel-rimmed, thick lens glasses—became amusingly apparent. Sitting as they did high up on the bridge of his nose, the glasses magnified the doctor's rheumy old eyes to comical proportions. Adding to his humorous appearance was the precarious way the arms of his glasses barely hooked over his elephantine ears. *Madre de Dios! I mustn't laugh* she thought, and quickly cut her eyes at Yury—who, with the hint of a smile on his lips, impishly winked at her in response. Teresa gave Vanin a sharp look that said, *You Devil. I know you're trying your best to make me lose it.*

Dr. Chusov missed the interplay between Lopez and Vanin and said, "Doctor Nicholas Fedotov is one of our most esteemed nuclear physicists." After everyone was introduced, Chusov helped Fedotov to return to his chair, asked Major Vanin to sit on Fedotov's right, and sat in a chair to the Fedotov's left. Landry and Lopez sat on the couch—much to Teresa's relief, because its odd-angled position enabled her to avoid eye contact with either Vanin or Fedotov. "We were having tea before you arrived. Will you join us?" Chusov inquired and nodded toward the teacart.

Vanin answered for the group, "Thank you, no, director. We are eager to hear what the good doctor has to tell us."

Chusov nodded and began, in deference to the Landry and Lopez, slowly speaking in Russian, so Vanin could translate. "Doctor Fedotov retired six years ago. He called me this morning in response to our inquires. He remembers speaking to a KGB officer in early 1991. The officer wanted to know about gun-type nuclear bombs—how they worked, and if we developed one in the early days of the program. Tell them doctor, what you related to me this morning."

"The colonel, I think he was a colonel, asked me to explain how a gun-type weapon worked. He specifically asked about the Little Boy. He really knew very little about nuclear weapons, so I began with nuclear reactions. Then I explained how implosion bombs compressed the atoms of plutonium closer together, forming a supercritical mass. I also told him how a gun-type bomb formed a supercritical mass by bringing two subcritical pieces of uranium together. *Da*, I remember telling him how America's Little Boy used a three inch naval gun to fire a uranium projectile into the target rings."

Fedotov scratched he right ear. "He was very interested when I told him the bomb consisted of a cannon, a cannon shell, and four rings. He asked if the bomb could be taken apart and reassembled. I assured him it could. I remember being amused when he said something like ... let me paraphrase. A gun-type bomb was easy to make. *Da*, a 'poor man's nuclear weapon,' is what he called it."

Fedotov scratched his left ear. "His next questions pertained to storage. Would weapons deteriorate in storage? I told him implosion weapons would, but a gun-type would not. The only two things that would deteriorate were the propellant and the neutron source. Both could be replaced. The last question he asked was whether we built a gun-type nuclear bomb, in addition to our first implosion bomb. When I told him no, we did not—not until much later— he smiled. And," Fedotov scratched his right ear again, "I remember thinking at the time that was odd. Why would he smile? Then he left," Fedotov concluded with a frown.

"Did he come back or contact you again?" Vanin asked.

"No, I never heard from him again."

"Can you describe him?"

"Yes, he was similar in build to you, Major, about one hundred-eighty centimeters, ninety kilograms, blonde, military haircut, blue eyes. He wore a KGB uniform."

"Do you remember the date?"

"No, only that it was cold, probably January or February 1991."

Standing Chusov said, "We are searching the visitor's records. I will let you know what we find, Major. Now Doctor Fedotov, I think we've tired you quite enough for one day. I believe your wife is waiting with my driver to return you to your residence." Escorting Fedotov to the door, Chusov said, "Thank you for coming. You have been most helpful."

Lopez and Landry followed Chusov to the door and said their goodbyes, wondering what had transpired, because Vannin had ceased translating in the middle of the interview to avoid distracting Dr. Fedotov. After the physicist departed, they returned to their seats. Chusov filled his teacup, and sat silently observing, while Vanin used his notes to recount Fedotov's statement to Teresa and Landry.

When Vanin completed his translation, Chusov rubbed his chin, looked at Lopez and Landry, and said, "The KGB colonel's interest in gun-type nuclear bombs, and our development of one in the late 1940s, raises intriguing questions. Perhaps your president's speculation has merit. If there was such a program, we will find it, now that we know what to look for. It's impossible to erase all traces of it. There will be discrepancies in records ... little things. Yes, we will find it."

"And I will find this KGB colonel," Vanin said with a determined look.

We will stay until you've identified him in the visitor's log."

Landry entered the conversation. "Director Chusov. I suggest you look at the U-235 production from several angles. Compare production records with power consumption and payroll. It would be easy to change the production records to reduce the amount of uranium produced. But, it would be very difficult to change the payroll and power consumption records. A gaseous diffusion plant requires hundreds of personnel to operate it, and it consumes a huge amount of electrical power."

"Chusov smiled, "My thoughts exactly, Doctor Landry."

The meeting ended with Landry inviting Director Chusov to dine at his house, when next he visited Los Alamos. Vanin and Lopez thanked Chusov for his assistance and walked side-by-side down the hall toward the building's entrance. Teresa looked up at Vanin who winked, causing both to laugh. "Yury Vanin you are incorrigible," she said, remembering Dr. Fedotov's ears.

The following afternoon the KGB colonel was identified as Alexei Valek, and the team returned to Moscow. Before departing, Vanin transmitted his report to his boss, Vladimir Melnikov. Colonel Valek's file would be waiting for him when he reached his office. The local FSB office would begin a search—starting in 1990—of old KGB records for any mention of Colonel Valek. The man must have left some footprints. On the return flight, Vanin said to Teresa, "Once we determine who Colonel Valek dealt with in Sarov, we'll return." Looking at Landry the major continued, "Chasing Valek's contacts is a job for Agent Lopez and me. I suggest you concentrate on uranium production with MINATOM. Hopefully, when we combine our findings we'll have a path to follow."

After an early dinner at the embassy, Teresa and George prepared a summary report for the president and designated Cabinet and staff members. Once the report was encrypted and sent, Teresa felt the need to be alone and sought out a secluded bench near a gurgling fountain in the embassy's garden. Thoughts of Julian and Yury filled her mind. Yury, a man of the world, was older than Julian. Yes, Yury excited her greatly, and she was physically attracted to him. *Julian and I got caught up in the moment. Now I understand why so many women have affairs during war. Do I love Julian? Does he love me? I don't know. We hardly know each other. Does our brief affair constitute a commitment? Getting involved with Yury is not a good idea. Julian and I could have a future. Is one possible with Yury, even if he wanted one with me? I ... I really should call Julian. I haven't spoken with him since Friday.*

Chapter 34

Patricia Manning was outraged. After being forcibly removed from the president's conference room, she, Pollock, and Jacobson were handcuffed and taken to a waiting aircraft that transported them to Nellis AFB located on the outskirts of Las Vegas. The following morning, accompanied by Zimmerman, they departed in an Air Force van for the 180-mile trip north on US-95 to Camp Alpha, located on the Tonopah Test Range, thirty-eight miles southeast of Tonopah, Nevada.

Upon arrival at the internment camp, Manning's personal possessions, including her clothes, were confiscated. She was forced to strip naked, bathe in a large, drafty, open shower area, don a paper hospital gown, and submit to an Army doctor's physical examination. After the exam, Marissa Brown, the female Army specialist assigned to guard her, issued Manning a laundry bag containing her internment apparel: four each orange coveralls, bras, cotton underpants; four pairs of white cotton socks; and one pair of white sneakers. When told to get dressed, Manning refused to wear what she called "those ghastly common rags." In response, Brown calmly stated that she could either get dressed, or go to the barracks wearing her paper hospital gown.

Patricia Manning was—to put it mildly—pissed. Underlings always did as she ordered. Now she was being ignored—demeaned. Screaming at the specialist, Manning ordered, "Get out, so I can change!"

Finally realizing Brown wasn't going to obey, Manning ranted and raved at the specialist for the next ten minutes. Eventually she ripped off the paper gown and donned the new attire. Bedraggled, with damp hair hanging in her face, Manning sat panting and glaring at the specialist, *"Now what?"* she snarled.

"Central supply, ma'am … after you," the younger woman said with a satisfied smile, as she opened the door and gestured for Manning to precede her.

"Stop calling me *ma'am*, damn you," Manning growled as she rose.

"Yes, ma'am," Brown solemnly responded, and then as an afterthought, pointed to the laundry bag containing Manning's standard issue lingerie, "Oh, and ma'am don't forget your *skivvies*," she added with a smug expression.

At central supply, the specialist greeted the private behind the counter with a nod, and then waited quietly, observing the private issue Manning's linens, bedding, and other personal items. When told she must carry her own linens—two towels, two washcloths, four sheets, two pillowcases, a pillow, and two blankets—to her new quarters, Manning became enraged. "You want me to do *what*?" she screeched at the private. "How the hell do you expect me to haul all this stuff? I'm already dragging this damn laundry bag."

"Yes, ma'am," the private replied with a bland expression.

For a moment, the older woman appeared on the verge of bursting into tears. But her temper got the best of her when the private unceremoniously handed her a small paper bag. "What the hell is *this*?" she screamed.

"It's your tooth brush, tooth paste, a bar of soap, and some deodorant ma'am," the private responded, pressing his lips together to keep from laughing.

"You've *got* to be kidding!" Manning sneered, "I brought *my own toiletries* with me. I *demand* they be brought to me immediately."

"Can't do that ma'am. You'll have to take that up with the sergeant," the private said, struggling to keep a straight face. Catching sight of an approaching corporal, the private returned to his other duties, leaving Manning to struggle with her belongings.

"Afternoon, Marissa. I'll take over from here," the corporal said to the specialist, who was doing her best to keep from laughing.

Turning to the disheveled older woman, who was sneering at him, the corporal said, "Ready to go to your new quarters? Right this way, ma'am," indicating Manning should precede him.

All the way to her new quarters in the barracks compound, Manning carped at the corporal. Huffing and puffing under the weight of her belongings, she stopped repeatedly to catch her breath. Each time she stopped, she demanded the corporal help her. "I'm not used to this treatment. I can't possibly make it carrying all this stuff. Be a gentleman and at least carry my laundry bag," she whined, but the corporal made no reply: instead, each time she stopped, he motioned her on toward the compound's gate.

About half way to the gate, Manning stopped to adjust her heavy load and to retrieve her dropped laundry bag. "Aughh! ... Help me ... *damn you*," she screamed, struggling to grasp the cord.

"Can't do that, ma'am," he responded, shaking his head, It's 'gainst regulations."

As they approached the compound gate, Manning stopped one last time. Gesturing with her head at the large, fenced-in, rectangular compound, she screamed at him. "You don't honestly expect me to live in that ... that *big cage* ... do you?" she added, still in denial of her predicament.

"Yes, ma'am. Here's where you and them other trouble-making

internees'll be kept for the duration. It's built to keep them terrorists in, so's they don't cause us no more harm. You see them two fences, topped with razor wire?" he asked pointing upward. "Well, they's 'lectrified. And you see the dirt area 'tween the fences?" he said rolling his eyes so mostly white was showing. "Well, ma'am ... that twenty or so feet's pretty much covered with anti-personnel mines. Yes, ma'am, any fool dumb enough t' get over the first fence most likely won't live to make it mor'n a foot or two 'fore bein' blowd clear up," the corporal told her with a hint of a smile. He was getting a kick out of messing with her—her acting so god-all-mighty uppity and all. "Then there's them guard towers located at each corner. No ... I don't rightly think nobody's ever gettin' out o' here for a looong time," he said, deliberately stretching out the word, rolling his eyes again, and chuckling.

Manning glared at him and hissed expletives unbecoming a lady of her exalted status.

Staggering up to the compound's entrance gate—half carrying, half dragging her belongings—Manning caught sight of Winston Pollock and Tom Jacobson sitting on the stoop of the nearest barracks.

Squinting in the glare of the setting sun, Pollock was the first to notice the scraggly looking woman approaching the gate. "Patricia ... Could that possibly be Patricia?" Pollock wondered aloud, amazed at the sight of Manning dressed in the same ill-fitting, orange jump suit he and Jacobson were wearing.

"Patricia? Is that you Patricia?" Pollock yelled, and gestured for Jacobson to follow as he hurried toward the gate.

"Of course it's me you nitwit. Who the hell else do you think it would be?" she screeched, while the corporal fingered the keypad to unlock the gate.

"Thank God you're all right. We've been worried about you," Pollock said, trying to help her struggle through the gate.

"Oh, shut up Winston," Manning snapped and flung back her mop of damp, tangled, grey hair. "Take this damn pile of junk, before I drop from exhaustion," she demanded and dropped her belongings in a heap on the ground.

"Now where the hell am I supposed to sleep?" she said, turning her venom on the corporal.

"Them other buildin's are available to you ma'am. If you don't want t' live in a co-ed building with these here two fellas," the corporal said, gesturing to the other barracks in the compound. " We're goin' t' leave segregation by sex up t' internees," he said smiling broadly.

"I'm not staying alone with the filthy ruffians you'll be bringing in here," she snapped, "I'll stay with Winston. He's perfectly capable of looking after my needs," she concluded and stomped off after Pollock and Jacobson, who were carrying her belongings to the barracks.

For several seconds the corporal stood chuckling at the comical sight they made clamoring up the steps to the building. Shaking his head, he turned to exit the gate, but stopped dead—sure that he'd heard a crackling sound and felt something pop beneath his right boot. *Sweet Jesus, what was that?* He thought, remembering his yarn about the land mines. Looking down to investigate, he was relieved to see the source of the noise was Manning's paper toiletries bag. Oozing from the bag and covering the toe of his boot was a glob of toothpaste. "Oh, shit," the corporal muttered, "Guess this here won't be doin' her no good after all." Laughing, he bent over to scoop up the crumpled bag and wipe off his boot.

Inside the building Manning was making it clear exactly how disgusted she was with her new home—a typical barracks with a row of cots running along the walls of either side of a long room. At the far end of the building, was a large bathroom with open showers and a latrine. Immediately confiscating her companions' four blankets, Manning fashioned a haphazard tent-like enclosure next to the bathroom entrance. There she positioned her meager belongings and set about making all three of their lives as miserable as possible.

For the next twenty-four hours, Manning pestered the guards, repeatedly demanding the return of her "personal toiletries," her cellphone, or the use of the camp's phone. Other than receiving a new paper bag of issued toiletries, her demands fell on deaf ears. After two days of being ignored and losing control over Pollock, who was fed up with her, she threw one of her trademark temper tantrums. For several hours, she disrupted the entire camp by screaming obscenities, turning over beds, and hurling objects. At the height of her rant, she smashed out a barrack's window with one of her sneakers, and finally obtained the attention she was seeking. Her punishment was to scrub every latrine in the compound. Naturally, she refused. Food was withheld until she complied. By the end of her first week's confinement, Ms. high-and-mighty Manning was positive things couldn't get any worse.

She was mistaken.

At 1:27 p.m., a five-bus caravan arrived at the camp. Alerted by the noise, Manning, Pollock, and Jacobson walked toward the gate to see what was happening. Men, shackled one-to-another, were being marched from the first bus into the internment processing building. All wore orange coveralls. Most had long hair and beards. Guards with loaded rifles and fixed bayonets watched them. A guard from the second bus carried a file box containing the internee's records into the processing building. Two hours later, the first batch of processed internees exited the building. Several armed guards marched them through the compound gate. Once inside, the guards removed their shackles and told the internees to find a cot in one of the buildings. When the few women in the caravan requested separate quarters, they were directed to select a barracks building.

Riyadh al-Fulani and five members of his Hamas cell, captured by the Michigan National Guard, were on the last bus. The Michigan Freemen's Militia had killed the other ten cell members. Once captured, it didn't take long for them to be classified as troublemakers, and culled for transport to Camp Alpha. After three days on a hot bus, the six terrorists were spoiling for a fight. Processing complete and freed from their shackles, Riyadh and his men surveyed their surroundings inside the compound. Three infidels, a woman and two men were standing on the stoop of the nearest barracks. Picking up his issued items, Riyadh led his fellow cell members toward the haughty looking *kafirs* blocking the barrack's door.

As the terrorists climbed the steps, Patricia Manning ordered the six bearded Middle Eastern men to, "Find another building."

For several seconds, Riyadh glared with loathing at the infidel woman, then viciously shoved her aside and entered.

Winston Pollock chased after the man, the apparent leader of the group, and managing to get ahead of him shouted, "Now see here. This is our building. Find another one. Ms. Manning doesn't want you in here."

Without warning Riyadh struck Pollock in the stomach with his fist, causing him to double up and fall to his knees. Stepping around Riyadh and Pollock, the man behind Riyadh kicked Pollock in the back, slamming his body forward, and his face into the floor. When Manning saw what was happening she screamed, ran at the second man, and clawed him across the face. In a flash, Riyadh whirled and punched her in the face, knocking her to the floor. The blow broke bones in her left cheek and shattered the expensive upper bridgework in her mouth. Reaching down, he grabbed her by the hair, lifted her off the floor, and viciously slapped her several times across her face. "Infidel whore, do not speak until you are spoken to. Cover your infidel face. Where is your *hijab*, headscarf?"

Shocked, for no one had ever struck her, Manning whimpered in pain. Tears from her swollen eyes ran down her face, and mixed with blood and drool from her mouth and split lips. Holding her by the hair, Riyadh forced her to look at his viciously scowling, bearded face. She couldn't avoid the pure hatred emanating from his dark, feral eyes. Still holding her hair, Riyadh shoved her down and began dragging her by her hair along the floor toward the barrack's exit. At the open door he pulled her body upright again so that her face was inches from his. Looking into her eyes, he spit in her face and screamed "Infidel whore," before throwing her bodily out the door and onto the ground.

Stunned and half conscious, Winston Pollock sat up in the middle of the barracks and looked on in horror. He knew he was no match for the six men.

Mortified and frozen in fear, he cowered when two of the men grabbed his legs, dragged him to the door, and heaved him out to land beside Manning. Jacobson, who'd been hiding under a cot, saw an opportunity to flee. Slipping out the door behind the two men, he ran to another building and hid.

Patricia Manning had met her poor misunderstood Muslims. Her education had begun.

Chapter 35

Currently known as Igor Shipilov, retired KGB Lieutenant General Valrie Yatchenko, watched the BBC news with concern. The United States' reaction to al-Qaeda's attack surprised him. It was not the hand-wringing, milk-toast reply he expected. No, a strong, decisive, leader had emerged and was doing what had to be done—what the old Soviet Union would have done. *Of course the world is accepting America's reaction. The world never stands up to strength. The Americans are acting like they did in WWII. No, they're angrier and have more resolve—understandable, after what the stupid Muslims are calling their "Day of Islam." The End of Islam might be a better term. I wonder if Usama approved the attack. I never met Mohammed, but Saladin II fits Alexei's description of him—the Cobra, a raving fanatic, a dangerous man. At some point Alexander is going to start looking for those responsible. Who can connect me to the bombs? The recovery team's orders came from the KGB, but not directly from me. Only Usama and Alexei can tie Gruppa and me to the bombs.*

In 1987, Yatchenko founded *Gruppa*, The Group, a secret network of Soviet KGB, military officers, and bureaucrats. Preparing for the collapse of the Soviet Union, *Gruppa's* scheme was to grab—while the grabbing was good—and sell anything of high value. Nuclear weapons topped their list of most wanted items. Arzamas-16, home of the Soviet's nuclear bomb development program, was one of the places to look. *Gruppa's* local agent was a KGB agent named Boris Glukhih. He was assigned the task of contacting engineers and scientists from Bureau-11. Glukhih told them he was looking for abandoned test equipment and radioactive materials—*orphelins*, orphans. Anyone with information pertaining to an orphan was given a phone number, and promised a reward if their orphan was recovered. Ivan Zeldovich, an elderly, retired, nuclear engineer, heard about the reward and used the phone number to contact the orphan hunter, KGB Colonel Alexei Valek.

Valek took Ivan's call in January 1991 and interviewed him in a hotel in Arzamas-16. The result was the equivalent of finding the Hope Diamond. Ivan revealed that he'd been a member of an undocumented second atomic bomb development team. His team was charged with duplicating the Little Boy. However, in 1949, when a competing team successfully detonated its implosion bomb, *First Lightning*, Ivan's team was disbanded and purged. All records of Ivan's team were deleted, and all but the lowest ranking team members and their families "disappeared." Ivan miraculously escaped the purge and for forty-two years kept his secret—the location of his team's five gun-type test devices. Valek formed a clandestine recovery team. With Ivan's help, Valek and the team found and removed the five devices from the secret bunker on the Semipalatinsk test range in Kazakhstan. Ivan was told the devices were being returned to Mother Russia. His reward for recovery of the orphelins was a considerable sum of money and comfortable retirement in Cuba. Valek and his team covertly transported the devices by train to Uzbekistan, where they were turned over to Mohammed al-Mihdar in the desert. Al-Qaeda paid $250 million USD for the five gun-type atomic test devices.

Ensenada, Argentina – Thursday, June 8th

For reasons Nancy could not fully understand, her partner in life, Ralph Eid had slipped into a deep depression. At first she thought it was the loss of his business, REM, Investments, Inc.: a holding company Eid used to build a chain of nuclear diagnostic facilities, providing the latest and best diagnostic services available. Under REM's umbrella, Eid established diagnostic centers in four major cities—Atlanta, Boston, Chicago, and New York. Centers in Dallas and Houston were added later. In Washington, DC, he formed a mobile diagnostic business to service downtown DC and rural areas. With the exception of DC, all the centers were located in high-rise office buildings in the center of the city they served. The Dallas and Houston centers were still operating, but Eid showed no interest in them. Despite Nancy's urging, Eid made no attempt to contact either center in the aftermath the attacks. He was therefore unaware Tom Braggs, REM's president, and his family survived the New York City blast and moved to Dallas. Braggs attempted to contact Eid, but no one knew his or Nancy's whereabouts. Braggs finally stopped looking for them. He suspected they'd been in either Chicago or New York and perished in the explosions.

Nancy had no way of knowing that the weight of ten million dead or dying Americans was crushing Ralph. Now, he had to face the added sorrow of the destruction of his religion, because he was certain America would annihilate Islam. Day after day, Eid sat staring at the Rio de la Plata River and brooding, *It's all my fault. I'm responsible.*

The morning's mail contained an invitation from the U.S. ambassador's wife to an embassy luncheon the following week. Bored and unable to raise

Ralph's spirits, Nancy decided to accept.

Peshawar, Pakistan – Thursday, June 8th

General Kamal Hussain, dressed in a tan, Western style, business suit, blue silk shirt, and brown tie, sat in a teahouse on the western side of Peshawar. Now 58, and in good physical condition, the former head of Pakistan's ISI—Inter Service Intelligence—wasn't ready for retirement. In fact, Hussain had high political ambitions. Sitting with him were two men dressed as local merchants. To outward appearances the three were visiting and enjoying a cup of tea.

In reality, Hussain's companions were far from innocent. They were in fact two leaders from Lashkar-e Jhangvi, a radical Islamic terrorist group. The purpose of the meeting was to finalize plans for a coup to overthrow the current Pakistani government. Their business complete, the two men wished Allah's blessings on Hussain and departed.

Hussain nodded good-bye and remained seated. Smiling to himself, he lit a cigarette, sipped his tea, and gazed at an old picture on the far wall—seemingly lost in reverie. Actually, he was gloating over his anticipated new position. Stubbing out the cigarette, he stood, placed several bills on the table, and departed. His bodyguards, two men sitting at a table by the door, followed him.

A waiter, standing near the table watched Hussain and his bodyguards leave. A long time employee of the teahouse, the waiter had observed many of the general's meetings. To Hussain, the waiter was harmless—an invisible part of the teahouse's furnishings. It was natural for him to stand near the table, waiting for a signal to serve. Anyway, the three spoke in Farsi, a language no poor, uneducated, Pakistani waiter would understand.

Outside, General Hussain looked westward toward the Khyber Pass. *This teahouse contains many memories.* A smile spread across his face. *I concluded many successful deals here. The most profitable one marked the beginning of what will soon be the new Islamic Republic of Pakistan. It was here, in 1988, I set in motion the events culminating in our Day of Islam, the destruction of the Great Satan's five cities. Mohammed had just become Usama's lieutenant, and I arranged his first meeting with Colonel Valek. Now Mohammed is Saladin II, Caliph of the Islamic Empire, and by Sunday, I will be president of Pakistan.*

Gloating, Hussain lit another cigarette and looked around to check on his bodyguards. Nodding to them, he turned his attention back to distant mountains, and thoughts of his personal wealth. *Usama paid me $5 million USD. Later, The Group paid me an additional $5 million USD. Since al-Qaeda requested no more nuclear weapons, and Mohammed disappeared, it's now obvious Valek provided the weapons used to destroy the Great Satan's* *cities. It's also obvious Mohammed planned the attacks and set them in motion. That explains how he became caliph. As soon as I'm president, Pakistan will join Mohammed's Empire. I will become his second in command. That leaves Usama. The old fool is still hiding in the tribal lands, fantasizing he is the head of al-Qaeda. I will have to eliminate him.* Stomping out his cigarette, Hussain signaled his bodyguards and driver that he was ready to leave. Entering the back door of his Mercedes, he glanced at his Rolex. It was time to find a safe place to ride out the coming storm.

As soon as Hussain left, the waiter quickly finished his duties and departed. Entering his small house, he immediately wrote out a report detailing what he'd heard. Placing the report in a soda can, he pedaled his bicycle to the main highway and made his emergency signal—a circle marked in yellow chalk on the end of a building facing the main road from the west. Next he placed the soda can behind a loose brick in another building one kilometer from the flag. He knew his controller from the Indian embassy drove past the building twice a day.

Pyongyang, North Korea – Friday, June 9th

Admiral Cheung and Kim Jung-il were in a private room in Kim's palace. For the last hour, Cheung sat impatiently listening to the little tyrant boast of his latest women and cars. Now it was time to get to the reason for the meeting. "The United States and its lackeys have captured the north coast of Africa. The first elements of U.S. armor will arrive on Sunday. When the full division is in place, I expect them to attack Egypt and capture natural gas fields, refineries, pipelines, and the Suez Canal."

Cheung watched Kim for a reaction. Kim nodded and smiled his goofy smile. Satisfied, Cheung continued, "As I predicted, America's attention is fully concentrated on the Middle East. The time for you to strike is at hand. The spineless capitalist dogs in the south will cower before your great army."

Not the complete fool Cheung believed him to be, Kim smiled before replying, "That appears to be the case. I have been waiting for you to seize Taiwan, before I issue the invasion order. When do you attack?"

Cheung hoped to avoid Taiwan. Now he must employ his own diversionary strategy. "I have been ready for the last two days," he said, giving Kim a deferential look. "Unfortunately, I am not a great powerful man like you. No, I answer to a spineless bureaucrat under the influence of a Western pissant. My hands are tied. Our great, leaderless country needs a strong man to show the way." Looking at Dear Leader with a feigned expression of awe, he continued his sales pitch. "You alone have the strength, purpose, and fortitude to pick up the torch and lead us to greatness. You must make the first move. When you do, I can force our weak-kneed leader to allow me to follow your example." Assuming his usual pose of mock deference, Cheung waited to see if he'd pushed the right buttons.

No matter their intelligence quotient, egotistical men and women usually respond when properly stroked. Kim was no exception. Unfortunately, egomaniacs often make monstrous decisions. Assuming his trademark grin, Kim snorted softly and replied, "I will issue orders for the invasion of the south." *But first, I must slap the arrogant Americans and teach them respect. I will launch two of my Taep'o-dong-2 missiles with nuclear warheads at their west coast.*

Pleased with Kim's commitment, Cheung said goodbye to Dear Leader and returned to Beijing to watch and wait. *If he succeeds, I will invade Taiwan, then take over the government. If he fails ... well ... there will always be another day.*

After Cheung departed, Kim Jung-il spent the remainder of the day scheming. Finally, he made his decision. *Yes, I will launch two of my Taep'o-dong 2 missiles—one at Honolulu and the other at Seattle. Now, all I have to do is decide when to attack. I don't think the West knows we've added a third stage to the missile ... My surprise package.* Curling his lips into an evil grin, Kim called his general and ordered two missiles to be armed. Each missile could carry a single nuclear warhead with a yield of 150 KT. "Keep the armed missiles on alert," he commanded.

"Yes, sir. We will require twenty-four hours to complete fueling before the missile is ready for launch."

Chapter 36

The previous day, the president had appointed two new members to his Cabinet: Christopher Newman acting Secretary of Homeland Security; and Congresswoman Betty Chatsworth, M.D., acting Secretary of Health and Human Services, and Surgeon General.

Newman, a sixty-four year old, retired Chicago Chief of Police with impeccable credentials, was an expert in border and port security. Five weeks before the attack, Alexander had interviewed him as a replacement for Ronald Jefferson. Of course Bloomberg blocked Alexander's plan. Newman, a stocky man, about five-feet-ten, and weighing around 190 pounds, had a full head of medium-length, neatly trimmed, silver hair that gave him a look of distinction and authority. Alexander knew the group would readily accept him. Newman radiated self-assurance and authority.

Chatsworth, on the other hand, was an unknown quantity. After yesterday's meeting with her, Alexander—despite certain misgivings—asked her to become part of the Cabinet. Chatsworth's comments during the interview, and her grief over Rodman's death, established her as an extreme liberal—a fact that vexed Alexander. By the end of the interview, he'd decided her assets outweighed her liabilities. He needed her expertise. Chatsworth was a medical doctor and a politician. Skills she'd need to do the job he had for her. And, she was elected to congress by her state, which gave her a right to be a member of the new government. Whatever ideological differences Alexander had with her could be worked out later.

Congresswoman Chatsworth, an Idaho Democrat, was a fifty-five-year-old, refined widow whose husband passed away in 1999. With a medical degree from Mayo Medical School, and credentials in the medical field equal to Newman's in law enforcement, Chatsworth was the perfect candidate for the demanding task of Secretary of Health and Human Services.

Extremely capable, always ladylike and unpretentious, the tall, thin, congresswoman, with grey streaks running through her hair, was a strikingly attractive woman. Quickly winning public favor, Chatsworth had won a landslide victory in her first bid for Congress. Her popularity with her Democratic constituency and fellow congressmen—along with her gift for fund raising—had not escaped President Hilda Rodman. Wherever Rodman went, Chatsworth was sure to be in tow. If Chatsworth hadn't been visiting her daughter in Boise, Idaho—for the birth of her first grandchild—she probably would have been at Rodman's side when the bomb went off. In the aftermath of Washington's total destruction, Chatsworth had no idea what to do. Learning of Alexander's survival and his ascendancy to the presidency, she'd decided to make her way by car to Albuquerque—the recognized center of government. Upon her arrival, and to her surprise and relief, Alexander had greeted her warmly. He had informed her of his take on the situation in the country and the world. After a relatively short interview, Alexander accepted her offer to help him form a new government.

During the meeting, Alexander had told her, "The American people are suffering physically and mentally. The number of victims from the nuclear attacks is staggering. The uninjured are clearly terrified they will become ill from fallout. Your number one priority will be to take command of the treatment and transportation of victims: first to temporary triage centers; and ultimately to permanent long-term care and recovery facilities. All available governmental and military resources will be at your disposal. Use them rapidly and unstintingly. When you leave, see my aide, Captain Julian Taylor, in the outer office. He'll help you find housing and assist in setting up your office and communication network. As a member of the Cabinet, you'll receive daily status briefings, including areas related to the country's defense. You'll be expected to report on developments in your area of responsibility. Time is of the essence. I expect you to act on your own without regard for protocol or approval. Do what has to be done." Alexander ended the interview by inviting her to attend the next afternoon's Cabinet meeting and wishing her God's speed.

I'll probably need it too. Judging from what I've heard about the fast track you have everyone on, she decided, recalling her earlier misgivings about working with a man many of her former colleagues described as overbearing and dictatorial.

Friday afternoon Cabinet meeting

Chatsworth's facial expressions told Alexander the reports of Muslim arrests weren't sitting well with her. *She's going to have a rough go of it with some Cabinet members. I can see it coming. But, someone has to help the injured, and she was the only person available with the political skills, knowledge, and ability to handle the enormous task ahead. A task she's already attacking with vigor. It's imperative I maintain as much continuity of government as possible. Chatsworth's a popular elected official. As such, she represents the will of the people. Having her at my side as the Secretary of*

HHS will send a signal to the public and the world that I'm first and foremost acting for the good of the people.

It pleased Chatsworth to be part of the new government, but she was concerned about working with Alexander. Watching the man in action, she remembered her mentor's opinion of him. *President Rodman always said he was a loose cannon—too conservative, too warlike, and too hardnosed. But I don't see him that way. The country doesn't seem to either. They like what he's doing. Everyone I talked to during my trip here praised him. But the way the Muslim population is being treated is hard for me to accept.*

A humanitarian by nature and profession, Chatsworth considered herself to be liberal through and through. Sustaining and preserving life—human, plant, and animal—was at the core of her beliefs. Anything resembling overt aggression and religious intolerance repulsed her. She'd spent the morning occupied with briefings containing unbelievable reports of domestic and foreign Muslim insurrections. Alexander's methods for controlling the insurrections presented a serious affront to her sensibilities. Now she wondered, *Should I voice my concern about the reports I've read of Muslim arrests and detention? Before the meeting, I heard what some of the other Cabinet members think about internment camps. They're so small-minded. It's disgusting.* Alexander interrupted her thoughts by asking SecWar Simpson for his report.

"Operation Flare is slightly ahead of schedule. The invasion of Egypt can begin in five days. So far we've incurred minimal losses. Mobs are rampaging throughout Europe, burning cars, buses, and buildings. Police are out-gunned. Citizens, police, and rescue workers are being killed. All of our personnel rescued from Kuwait are back in the U.S. Foreign personnel are being returned home as quickly as possible. Debriefings of the rescued personnel revealed an unparalleled scale of atrocities in the Middle East—mostly mindless killing by mobs—pure hatred. There have been crucifixions of Christians and Jews—a punishment authorized in their Qur'an," Simpson concluded with a grimace.

Alexander gestured for Keese to begin.

Before Keese could speak a visibly shaken Chatsworth blurted out, "Do you mean actual crucifixions, like in the Bible?"

"Yes," Simpson and Keese answered together.

"Crucifixion is one of the most inhuman forms of execution ever devised—possibly the worst," Chatsworth said with a visible shudder.

"This is the nature of the enemy we face," Keese told her in a cold voice. "Each country making up the Islamic Empire is governed by a council of clerics. Religious courts, similar to ones held during Iran's Islamic Revolution, are trying natives, infidels, and diplomats. People are being imprisoned or executed. Any violation receives the maximum punishment.

For women, accusations of adultery result in stonings. A French diplomat's wife has been stoned to death in Saudi. Homosexuals are being beheaded. These Islamic courts only recognize *sharia,* Islamic law. The laws of other countries, which differ from *sharia*, are summarily dismissed as the work of *kafirs*, infidels."

"Are reports of these events being released to the press?" Alexander inquired.

"Yes," Keese replied. "Our two-faced French friends are in an uproar over the stoning."

Chatsworth frowned. She wasn't used to derogatory remarks being made against a country she'd always considered an ally. Both Keese and Alexander noticed her expression.

"Speaking of our French friends, Harry, did you have any problem obtaining clearance for our bombers to over fly France on Sunday?" Alexander asked, with a sly smile and a quick glance at Chatsworth.

Simpson grinned, "Oh, yes. I informed them of the flights and requested they place a ceiling of 15,000 feet on all their aircraft. A short time later, the Defense Minister called to tell me our request was *eem-pos-ee-ble*. I told him nothing was *eem-pos-ee-ble*. Then I clarified the situation. Our fighter aircraft would engage and destroy any French fighter that interfered. If missiles were fired, the bombers had orders to drop their bombs on the nearest French city. The Minister said he didn't believe me. I asked him if he wanted to challenge us and find out." Simpson laughed, and then added, "He didn't."

Everyone, except Chatsworth, had a good laugh. As soon as things quieted down Keese continued, "An hour later, I got a call from the French Foreign Minister, who asked if we needed French assistance. I told him we had experience with French assistance and didn't need any more. The minister told me he was insulted," Keese said with a feigned expression of indignation, then continued allowing his voice to resonate through his nasal cavity, "I told him I was glad he felt zat way."

Keese's last statement cracked up everyone but Betty Chatsworth who was indignant. "The French are our friends. Is this any way to talk about them? Surely you wouldn't have done such a ghastly thing," she said in a huffy manner.

Wellington turned to Chatsworth whom she was beginning to suspect was a liberal fool and said, "Betty, whatever gave you the idea the French were our friends? A better way to put it is, with friends like the French who needs enemies?"

Chatsworth's face morphed into a classic liberal smirk. Holding her head high and looking directly at Wellington, she shot back, "Martha, the French are important members of the European community. We'll need their support. We mustn't give the Europeans any more reasons to dislike us. We have to be careful not to offend."

Oh boy! This is going to be good, a grinning Colonel Young thought. He knew Wellington had a short fuse. But to his surprise, Wellington said nothing. Instead, she'd sat back, grasped the arms of her chair and rolled her eyes up to the ceiling. Ignoring what she considered foolishness, she waited for the inevitable—Alexander's comment.

Still smirking at Wellington, Chatsworth suddenly realized everyone in the room was looking at her. Most had amused expressions. *What's so funny? Are these guys on a testosterone trip or something?* No one spoke. Finally, she broke the silence by cryptically asking, "Am I *missing* something?"

The president, observing the exchange with his usual unflappable demeanor, slowly allowed his expression to soften. Sitting forward in his chair with a solemn expression, he said, "Betty, the world as you know it has changed. The UN is *gone*, never to return. We're the *biggest* and *baddest* dog in the pack, and it's past time for everyone understand it. The only thing Europe—and for that matter the rest of the world—has to worry about is *not pissing us off*. Our interests come *first*, followed by those of our true allies— the few who have demonstrated we can count on them, and they in turn they can count on us. It will take you some time to catch up with events. The war is just beginning. Many changes lie ahead."

Well I've just had my comeuppance. A red-faced Chatsworth thought as she'd swallowed hard and returned Alexander's look. *There's clearly no question as to his position in all of this. I'm expected to get with the program, whether I like it or not. Just how this will play out is still up for debate, but ... I do have a job to do ... and like it or not I'll help those who need me— personal and political opinions aside.*

Sensing the palpable tension in the room, Keese suggested a recess. Alexander agreed.

During the recess, Chatsworth sat alone at the conference table, reflecting on what she'd seen and heard. Looking around, she studied her fellow Cabinet members. *I've never in my life been exposed to such hardnosed, inflexible people. No one seems to want to find a peaceful solution to this Muslim conflict. Muslims can't all be bad. Dare I speak up? It's obvious they all support Alexander's view—and he clearly believes all Muslims should be eliminated.* Chris Newman's laughter interrupted her disturbing thoughts. Watching Newman, she tried to hear what he was saying. The others were warmly accepting him. She could tell from all the backslapping and smiling. He was "in"—accepted. *He walks the walk and talks the talk.* The group moved closer, and she was able to hear Newman's last comment. "I fully agree, Martha, round them all up. Sort out the troublemakers and put them in separate detention camps."

At first Chatsworth had been glad to find another woman in the group.

But now, watching and overhearing Wellington's banter with Newman, Chatsworth realized she and Wellington had nothing in common. *Martha Wellington is one hard-nosed woman. She acts and talks like a man,* Chatsworth thought with a self-righteous sniff. Directing her attention to Alexander who was talking quietly with one of his assistants, she continued to mull over all she had seen and heard. *I've always felt everyone has a right to their own opinion—certainly people have the right to worship as they please. I've always assumed Muslims were gentle people with a few fanatics among them. Now I'm being shown that Islam is just the opposite—a religion of fanatics with a few gentle members. Everything I'm hearing goes against what I believe. But the facts support the Cabinet's position.*

Deeply conflicted, Chatsworth knew she could not accept violence on either side. *Dear God, the videos they showed me this morning of atrocities committed in the Middle East speak volumes as to the vicious behavior of jihadists. Coupled with the damage and injuries caused by the terrorist's attack on our cities ... I can no longer deny the truth of what I've seen and heard.* Chatsworth continued to sit alone, reflecting on the embarrassment she felt in the minutes before their break. *I think I may have made a complete and utter fool of myself—time will tell.*

In fact, Chatsworth's behavior during the first half of the meeting was pretty much what Alexander expected. Now, near the end of the break, Chatsworth sat looking woebegone, trying to salvage her wounded pride. To her surprise, she caught Alexander looking at her and smiling. What happened next surprised her even more. The president gestured for those standing to return to their seats, and said, "So much for initiating our newest members to the woes of the world."

Chatsworth realized the president's comment was meant for her. *What a nice thing to do. I think it's his way of telling the others to give me time. I'm new at this. Thank you, Mr. President.*

Taking his seat, Alexander smiled at Chatsworth, and said, "Let's get on with it. Allan, you're still at bat."

Keese picked up where he'd left off. "Let me summarize the present international mood. It's apparent the Muslims' barbaric behavior has turned the entire non-Muslim world against them. At this point, whatever we do will not be challenged. Russia is cooperating. I assume most of you have received the report from Lopez and Landry."

The president interrupted. "Some of you aren't cleared for the details, so I'll give you the big picture. Russia is working with us to identify the source of the fissionable material used in making the bombs that destroyed our cities. FBI Special Agent Teresa Lopez and DOE's Doctor George Landry are in Russia. They're working with their counterparts, investigating the possibility al-Qaeda got hold of Soviet era highly enriched uranium. We're all working on the assumption this occurred in the late 1980s or early 1990s, when the Soviet Union was breaking up. Details will be on a need-to-know basis. We're after the people responsible, not the new Russian government. There will be no discussions about this operation outside of this room." Everyone nodded in agreement, and the president continued.

"Our team reports total cooperation from the Russians, who allowed them to land our embassy airplane at their most secret city. Very few Russians are allowed to go there. This demonstrates President Karpov's commitment." Looking at Keese, the president paused, chuckled, and said, "That reminds me, Allan, what *are* you going to do with Ambassador McGill?"

Everyone in the room turned to look at SecState. Other than Chatsworth and Newman, everyone knew about McGill's recall. Chatsworth and Newman looked questioningly at one another, both wondering who McGill was, and what Alexander meant by secret cities. Alexander caught their reaction, but decided that now wasn't the time to explain.

Keese grimaced, "After meeting with him … well … I sent him back to the minors." Surprised by Keese's use of a baseball term, both Simpson and Wellington chuckled.

Alexander tried to suppress his laugh. *Good call. He always was a minor league player.* "Who's his replacement?"

"Igor Mikhailov. He's a U.S. citizen, raised by Russian grandparents in New York, speaks Russian like a native, knows Karpov and many of the other key Russians. He's solid. He'll make a good addition to our team."

"I know the man. Good choice," Wellington commented. Simpson nodded his agreement.

"I've met him. I agree. Good choice," The president said, setting his stamp of approval on Keese's action. "Anything else, Alan?" Keese shook his head no. "Okay, Barry, you're next."

Clark reported relative peace and quiet throughout the states. "We've had some problems at the borders, but Chris," he said, nodding at Newman, "is getting a handle on those. He'll assume control on Monday. We did have a problem at Camp Alpha. It seems Ms. Manning attempted to order some new arrivals around and was badly beaten—lost a bottom tooth and had her dental bridge broken. The camp physician brought in a dentist from Edwards Air Force Base to repair it. Manning's now in the women's barracks and not a happy camper," he said with a sigh.

The room was quiet. No one was pleased that the inevitable happened. Again Chatsworth and Newman looked each other. Newman shrugged, but Chatsworth frowned and made a mental note to ask about the Manning woman. She thought the name sounded familiar, but couldn't place it. From the sound of things, Manning had gotten innocently caught up in some sort of Muslim arrest. *Poor soul, I wonder who beat her up. Just more unnecessary brutality. God grant me patience—*

Chatsworth's musings were interrupted by Alexander saying, "Anything else, Barry?"

Clark shook his head and said, "No."

"Okay, Martha, your next."

"Several problems exist. First, Iran has installed nuclear warheads on a Shahab-3D and its experimental Shahab-5 missile—they have named it the Kosar. We have reports indicating their last Soviet Granat has been armed with a nuclear warhead. Unconfirmed reports say it's enroute to Bandar Abbas.

"There is much concern in Tehran about the explosion of the first Granat. It appears they bought our deception," she said smiling at Alexander, "and, an interesting bit of raw intelligence has come to light. An agent reports hearing a story—second or third hand—that the caliph asked technical questions about the detonation. Another story says the caliph has a degree in physics from an American university. No one knows where he came from. He just appeared out of nowhere on the two TV tapes, and then suddenly became caliph.

"The second problem concerns North Korea and China. Admiral Cheung made an unannounced visit to Dear Leader this morning. It appears to have been a secret visit. I'm wondering if the admiral has his own agenda. He's been pushing for in invasion of Taiwan for years. He may see this as an opportunity."

"Worse," Keese added. "He may see this as an opportunity to pull off a *coup d'état*."

Alexander frowned. *Just what I need—a hardliner running China.* "Keep an eye on him. Try to ascertain if Wu knows about his trip. If he doesn't, I'll let something drop the next time I speak with him. Anything else, Martha?"

"Yes, Indonesia and Pakistan. Indonesia has a civil war brewing— Islamic extremists against the government. I think China and Japan are going to intervene. If they do, we can say goodbye to Indonesia. They'll split it up as territories." Keese paused for a couple of seconds, then continued.

"Pakistan is ready to blow. It could happen this weekend. Allan, Harry and I think a General Kamal Hussain is ready to take over. He had ties with the old KGB, and supplied the Afghanistan mujahedeen with Soviet arms to fight the Soviets."

"When it starts," Simpson added, "India's first target will be Pakistan's nuclear storage facilities and missiles."

"How good is our intelligence?" Newman asked. *Damn, I've been thinking about border problems. They're minor compared to what I'm hearing. Now I know what Alexander meant, when he told me to take charge and do what had to be done. He doesn't have time to worry about every detail. By God I'll get the job done, so he can concentrate on the bigger problems.*

"Not the best." Wellington replied, "Diplomatic personnel are fleeing. Indian armed forces are on a high state of alert. We've pulled all of our diplomatic personnel out. We have no HUMINT, human intelligence gathered on the ground. However, I'm sure India does. There's no way India is going to tolerate another Islamic conquest."

"What are we getting from India?" Clark asked, familiar with the history of the Islamic invasion that destroyed India's advanced civilization.

"Nothing important," Wellington answered. "They've clammed up. I think they're preparing to intervene."

Alexander let the discussion continue for a few more rounds of questions, then brought the subject to a close. "If a revolution begins and the nuclear sites are in danger, India will launch a nuclear strike. If they don't, China or Russia may ... although they have other problems. Neither country can afford to let Pakistan's nuclear stockpile fall into the hands of the Islamic Empire. For that matter, neither can we. Martha, set up 24/7 satellite surveillance ... and let your counterpart in New Delhi know we'll understand if they take out Pakistan's nukes. Harry, target two ICBMs on key locations in Pakistan—include the tribal area. If India, Russia, or China fails to act, we'll clean up the mess." Looking around the table, Alexander got nods from everyone but Chatsworth, who appeared to be in a trance.

Actually, Chatsworth was stunned. *My God! They've just approved a nuclear strike on Pakistan as if it was an order for a new desk. The men and women in this room have the power to wipe out a nation with a simple command.* Shocked by the thought, Chatsworth closed her eyes, trying to resolve the conflict raging in her mind and come to grips with the new world. Opening her eyes, she looked at the others in the room. *They're pulling the country back together. I don't approve of everything they're doing, but I can see all of them, including Wellington, are dedicated to saving the country. On the way here, I heard nothing but praise for President Alexander. The people are behind him. Our interests first ... now that's a novel thought. I have some serious things to consider about the rightness of my position.*

Chatsworth's thoughts were interrupted when Fobbs reported success was at hand. Credit cards were working. Banks were open. Fuel rationing was working. The country was recovering.

Henniger was next. "Our biggest problem is determining ownership of property. So many have been killed. Records have been destroyed. There'll be claims and counter claims. Lawsuits will clog our court system for decades. Once the legal ball starts rolling, there'll be no stopping it."

Alexander remembered thinking about this problem, it seemed like years ago—no, it was last week. *Jay is correct. The legal system can't cope with the size of the problem. It'll have to be solved by legislation ... no Congress ... and that may be a blessing. The old Congress would be less capable than the courts. Hmmm ...* "Jay, this isn't a problem for us to solve. The solution must be debated, but not debated forever. "I'll ask Kurt to form a governor's committee, with a couple of senior federal judges, to start working on solutions. Once ideas are drafted, they'll be presented to our citizens. Next will come public debates, then a national vote. The final solution must have the majority of our citizens behind it. Jay, draft an executive order banning litigation pertaining to property and assets until a national policy is established."

The meeting continued, dealing with administrative issues, for another thirty minutes before Alexander called for adjournment.

Chris Newman left the meeting feeling as though he'd attended the most important meeting of his life. Betty Chatsworth left in a daze. She didn't agree with much of what had transpired, but felt a newfound respect for her fellow Cabinet members. She approved of Alexander's position on public debates. *There's a rightness in the man—his actions, his thinking, his "Our interests first" philosophy. Yes, I have much to think about.*

Martha Wellington followed the president into his office and closed the door. "Sir, there's another problem I thought I should discuss with you in private. I assume you're aware Islamic terrorists have established a presence in our hemisphere. The worst area is the tri-border area where Argentina, Brazil, and Paraguay meet. Three cities, Ciudad Del Este in Paraguay, Foz do Iguaçu in Brazil, and Puerto Iguaçu in Argentina, are known as the "triangle." Al-Qaeda's main source of funding is narcotics, and the triangle is al-Qaeda's and Hizbullah's center of operations in South America. In 1983 Hizbullah arrived in Foz do Iguaçu to raise money for the jihad against Israel's and America's intervention in Lebanon. Hizbullah—the Party of God—was created by Ayatollah Ruhollah Khomeini in 1982, and trained by Iranian Revolutionary Guards. Brazil recognizes Hizbullah as a political party. Usama bin-Laden visited Foz do Iguaçu in 1995 and established a working relationship with Hizbullah and local drug lords. Sir, we're going to have to deal with the terrorists in South America."

"Yes, but they'll have to wait until we have total control in the Middle East."

"I understand, however, Hugo Chavez is preparing to cause more trouble. Do you recall the accusations he made against Bush I? He accused the president of planning to assassinate him and mount an invasion of Venezuela. Now he's leading a popular movement, known as the 'Bolivarian Revolution,' challenging 'U.S. domination' of the region. The day after 9/11, Chavez's supporters celebrated the attack by burning our flag in Caracas' Plaza Bolivar. After that, he donated one million dollars to al-Qaeda. Chavez has allowed al-Qaeda to establish a training camp on Venezuela's Margarita Island. And, his government provides *cedulas*, identity papers, and passports to people we classify as terrorists. During state visits to Libya, Iran, and Iraq, he pledged to help bring America to its knees. I am sure he is planning to cozy up to the Islamic Empire."

Pausing for a moment, Wellington waited for her revelations to sink in, before dropping the next bombshell. "The CIA has credible reports that Chavez's buddy and idol, Fidel Castro, has set up a bio-weapons facility in San Antonio Los Altos, near Caracas." Wellington paused, then continued, "North Korea is supplying Venezuela, and through them al-Qaeda, with modern weapons, including surface-to-air missiles. This morning I received reports that Chavez plans to make a move against us in the next two weeks. Specifically, he plans to nationalize the oil industry, raise the price of oil, and then impose a 100% tax on exported oil. He sees this as his opportunity to become the dominant political force in South America—the next bigger and better Castro."

Alexander leaned back in his chair and folded his hands. "What do you suggest?"

Wellington who was still standing quickly took a chair facing his desk. *Well, now's the time to see just how far he's willing to go.* Mr. President, if we let Chavez get by with this, he'll spread socialism throughout the hemisphere. Under the present circumstances, I don't believe we can live through another Castro, especially one with oil and drug money." Wellington studied the president, trying to read him. Responding to his gesture to continue, she said, "Sir, we should take him out."

Alexander sat quietly for several seconds, then asked, "How? When?"

Wellington relaxed. *God, I love this man. No bullshit. He deals with problems and seeks solutions.* "Sir, the *when* depends on when he makes his move. The reason for our action will be easy for the rest of the world to understand. The *how* must send a message." Wellington continued to study the president who showed no visible reaction to what she was telling him. "The how will have to be worked out. As I said, it must make a statement. One that can't be misunderstood ... Don't screw with Uncle Sam," she emphatically concluded.

The president appraised the intense woman sitting before him. *She was a good choice. Not one of the liberals who were taking over the agency.* "Prepare a plan. I'll authorize the sanction if it becomes necessary."

Chapter 37

Islamabad, Pakistan – Friday, June 9th

Triggered by the Peshawar waiter's report, Indian embassy personnel began their exodus from the city. Most foreign embassies were closed, or were operating with a skeleton staff. By nightfall, the Indian embassy was closed. At 7:00 p.m., the special train, sent by India to evacuate embassy personnel, departed the station. The waiter and his wife, standing on the rear platform of the last car, watched Islamabad disappear into the twilight.

Reports of unrest in Pakistan had been pouring into India's Intelligence Bureau all day. Intelligence expected Pakistan's civil war to begin in the next twenty-four hours. India was preparing for the worst. Northern and Western Commands were on full alert. Western Command's II Corps, called "Strike Corps," was moving closer to Pakistan's border. Strike Corps was armor intensive and represented half of India's offensive capability. Its mission—cut Pakistan in half.

☆   ☆   ☆

While Muhammad's successors were spreading Islam, India was becoming one of the world's great civilizations. By the tenth century, India's civilization equaled Eastern and Western civilizations in science, mathematics, and philosophy, while its artisans created sculpture and architectural wonders that are unequaled in human history.

The green wave of Islam spread from Mecca like a tsunami created by a massive underwater earthquake. In the early eighth century, the green wave reached the shores of India. Moslem invaders began sweeping through India's provinces, perpetrating some of the greatest massacres in human history. Some of the worst occurred when Sultan Mahmud devastated India in the eleventh century, ordering all Buddhist and Hindu temples to be razed and mosques built on their ashes. Following the Qur'an's teaching to "Slay the idolaters wherever you find them, and take them captive and besiege them … ." Mahmud ordered 50,000 Hindus put to the sword at Sommath.

City after city, temple after temple, and palace after palace was plundered and destroyed at the hands of Allah's warriors bent on looting, raping, and spreading Islam through jihad. Marauding Muslim forces crushed and torched everything of beauty they encountered. Golden statues—idols to the followers of Muhammad—were melted, decorative precious jewels adorning temple walls removed, and women and children sold into slavery—all booty for Allah's warriors and their leader.

Gentle Buddhists were also targeted for slaughter and slavery. Muhammad Khilji burned the great Buddhist library in 1193. In 2001, the Taliban followed Sultan Mahmud's example and destroyed the four giant statues of Buddha in Afghanistan.

India, like Spain and Portugal, had no desire to join the new Islamic Empire.

Beijing, China – 8:30 p.m., Friday, June 9th

President Wu was two hours into a meeting with his ministers in the Council of Ministers building. They too were concerned about a nuclear Pakistan joining the Islamic Empire. The Minister of State Security completed his summary of intelligence gathered by his Ministry's Second Bureau, and the PLAN General Staff's Second Department, responsible for collecting military intelligence in foreign countries. The minister's report, based upon satellite photos and HUMINT, predicted civil war starting in the morning.

"Will India attack? Will they use nuclear weapons?" Wu asked.

"I cannot answer either question with one-hundred percent certainty. India has activated its National Security Council—something rarely done. Their military is on full alert, and their Strike Corps is moving toward the border. We consider a nuclear strike probable," the minister replied. Admiral Cheung voiced his agreement.

Still concerned, Wu asked, "Should we make a nuclear strike on Pakistan's nuclear weapons, if India doesn't?"

Cheung answered with a question. "Will the United States strike, if India doesn't?"

Paul Xi decided to answer both questions. "Admiral, President Alexander specifically referred to 'our part of the world.' I think he will give India and China a chance to deal with the Pakistani problem. If we do not, he will. Then it will be *his* part of the world. Therefore, if India does not take out Pakistan's nukes, we must. We cannot allow the Islamic Empire to acquire more nuclear warheads. If they do, we may be their next target."

President Wu didn't want to think about launching a surprise nuclear strike on anyone, but events were forcing him to do so.

Unknown to Wu, Admiral Cheung had other plans, and attacking Pakistan would interfere with them. On the other hand, allowing the Islamic Empire to obtain Pakistan's nuclear warheads and missiles was not a pleasant thought. *We created the Pakistani monster when we sold them M-11 and M-18 missiles and launchers, and plans for an early 1960s uranium-235 implosion device. The fools will use them. They have dreams of a worldwide empire, and I have no intention of becoming a Muslim. Xi is correct. If India conquers Pakistan, it will not affect us. The Indians are rational, and we can live with them as a neighbor.* "I suggest we inform India we'll approve of any actions they take against Pakistan, including a nuclear strike."

Xi and Cheng had found something to agree on. Xi decided to broach another sensitive subject—Indonesia. Addressing President Wu, he asked, "How are your discussions going with Japan's Prime Minister, regarding the coming Indonesian civil war?"

President Wu grimaced. "Prime Minister Fukui also believes it is time to contain, if not eliminate, Islam. He implied Japan would cooperate with us in subduing Indonesia. He said something to the effect that the world would be more stable if these rebellious areas became our possessions."

Wu's last statement got Cheng's attention. *Hmmm ... Dividing up Indonesia is a pleasant prospect ... no interference from the United States. Taiwan can wait. If we get Vietnam, Cambodia, and Thailand—why not wait. My opportunity will come. Best not to do anything at this time. If the crazy fool in Pyongyang attacks the U.S., they will take care of him for us. My invasion fleet is ready. It doesn't have to invade Taiwan.*

The Arab Street

The Great Satan's seizing of Islamic assets ignited the "Arab Street." More riots erupted in Germany and France. Other European countries with smaller Muslim populations were experiencing a new surge of jihads. Even Switzerland felt the effects.

Indonesia was in turmoil. Jihad or civil war was imminent.

Chaos ruled in Turkey. Fanatical Islamic clerics were demanding Turkey join the Empire, which meant becoming a theocracy. Government leaders had no illusions as to the eventual fate of the Empire—the U.S. was going to destroy it. Turkey had three choices: join the Islamic Empire and eventually be destroyed; abandon Islam, and have a civil war; or, attempt to maintain the status quo by containing and suppressing the Islamic fanatics. Turkey's government chose the third option, but its Islamic fanatics were already out of control.

The invasion of North Africa whipped Muslim fanatics into a frenzy. Shouting, "The crusaders have returned," the clerics issued a worldwide call for fighters to defend the holy lands. Chanting, "Death to the crusaders, Allah is the greatest, Death to the Great Satan, and Death to the Little Satan," fighters from all over Europe, the Middle East, Asia, and Indonesia headed for

Mecca and Medina. African fighters headed for Cairo and Khartoum. Millions of fanatical mujahedeen began arriving at each site.

Word of the pending Pakistani civil war further emboldened the Arab Street. Soon the Empire would have more nuclear weapons. Fanatical warriors with 9th century mentalities prepared to attack 21st century "crusaders."

In Albuquerque, Alexander, the grand master, studied his chessboard and smiled. His gambit was working.

Pakistan – 4:00 a.m. Saturday, June 10th

General Kamal Hussain was on his way to pick up Abdul Qadeer Khan, the father of Pakistan's nuclear bomb, and former head of an international nuclear smuggling consortium. They would take refuge in a bunker near the warhead storage area. The civil war would begin when rebel air force pilots bombed the presidential palace. Infantry troops supported by tanks would follow. Hussain planned to personally take command of the weapons storage depot. If things went according to plan, the country would be his by Sunday afternoon.

A man riding a bicycle, apparently an ordinary worker on his way to work, observed the black Mercedes sedan pull into Khan's driveway. Without being seen, the man stopped in the shadows, and removed a pair of night vision glasses from his backpack. Focusing on the sedan, the man watched intently, while Hussain greeted Khan, and the driver placed a suitcase in the trunk of the car. After the car disappeared into the darkness, the man opened his cellphone and made a call. His report quickly made its way through India's Research and Analysis Wing (RAW), to the Intelligence Bureau, and then to the Joint Intelligence Committee (JIC). The JIC compared the report with other data and concluded civil war was imminent. Recommendations were forwarded to the National Security Council (NSC).

The NSC, established on 24 August 1990, included the prime minister as chairman, and ministers of Home, External Affairs, Defense, and Finance. Now it was up to the NSC to decide how to deal with the immediate threat of Pakistan becoming a radical Islamic state with nuclear weapons. There was only one rational choice. The Islamic Empire could not be allowed to obtain Pakistan's nuclear arsenal.

The NSC issued orders to the 555th Missile Group at 7:07 a.m. Nine Agni-II IRBMs were put on alert. The Agni-II—a two-stage solid propellant, intermediate-range ballistic missile, capable of carrying a 1,000 kg warhead 2,500 km—could be launched fifteen minutes after a launch command was received. Three Agni-IIs, armed with 200 KT boosted nuclear warheads set for ground burst, were targeted on: the Pakistani nuclear weapons storage site; the Ghauri-V missile launch complex; and the Shaheen-II depot. Pakistani Air Force bases and major tank loggers were the target of the remaining six Agni-IIs, carrying fifty KT implosion fission warheads, fuzed for airbursts. Launch of the Agni-IIs would be the signal for Strike Corps to attack. Other corps would attack along the border, and the Indian Navy would attack the Pakistani Navy and blockade the coast.

The expected destruction of Pakistan's command and control network—brought about by the civil war—was a key element of India's war plan. The Shaheen-IIs would be in their depot. General Hussain would make sure of that. Otherwise, he might lose control of them. The CIA station chief was unofficially informed of India's plan.

India planned to settle a centuries old score with Islam by recapturing the lands taken from it by Muslim conquerors. When the radiation dissipated, Pakistan and Afghanistan would again belong to India. Hindu and Buddhist temples would be rebuilt on their original sites.

Mushaf Air Force Base, Pakistan – 0545 Saturday, 10 June

Captain Harun Mamood eased back on the stick of his F-16B. The Pakistani fighter lifted off from Mushaf Air Force Base and began a climb to 25,000 feet. Looking to his right, the captain saw his wingman give him a thumbs up. Their mission was to relieve a flight of two F-7PG fighters—Chinese copies of the MIG-21—providing air cover over Islamabad. Both F-16s were armed with two AIM-9L Sidewinders on the wing tip rails, and two older AIM-9P2 Sidewinders on the outermost under wing racks. Five minutes into the flight, the wingman's sabotaged oxygen system malfunctioned, and he returned to base.

A flight of four Pakistani Mirage V fighter-bombers cruised north, paralleling the Indian border, 125 kilometers southeast of Islamabad. Each carried four Atlas 2,000-pound guided bombs, and a Thompson CFS guidance pod. As soon as the F-7PG fighter cover over Islamabad was eliminated, they would attack the president's residence and other designated targets. The civil war would begin when the first bomb detonated.

Captain Mamood whispered a silent prayer to Allah as he positioned his aircraft directly behind the two F-7PGs. Mamood selected the two older Sidewinders, and received a tone from each. He chose the two older Sidewinders, because they could only acquire the infrared signature of his targets from the rear. If he missed, he still had two of the newer Sidewinders, which could acquire from the front. "Allah be praised," he muttered as he launched both Sidewinders from two kilometers. The time was 0629 hours. Neither pilot of the F-7PGs had any warning and both died in the name of

Allah. Pilots in the Mirage Vs heard Mamood's code word for the attack to begin, "Allah has prepared the path."

Twenty minutes later, Atlas bombs killed the president, members of parliament and destroyed the main command and control center, which was loyal to the current government. Chinese, Russian, Indian, and U.S. satellites reported the attack. An hour later, in New Delhi, the launch order was issued.

Southwestern White House – 2000 Friday, 9 June

Martha Wellington entered President Alexander's quarters to inform him the Pakistani Civil War had begun. Turning to his wife, Alexander said, "I'll be gone all night. I love you. Don't worry. We're going to watch this one from the sidelines. Our turn at bat will come later."

"God bless you. God bless all of us," Jane replied with tears in her eyes, when her husband kissed her goodbye.

Entering the staff car, the president asked Wellington, "Have you discussed the situation with your Indian counterpart?"

"Yes, and he agreed. Islam must be expunged from the planet. India has received tacit approval from China and Russia to take out the Pakistani nukes. He was happy we concurred. I expect a missile launch in the next hour."

"It's difficult to believe General Hussain doesn't realize none of the major powers will allow him to turn Pakistan's nuclear arsenal over to the Islamic Empire. Are all of these Muslims crazy?"

Wellington turned to look at the president. "No, not crazy, spoiled. They've been getting away with their bullshit for so long they believe that's the way things are. For the past sixty years they've been getting by with telling us—the West—one thing and doing the opposite. Hell, Yasser Arafat would give a speech in English making grandiose promises, then the same day give a speech in Arabic saying the opposite. No one ever publicly called him on it. Members of the Saudi Royal Family funded al-Qaeda, as did princes from other Arab countries. President Clinton held up an air strike on bin Laden at a hunting camp in Afghanistan, because a prince from one of the emirates was also there. Of course Hussain expects to get away with it. Why wouldn't he?"

Alexander shook his head in resignation and sighed. "I spoke with President Karpov. His government has reached the same conclusion we have. Islam cannot co-exist with the rest of the world. Islam has to make radical changes, or it must be eliminated. I had a similar conversation with President Wu. He's having discussions with Japan's Prime Minister Sadakazu Fukui. Indonesia is about ready to explode into civil war—a major problem for China and Japan. They're discussing how to deal with the civil war if it begins.

"All of us recognize we have to live together ... make allowances for each other. We all agree that possession of nuclear weapons must be limited. They must be taken away from North Korea and Islamic states. We must not allow any new nation to develop or purchase them. So far the world has only seen the effects of Hiroshima size weapons. The damage done by larger weapons with yields in the hundreds of kilotons is beyond the average person's ability to comprehend. Films of the damage done to Damascus by the Israeli one hundred fifty KT warhead haven't been released. When the yields are in the megatons, it's beyond imagination."

Alexander sighed, and continued with a grimace, "Russia detonated the world's largest thermonuclear bomb in 1961. They named it 'Tsar Bomba.' The reported yield was fifty-two megatons—some estimates were as high as seventy megatons. Tsar Bomba was a prototype for a one hundred megaton city buster—totally impractical from a tactical point of view. It was designed to intimidate the world. After the test, they dropped the project. I suspect the results scared the hell out of them. I know it did me. Our largest tactical thermonuclear bombs had yields of twenty-five megatons. They were too large and heavy. A B-52 could only carry two of them. They're no longer practical. One or two megatons is more than enough. ICBMs have multiple independently targetable reentry vehicles (MIRVs), each with a yield in the high kiloton range. Hitting a target quickly is what's important, and nothing beats a missile. High yield thermonuclear bombs are only good for intimidation."

The staff car arrived at Building 600. Accompanied by Wellington, the president, wearing blue jeans, a tan crew neck shirt, and Reeboks entered the situation room. SecWar Simpson and General Blankenship were already there. SecWar looked up and greeted the president. "Good evening, sir. India just launched three missiles. We expect more launches in the next few minutes. We think they're nuclear."

With a grim expression, Alexander acknowledged the report with a nod. "I expect Pakistan will cease to exist as a nation in the next hour. India will invade and conquer them."

Thirty minutes later General Hussain, Abdul Khan, and three million other Pakistanis were dead or dying—all in the name of the one god, Allah.

Pyongyang, North Korea – 7:30 p.m., Saturday, June 10th

Dear Leader was watching European, BBC, and FOX news. All were reporting India's nuclear attack on Pakistan. The BBC and FOX reports stuck to the facts. There'd been a change of management and reporters at the BBC.

The Brits were getting real news for a change—not propaganda. Not so in France. The French news network was heaping criticism on India. The French still hadn't grasped the fact that no one cared what they thought, said, or did.

Dear Leader was elated. Now was the time for him, as Shakespeare said in *Macbeth*, "To strut and fret ... his hour upon the stage ..." Unfortunately, Dear Leader forgot the last part of the quotation. "And then [be] heard no more ... A tale told by an idiot, full of sound and fury, signifying nothing."

Kim Jung-il issued orders to prepare two nuclear tipped Taep'o-dong 2 missiles for launch at 8:00 p.m. Monday. One missile would be targeted on Honolulu and the other on Seattle. Dear Leader planned to catch the end of Seattle's morning rush hour. The other missile would strike Honolulu at 6:30 a.m.

At 8:17 a.m. local time, Sunday, a U.S. satellite, tasked to monitor North Korea, reported activity at the Todsong-gun North Korea missile base. The report to STRATCOM and NORAD stated two Taep'o-dong 2 missiles were being fueled at a suspected nuclear missile base. Alert orders were issued. A launch could occur anytime after 1800 hours Monday, North Korea time.

Chapter 38

U.S. Embassy, Moscow – Sunday, 11:30 a.m., June 11th

The embassy staff was in a state of turmoil. The majority of the personnel couldn't believe India decimated Pakistan in a matter of minutes. Nuclear wars are won in minutes and hours, not months or years—something known on an intellectual level, but not really understood. It also seemed most Westerners were still trying to grasp the root cause of the conflict sweeping the globe. The Great Jihad was forcing the West to confront the issue—Islam was at war with the world.

George Landry, Teresa Lopez, and David Tuttle were having brunch in the embassy dining room. Teresa, casually dressed in a blue blouse and white slacks, decided she liked her new life style. Eating a Belgian waffle on a china plate, emblazoned with the U.S. Seal, was intoxicating for a young Hispanic woman from south Florida. Her father had worked in the Panama Canal Zone until it was turned over to Panama. The family emigrated to the U.S., and Teresa was born in Miami. She graduated from the University of Florida with a degree in finance. After working for the Florida Attorney General for two years, she joined the FBI. Now she was on a special mission for the President of the United States, and had met with the President of Russia twice.

Tuttle, who had just finished his omelet with gusto, enjoyed the relaxed atmosphere on Sundays. He too was casually dressed in a sport shirt and jeans.

Landry wore in his usual blue, button-down, short-sleeve, dress shirt, grey slacks, and loafers. Unlike others in the embassy, he had taken the morning news in stride. He knew India's action was anticipated. Now, as he sat enjoying his bowl of Wheaties topped with blueberries, he realized he had insight into Alexander's vision. Pushing aside his empty bowl, he sipped his strong coffee, and listened to Teresa and David discussing the ramifications of India's action. After listening to what both had to say, it was obvious to him they were missing the big picture. Setting his empty coffee cup aside, he interjected, "I think you're both missing something in the grand scheme of things. We're still in the early stages of a worldwide realignment. Islam is going to be eliminated. Can't you see it's in everyone's best interest to do so? World leaders have finally reached the conclusion that Islam will always be a source of unrest, discontent, and terrorism. Islam will never consider reforming itself. So, it's being eliminated. When this is over, the world map will be redrawn. Many countries will disappear and become part of … of new," he paused to think, "new empires," he hesitated, "Yes … *empires.* Islam started it, with its Islamic Empire, but there will never be another Islamic Empire."

Tuttle, who'd been listening intently, slowly began seeing the picture Landry was painting. Picking up on Landry's statement, he responded, "If I follow your thoughts, George, you're saying the big powers are going to swallow up the weaker ones."

"No, not the weaker ones—the Islamic ones. President Alexander will not allow our friends—countries historically allied with us—to be taken over. What I mean is the Big Three—the United States, Russia, and China—realize the danger of smaller countries having nuclear weapons, or the ability to purchase them. Great Brittan is really part of us. So is Australia and Canada. Only the fanatical Islamic countries are going to be absorbed, and the threat to world peace eliminated." Landry frowned, and then added, "At least the Islamic threat."

"What about India?" Tuttle asked leaning forward.

"I'm not stating our policy. I don't know what our policy is. However, it makes sense for India to claim Pakistan, and probably Afghanistan as its territory. India like Japan is becoming a major power," Landry answered.

"Yes … that makes sense. After all, India will only be reclaiming territory taken from it by Muslim conquest," Tuttle replied, rubbing his chin.

Teresa who'd been intrigued by the importance of the concepts they were discussing suddenly began to understand. "Then you expect Russia to take back all of the Islamic Republics—the 'stans?' " she asked, looking intently at Landry, who nodded yes. *The Muslim conquest of India? I was never taught about that. Madre de Dios, they are talking about a worldwide realignment of nations.* "What about Indonesia?"

"President Alexander told President Wu that Kim Jung-il was in his part of the world, and Wu should deal with him. My guess is Japan and China will clean up, then divide up Indonesia," Landry replied.

Teresa, amazed at the thought, exclaimed. "What about the U.S. and the U.K.?"

Tuttle's mind was racing. "Well, there's the Monroe Doctrine … our hemisphere. Then there's the heart of the Islamic Empire—Iran, Iraq, and Saudi Arabia … We can claim them as part of our retribution. England gets Egypt and the canal. Spain and Italy get Algeria and Libya. Yes, it's all starting to make sense."

"You know this would never have happened, if Islam hadn't started a war they never had a chance of winning," Landry said, pressing his lips together and shaking his head.

A Marine private interrupted the conversation. "Miss Lopez, you have a call from Major Vanin."

Following the private to a telephone near the entrance to the dining room, Teresa answered, "Good morning, Yury."

"Good morning, Teresa. I have news," he announced, but suddenly realized she'd probably think he was talking about Pakistan, and quickly added, "No, not about Pakistan. We've identified and located Colonel Valek's contact in Sarov. His name is Boris Glukhih. If you can arrange for us to use the embassy's airplane, we can fly to Sarov this afternoon. Otherwise, the only way to get there is an overnight train, which arrives early Monday morning."

"I'll call you back as soon as I determine the plane's availability.

Half an hour later, Teresa informed Vanin that the plane would be ready for takeoff at 2:00 p.m.

Major Elistratov from the Sarov FSB office met Major Vanin and Special Agent Lopez. Prior to their arrival, Major Elistratov had been in a quandary. He'd received a call from Colonel Girgidov telling him to pick up one Boris Glukhih and take him to headquarters. Then his orders called for him to meet a U.S. aircraft at the Sarov airport and take the two passengers back to headquarters, where *they* would interview Glukhih. The colonel had referred to the arriving FSB officer in a highly respectful manner. It was all very strange. Why was a U.S. aircraft landing at the restricted airport? Why was a FSB major on the aircraft? He had expected the officer to be a general. Why was a female FBI agent, a good-looking one to be sure, being treated like a VIP? It appeared the aircraft they arrived on belonged to her. Did all American FBI agents own beautiful jet aircraft? After all, this was his first experience with Americans.

Following introductions, Elistratov learned that his visitors planned to return to Moscow after the interview. During the drive into the city, Vanin asked Elistratov to have an interrogation room ready, "I will conduct the interview. One recording of the interrogation will be made and I will take it with me. Special Agent Lopez will make the recording and observe the interview from the viewing room. She does not speak Russian, so I will translate the recording for her during the return trip. Show Special Agent Lopez how to operate the recording device. There will be no written record of our visit, nor our interrogation of Boris Glukhih."

"I am not to be included in the interrogation? No records?" Elistratov asked in strained voice. "I will need approval from the colonel." *What is going on? I'm dealing with a major, and the American is very young. How can they make such a request?*

Vanin heard the concern in Elistratov's tone of voice. Laughing, he replied, "No reason to get upset. Your colonel is aware of our requirements. Why don't you call him at home? He will confirm my request."

Teresa sat quietly in the back seat, trying to figure out what was going on.

With great reluctance, Major Elistratov placed a call to Colonel Girgidov's residence, repeated Vanin's request, and asked for instructions. Colonel Girgidov told him to treat Vanin's requests as though they from the colonel himself. Slowly closing his cellphone, Elistratov turned to Vanin and said rather sheepishly, "*Da*. It will be as you requested."

Judging from the somewhat cowed look on Elistratov's face, Vanin realized it was time, as the Americans liked to say, to smooth ruffled feathers. "You did exactly what I would have done. One should always verify requests such as the one I made," Vanin said patting the major on the shoulder.

Vanin and Lopez waited in Elistratov's office, while guards took Glukhih to an interrogation room with bare, white, walls, and three pieces of furniture—a table and two chairs. Bare florescent tubes lit the room. Glukhih was very concerned. The guards made him take the chair facing the large mirror. As he sat there looking at his reflection in the mirror—which he knew was two-way for observation—his hands began to sweat and he worried, *Why am I here? I have done nothing wrong ... recently.*

Glukhih's troubled thoughts were interrupted by the click of the door lock mechanism. Turning his head to the right to see who was entering, Glukhih saw a casually dressed, handsome man, carrying a leather briefcase. A chill ran down his spine. *My God, he looks like a young Colonel Valek. Could this have something to do with him?* The unbidden thought completely unnerved him.

The man walked over to the table and extended his hand in greeting, "Good afternoon. My name is Yury."

"Good afternoon, sir," Glukhih replied, attempting to calm himself.

Yury pulled out the chair opposite Glukhih's and placed his leather case on the table, but did not open it. Smiling pleasantly, Yury began the interrogation, "Would you care for tea?"

"No, thank you. I am fine," Glukhih replied, knowing the technique.

Vanin smiled again, "Boris Glukhih, you are an experienced agent, so I will dispense with the usual questions and get to the point. Do you know a Colonel Alexei Vanin?"

Glukhih blanched and closed his eyes. *I knew it. I'm in trouble.* For several seconds he sat perfectly still, trying to compose himself. Finally, he sighed, looked up at Yury and said, "I–I performed some duties for him on occasion a long time ago."

"When?"

"Let me think. Oh yes, it was in 1988 and 1989. Maybe even in 1991."
This must have something to do with the orphelins.

"What *kind* of duties? Tell me *exactly* what you did for him."

"Uh, let me think—uh, nothing specific. I followed up on things he had
questions about. Talked to local people," Glukhih answered with a shrug.

"Did you file written reports? If so, to whom?"

"Uh, no ... only one written report, which I handed to him—the rest
were verbal reports."

Vanin scrutinized Glukhih. He'd started to sweat and—clearly
frightened—his eyes were darting about. *He is scared as hell about
something.* "When was the last time you did work for him?"

Squirming in his chair, Glukhih stared at a spot on the wall. Finally he
replied, "I think it was in early 1991." *He must know the colonel visited here.*
"He would take the train to and from Moscow. Yes, I am sure it was in 1991.
It was very cold, and he complained about the heater in his own
automobile ... and the heater in the car we provided for him."

The questioning was interrupted when Major Elistratov entered and
motioned for Vanin to step out of the room. In the hall Elistratov whispered,
"It appears Boris Glukhih lives very well on what we pay him. My men have
visited his house—a very nice house I'm told, with color TV, high quality
furniture, and ... a new car," he added, raising his eyebrows.

"*Da*, very interesting. Good work. Thank you," Vanin replied with a
smile, then reentered the interrogation room. Walking to the table, Yury sat
and studied Glukhih with a cold expression for what seemed like an hour.
Actually, it was twenty seconds. Finally Yury spoke. "Working for Colonel
Valek must have been very rewarding," he observed, and let his statement
hang for another ten seconds before continuing. "You seem to live *very
well* ... too *well* for your position. Tell me how do you do it?"

By now Glukhih was sweating profusely and squirming in his chair. *Are
people still taken to the basement and shot in the small room with a floor
drain?* He wondered with a gulp. He'd never seen the room, but everybody
knew about it. Finally he responded, knowing before he spoke it was futile, "I
don't understand. How do I do what?"

Yury slammed his hand down on the tabletop so fast it made Glukhih
jump. "*Enough of this!* I know you took *bribes*. I know Colonel Valek *paid
you* to do special work. Now tell me *exactly* what you did for him. Then, I'll
decide your punishment," Yury snarled, and leaned across the table, glaring at
the cowed, over-weight man who'd pushed his chair so far back it was
jammed against the wall.

Completely intimidated, Glukhih began rapidly blurting out the story.

"Colonel Valek *ordered* me to interview engineers and scientists from Bureau-11 ... ask them about weapons and materials. The Colonel told me to tell them we were looking for items abandoned or lost uh ... fissionable materials, parts of nuclear weapons, things of value. We referred to them as *orphelins*."

"You mean items belonging to the state that could be sold for a high price, don't you?"

"Yes. You are correct. I told the scientists and engineers there was a reward."

"Did you find any orphans?"

"I don't know. I had several leads. I would get preliminary information and report it to ... to the colonel's office."

"Whom else, beside Colonel Valek, did you speak to?"

"I don't know. I called a phone number in Moscow and reported to whomever answered the phone."

Yury sat studying Glukhih. It was obvious he was hiding something. "Valek paid you commissions for your work." It was a statement, not a question. Yury continued to glare at Glukhih, forcing him to answer.

"Yes, I received a bonus."

"One. Just one?" Yury snapped.

Glukhih swallowed hard, gulped, and finally replied, "Several small ones, and one large one."

Yury leaned back in his chair, a satisfied smile on his face, and said, "Tell me about the large bonus. What did you do to earn it?"

Glukhih squirmed in his chair, desperately seeking a way to escape the question. Looking up at Yury, he asked, "May I have some tea?"

Turning toward the mirror, Yury spoke in a foreign language—Glukhih thought was English—"Have someone get us some tea," he requested, before turning back with a scowl on his face and saying, "Continue. What *did you do* to earn the large bonus?"

At a loss for words, Glukhih frowned, and lowered his head to look at the tabletop. Finally he muttered, "I am not sure, sir. Colonel Valek called and instructed me to have a file ready for him. The file was on a low-level retired engineer from Bureau-11 ... a Comrade Ivan Zeldovich. It was the first time I heard his name." Glukhih looked up and Yury motioned for him to continue. "I had dinner with the colonel the night he arrived. He asked if Zeldovich was one of my contacts. He wasn't. The colonel informed me that Zeldovich had called and said he knew about an *orphelin*—said a friend told him about our search for *orphelins*. The colonel wanted to verify whether or not Zeldovich's friend was on my list of contacts." Glukhih paused, remembering the event. "Comrade Zeldovich met the colonel at his hotel the next morning. I was ordered to wait in my office until the meeting was over. Colonel Valek called me before noon and gave me the name of Zeldovich's friend, I don't remember it, but he was on my list of contacts. The colonel told me to arrange for a secure phone line so that he could call the general."

"*Which general?*" Yury demanded.

Startled, Glukhih jumped, his hands were shaking. Desperately seeking a way to avoid answering the question, he was saved by a knock on the door.

Yury, irked because the tension had been broken, snapped, "*Come in!*"

A woman entered with a tray holding a pot of tea and two cups. Without a word, she placed the tray on the table and left, closing the door behind her. Yury slowly poured the tea into the two cups. Setting one down in front of the now terrified Glukhih, he raised the other to his lips and sipped the hot brew. Neither man spoke. Glukhih picked up his cup and gulped down a mouthful. His throat was dry, his lips parched. Even though it burned his tongue, the hot tea helped him calm down.

Suddenly, Yury leaned forward, pounded his fist on the table, forcefully demanding, "*Which general?*"

The ploy worked, and a terrified Glukhih blurted out, "Lieutenant General Valrie Yatchenko."

Yury knew the name. *I should have known. Yes, this is beginning to make sense. Yatchenko headed Gruppa. Valek was a member. I wonder if this is the source of the HEU?* "So, Colonel Valek worked for General Yatchenko?"

"Yes. I sent envelopes to Comrade Colonel Vanin at the general's office."

"What envelopes?"

"Uh … envelopes from Zeldovich. After their meeting, the colonel called the general. The next morning the colonel visited VNIIEF. I arranged for him to meet with Comrade Zeldovich at a cabin later that afternoon. A non-Russian-speaking cook prepared a grand dinner. After the meeting, the colonel instructed me to take care of Comrade Zeldovich and his sick wife. They were living in an unheated apartment—five flights up. They had little food. They were in a bad way. I provided food, a warm coat and hat for Ivan, and medical attention for Anya. Oh yes, I also provided coal, so they could heat the apartment." Looking down at his teacup, Glukhih was beginning to relax, *God how I hated those stairs. Best not tell him about the vodka I gave them. Poor old things, I wonder what happened to them?* Recounting the story had somehow relieved him—like getting rid of a heavy burden.

"Did Colonel Valek return?"

"Yes, one more time. He met Ivan in the same cabin … but I uh, used a different cook," Glukhih added as an afterthought. "Before he left, Valek told me to deliver an envelope, a thick envelope, to Ivan, which I did. The following day I returned, and Ivan gave me a sealed envelope for the colonel.

I sent the envelope to the colonel by courier."

"Do you know what was in the envelope?"

"No. I was just a messenger."

"Where can we find Ivan Zeldovich?"

"The colonel arranged for Ivan and his wife, Anya, to be sent to Leningrad. Anya's sister lived there. I do not remember the sister's name. Anyway, they were all old. I am sure they are all dead by now."

"One final question … for now. What was Zeldovich's *orphelin*?"

"I was never told. The day after I sent Anya to Leningrad, Ivan traveled by train to Moscow and met Colonel Valek. I believe they were going to Kazakhstan." Glukhih looked up and shrugged, indicating he had reached the end of his story. Then as an afterthought he muttered, "I became fond of Ivan and Anya. So did Colonel Valek. Do you think they're still alive somewhere?"

Yury Vanin sat quietly contemplating Glukhih's story. *Yes, it fits. Whatever Zeldovich's orphelin was, it had to be important for General Yatchenko to be involved. What did Ivan Zeldovich work on? Was he part of the mythical gun-type bomb program? If so, the testing would have been done at the Semipalatinsk test range in Kazakhstan … time to wrap this up.* Giving Glukhih a hard look, he said, "You may return to your home. You will *not* repeat what you've told me to anyone … even to the colonel in charge here. If anyone asks, tell them I ordered you to remain silent."

"Yes, sir. Am I going to be punished?"

"I have not decided. If you continue to cooperate, I may overlook your … shall we say, extracurricular activities."

During their return flight, Yury played the tape and translated the interview for Teresa. After answering her questions, he said, "I will start a search for Ivan and Anya Zeldovich and her sister. I'm afraid Glukhih is correct. They're probably all dead. Tomorrow I will ask Doctor Chusov to investigate Ivan Zeldovich. If he worked on the phantom gun-type bomb team, it may show up in his file."

Teresa nodded. "Yes, there may be a gap in his records. If the team's records were destroyed, he will have disappeared for a period of time. What about General Yatchenko?"

Yury frowned. "General Yatchenko is already a person of high interest. I think he just went to the top of the list."

The Caliph's Palace, Tehran, Iran – Sunday, 6:50 p.m. June 11th

The council of clerics was in session. Saladin sat at the head of the table, with Grand Ayatollah Khomeini seated to his right. The two generals sat at the far end of the long table. One general was completing his report on the infidel's scurrilous, sneak attack on Pakistan. "Fighting around all of their nuclear weapons sites prevented a counter strike. Anyway, there was no one alive to authorize a counter strike." The general carefully avoided mentioning that Hussain had started the civil war, which caused a breakdown in Pakistan's chain of command. One did not criticize a Muslim leader fighting infidels. "Indian infantry and armor have driven deep into Pakistan. Most of Pakistan's aircraft and armor were destroyed in the first few minutes of the attack."

"We must send our great army and air force to drive the infidels out of Pakistan," the shrill-voiced cleric said. "Allah will provide us with the means to destroy the infidel Indians."

The general looked down. He knew there was no reasoning with fanatics. *Grand Ayatollah Khomeini and our caliph are being unusually quiet. I wonder if they're beginning to understand how bad our situation is?*

Saladin interrupted the general's thoughts by asking, "Are we sure all of Pakistan's nuclear weapons were captured or destroyed? If not, can we get them?"

The general answered, "Praise Allah. Oh, Great Caliph, if only that were so. Alas, there is little we can do. Our forces are moving into Iraq. We are integrating the Iranian and Iraqi armies to repel the crusaders—to keep the infidels from entering Egypt and Saudi Arabia. In order to aid our brothers in Pakistan, our army would have to turn around, and then pass through Afghanistan to reach Pakistan. It would take weeks. By then India would have totally occupied Pakistan." The general paused, glancing around to see if anyone was listening. He was surprised to see all eyes were on him. Taking a deep breath, he continued. "We must consider the possibility of the Great Satan making an amphibious landing on the shore of the Persian Gulf. They are very skilled at doing this."

"Our Granat missile will keep them from entering the Strait of Hormuz. If they come close, we can destroy their fleet," the shrill-voiced cleric interjected. "Allah will destroy them."

"Where is the Granat?" Saladin asked, mainly to shut up the cleric.

"Oh, Great Caliph, the Granat missile has arrived at Bandar Abbas. Our technicians are making sure it's in operating condition," the second general answered. He was relieved to have something positive to report.

"When will it be ready?" the shrill-voiced cleric asked, then, as an afterthought added, "Praise be to Allah."

"Is the Great Satan's fleet in range?" Khomeini asked.

Bowing to the scowling old man with the black turban, the general answered, "Esteemed One, may Allah bless you. We don't know. To target the aircraft carrier—the heart of the fleet—we must have a precise location.

Such information is no longer available from the Chinese or Russians."

Saladin interrupted before the questioning got out of hand. He realized such information came from satellites. "General, I understand we do not have satellite data needed to pinpoint the carrier's location. How else can we get the location?"

May Allah bless him. "Oh, Great Caliph, the only way is to send out reconnaissance planes. Most, if not all of them will be destroyed by the carrier's fighters."

"We must do so immediately," the same shrill-voiced hyper cleric screeched. "Allah will protect our aircraft. Anyway, if some of them are destroyed, the pilots will go straight to paradise."

Saladin waved his hand to silence the cleric. "I do not think it is wise to waste our pilots, aircraft, and our only Granat missile, by shooting at a distant target. Our nuclear warheads for our Raad missiles are not ready for use. We must wait until we're sure the Great Satan's fleet is coming toward us. The closer it is, the better our chance to destroy it."

Khomeini, who was not following the technical aspects of the discussion, and wanted to move on to more important issues, said, "Our Caliph is correct. What is important is striking back. We're not shipping oil, and our gasoline reserve is low. Our bank accounts have been stolen. We must hit the infidels, show the power of Allah. Use the power Allah has given us. It is time to use our Kosar and Shahab missiles."

Both generals looked down at the tabletop. *If we do, we're committing suicide,* they both thought. Neither spoke.

Reading their minds, Khomeini glared at them. *Spineless cowards. They will burn in hell with the infidels.* Looking at both generals he ordered, "Target one missile with a nuclear warhead on Tripoli. We will burn the crusaders out of our land. The other missile will be targeted on Tel Aviv. How soon will you be able to launch them?"

Bowing to the holy man who held the fate of Iran and the Empire in his hands, the senior general answered, "As Allah wills, Esteemed One. We will be ready in two days." *We could launch tomorrow. Perhaps the additional day will save us.*

Chapter 39

Dear Leader was strutting back and forth in his palace command center, sipping the glass of bourbon, and anxiously watching the clock. Dreams of conquest filled his mind. *Soon I shall accomplish what my father failed to do—unite Korea,* he fantasized. *Soon the world will recognize me as a world power.* Events would soon prove him to be partially correct.

At 7:30 p.m. the little egomaniac flopped down in his favorite swivel chair, and studied the TV monitors lining one wall of his lavish communications room. Lighting a *Bolivar Coronas Gigantes*—a recent gift from his new best friend Hugo Rafael Chávez—he settled back in his chair to revel in the full-bodied taste of the heavy cigar. At precisely 7:40 p.m. he reached for the communication console next to his chair, flipped the switch connecting him with control center at the Toksong-gun missile base in South Hamgyong Province, and gave the launch order. Twenty minutes later, the first Taep'o-dong 2 missile began rising from its silo.

One hundred fifty miles off the North Korean coast, America's YAL-1A Airborne Laser (ABL) aircraft, was orbiting in a racetrack pattern over the Sea of Japan. Colonel Helen Powell studied the images on her console in the command center. Feed from a satellite, in a synchronous orbit over North Korea's Toksong-gun missile site, showed fueling activities around the silos had ceased. "I don't like the looks of this," Powell said. Several Boeing, Lockheed Martin, and Northrop Grumman engineers, watching their consoles in earshot of the colonel, nodded in silent agreement.

❀   ❀   ❀

Intercontinental ballistic missiles (ICBMs) can deliver a nuclear warhead to targets located thousands of kilometers away. They have three phases: boost, or launch-phase; midcourse, or out of the atmosphere phase; and terminal, or reentry phase. An ICBM, especially a liquid fueled one, is most vulnerable during its boost phase. Liquid fueled missiles have thin skins covering piping, wiring bundles, pumps, and two tanks containing the propellant and oxidizer. Solid fueled rocket motors require thick walls to contain the high pressure generated by the burning propellant inside them. Obviously, it is easier to destroy a liquid fueled missile.

An ICBM propels a reentry vehicle (RV) out of the earth's atmosphere. The missile's angle and velocity at burnout of the final rocket motor determines its range. RVs are rugged, hard to kill. They have to be to survive reentry into the atmosphere at speeds up to 20,000 miles per hour. Advanced ICBM's contain multiple independently targeted reentry vehicles (MIRVs). Each MIRV can be individually targeted. So far, MIRV technology is beyond the capabilities of countries like North Korea, Pakistan, and Iran.

The arming sequence for a nuclear warhead mounted in an RV is complicated. It is not uncommon for a missile to unexpectedly explode during launch: so it's a good idea to design the warhead in such a way that it will not produce a nuclear explosion over the launch site. To accomplish this, a series of events—built-in safeguards—must take place in a specific order. These events, called the "arming sequence," can be thought of as "gates." A signal from a sensor tells the warhead's fuze that the required event has occurred. When the fuze receives the proper signal, the first gate opens. The fuze then waits for a signal telling it the next required event has occurred, prompting the opening of the second gate. This process continues until all gates have opened and the firing circuits are activated. If events occur out of sequence, the firing circuits are automatically disabled.

North Korea's Taep'o-dong 2 (TD2) missile is a 115-foot, three stage, intercontinental ballistic missile capable of striking Hawaii and parts of the U.S. west coast. When propelling an RV with a single nuclear warhead out of the atmosphere, the TD2 places the warhead on a ballistic path toward its target. The TD2 is launched from its pad by its first stage, a fifty-three foot liquid fueled rocket engine, with a burn time of 125 seconds. After separation of the first stage, the forty-six foot liquid fueled second stage motor ignites and burns for 100 hundred seconds. After second stage burnout and separation, the thirteen foot third stage solid rocket motor ignites and burns for an additional 100 seconds, propelling the third stage and nosecone out of the earth's atmospere. When third stage burnout occurs (end of acceleration), the nosecone releases the RV.

Warhead arming sequence begins with an accelerometer measuring the force produced by the rocket motor during launch. After the preset acceleration force is measured for the preset period of time (100 seconds), the first gate in the arming sequence opens. Next, a barometric sensor tells the missile's computer the warhead is at or above a preset altitude—say 50,000 feet. If it is, the second gate opens. Release of the RV from the missile's nosecone opens the third gate, and the launch-phase is complete. After the RV has completed its midcourse, out of the atmosphere phase, it begins its reentry or terminal phase. Deceleration caused by the vehicle's reentry into the atmosphere is measured, opening the fourth gate. The last gate is altitude. The RV must be above a predetermined altitude—say 40,000 feet. At this point the warhead is armed, and the detonation sensors activated. Detonation will be triggered by either a barometric sensor, an altitude-measuring device—such as a laser or radar—or by both. When the triggering device sends its signal, energy stored in capacitors is dumped into the wires leading to the detonators' exploding their bridge wires. The implosion sequence begins, resulting in a nuclear detonation.

A minimum time gate for the midcourse phase should be included as a safety measure. This gate would measure the elapsed time between the RV release gate and the reentry deceleration gate—a period of time lasting several minutes. If this safety gate is not included ... Well, it should be.

❋   ❋   ❋

Cruising at 40,000 feet over Sea of Japan, the big Boeing 747-400, was about to begin a 180-degree turn to the south, when its two port infrared sensors recorded the thermal energy from the first TD2 launch. The missile was only a few meters in the air, accelerating on a plume of fire. "Missile launch," a tense engineer reported, his voice half an octave higher than usual. Everyone knew what to do. Lockheed Martin's automatic target acquisition and beam control/fire control systems activated. A laser mounted on top of the aircraft—one of three targeting lasers—began searching for the missile.

Ten seconds later, an air force sergeant monitoring satellite feed reported in a calm, clear, confident voice, "Confirmed launch from Toksong-gun." A few seconds later the target acquisition laser acquired the missile and began providing accurate targeting data to the control systems. The Boeing's pilot immediately began a climb to maximum altitude.

Twenty seconds later the second targeting laser, the Track Illuminator, locked onto the missile and selected the aim point for the main laser, the Chemical Oxygen-Iodine Laser (COIL). Next, the third targeting laser, the Beacon Illuminator, locked onto the missile, and began measuring atmospheric disturbance between the aircraft and the rising missile.

Waiting for the missile's flight path to be calculated, the engineer monitoring the Target Acquisition laser studied the data. Thirty seconds after TD2 launch, he pressed the intercom and gave the pilot the intercept vector.

Three Lockheed Martin engineers were monitoring the acquisition, tracking, and targeting lasers. Four Northrop Grumman engineers began preparing the COIL for firing.

Events occur rapidly when a missile is launched. Two minutes after launch, first stage separation was reported. The COIL was charged and the 747, climbing through 43,000 feet, turned eight degrees to port. A long-range high-energy laser must be fired at high altitudes in order to kill a large missile. Atmospheric disturbance was decreasing, but not enough for a kill shot. Sixty more seconds passed, while the big Boeing clawed for altitude, and the targeting system tracked the missile. "Cleared to fire," the Lockheed Martin engineer monitoring the Beacon Illuminator laser said. The missile was now at 62,000 feet and accelerating.

For the past ninety seconds, the 747's main computer had been constantly adjusting the "deformable" mirror that aimed the main laser. All that remained was the command to fire. That honor belonged to Project Director, Colonel Helen Powell, who with the simple command, "Fire," became the first person to order a high-energy laser to be fired in anger.

The acronym LASER stands for light amplification by stimulated emission. Light consists of packets of energy called photons, which travel with the characteristics of a wave. The human eye can see a spectrum of wavelength called "visible light." Color is defined by a specific wavelength. A light bulb emits photons in every direction. Flashlights use reflectors to concentrate the beam of photons in one general direction. A laser produces a monochromatic beam, a beam of one wavelength directed in a single direction. Unlike a flashlight's beam, the laser beam does not spread out. A good example is the small beam of light from a ruby laser pointer. The size of the projected small red dot hardly changes in size as the distance increases from the laser pointer. A laser beam can be reflected by a mirror, which is the way the deformable mirror aims the COIL's laser beam.

Moisture and other materials in the atmosphere cause the laser beam to diffuse or spread out. A laser weapon inflicts damage by applying energy to its target. A narrow laser beam produces a small circle of energy on its target. The smaller the circle, the more concentrated the energy. Diffusion weakens the laser beam. For this reason, the missile must be attacked at high altitudes, where the atmosphere is thin.

The chemical oxygen-iodine laser is the world's shortest wavelength, high power chemical laser. Like the deformable mirror, it too was developed at Kirkland Air Force Base. The COIL emits light with a wavelength of 1.315 micrometers (μm)—invisible to the human eye.

COIL's megawatt beam is produced by mixing molecular iodine with molecularly excited oxygen. The mixture of oxygen and iodine gases is then accelerated to supersonic velocity and injected into the laser cavity. Energy from the excited oxygen atoms is transferred by resonance to the iodine atoms, causing the electrons in the iodine atoms to move to a higher orbit (shell). When the electrons drop back, photons of energy are released. The result is a high-energy beam of monochromic light, which is pointed at the target by the deformable mirror.

Less than a second after Powell gave the order to fire, an invisible beam of light lanced upward from the nose of the climbing 747. Traveling at 186,000 miles per second, it produced a spot of intense energy on the skin of the TD2's second stage motor. The beam moved as the missile moved, keeping the intense energy on the same spot. In less than a second, the beam of intense energy burned a hole through the missile's thin skin and fuel tank beneath it. Pressurized fuel was released, and the missile exploded in a spectacular fireball. A TV camera mounted on the aircraft's nose recorded the missile's explosion. When the image was displayed on monitors located throughout the aircraft, the crew erupted in cheers.

The Korean TD2 was in a near vertical angle, when the hole in its second stage caused it to suddenly lose of thrust. The ensuing explosion caused premature second stage separation, and the third stage failed to ignite. Lacking a sophisticated control package, the TD2 interpreted the end of acceleration to be the signal for the nosecone to release the RV. The RV continued rising, until the pull of gravity—deceleration—reversed its direction, and it began falling back to earth following a parabolic path leading directly toward the North Korean port of Wonsan. Within the RV, the warhead's arming sequence continued without interruption. The first three gates had opened. As soon as deceleration was sensed, the forth gate opened, which meant there was one more gate to go. When the barometric sensor in the RV reported its altitude was above the preset minimum, the fifth and final gate opened, switching on its detonation circuit and arming the warhead. Now the fuze waited for the falling, armed warhead in the RV to reach 600 meters, the programmed detonation altitude.

In the control room at Toksong-gun, the second TD2 was two seconds from launch, when the first missile appeared to explode. Launch of the second missile occurred before the shocked controllers could stop the sequence. Everyone in the control room panicked. They knew a U.S. reconnaissance plane, accompanied by two fighters, had been flying 241 kilometers off the coast for the past three hours. "Did they launch a missile?" the launch commander shouted at the radar operator, indicating the U.S. aircraft.

"No. Nothing," the operator replied. The invisible laser beam did not show on his radarscope. He failed to mention that after the first launch, the reconnaissance aircraft began increasing altitude. It didn't seem important.

Back in the 747, the airborne laser crew was celebrating success when a Lockheed Martin engineer announced in a strained voice, "Second missile launch." His announcement galvanized the crew into action. Again, the three fire control lasers locked on. This time the missile pitched over into a different trajectory, and the big Boeing turned toward the missile. Range to target was increasing. Everyone knew his and her job. "Set fire control on auto," Powell ordered.

The 747 was struggling to maintain the maximum altitude needed to compensate for the increasing range to the missile. Three and a half minutes later the COIL fired. Monitors still showed the missile's flame plume. "We hit it, but we didn't kill it," the engineer monitoring the fire control laser reported.

The second stage of the missile had indeed been hit. A control cable was cut, causing the guidance computer to initiate premature second stage separation. The second COIL beam hit the separated second stage and produced a fireball.

"Oh my God," the engineer at the targeting laser console shouted. "We've hit the second stage after separation."

The targeting laser found the missile and provided data to the targeting computer. COIL fired a third time, the beam hitting the outside of the third stage rocket motor nozzle. Already at a very high temperature, the added energy from the laser beam caused one side of the nozzle to split. Some of the hot gases, flowing through the damaged nozzle, vented through the crack. The thrust of the rocket engine changed, making the missile unstable. It began to corkscrew. Burnout occurred before programmed velocity was achieved, and the RV was released on an unplanned course.

Two SM-2 missiles fired from the *Lake Erie*, a U.S. Navy cruiser in the Sea of Japan, chased the second TD2. One locked onto the second stage and detonated in its fireball. The other chased the third stage and RV, but couldn't catch the out-of-control missile.

When premature stage separation occurred, the North Korean commander in the launch control bunker at Toksong-gun yelled, "What the hell happened?"

"Sir, a U.S. Navy cruiser fired two SAMs at our second missile. As far as I can tell, one SAM hit our second stage after it had separated, and the other missed our missile."

"What about the warhead? Where is the RV headed?" the commander shouted. *What am I going to tell Dear Leader? He will have me shot ... if I'm lucky.*

"Sir ... the RV is off course," the North Korean engineer hesitantly informed his commander, "I'm trying to calculate its new trajectory."

Dear Leader already knew. Furious, he too was wondering what the hell had happened. He'd been monitoring the launch in his media room and erupted in a fit of anger at the sight of the first missile's explosion. When the second missile rose, followed by another explosion, he raged at the wall of TV monitors—until he realized the missile was still going. Then squinting through his cigar smoke at the monitors, he realized that something worrisome had occurred. The solid rocket had begun to fly in an erratic pattern. "What's the fucking thing doing?" he screamed, springing up from his chair. "The fucking thing's off course," he screamed again—this time throwing his glass of bourbon at the monitor and biting the end off of his cigar.

Indeed, the missile was off course. To make matters worse, while Dear Leader helplessly chaffed in his palace, the RV continued on its erratic course toward an unknown destination. Inside the RV's warhead, its arming sequence had passed through the first three gates. Soon the RV would begin reentry, and the arming sequence would arm the firing circuit.

In the control bunker, the North Korean crew watched helplessly as the first missile's RV and third stage began to fall back to earth on their radar screen. The airborne laser crew in the 747 was also watching.

"Why don't they destroy it?" one of the Northrop Grumman engineers asked.

Turning toward him, Powell answered in a hushed voice, "War shots don't have self-destruct systems." At that moment, a sudden thought occurred to her. Punching the intercom, she quickly ordered the pilot, "Jake, get us out of here *now*. The warhead from the first missile may detonate."

Major Jake Quinn needed no further orders. Banking the big bird hard to starboard, he pushed the throttles to the firewall and dove to gain speed.

Five minutes later, the port city of Wonsan and USS *Pueblo* disappeared in a million degree fireball. Dear Leader has lost his tourist attraction, but soon that would not matter.

Southwestern White House – 0700 Monday, 12 June

President Alexander was sitting at his desk, enjoying a cup of coffee, reading reports from Libya. At 0722, his direct phone line from STRATCOM rang. *Now what?* he thought as he answered, "Alexander."

"Mr. President. This is Colonel Wright speaking. North Korea launched two missiles eleven minutes ago, at 0715 and 0718. The Airborne Laser aircraft destroyed the first one. We're not sure what happen to the second one. Its second stage separated early and blew up. The third stage lit off, but something caused it to become erratic. *Lake Erie*, an Aegis cruiser operating in the Sea of Japan, fired two SM-2s at the second missile, but neither hit it. Sir, it got away, but not on its original course. Looks like it will impact at Cape Newenham on the Alaskan coast." Pausing to take a deep breath, the colonel continued. "Sir, the warhead, from what we think was the first missile, detonated over Wonsan. Yield is estimated at one hundred fifty KT. Sir, Wonsan is gone."

For Alexander time seemed to stand still. *The crazy SOB did it. Harry said he would. Now I have to take action.* "Colonel, I assume you've alerted Fort Greely to intercept the RV."

"Yes, sir, they're tracking it. The Cobra Dane Radar on Shemya Island in Alaska's Aleutian chain has it. They've launched one Ground Based Interceptor. A second GBI should be launched in the next two minutes. We assume the RV has a one hundred fifty KT nuclear warhead."

"Good work. I'm sure your assumption is correct. How much time 'til intercept?"

"Sir, the exoatmospheric kill vehicle has been deployed. First intercept in three minutes." A few seconds later the colonel announced, "Sir, the second GBI has been launched. There may be time for a third shot."

Alexander sat staring at the wall thinking, *Everything's in the hands of technology. The value of our ballistic missile defense system is being put to a real test. Now we're going to find out just how well it works. We'll have the first results in a few seconds.*

One hundred and twenty seconds later, the colonel said, "Sir, the first EKV missed. Time to impact for the second EKV is three minutes and thirty-nine seconds. The third GBI has been launched."

Waiting during a crisis makes minutes seem like hours. Alexander's door suddenly opened, and Martha Wellington practically ran into the office, followed by Harry Simpson. Both had been notified of the North Korean missiles. The president pointed to two chairs in front of his desk and pushed the speakerphone button, while telling them, "The first EKV just missed ... second intercept's in about three minutes. This is an open line to STRATCOM. Colonel Wright is calling the plays." The three sat in silence. Somewhere in space were two small objects, each traveling at speeds over 16,000 miles per hour—one trying to have a head on collision with the other.

A Ground Based Interceptor missile is contained in a silo ready for immediate launch. The missile consists of three solid rocket motor stages. After launch the GBI receives in-flight guidance commands, based upon radar and satellite inputs. The idea is to get the third stage and nosecone containing the EKV into outer space as fast as possible. Seconds after GBI launch, the EKV becomes active and initiates its cryogenic cooling process. Krypton gas surrounds the EKV's infrared sensors, cooling them to hundreds of degrees below zero. Three minutes after launch, the third stage has propelled the nosecone into outer space. Four springs separate the EKV from the nosecone. The EKV immediately implements a course change to gain separation from the nosecone, and then assumes a second course designed to impact the onrushing RV. In effect, when released, the EKV becomes a rifle bullet, aimed at the incoming RV—except this bullet has the ability to alter its course. The EKV's super cooled infrared sensors are able to pick out the still warm RV silhouetted against the cold of space. Rushing toward each other, each traveling several times the speed of a rifle bullet, the EKV continues to make course corrections until impact.

Somewhere in outer space, the second EKV made its final course correction. Ten seconds later it struck the incoming RV. Kinetic energy is a function of mass and velocity squared. The impact vaporized the RV, causing the high explosive in the warhead to detonate. Several kilograms of plutonium-239 turned into fine dust particles, spreading away from the point of impact at thousands of miles per hour.

"We got it," Colonel Wright shouted and suddenly realized his left hand was painfully numb. He'd been squeezing the phone so hard he'd cut off circulation.

"Uh ... sorry sir," Wright apologized, while flexing his tingling hand. "Didn't mean to blow you away."

"Don't apologize Colonel, the hit deserved a good shout," the president replied, exhaling the breath he was holding. "Give everyone associated with this effort a 'well done' from me."

"And a well done from SecWar too," Simpson said.

"And another one from the CIA," Wellington added.

"Yes, sirs ... er, and yes, ma'am," Wright replied, realizing his hands were shaking.

For the first time, the three noticed Colonel Young, Captain Taylor, and several enlisted men and women quietly standing near the door, listening. "Sorry, sir," Sergeant Troy said for the group.

Alexander smiled and said, "It's okay. We understand your concern." Then, motioning for Young to stay, he added with a big smile, "Now, the rest of you get back to work."

A chorus of "Yes, sirs," flowed from smiling faces of the onlookers.

"That was a close one," Wellington finally said with a big sigh, followed by a shudder.

"Yes, it was. Kudos to Harry," Alexander commented, starting to come down from his emotional high. "It was his idea to move the Airborne Laser aircraft to Japan, so it could cover North Korea. Now, what to do about Dear Leader."

"We have to take him out," SecWar snarled. "The only question is how."

"Taking him out is easy," Alexander said, hitting the palm of his left hand with his right fist. "It's what comes next that's hard. We don't have the time or resources to invade North Korea. Why should we? No! After we do what we have to do, it will be up to South Korea. If they don't immediately invade, then China or Japan will. Don't forget, the little SOB shot one nuclear armed missile over Japan, and planned to shoot two. It's pure luck the missile's warhead didn't land on Japan instead of Wonsan."

"Well, one good thing came out of this," Wellington commented, knowing it was time to break the tension.

"What's that?" Simpson grunted, his tone betraying his pent-up emotions.

"Well, the *Pueblo* issue is finally settled," she replied with a grin. Her remark cracked up the president, and snapped Simpson out of his dark thoughts. All three spent the next minute heartily enjoying the benefit of laughter, while they let down from the high-stress event.

After the laughter subsided, a now serious Alexander said to Simpson, "Prepare a nuclear cruise missile strike. Flatten Pyongyang and their nuclear sites.

"Everything is in place. All you have to do is give the command," SecWar replied.

"Do it! Do it now," Alexander replied with a scowl, his voice as cold as liquid nitrogen. "An example is required."

Colonel Young, standing behind the president, shuddered.

Beijing, China – 9:28 p.m. Monday June 12th

A phone rang in President Wu's residence. It was the special phone. The one only answered by designated people. Wu answered, "President Wu. What's the problem?"

"Sir, two missiles have been launched from North Korea. The first one exploded in flight, followed by a nuclear detonation at Wonsan. A second missile was launched after the first one exploded, but before the nuclear detonation. The second missile appeared to have a problem, but it continued on its flight."

The crazy fool didn't heed my warning, Wu though, his stomach turning to acid. "Where is the missile headed? What's its target?"

"Sir, it will impact on Alaska's coast. We'll have more information shortly. Based upon the first missile's initial trajectory, the only possible target was Hawaii."

"Summon all of the ministers for an emergency meeting—*now.* I will be there shortly. Keep me posted."

Admiral Cheung had received word of the attack before President Wu. *The crazy little bastard didn't waste any time. Now we'll see just what the new U.S. president is made of.*

America's retaliation was under way by the time President Wu reached the Hall of Ministers. Six Tomahawks, each carrying W-80 nuclear warheads set at maximum yield, 200 KT, were traveling toward North Korea. All but one were fuzed for surface burst.

As Wu entered the huge conference room, a PLAN general, holding a phone, reported to the room, "The U.S. Navy launched six cruise missiles. One just detonated over Pyongyang. It was a nuclear detonation. We must assume the others will be too."

Wu sat slumped in his seat. He couldn't believe what he was hearing. Yet he knew it to be true. *I must call the American President.* Realizing he needed a better understanding of the situation before placing the call, he asked the PLAN general, "What is the status of the missile aimed at Alaska?"

"Sir, the Americans destroyed it with their anti-missile system," the general replied.

Admiral Cheung, sitting at the far end of the conference room, was surprised. *So, their system does work. I didn't think it possible.*

Feeling less anxious, Wu relaxed and sank back in his chair. "Well, that explains the cruise missile attack. If Kim's missile had struck its target, we would be watching their ICBM's instead of cruise missiles. Place a call to President Alexander."

Two minutes later the call went through, and Wu turned on the speakerphone. "President Alexander, I wish to express our concern. We had no warning, or any indication Kim Jung-il was planning to launch an attack." Wu paused, quickly reading a note passed to him—five more nuclear detonations in North Korea—then continued, "We fully understand the need for your action." Wu passed the note to one of his ministers who read it and passed it on. The room was filed with whispers, grumbling, protests, and shuffling of feet and papers.

Holding the receiver to his ear, Alexander scowled at the noise Wu's generals and ministers were making. *Sounds like they're not all in agreement over there. I wonder if Wu doesn't know of Cheung's visit. Well, it's time to let him know we know.* "Thank you for your concern. However, I have to wonder about your not knowing ... since Admiral Cheung visited Kim on Friday."

Wu blanched. Everyone in the room had heard Alexander's remark. Now they all turned to look at Cheung. Seconds passed, while Wu contemplated the situation and turned off the speakerphone. Finally, having collected his thoughts, he abruptly said, "Mr. President, please excuse me. I will have to call you back."

So, he didn't know, Alexander thought with a snort. *How he handles this will provide a measure of the man.*

Knowing the game was up, Cheung decided to call the hand. Standing, he intended to bluster his way through a takeover. Before he could speak, Wu snarled at him, "*Is this true?*"

Paul Xi, sitting next to Wu, watched the other officers of PLAN intently. *Will PLAN back our president, or will we have a coup? I think we're about to find out.*

President Wu who was thinking the same thing decided to throw caution to the wind. Standing and looking Cheung in the eye, Wu confidently announced, "Admiral, you are relieved!" Quickly turning to look at the most trustworthy of the officers in the room Wu said, "General Tao, I now appoint you Commander of the Peoples Liberation Army and Navy." Stunned at the speed with which Wu acted, and unable to voice any justifiable dissent, the other ministers wisely voiced their approval.

Cheung remained standing, glaring at the others in the room—furious because none of his subordinates had supported him. Everyone in the room was dumbfounded at the speed with which events had unfolded. America's instantaneous response to Kim's attack left no doubt in their minds as to what would happen if they supported a coup. Suddenly Paul Xi's explanation of the new American president's power and personality made sense. It was not wise to piss-off a 4,000 kilogram gorilla—especially if he was already pissed.

Cheung stood alone, everyone in the room was staring at him. Finally, he got the message. His shoulders slumped and his head lowered. He had lost.

Turning to the security guards, President Wu ordered, "Place Admiral Cheung under arrest."

Wu watched Cheung being escorted out of the room, then asked the others, "What course of action do you recommend?" After several minutes of debate, no clear course of action emerged. Finally, Wu turned to Xi and repeated his question.

"President Wu, a power vacuum has been established. Someone must fill it. The most logical choice is South Korea. They can reunite Korea, and they will have to pay for cleaning up the damage. If they don't and we don't, I think Japan will seize the opportunity to reclaim part of the Korean peninsula."

After considering Xi's comments, Wu nodded and graciously said, "Thank you. Sage advice as always," and then promptly directed his assistant to place a call to the president of South Korea.

"I will inform him China will assist South Korea in forming a new country," he told the others in the room, "President Alexander was correct. A united Korea is in all of our best interests."

As soon as both countries agreed on a reunification concept, President Wu called Alexander and cordially informed him of the details of the plan.

Chapter 40

General Ross opened the noon press conference. The media was there in force. Press releases had kept them up to date on the attempted coup in Pakistan, and India's nuclear attack. First reports of a U.S. attack on North Korea were dribbling in from the BBC and Asian news sources.

Raising his hand to quiet the excited mob of reporters, Ross began, "This conference was originally scheduled to answer questions regarding the war between Pakistan and India. The war started at 11:00 p.m. last night, which was 10:00 a.m. Saturday in Pakistan." Before he could continue, four new, young, liberal, reporters from California jumped to their feet and began shouting questions. Informed of their presence, Ross was prepared to be peppered with the usual far left questions. Unwilling to tolerate such behavior, he gave the newbie's a hard look and allowed them to make fools of themselves. Other reporters around them looked on in amazement. Most were laughing to themselves at what they knew was coming. They all knew such behavior was unacceptable, and Ross had a no nonsense reputation.

Finally raising his hand, Ross waited for the four who stood side-by-side on the same row to quiet down, "I see some of you are new," he told them, "Press conference rules are simple. Raise your hand when you want to ask a question, and wait until you're called upon. Otherwise you'll be escorted out of the auditorium and your press credentials revoked."

Momentarily dumbfounded by Ross's remarks, the four offenders looked around at the regular reporters for support, but they simply shrugged or nodded in reply to the unasked question—yes, this is how things are done. Three reluctantly took their seats, but one—a young man with stringy blonde hair pulled back in a ponytail—remained standing, belligerently glaring at Ross. Recognizing the challenge, Ross demanded, "Identify yourself and who you represent."

The twenty-nine years old, defiant reporter, dressed in dirty blue jeans, and a soiled T-shirt bearing Fidel Castro's photo, replied, "I'm Andrew Fairley, and I represent Movealong.org, an internet website." He began stepping over his fellow newbie's legs and trampling the feet of several regulars on his way to confront Ross. At the center aisle he abruptly turned and stomped threateningly toward the stage shouting. "We're not going to stand for fascists like you suppressing the truth. I demand that you answer the—"

Before he could finish, two large senior airmen from Kirkland's 377th Security Force Squadron, standing on either side of the stage below Ross, quickly moved forward, grabbed the belligerent young man under the armpits, and hauled him forcibly out of the auditorium.

Shaking his head, Ross said for the benefit of the remaining three radicals, "The purpose of the press is to report the news, not to run the country. If anyone wishes to obtain an interview to debate policy, forward your request to me. News conferences are just that—conferences to dispense information and answer relevant questions. The press reports the news. It does not *make* the news. Does anyone *not* understand this?"

No one moved nor spoke, and the conference proceeded as planned. Later Ross would interview the four activists and determine if further actions were required. If necessary, one or more of them would join Ms. Manning at Camp Alpha.

"As I was saying," Ross continued, focusing his attention on the cameras, "the war broke out, because of an attempted coup in Pakistan led by General Kamal Hussain, Pakistan's former head of intelligence. He planned to take over Pakistan, and then join the Islamic Empire. Pakistan possessed approximately one hundred nuclear warheads. India acted to prevent the nuclear warheads from falling into the Empire's hands." Ross paused, and directing his attention to the reporters said, "Now I'll take your questions."

Before any of the regulars could raise their hand, one of the three remaining newbies jumped up, but did not shout. Ross decided that was good enough and pointed to him.

"General Ross, I'm Sylvester Greer with the *San Francisco Herald*." Like the expelled reporter, Greer was also in his late twenties, but better dressed and groomed than his companion. "Does the administration condone India's scurrilous sneak attack?" he asked with a sneer.

"Mr. Greer, I can't answer your question as phrased. Did you mean to ask if our government approve of India's actions?" Ross's rebuke prompted some laughter and a couple of snorts from several regulars.

Greer's face turned red. He and his three friends came for a confrontation, and things weren't going according to plan. "*No, General*," he said in exasperation, "my question *was* properly phrased. Not *everyone* agrees with the current administration's position. Our government's job is to prevent conflict."

Ross leaned forward on the podium, staring at the young activist. "Mr. Greer, I must have made a mistake. I thought you said you were a reporter. You are acting like an elected official. Please tell us who elected you and to what position you were elected."

Greer clenched his fists at his sides. Most of the regular reporters were either laughing at him or staring at him as though he had the plague. Seething, he replied in his most sarcastic voice, "I *am* a reporter. I answer to the *people*. It's my job to make sure *madmen*—like your *Mr. Alexander*—don't destroy our country."

Ross gave a dramatic sigh, and slowly shook his head in disgust, prompting more snickering and a few hoots from the others in the audience. Greer wasn't getting the reaction he sought. Something was wrong. The regular reporters hadn't joined his attack: the way they normally would against a conservative or a member of the military. Then after several more seconds of palpable silence, during which Ross continued to stare at him, several regulars sitting next to Greer stood and moved away from him. Embarrassed and feeling compelled to say something, Greer finally whined, "I demand an answer!"

Ross didn't immediately respond. Instead he smiled, looked around the audience, and allowed the tension to build and Greer to squirm a little bit longer. Knowing Alexander would approve, Ross decided to use this opportunity to make it clear to the media and the public that Greer's behavior was unacceptable.

Finally breaking the silence, Ross elicited more snickers by sarcastically asking, "Mr. Greer, did you by any chance skip most of your journalism classes?"

When Greer looked down at his feet and failed to respond, the general continued in a commanding tone, "Young man, look at me and listen to me carefully." Ross paused, while Greer did as he was told. "The president of the United States and his appointed Cabinet make policy for the country. Reporters report the policy and newsworthy events. Reporters *do not* make demands. Reporters *do not* tell the president how to do his job. The president *does not* tell reporters how to do their jobs. This relationship is based upon the assumption that all parties know their job description. Now, I suggest you leave and take a refresher course in journalism. Next question."

Greer looked around and realized two things: one, he was not going to get any support; and two, he was about to be forcibly removed. "Forget it," he muttered to himself. Then hanging his head, he jerked up his shoulder bag and stomped out of the auditorium.

After Greer cleared the doors, quiet returned, and Ross continued. "Over one hundred Pakistani nuclear warheads were hours, if not minutes, away from falling into the hands of Islamic fanatics—fanatics who would use them—use them against India, the U.S., and probably China and Russia.

"India did what *had* to be done."

Ross's statement prompted a buzz among the regular reporters, and comments of disgust from the two remaining activists. Holding up his hand for quiet, Ross continued, "Another important event occurred this morning. At 7:15 a.m. local time, North Korea launched two intercontinental ballistic missiles with nuclear warheads at the U.S. Both were destroyed."

This announcement stopped the buzz. In its place came a chorus of anxious gasps." Holding up his hands, Ross calmed the group. "President Alexander is going to join us and relay the events as they occurred."

The president walked onto the stage. Casually dressed in an open-collar, short-sleeved blue shirt, gray slacks, and black loafers, Alexander stood confidently behind the podium. His gaze first swept the assembled reporters, then found the TV camera with the red light. "Fellow citizens, members of the press. At seven fifteen this morning, North Korea launched two ICBMs—one was aimed at Honolulu, Hawaii, the other aimed at Seattle, Washington. Fortunately our Secretary of War, General Simpson had anticipated Kim Jung-il's actions, and pre-positioned assets to counter any hostile move by North Korea. As you may already know, the U.S. has spent years developing a layered ballistic missile defense system. Kirkland Air Force Base plays a major role in this system. The Airborne Attack Laser Program is managed by Colonel Helen Powell, whose office is here on the Base. The Attack Laser is a high-energy test weapon, mounted in the YAL-1A aircraft—a modified Boeing 747-400 Freightliner. The main laser is a megawatt-class Chemical Oxygen-Iodine Laser, referred to as COIL. Details will be provided to you after today's conference. COIL's purpose is to shoot down missiles during their launch phase.

"This morning, when the North Korean missile launches occurred, Colonel Powell was onboard the Airborne Laser aircraft, flying 150 miles off the North Korean coast. The COIL destroyed the first missile by causing its second stage to explode. The missile warhead fell back to earth and detonated over the North Korean Port of Wonsan. The detonation was estimated to be one hundred fifty kilotons." Alexander held up his hand to quiet the reporters who were becoming more and more excited.

"While the first missile was being destroyed, North Korean launched a second ICBM. The COIL hit the second missile three times. The first shot caused premature second stage separation. The second shot hit the second stage after separation. The third shot struck the solid rocket motor's nozzle, causing the missile to become erratic, but *did not destroy it*. The second missile's reentry vehicle was knocked off course, and headed for the Alaskan coast."

The reporters were excited. Forgetting the rules, they began to shout questions. Alexander raised his arms to quiet them. "Another element of our layered ballistic missile defense system is the GBI, Ground Based Interceptor. GBIs are high acceleration, solid fuel missiles that can be fired from their silos with no preparation. Three GBIs were launched from Fort Greely, Alaska. Three minutes after launch, the GBI reaches outer space and releases its EKV, Exoatmospheric Kill Vehicle. The EKV is a solid object designed to have a head-on collision with the on coming RV," the president said, bringing his two index fingers together in front of him. "The first EKV intercepted at maximum range, but missed the RV by a couple of feet. Our second EKV made a direct hit on the RV and destroyed the nuclear warhead in outer space. There was no nuclear detonation." The president smiled and the reporters erupted in applause. After the applause died down, he continued.

"North Korea launched a surprise attack against the United States. We received no warning prior to this deliberate attack. Surprise attacks are something North Korea is good at. In 1950 they invaded South Korea without warning. President Truman and the UN defended South Korea in a conflict they called a Police Action—a politically correct term for war." The president paused, and after slowly looking around the room asked, "Questions?"

Roberto Gonzales, AP, got the president's nod. "Mr. ... President ... " Gonzales faltered, struggling to phrase his question in the face of what he'd just heard. *Realizing your country just dodged two nuclear tipped missiles tends to have that effect.* Finally having gathered his thoughts Gonzales asked, "Mr. President, how will America respond? Will there be another police ac ... uh, another war?"

Alexander's face showed a thin smile.

Some of them are finally beginning to come around—no more political correctness bullshit. "Yes, Roberto, we've already responded. North Korea ceased to exist as an independent nation at eleven minutes after eight this morning. Six of our cruise missiles armed with nuclear warheads destroyed Pyongyang, along with five missile and nuclear weapons sites."

Amazed, Gonzales froze, trying to digest the enormity of the president's statement. *He nuked North Korea a few minutes after the ICBM was destroyed. Wow! He just gave the old saw, "Don't mess with Uncle Sam," a whole new meaning.* Finally regaining his composure, Gonzales studied the faces of other reporters around him. What he saw shook him even more— shock, disbelief, and confusion. *From the expressions on some of their faces, I can see they haven't grasped the significance of his statement. Like me they're asking themselves—how could a war start, be fought, and end in less than an hour? Well, welcome to the 21st century.* Looking up at the president, he said "Follow up question if I may, Mr. President."

"Go ahead."

"What will China ... and South Korea do?"

Alexander smiled, "China will collect and remove all nuclear weapons materials and nuclear weapons from North Korea. Facilities used to make nuclear weapons will be destroyed. South Korea will absorb North Korea, forming the nation of Korea."

Amazed, and filled with growing admiration, Gonzales pondered Alexander's response. *He has solved a fifty-six year old problem in ... what ... two or three hours. This man is now the undisputed leader of the world. He redefined the word statesman,* Gonzales thought before slowly sitting down in a daze. "Thank you, Mr. President," he said softly.

The remainder of press corps was unusually quiet, while they tried to comprehend the enormity of the news and frame their questions. Allan Graham, representing FOX News, raised his hand. Alexander recognized him. "Mr. President, how are other world leaders reacting to these events—France, Germany, Great Britain?"

"Japan approves of Korea's reunification, especially removal of all nuclear weapons and facilities. Russia who shares a small border with the new Korea is also pleased. Leaders of other countries have been informed of our actions and the reunification plans," Alexander responded.

One of the two remaining radical, California journalists stood and raised her hand. Alexander pointed to her. "Mr. President, I'm Maria Zapata, *The Berkley Voice.* My question is, what right do you have to order an attack on a smaller nation? An attack, which according to your own words, destroyed North Korea. How many innocent North Korean people did you kill—*Mr. President?*" she asked, sarcasm dripping for her last words.

Alexander studied the young, five-foot-seven woman whose flushed face radiated anger. Frumpy looking and heavyset with a mop of wild dirty-blonde hair, she appeared to be in her early thirties. Her sour expression and bedraggled appearance belied her twenty-four years, and made her look shrewish and irrational. *Another radical, probably from the University of California, a university that operates our nuclear weapons labs. It's always been a breeding ground for left-wing radicals. They're almost as bad as the jihadists. Something has to be done about this.* Slightly shaking his head and looking at her in disbelief, he replied, "Ms. Zapata, if I heard you correctly, you've just voiced the most idiotic question I've ever been asked."

Zapata gasped, clenched her fists by her sides, and glared at Alexander who continued, "Without provocation and without warning, North Korea, Kim Jung-il to be specific, attempted to *destroy* Honolulu and Seattle. The man was a dictator. He and North Korea were one in the same. So to answer your ridiculous question, I performed my duty as Commander-in-Chief. I defended our country by eliminating a nuclear threat. Any country that attacks America with weapons of mass destruction can expect to be destroyed." For several seconds, Alexander continued looking at her as though she was insane, before bluntly adding, "Now, with respect to your comment about innocent people being killed, understand this—when anyone launches a nuclear weapon at a country, innocent people are going to die. The real question you should ask is, which innocent people most *deserve* to die? The people who launched the weapon or the people at whom it was aimed."

Finally realizing she was the center of attention, Maria Zapata flinched. All the TV cameras were trained on her, and the other reporters were staring at her. Seething with anger, she slowly sank into her chair, desperately trying to understand the attitude of those around her. *What's wrong with these people? After all, the missiles didn't hit any cities. We stopped them. So what's the big deal?*

Once Zapata was finally seated, the president continued. "Next question," Alexander said, then recognized the reporter from NBC.

"Mr. President, I've heard reports saying millions of fighters are assembling in Egypt and Saudi Arabia. Will our troops in Libya be able to hold them off?

Alexander frowned. "I understand your concern, however, your question involves national security issues—military matters that I'm not going to discuss. As to our activities in North Africa, I *can* tell you everything is on schedule."

The press conference lasted another fifteen minutes.

Simpson accompanied Alexander back to his office, where they found the two newest Cabinet members waiting after viewing the news conference. Betty Chatsworth was agitated. Christopher Newman was concerned. Both stood when Simpson and the president entered. Simpson joined the two sitting in the cluster of comfortable chairs near the president's television set. Alexander decided to sit in the fourth chair. Newman was the first to speak. "Mr. President, General Simpson, nice work. I had no idea we had a functional laser weapon."

Alexander chuckled. "Neither did Dear Leader. Actually, it's a test vehicle." Smiling, he added, "I guess we can say it passed its first operational test. Same goes for the Ground Based Interceptors. Do you know we only have one other missile interceptor installation—a smaller site at Vandenberg in California?" Suddenly turning serious, he continued. "If the laser hadn't stopped the first missile, Honolulu would have been destroyed. We have no land-based missile defense system in Hawaii, and the Navy's ships with SM-3s were at sea. Harry had the foresight to move the Airborne Laser aircraft to Japan, because he thought Kim might try to take a shot at us. After it was over, I called Governor Kaneshiro in Honolulu. He found it hard to believe just how close he and his city had come to death. I explained to him the only reason Honolulu still exists was the Star Wars program most people in Hawaii had opposed. His only comment was 'Oh!' " Smiling, Alexander added, "I think he's now a supporter."

Betty Chatsworth sat in sullen silence, feeling that her whole world was in total disarray. As a medical doctor she must cope with the horrific injuries caused by the nuclear attacks on the U.S. Bringing more misery with another such attack was unimaginable, yet one had just occurred. The use of nuclear weapons was escalating—first Israel, then India, now North Korea and America's swift counterattack. When would it to stop? "Mr. President. Was it really necessary for us to use nuclear weapons on North Korea? Couldn't we have used conventional weapons?"

Watching the others turn to stare at her, Alexander reached a decision. The time had come to confront Dr. Chatsworth's liberal views. Either she got with the program, or he'd have to find another doctor to fill her position. Looking directly at her, Alexander said in a stern voice. "Doctor Chatsworth, please present your plan for a conventional response."

Surprised by the president's blunt demand, Chatsworth stammered, "I–I don't understand."

"You questioned why we didn't use conventional weapons to respond. Now I'd like you to explain what you would have done."

Bewildered and a bit intimidated by the president's uncharacteristically sharp tone, she hesitantly replied, "Well," she sighed, "the attack was foiled. We could have called on other leaders to impose sanctions—"

"How do you know he wasn't going to launch more missiles?" Simpson cut in.

"Well, I … I hadn't thought about that," she answered with chagrin.

"Did you think about Kim launching a nuclear attack on South Korea—killing South Koreans and our men, women, and children? America has a large population of military, State Department, missionary, and private citizens living in South Korea," Simpson persisted.

Grasping at straws now, Chatsworth replied with what sounded like a question, "We could have used conventional bombs, and … and missiles?"

Simpson frowned and responded. "Planning such an attack would have taken weeks. It would have put American citizens and South Koreans at risk. Kim was prepared to attack South Korea. He would have done so at dawn, forcing us to fight another Korean war. Be assured, Kim would have used more nuclear weapons. Your plan would not have stopped a war. It would have started one. Thousands of men, women, and children outside of North Korea would have been killed. President Truman tried it your way. He got a lot of people killed, and we still had the *cancer* in North Korea," Simpson concluded, staring at Chatsworth who appeared to be frustrated and embarrassed.

Alexander let her suffer in silence for several seconds. Finally, he looked her straight in the eye and said, "Betty, I'm well aware liberals and well meaning do-gooders always have quick answers for our problems. The real problem is, most of them never have to make their half-baked schemes work.

For years our country allowed Monday morning quarterbacks to set policies. Policies that made us appear vulnerable and encouraged Islam to attack us. Policies that made Dear Leader think he could get by with another sneak attack. I'm afraid there are still fools out there harboring the same delusion—fools waiting for the chance to catch us unaware. That includes the leaders of the so-called new Islamic Empire: fanatics who wouldn't hesitate *one second*, before slitting the throat of every man, woman, and child who refused conversion to Islam."

Cornered and angry, Chatsworth glared at Alexander and Simpson, and shot back, "How can you include all of Islam as the enemy. Islam is a peaceful religion—"

"I thought by now you'd know better." Alexander cut her off, and frowning in disgust came to a decision. *I must confront this and put and end to it. We can't afford the time it's taking, and I don't have patience for this nonsense,* "Betty, before we have our next discussion on this matter, I want you to meet with our three religious advisors. Don't take my word for it. Learn the truth about Islam. Then I think the time will have come for you to decide if you think you *can* be a member of my team. Colonel Young will set up a meeting with them."

Simpson was also fed up with Chatsworth's liberal nonsense. Leaning forward and scowling, he said, "Betty, under *sharia* any Muslim who renounces Islam can be executed! Abdul Rahman was arrested in Afghanistan in March of 2006, charged with rejecting Islam—converting from Islam to Christianity. He is in prison waiting to be tried."

Chatsworth didn't respond. She knew by now it was pointless to continue their discussion. *Mr. President, I'm afraid you and I may never agree on Islam—and many other issues as well. I respect you, but you'll never convince me war is a good thing, s*he pouted and determined to keep quiet for the rest of the meeting.

Annoyed with her and ready to move on to more productive matters, Alexander shifted in his seat and turned his attention to Christopher Newman. "Well Chris, are you getting up to speed?"

"Yes, Mr. President," Newman answered, trying not to show his own disgust with Chatsworth. "Undocumented workers—illegal aliens—present a dilemma of our own making. Sure, they broke the law, but we sanctioned their actions by turning a blind eye to them doing so. A practical solution is required." He then began avidly describing his plans for border control. "I would like to implement a modified, scaled-back version of your 'Homeland Security Undocumented Worker Plan.' Starting with three border towns, my plan will allow Mexicans with verifiable jobs and no criminal record to apply for a five-year photo ID worker visa card. The ID number will be used like a social security number to collect taxes. Workers with a clean history can apply for citizenship in the approved manner. At the end of five years they can apply for a ten-year card. This way, workers can move freely through border crossings. If both husband and wife have worker visa cards, they can bring their dependant children with them, however, children born in the U.S. will not be citizens. They must keep their address and the name of their employer current. If not, they will be deported. Men or women seeking employment can apply for a thirty-day temporary photo ID visa. Thirty days should be sufficient time for them to find a job. Once the plan is implemented, anyone caught illegally entering will be treated as a criminal. Criminals will be deported. If they return they will be sent to work gangs."

"All right. Give it a try. I suggest Tijuana, Mexicali, and Juarez."

"Thank you, Mr. President. Those were my choices. I plan to crack down on the real problem areas like Nuevo Laredo. I want your approval to use extreme force to stop drug shipments. I want authority to shoot down aircraft refusing to land, and to sink boats attempting to escape from our Coast Guard. Trying to hit an outboard motor on a speeding boat with a rifle from a helicopter is not working."

Alexander smiled. *The very things I wanted to do. But Madam President wouldn't hear of it. Well, now I'm making the decisions.* "Approved."

Earlier, during his conversation with Chatsworth, the president had noticed Martha Wellington, Alan Keese, and Colonel Young standing in the doorway listening. Realizing they didn't want to interrupt his discussion with Chatsworth, he hadn't acknowledged their presence. Now he motioned for them to enter. Joining the group, they took seats on the couch.

"What's up, Martha?" Alexander pleasantly asked with a smile.

"Sir, we have new intelligence, confirmed by HUMINT and satellite. The second Granat missile is at Bandar Abbas. Do you think we can pull off the same trick again?" Wellington asked, noticing Chatsworth's confused expression, *She has no idea what we are talking about.*

Wellington was right in her assessment, but Chatsworth wasn't about to own up to it. *I've had quite enough rebukes for one day, thank you,* she thought continuing to pout, trying to remember what HUMINT stood for, and wondering what Wellington meant by the trick. With this group it could mean anything. She was about to find out.

Alexander answered both of her questions. "Betty and Chris don't know about our little deception. Through HUMINT, which refers to intelligence obtained from humans on the ground, we learned that the Empire was moving one of Iran's two nuclear-armed Granat anti-ship cruise missiles toward Lebanon's coast. They planned to use it to attack our Mediterranean fleet. With help from a couple of our friends, we found the missile in a small Iraqi village. The Granat's warhead had a yield of two hundred KT. So we set the warhead on one of our ALCMs, an air launched cruise missile, to two hundred

KT and took out the Granat. The Empire thinks its warhead exploded."

Newman started laughing. But Chatsworth, who'd never been exposed to such actions and tactics, was astounded. The things they did were beyond her imagination. She sat with her mouth hanging open while Wellington expounded on the trick idea.

"We think that's why they haven't launched any missiles at Israel or us. Why not give it another shot? If we launch from a submarine they may not detect the Tomahawk."

When Wellington caught sight of Chatsworth's slack-jawed, wide-eyed response to her last comment, she decided to take pity on the confused woman and explained, "Betty, the Air Force and Navy both use the same basic cruise missile. Configurations are different to accommodate launch procedures. An ALCM is dropped from an airplane. A Tomahawk is launched from a torpedo tube or vertical launcher on a submarine or ship. Both have air breathing turbofan engines, developed by Williams Research."

Chatsworth's mind was in turmoil. "Do you mean—"

Before she could go on, Alexander cut her off by telling Simpson, "Make it so."

"One more thing," Keese interjected. "I received a request from the French Foreign Minister. Ten ships filled with Muslim *refugees* are scheduled to depart Marseille tomorrow morning. They're bound for Jidda. The French have requested safe passage for them through the Suez Canal."

"Bullshit," Wellington snorted, causing Chatsworth to flinch. "They're filled with Islamic fighters answering the call for jihad. I say we sink them in the Med."

Chatsworth inwardly cringed. *Sink a ship loaded with women and children?* She couldn't help herself, despite her determination to keep quiet, she had to protest this despicable suggestion, "How do we know they're fighters? The ship could be filled with innocent women and children." *What kind of people are these? They're as barbarous as they accuse the Islamic fanatics of being.*

Young answered. "Betty, you still fail to grasp the Muslim mind set. Their leaders are fixated on converting the world to Islam. Women ... children ... Why do women and children matter? Killing infidels is all that matters. Their children are taught to hate us as soon as they learn to talk."

"Besides," Keese agreed, "if France is providing the ships, you can be sure they're filled with the most undesirable elements ... which may well include women and children."

Alexander said nothing, but appeared pensive when Wellington cautioned, "You know they'll join the forces at Cairo, Medina, and Mecca." Everyone looked at him, wondering what he was thinking and waiting for his response, but appearing to be lost in thought, he said nothing. A moment or so later, after pursing his lips and rubbing the stubble on his chin, Alexander smiled, looked at Keese and said, "Approve the French request."

Chapter 41

Amerca's new ambassador to Russia, Igor Mikhailov, had arrived in Moscow Monday evening. His plane had been diverted to London after the North Korean attack. Before departing Albuquerque, Mikhailov was cleared for and briefed on Landry's and Lopez's mission. At 9:00 a.m., he presented his portfolio to the Kremlin. President Karpov gave him a warm welcome at the obligatory ceremony. When the formalities were concluded, Karpov invited the ambassador to his office for a half-hour briefing on certain security matters by Major Vanin. Mikhailov invited Vanin to return to the American Embassy with him.

When Teresa Lopez and George Landry entered the new ambassador's office, they were both surprised to find Vanin present. Standing, Ambassador Mikhailov introduced himself and indicated for them to take a seat. "Major Vanin has new details regarding your assignment," Mikhailov told them.

Vanin stood and warmly greeted them, while a steward served coffee and placed a tray of pastries on a table. Smiling, Vanin held up his cup and jovially announced, "I'm beginning to acquire a taste for coffee." Mikhailov, who never acquired his Russian grandparents' taste for tea, smiled and sipped his coffee.

While everyone enjoyed their coffee and pastries, Vanin brought them up to date. "As you know, we've been searching for any trace of Ivan Zeldovich and his wife Anya. I'm pleased to report we located Anya Zeldovich's sister, Valya Golovko, in Saint Petersburg. Unfortunately both Valya and her husband have passed away. Their only living daughter remembered Ivan and Anya. They came to visit in the spring of 1991. For some strange reason, Anya thought Valya was ill. Somehow, Ivan arranged for them to move to Saint Petersburg. They were there about a month, when Ivan was unexpectedly recalled to Sarov. An official car collected both of them. Valya wrote to Anya's Sarov address several times. The daughter remembered her mother being concerned about how long it took for Anya to respond."

Vanin paused to take a bite of his pastry and a sip of coffee. "In truth, it appears Ivan Zeldovich never returned to Sarov. He and Anya simply vanished. We've located records showing both of their 1991 departures from

Sarov to Moscow. Anya continued on to Leningrad, the Soviet name for Saint Petersburg. We did find a record of Zeldovich flying from Semey, Kazakhstan, to Moscow. From Moscow, he took a train to Saint Petersburg—it was Leningrad then—but there is no record of how he originally got to Semey. We've sent an agent to Kazakhstan to look through the records at the Semipalatinsk test range for any trace of Ivan and Colonel Valek. We may find some footprints there. It's doubtful, but possible."

Vanin paused to see if there were any questions. There weren't any. After taking another sip of coffee, he continued. "Ivan Zeldovich has become a man of mystery. There are housing records for him beginning in 1945 and continuing through June of 1991. His employment record shows he was a nuclear engineer assigned to Bureau-11 through 1947. Ivan and Anya Zeldovich ceased to exist from January 1947 to December 1949, when Ivan's name once again appears as a low level engineer on the official payrolls. He remained in the same position, until his retirement in 1985."

Vanin frowned and leaned forward in his chair, "I'm starting to believe the phantom gun-type bomb program really existed. At George's suggestion, MINATOM is comparing uranium-235 production records to worker records and electrical consumption at Sverdlovsk-44 from 1947 to 1949. If they don't match ..." he paused with a shrug, "we may have found the source of the highly enriched uranium we're looking for."

Following the meeting, Teresa and George invited Vanin to join them for lunch in the dining room. The Embassy's Point Four Program Director, Paul Eckard, whose title was cover for his CIA position, and FBI Special Agent Dave Tuttle, the embassy legat, joined them. As the two agents took their seats, Vanin smiled at Eckard and asked with a knowing smile, "Do you find your Point Four duties stressful? I found being a Cultural Attaché dreadfully boring."

Eckard laughed. *Of course he knows who I am. I guess I have to keep up the farce.* "Oh, not *too* boring," he responded, "It leaves me plenty of free time for ... shall we say, *personal* activities."

Both men laughed. It took Landry and Tuttle a couple of seconds to catch up, and then they joined Eckard in the merriment. Teresa remained silent, observing and learning.

Now serious, Vanin continued, "America's handling of that idiot Kim's sneak attack was very impressive. I never believed a portable laser weapon was practical, much less operational. I'm sure you know we've spent a lot of time and money on an anti-satellite weapon—lasers and beam weapons. Even more impressive was your ability to intercept a missile RV in space. Getting two objects to collide in space is quite a feat."

"You sound like one of our congressmen," Tuttle quipped. Vanin, Landry and Eckard laughed. Teresa, still new to the game, was unsure how to react when someone poked fun at a congressman.

Serious once more, Vanin said, "I can't wait for your president's next slight of hand. He keeps pulling rabbits out of his wool hat. We're all wondering when he plans to deal with the Empire."

"So are we," Eckard answered for all of them. "When he does, I'm sure it will be spectacular."

After lunch, Teresa, chuckling, whispered to Yury, "Magicians use silk hats, not wool ones."

Gulf of Oman – Wednesday, 14 June

At 0142, the *New Mexico*, SSN 779, a Virginia class attack submarine, rose to periscope depth in the mouth of the Gulf of Oman. The captain scanned the area for hostile ships, aircraft and electronic emissions. Satisfied no threat was present, the captain issued the command to fire tube three.

Compressed air ejected the UGM109-A TLAM-N (*Tomahawk* Land-Attack Missile - Nuclear) missile nestled in its transport canister. Once clear of the torpedo tube, the canister opened, and the rocket booster motor ignited, propelling the missile to the surface and into the air. As soon as it was fully airborne, the missile's remaining protective covers fell away. Four tailfins and two straight wings extended, followed by the air intake scoop for the Williams F107-WR-400 turbofan engine. Having done its job, the spent booster separated and fell into the sea. The turbofan engine started, and the Tomahawk was on its way to Bandar Abbas—some three hundred miles away—its W-80 boosted nuclear warhead set for a 200 KT surface burst.

The captain watched the Tomahawk through the periscope until booster separation, and engine start. Satisfied it was a clean launch, he turned to the XO and ordered, "Make your depth two hundred feet, course one-three-five, ahead two thirds." Like a ghost, the *New Mexico* silently descended into the dark water and headed for the open sea.

Flying at 450 knots, the Tomahawk dropped to fifty feet and headed north toward the coast of Iran. Soon it would cross the coastline between the villages of Jask and Gabrih, then follow a northwesterly course until it was north of its target. Turning west, the missile would continue—flying fifty to one hundred feet above the ground—until it was due north of Bandar Abbas. At which point it would turn due south and finish its journey by plunging into the building containing the Empire's Granat missile. Altogether, the Tomahawk's journey would take seventy-two minutes.

The Tomahawk is guided to its target by a McDonnell-Douglas AN/DPW-23 TERCOM (Terrain Contour Matching) system, combined with an inertial navigation system called TAINS, (TERCOM Assisted Inertial Navigation System). Altitude information obtained by a radar altimeter is continuously matched to a preprogrammed radar map of the area below the missile. The *Tomahawk* follows a detailed predetermined flight path. Several waypoints tell the missile when to change altitude and direction, in order for it to fly around hills and avoid detection by point-defense installations around the target.

Bakhit was asleep near his herd of goats, in an isolated valley south of Khue Kuhran, a 2,161 meter mountain, seventy miles north of the coast of Iran. A river flowed from the mountain, through the valley below, and on toward the sea. Bakhit's goats were bedded down and sleeping around his simple camp. Slowly awakening to the sound of a strange rumbling noise, the gentle shepherd sat up trying to determine the source and direction of the frightening noise. The ground beneath him was shaking. All around him the goats began springing to their feet, bleating and milling about. Bakhit stood to quiet them. The rumbling noise grew louder. Bakhit's heart beat faster.

Suddenly, out of the blackness, a roaring demon flashed across the sky above him. To the trembling shepherd, the thunderous roaring sounded like an aircraft. But this noise was different. The demon flew so low its roar hurt his ears and caused a terrible wind that knocked him to the ground. His terrified goats frantically scattered in every direction. Wild eyed and breathless with fright, Bakhit momentarily lay where he fell. As the demon roared off into the night, Bakhit rolled over onto his knees and began lowering his head to the ground, begging Allah to protect him.

One hour and forty-six minutes later, the BBC announced another 200 KT explosion. This one was at Bandar Abbas in Iran.

The Caliph's Palace, Tehran, Iran – 4:05 a.m., Wednesday, June 14th

Once again a terrified Omar entered the caliph's bedchamber to awaken him. Tiptoeing cautiously, he approached the bed and found his master, Saladin II sound asleep, his young companion next to him. Both were snoring. Shaking with fear, Omar stood by the bed and anxiously called out, "Excellency ... Excellency," he whimpered, "Your presence is requested by the *Shura* and your generals." On his fourth attempt, Omar jumped, then prostrated himself on the floor when the caliph responded with a grunt.

"Is it six o'clock already?" Saladin asked, remembering he had planned to rise an hour before the scheduled launch of the Empire's Shahab-3 and Kosar missiles.

The *Shura* should have learned a lesson from America's devastating response to North Korea's attempted nuclear attack. Unfortunately, fanatical clerics are not fast learners. After all, Allah doesn't protect communists.

"No, Excellency. It is four-o-six o'clock," Omar replied, still lying on the floor.

Shit! Now what's gone wrong? This fool won't know. "Stop groveling and help me dress," he screamed at the servant, before lunging from the bed and kicking the sniveling man in the ribs.

Twenty-five minutes later, the caliph entered the conference room. Taking his place at the head of the table, he barked at the generals, "Report! What's important enough to required me to be awakened at this hour?"

"May Allah be praised. Excellency, we've lost contact with Bandar Abbas. They failed to report at 3:45 a.m. Then the BBC issued a news bulletin announcing that satellites had recorded a two hundred kiloton explosion at 3:36 a.m. at Bandar Abbas."

The clerics sat in silence. The caliph stared at the general, then slowly said in a menacing voice, "Our Granat cruise missile is there. I thought you told us the technicians checked the missile."

"Praise be to Allah. It *was* checked. It was scheduled to be moved to its launch position on Qeshm Island today."

Are the missiles defective? The caliph's mind screamed. *The other one detonated while being moved.* After calming himself he asked, "Was there any indication of an attack on the base?"

At least he is capable of thinking things through, the general noted. *More than I can say for the others.* "No Excellency. We've received no reports of an attack by the Great Satan or the Little Satan," the general replied, hoping this would end the affair.

"Allah is merciful. Bring the survivors here for questioning. Surely some of them know what happened," the overexcited shrill-voiced cleric screeched.

The general was dumfounded. *Survivors! These old men have no concept of what they're dealing with.*

The caliph interrupted by sarcastically asking, *"What survivors?"*

Grand Ayatollah Khomeini was tired of the problems. *"Insha'Allah.* All things are Allah's will. Are you prepared to launch our missiles at seven o'clock?"

Before the general could frame an answer, the caliph took charge. "The missiles will not be launched! Not until they have been *thoroughly* checked. Apparently, someone or something has caused the nuclear warheads of both Granats to detonate. It may be the Granat, or it may be the warhead." Slamming his hand down on the table he snarled, "We *must* find out before we have *another* accident."

Khomeini bristled. *How dare Mohammed countermand my order.*

Saladin, observed Khomeini's expression. *It's time for me to truly become caliph. I've had enough of being his puppet.* "I repeat, the Shahab and Kosar missiles *will not* be launched. Not until we're *sure* there is no defect in the warheads." Pausing to look around the room, he focused on the generals and asked in a low, menacing voice, "How long will it take to inspect them?"

"Allah be praised," the general responded—this time really meaning it. "The warheads will have to be removed, disassembled for inspection, then reinstalled. It will take nine days."

Looking at the generals through half-closed eyes, the caliph said with an evil smile, "You have ten days counting today. We will launch the missiles at seven o'clock the morning of the tenth day."

Khomeini, still seething with anger, nodded and said, *"Insha'Allah." My puppet is getting out of control ... However, for once he may be right.*

Chapter 42

Nancy Hatterson was glad she decided to attend Ambassador Gorman's wife's luncheon. She and Ralph had always enjoyed an active social life when they vacationed in Argentina. This time Ralph wouldn't leave the hacienda. He was moody, and she was unable to snap him out of it.

The luncheon was held in a private dining room with six lavishly appointed tables. Magnificent vases of roses, their fragrance filling the air, sat atop ornately carved pedestals, adorning each corner of the room. A well-known classical guitarist softly strummed Spanish flamenco melodies. Nancy relaxed, and for the first time in the last two weeks began to enjoy herself. After introductions and the usual women's chitchat, the conversation at her table and others around her turned to world events. The latest attack by North Korea, and America's devastating, instantaneous response frightened the American community.

Waiting for dessert to be served, Nancy, and one of her table companions, overheard comments from a table next to their's. A woman was saying she expected Hugo Chavez to double the price of oil. "After he doubles the price, he'll add a hundred percent export tax to the new price," the woman continued.

Nancy raised an eyebrow and looked at her companion who was toying with her dessert. "Could that possibly be true?"

"It probably is," her companion answered, before leaning forward and whispering, "She should know, her husband is an executive with Royal Dutch Shell." Both women continued to eavesdrop, while the oil executive's wife prattled on.

When questioned about how soon Chavez might make the announcement, the woman responded, "Friday." Nancy, ever mindful of finances, made a mental note to tell Ralph they needed to buy oil futures.

After the luncheon, Judy Gorman invited Nancy to join her for an afternoon of shopping. Sitting in a small waiting room while the ambassador's car was being brought around, Nancy passed the time by picking up a magazine. Turning it over she saw a picture of an intense looking, bearded, Muslim man, glaring fiercely at her from the cover photo. In an instant her blood turned to ice. Her breath caught in her throat. Her hands began to shake. She would never forget those evil looking eyes. The caption in Spanish read, "*¿Quien es Saladin II?*" Who is Saladin II?

Nancy remained sitting, staring at the photo, until finally the ambassador's wife came looking for her. Entering the room, Judy found a clearly distraught Nancy, her face drained of color, and her eyes riveted on the magazine. Worried by Nancy's appearance, Judy asked, "Whatever's wrong dear?"

Without moving, Nancy hoarsely whispered, "I know who he is."

Judy Gorman approached the younger woman, took the magazine from her trembling hands, and looked at the image, "You do?" She gasped.

"Yes," Nancy moaned. "His name is Mohamed al-Mihdar ... He's Ralph's business partner."

Shopping forgotten, Judy Gorman picked up a phone on the table near the door and called her husband. "Charles, I must see you immediately. Get rid of whoever's with you. I have a woman with me who knows the identity of Saladin."

Judy Gorman stayed with Nancy while she was being ushered into the ambassador's office. Tony Wilson, the embassy's Legat, was present. While Judy introduced Nancy and got her a snifter of brandy, the ambassador took a seat beside her. Quickly coming to the point, Ambassador Gorman gently said, "Judy tells me you know who Saladin II is."

"Yes," Nancy bitterly replied, with tears running down her cheeks. "Yes, I know him," she said and took a gulp of brandy, "He is a Saudi, a director of Ralph's company, REM Investments, Inc.," she softly sobbed.

"There, there dear," the ambassador softly said, while patting her hand. "We're all here to help you," he coaxed, "Now tell us everything you know about Saladin—starting from the beginning."

Ralph was wondering where Nancy was. It was getting late. Security called, "Senor Eid, there are several men here from your embassy. They are demanding to see you."

Eid flipped to the TV monitor showing the entrance gate, where three black SUVs awaited entry. Time seemed to stand still. Darkness descended on him. His mind and body became numb. His nightmare had become real. *They've found out,* his frenzied mind screamed. *It had to happen!* Acting as though in a trance, he spoke into the intercom, "Jose, tell them to wait while I get dressed." Standing, Eid walked out a rear door and got into his golf cart. Exiting the grounds by the rear gate, he drove the cart to a small building on a hillside overlooking the broad river.

An agent circling the grounds reported seeing Eid exit through the rear gate. The senior FBI agent drew his pistol and ordered Jose to open the gate.

Two of the sedans sped inside the walled compound—only to find no way to exit the rear. The heavy steel gate required a keypad code to open it.

Reaching the small building, Eid quickly opened the rollup door and pulled out his motorized hang glider. He'd never consciously planned what he'd do when they came for him, but perhaps his subconscious had. Strapping on the light glider, he quickly started the motor, and ran across the hilltop. The wind caught the sail for an easy launch. Off he flew over the wide, muddy-brown *Rio de la Plata*. Mindlessly soaring aloft, Eid turned the glider for one last look at the paradise he shared with Nancy. At last, after gaining sufficient altitude, he headed east, toward the sea. Drifting aimlessly along, mesmerized by the beauty of the clouds, a final thought emerged from his muddled, tortured mind, *I wonder if I can reach South Africa?*

He couldn't.

Nancy Hatterson and Tony Wilson boarded American Airlines Flight 900, nonstop to Miami. The Boeing 767 departed Ezeiza International Airport at 8:45 p.m. and landed at Miami International Airport at 5:00 a.m. the next morning. They were met by customs officials and immediately transferred to an Air Force C-37A jet. Twenty-five minutes later the G-V departed for Albuquerque.

Teresa Lopez had received an immediate recall order from Director Clark. She was enroute to Albuquerque, via London and Philadelphia. Important new information had been obtained. Dr. Landry would remain in Moscow until the uranium-235 production questions were answered. Major Vanin decided to go to Kazakhstan.

Caracas, Venezuela – Wednesday, June 14th

A black Mercedes sedan pulled through the hacienda's large, wrought iron gates. Located on a hill, the main house overlooked Caracas to the north. Herr Ludwick von Graften observed the automobile from his upstairs office window. It was a government vehicle. Von Graften descended the impressive marble staircase to the entrance hall and watched his servant and bodyguard open the massive front door.

Colonel Manuel Garcia, holding his military hat under his left arm, pressed against his side, strutted through the doorway. "*Buenas tardes, Señor*," Garcia said clicking his heels and standing at attention. Garcia was a fan of WWII German movies.

"*Buenas tardes*, Colonel," Von Graften replied with a slight German accent, then added, "Manuel, *por favor*, would you join me on the patio for a drink?"

"*Si señor, gracias. Una cerveza.*"

Turning to his servant, von Graften said, "Hans, please bring us two Becks."

"*Ja. Zwei Becks mein herr.*"

Von Graften led the colonel through large, open, double doors onto a bougainvillea-covered loggia and out onto a terraced patio. Walking across the expansive, tiled patio to a marble table, von Graften and Garcia seated themselves in cushioned chairs. After politely inquiring about Garcia's family, von Graften inquired as to the reason for the colonel's visit. Garcia was an aide to President Hugo Chavez.

"*El Jefe* would like you to be his guest Friday afternoon at the *Brigido Iriarte Stadium*. He will give a very important speech," Colonel Garcia said.

Von Graften inwardly winced. *Another long-winded speech,* he silently moaned. *My ass went to sleep during Chavez's last speech and didn't wake up for three days. What is it with these two-bit dictators? I think Chavez is trying to out-talk Castro. This could go on for hours.* "Can you tell me the subject of this important announcement?"

"*El Presidente* plans to assert his leadership in the Americas. He will chastise the reckless actions of the self-appointed *El presidente de los Estados Unidos*. He will present his vision for the Americas. And, he will also announce a new price for our oil."

"Do you think it's wise to do so? The United States invaded Libya and Algeria to get oil. Aren't you inviting them to do the same here?"

Garcia stiffened in his seat. One did not question the wishes of *El Presidente*. "No, they wouldn't dare. Anyway, they are involved in North Africa. They do not have the ability to invade Venezuela," Garcia sneered.

Von Graften frowned, but did not disagree. His life style, purchased through generous "donations" to President Chavez, depended upon the unstable dictator's protection. "Please tell President Chavez I will be honored to be his guest."

After the colonel departed, von Graften returned to the patio. Hans brought him another beer, along with a Cuban cigar. Gazing over the lusciously landscaped lawn below, von Graften wondered, *Where could General Yatchenko be? The Cobra has certainly stirred up a hornet's nest. How did he pull off becoming caliph? Somehow I think his career is coming to an end.*

In another life, von Graften was known as Colonel Alexei Valek.

A worker preparing the 25,000-seat stadium for Chavez's speech approached the podium. Casually looking around to see if he was being observed, the worker took a small device, smaller than a cellphone, from his pocket. After checking to see if it was functioning properly, he punched the "Store" button and quickly returned the device to his pocket.

Basel, Switzerland – Wednesday, June 14th

Herr Igor Shipilov was not a happy man. It seemed as if someone had disconnected his phone. He'd received no calls. Worse, no one was returning his calls. He knew something was wrong. The thought of U.S. agents running around in mother Russia was bad enough. Karpov, the spineless dog, had given them access to Sarov, of all places, and allowed them to fly their aircraft into the secret city. Shipilov's last report said the agents had returned to Sarov on Sunday. After that there was only silence.

Dining alfresco in the garden of *Stucki's*, one of Basel's well-known restaurants, Shipilov nibbled on a wedge of Brie cheese, and sipped a glass of fruity white wine. *They must have found Glukhih. I planned to eliminate him, but the collapse came too quickly. He can identify Colonel Valek, and Valek could lead them to me. Of course I can deny any knowledge of Valek's activities. Not that they will believe me. Anyway, I do not know where Valek is, and if I don't, I doubt anyone can find him.* Shipilov gazed at the people walking by and sipped his wine. *Yes, Glukhih can tell them about Ivan, but he never knew what Ivan's orphelin was. Ivan is dead. Unless they discover the Little Boy team, they will never figure out what happened. I must not panic. I'm still safe.*

Baghdad, Iraq – Wednesday, June 15th

Leading elements of Iran's *Artesh*, army, arrived on the outskirts of Baghdad. Commanders of the *Artesh* and Iraq's reconstituted Republican Guard began the arduous task of integrating two armies. By Sunday, most of Iran's Army would be in the Baghdad area. After a couple of weeks of joint training, the new Army of the Islamic Empire would sweep west and eliminate the Little Satan. After the destruction of the Jews, the army's ranks would swell, when it combined forces with fighters from Khartoum, Cairo, Medina, and Mecca. The now unstoppable army of Allah would crush the crusaders—throw them back into the sea. The Empire's war plan was impressive. At least it was on paper.

Kirkland Air Force Base – Thursday, 15 June

Nancy Hatterson and Tony Wilson arrived at 0834. Nancy was emotionally and physically exhausted. After meeting with them, Clark decided to allow Nancy time to recuperate, while they awaited Teresa Lopez's arrival. Clark spent several hours with Wilson going over everything Nancy had said at the embassy and on the plane. Teresa received a summary of the debriefing when she landed in Philadelphia.

Captain Julian Taylor was at the airport to greet Teresa, when she deplaned in Albuquerque at 1625 hours. Grabbing her around the waist, he lifted her off the ground and swung her around. "Welcome back. I sure missed you."

Suddenly realizing she had missed him too, Teresa stood on tiptoes and gave him a very long, very passionate kiss.

"Whoa! Looks like the captain has a winner," Sergeant Troy said to the driver. After giving the two lovers a few more minutes, Troy said, "Sir, Director Clark is waiting for Agent Lopez. We'd better get a move on."

Entering Clark's office, Teresa found an oriental man sitting with the director. "Welcome back, Teresa. Sorry about the hurried recall. I don't think you've met Secretary Chin."

Teresa acknowledged SecEnergy, and replied, "I am pleased to meet you, sir."

Clark got straight to the point. "Ms. Hatterson has told us a shocking tale. We sent you a summary. The report didn't include the following information. Doctor Ralph Eid was a native-born U.S. citizen who earned his Ph.D. in nuclear physics at the University of California. He then gained employment at Livermore National Laboratories, where he had access to nuclear weapons technology. Doctor Eid inherited a great deal of money from an uncle in Egypt. Money he used to start a series of radiological diagnostic centers in the same five cities destroyed in the nuclear attacks. Each center was in a high-rise building."

Teresa sat quietly digesting Clark's statements before saying, "I think I get it. Where better to hide a nuclear weapon than in a radiological center. The high-rise provided an airburst. Damn!"

"Yes, *damn* is appropriate under the circumstances," Chin commented. "Ms. Hatterson has told us she and Eid owned a house in Livermore, where they entertained the laboratory's scientists."

Clark picked up the conversation, "Ms. Hatterson was a venture capitalist, a very successful one. She used the Livermore scientists as technical consultants to evaluate business plans, then gave them the opportunity to buy into IPO's. From what she said, she made several of the laboratory's scientists very rich. After we finish going over the details, I want you to spend time with Ms. Hatterson. Get to know her. Take her to dinner tonight. She's not a terrorist. She's just learned the man she has lived with for several years—a man she loved—was a terrorist. I want you to make her understand that she is not an outcast. You know the drill. People know things they don't know they know. Keep her talking, and you'll pick up valuable information. Secretary Chin has spoken with the director of Livermore. You and Ms. Hatterson will fly to California on Sunday. She and Doctor Eid lived in a condo in San Jose. The Livermore house was for weekend retreats. I want both of you to go through everything in Eid's office, the condo and the Livermore house. After you leave, we'll send in a team to take the places apart."

Dr. Chin spoke up, "We want Ms. Hatterson to introduce you to every one she had contact with at Livermore. She has agreed to tell them Doctor Eid was killed in a sailplane accident in Argentina. Find out what Eid was interested in—who he talked to and what about. I'm sure he used information and technology he obtained from the lab. We need to know what it was."

"Okay, it's time for you to meet Nancy Hatterson," Clark said and escorted Teresa to a small conference room where they found Nancy sitting with Captain Taylor. She was crying. Introductions were made and Clark and Taylor left the two women to get acquainted.

Chapter 43

Dallas, Texas – Friday, June 16th

It was 9:03 a.m., when two clean-cut FBI Special agents, wearing dark suits, stepped of the elevator on the 38th floor in a new downtown Dallas high-rise office building. Turning to the right, they walked a short distance down the hall and stopped before massive, wooden, double-entry doors. "Dallas Nuclear Diagnostics" was displayed on the doors in large gold letters. Entering through the left door, the two men found themselves in a plush lobby. Two well-dressed women were seated on a leather couch. A distinguished, fiftyish looking gentleman, reading a copy of *Barron's,* relaxed in a matching chair. The strikingly attractive, sophisticated, young woman at the reception desk rose to greet them.

"Welcome to Dallas Nuclear Diagnostics. How may I help you?"

Both agents nodded in greeting and one replied, "Good morning. We're looking for Mr. Tom Braggs."

The aloof expression on the brunette's face did not change as she somewhat patronizingly asked, "May I inquire as to your business with Mr. Braggs?"

"Yes, Ma'am, we understand he's the president of REM Investments. We have news regarding Doctor Ralph Eid." Both agents noted a change in the poised receptionist's cool veneer.

"Oh," she sighed. "Oh, Doctor Eid is our founder. We've been *so concerned* about him. No one has heard from him since the awful attacks. Do you know where he is?"

"I'm sorry. We must discuss this with Mr. Braggs. Where can we find him?"

"He has an office on the 22nd floor, Suite 2218. I'll let him know you're here."

Smiling, the second agent said, "Please tell him we're on the way down," and the two turned and left before the receptionist could ask their names.

Both men headed for the elevators. Three minutes later, they opened the door to suite 2218 and found a pleasant looking man waiting for them. He was in shirtsleeves with his collar unbuttoned and his tie pulled down.

"Good morning, I'm Tom Braggs," the man said, offering his hand.

The receptionist in the simply furnished, functional office was sitting at her desk doing data entry. She looked up briefly when Braggs greeted the men, and immediately returned to her work. Turning his back to the woman, one of the men discretely opened his wallet and showed Braggs his FBI identification. "Mr. Braggs, do you have a place where we can talk privately?" the agent asked.

A bit taken aback by the man's FBI identification, Braggs hesitated, "Uh, yes ... of course." Frowning, he turned and opened a door leading into the rest of the suite. "My office is this way."

Proceeding on down a hall, Ross led the two agents to a large corner office. Once the men were inside, Braggs closed the door and said, "Please have a seat," indicating two office chairs in front of his desk. "Can I offer you a cup of coffee or a soft drink?"

Both agents declined his offer. Settling into his chair, Braggs picked up the phone receiver, dialed a two-digit number and said, "Sheila, please hold my calls." Then looking at the agents, he asked, "Now, gentlemen, what can I do for you?"

The senior agent began, "Are you acquainted with Doctor Ralph Eid?"

"Yes, of course. He founded our company. He's our CEO and director. Do you have any idea where he is? We have been so worried—"

"Yes," the agent interrupted. "I'll get to his location later. Do you know a Mr. Mohammed al-Mihdar?"

"Yes. He is a director." Braggs looked perplexed. "You know," he said with a thoughtful expression, "I never met him."

"So you don't know what he looks like. Besides Doctor Eid, who would?"

"Doctor Bhatti and Doctor Wesley Murdock III worked with him. Both of them were in Boston. Doctor Murdock was the center director of Boston Nuclear Diagnostics." Braggs paused, squinting his eyes. "Oh yes, and Doctor Qaiser Ahmad, he was the Chicago center director."

Both agents frowned. "Anyone else? Anyone who might be alive?" the second agent prompted.

"No. I don't think so. Can you tell me what this is about?"

Ignoring the question, the first agent continued, "What do you know about Mr. Al-Mihdar?"

"He was a Saudi—very wealthy. As I told you I never met the man, but I always assumed he was an investor." Braggs frowned, looking thoughtful, then continued, "I was REM Investments' account manager at Arthur Anderson. Doctor Eid offered me the job as president. The company was fully funded when I joined. I never knew the source of the funds, other than they came from the Middle East. Doctor Eid inherited a fortune from an uncle in Egypt. Doctor Eid and Saudi Arabian investors owned REM Investments.

Each of our diagnostics centers was a separate company, with REM owning the majority of the stock. The center directors and I owned stock in the subsidiary companies. REM Investments was very profitable."

The two agents looked at each other. An unspoken exchange took place. This man was not involved. Looking back at Braggs, the senior agent said, "You asked if we knew where Doctor Eid was and what this inquiry is about. I regret to tell you that Doctor Eid is dead. We think he committed suicide."

"What!"

"Mr. Braggs, Mohammed al-Mihdar has been tentatively identified as Saladin II, the caliph of the Islamic Empire. The man who claimed responsibility for the atomic bombs that destroyed our cities. Cities where REM had established diagnostics centers."

Braggs, slumped in his chair, his mind racing. Finally, he looked up with a shocked expression and whispered, "Oh my God!"

The three sat in silence. Finally, the senior agent placed a small recorder on Braggs' desk and said, "Tell us everything you know about REM Investments. Start at the beginning—names, companies, and affiliates—everything."

After Braggs finished his story, the two agents thanked him and gave him their business cards. "You must tell no one what we've told you," they instructed him before leaving, "The official story is that Dr. Eid crashed his sail plane somewhere in the mouth of the Rio de la Plata River—out of sight of land—and drowned. The river is 125 miles wide at its mouth."

Albuquerque, New Mexico – Friday, June 16th

Nancy Hatterson and Teresa Lopez were finishing a late breakfast in the Marriott dining room. Nancy was still an emotional wreck. The previous evening Teresa allowed Nancy to babble. She'd talked about her life on the farm, Harvard, her job as a Venture Capitalist in Boston, and her early affair with Ralph. During the conversation, she mentioned the death of Ralph's parents, and how it affected him. Teresa recognized the importance of this comment. *Bingo. Revenge, not religious fanaticism drove Eid to become a terrorist.*

Now it was time to get the details of Eid's parent's death. "Nancy, tell me everything you remember about how Ralph's parents died."

Nancy shuddered. Frowning, she began, "We, Ralph and I, were at Harvard. His parents were returning from some friend's house on Long Island. A teenager, driving very fast, lost control of his car and hit them. Then their car was hit by a semi and rolled several times. Both of his parents died in the resulting fire. The kid was drunk. He was also the son of a powerful state senator. The politician pulled strings. When his son got off with one hundred days community service, Ralph nearly lost it. He vowed he'd get the kid and his parents, if it was the last thing he ever did. He became moody, and we decided to part. Several years later he called me. We started dating and … well," she paused fighting back tears, "It was like old times. Ralph was a successful businessman. He was happy. We were happy. He talked me into quitting my job and starting my own venture capital firm, PC Capital, in Livermore.

"He introduced me to his laboratory associates at a dinner party I helped him give at his Livermore house. Later, after I moved in with him, I became friends with many of the scientists he'd worked with. They advised me on new technology. In return I got them in on hot IPOs. We all made a lot of money. The only problem in our lives was Mohammed. He didn't like Western women, especially me." Nancy paused, her thoughts drifting, and then continued, "You know, I don't think he liked women period. He was always jabbing Ralph about me." Suddenly her expression changed, "No wonder Mohammed hated me. I was his competition. I suspected he was gay, but … damn, I never put the final piece of the puzzle together. He wanted Ralph."

"What makes you so sure?" Teresa asked.

"The one and only time I encountered Mohammed was at a dinner party in Boston. He started putting me down in front of the other guests. I took it for a while, and then went back at him. I still get a chill when I think of the evil way he glared at me. After dinner we were outside, waiting for a cab and Ralph and Mohammed had words. From that point on, Ralph's relationship with him was strained. There were occasions after that that I wondered if Ralph wasn't afraid of something or someone. He always had a tendency to be moody and often had nightmares. He blamed them on reoccurring memories of his parent's death. Then he bought a gun. He said it was for protection after he'd almost been mugged. But now I wonder if Mohammed hadn't somehow forced Ralph into conspiring with him and threatened to harm us in some way. They must have continued to communicate, because they were in business together. He seemed to disappear. Ralph did not mention him for a long time.

"Then a couple of months before the attack he surfaced. Ralph met him in New York for a conference of some sort. I heard nothing about him again, until a couple of weeks before the attacks. Ralph was on one of his annual tours of REM's facilities. I remember Ralph calling me from Boston. He told me he was going to New York to meet Mohammed. They were going to visit the New York center, then Atlanta,"—Nancy's forehead wrinkled in concentration—"Yes, then they were going to drive back to Washington. Ralph called to say he planned to fly back to California from Washington on Tuesday. He sounded tired and suggested we go to Argentina on Thursday for a holiday. We left the day before the attack. After the attacks, he went into a shell. I thought he was depressed over losing the diagnostic facilities," she concluded with a sigh and tears in her eyes.

The conversation continued for another hour. Later, Nancy helped Teresa write a summary of their discussions, and placed calls to several of the scientists at Livermore. She invited them to Ralph's Rancho Nuevo house— now it was her house—the following weekend for a memorial service. The death notice said Dr. Eid drowned after crashing his sailplane in the Rio de la Plata River. Clark asked Nancy and Teresa to fly to Oakland the next day. They would spend a couple of days at the San Jose condo and Ralph's office, then drive to the house in Livermore.

Honolulu, Hawaii – Friday morning, 16 June

The YAL-1A Boeing 747 was on final approach to the Honolulu International Airport. The crew was looking forward to the two-day layover before departing for Edwards AFB. Colonel Helen Powell was a happy camper. Her baby had proved itself. She wasn't sure why they were stopping in Hawaii, but hey, why look a gift horse in the mouth. Major Jake Quinn didn't have any problems with the Honolulu layover either. *Boy, I can't wait to get on the beach at Waikiki.*

Quinn set the big bird down like a baby. Following tower instructions, he turned off the runway and taxied behind the "Follow Me" truck. As expected, they were headed toward the Hickam AFB portion of the airfield. As they approached the hanger, Quinn couldn't believe his eyes. Picking up the intercom he said, "Colonel, you'd better come up here ASAP."

"What's the problem, Jake?"

"We got a reception committee waiting for us."

The big Boeing came to a stop as directed by the ground spotter, and the ground crew deployed and secured the mobile staircase. A short time later, an air force sergeant thumped on the front door to indicate it was safe to deplane. Immediately after the door opened, Colonel Helen Powell stepped out onto platform, and the Hickam Air Force band struck up the "Washington Post" march. Standing at the foot of the stairs was the Governor of Hawaii, the Mayor of Honolulu, the Commander-in-Chief Pacific Fleet (CINCPACFLT), the Commanding Officer of Hickam, reporters, TV cameras, and a sea of people. The cheering was deafening. People appreciate heroes, especially ones who have just saved their lives.

Colonel Powell, followed by the crew, which deplaned in no particular order, descended the stairs. The governor grabbed her hand, and began pumping it up and down, trying to tell her over the noise how much Hawaii appreciated her actions. Powell managed to salute CINCPACFLT and

Hickam's commanding officer, before being surrounded by more politicians. The Governor and Mayor continued extending their greetings and gratitude to the pilot and crew, as well as the civilians from Boeing, Northrop Grumman, and Lockheed Martin. All three companies received incalculable amounts of free publicity, because their engineers and technicians were wearing T-shirts emblazoned with "Airborne Laser" and their company's name.

After everyone had been greeted and garlanded with traditional Hawaiian leis, they were honored with the equivalent of a New York City ticker-tape parade. Cheering people lined the H-1, Nimitz Highway, Ala Moana Boulevard, and Kalakaua Avenue leading to the Royal Hawaiian Hotel. Festivities lasted two days. The Airborne Laser's crew were Hawaii's honored guests. Quinn was informed his next stop was Seattle, where similar events were planned.

Chapter 44

Hugo Rafael Chávez Frías was born on July 28, 1954, in the town of Sabaneta, in the State of Barinas, Venezuela. His father, Hugo de los Reyes Chávez, was a former regional director of education, a former member of the rightist Social Christian Party, and a past governor of State of Barinas. His mother, Elena Frías de Chávez, was also an educator. Chavez graduated from the Venezuelan Academy of Military Sciences on July 5, 1975, with a master's degree in military science and engineering. He began work on a master's in political science at the Simón Bolívar University in Caracas, but did not complete the program. Instead, he entered the army, became a paratrooper, and rose to the rank of lieutenant colonel. On July 24, 1983, the 200th anniversary of South American Liberator Simón Bolívar's birth, Hugo Chavez and fellow officers founded a group they named Revolutionary Bolivarian Movement-200. On February 4, 1992, a group led by Chavez parachuted into the presidential palace in Caracas and attempted unsuccessfully to remove then President Carlos Andrés Pérez from office. The plot failed and Chavez surrendered. Nine months later, while Chavez was in jail, his group staged a second coup attempt. This time they succeeded in capturing a TV station, and broadcast a video made by Chavez announcing the fall of the government. The second coup attempt was also crushed. After two years in prison, Chavez received a pardon from President Rafael Caldera. Instead of attempting a third coup, Chavez formed a left-wing political party called the Fifth Republic Movement, which helped elect him president in 1998 and 2002. When Chavez became president, Venezuela was a typical "Banana Republic," with oil instead of bananas. Corruption and poverty were rampant, making the country an ideal breeding ground for socialism.

Chavez wasted no time in starting reforms, most of which were needed. Soon after taking office, he sponsored a series of referendums aimed at giving him more presidential powers. Through the referendums, he established procedures for electing delegates to a Constitutional Assembly that would have the power to rewrite the Venezuelan constitution. Sitting legislators were barred from being chosen as delegates. Chavez's widespread popularity allowed his supporters to win 120 of the 131 delegates' seats in the new Constitutional Assembly, which prohibited Congress from holding meetings of any sort. In a national radio address, Chávez warned Venezuelans not to obey opposition officials, stating, "We can intervene in any police force in any municipality, because we are not going to permit any tumult or uproar. Order," he ranted, "has arrived in Venezuela." The new constitution renamed the country the "Bolivarian Republic of Venezuela;" and among other things, increased the presidential term of office to six years, while providing for a new procedure to recall a president, and providing term limits to the president of two terms. A socialist party had replaced the old dictatorial one. But Venezuela's president retained his dictatorial powers.

Fidel Castro supported Chavez's vision of a Bolivarian state. Castro became Chavez's hero. Like Castro, Chavez resented and opposed U.S. domination of the hemisphere. Chavez's revolutionary socialist policies and combative personality placed him at odds with the church and the middle and upper classes. Chavez continued his socialist reform program, passing laws by decree and giving land to the peons. After attempting to take control of the oil industry on April 12, 2002, Chavez was briefly deposed and arrested in a media-military coup d'état. Pedro Carmona was installed as the interim president. Within two days, the poor took to the streets and returned Chavez to power. His presidential guard captured *Miraflores*, the presidential palace, and returned him to office. Chávez repeatedly accused the first Bush Administration and the CIA of attempting to orchestrate a coup. In an interview with Al-Jazeera, he added Israel's Mossad to the list of coup plotters. Starting December 2, 2002, Chavez's actions resulted in a two-month business strike led by the oil industry. The strike forced Venezuela to import oil. Chavez retaliated by firing about 18,000 employees of the state-owed PDVSA oil company. A court ruling in favor of the dismissed workers was never enforced.

Chavez rewarded Castro by providing Cuba with 90,000 barrels of oil a day in exchange for the services of 20,000 physicians, teachers, and other professionals. A deal that revitalized the Cuban economy, and improved health and literacy conditions in Venezuela. Chavez who openly declares his hatred for the U.S. was the first elected government official to visit Saddam Hussein after the 1991 Gulf War.

Brigido Iriarte Stadium

Warm-up speeches by party hacks, followed by Harry Bellicose's rendition of "Night-O," had worked the crowd of 25,000 socialists to a near frenzy. *Presidente* Alexander and the *Estados Unidos* were painted as warmongers, who used the terrorists attack as an excuse to invade and conquer peaceful Arab lands. The crowd roared for *El Presidente* to speak. After suffering through an hour and a half of warm-up ravings, Von Graften was faced with hours of Chavez's ranting. *I hope the fool doesn't go too far. He is not dealing with the old U.S. The new one has shown its willingness to take swift, decisive, action. That idiot Kim didn't last an hour after he launched his ICBM's.*

The latest speaker finished with a flourish and began his grandiose introduction of *El Presidente*. "It is now my great pleasure to welcome the president of the Bolivarian Republic of Venezuela, His Excellency ... *Hugo Chavez!*" he shouted, sounding like a boxing match announcer.

The crowd roared its thunderous adulation. Waving small Venezuelan flags they chanted, "*Viva* Chavez, *Viva* Venezuela."

Chavez swaggered to the podium, wearing his red, long-sleeve, open-collar, shirt-jacket, over a red T-shirt. The same outfit he wore at the PetroCaribe Summit in Montego Bay, Jamaica. As usual, the shirt wasn't tucked into his dark pants. Standing behind the podium, he let his gaze sweep over the standing, shouting crowd. Chavez was in his element—a petty dictator basking in the adoration of his subjects.

Looking at Harry Bellicose, who was standing and shouting '*Viva* Chavez' with the crowd, Von Graften inwardly groaned, *It's going to be a long night, and my hemorrhoids are already on fire.*

Finally, Chavez raised his arms to quiet the crowd and began, "*Buenas tardes.*"

"*Buenas tardes El Presidente,*" the crowd shouted back.

"Venezuela has made great progress. Under my leadership, the living conditions of the poor have improved. We have established trade agreements with other Latin American countries for our mutual benefit. My good friend, Fidel Castro, has provided us with doctors and medical facilities. We have followed his glorious example and established a worker's paradise here in South America. Venezuela is the model for our socialist revolution ..."

Von Graften shifted in his seat. Chavez had been raving for almost two hours. Now he was speaking to the crowded stadium in somber tones, beginning his Simón Bolivar routine.

"Eight days from now, on June 24th, the Battle of Carabobo Day, our great country will commemorate the victory of a great man. On that day, 187 years ago at Carabobo—just two hours from here—a great man led our country's war weary patriots, along with Irish, Welsh, and English settlers, in a final decisive battle." Chavez slowly increased his intensity and volume, building up the final shouted statement, "*The battle for Venezuela's libertad.*

"*Si,*" he shouted. "I said *libertad* ... freedom from years of tyranny under Spanish rule."

"*Libertad, libertad,*" the excited crowd shouted back, the reply becoming a chant.

Chavez quieted them with raised arms. "All of you, even the youngest *estudiante,* know the great man. He, who was our greatest patriot. He, who became known as the towering genius of the Hispanic-American world. He, whose deeds as a warrior, political thinker, sociologist, writer, and prophet are unsurpassed among our people. Who can tell me the name of the man who is my inspiration?" "*Who is the soldier-statesman we most venerate?*" Chavez's question ignited the crowd.

From every corner of the stadium echoed back the thunderous response "*El Li–ber–a–tor-or-or! El Li–ber–a–tor-or-or!*"

"WHO?" Chavez shouted back, and then to the delight of his fans, he began his favorite method of inciting a crowd—jumping up and down on the balls of his feet like a jumping jack.

"*El Liberator–or-or, El Liberator–or-or,*" roared the crowd again and again.

"*Si! Si, El Liberator,* The Liberator ... *Simón Bolívar,*" Chavez yelled back to the crowd, continuing to jump up and down.

"*Simón Bolívar, Simón Bolívar,*" the crowd roared again and again.

"*Simón Bolívar,*" Chavez continued, leading the thunderous chanting of the frenzied crowd. "*Bolívar, Bolívar.*" The shouting could be heard for kilometers around the stadium.

So began Chavez's tribute to his idol, and the ensuing two hours of Von Grafton's torment. For the next 120 agonizing minutes, Grafton smiled and squirmed on the hard wooden seat to ease his hemorrhoids, and politely applauded while Chavez continued to extol the endless virtues of his idol.

Simón Bolívar was indeed a man to be respected and venerated. He had, during his illustrious military career, accomplished what thousands of multinational colonists and slaves thought was a miraculous feat. He had, through sheer self-determination, freed the poor and starving masses from Spanish tyranny, and brought constitutional rule to six South American countries. Venezuela, Columbia, Peru, Bolivia, Panama, and Ecuador all owed their independence to Bolivar's unwavering determination to free his homeland.

Finally, to Grafton's relief, it appeared as though Chavez might be about to wrap up his speech. He'd allowed the applause to die and was standing quietly gazing over the stadium, when suddenly he burst into a tirade berating the United States and its new president.

"*Estados Unidos* is an evil country," Chavez shouted. "President Bush planned to invade our country, just as President Alexander has invaded North Africa. The Bush invasion plan had a name. It was called 'Balboa.' Bush planned to invade us with aircraft carriers and planes. Their soldiers landed on our island of Curaçao to scout out a landing beach. My denouncement caused them to scrap the plan." *El Jefe* was interrupted by more applause.

"The United Nations kept *Estados Unidos* under control. Now, the UN needs a new home—a home in a free, neutral, country. Today I am offering the city of *Caracas* as the new home for the United Nations." Assuming an arrogant stance, Chavez paused, letting his eyes survey the crowd, while he received a standing ovation.

"The Organization of American States is dominated by *Estados Unidos*. No more! It is time for a change. It is time to *expel* the capitalist dogs. It is time to rename the organization. It must be renamed the 'Organization of Socialist Spanish American States.' " More shouting and applause came from the overexcited crowd. The speech went on for another hour before Chavez finally got to his main message.

"Capitalism is destroying Latin America. The people are poor. Something must be done. Cuban-style socialism is the best alternative to capitalism. We need a new Simón Bolívar, a man of vision and an economic liberator for the twenty-first century—a leader who will free our economically oppressed people. We need a leader who will bring socialism to Latin America."

Holding both arms up over his head, Chavez strutted and basked in shouts and applause from his audience. He was experiencing a high few men would ever know. The euphoria that comes from being worshiped. Now was the time for the *coup de grâce*.

"Tonight I am changing the PetroCaribe oil agreement. Member countries of the agreement will no longer pay $70.00 a barrel for our oil. Their new fee is $40.00 a barrel. Other Spanish speaking nations of the Americas are invited to join PetroCaribe." Chavez paused, looking at the crowd with his usual idiotic expression.

"*Estados Unidos* is excluded. It will *not be allowed to join* PetroCaribe," he shouted. The crowd went wild as Chavez once more began childishly hopping up and down. Finally, with an evil grin on his face, he raised his arms for quiet and continued, "We will join with our Muslim brothers. Our new terms for oil will be similar to those of the Islamic Empire. Our new price for *non*-PetroCaribe members will be $150.00 per barrel. *Estados Unidos* will be charged an export tax of 100 per cent. If he wishes to purchase our oil, President Alexander will have to recognize me as the leader of the Organization of Socialist Spanish American States."

Von Graften slumped in his uncomfortable chair. *Oh, shit. Now he's done it. The fool has thrown the glove down in such a manner Alexander will have to pick it up. I think I'd better start looking for a new home. I wonder how much time I have?*

Chavez continued ranting about his new Organization of Socialist Spanish American States.

Southwestern White House – 2034 Hours, Friday, 16 June

Ironically, President Alexander, who was watching the end of Chavez's speech in the situation room in Albuquerque, agreed with Von Graften's assessment. *That tears it. Wellington's right. He's left me no choice—I have to take him out.*

Martha Wellington, Ross, Young, Newman, Keese, and Simpson, sitting near the president, sat shaking their heads, while privately wondering—*How can the man be such a fool?* Finally, Keese said, "Jacking up the price of oil is bad enough. But, what really concerns me is his call for revolution in Central and South America. He is attempting to plunge our hemisphere into total chaos. Hell, it may even destabilize Mexico."

Wellington agreed. "Mr. President, his speech is going to trigger revolution in several unstable governments. You have to do something to stop him. We don't have time for diplomatic niceties."

Finally Alexander spoke. "He has given me no choice." Looking directly at Simpson, he said, "Harry, give the order."

SecWar Harry Simpson picked up a phone sitting in front of him. Admiral Robert Vazquez, CINCSTRATCOM, answered. SecWar said, "Bob, Operation Cortez is authorized. Execute."

A B-2 bomber, loitering 100 miles offshore over the Atlantic, turned toward the coast of Venezuela. Approaching Caracas at 42,000 feet, its bomb bay doors opened, and four JDAM Global Positioning Satellite (GPS) guided bombs, each programmed with the exact coordinates of Chavez's podium—provided by the worker two days earlier—were released. Chavez's socialist revolution ended with a bang at 2107 hours.

New elections would be held in three months, and Venezuela would again be free.

Chapter 45

Kirkland AFB – Thursday, 15 June

War quickly develops its own dynamics. U.S. led forces were consolidating their position in Libya. Iran's Army was moving into Iraq to form the Army of Islam—a matter of concern to U.S. commanders. Wars are won through decisive action, not by playing defense. CINCSTRATCOM called SecWar to discuss the situation.

"Harry," Admiral Valquez said, "We have to disrupt the Empire's troop movements. If we allow the armies of Iran and Iraq to combine, we have a problem."

I agree, Bob. I've discussed this with the president. He's aware of the problem. What do you suggest?"

"I think it is time for a council of war. I suggest a meeting with the British in Eisenhower's old headquarters at Gibraltar. The president will be safe in the tunnels. It would take a large nuclear warhead to destroy 'The Rock,' and it is guarded by the Royal Gibraltar Regiment."

"Good idea. I'll suggest it to the president."

President Alexander and Martha Wellington were on Air Force One, one of three C-37As that touched down at Gibraltar on Saturday at 2000 hours. SecWar Simpson and LG John Blankenship, Deputy Commander STRATCOM were on the other two C-37As. When they landed, Simpson pulled General Letterman aside and inquired about the status of the *Ibrahim-al-Ibrahim* Mosque, built in the South area of Gibraltar by Saudi Arabia's King Fahd in 1997. Letterman assured SecWar the mosque had been sanitized and its minaret was being used as an OP.

The secret meeting to finalize plans to destroy the Islamic Empire convened early Sunday morning in a chamber located off one of the tunnels deep inside The Rock. It surprised Alexander to find Britain's Prince Harry in attendance with the country's Air Marshal, Sir James Murrell. General Letterman, Commanding General for Operation Flare, opened the meeting by reporting oil production in Algeria and Libya was restored, and would soon be above previous levels. A steady stream of ships carrying troops and equipment from Europe were arriving at Libyan ports, faster than they could be unloaded. Several additional ports were being opened to speed up the unloading process. "In another week I'll have sufficient forces on the ground to invade Egypt. Air power is in place. Italian, Portuguese and Spanish troops will occupy Algeria, Libya and Tunisia, freeing U.S. and British troops for the next phase," the general concluded.

Over the next few hours, the order of battle and timetable for the second phase of Operation Flare were discussed and finalized. After a thorough review of strategies for attacking Egypt, Syria, and Saudi Arabia, plans for invading the three countries were finalized and approved.

The meeting was progressing well, but they still hadn't set a kickoff date for the second phase. One big question still remained unanswered in everyone's mind—when would the president authorize the other part of the war plan, Operation Brimstone, the main attack on the Islamic Empire. Details of Brimstone's opening phase hadn't been revealed. Only the president and SecWar knew the exact plans. And SecWar would say no more about the plans than to advise General Letterman, that six B-1B Lancer bombers and a squadron of F-22A Raptors would arrive at Wheelus on Thursday. "Each Lancer is to be placed in a guarded hanger," Letterman told him, "The command pilot of each plane will have sealed orders. The Raptors are tasked to provide fighter cover for the Lancers." Letterman, Murrell, and the prince all looked at Blankenship for an answer, but he responded with a slight shrug. SecWar noted the exchange and smiled. The president kept his secrets close.

After a brief break for a catered lunch and some discussion about Eisenhower's cramped quarters—a damp eight foot by five foot chamber deep in the Rock—the meeting reconvened. Alexander began by announcing the kickoff date for Operation Brimstone, the main attack on the Islamic Empire, "A special cruise missile strike will be launched to take out TV stations and transmitters at 1900 Zulu Friday, 23 June. The main cruise missile attack will be launched to simultaneously attack the Empire's Air Force and missile bases at 0200 Zulu Saturday, 24 June. Following the cruise missile attack, the B-1B Lancers and the Raptors will execute simultaneous attacks according to their special orders. Additional data will be provided before the strike. In addition, we'll launch one ICBM at Iran. Phase II of Operation Flare, the land invasion of Egypt will begin the following day. Once Saudi Arabia is conquered, we will continue into Iraq and Iran.

"Marines will land in Israel and Lebanon. Israel controls the area and no resistance is expected. The *Truman* Strike Group will eliminate any remaining Iranian resistance and move into the Persian Gulf. Marines will land in Bahrain, Qatar, and the UAE. Reinforcements have sailed from our east coast. When they arrive, we'll occupy key locations in Oman and capture the main port in Yemen. Next, Kuwait will be occupied as our staging area for the invasion of Iraq. So far, Bahrain, Qatar, Kuwait, and the UAE have avoided joining the Islamic Empire. Unless resistance is experienced, they and their citizens will be treated as allies."

Alexander looked at each person to make sure his orders were understood. Satisfied, he continued. "If we encounter any resistance in these countries, eliminate it in a manner that will discourage further opposition. Mosques will be closed and destroyed. Copies of the Qur'an will be confiscated and burned. Men and women will be forbidden to wear Muslim clothing. We're going to break the back of the Islamic religion. I expect resistance from the clerics. Round them up. Eliminate them if necessary. If a mosque becomes a base for resistance, turn it into a pile of sand. The rulers of each country will be informed of the rules. It they cooperate, they will remain independent countries. If not, they will become our possessions." His last statement was greeted with grunts and nods of approval. Standing, Alexander said, "Let's take a break."

When the meeting reconvened, Alexander turned the meeting over to Lieutenant General Blankenship. Planning and briefing continued until 2000 hours.

Early Monday morning the president and his party departed for Albuquerque. As he watched Air Force One lift off from Gibraltar's airport, General Letterman smiled. *The Commander-In-Chief knows how to keep a secret. He didn't specify the B-1B's ordnance or targets. One thing's for sure, he isn't afraid to use overwhelming power. It's nice to work for a man who worries about our men and women, not the enemy's.* Laughing, he remembered the opening scene of the movie *Patton*. George C. Scott, playing Patton, said something to the effect "I don't want you to die for your county. I want you to make the other SOB die for his country." *Something our politicians either never understood ... or if they did, they forgot it. I will be told what the Lancer's targets are when the time comes. His orders to allow the French ships to pass opens some interesting areas for speculation.* "Hmmm."

Los Angeles, California – Friday, June 16th

Reverend Smyth left Dream Maker Studios carrying a box full of his "Message to Islam" DVDs. It had taken five days to record, edit, and add the special effects. At first he'd found it difficult to preach from a stage that was set in front of a green screen. On the fourth attempt he got it right, and the final results were ... well ... they were. He would show it to President Alexander as soon as he reached Albuquerque.

During the flight to Albuquerque, Smyth gazed out the window at the towering cumulous clouds. It appeared the plane was flying through huge canyons formed by massive clouds rising out of sight on both sides of the aircraft. The "New World Symphony" was playing through his earphones. Settling back in his leather seat, he began reviewing events. *The Interfaith Advisory Committee was almost finished drafting its recommendations on what to do with the domestic Muslims. Questions still remained— unanswerable questions. Will domestic Muslims accept revisions to or elimination of their faith—their Qur'an, Sunnah, and sharia? Do they have a choice? The alternative is too horrible to contemplate.*

Will the millions of illiterate, impoverished Muslims throughout the world—brainwashed since childhood in madrasaes, fed propaganda in mosques by illiterate mullahs and ayatollahs—accept major revisions to their faith? They carry a book—the Qur'an—most of them can't read. They memorize scriptural passages and repeat them over and over, until they've become holy ritual. Millions are being manipulated by a few educated clerics who selectively tell them what to believe. The result is hundreds of millions of brainwashed fanatics. The only real solution is to separate and educate the young children, thereby creating a generation of orphans. What a terrible solution, but is there an alternative? So far none's been found. Time is running out.

In the sky over Northern California – Saturday morning, June 17th

Taking off her reading glasses and rubbing her eyes, Acting Secretary of Health and Human Services, Dr. Betty Chatsworth tried to ignore the headache throbbing in her temples. She'd been reading a brochure describing a series of CD-ROMs developed over a two-year period by the Navy to train medical professionals in ways to treat victims of nuclear attacks. According to the brochure, a FEMA training specialist had stated that experts trained in treating victims of nuclear attacks were few and far between. *Tell me something I don't know.* Chatsworth frowned. *We're doing the best we can to care for the victims of this attack, but we have nowhere near enough knowledgeable people to cope with a disaster of this magnitude. We've failed miserably to prepare for this kind of attack, and now I'm at the epicenter of dealing with someone else's failure to recognize the danger.*

Setting the brochure aside, she tried in vain to fall asleep. Every time she closed her eyes, she saw images of horribly burned and maimed radiation victims. Whimpering softly to herself, she gave up fighting her headache and reached in her purse for her pain meds. *I've got to get a hold of myself. We land in forty-five minutes and I'm a wreck,* she told herself and gulped down two pills with a sip of water.

The stress of her new job and a lack of sleep during the last forty-eight hours were beginning to show. Even now, sitting in the comfortable leather chair of a C-20 Gulfstream III jet, cruising at 30,000 feet, she couldn't relax and shut off her troubled thoughts. Today she was on her way to Seattle: the last stop on her cross country tour of treatment centers dedicated to the care of survivors from the five cities.

Sighing deeply and choking back tears, Chatsworth felt completely overwhelmed and sick at heart—crushed by the mind-numbing magnitude of the suffering she'd witnessed at every stop along the way. Thousands upon thousands of injured and dying were being treated at civilian and military hospitals, military triage centers, field hospitals, and Red Cross emergency centers. More victims were arriving every day, and would continue to arrive over the next weeks and months to come. It would be years before the exact death toll and the scope of human suffering would be known.

Early on in the tour, she'd been devastated to learn that initial efforts to get aid to the injured had been seriously hampered. Local hospitals had been reduced to radioactive dust and regional and local emergency transport vehicles destroyed. First emergency responders reported finding roads clogged with survivors. Desperate people were driving themselves or family members in personal vehicles to nearby towns and cities for help. Thanks to the National Guard taking over, major highways were kept moving and survivors directed to predetermined temporary evacuations sites.

If not for the fast response by the combined military services—thanks to the fast action by Charles Young, Alexander's Chief of Staff—field hospitals and staff to run them wouldn't have been quickly set up to receive the injured. Triage stations determined which survivors would be sent on for treatment and which would be sedated and housed in hastily set up tent cities until they died. Faced with the enormous number of dead and dying the military abandoned the idea of setting up temporary morgues. There was no time for identification of the dead. After being photographed and fingerprinted, the dead were placed in body bags then stacked like cord wood, waiting for transport by the military for mass burial or cremation.

There was no end to the tales survivors were telling about their horrifying experiences during and after the blast. Some told of being blinded by a brilliant light; others of being blown through the air by the shock wave. Still others recounted how their clothing spontaneously ignited leaving them horribly burned. Then there were those brave souls, who, even though injured, went back into the inferno to try and free fellow victims from the radioactive rubble of collapsed buildings. And finally, there were the ones who watched helplessly as loved ones perished in agony before their eyes.

The greatest concern among medical staff and emergency responders was the lack of pharmaceuticals and plasma. The national blood supply had been almost depleted. But thanks to domestic and foreign Red Cross efforts, citizens around the world were rolling up their sleeves to fill the void. Drug companies were donating millions of dollars worth of medications to help with the relief. But all of this needed to be coordinated and channels of distribution established.

Once more choking back tears Chatsworth swallowed hard, frustrated by her lack of training in dealing with a crisis of this magnitude. Her only experience with A-bomb disease, a term given for the medical conditions experienced by Hiroshima and Nagasaki survivors, had been a seminar she's attended at NIH. In response to a request by American physicians and emergency providers for training in caring for A-bomb survivors, the Hiroshima International Council for Health Care of the Radiation-exposed, HICARE, had conducted the seminar. Many of the medical professionals she'd met on her tour had received training through similar programs. Using records of the treatment and study of Hiroshima and Nagasaki A-bomb survivors, HICARE was a leading authority on the care of radiation victims.

Closing her eyes, Chatsworth gradually began to relax. Her headache had eased and somehow recalling all she'd witnessed, was helping her to feel a bit more optimistic. *It really is comforting to see the marvelous way so many American citizens and people from around the world are responding to the crises. Doctors and nurses from many countries have come to help. Medicine is pouring in from Asia, England and Europe. Millions of people are displaced. Their homes and cities are gone. But others throughout the country are pitching in to help, accepting displaced families into their homes. Families are being reunited and kept together. Closed military bases have been opened to house refugees. The president's given the Corps of Engineers responsibility for planning and reconstructing the five cities. Radiation is still too high to allow entrance into the center of the bombed cities. Victims are receiving the best available treatment. We have almost unlimited funds to pay for the treatment ... but the source of the funds. We stole the funds,* she snorted in disgust. *We simply reached out and took the money ... spoils of war? That's what most are calling it. Almost everyone I speak to praises Alexander's actions. If they held elections today he would be a shoo-in. The injured and their families want retribution—retribution against Islam.*

Oh, God, what are we to do? Chatsworth wondered as her thoughts turned to her meeting with the IFAC. *After reading surahs from the Qur'an, and passages from what they called the Sunnah, I don't know what to think— the message is the opposite of what my friends, colleagues, and the media have been saying. How could society have failed to recognize the truth? It was right there in the teaching of Islam, in the* Qur'an, *and the words and deeds of Muhammad.* Nonetheless, Betty Chatsworth was struggling to accept what facts and logic told her. Emotions do rule logic. People believe what they want to believe. Denial is the most convenient way to deal with unpleasant facts.

Chatsworth continued her thoughts as she gazed out of the window, attempting to reconcile them with her emotions. *How could people we've tried so hard to help hate us so much? How could a religion founded on war, oppression, piracy, slavery ... a religion that celebrates death be accepted by one-and-a-half-billion people? Perhaps the name provides a clue. After all, the committee did tell me Islam means submission.*

Each day of her tour she'd been plagued by memories of what the IFAC had told her. Why had so many European countries sheltered Islamic fanatics who were bent on destroying them? And now according to briefings she'd received after her arrival in Albuquerque, several South American countries had joined forces with the jihadists. Even Fidel Castro had supported Iran.

Castro surprised her when he called with an offer to send a team of doctors and nurses to help treat Spanish-speaking victims from the five cities. *What on earth was he trying to achieve by that act of kindness?* Even more surprising was the president's reaction when she spoke to him by phone about Castro's call. "Accept the offer," he'd told her, leaving her even more confused as to both leaders' motives.

What Chatsworth didn't know—because she couldn't see the president's face—was how Castro's offer to help had pleased him. She couldn't see the broad smile on his face, or know the reason for it. Alexander was glad to know Fidel understood the message the U.S. delivered at the Brigido Iriarte Stadium.

San Jose, California – Saturday afternoon, June 17th

Teresa Lopez and Nancy Hatterson entered the private elevator in Nancy's eight-story condominium building. Stepping out of the elevator into the entry foyer of the penthouse, Teresa marveled at what she saw, *Wow! I guess she was successful. This place is worth millions.*

Still wide-eyed with wonder, Teresa followed Nancy through an opulent living room, down a long hallway, and into an elegant room Nancy called the guest bedroom. Taken aback at the size of the room—actually a suite of rooms—Teresa couldn't help comparing it to her small BOQ apartment in Albuquerque. After she'd unpacked, Nancy gave her a tour of the penthouse. Together, they went through Ralph's personal effects. Another bedroom served as a study, with a small desk, telephone and computer. The hard drive contained nothing of interest. Nancy explained they used the computer to monitor the markets, news websites, and to check e-mail. "I keep all my files on a small portable hard drive. Ralph kept his on a mini-portable hard drive—it was always with him. Perhaps you'll find something of interest in his office tomorrow. Our offices are on different floors."

The last room on the tour was a fully equipped gourmet kitchen. "We both loved to cook. Ralph spent a lot of time in here helping ...." Nancy started to cry again, and Teresa suggested they go out for dinner. There would be time for her investigation tomorrow.

The next morning they entered an impressive looking office building and took the elevator to the third floor. Nancy led Teresa to a door displaying only the suite number, 320. Inside, Teresa discovered a suite with a reception area, two apparently unoccupied twelve-by-twelve furnished offices, and a large, richly appointed, corner office. A custom-made leather executive chair stood behind a large teak desk. Behind the desk and against the wall was a matching credenza. After showing Teresa around and answering her questions, Nancy gave her a sheet of paper containing notes and her office phone number, and left for her office on the fifth floor.

Teresa decided to start in Ralph's office. A 20-inch LCD display screen was located near the center of the desk. Taking a seat in Eid's chair, she quickly discovered a computer keyboard on a pullout shelf under the desktop. The desk was locked, but Nancy had given her Ralph's spare key. An indexed business card file box sat next to the telephone on the left side. Carrying the small box to the outer office, she began copying the cards on a Canon copier—starting with the A's—carefully replacing each one in its original order.

Returning to the desk, she began going through the drawers, finding nothing of interest in the top drawer on the left. The two mock drawers below—actually one large hanging file drawer—held ten folders containing financial reports from each diagnostic facility. After scanning the first three reports, Teresa shook her head in admiration, *Yeah, the facilities were definitely cash cows.*

The top right desk drawer contained Ralph's checkbook, a current bank statement for his personal account, a phone book, pens, pencils, and a small note pad. The bottom right mock double drawer concealed the HP computer's CPU. The matching teak credenza held a color laser printer, and two framed photos of Ralph and Nancy. *Boy! He sure was handsome.* Opening the sliding doors on the front of the credenza, she found nothing of interest, just a variety of technical books and manuals.

Teresa got up from the desk and began examining the rest of the room. Against an inside wall, two large Danish modern leather chairs, separated by a teak end table with a door on the front, sat at an angle to one another. In front of the two chairs was a teak coffee table topped with several copies of *Fortune* magazine and a replica of Aguste Rodin's sculpture, *The Thinker*. When she opened the front door of the end table, Teresa was surprised to find a safe. *This is no home safe you buy at Lowes. This baby's bolted to the floor and has a biometric fingerprint lock. It will take an expert to open it.* Closing the table's door, she took another look around the room. *There's nothing more of interest in here, but I will ask Nancy about the safe. Maybe she can open it.* Teresa decided to continue her search in the reception area.

Walking toward the receptionist's desk Teresa noticed something she'd missed when she'd entered with Nancy. On the floor next to the desk sat a cardboard box. When she bent to investigate its contents, she discovered that someone, perhaps the cleaning staff, had placed mail in it. She picked up the box, emptied it on the desk, and began going through the pile of mail—mostly junk, a few credit card bills, letters from the center directors, two letters from a New York law firm, and a letter from REM Investments, Inc., with a New York address. *This must be from Tom Braggs' office*, she thought and continued sorting. Then she found something odd: something out of place, something that might just be the clue Clark told her she'd stumble across. *Could this be the trail marker along the path leading to the solution of the mystery?* she wondered as she looked at the envelope in her hands. The name on the return address was Mail Boxes, *Etc.* Why would Ralph Eid have a mailbox in Oakland? Using the receptionist's letter opener, Teresa carefully slit open the envelope and found an invoice addressed to Mr. Ralph Eid for what appeared to be a personal mailbox. *So, Doctor Eid had a postal address in Oakland. Why would he need another mailing address? I wonder what we'll find there, and if Nancy knows anything about it?* Teresa thought, smiling as she placed the invoice in her briefcase.

Having found nothing more of interest in the mail, Teresa made a quick search of the receptionist desk but found nothing. *Perhaps I'll get lucky and find something on Ralph's computer.* Seated in the large leather chair at Eid's teak desk, she booted the computer. Of course it required a password. Looking at the piece of paper Nancy gave her, Teresa picked up the receiver and dialed Nancy's office. "Nancy, can you open the safe, and do you know the password for Doctor Eid's computer?

"No, I can't open the safe, but the password is 'ringsofallah,' all lowercase."

"Teresa spent the remainder of the morning going through Eid's hard drive. She found nothing of importance. *The techies will spend hours dissecting this. Maybe they'll find something. I suspect all the good stuff is on his mini-portable hard drive, and it should be in their house in Argentina.* Flipping open her cellphone, she pushed the speed dial button for Director Clark. When he answered, she provided him with a concise report. Shortly thereafter, a team from the Buenos Aries embassy was on their way to the hacienda to search for Eid's mini-portable hard drive. Before leaving Eid's office, Teresa faxed a copy of the Mail Boxes, *Etc.* invoice and a short report with recommendations to Barry Clark and Sean Kilpatrick, the SAC of the San Francisco Bay FBI office.

Late Monday afternoon, Nancy and Teresa drove to the Livermore house. Ralph's Mercedes SL 500 was in the garage. "I guess it's mine now," Nancy said with tears in her eyes. After a tour of the house, the two sat on the patio, and Nancy began crying. Memories of the pleasant times she and Ralph shared came rushing back. Teresa encouraged her to talk. Names of Livermore scientists emerged during Nancy's recollections. The next morning, Tuesday, Nancy would begin calling the rest of their contacts and friends at Livermore National Laboratories to invite them to Doctor Eid's memorial service to be held at the house on Sunday afternoon.

Kirkland AFB – Tuesday, 20 June

Starting at 0100, several convoys of heavily guarded trucks departed Kirkland's Underground Munitions Storage Complex (KUMSC) and made their way across the base to guarded hangers containing six B-1B bombers. After unloading their cargo, they returned for another load. Lieutenant Colonel James Harley, 898th Munitions Squadron of the 377th Air Base Wing, supervised the operation.

That evening, Jane Alexander and the president were relaxing in their recliners. Reverend Smyth, and Martha Wellington sat on the couch, and Harry Simpson and Alan Keese occupied dining room chairs. They'd all been watching Smyth's Dream Maker DVD. The music and final image on the forty-two inch LCD screen faded away. No one spoke for several long seconds. Finally, Jane said, "Awesome."

Smyth added, "I've seen it several times, and I'm still awed by my own performance. Boy, Dream Maker really did a good job."

"What are you going to do with it?" Jane asked, getting up.

Standing, Alexander smiled, walked over to Jane, placed his arm around her and gave her a hug. "You'll have to wait and see. I don't want to spoil the surprise," he replied with a grin

"Oh, you and your surprises, you're just awful. I'll bet even the reverend doesn't know what your plans are," Jane replied with a smile.

Reverend Smyth squirmed on the couch. "You're correct, Mrs. Alexander. But I can't wait to find out," he added looking at the president who laughed.

Twenty minutes later Reverend Smyth, Simpson, Keese, and Wellington left and the Alexanders were able to enjoy a rare hour of quality time. After Jane went to bed, the president entered his bedroom office, opened his briefcase, and extracted a memo from Colonel Young, which read, "B-1B modifications complete. Aircraft will arrive Kirkland, 20 June to load special ordnance. Scheduled for departure at 0530, 21 June." Replacing the memo, Alexander picked up the DVD they had viewed earlier, and placed it in the briefcase with the memo. Smiling, he prepared for bed.

FBI Office, San Francisco, CA – 8:00 a.m., Wednesday, June 21st.

Teresa Lopez was ushered into SAC Sean Kilpatrick's office. Kilpatrick stood and walked to greet her. "Good morning, Special Agent Lopez. Good job with the terrorists."

"Good morning, sir. Thank you, but I had a lot of help," Teresa replied, sizing up Kilpatrick. *Now, he's exactly what a SAC should be—nothing like The Twit. Pleasant, but no bullshit allowed. Another one of Clarks and the president's instant appointments, boy, they sure know how to pick 'em.*

Taking the indicated chair, Teresa waited for Kilpatrick to return to his chair, and then said, "I suspect we may find some interesting things in Doctor Eid's Oakland mailbox. Do you have the search warrant?"

Kilpatrick smiled. *Good, she gets right to the point. Clark's very impressed with her.* "Yes. At first Judge Ginsberger was reluctant to issue it— said it was too broad. I had to point out we were after the man who planted the five atomic bombs. Getting in the way of our investigation would lead to early retirement. In light of Judge Kennedy's 'early retirement,' Ginsberger reconsidered. Our warrant to search the mail box is good for the next six months—plus it includes any other location identified from materials obtained in the search."

Teresa laughed. *Yeah, this man gets things done.* "Wonderful! Okay, let's go to Oakland and visit Mail Boxes, *Etc.*"

An hour later, Kilpatrick parked his car in the Jack London Square lot. Teresa parked her FBI Chrysler 300C two spaces away. She'd been issued a car, because she planned to return to Livermore after the day's investigation to help Nancy, who was busy arranging the Sunday memorial service.

Inside the store, Kilpatrick presented the search warrant to the owner, who reviewed the document and gave them a box of mail. "Mr. Eid hasn't collected his mail since May 13th. I'm afraid he might have been in one of the bombed cities. I know Mr. Eid frequently flew to Chicago and New York."

"No, Mr. Eid was killed in a sailplane accident. Please keep the mailbox active. One of our agents will come by every week to collect the mail," Kilpatrick said, handing the man his card. "Call me if you have any questions. Can we use your office to go through the mail?"

"Yes. This way."

While sorting through the box of mail, they found statements from five different banks. Each statement was for a different company. Then they found an invoice for a safe deposit box in the name of Ralph Eid. While piling the mail back in the box, Kilpatrick made a decision "Let's go to our Oakland office. I think we found a gold mine." Picking up the box of mail, they thanked the storeowner and departed.

Chapter 46

Operation Brimstone

Phase I

Dora, Qatar – Thursday, June 22nd.

William Finch, America's ambassador to Qatar, received coded instructions from the Secretary of State. The content shocked him. Shortly thereafter, Lieutenant Colonel Jim Ryder, USA, the embassy's military attaché, received a call from Colonel Young. Young briefed Ryder on America's plans for the next twenty-four hours, and on Ryder's role in implementing the president's directives—particularly those involving the ambassador. After receiving his orders, Ryder called the ambassador to confirm he had obtained an immediate audience with Emir of Qatar. Ryder also mentioned that he would accompany the ambassador to the meeting. Ambassador Finch was not pleased.

The pair arrived at the emir's palace at 2:45 p.m. After the usual diplomatic protocols, Finch attempted to subtly broach the subject of the interview. "Excellency, the United States appreciates the warning you provided before the atomic attacks, and the copy of the second al-Qaeda video. We believe that your actions indicate your commitment to support our country's efforts to defend itself. Therefore, acting on my government's instructions, I am requesting that you order Al-Jazeera to cease broadcasting all programs at 10:00 p.m. Friday. In addition we ask that the network begin continuously playing this DVD until 7:00 a.m. the following morning." Finch said, offering the emir a DVD in a plastic case. "President Alexander will address the world beginning at 7:00 a.m., and Al-Jazeera will carry his address."

The emir bristled. Scowling, he replied, "Such a request is out of the question."

"Excellency, my government makes this request as a friendly ally of your country. Honoring our request will be—"

The emir stood and glared at them. Then waving his hand in a dismissive gesture, he turned his back on them to indicate the interview was over.

Both Ryder and Finch quickly stood. Ambassador Finch was about to make an apologetic statement when Ryder stepped in front of him. Boldly addressing the emir's back, Ryder said, "Sir, honoring our request will mean you will remain emir. Not doing so will result in your untimely death."

Whirling back to confront the colonel, the emir snarled, *"You dare to threaten me in my palace."*

"No, sir. I'm not threatening you. I'm stating a fact. The United States is at war. We plan to crush the Islamic Empire and take its territories as our possessions. Qatar, and the other small Arab countries that have not joined the Empire, will be spared destruction. Islam, however, will be banned. If your TV station does not broadcast our DVD as requested—the station will be destroyed, and we'll broadcast on its frequencies."

Ryder's effrontery stunned the emir. Following his initial flash of anger, the emir remained quiet for several seconds, considering the seriousness of his situation. After assessing the nervous ambassador, he looked into Ryder's steely eyes, and faced reality, "I think you are serious."

Returning the emir's contemptuous look, Ryder replied, "Yes, your Excellency, we are *deadly* serious. If you cooperate, no harm will come to you or your country."

Ambassador Finch was panic-stricken. Diplomats did not speak to the ruler of a country in this manner. Yet, this Army light colonel had just done so. With his face flushed and sweating profusely, Finch remained quiet. He'd been given specific orders not to interfere if Ryder chose to intervene. Now he was petrified at the thought of what would happen next. *We're about to be thrown out of Qatar,* he worried, fighting hard to control his anxiety.

Suddenly, to Finch's relief, the emir broke the tension by returning to his chair. For several seconds he sat staring at Ryder, obviously considering the implications of what the military attaché had said. "What do you mean by your statement that Islam will be banned?" he finally asked.

"Sir, the president and his Cabinet consider Islam the root cause for the attacks on the West. Detonating atomic bombs in five of our cities placed Islam at war with the United States. After the detonations, Muraaqibu al-Khawaatim, who is now Saladin II, took credit for the attacks and founded the Islamic Empire. Islam declared war on the United States and the West. In this war, there will be one winner and one loser. The loser will be Islam. In order to prevent a future war, Islam will be expunged from the planet—no matter how long it takes."

The emir made no immediate reply. Instead, he sat looking at Ryder for several seconds, pondering his words. *It had to happen. The fanatics would have nothing less. Perhaps this is a good thing. After what the U.S. did to North Korea, I have no doubt they're serious. My religion has prevented me from instituting many changes. Islam destroyed Iran and Pakistan and is destroying Afghanistan and Iraq. Yes, the Army colonel is correct. The West will win this war. And this time they're going to stay as conquerors. These are probably the last days of Islam. Best not to be one of the conquered.* Standing, he walked over to the ambassador and held out his hand for the DVD. "It will be as you requested."

"Thank you, sir. President Alexander requests that you refrain from discussing our request with anyone," Ryder said, saluting the emir. It wasn't protocol, but it had the desired effect.

Other U.S. ambassadors and their attachés were having similar meetings in Kuwait and Bahrain. The UAE proved to be recalcitrant, but finally came to grips with the situation.

After returning to the embassy, Lieutenant Colonel Ryder placed a call to Khalid Ali at Al-Jazeera. "Good afternoon, Ali. I'm calling to return a favor. I suggest you have teams in place by nine a.m. tomorrow morning to cover the al-Aqsa Mosque and the Dome of the Rock. Place your teams where they can film the sites from a distance. Tell no one of this conversation. Just have your cameras in place."

"Colonel Ryder, what is going to happen?" a worried Ali asked.

"Sorry, I can't tell you. You'll have to trust me, as I trusted you when you told me about the first al-Qaeda video."

"It will be as you say. Thank you."

Tel Aviv, Israel – 10:00 p.m., Thursday, June 22nd.

Israel's Prime Minister Wurtzel received a phone call on a secure line from President Alexander. The president briefed Israel's leader on his plans and then made a request. Wurtzel was shocked. After a long pause, he replied, "Mr. President, I am sure you understand exactly what effect our carrying out your request will have in the Arab street."

A smile tugged at Alexander's lips, "Yes, I'm counting on it."

At ten o'clock the next morning, two convoys of Israeli military vehicles arrived at Islam's "Noble Sanctuary," the site surrounding the Dome of the Rock and the al-Aqsa Mosque. Heavily armed Israeli Defense Forces (IDF) quickly encircled the both the structures, and began forcefully routing Palestinians from the two holy sites. Perimeters were set up around both sites to keep all civilians out.

☆   ☆   ☆

The Dome of the Rock is located in what Muslims call the "Noble Sanctuary." A shrine, not a mosque, the building was constructed to commemorate *Isra*, Muhammad's fabeled Night Journey from the Ka'aba in

Mecca to *Masjid al-Aqsa,* the furthest mosque, in Jerusalem.

According to Hadith[*] tradition, Gabriel brought Muhhamad a winged steed, *al-buraq*—a white animal, larger than a donkey, and smaller than a mule, with a stride equal to the distance of one's range of vision to the horizon. Al-buraq carried Muhammad to Jerusalem—a journey of 900 miles—and back to his bed in Mecca the same night. In later descriptions, the winged steed, had the tail of a lion, body of a horse, and the torso and head of a woman.

Upon arrival in Jerusalem, Gabriel called forth 144,000,000 angels to hold a wooden ladder, which he and Mohammed used to ascend to the seven heavens. A rock in the center of the Dome of the Rock is believed to be the spot from which Muhammad and the angel ascended.

In one of the lowest heavens the pair met Adam who welcomed them. After greetings and prayer, they ascended to the second heaven, where Jesus and John waited to pray with them. Their upward journey continued to the third heaven, where they met Joseph who also prayed with them. They ascended higher to the fourth heaven and met and prayed with Enoch. Ascending once again, they reached the fifth heaven, where Aaron also prayed with them. Moses awaited them in the sixth heaven. After prayer and consultation with Moses, they made the final ascension to the seventh heaven and Allah, who after much discussion gave Muhammad the obligatory Islamic prayers—to be prayed to Allah as much as fifty times a day. Troubled by the burden of praying so often, Muhammad descended to the sixth heaven to ask Moses for advice. Moses suggested Muhammad ascend back to Allah and ask him to lighten the load. Muhammad continued back and forth many times, until Allah finally agreed to five prayers a day. Relieved to be rid of his burden, Muhammad descended back to earth and rode *al-buraq* back to Mecca.

Considered by Muslims to be the center of the earth, the Dome of the Rock shrine was completed in 691 CE. The 9th Umayyad Caliph, Abdul al-Malik spent all the taxes collected from Egypt for seven years to finance the structure. The building was constructed from wood on an eight-sided marble base, with exits leading north, south, east, and west. Marble and mosaic tiles richly decorate the facade. Inside, sixteen grilled windows illuminate the shrine's walls and dome, which are covered with glittering, golden mosaics and depictions of jewels. Atop the structure is a gold-capped cupola, twenty-five meters in diameter, and thirty-five meters high.

The geographic location of the shrine is important to Muslims, Jews, and

---

[*] There are several versions of the Night Journey in various Hadith. Only a small part of the story is told here. *Isra* appears to be the basis for the Islamic claim on Jerusalem.

Christians alike. For Muslims, it not only represents the place of the Prophet's *Mi'raj*, ascent to Allah, but it's also the place where Umar, the second caliph, prayed after he conquered Jerusalem. For Jews and Christians it's the place where an angel freed Abraham from obeying God's command to sacrifice his son, Isaac. Because Abraham obeyed, Isaac would become the father of many nations.

The Knights Templar used the shrine as their spiritual headquarters during the crusades. It also became the model for Templar churches across Europe. Modern day Christians believe the location to be the site where Christ was crucified. Long before Muhammad, King Solomon built his temple on the site to replace Moses' traveling tabernacle, which contained the Ark of the Covenant. Destroyed by the Babylonian King Nebuchadnezzar (605-562 BC), Solomon's Temple was rebuilt on the same site by the Roman King Herod (37-25 BC)—only to be destroyed by the Roman Army under Titus some forty years later in an effort to quell a Jewish uprising.

The Noble Sanctuary's other holy structure, the black domed, *Masjid al-Aqsa*, or al-Aqsa Mosque, was built near the Dome of the Rock—on the site of Solomon's Temple—by the Umayyad dynasty's Caliph al-Walid, during the years 705-715. Muslims consider the mosque to be the third most holy place in Islam. Damaged by earthquakes and time, nothing remains of the original structure. Caliph al-Dhahir rebuilt the mosque in 1033. Muslims believe Muhammad visited the mosque during his miraculous Night Journey—an historical impossibility, because the mosque wasn't constructed until eighty-three years after the Prophet's death.

According to Islamic law, al-Aqsa Mosque is the "Cradle of Religions." Muslims worldwide consider it sacrosanct—their Noble Sanctuary, not to be tampered with. Therefore, it's ironic that this site—holy to three religions—has become the symbol of never ending conflict. All attempts to create an open city where Jews, Christians, and Muslims can peacefully worship at the same location have failed. Why? Perhaps because Muslims' believe the presence of non-believers in the Noble Sanctuary is an affront to Allah.

For Muslims, it has always been their way or the highway. Now the road was beckoning to them—but did it lead to paradise or hell?

Thanks to Al-Jazeera's broadcast, word of the Israeli military occupying the shrine and mosque quickly spread. In a matter of minutes, mobs of angry Moslems shouting *Allahhh-u Akbarr, Allahhh-u Akbarr* surged through the narrow streets of the old city heading toward the Noble Sanctuary. In the sky above Jerusalem, Israeli F-16 pilots observed the rampaging mobs. Swooping low over the raging fanatics, they began dropping cluster bombs and napalm. The ensuing conflagration consumed the first waves of rampaging fanatics in a horrific inferno. Israeli attack helicopters and tanks followed. Those remaining rioters still seeking Allah quickly found Him in the hail of machine gun and cannon fire from helicopters, and flechette rounds (tiny arrows, the size of a small nail) fired by tanks. Al-Jazeera broadcast the gruesome battle scenes to the Arab world.

By 3:00 p.m. the main battle was over, and Israeli soldiers began carrying crates into the two structures. Four hours later, after all of the soldiers had left the two buildings and expanded their perimeter around the Noble Sanctuary, a few fanatics broke through the lines. Desperately racing toward the mosque, two Moslems had just reached the entrance when the explosives planted around the perimeter began detonating. Horrified Al-Jazeera viewers watched as detonations rippled around the structures, collapsing them into a pile of rubble. TV coverage of the detonations and the resulting fires enraged the Islamic world. Indonesia exploded into jihad and the government fell. Turkey erupted in civil war.

Southwestern White House – 1000 Friday, 23 June

While Israel subdued mobs in the streets of Jerusalem and other cities, President Alexander placed a series of calls to President Wu, President Karpov, the Prime Minister of Japan, and finally to King Ali. Allies received notice of the America's war plans through military channels, with details limited according to need-to-know. Other nations would receive two hours notice through diplomatic channels.

Shortly after Alexander's call, President Wu was pleasantly surprised to discover Admiral Cheng's invasion fleet was ready to depart for Indonesia. Japan was also prepared: the 1940s co-prosperity sphere concept—create a self-sufficient block of Asian nations—had not been forgotten.

At 1120 hours, Alexander received a call informing him Reverend Smyth's *"Message to Islam"* was being broadcast by all Islamic controlled TV stations.

Message to Islam

At 10:00 p.m. in Qatar, 1:00 p.m. in Albuquerque, Al-Jazeera and other TV stations in friendly or conquered Arab lands ceased broadcasting pictures from Jerusalem. Instead, for several minutes the stations transmitted no sound, and only broadcast their channel's logo.

Suddenly, without warning, viewers were startled by the ominous sound of rolling thunder. A sound so loud those with good sound systems were nearly deafened.

Thousands of bewildered viewers, desperate to understand what was happening, scrambled to gawk at their TV screens. Within seconds of the first roll of thunder, there appeared an image that terrified some and intrigued others. Flashing across the screen were powerful lightning bolts, superimposed against a backdrop of roiling, muddy water, and dark, foreboding clouds. A howling wind joined the booming thunder and crashing lightning. The effect was hypnotic, leading the impressionable to think they were about to die in the violent storm.

Then just when it seemed the storm could get no worse, the thunder and wind suddenly abated. Only the flashing lightning remained. After a few seconds, a new sound could be heard. At first the sound was only a low tone, but as it slowly grew louder, listeners realized it was the deep resonating voice of a man: a man who was speaking in the viewer's local dialect.

BROTHERS AND SISTERS OF ISLAM,
YOU HAVE BEEN DECEIVED!

The voice came booming out of the speakers, repeating its ominous message several times—each time louder than before. Befuddled viewers gaped in terror at the growing storm, frantically seeking some manifestation of the invisible speaker.

At last, viewers began to see a faint, ghostly image in the clouds. A man's scowling face and upper body began materializing in the midst of the lightning. Along with his barely discernable torso, viewers could see his raised, muscular arm: his hand and forefinger pointing heavenward. For the learned, the pointing finger was reminiscent of Michelangelo's paintings of man's creation and the end of the world. For the superstitious, the image held the terror of an omen fulfilled.

All at once, the hypnotic lightning bolts began gravitating toward the tip of the man's finger. Again the deafening thunder rolled. Now the lightning bolts were flashing skyward from the end of the man's finger. The effect of the cinematography, with the lightning reflecting off the dark foreboding clouds, was breathtaking. For what seemed an eternity, the ghostly apparition and its extended finger appeared to wax and wane in the brilliance of the flashing lightning bolts. The overall result left the viewer trembling in anticipation, awaiting some unforeseen, horrifying event.

The storm raged on, while the apparition repeatedly faded and reappeared. Suddenly, the thunder ceased, and the image materialized once more—this time into the clear image of a clean-shaven man dressed in a white robe. For several seconds, the man's scowling visage glared menacingly from the screen. Viewers watched in breathless anticipation of the man speaking.

Instead, in the blink of an eye, another flash of lightning lit up screen: followed quickly by the image of the man floating forward. A horrific clap of thunder boomed from the speakers. The man dramatically dropped his raised arm and pointed his finger—with its flashing lightning bolts—directly into the face of the viewer.

Once more the deafening thunder rolled, the hypnotic lightning flashed, and the man silently glared at the viewers. Suddenly the roaring sound of the thunder stopped. In its place came, yet again, the booming, foreboding tones of the man's ominous declaration.

YOU HAVE BEEN DECEIVED.

Thunder roared, lightning flashed, and the screen appeared to shake. Just as it would after each of the man's following pronouncements.

YOU HAVE BEEN DECEIVED by a camel driver with delusions of grandeur.

YOU HAVE BEEN DECEIVED by a pirate, a man who robbed caravans.

YOU HAVE BEEN DECEIVED by a mass murderer. A man who conquered a peaceful Jewish tribe, beheaded all the men, raped their wives and daughters, then sold them into slavery. It took all day … to behead the 1,000 men.

YOU HAVE BEEN DECEIVED by a man who claimed to have been visited by the angel Gabriel. Who claimed Gabriel revealed to him the message of the one god, Allah, and told him to recite the message to others.

Did anyone else claim to have seen the angel? … NO!

Did Allah reveal his message to anyone else? … NO!

Did Allah or Gabriel grant Muhammed the ability to read and write, so he could write down the words of your one god? … NO!

What do you know of your Prophet's history? Do you know Mecca was a place of pagan worship? Your ancestors came to Mecca to worship rocks. That's right, **ROCKS** … 360 rocks. One of them was a black rock, the MOON GOD.

Did you know Muhammad's grandfather and father were the keepers of the god rock garden?

Muhammad created the Qur'an to justify his lust for power and money. All of your great caliphs expanded their dominion by conquest. Islam's empire was financed by booty. Muhammad divided the booty—including captured humans—among his followers. He allowed Jews and Christians, his so-called 'people of the book,' to keep their religion … if they paid a tax called *dhimmis*, a tax of *submission*. Muhammad was only interested in booty, young girls, and collecting taxes.

Islam celebrates death. The Prophet and his **god** approve of torture, slavery, and robbery.

How many religions encourage children to blow themselves up in the name of their god? *Only one. Islam.*

Did the angel Gabriel visit Muhammad in the cave near Mecca? I do not think so. No, Gabriel is a good angel. The angel of a good, kind, loving God. The true God.

Who then, was the angel who visited Muhammad? The bright, seductive angel who put the verses of the Qur'an in Muhammad's head?

The angel's name was **LUCIFER**. The angel cast out of heaven by the only true God.

An **evil** angel. An angel you know as the **SATAN** ... *the* **DEVIL**.

That's right, you poor misguided souls.

YOU ARE WORSHIPING THE DEVIL.

The man's image slowly faded from the screen. In its place appeared a new scene—a backdrop of distant hills, surrounding a verdant valley, under a brilliant, blue, sunlit sky. Slowly the sky above the hills filled with billowy, white clouds, against which arched the radiant colors of a rainbow. Adding to the beauty and serenity of the panorama were the distant voices of a magnificent choir singing in unison, "Glory to God in the Highest."

Again, the scene on the screen faded, as did the sound of the heavenly choir. In its place came a new image—a magnificent stained glass window, upon which was superimposed the smiling visage of the previously scowling man. Slowly, the smiling face morphed into a full body image of Reverend Harold Smyth, resplendent in a white, gold embroidered robe. Standing with open, outstretched arms, Smyth appeared to be beckoning the viewers to join him. As an organ played and a choir sang "Glory to God in the Highest," Smyth walked forward. Behind him, the scene of the stained glass windows changed to reveal the interior of the Crystal Tabernacle and its enormous choir. Smyth smiled and looking directly into the camera spoke with deep emotion.

Brothers and Sisters of Islam. Hear my words and know they are true. The Christian and Jewish faiths are based on peace and love for their fellow man."

The camera pulled back, revealing Monsignor Morani and Rabbi Steinberg standing on either side of Smyth, also dressed in robes.

I am a Protestant Christian.

Smyth gestured to his right.

Monsignor Morani is a Catholic Christian.

Then, he gestured to his left.

And Rabbi Steinberg is a Jew. We each have different beliefs, just as the Shia' and the Sunni have different beliefs. The difference between our faiths and Islam's is great. Our God does not tell us to fight, terrorize, and kill one another.

Smyth opened his arms in a gesture that included Morani and Steinberg.

We live together, work together, eat together, and love one another, for we all worship the same God.

Allah has predetermined a Muslim's life. Muslims do not have free choice.

Our God allows men and women to have free choice.

Our faiths do not tolerate forced conversion. We do not make war on other faiths. Our faiths teach respect for all men and women. Our commandments forbid killing. We do not believe the way to heaven is through death while making jihad. Our way to heaven is through love for our God, and by following His commandments.

Our God loves you. He will accept you if you love Him.

This is your last opportunity to save your souls. Cease placing your head on the ground. You are praying to the Devil, who will one day burn in hell. Do you want to join him there for eternity? Stand with us now and pray in the presence of our loving God.

Side by side, the three men of God stood by the podium.

Raise your faces toward heaven. Close your eyes and embrace the one, true God. If you want to save your immortal souls pray with us.

As the three men of God joined hands and raised their faces towards the heavens, Reverend Smyth offered a prayer of forgiveness for all Muslims who would join them.

Oh heavenly Father,

Forgive these deceived men, women and children who have unknowingly worshiped Satan. They did not know what they were doing.

Oh heavenly Father,

Allow them to renounce their false god and embrace You— love You. Grant them the opportunity for salvation, for their time on this earth is short.

Oh, thank you God, for your mercy.

We give you all the glory,

Amen.

Yes, your time in this world is short. You have but hours to accept the true God. Save your souls; lift your eyes toward heaven and tell God you love Him. He will accept you into his holy kingdom. Say to the Lord God Almighty, "I accept you as my God. I love You. Please forgive me, for I did not know I worshiped a false god."

The reverend concluded and the scene slowly faded. In its place came the earlier scene of the verdant valley, but now it was filled with multitudes of people—all slowly walking side by side toward the rainbow.

Chapter 47

Operation Brimstone

Phase II

Friday, June 23rd

The CIA had commandeered United States' and United Kingdom's satellite networks serving the Middle East and Indochina. AGM-86C Conventional ALCMs (CALCMs) with high-explosive, blast-fragmentation warheads—targeted on TV transmission towers and broadcast centers in Egypt, Yemen, Oman, Saudi Arabia, Iraq, and Iran—had been launched from B-52Hs flying over the Mediterranean and Gulf of Oman. Each missile was programmed to reach its target at 1900 Zulu Friday—1:00 p.m. Friday in Albuquerque, 10:00 p.m. in Mecca, 11:00 p.m. in Baghdad, and 10:30 p.m. in Tehran. Al-Jazeera and other stations, broadcasting the "Message to Islam," remained on the air in Syria, Algeria, Libya, Israel, Lebanon, Jordan, Bahrain, Qatar, and the UAE.

Friday evening in the Middle East (1900 Zulu), TVs in Egypt, Yemen, Oman, Saudi Arabia, Iraq, and Iran lost signal from most popular local stations. A few minutes later, confused viewers watched in wonder as—courtesy of U.S. satellites—Reverend Smyth's "Message to Islam" abruptly appeared on all channels. The message repeated over and over again, prompting some viewers to watch in rapt silence as if hypnotized by the message. A very few got the message and joined Smyth in prayer to save their mortal souls. Most changed channels in frustration seeking an answer to why this annoying program was being telecast. Others became furious, raged at the screen, and turned off their TVs—only to turn them on again later and hear the same message. Why were Islamic TV stations urging the faithful to seek forgiveness and to love the kafir's God? It was all very disturbing. Something was wrong. After years of watching nothing but hate filled Islamic rhetoric, now the Prophet's followers were being told Allah was a false god, and the kafir's God loved them. If they loved Him in return they wouldn't have to kill someone or blow themselves up to go to paradise. What was all this heresy about?

If that wasn't unsettling enough, they were further mystified, when suddenly, at 0400 Zulu Saturday—7:00 a.m. in Mecca, and 10:00 p.m. in Albuquerque—a Western looking kafir appeared on the screen. Dressed in a dark blue suit and red tie, the man was obviously giving a speech. But his words—translated into the local dialect—made no sense. Why, the viewers wondered, was this infidel, with the emblem of the Great Satan on his lapel, talking about their caliph's attack on the infidel's cities—their great Day of Islam? In home after home across the Middle East, Islamic viewers changed channels time and again searching for answers—only to discover that the infidel was speaking on all channels.

Wheelus AFB, Libya – 0200 Saturday, 24 June

Major Bobby Kilgore, piloting *Heavy Metal*—the last B-1B Lancer bomber to take off from Wheelus—was thinking to himself, *Well, old girl, you certainly are well named. We definitely have heavy metal on board today.* Leveling off the Lancer at 45,000 feet, Kilgore checked the time. He was due to meet his fighter escort—four F-22A Raptors—in thirty minutes. Scanning his instruments, he saw that all four General Electric-102 turbofan engines were performing as designed. Kilgore loved his *"Bone,"* the name given to B-1B bombers by their crews. Bones are the only supersonic heavy bombers in the U.S. inventory.

Bobby Kilgore was the command pilot on this history-making flight. His crew consisted of a copilot, a defensive systems officer, and a new offensive systems officer. Having a last minute replacement crewmember wasn't unusual, but it was disconcerting. Activating the autopilot, Kilgore allowed his mind to drift over events of the past two weeks. *First, there were the mysterious modifications to my plane's bomb bays. Then Major Barrett inexplicably replaced Captain Bennington as my offensive systems officer. But things finally began to make sense the day I landed the Heavy Metal at Kirkland AFB and met five other* Bone *crews. I knew something big was up. Why else would all six of us have altered bomb bays and new offensive systems officers?*

That evening members of the six crews had attended a private dinner at Kirkland's Officers Club hosted by Colonel Charles Young. Kilgore and the others realized they were part of something very important when Colonel Young was introduced as the President's Chief of Staff. After dinner, they'd been taken to a guarded conference room, where Young briefed them on their mission and payload.

None of Kilgore's crew, with the exception of Barrett, had ever carried a nuclear bomb. Now they were flying with three thermonuclear bombs: one B-53-Y2 in the forward bomb bay; and two B-83s in the aft bomb bay—the latter were backups for the B-53-Y2, or to be used to attack targets of opportunity. The B-53-Y2 was undoubtedly the biggest bomb Kilgore and his crew had ever seen.

Manufactured in 1964, only fifty B-53-Y2 TN bombs remained in the enduring stockpile. Weighing 9,000 pounds, the B-53-Y2 measures twelve and a half feet long, and is slightly over four feet in diameter. A true two-stage thermonuclear weapon, the B-53 is the only U.S. thermonuclear weapon to have a uranium-235 primary. Its secondary is a standard lithium deuteride–uranium-235 layer cake design. The bomb has four fuzing options: laydown delayed surface burst, immediate contact surface burst, parachute retarded air burst, and free fall air burst. Burst option must be selected prior to take-off. Kilgore's B-53 was set for parachute-retarded air burst.

Kilgore had commented on the size of the bomb when it was loaded into the *Heavy Metal* at Kirkland. The senior master sergeant in charge of the loading detail had laughed and replied, "If you think this one's heavy, Major, you should've seen the MK-17. It was over five feet in diameter and weighed 42,000 pounds. Our old MK-41 had the biggest yield. It was a three-stage thermonuclear bomb, about the size of the B-53, with a yield of twenty-five megatons. Hell, sir, this B-53's only nine megatons."

Well, a nine megaton detonation is larger than I can imagine. Kilgore chuckled. *I guess I won't have to imagine after this baby goes off. This is my kind of proportional response. The rag-heads hit us with fifty kiloton bombs. I sure hope they appreciate our using nine megaton ones in return.* Kilgore would have no regrets. His parents died in the Boston blast. Every crewmember on the six B-1Bs had lost relatives or loved ones in one of the five cities.

Over the Mediterranean Sea and Gulf of Oman

B-52Hs began launching CALCMs targeted at Saudi Arabian, Iraqi, and Iranian Air Force bases, and surface-to-air missile installations. Strikes were timed for simultaneous impacts Saturday at 0200 Zulu—5:00 a.m. in Riyadh, 6:00 a.m. in Baghdad, and 05:30 a.m. in Tehran. The B-52 assigned to attack the Bakhtaran missile site, 460 kilometers southwest of Tehran, experienced launcher problems. Two hours later, the backup bomber launched its CALCMs.

The six Lancers, each with a separate target, would enter hostile air space after the ALCMs reached their targets. Radar would only show a single bomber. The stealthy Raptors would be an unpleasant surprise for any hostile fighters.

Indian Ocean

Following orders, the *West Virginia*, a 560-foot fleet ballistic missile submarine (SSBM), armed with twenty-four Trident II D-5 fleet ballistic missiles, rose to antenna depth at 0000 Zulu. She'd departed Kings Bay, Georgia nine days earlier, and was at the coordinates specified in her sailing orders. As soon as burst transmissions were sent and received, Commander Joshua Stern, the *West Virginia's* captain, turned to his executive officer and said, "XO, make your depth four hundred feet." Five minutes later, Stern received a decoded message. After carefully reading the message and showing it to his XO, he ordered, "XO, proceed to the designated launch coordinates. Be on station at launch depth by 0430 Zulu."

Officers Club, Kirkland AFB – 1830 Friday, 23 June

The president and first lady were eating dinner in a private dining room. SecWar and Martha Wellington were with them. Alexander had just tasted the first piece of a thick, rare, porterhouse steak. "Ummm, this is good. You should have ordered one," he told the first lady.

"George, you know you shouldn't be eating red meat. Chicken would be much better for you," Jane Alexander replied with a smile. *I'm glad he's enjoying himself ... getting his mind off the terrible speech he has to give in three and a half hours. It's amazing what we Americans have accomplished in less than a month under his leadership.*

The president replied by eating a large fork full of baked potato, loaded with butter and sour cream. Before Jane could continue her good-natured lecture on healthy food, Wellington's cellphone softly chimed. Flipping open the phone, she answered, "Wellington," listened, frowned, and flipped her phone shut. "Mr. President, all activity has ceased at Bakhtaran, the Iranian missile launch complex. As you know, they re-installed their warheads yesterday. Two missiles are erected on their launch pads. It looks as though they're getting ready to launch."

Addressing the president by his first name—the only Cabinet member to do so in private—SecWar Simpson said, "George, we can still hit them with a Minuteman if we launch it now."

"No, Harry, I don't want to tip our hand. ALCMs targeted on the base should disrupt any launch plans they have. Even if they do launch, I'm confident we can handle the threat. Martha, has everyone been alerted, including the Israelis?"

"Yes, sir."

"Okay, let's enjoy our dinner. It's going to be another long night."

Three hours would pass before Simpson was informed of the delayed CALCM launch.

The Caliph's Palace, Tehran, Iran – 6:30 a.m., Saturday, June 24th

Dreading his task, Omar once again entered the caliph's bedchamber to awaken his master. But this time he was surprised to find both men out of bed. Saladin had already bathed, and Yosif was using a large towel to dry him. "Excellency, may I b–be of assistance?" Omar stammered.

"Yes, lay out my clothes. Then get a pot of coffee," Saladin replied, leaning back into Yosif.

Thirty minutes later found Omar straightening the bed sheets, Yosif in a bathrobe, and his master preparing to leave his bedchamber. However, just as Saladin was about to reach the door, he stopped abruptly. Turning to look back at Yosif, he frowned at the sight of the boy's doleful eyes brimming with tears.

"You did not bid me farewell, my master," the youth whimpered and trembled from some inexplicable sense of dread.

"I will return shortly," Saladin replied and held out his arms, beckoning Yosif to come to him. While Omar busied himself with the bath towels, Saladin embraced Yosif's slender body. Ill at ease, Omar quickly averted his eyes and quietly fled the room.

When, a short time later, Saladin finally emerged from his bedchamber and walked past Omar without appearing to notice him, Omar grew curious. Always cautious, he waited a minute or two after Saladin left, before tiptoeing to the door to peek into the bedchamber. There he saw Yosif, lying naked on the bed, softly weeping.

Caliph Saladin II walked into the Shura's main conference room at 7:30 a.m. A 64-inch plasma TV monitor was showing various images of the underground Bakhtaran missile launch complex: home to the al-Hadid Missile Brigade, a division of the Islamic Revolutionary Guard Corps. Anxious for proceedings to get underway, and annoyed with the prattling clerics who were milling around, Saladin sneered with revulsion when the shrill-voiced cleric pointed the large TV screen and began shrieking "*Allahu Akbar, Allahu Akbar.*"

A menacing looking, three-stage *Kosar* missile, known to Western militaries as the Shahab-5, filled the screen. The Kosar, which means "Stream of eternal life in paradise" in Farsi, is a variant of North Korea's Taep'o-dong 2 missile. Its first two stages are liquid rocket motors, and the third stage is solid propellant. In the background, approximately two hundred meters distant, viewers could see a Shahab-3D two-stage missile, mounted on a mobile transporter-erector vehicle. The Shahab-3D, which means "meteor or shooting star" in Farsi, was elevated and ready to be launched.

Three minutes later, the scene on the monitor switched to the missile launch control room in the blockhouse, where several uniformed men sat at consoles. A countdown clock showing 0:02:24 appeared in the lower right corner of the screen. Realizing the Kosar was about to launch, Khomeini directed the *Shura* to take their seats, facing the monitor along one side of the large conference table

Tired of drinking from small, handleless cups, the caliph picked up a mug of hot coffee and settled back in his chair to watch the countdown clock. Sipping his coffee and trying to ignore a sudden sinking feeling in the pit of his stomach, Saladin looked at the expectant faces of the ignorant clerics in disgust, *Do any of them understand what's going on?* he wondered, frowning when it suddenly occurred to him the generals weren't there. *Oh well, they probably have important duties elsewhere,* he decided, but once more felt a knot in the pit of his stomach. Shaking his head in an effort to dispel an overwhelming premonition of doom, he closed his eyes tightly. About to gain some modicum of control, Saladin's peace was shattered by the shrieking of the hysterical shrill-voiced cleric, who was pointing at the TV monitor showing the Kosar on its launch pad. Lift off was imminent, and Saladin held his breath. Joining the shrieking cleric, the remaining clerics counted down in unison with the launch control clock as it slowly ticked down to zero.

As soon as the missile's first stage liquid fuel motor ignited, Khomeini dramatically intoned, "Praise be to Allah," and the clerics began chanting *"Allahu Akbar, Allahu Akbar."* The chanting grew louder and louder as the Kosar, trailing smoke, rose on a pillar of fire into the clear morning sky.

Saladin, who had been holding his breath, relaxed. *So far so good, I was afraid the damn thing was going to blow up.*

Relieved by the Kosar's successful liftoff, Saladin sighed heavily and directed his attention to the new image on the screen—the second missile was about to launch. Sixty seconds later, the Shahab-3D's first stage liquid motor ignited. Suddenly several small explosions began occurring near the missile. Startled, Saladin watched in horror as streaks of fire radiated away from each of the explosions. Then, as the Shahab-3D began lifting off its launcher, he cringed when he saw another small explosion occur two meters from the missile. *Shit! I knew it ... it's going to blow up.*

Everything happened in the blink of an eye. Fiery streaks from the last explosion reached upward toward the side of the missile, causing the first stage liquid motor to dissolve into a giant fireball. As the missile broke apart, the fireball entered the nozzle of the second stage, igniting the solid rocket grain. The second stage—still connected to the nosecone and now almost parallel to the ground—took off across the desert. Sensing acceleration, the warhead began to arm and its first gate opened. The altitude sensor determined the altitude was below preset parameters, and the arming process stopped, waiting for the correct altitude reading. When the second stage and its attached nosecone buried itself in a small hill, the impact detonated the warhead's explosive sphere, creating a cloud of plutonium oxide that would contaminate the downwind area of the site.

In the minutes that followed, no one moved, nor spoke, not even the shrill-voiced cleric. Khomeini and the clerics sat gaping at the screen in disbelief, all wondering, *What the hell had just happened?*

Unknown—and forever to remain a mystery to them—was that the explosions were caused by combined effect bomblets released by the tardy CALCMs—the ones launched two hours late by the backup B52 bomber. The fiery streaks they'd seen radiating away from the explosions were actually pyrophoric metal fragments from the bomblets.

An orbiting satellite observed the Kosar's launch and the Shahab-3D's subsequent explosion on an adjacent pad. Analysts monitoring satellites at the 480th Intelligence Wing, located on Langley AFB, Virginia, issued a launch warning to USCENTCOM (United States Central Command), which relayed the warning to all forces in Operation Flare and Israel. Ninety seconds later the Kosar's trajectory was calculated. It was headed for Libya. Patriot missile batteries on the Libyan coast, equipped with new Patriot-3 missiles, prepared to engage.

Israeli missile tracking crews breathed a sigh of relief that the Shahab-3D was destroyed, but felt remorse when notified the Kosar was targeted on Tripoli. Then USCENTCOM reported two additional Shahab-3B missile launches from remote sites in western Iran. It was quickly determined their targets were in Israel. Personnel at Palmachim air base and missile test site, south of Tel Aviv, began tracking the two Iranian missiles. "They'll have chemical or biological warheads," the commanding officer observed.

USS *Vella Gulf*, a Ticonderoga class Aegis cruiser, was on station off the coast of Libya in the Gulf of Sidra. When satellite feed showed the Shahab-5 launch, and the cruiser went to battle stations. Alarms sounded throughout the ship, and a female voice began repeating over the intercom, "General Quarters, General Quarters, this is not a drill." The ship's captain, CDR Neil Robertson entered the CIC.

"Sir, the satellite shows a missile headed our way from Bakhtaran. It can't be a Shahab-3—it doesn't have the range. It may be their experiential Shahab-5 ... and it's probably a nuke."

"Yeah, Chief, you're probably right. Do we have it on radar?"

"Not yet, Skipper. It should come over the horizon in the next couple of minutes."

The ship had already turned toward the incoming missile. Its AN/SPY-1 radar, capable of tracking one hundred targets at the same time, was scanning the sky. One hundred and thirty-one seconds later the chief reported, "Skipper, there she is ... She's in her midcourse phase."

"Captain, the system is up," the weapons officer reported. "SM-3s in the aft launcher have been selected. Fire control is set on auto. We're ready to fire."

Robertson leaned over and inserted his key in the fire control panel. Turning his key, he armed the system, and the computer took over. Seconds later the ship vibrated as the first SM-3 lifted out of its storage container, located in one of the aft missile cells, and quickly rose on a column of fire.

"One away ... clean launch," the chief reported. The CIC was deathly quiet. Everything was now in the hands of technology.

Two minutes later a second SM-3 launched, and the chief reported, "Clean launch."

The SM-3 is an evolution of the SM-2 Block IV interceptor. It's a hit-to-kill, three stage missile that propels its warhead on a course calculated to impact the incoming missile. The third stage is a dual-pulse rocket. The solid rocket motor can be ignited twice—thereby increasing its accuracy. The SM-3 climbs rapidly as each of its three solid rocket motor stages burn out and separate. During flight, its inertial guidance system receives information from the ship's radar and GPS module. As soon as the nosecone reaches outer space, it releases its kinetic warhead. Like the GBI missile launched earlier from Fort Greely, Alaska, the warhead would immediately begin searching for its target. Once acquired, the high-resolution seeker would steer the warhead toward the oncoming RV. Kinetic energy at impact would destroy the incoming warhead.

Captain Robertson stood quietly watching as the two symbols on the screen closed on each other at a combined speed of three-point-three miles per second. The symbols appeared to merge, then passed each other. The ship shuddered as a third SM-3 launched. Now the captain watched the second interceptor warhead on the screen as it closed on the incoming RV. Again the two objects passed each other. A fourth SM-3 launched, then a fifth. The RV was getting uncomfortably close. Tension built in the CIC. No one spoke. Everyone knew his or her job and was doing it. Soon the Iranian missile would be in range of the Patriot-3 batteries on the coast.

"Time to impact six seconds," the calm voice of Chief O'Donnell reported. "Three, two, one ... missed. That one was very close."

Each second seemed longer as they watched the fourth kinetic energy warhead approach the on-rushing Iranian RV. "Another miss ... Our last chance coming up," O'Donnell said. "The Patriots will begin launching in a couple of minutes. Okay ... three–two–one." The two symbols on the screen converged, and then appeared to change into hundreds of tiny objects that faded away. "We got it!" O'Donnell shouted, showing emotion for the first time.

"We sure as hell did!" the captain added with a grin. "Well done!"

In Israel, the Arrow 2 Theatre Ballistic Missile Defense System was on full alert. Green Pine EL/M2080 L-band long-range acquisition radar began searching for the Iranian missiles. Two operational Arrow batteries waited to intercept the inbound Iranian missiles—one at the Palmachim base to provide cover for Tel Aviv, and the other near the city of Hadera.

Each Arrow 2 battery consists of four elements: a trailer mounted Citron Tree fire control center, and elements of the mobile Green Pine radar system; a truck mounted Hazelnut Tree Launch Control Center; a truck mounted communications center; and either four or eight missile launch trailers—each with six launch tubes and ready-to-fire missiles. Green Pine radar can detect and track incoming missiles at 500 kilometers. Each Arrow 2 missile is sealed in a container, installed on the erectable truck launcher. When the launcher is in position, a large hydraulic cylinder raises six clamped-together missile containers to a vertical position.

Things were quiet in the launch control center at the Hadera battery. The sky situation coordinator, intelligence officer, post mission analysis officer, resource officer, senior engagement officer, and commander sat at their workstations, waiting for the missile to appear on their screens. "Set threat vector at eighty degrees, and place system in automatic mode," the Hedera battery commander ordered. A second later the first seven meter long, 800-mm diameter, Arrow 2, rose from its sealed container. Rising on a column of fire produced by its first stage solid rocket motor, the Arrow accelerated vertically, then pitched over toward the east. A short while later the first stage burned out and separated. The second stage ignited and propelled the missile upward, achieving a velocity of mach-9. Objects traveling thousands of miles per hour have a very small window of engagement. In order to achieve the engagement at maximum range, the first Arrow missiles are launched before the incoming enemy missile's trajectory and intercept points are accurately calculated.

Two minutes later, the second Arrow was launched. Trajectories of the Arrows appeared on the workstation screens. Each missile was identified with a symbol labeled AH-1 and AH-2, indicating Arrow Hederas one and two. Three minutes later, the first Shahab-3 appeared on the workstation screens as a red symbol TR-1—T for target missile, and R for red, the color code assigned the missile's launch site in Iran. A red colored cone from the missile's position was projected on the screen. The cone indicated the missile's projected path and its impact point as an ellipse on the ground—the red ellipse included Haifa. The projected impact ellipse would shrink as the incoming RV grew closer and the computer received additional radar data.

A third Arrow was launched. Then the second incoming missile appeared on the screen as a blue symbol, TB-1. Everyone in the trailer let out a gasp, when the inbound missile's blue ellipse fell over Jerusalem.

"Why would they attack their holy city?" the pert, brunette, female sky situation coordinator asked.

"If we assume the Shahab-3 destroyed at Bakhtaran had the nuclear warhead, then these two will have chemical or biological warheads. They will not destroy the holy city ... just kill the Jews infesting it," the intelligence officer sardonically replied with a scowl.

"But, they'll also kill all the Muslims in the area," she responded.

"*Insha'Allah*," the commander scoffed, "Anyway," he sarcastically added, "I'm sure the crazy ayatollahs would tell them they were doing God's work."

Everyone was quiet, their eyes glued to the screens showing the battle developing in space.

"Arrow one is out of position for an intercept on the red RV. But it has a chance to engage blue one," the brunette reported, her voice still calm.

The fourth Arrow launched. Each Arrow's position, trajectory and the predicted impact point were displayed on each screen's electronic map. Intercepts can begin at a distance of 100 kilometers. Arrows are steered during their first and second stage motor burn. When second stage burnout occurs, the second stage separates, and the nosecone leaves the atmosphere. Once clear of earth's atmosphere, the high explosive fragmentation warhead is released. Terminally guided by a passive infrared seeker, the warhead has an effective radius of 130 feet. However, if the warhead detonates behind the RV, its effectiveness is reduced.

"The Tel Aviv battery has engaged the blue RV. I have crossed linked with them," the engagement officer said. A few seconds later the display on the screens showed AT-1 and AT-2. Tel Aviv battery Arrows were designated AT.

The red and blue impact ellipses surrounding Haifa and Jerusalem shrank as additional tracking data was received.

Hedera Arrows five and six launched ten seconds apart.

"Hedera Arrows one and two missed ... three and four are closing on red RV," the engagement officer reported. Hedera Arrows five and six appeared on the screens.

When a fragmenting warhead explodes, metal fragments are propelled outward at a velocity near the detonation velocity of the explosive. As the distance from the point of detonation increases, the distance between fragments increases. A good example would be a shotgun firing No. 4 shot at a paper target. If the target is twenty yards away, the shot pattern on the target is tight. When the target is sixty yards away, the shot pattern is thin—dispersed. A hunter, shooting at a duck at sixty yards, may be aiming correctly, but the pellets in the shot pattern pass over the duck without any pellets hitting it. This is called flying through the pattern. The same principal applies to hitting the RV.

Hedera Arrow three detonated behind the incoming red RV. The RV was traveling west at 10,000 feet per second. AH-3 was traveling east 9,000 feet per second. Fragment velocity from the AH-3 warhead was 20,000 fps. Because the two warheads were separating at a rate of 19,000 fps (10,000 + 9,000), the fragments overtaking the Iranian warhead had an effective velocity of 1,000 fps (20,000 - 19,000). Only one fragment struck the RV, and it lacked sufficient energy to cause damage.

Hedera Arrow four detonated slightly behind the red RV, causing minor damage. Hedera Arrows five and six were closing on the RV. This time the missiles were on a near collision course. The fifth Arrow detonated next to the red RV at a distance of twenty feet, causing severe damage, and diverting it into the path of the sixth Arrow which destroyed it. Cheering erupted in the control center for a few seconds, but quiet returned quickly as personnel breathlessly watched the blue RV intercept drama being played out on their screens.

The first four Tel Aviv Arrows targeted on the blue RV missed. All were targeted at, or beyond, maximum range. Arrows five and six were approaching the incoming blue RV. The Tel Aviv battery launched their seventh and eighth Arrows. The fifth Arrow detonated behind the blue RV. Six detonated slightly ahead of its target at a distance of seventy-five feet, damaging and deflecting the RV. The sudden course change caused the remaining two Arrows to miss. The damaged, but functional RV, with its cargo of anthrax bomblets, was now heading south of Tel Aviv.

Tel Aviv was on alert, as was most of Israel. Citizens wearing gas masks were unaware of the drama being played out in the sky above them. Some saw the missile trails as the Arrows streaked skyward. None knew what to expect.

A building, with a dome resembling an observatory, was located in a restricted area of Palmachim Air Base. The dome was retracted, exposing a strange looking telescope-like device. Mounted on a metal frame, the device had a large lens-like opening that glowed like a giant red eye when light entered it. A metal frame, attached to two large metal pillars by brackets, allowed the device and metal frame, or yoke, to rotate up and down. A careful observer would realize that the columns were mounted on a turntable, so the device with its red eye could both rotate and pivot. If the observer surmised the device might be a searchlight, he would be close to the truth. Mounted on top of the metal frame were two small boxes with green lenses, looking something like the green light in a traffic signal. Next to them, on one side, was an odd looking box with a lens protruding—perhaps a TV camera.

Suddenly a warning horn blared, and a flashing yellow light began revolving on a pole near the device. The turntable rotated, pointing the device toward the east. Then the device elevated to an angle of approximately 70°. Inside the domed building, in a room resembling a missile launch control center, tense men and women sat around computer workstations linked to the Green Pine radars. The damaged blue colored TB-1 RV was spiraling down toward them.

"Range, 58,251 meters. Altitude, 31,089 meters. Velocity, 3,387 meters per second," a man in civilian clothes said in a calm voice.

"Set fire control computer to automatic and commence firing," a tall woman, wearing a white blouse and khaki skirt said.

Outside the building, the two small boxes with green lenses on top of the metal bracket began to glow, projecting narrow beams of green light, which quickly found the incoming RV. The beams were the tracking and targeting lasers. The red-eyed device was a Tactical High Energy Laser Advanced Concept Technology Demonstrator (THEL/ACTD)—identical to the one located in the U.S. at the White Sands Missile Range in New Mexico. Seconds later, the object, resembling a search light with a red eye, seemed to momentarily flicker when it sent a beam of intense energy—invisible to the naked eye—toward the descending RV. The Mid Infrared Advanced Chemical Laser (MIRACL) had fired. Atmospheric distortion would have little effect on the main laser's beam when the target was twenty-five miles distant and closing. In fact, the first beam would burn a hole through the atmosphere for the second beam—providing the second beam was fired a short time after the first. It all has to do with the change of angle to the RV.

The first and second high-energy laser beams struck the heat shield of the RV, doing little damage. Fragments from the Arrow warhead had damaged the heat shield, and the blast had caused the RV to oscillate. THEL's third shot found the damaged spot on the heat shield, and the intense beam of energy burned through it and into the cargo of bomblets. Temperature rose, gases expanded, and pressure increased in the RV's bomblet containment vessel, causing it to rupture and release its bomblets. Released above the proper altitude, the still-intact bomblets functioned and released their charge of anthrax into the atmosphere at 65,000 feet. UV and IR radiation from the sun quickly destroyed the deadly anthrax spoors.

Cheers broke out in the Arrow and THEL/ACTD control rooms.

In Tehran, Saladin, Grand Ayatollah Khomeini, and the clerics, chanting *Allahu Akbar, Allahu Akbar,* had been watching with glee when the Kosar lifted off. The chanting resumed when the motor of the Shahab-3D ignited. When the missile exploded, they sat in stunned silence. Suddenly, Saladin had a second thought, *Shit! Where the hell are the generals?*

The two men in question were—much to their relief—far removed from what they knew was imminent disaster. Several hours prior, both beleaguered generals had wisely packed up their families and headed toward the Turkmenistan border. U.S. dollars and gold coins were still the best entry visa in that part of the world.

Breaking the silence, Khomeini ordered, his voice cracking, "Call the commander at Bakhtaran."

Four minutes later, the commander reported they'd been attacked by the Great Satan's cruise missiles. Radars tracking the Kosar in Iran, Iraq, and Syria were displayed on the large screen in Tehran. New tracks began appearing, heading toward the Kosar.

"What are they?" Khomeini screeched, standing and pointing at the screen.

"Excellency, they are interceptor missiles," the commander replied from Bakhtaran.

Regaining control, Khomeini pronounced in his usual calm, all-knowing manner, "Allah will protect our Kosar."

Saladin, also staring at the screen, was losing faith in Allah's protection. *They shot down the North Korean missiles ... They may be able to shoot down our missile too. If they do ... Perhaps I should start thinking about retiring ... Damn. Maybe that's why the generals aren't here.*

Was retirement included in Allah's plans for the caliph?

Insha'Allah.

Chapter 48

Southwestern White House – Friday, 23 June

News bulletins broadcast throughout the day announced the president would address the nation and the world at 10:00 p.m. MDT. Live coverage from Kirkland's main auditorium would begin at 9 o'clock. All networks were requested to carry the address. Guests and reporters were advised to arrive by 8:45 p.m. Reporters scoured their sources for tips, but no one knew—or would admit to knowing—what was up. Why so late, they wondered?

When Governor Richards and his wife, Nora, arrived at the auditorium, they were mobbed by anxious reporters, hungry for information about the president's speech. The governor politely declined to comment, primarily because he didn't know what the president was going to say. Nora Richards had been shaken by their encounter with the press. Sitting with his wife in the reserve section next to the First Family, the governor was still annoyed. *Damned fools, she's not used to being jostled around like that. I'll stay with her until it's time to join the Cabinet back stage.* He relaxed somewhat and smiled, when the "Pride," University of New Mexico's celebrated marching band, began playing a lively version of the state song, "Asi es Nuevo México." While Nora chatted pleasantly with Jane Alexander, Richards' thoughts returned to the reporter's questions. Tapping his black Caiman gator cowboy boots to the music, the governor asked himself. *What will Alexander say? I haven't a clue. One thing's for sure. He does love surprises, and I have a feeling this is going to be a beaut.* Richards chuckled.

Checking his watch, the governor saw it was time for him to join the Cabinet waiting backstage for the event to begin. After giving Nora's hand a reassuring squeeze he rose, and, followed by an aide, walked briskly to the back stage entrance. As he did, several reporters representing major news services jumped up and shouted questions from their seats in the press section. Smiling pleasantly Richards shook his head in the negative and surveyed the capacity crowd filling the auditorium. *They can't wait to find out what the president has to say.* Laughing to himself, he passed sound techs making final checks on radio and television mikes, and cameramen waiting patiently for their cues to begin.

In the auditorium, the band was playing a medley of light classics, and the murmuring audience grew antsy. At precisely one minute before nine o'clock—to everyone's delight—the house lights dimmed and the stage lights came up, illuminating the podium and a row of empty chairs awaiting arrival of the president's cabinet. One minute later, red lights on three TV cameras blinked on, and General Ross, looking handsome in his dress uniform, walked across the stage. Live international coverage of the event had begun.

When Ross reached the podium, the conductor gave the "cut" signal to stop the band, the house lights brightened, and the audience turned to watch the University of New Mexico's Air Force ROTC Color guard march down the center aisle. After smartly presenting the colors, the guard marched out, Ross faced the audience and TV cameras and announced, "Please stand for the Pledge of Allegiance and our National Anthem." A hush fell over the auditorium as the audience stood, recited the Pledge of Allegiance, and then joined a soprano from Albuquerque's Civic Light Opera Company in singing the National Anthem.

After the conclusion of the National Anthem, Ross addressed the seated audience and the TV cameras, "Ladies and gentlemen, fellow citizens, honored guests, and members of the press, good evening. At 10:00 p.m., the president will make a major address concerning the war and the state of the union.

"For the past two weeks, the press has reported the gathering of millions of Islamic fighters at Cairo, Khartoum, Mecca, and Medina. For security reasons we have refused to comment on these reports. This evening I am at liberty to confirm the reports are true. The president will address this threat in his speech."

Waiting for murmuring in the audience to die out, Ross paused for a moment, before raising his right hand to indicate a large screen descending from the ceiling above him.

"While we're waiting for the president's speech, we'll be showing a video production from Dream Maker Studios.

"Before starting the video, I want to remind you to that wars are fought with both weapons and propaganda. Normally, propaganda focuses on undermining the political beliefs of the enemy. The war we're being forced to fight is far more insidious. Our enemy is both religious and political. Islam is both a religion and a form of government—a theocracy. For years the Islamic press and TV have fed the Muslim people a steady diet of hate-filled rhetoric, pictures, and written word. We're about to change the menu, and you're going to partake of the first course. We've targeted the following video at Muslims around the world, and it's being broadcast—as I speak—on all major Islamic television networks. Some stations are doing so voluntarily. Others"—the general smiled a cold smile—"are off the air, and we're using their frequencies. The dialogue in the video has been voiced-over in local dialects appropriate for the viewing audience. We call this video, our 'Message to Islam.' Copies will be provided to the press after the president's address."

While the lights dimmed and Ross withdrew across the darkened stage, the audience waited in anticipation. The video began, with networks receiving direct feed.

Complete darkness descended over the auditorium. Suddenly, to the audience's consternation, the ominous sound of rolling thunder boomed from the surround-sound speakers. So unexpected, and so loud was the thunder, it caused most of the audience to jump in fright and cover their ears. Within seconds of the first roll of thunder, a realistic and terrifying image appeared on the screen. Flashing across the screen were powerful lightning bolts, superimposed against the background of a terrifying storm.

Roiling muddy water surged to the forefront of the scene, giving the appearance of a horrific flood, consuming everything in its wake. Flash after flash of lightning streaked across the screen, followed by booming thunderbolts, so loud the speakers seemed to rattle in the aftermath. From behind a side-stage curtain, General Ross watched the audience's reaction with interest. Illuminated by the lightning flashes on the screen, the people cringed and jumped with every crashing thunderbolt. *They're really getting into it. Most of them are jumping like scared rabbits. Some of them are so still they almost look hypnotized. Other's look like they wonder what the hell is going on. If their reaction is any indication of what's happening to the Muslims, Dream Maker deserves an Oscar for Best Short Film.*

Just when it seemed the storm could get no worse, the thunder suddenly abated as quickly as it had come. In its place, out of the speakers came a new sound—the deep resonating voice of a man.

BROTHERS AND SISTERS OF ISLAM,
YOU HAVE BEEN DECEIVED!

The message boomed over the speakers. Some audience members were smiling and nodding their heads in the affirmative. They obviously understood the intent of the dramatization. Others continued to look on in consternation. The voice repeated the message several times, each time louder than before. Transfixed by the fury of the terrifying storm, the audience sat in anticipation of some manifestation of the invisible speaker.

Twenty minutes later, when the "Message to Islam" ended and the house lights came up, most of the audience sat spellbound. No one uttered a word. Ross returned to the podium and said, "The video you've just seen has been continuously broadcast throughout the Middle East for several hours. We want to make absolutely sure the Muslims have gotten the message."

Looking from his watch to the left side of the stage, Ross saw the

Cabinet waiting behind the curtain for his introduction. Then assuming his most dignified stance, he announced, "Ladies and gentlemen, and members of the press"—Ross turned and gestured toward the empty chairs on the stage— "the president's Cabinet and honored guest, New Mexico's Governor Kurt Richards." The university band began playing "God Bless America" as the Cabinet and Governor Richards filed on stage and took their seats.

For several awkward minutes, the audience, many of whom were still agitated by the video, continued talking—apparently unaware of the dignitaries' arrival. Only scattered applause greeted the Cabinet as they took their seats. Most audience members had failed to hear Ross's introduction. Finally, pockets of applause broke out in the auditorium, along with shouts of praise for the spectacular performance Dream Maker Studios and Reverend Smyth had presented. Others were finally acknowledging the dignitaries. A few, like Dr. Patricia Chatsworth, looked worried—conflicted about the rightness of what was happening.

Coverage for the president's address was scheduled to begin in three minutes. As the remaining minutes ticked by, the network's talking heads chattered about the video, the Arab street, Korean unification, and Chavez. One commentator wondered if the U.S. had anything to do with the explosion that killed Chavez near the end of his recent speech.

Jane Alexander looked at her two children and marveled at their resiliency. Both brother and sister were unaccustomed to the attention they were receiving. Yet, they calmly accepted the change in their lives without complaint. Both expressed nothing but loving pride in their father and support for his actions. Jane was also proud of her husband, but couldn't stop worrying about the toll his work was taking on him. *I have to make him take a day off. He can't keep going at this pace. No man can.*

General Ross, who'd been standing to the side of the stage waiting for the Cabinet to be seated, returned to the podium. Alternately checking the TV cameras and his watch, Ross waited as the second hand ticked down the remaining seconds. Finally, the red light on several TV cameras came on. "Fellow citizens, honored guests, and members of the press, tonight the president will address the nation and the world, including the Islamic Empire. I now present to you, George Robert Alexander, President of the United States of America."

Trumpets in the band began playing "Ruffles and Flourishes, followed by "Hail to the Chief," and a dignified Alexander entered the stage and walked to the podium. Applause from the standing audience greeted him and continued for several minutes. Alexander gazed at the audience, smiled and acknowledged his family with a nod. Standing erect, the president presented a formidable picture. His navy blue suite was cut to perfection, and his red tie provided color against his light blue shirt. An American flag pin adorned his left lapel. To the audience in the auditorium and to viewers around the world, Alexander presented the image of the confident world leader that he was. Lifting his hand to silence the applause, he waited for the music to stop and for everyone to be seated before speaking.

"My fellow Americans, distinguished guests, and members of the press, good evening. Twenty-eight days ago, I informed the nation the United States had been attacked with nuclear weapons. We did not know who was responsible, but I promised to find out how we were attacked, and we are doing so. I warned leaders of other nations not to try to take advantage of us. Some failed to heed my warning. I told you your government was still functioning, and so it is. I pledged the government would give top priority to caring for the injured, and so it has. I pledged to maintain order, and order has been maintained. Finally, I pledged that after we reorganized and bandaged our wounds, we would determine who was responsible for the attacks … and then seek retribution."

Alexander paused, allowing his last words to impact the spellbound audience. Then centering his eyes on the TV cameras, he continued.

"Much credit for our recovery lies with our state governors. Our guest this evening, New Mexico's Governor Kurt Richards, has acted as chairman of governors. He has done an outstanding job of interfacing with them. We owe him a debt of gratitude for his service in restoring domestic order to our country. Governor Richards, please stand."

Turning toward Richards, the president motioned for the governor to stand. After the applause died, Alexander resumed speaking.

"Next, I wish to introduce two, new, acting Cabinet secretaries. I have appointed Doctor Betty Chatsworth as acting Surgeon General and Secretary of Health and Human Services. Betty, please stand up."

Smiling, Alexander gestured toward her.

"Doctor Chatsworth, a physician, is the congresswoman from Idaho. I have given her the grave responsibility for overseeing care and treatment of our injured. A job she has undertaken with outstanding professionalism and compassion. She has just completed a tour of hospitals and emergency treatment centers throughout the country."

The audience stood, applauding Chatsworth. After a few seconds, the president signaled for the applause to end by raising his hand.

"I have also appointed Christopher Newman, to replace me as the acting Secretary of Homeland Security. Stand up Chris."

"Secretary Newman is a former Chief of Police for the City of Chicago. His extensive experience with border and port security makes him ideally suited to replace me as Secretary of Homeland Security. Securing our borders is one of our most challenging responsibilities—one that Chris has aggressively undertaken by implementing much needed changes to border security. I am pleased to report a significant drop in illegal drugs entering the country."

Again, the audience was on its feet and applauding. Alexander smiled and waited for a few seconds, then signaled for the applause to end.

"Now I'd like to begin my address by commenting on actions I've taken since assuming the presidency. Leaders of other nations were warned not to try to take advantage of us. Two failed to heed my warning. North Korea launched a nuclear missile attack on us … and we destroyed them.

"A petty dictator in South America attempted to start a Socialist Revolution in our hemisphere … and he failed."

Alexander waited for the buzz to die.

"Who was responsible for the nuclear terrorist attack on our cities? A man, identifying himself as the 'Keeper of the Rings' claimed responsibility. The rings he referred to were components of a gun-type atomic bomb. The same type of bomb the U.S. dropped on Hiroshima. A bomb named the Little Boy. His claim to have hidden the bombs in our cities appears to be correct. This man, this self proclaimed 'Keeper of the Rings,' has changed his name. He now calls himself Saladin II, caliph of the Islamic Empire. An evil empire that celebrates the attack on our nation … calling it their 'Day of Islam.' "

Again, the president was interrupted by a buzz in the audience.

"When we were attacked, there was no Islamic Empire, and no caliph. So, who *was* responsible? Events that occurred around the world after the attack provide the answer. Saladin II, the Keeper of the Rings, made two videos. Both were made in the name of the Muslim god, Allah. Both called for the destruction of Israel, the Little Satan. Both called for the conversion of the United States, the Great Satan, to Islam … and both called for jihad, a Muslim holy war to impose worldwide conversion to Islam, which means *submission*. According to the Qur'an and Muhammad, jihad is the duty of all able-bodied Muslim men.

"Saturday morning, the day after the nuclear bombs exploded in our cities, that worldwide jihad began. We all know what happened here. Churches and synagogues were burned. Christians, Jews, and other non-Muslims were killed. Citizens and militia groups joined police in quelling the jihad. Finally, the National Guard was required to restore order. Other than a few previously known criminals, who was responsible for the jihad? Muslims! In an effort to restore domestic order, I issued orders for all Muslims to be interned—and they have been.

"Several additional terrorist attacks in this country have been thwarted—not so in Europe, where Lisbon, Frankfurt, Paris, Rome, and the Vatican have been contaminated with radioactive isotopes. Who was responsible for these attacks? Who was responsible for past attacks against the United States in Saudi Arabia, Lebanon, Yemen, Africa, the Pentagon, and twice at the World Trade Center? We know them by many names: al-Qaeda, Hamas, Hizbullah, al-Aqsa Martyrs Brigades, to name the most infamous. But these are only names. No, we must look deeper to find the real enemy.

"What do all terrorists acts have in common? What motivates people to encourage their children to strap explosives to their bodies to kill themselves and people they do not know?"

Alexander placed both hands on the podium and leaned forward, looking earnestly into the TV cameras.

"What motivates men and women to commit atrocities against other humans ... to dance and clap, while a live human being's head is cut off ... or while a person is being disemboweled? What motivates men and women to seek death ... to *celebrate* death? What motivates the inhabitants of Muslim cities to celebrate the destruction of five of our cities?

"There is only one answer to these questions. The answer is a *religion*. The answer is *Islam*."

Alexander stared into the TV cameras with a hard expression—the angry leader of an angry people demanding retribution.

"I am now going to show you and members of the viewing audience a series of photographs and video clips. I'll warn you in advance—what you are about to see is extremely gruesome ... but, we must know our enemy. First, you'll see the damage done to our cities."

Once again the large over-head screen descended. Video of the destruction of each city was shown. Scenes, not previously released, showed the extent of the incomprehensible damage.

"Next are images of some of the injured. The first were taken during the evacuation of the bombed cities."

The screen was filled with images of horribly burned individuals—little children, old men and women all suffering burns from thermal and radiation energy. Two people in the audience were overcome with nausea and had to leave. Others looked on in horror as, ravaged by pain and despair, victim after victim looked out at them from stretchers and hospital beds.

"The next footage was filmed during Doctor Chatsworth's tour. You'll see men, women and children in hospitals. Many will never recover. They're waiting to die.

"All of these people ... *our people* ... *our loved ones* ... were *murdered* and *maimed* ... *IN THE NAME OF ALLAH!*"

Alexander banged his fist on the podium, as he thundered the last statement. For several seconds viewers witnessed heart-rending scenes of Chatsworth comforting person after person—many burned beyond recognition. Visibly shaken and interrupted by sobs from the audience, Alexander waited for their mutual anguish and anger to subside. Then, with a look of fierce determination, he continued.

"I know what you've just seen is horrible. It gives me no pleasure to have you exposed to such gory images. Too often in the past, our government chose not to inform you of the true nature of the enemy we are dealing with. But now it's time for you and the rest of the world to see exactly what our enemy is capable of. What they've done to our people is horrific. Now I must show you how non-Muslims have been treated in the lands of the Islamic Empire."

The carnage viewers saw next was too horrible for most to endure. Many covered their eyes to avoid the gore before them, as picture after picture of slaughtered American, British, French, German, Italian, and Spanish embassy personnel appeared on the screen. Bodies hung from embassy gates, some with intestines dangling form their gaping bellies. Again, nauseated audience members rushed for bathrooms. Others, unable to endure what they were witnessing, rose and solemnly left the auditorium.

Prompted by sobs from Governor Richard's wife, Jane Alexander put her arm around Nora's shoulders to comfort the shaken woman. Jim Alexander put his arm around his younger sister, Jenna, who, unable to watch any more, had lowered her head and was softly mumbling, "Why? Why would anyone do such a thing?"

Throughout the auditorium, people began to grumble in anger. Several stood and cursed at the screen, "Bastard, animals, they deserve to die."

Others demanded retribution, crying "Kill them! Kill them all," and shook their fists at the screen.

The audience's fury grew more intense when they witnessed the next scene, in which a woman cowered before a screaming mob. With her hands tied behind her back, the women pitifully begged for help, while Moslem men dragged her toward a wooden pole. When they reached the pole, one of the men grabbed her by the hair, while another bearded, black-turbaned man painfully jerked her bound wrists up behind her. As others lifted her body, the man hooked her bound wrists over a spike driven into the pole. When the men released her, her weight forced her arms up behind her and dislocated both shoulder joints. Screaming in agony, with her toes barely touching the ground, she slumped forward—held upright by the spike. Then a number of women and children joined the angry mob in front of her. Straining to hold her head up, the woman watched in horror as each member of the mob picked up medium-sized stones from a pile previously dumped before her. "*Pitié ... Pitié*," she pleaded in French, for she could see her death was eminent. They meant to stone her—a traditional Moslem punishment for breaking some archaic Islamic tradition.

When the first rock hit her with a resounding thud, some members of the audience groaned. With each successive blow, they winced. On the screen, the Muslim throng jeered, waived their hands and arms, and shouted *Allahu Akbar* over and over. Finally, a large rock burst open her skull, and her bloodied body mercifully went limp. But, the vicious, shouting crowd wasn't satisfied. They continued to pummel the woman's blood soaked body long after she died. Finally, to the collective relief of the audience the scene faded and they heaved a sigh of relief. While the audience was watched the stoning, Young had joined Alexander at the darkened podium. After quickly briefing the president on the Iranian missile battle that had just concluded, Young departed unnoticed across the stage. When the last scene ended, Alexander continued.

"You have just seen the stoning of a French diplomat's wife. What you are about to see is worse!"

The audience gasped and someone cried "God in Heaven," when three crosses appeared on the screen. Upon each cross hung three, horribly mutilated, naked men.

"These photos are *real*," Alexander said, his voice raw with emotion. "The three missionaries in this picture were crucified in Saudi Arabia for nothing more than exposing Muslims to Christianity. Yes, crucifixion is approved in the Qur'an and by Muhammad. Other crucifixions have occurred in Iran and Saudi Arabia. Crucifixion is one of the most inhumane forms of execution known to man.

"There is much more, but I think we've all seen enough to understand the nature of our enemy ... an enemy that is a *religion*. A religion that is responsible for the deaths of over thirteen million of our people—our fellow Americans.

"OUR ENEMY IS ISLAM."

Alexander thundered, striking the podium with his fist for emphasis: a gesture he would repeat after each of the following statements.

"The world's enemy is *ISLAM*.

"We are at war with a religion—ISLAM—which means *SUBMISSION*."

Pausing briefly, he looked at the audience with steely resolve, then glared into the TV cameras.

"A religion that requires its practitioners to blindly obey the will of their unspeakably cruel god, Allah. In reality Islam means they must submit to whatever a cleric tells them is Allah's will. We are engaged in a religious war. Our choice is surrender and submit to Islam ... *or destroy Islam*."

Alexander spoke the last phrase in a slow, measured, menacing, cadence, then paused again to allow his final words to have their full impact. Finally, he returned his gaze to the TV cameras and resolutely continued.

"At ten minutes after ten this evening, the Islamic Empire launched one Shahab-5 and three Shahab-3 missiles from Iran. Two had nuclear warheads. The other two had chemical and biological warheads. The Shahab-5 nuclear tipped missile was targeted on our base in Tripoli. A Shahab-3D with a nuclear warhead was aimed at Tel Aviv."

Again, the president was interrupted by gasps from the audience.

"At the same time, United States forces were conducting a cruise missile attack against Iran. One of our cruise missiles destroyed the second nuclear tipped missile, the one targeted at Tel Aviv, as it was being launched. The other three missiles were launched before our attack began. A U.S. Navy Aegis Cruiser, equipped with our new Standard Missile-3, destroyed the first Iranian missile aimed at Tripoli. Israeli Arrow missiles intercepted and destroyed the third Iranian missile. The fourth and last missile, with a biological warhead, was damaged by an Arrow and destroyed by a ground-based laser developed by Israel and the United States. No other details are currently available."

The president paused again to allow the murmuring in the audience to die out. After surveying the audience, his gaze returned to the TV cameras.

"Twenty-eight days ago, I pledged we would have retribution.

"*Now we shall have it.*"

Again the president used a slow, measured, menacing cadence to emphasize his last statement. A hush fell over the large auditorium. No one was sure what was coming next.

Alexander paused to look at his watch and consider the timing of events in the Middle East. *It's 2246. By now all of the TV stations in Iran, Iraq, and Saudi Arabia have been destroyed. Reverend Smyth's "Message to Islam" has been broadcast on all of their frequencies. Now my address is being broadcast.* Looking quickly to his left, Alexander locked eyes with Colonel Young who stood behind the curtain—out of sight of the audience and TV cameras. In response to the president's look, Young held out his right fist, thumb up. *Good, everything is on schedule.* Alexander sighed and continued.

"For the past fourteen hundred years Islam has been at war with the West. When they weren't fighting us, they were fighting each other—Shia' verses Sunni. For the past sixty years, Israel's existence has been used as the excuse for conflict. All attempts to reach a reasonable settlement have failed. Jerusalem is a holy place to Christians, Jews, and Muslims. The Dome of the Rock and the al-Aqsa mosque were built on the site of King Solomon's Temple—the Temple Mount. Muslims have refused to share the site. They've been so cruel as to drop stones from the top of the Wailing Wall onto Jews praying below.

"I pledged we would determine who was responsible for the attacks on our five cities, and then seek retribution."

Alexander paused, his gaze sweeping the enthralled audience.

"Our retribution has begun!"

The president's voice was cold and ominous. After a short pause, he pointed to the screen.

"On the screen above you will see a video, shot today in Israel, of the Dome of the Rock and the al-Aqsa mosque."

Images of the shrine with the gold dome and the mosque with the black dome appeared on the screen. Suddenly, a ring of explosions rippled around the base of both structures: their walls slowly collapsed and their domes fell onto the piles of rubble. Fire erupted in the ruins. Smoke billowed upward. The Dome of the Rock and the al-Aqsa mosque had been destroyed, and the audience's pent up emotions—hanging by a fragile thread—spontaneously erupted. Shouts of approval reverberated throughout the auditorium. Raising his voice to get attention, Alexander shouted over the cheering crowd,

"All traces of Islam will be destroyed.

"We will begin with Mecca."

A satellite view of Mecca appeared on the large screen, and the auditorium became as quiet as a tomb.

"You are now looking at real time images of Mecca."

The camera zoomed in.

"This is Mecca's *Masjid al-Haram* Mosque."

The camera zoomed in again.

"And now ... the *Ka'aba*."

The Ka'aba's image filled the screen.

"The Ka'aba is supposed to be a model of Allah's house in heaven.

"They call it called the "*Bait-ul Ma'amoor*,

"Now ... "

Alexander paused dramatically, looking directly into the camera.

"I now address my following remarks to all Muslims worldwide.

"Let *Allah* protect Mecca.

"If your god is false ... I will destroy Mecca."

Alexander's emphasized his last statement by raising his arm and pointing dramatically to the image on the screen above him. On cue, the camera pulled back to show the satellite view of Mecca and the surrounding area. Many members of the audience gasped at the sight of millions of Islamic fighters encamped around the city. When the satellite camera zoomed in, furious hordes of fighters could be seen waving their arms and firing weapons into the air.

❂   ❂   ❂

Flying his Lancer at 40,000 feet, Major Kilgore turned the *Heavy Metal* onto his attack vector. Earlier two Saudi F-15s had risen to intercept the lone bomber. They never saw the two Raptors that killed them. The flight of the four Raptors and the Lancer were approaching Mecca from the east at 575 knots. Major Barrett activated the bombing computer and initiated the arming sequence of the B-53 thermonuclear bomb. Energy flowed from the aircraft through an electrical cable into the bomb's capacitor bank. Inside the bomb bay, two solenoids closed locking jaws onto a thin metal rod—the bomb's arming cable. The forward bomb bay doors opened. Seconds later, clamps holding the heavy bomb released, and two propellant activated pistons thrust it out of the bomb bay. When the bomb separated from its rack, the electrical cable disconnected. The arming cable held by the clamping jaws pulled out of the bomb's body, removing the mechanical block that prevented the fuze from arming.

As soon as the heavy bomb was released, the Lancer jumped upward. A green light on the control panel told Kilgore the bomb bay doors had closed. Kilgore keyed his mike, "Brimstone Flight, burners now." He heard four clicks as the four Raptor pilots pushed their throttles to full military power—Raptors do not require afterburners to exceed mach-1.

Getting as far away as possible from a nine megaton explosion is prudent.

❁ ❁ ❁

Alexander looked at his watch, and then glanced at Colonel Young, who, while carefully cuing the president, was also listening intently to reports through an earpiece. Noting a change of expression in Young's face, Alexander shot him a questioning look. Then to Alexander's relief he saw Young nod and once more hold out his right fist, thumb up. The bomb had been released. It was time for the *coup de grâce*. On the screen above the president, the satellite view of Mecca pulled back, showing the coast of Saudi Arabia and the Red Sea.

"What your are about to see is happening in real time. One of our bombers has just released a large thermonuclear bomb, targeted on Mecca. Detonation will occur in approximately three minutes."

Excited murmuring rippled through the audience. For once, the network talking heads were speechless. For several seconds the president waited, allowing his words to sink in. Finally he continued,

"While this bomb is falling over Mecca, other bombers are releasing the same type of bombs on Medina—the second holiest place in Islam—Cairo, and Khartoum. Millions of mujahedeen fighters have gathered at each of these locations.

"Tehran is the capital of the evil Islamic Empire. For the past two weeks, the combined armies of Iran and Iraq have been forming around Baghdad. Both cities are also being destroyed by the same type of bomb."

Gesturing at the screen above him, Alexander continued.

"The destruction of Mecca will appear as a bright flash on the screen."

❁ ❁ ❁

As the B-53 plummeted on its calculated ballistic path toward the Ka'aba, its computer checked altitude and found it to be above the set minimum. The bomb continued to fall until it reached 20,000 feet and the parachute deployed. Deceleration was measured and the deceleration gate in the fuze opened, arming the warhead. Ground sensing radar was activated, and the computer began checking altitude, comparing it with the preset detonation altitude. When the altitude reached 7,000 feet, the fuze sent the detonation command. Q-switches closed, simultaneously dumping the electrical energy stored in the large capacitors into wires leading to exploding bridge wire detonators, mounted in the center of each explosive lens of the sphere of explosives surrounding the pit. The high voltage caused the thick bridge wires to explode with enough force to detonate the booster explosives. Detonation of explosive lens in the sphere began. The explosive wave traveled inward, striking the tamper, compressing it into an even smaller shell. Finally, the tamper, driven by the explosive wave, closed on the pit—the sphere containing alternating layers of U-235 and lithium deuteride. Now, the neutron source was triggered, and a combination fission-fusion reaction began. Temperature rose in a few billionths of a second. The combination of neutrons, gamma radiation, and temperature generated by the primary, ignited a fusion reaction in the secondary, resulting in a thermonuclear explosion.

An unbelievably bright light illuminated the cockpits of the *Heavy Metal* and its escorts as they raced westward at mach-1.2. When the ensuing three-mile-plus-wide fireball kissed the earth, Mecca and the surrounding area was transformed into molecules of ash. An eight-mile wide column of hot gases began rising heavenward. Ice crystals forming on the column's exterior made it made it appear to be white.

"Holy Mother of God," Major Kilgore whispered. Thankfully, the blast wave could not catch the supersonic planes.

❀   ❀   ❀

The president stood quietly, while all eyes remained riveted on the screen. Suddenly, the screen turned white. Slowly, a round white expanding sphere became visible. For an instant, vivid colors appeared in the sphere. A ring suddenly radiated outward from the center. The sphere slowly grew, becoming a giant white mushroom. Temperature in the center of the sphere matched the sun's core. The city of Mecca and its surrounding area was instantly transformed into a shallow, broad crater. The satellite continued to transmit the image of the expanding thermonuclear detonation. Higher and higher rose the column of superheated gases that formed the giant mushroom. Glittering white ice crystals formed on the column's exterior as it rose with its mushroom cap reaching upwards to the stratosphere. A thermonuclear detonation is both beautiful and frightening. Awesome does not adequately describe it. When the cloud finally dissipated, satellite photos would show a large circular area some ten miles across completely devoid of life and structures. No trace of the city or surrounding towns would remain—only barren desert and glass fused from the silica in the sand where the Ka'aba once stood. The audience was deathly silent, overwhelmed by what they'd just witnessed. Alexander waited several seconds after the satellite image had faded from the screen before continuing.

"Tonight the Islamic Empire and Islam—as we know it—will come to an end. But Iran's nuclear program still poses a threat—a threat that must be eliminated. Iran has several nuclear weapons facilities scattered throughout the country. These must also be destroyed."

With the wave of his hand Alexander cued a new video. For a second or two, the scene on the screen above showed a calm patch of ocean. Suddenly the surface of the water bulged upward, then violently erupted as the nose of a missile broke the surface. Quickly rising out of the geyser of water, the missile burst through the surface of the sea, on a column of fire.

While the camera followed the three-stage, solid propellant, inertially guided, fleet ballistic missile as it climbed skyward, an announcer in the video described the action, "When the third stage motor separates, the nosecone will enter outer space, and six MK-5 Multiple Independently Targetable Reentry Vehicles and decoys will be released. Each MK-5 RV, traveling at twenty thousand feet per second, contains one W-88—a four hundred seventy-five kiloton boosted nuclear warhead."

The scene faded and the large screen was being retracted, the president continued.

"What you've just viewed was an informational video showing a Trident II D-5 fleet ballistic missile launch. While you were watching, an Ohio class Trident class submarine launched a similar missile, targeted on the nuclear weapons sites in Iran. Thirty minutes from now nuclear sites at Arak, Busheir, Isfahan, Natanz, Lashkar Abad, and the tribal lands in Pakistan will cease to exist."

Alexander paused, and stood staring at the TV cameras, then at the audience. The auditorium was deathly quiet. One could hear one's heart beat. The magnitude of what they'd just witnessed was incomprehensible. People in the audience and throughout the world were stunned, awed. Looking at the audience staring up at him, Alexander saw the first glimmer of realization on some of their faces. *I pray to God this will end it and that remaining Muslims will understand what has happened—what they caused to happen. If they don't* ... He sighed deeply. It was time to continue.

"As soon as the radiation dies down, U.S. and British forces will invade, and conquer Egypt, Saudi Arabia, Iraq, and Iran. Once the populations have been subdued, and all traces of Islam removed, Egypt will become a possession of Great Britain. Saudi Arabia, Iraq, and Iran will become possessions of the United States.

"Smaller Arab nations that did not participate in the attack on our country, and did not join the Islamic Empire will remain free states—provided they remove all traces of Islam from their lands. The same is true for Turkey. The United States and other countries are prepared to aid the government of Turkey in eliminating the Islamic fundamentalists who have started a civil war—and with them all traces of Islam.

"China and Japan are preparing to deal with the Islamic problem in Indonesia. Russia will deal with Islam in its former republics.

"Islam will be purged from the earth. It may take decades to find all of the small pockets, but find them we will.

"The world cannot allow another dictator, or religion, to drag it to the edge of the abyss. This time, humanity came very close to falling in. There must never be a next time."

Alexander paused to take a drink of water, as he waited for the applause to die down before continuing.

"We have much to accomplish in the weeks and months ahead. We're faced with seemingly insurmountable problems here at home, however, I am confident that the American people are up to the challenge. After the attack on our five cities, men and women lined up to volunteer for our military. I asked them to wait until their country needed them. Now, that time has come.

Your country needs you: to occupy our new possessions; to join the Corps of Engineers in cleaning up and rebuilding our damaged cities; and to begin rebuilding the infrastructures of our new possessions. Later, we will need teachers to start the task of properly educating the children of our new possessions. Once freed from the chains of Islam, the young can be properly educated in art, philosophy, mathematics, science, and history. It may take a generation to rid the world of Islam. It may even take more than a generation ... but, the process starts now."

Alexander stopped speaking, slowly looked over the audience, and clearly indicated by his expression he intended a change of pace.

"The world must look to the future. We must learn from our mistakes. The forgotten war in Korea established a dangerous policy. The aggressor was not punished ... The aggressor was not destroyed ... Thousands of our citizens, and citizens of other nations died without achieving an absolute victory. As a result, history repeated itself in Viet Nam, Somalia, and twice in Iraq.

"*Never again* ... Never again will we leave the job half finished. From this day forth, if the United States sees the need to defend a country, as we did for Kuwait, we will destroy the aggressor and seize its property and land. The United States will not start a war ... but it will always finish one."

The auditorium erupted with shouts and applause, which continued for over a minute. Finally, the president was able to continue.

"The United Nations, like the League of Nations, was a failure. A new approach is required.

"As soon as ongoing military operations end, I will call a conference of the major world powers to begin forming a new world organization to replace the United Nations."

Again, the president paused and changed his demeanor and body language to indicate a change of subject. His gaze returned to the TV cameras.

"Now, I wish to direct my comments to my fellow countrymen. Soon we must begin forming our new government. But, before the process begins, we must identify the defects in our old government.

"What went wrong?

"How did we allow ourselves to be attacked?

"Part of the answer is the emergence of a political philosophy whose practitioners refer to themselves as *'secular-progressives'* and *'elitists.'* People who scorn patriotism. People who claim moral superiority by identifying with humanity at large and some Utopian New World Order. People who will not stand for our National Anthem. People who refuse to pledge allegiance to our flag. People who use our legal system to enforce their beliefs on others. People who have used every stratagem to remove any reference of God from our buildings, the Pledge of Allegiance, and our money. People who approve of desecrating our flag.

"These elitists showed their disdain for our country and flag during the Viet Nam war—even though the war was started by one of their own—President John F. Kennedy. Elitists disavowed their country ... They gave aid and comfort to our enemy. Actions by elitist students, academicians, politicians, and our news media encouraged the North Vietnamese to continue the war, resulting in the deaths of thousands of our citizens, and tens of thousands of South Vietnamese.

Again, Alexander allowed his gaze to sweep the audience before addressing the cameras.

"Elitists have encouraged others to attack us, because they portrayed us as being weak. Their philosophy encouraged al-Qaeda to attack our five cities.

"The words liberal and elitist have become synonymous terms. Elitists introduced the concept of political correctness. A socialistic concept meaning 'go along to get along.' A concept used to stifle the expression of free thought. A concept alien to America.

"Political correctness *has no place in America!*

"How can we prevent history from repeating itself?

"Citizens of the United States owe their allegiance to the nation—to its Constitution as symbolized by its flag and National Anthem.

"If a person will not stand for our national anthem, will not stand and repeat the Pledge of Allegiance to our flag—this person *is living in the wrong country*."

With a few exceptions, the audience was on its feet, cheering and shouting. Citizens—wherever they were—in their homes, churches, bars, across the nation, across the planet, joined the audience in cheering. Smiling, the president waited for the cheering to end, and then slowly looked around the audience. It was time to close. Still smiling he looked back at the TV cameras before continuing.

"In conclusion I'd like to thank all of you, our citizens, those in the private sector, the care givers, state and federal employees, state governors, and the military for your hard work and untiring support during these difficult days. God only knows what your prayers and letters have meant to me, to my family, and to the members of my Cabinet.

"Yes, I'm grateful to you, but I'm not surprised. America has always been at its best during crisis and adversity.

"We have suffered a grievous attack.

"We have supported each other.

"We have survived.

"And with your continued help, we will go forward and build a better and stronger republic.

"America still has *the right stuff*.

"Good night, and God bless America."

For over a minute, the president stood at the podium, smiling to acknowledge the audience's standing ovation, while the large screen above him descended unnoticed. Then he turned and motioned for Richards and the Cabinet to stand. After another two minutes of cheering, the president gave a signal. The band struck up John Philip Sousa's greatest march, "The Stars and Stripes Forever," and a beaming Alexander turned and proudly marched instep with the music across the stage. The Cabinet and Governor Richards followed.

When the president turned to exit the stage, a large billowing American flag appeared on the screen above. Slowly the rippling flag faded and in its place came scene after scene of memorable historic and patriotic images: the rocky coast of Maine; the Liberty Bell, the Constitution and Declaration of Independence; The Wright Brother's airplane flying over the sand dunes of Kitty Hawk; Marines lifting the flag on Iwo Jima; a Saturn rocket blasting off from Cape Canaveral; a man walking on the moon; the space station and space shuttle in orbit above the earth; the St. Louis arch; fields of waving golden grain; buffalo on a grassy prairie; a southwestern desert; towering mountains, lakes, rivers, a city overlooking a bay; the Pacific coastline; herds of elk on the Alaskan tundra; and finally the Hawaiian islands.

Citizens in the auditorium, across the nation, and in other countries sat spellbound, many with tears in their eyes.

When the band reached the second stanza of the march, the brass section thundered, thundered again, and then cascaded down the scale like rolling thunder.

Without conscious thought, men and women in the viewing audience began to stand, most with their hands over their hearts. As suddenly as it came, the stirring notes from the brass section faded, and were replaced by the haunting refrain played by a piccolo. Now everyone was standing—tears running down their cheeks—in the auditorium, in their homes, wherever they were.

The band was on its feet, giving the performance of a lifetime. The second stanza of the march repeated and the brass section thundered again.

Pride swelled in every breast.

Yes, America still had *the right stuff.*

America had been re-born.

A new, determined America locked step with its leader and marched bravely forward into the new world.

References

Allison, Graham, *Nuclear Terrorism*. New York: Times Books, 2004.

Anderson, Paul, *The Al Qaeda Connection*. New York: Prometheus Books, 2005

Coalition to Reduce Nuclear Dangers, Chronology of Key Events in the Effort to End Nuclear Weapons Testing: 1945-1999.
http://www.clw.org/coalition/ctch4050.htm

Corsi, Jerome R., *Atomic Iran*. Nashville, TN: WND Book, 2005.

Defense Threat Reduction Agency, *Defense's Nuclear Agency 1947-1997*. Department of Defense, 2002.

Emerson, Steven, *American Jihad*. New York: The Free Press, 2003.

Evans, Michael D., *Beyond Iraq*. Lakeland, FL: White Stone Books, 2003.

Gabriel, Brigitte, *Because they hate: a survivor of Islamic terror warns America*. 2006. New York: St. Martin's Press.

Ishaq, Ibn, S*irat Rasul Allah*. Edited and abridged by Ibn Hisham, translated by Alfred Guillaume, published by the Oxford Press in 1980, and 2002 under the title *The Life of Muhammad*.

Price, Randall, *Unholy War*. Eugene, OR: Harvest House, 2001.

Rashid, Ahmed, *Jihad*. New York: Penguin Group, 2003.

Soviet and Russian Nuclear Weapons and History.
http://nuclearweaponarchive.org/Russia/

Spencer, Robert, *The Truth about Muhammad*. Washington, DC: Regnery Publishing, Inc., 2006.

Timmerman, Kenneth R., *Countdown to Crisis*. New York: Crown Publishing Group, 2005.

Trifkovic, Serge, *The Sword of the Prophet*. Boston, MA: Regina Orthodox Press, Inc.

Walvoord, John F., *Armageddon, Oil and the Middle East Crisis*. Grand Rapids, MI: Zondervan Publishing House, 1990 (Revised).

Warraq, Ibn, *Why I Am Not a Muslim*. Amherst, NY: Prometheus Books, 2003.

Weldon, Curt, *Countdown To Terror*. Washington, DC: Regnery Publishing, Inc., 2005.

Williams, Paul L., *Osama's Revenge*. Amherst, NY: Prometheus Books, 2004., and *The Al Qaeda Connection*. Amherst, NY: Prometheus Books, 2005.

Winn, Craig, *Prophet of Doom*. Cricketsong Books, 2004

Appendix

Basic Nuclear terminology

Atom

An atom consists of three main parts: a proton, which has a positive electrical charge; a neutron that has no electrical charge; and an electron that has a negative electrical charge. The proton and neutron are located in the nucleus or center of the atom, and the electron orbits around the nucleus much like the planets orbit around the sun.

Element

An element is a substance that cannot be separated into simpler substances by chemical means. An atom is the smallest unit of an element that possesses all the characteristics of the element. A substance that consists wholly of atoms having the same atomic number is called an **element**, and is given a chemical symbol.

Atomic number

The number of protons in the nucleus of an atom is referred to as the element's **atomic number**. Hydrogen, the lightest element consists of one proton in the nucleus and one orbiting electron, has an atomic number of 1 and is written $_1$H. Helium, the second lightest element, with 2 protons and 2 neutrons in its nucleus and 2 orbiting electrons, is written $_2$He. Uranium (depletealloy), a very heavy element, has 92 protons and 146 neutrons in the nucleus, and it's written $_{92}$U.

Atomic mass number

The total number of protons and neutrons is called the element's **atomic mass number**. Hydrogen has one proton and no neutron, and its atomic mass number is written ^{1}H. Helium that has 2 protons and 2 neutrons in its nucleus and its atomic mass number is written ^{4}He. Uranium has 92 protons and 146 neutrons and is written ^{238}U. Electrons are not counted when determining the atomic mass number because the electron's mass is so small it's insignificant—approximately 1/1837 of the weight of a proton or neutron. One proton weighs approximately .00000000000000000000000017 grams.

Combined atomic notation

The chemical symbol, atomic number and atomic mass number can be combined and written as follows: $_1^1$H, $_2^4$He, and $_{92}^{238}$U.

Isotopes

Elements can have variations caused by a different number of neutrons in their nucleus and are called **isotopes**. An isotope of an element always has the same number of protons but has different numbers of neutrons. Hydrogen has one proton. Hydrogen's second isotope, deuterium, has one proton and one neutron. Hydrogen's third isotope, tritium, has one proton and two neutrons. Helium has two protons and two neutrons in its nucleus

The two important uranium isotopes are $^{238}_{92}U$ (depletealloy) and $^{235}_{92}U$ (HEU or Oralloy).

Large amount of uranium-238 hexafluoride residue from the uranium separation processes was accumulated as waste at gaseous diffusion plants. Some of the residue was converted back to depletealloy and used to make the tamper in fission bombs. Later depletealloy was used to make "Depleted Uranium Kinetic Energy Penetrators" used in American anti-tank and anti-armor ammunition. The effectiveness of DU penetrators was demonstrated in the 1991 Gulf War and later battles.

Nuclear fission and chain reactions

The nucleus of fissionable isotopes of uranium or plutonium captures a neutron, causing it to divide into two new atoms of lighter elements called fission products. The phenomenon is called fission. U-235 and Pu-239 atoms can only capture slowly moving neutrons, called thermal neutrons. Neutron velocity or speed is measured in units of energy, electron volts, instead of usually terms such as miles per hour. Fast moving neutrons are measured in million electron volts (Mev). Think of a cue ball breaking the balls on a pool table. Every time the cue ball strikes another ball it loses energy, slows down. The same thing happens to a neutron released when an atom splits. A neutron released from the fission of a U-235 atom must collide with other atoms, slowing down until it has slowed enough (becomes a thermal neutron) to be captured by another U-235 or Pu-239 atom, causing it to split. The fission equation for uranium-235 is written:

$$^{1}_{0}n + ^{235}_{92}U \rightarrow 2 \text{ fission products} + 2.43\,^{1}_{0}n + \text{energy.}$$

The number of neutrons released depends on how the uranium atom divides—which pair of fission products it creates. Different product pairs release different numbers of neutrons. Typical fission product pairs are $^{94}_{38}Sr$ and $^{140}_{54}Xe$, or $^{96}_{40}Zr$ and $^{138}_{52}Te$. In reality there are hundreds of fission products. The average number of neutrons released is 2.43 neutrons per fission. Neutrons fly off in various directions, collide with the nuclei of other uranium atoms, and if captured, cause the atom to split, releasing more neutrons.

An atomic bomb or atomic device requires a rapidly increasing chain reaction called a "supercritical reaction." While a nuclear reactor requires a self-sustaining reaction called a "critical reaction." Only highly enriched uranium-235 and plutonium-239 will sustain a supercritical reaction.

Subcritical reaction

A subcritical reaction is one in which the chain reactions die out. In other words, one fission does not produce another fission, and the chain reaction is not maintained. Random fissions will continue, producing small amounts of radiation.

Critical reaction

A critical reaction is a self-sustaining nuclear chain reaction. When one fission produces one fission that produces one fission—a self-sustaining critical reaction has occurred. A nuclear reactor is said to have "gone critical" when a self-sustaining chain reaction is achieved.

Prompt critical reaction

A prompt critical reaction is an increasing chain reaction in which one fission produces more than one fission in a controlled manner. In a nuclear reactor, control rods that absorb neutrons regulate the prompt critical fission reaction. A prompt critical reaction occurs when a nuclear reactor increases its power level. Once the new power level is achieved, control rods are adjusted to bring the reaction back to critical. Without control rods, the fission reaction increases (runs away) until the uranium core of the reactor melts and deforms: leaving highly radioactive molten metal slag. If the reactor's containment vessel ruptures, fission products can be released. Such a runaway is popularly referred to as "The China Syndrome:" a name coined from the title of a movie depicting a fictional account of runaway reactor. An event that later became a reality when Russia's Chernobyl nuclear reactor went into an uncontrolled prompt critical reaction and melted, rupturing, the containment vessel.

Nuclear reactors use enriched uranium (EU), which cannot sustain the supercritical fission reaction required to produce an atomic explosion. Nuclear reactors cannot blow up and make an atomic explosion, because they do not contain HEU (weapons grade fissile material). The international community considers reactor grade enriched uranium—up to 20% U-235, to be HEU. The dual definition creates confusion.

Supercritical reaction

In a supercritical chain reaction, one fission produces, for example, three fissions, each of which produces three more for a total of nine—nine produces twenty-seven, twenty-seven produces eighty-one, *etc.* These chain reactions result in a nuclear detonation. The yield of the detonation will depend on the length of time the fissile material remains in a supercritical mass configuration—measured in nanoseconds. One nanosecond is one billionth of a second, or 1×10^{-9} second. A typical implosion device will complete its supercritical chain reaction in thirty nanoseconds. Most fission products—fallout—are unstable isotopes that are radioactive and decay to form new atoms by releasing one of the following: a positive charged alpha particle (two protons and two neutrons), a negatively charged beta ray (an electron discharged from the nucleus), a neutron, or gamma radiation (similar to but more powerful than X-rays). Fissile material referrers to isotopes that will sustain a supercritical fission reaction: uranium-233; uranium-235, and plutonium-239.

Neutron source

Fission is caused by the U-235 or P-239 atom capturing a thermal neutron. Introducing neutrons will increase the number of initial fissions, the first generation. One fission produces three fissions, three produces six, six produces twelve, *etc.* Increasing the number of fissions in the first generation will increase the yield—one million produces three million, and so forth.

Polonium-beryllium neutron sources were used in early nuclear weapons. They were constructed by combining polonium-210 ($^{210}_{84}Po$), and beryllium-9 ($^{9}_{4}Be$). Polonium-210 is radioactive and decays by emitting an alpha particle and decaying to lead.

$$^{210}_{84}Po \rightarrow {}^{206}_{82}Pb + {}^{4}_{2}\alpha + energy.$$

The alpha particle reacts with the beryllium to release neutrons and the beryllium decays and becomes carbon.

$$^{4}_{2}\alpha + {}^{9}_{4}Be \rightarrow {}^{12}_{6}C + {}^{1}_{0}n$$

Polonium-210 has a half-life of 138 days, which means half of the polonium will decay in 138 days, half again in the next 138 days. Polonium-beryllium neutron sources have to be replaced every two half-lives or every nine months, which is incorrectly referred to in the media as replacing the nuclear components. Polonium-beryllium neutron sources have been replaced with electronic one in modern nuclear weapons.

Another method of providing source neutrons is through a pulsed neutron emitter, which is a small ion accelerator with a metal hydride target. The ion source is turned on by applying a high voltage electrical current that creates a plasma of deuterium or tritium. The electrical field accelerates the ions into tritium rich metal (i.e., scandium), producing a nuclear fusion reaction. The deuterium-tritium fusion reactions emit a short pulse of high energy neutrons sufficient to initiate the fission chain reaction. The timing of the pulse can be precisely controlled, making it better for an implosion weapon design.

Fusion Reaction

Neutrons from U-235 fission combine with the deuterium ($_1^2H$), the second isotope of hydrogen contained in lithium deuteride to produce tritium ($_1^3H$), the third isotope of hydrogen. Sufficient temperature and pressure is produced by the uranium fission reaction to start the deuterium-tritium fusion reaction. The two isotopes of hydrogen combine (fuse together) to make a new element, helium ($_2^4H$), releasing energy.

The neutron from U-235 fission combining with deuterium is written:

$$_0^1n + _1^2H \rightarrow _1^3H$$

The deuterium tritium fusion reaction is written:

$$_1^2H + _1^3H \rightarrow _2^4H + _0^1n + energy$$

The neutron released can cause conversion of deuterium to tritium or the fission of a U-235 or Pu-239 atom.

Basic types of atomic bombs

Gun-type

Two or more pieces of HEU are brought together to form a supercritical mass. The Little Boy atomic bomb dropped on Hiroshima used a 3 inch naval gun tube to fire a U-235 projectile into a U-235 hollow cylinder called the target. The cylinder was actually several rings that resembled large washers. An external neutron source was used to accelerate the supercritical reaction.

Implosion type

A subcritical mass of plutonium-239 is compressed to form a supercritical mass by an explosive charge. An external neutron source is used to accelerate the supercritical reaction. The explosive charge is constructed of pieces of high energy explosives configured to fit together to form a sphere around the subcritical plutonium mass, called the pit. The explosive components are referred to as lens because they are machined to tolerances associated with camera lens. Each lens must be detonated at exactly the same time. The explosive pressure waves must reach the surface of the pit as exactly the same time in order for the pit to be compressed in a uniform manner.

Boosted Fission Type

The pit is a sphere with a uranium-235 center. A layer or shell of lithium deuteride coats the small ball of U-235 in the center. A third layer of U-235 coats the layer of lithium deuteride. This process is repeated several times. Detonation of the explosive lens compressed the layer producing a uranium supercritical fission reaction. Neutrons from the fission reaction initiate the fusion reaction, producing a limited amount of fusion—a fission reaction created by implosion, augmented by a fusion reaction—a fission-fusion-fission reaction. The U.S. employ's a different method to boost its fission warheads. Boosted fission warheads can achieve yields in the hundreds of kilotons.

Tamper

A tamper is a layer of very dense material (*e.g.*, depleted uranium or tungsten) surrounding the pit. It's located inside the explosive lens system. When the explosive lens detonates, the shock wave compresses the tamper shell, accelerating it inward toward the surface of the pit. The inertia of the dense material contains the expanding pit for a very short time, allowing one or two additional fission generations, thereby increasing the yield—each generation is more than double the number of fissions in the previous generation.

Neutron reflector

The neutron reflector is a layer of beryllium metal surrounding the pit. Neutrons reflected back into the pit increase the number of fissions, increasing the yield. The tamper also acts as a neutron reflector, which increases the number of fissions.

About the Author

Lee Boyland is well qualified to write about all types of weapons: nuclear, chemical, biological, and conventional. He has a degree in Nuclear Engineering. He served three years in the U.S. Army as an explosive ordnance disposal officer, assigned to the Defense Atomic Support Agency (DASA), Sandia Base (now part of Kirkland AFB), Albuquerque New Mexico. DASA controlled the development and stockpiling of all nuclear and thermonuclear weapons, providing Lieutenant Boyland access to the design details of every nuclear and thermonuclear warhead developed by the United States up to the Mark 63 warhead. His primary assignment was the DASA Nuclear Emergency Team, responsible for nuclear weapons accidents and incidents. Other duties included providing bomb disposal support to the local authorities, participating in tests at the Nevada Test Site, and teaching training courses provided by DASA.

After three years of active duty, Lee spent the next thirteen years designing conventional and special ordnance. He also applied aerospace combustion technology to incineration of Agent Orange for the Air Force, and demilitarized chemical weapons at Rocky Mountain Arsenal and Tooele Army Depot for the Army. He transitioned into the hazardous waste industry and started the first full service medical waste management company in the Midwest.

Lee and his wife and co-author, Vista, live in Florida where he consults in waste management and writes. As a member of a U.S. technology exchange team, he traveled to Shanghai, Beijing, and Tianjin China in 2003. His published works include technical articles, a chapter in the Biohazards Management Handbook, and the Occupational Exposure to Bloodborne Pathogens Training Series marketed by Fisher Scientific.

Schools

North Carolina State University, BS Nuclear Engineering, commission, Second Lieutenant U.S. Army

U.S. Naval School, Explosive Ordnance Disposal

U.S. Naval School, Nuclear Weapons Disposal

Defense Atomic Support Agency, tri-service Nuclear Emergency Management (instructor and member of DASA Nuclear Emergency Team)

U.S. Army Ammunition and Explosive Safety Course

U.S. Army, Advanced Chemical Weapons, Dugway Proving Ground

Contact Lee and Vista Boyland at: http://www.LeeBoylandBooks.com